Also by Sarah Micklem

Firethorn

Wildfire

A NOVEL

Sarah Micklem

Scribner

New York   London   Toronto   Sydney

SCRIBNER
A Division of Simon & Schuster, Inc.
1230 Avenue of the Americas
New York, NY 10020

This book is a work of fiction. Names, characters, places, and incidents either
are products of the author's imagination or are used fictitiously. Any resemblance
to actual events or locales or persons, living or dead, is entirely coincidental.

Copyright © 2009 by Sarah Micklem

All rights reserved, including the right to reproduce this book or portions thereof
in any form whatsoever. For information address Scribner Subsidiary Rights Department,
1230 Avenue of the Americas, New York, NY 10020.

First Scribner hardcover edition July 2009

SCRIBNER and design are registered trademarks of The Gale Group, Inc.,
used under license by Simon & Schuster, Inc., the publisher of this work.

For information about special discounts for bulk purchases,
please contact Simon & Schuster Special Sales at 1-866-506-1949
or business@simonandschuster.com.

The Simon & Schuster Speakers Bureau can bring authors to your live event.
For more information or to book an event contact the Simon & Schuster Speakers Bureau
at 1-866-248-3049 or visit our website at www.simonspeakers.com.

DESIGNED BY ERICH HOBBING

Manufactured in the United States of America

1 3 5 7 9 10 8 6 4 2

Library of Congress Control Number: 2008032779

ISBN 978-1-4516-4648-1
ISBN 978-0-7432-9369-3 (ebook)

This book is for my mother,
Carolyn,
who always asks for news of Firethorn—
how is she, and what is she up to now?
Often, by telling her, I discover the answer.

And for Cornelius,
who gave me time to write,
the most generous gift
one writer can give another.

THE DIVINING COMPASS

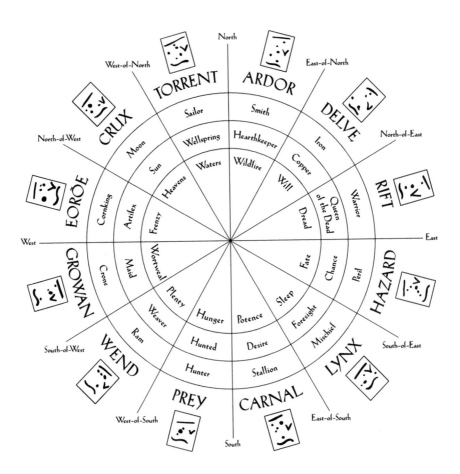

Wildfire

Wildfire

 disobeyed. I followed Sire Galan to war, though he had commanded me to go home. He'd been generous, granting me the use of a stone house on a mountainside for all of my days to come. But how could I call it home, a place I'd never seen? A blanket and the ground to lie on with Galan beside me, that was the home I claimed. It didn't suit me to be put aside, judged too weak to endure what lay ahead. I set my will against Sire Galan's, hazarding that if I did as I pleased, I might also please him.

He'd charged his horsemaster, Flykiller, with the duty of herding me home, along with the warhorses Galan had won in mortal tourney and was forbidden to ride—all of us to be turned out to pasture. But I gave Flykiller the slip during the army's embarkation: two days of shouting and cursing, mules balking on gangways and men falling overboard, baggage and soldiers gone missing. In such confusion only thieves had been sure of their duties. I took refuge with my friend Mai, and set sail under the copper banners of the clan of Delve.

So I found myself now aboard a ship crossing a sullen green sea. Wretched, queasy, beset by misgivings. I lay curled up on deck, one leg heavy on the other, the bones bruising the flesh. My sheepskin cloak was sodden, and from time to time a drop of seawater crawled down my back. The ship creaked under us like an old alewife's hip joints, and stank of bilgewater, dung, salted fish, and the pungent pitch that coated the planks and rigging.

Before we left Corymb, the priests had prayed for a wind from north-of-east, the domain of Rift, and the god of war had been pleased to send it. For four days this strong cold wind had driven the fleet apace toward the kingdom of Incus. The ships went heavy laden, but we rode no lower in the water for bearing the weightiest cargo of all, Rift's banes: war, dread, and death.

Yet the war had commenced without us. A tennight ago King Thyrse in his wisdom had sent a small force of men ahead across the Inward Sea to

1

make landfall at the port of Lanx; Sire Galan and his clansmen of Crux were among them. The king had called them a dagger. A dagger is your best weapon for treachery, and by treachery they were to pass the city's gates, for the king's sister, Queenmother Caelum, had allies to let them in. By now they'd taken Lanx or failed in their purpose. In two or three days, if the wind stayed willing, we'd know their fate, and therefore our own, whether we would face a sea battle and siege, or the grudging welcome owed to conquerors.

The ship was crowded. Idle foot soldiers sat on the rowing benches, dicing and quarreling for amusement. Mai and I had laid claim to a small space behind the mainmast, between great baggage chests fastened to the deck, and we'd stretched a canvas overhead to make a shelter. Two of her nine children accompanied her on this campaign: her only son, Tobe, and third-daughter Sunup to look after him. We all suffered from Torrent's hex, seasickness, which made Sunup listless, and Tobe fretful, and gave me a qualmish stomach. Mai suffered the most. She'd always seemed to me as strong as she was stout, and she was stout indeed. But her strength had dwindled quickly at sea, and I was more troubled than I was willing to show.

I sat up beside Mai and leaned against a baggage chest. She was white about the nostrils and her round cheeks had turned yellow as an old bruise. There was sweat on her brow despite the wintry chill in the air. She had her arms clasped over her midriff. She grimaced at me and said, "I think Mouse is trying to thump his way out."

I put my palm against the hard hill of her belly and felt the kicks of the child she carried within. A boy, Mai claimed, for the way he rode high, and she thought he'd come about the time of Longest Night, nearly a month away. She'd named him Mouse because she swore he had too much Mischief in him—Mischief, the boy avatar of the god Lynx, who goes everywhere accompanied by a scurry of mice. I knew she dreaded this birth, for her last child had been stillborn after a long and dangerous travail, and it seemed to me the name was a poor jest and an ill omen. But Mai's wit was ever on the sharp side.

I leaned over and whispered to Mouse, "Too soon, little one. Have patience."

"Let him come, I don't care," Mai said. "He'll split me in two if he gets any bigger. Besides, sick as I am, I couldn't feel worse."

"Hush." I nodded toward Sunup, who lay next to me with her head under a blanket. She was not yet eleven years of age, and such talk might frighten her.

"She'll know a woman's travail soon herself. Time she learned about it."

Tobe was cradled in a coil of tarry rope covered with old grain sacks, with Mai's old piebald dog dozing beside him. Now the boy sat up and began to wail. I took him on my lap and wrapped his cold feet in a fold of my kirtle. Mai had suckled him for two years and only just weaned him, and he still clamored for the tit. I gave him a bit of dried apple to chew, and hugged him. Spoiled or not, he was sweet enough to nibble on.

Sire Torosus came to see Mai, walking along the narrow gangway where whiphands paced to make the oarsmen keep the beat when the winds were not so obliging. He jumped down beside us, and the piebald hound bowed before him and wagged his mangy tail back and forth. Sunup and I moved over so that Sire Torosus could sit beside Mai. He was narrow where Mai was broad, and she was taller by a forehead. But if a man dared say to Mai's face that they were mismatched, she would wink, saying Sire Torosus was big where it counted. And when the man made some lewd boastful answer, as he always did, she'd chase him away with her raucous laugh, saying, "It's his heart that's big, lad—I wager yours is the size of a filbert, and just as hard!"

Sire Torosus put his hand on Mai's leg. She kept her face averted and said, "I beg you, go away. I'm not fit to be seen."

"You're too vain." He gave her a buss on the cheek, and she flapped her hand at him.

Tobe squirmed in my lap and reached out for Sire Torosus, who let him stand upright on his knees and use his beard as a handhold.

Sire Torosus said to me, "Is there nothing you can do for Mai?"

It pained me to have to show him my palms, empty of comfort. All my remedies, all my herb lore, had failed. I could cool a fever with my hands, but the hex of Torrent Waters was a cold, wet malady, and I was powerless to draw out the chill that had settled deep inside Mai.

Sunup asked her father, "Is she going to die?" She had the pinched look of fear.

"Of course not," he said, and I met his eyes for a moment.

I said, "I never heard seasickness was mortal, only that it made folks wish they were dead."

Sire Torosus said to Mai, "Won't you come to the cabin, my dumpling, and lie on the featherbed?"

He had a berth in the sterncastle with the other cataphracts and armigers of the Blood. Mai had told me she was made to feel unwelcome when she tried to stay there with the children. She touched his arm, but still she wouldn't look at him. "It's stifling inside. Not a breath of air that doesn't stink."

He sighed and gave Tobe back to me.

Fifteen years they'd been together, Sire Torosus and Mai. He had a wife, of course, and an heir of his Blood—just as Sire Galan did, who had married a year ago and promptly sired a son. But Sire Torosus was never long from Mai's bed, and they had nine living children to prove it. She was his sheath, and I daresay a truer wife to him than the one he'd left at home.

Sheath had a filthy sound in men's mouths, being another byname for a woman's quim, like mudhole or honeypot. But that was the name we went by, those of us who had taken up with a warrior of the Blood or a mudborn soldier and followed him to war, each of us sheath to a blade. From sheath to whore was but a little slip. Often it happened that a woman took a chance on some likely man who lured her with fine promises and caresses, only to find herself at his mercy, lent or sold to his companions. I'd taken such a chance, and it was my good fortune that Sire Galan had proved jealous rather than generous when it came to sharing my favors.

A two-copper whore, without even a blanket of her own, envies a harlot who serves only men of the Blood, who in turn envies a sheath who must please one man only, and above all the sheath of a cataphract such as Sire Galan, the most admired hotspur among the hotspurs of the army. I had merely to stand near him to shine by reflection. I didn't pride myself on this—to be eminent among the despised was still to be despised. But I'd chosen to be Galan's sheath and I would do the same if it were mine to do over; I ought to be brazen, and wear the word *sheath* proudly, and never flinch at it.

Why then did I suffer a pang of envy to see Mai with Sire Torosus, to think of their many years together, when my time with Sire Galan could be measured by the month? It was foolish of me. She might hoard in her memory years gone by, to be sure, but no more than I, no more than any sheath, could she store up years that might not come to pass. A warrior is a prodigal spender of his days, and not a miser of them.

I knew this, yet I went on as if Galan would live forever. He might be dead already.

But that thought was dangerous, it could not be borne or believed. I felt the bond stretched taut between Galan and me, anchored by a hard knot under my breastbone. I would know if that bond were severed. Surely I would know.

That night we huddled together under our cloaks, Sunup and I with little Tobe between us. The dog put his head over my ankles. I was weary, my bones ached, and I drowsed and dreamed. When I woke, the dream was gone and there was nothing left of it but the sure knowledge that I'd lost something sweet.

Wildfire

Tobe squirmed in his sleep until he twisted my old sheepskin cloak about him and pulled it off my back. Greedy boy. Now he kicked as if he were too hot, and I gently tugged the sheepskin away from him and covered us again.

We'd dallied autumn away in the Marchfield, preparing for war, and already the Crone had visited with her winnowing basket full of snow. Winter wasn't a fit season for campaigning, it was a season for making and mending. When I'd served in the Dame's manor, even the shortest days of winter had seemed ample: time enough for the Dame to weave a common jillybell in a tapestry, or for me to steep skeins of wool in a dyebath until the color sang. Time enough for the Dame's housekeeper, Na, to tell stories when there was a pile of stitching for our chapped fingers; time enough for singing the longest ballads.

There was sweet pain in recalling the hands of the Dame and Na busy about their work, for they were dead, and all I had of each was a finger bone that I kept hidden in a pouch under my skirts. They had raised me, a motherless child, so well that I never pined for the mother I couldn't remember. Now they were shades, each on a solitary journey, yet sometimes I called on them for counsel.

With numb fingers I untied the pouch from the cord around my waist, and I ducked out from under the awning and climbed to the top of a storage chest. While I'd slept, clouds had descended; they hung so low that the ship's masts scraped their underbellies, and we sailed through the narrow crack between sea and sky. Nothing could be seen of the full Moon but a faint glow. The three galleys of Delve sailed in close company, and beyond them the rest of the fleet was scattered over the sea. As we bobbed up and down, their lanterns seemed to blink, hidden and revealed by the endless swells. I had gotten used to the motion at last; just the faintest flutter in my belly, nothing troublesome.

I was as alone as I could be aboard ship, with only the sailors on watch and the helmsman high in the sterncastle. I took my treasures from the pouch: the two finger bones and Galan's pledge to me of a house and lands on Mount Sair, inked on a linen scrip that I kept folded in a neat knot. I'd turned my back on his gift when I chose to follow him, but I cherished it nevertheless. I tucked the scrip in my sleeve for safekeeping.

The pouch was a circle of leather fastened by a thong, and I loosened the drawstring and smoothed the pouch flat on my lap to show the divining compass painted inside. After my first divining compass had been destroyed in the fire that burned Galan's tent in the Marchfield, I made this one myself, using an awl and string to scribe the three circles, one inside the other, for the three kinds of avatars, male, female, and elemental. I'd crossed the compass with direction lines to divide it into twelve arcants, each the realm of a god. Then I'd labeled the arcants, painting the godsigns as neatly as I could around the horizon of the compass, setting the twelve gods in their places one beside the other in the same succession that their constellations appeared in the Heavens. I'd been pleased, in the making, to see how well the compass reflected the order of the world.

I held the bones in my palm: the Dame's was dyed blue, and Na's had a red tip. They were tiny things, these bones, the topmost joints from the pointing fingers of their right hands. Na's sister Az had given them to me, though it was forbidden to keep relics of the dead. She was a skilled diviner, but I'd seen her throw the bones only once, and after that had to find my own way with them.

No doubt it was selfish to ask the shades of the Dame and Na to tarry on their journey, and strive so hard to speak to me when I understood them so imperfectly. But I believed—I hoped—they wouldn't begrudge me an answer, for they'd been fond of me when they were alive. I closed my hand around the bones and whispered into the hollow of my fist: Will I see Galan again?

I threw in haste and the ship tilted, mounting the slope of a wave, and the bones nearly tumbled from my lap. I snatched them up before they could roll away, and cast again, three times in all, just as Az had shown me, the first for character, the second for time, and the third for the gods who governed the question and must be honored or appeased. I mulled over the signs, wishing—as often I'd wished before—that I had Az's knowledge of the avatars, that I might understand how each sign bore upon the others. They could not be understood singly.

The Dame touched Crux Heavens on the first throw, which I took to be her judgment of Sire Galan's character. In ancient days Crux Sun bore seven sons to mortal men, who founded the seven houses of the clan of Crux, and one of those sons was Sire Galan's forefather. So it was no wonder that with the god's Blood in Galan's veins, he partook of Crux's attributes. Yet of the three avatars of Crux—the Sun, Moon, and Heavens—I'd always thought Galan most akin to the Moon in his fickle nature. He'd given me reason enough to think so. Had I misjudged him? Perhaps he was indeed more like the Heavens: constant as the stars when he gave his word, and changeable as the weather in his moods. I prayed now for fair skies sailing to him, and a fair welcome when I arrived, but if he greeted me with storms, I was determined not to be daunted.

In the second cast the Dame landed on Hazard Peril, in the outer ring of the compass that represents the future, and Na touched the Heavens. Galan—the Heavens—in Peril. It was not as ominous as it sounded. If

Wildfire

Galan was in peril, he was still alive. And Peril could mean a shield against danger, rather than danger itself. Either way, I took the two signs together as good tidings, and I would have been content with that—more than content—if not for the third cast, for the gods.

Both finger bones landed in Ardor Wildfire, but they pointed in contrary directions: the tip of the Dame's bone touched Torrent Waters, and Na's touched Delve Will. It was common sense that I should pray to the Waters to permit my crossing, and to Will to protect Delve's ship that bore me. But I was uneasy that both the Dame and Na insisted on Wildfire, Ardor's most unruly aspect: capricious, greedy, and wrathful.

A sign so emphatic must be a warning, and I feared it was meant for Sire Galan. In the Marchfield he had sparked a discord between the clans of Crux and Ardor that had grown into a conflagration. King Thyrse had commanded the clans to satisfy their honor by mortal tourney, and put an end to the feud. Crux had won, and Sire Galan had made enforced peace with the clan of Ardor, but had he made peace with the god Ardor?

I had my own reasons to propitiate the god. Ardor had saved my life twice—or rather, spared it twice—and also granted me small blessings: a healing song from the firethorn tree, the knack of seeing in the dark, and the gift in my hands of drawing fire from fevers and burns. I was grateful; at times I was even flattered. And yet it was no great boon to become one of the god-bothered. I would rather creep the rest of my life beneath the notice of gods than receive more such attentions.

I thanked the Dame and Na for their warning, and sacrificed to the gods as they'd advised. I made a small cut on my arm and sprinkled blood on the deck, and prayed to Torrent and Delve. To Ardor Wildfire I gave a hank of hair from my forelock, burning it with a coal from my fireflask. The singed hair smelled foul. I prayed to Wildfire that Sire Galan be spared Ardor's wrath, for he'd done his best to make amends. Furthermore I vowed that when I got to shore, I would burn at Wildfire's altar as much myrrh as I could get for a golden coin, which was all the gold I had, and I'd see that Sire Galan did the same.

Before dawn the sailors began their daily commotion. I was too restless to try to sleep anymore in our little shelter, which was rank with sickness. I took Mai's pot to empty it over the side, and leaned on the rail behind the forecastle to watch pleats of foam unfolding in the ship's wake. I'd left my cloak behind with Tobe, and the wind twisted my gown and yanked at my headcloth as it drove us along.

They were a noisy lot, the sailors, always shouting. I'd heard some of them call their ship Jouncy, and name her a wanton and a slut; they said she was the fastest whore that ever lived, and the quickest to capsize for a likely lad. There was pride in their insults. Indeed the ship was hasty, and she moved like a whore who enjoys her business, side to side and up and down. Her body was lean and her prow was sharp and at the rear she was high and round. Bright paint made her look a bawd. Her sails were striped like a harlot's skirts, and bellied out as if she'd been gotten with child by the wind.

Between night and morning I'd found my sea legs, and I felt I was astride the ship, riding her. I leaned over the rail to put my hand on her flank as she plunged forward. I adored her just then, the trull, and I felt a kinship with her too, for she came from the Kingswood where I was raised. No doubt her great keel had grown there in a grove of ship oaks, in a tree patiently shaped into the proper curve by woodsmen with cables and stakes, over the course of half a hundred years or a hundred. Her planking was of larch and her three masts of fir. The shipwrights had made a new living thing from these felled trees, and now her sheathing and pegs swelled in the water, her mortises and tenons strained, and she moaned. She was as much a wind creature as a sea creature.

The Sun rose behind us and colored the sky and sea red. The clouds overhead had lifted, or perhaps they had outpaced us to gather in the west, where a dark shadow hovered over the sea; the Sun's light did not seem to reach there. We raced toward those clouds, or perhaps they raced toward us, and as we came closer they reared up thunderheads like a range of sky mountains, and their shadows turned the silver water dull as hammered pewter. The clouds let down a billowing gray curtain and the horizon vanished.

Our sailors hailed the other galleys of Delve, using their own sea language that even the foreigners among them understood, but I did not. There was a great bustle as oarsmen—half of them mud soldiers, for there weren't enough seasoned mariners in the fleet—ran out the oars. The whiphands played their shrill whistles and the ships drew farther apart. Sailors took down the huge mainsail and hoisted a small square one, so we ran with just the storm sail and the smaller sails fore and aft.

A sailor went by on his way up the ladder of the forecastle, and said to me, "You might ought to go below."

I said, "Will it be bad?"

"We're in for a bit of a squall," he said.

No doubt the warning was kindly meant, but I was too ignorant to be afraid. I found it exhilarating, the shrill windsong in the rigging, the changeable light on the sea. A priestess of Delve and her attendants were on the high deck of the sterncastle, chanting and shaking copper disks. Cataphracts and armigers of the Blood joined them in prayers to ward off the storm and call down Delve's blessings to strengthen the metal that held the ship together. Waves rose higher, sharp edged, with frills and streaks of foam. We came thumping down into a trough and cold spray doused me, and I shivered and licked my lips and tasted salt. The pigs and cattle penned on deck were restless, and in the hold mules brayed and horses thumped against their stalls.

I made my way back to Mai and found Tobe and Sunup sheltered in her embrace. The awning overhead was flapping and I took it down. Mai said, "We're going in," shouting to be heard above the wind. I took Tobe in my arms and he began to cry. It was hard for Mai to get up, and Sunup and I both braced ourselves to help her. We staggered toward the hatch just behind the mainmast, weaving between the rowers' benches and the wall of baggage chests.

Rift's wind betrayed us, vanishing in an instant. A wind came from straight ahead and the sails fluttered against the masts and sent us lurching back until I thought we might tip over. But the ship righted herself and slid sideways down the face of a wave. And now wayward gusts came from here, from there, and the ship flew before them, running wherever they'd have her go.

Bagboys and jacks and foot soldiers jostled in the open space around the mast, waiting to go down in the hold with the horses. Mai and her children entered the dark hatch, but I hesitated. We had reached the cloud curtain, and we passed through into a new realm of white and gray, the water dark as charcoal, the air filled with hard grains of snow that skirled around us, snow sprites turning widdershins over the deck and sea. The other ships had vanished. I think Mai called me to come below, but sailors had already lashed down the hatch cover.

I heard rumbling in the distance, a muffled roar I didn't recognize until it careened closer. Thundersnow. The whiteness around us flashed as if the Sun had winked. I thought of Na clutching me tightly during thunderstorms when I was little, for her comfort more than mine. She used to tell me thunder was the sound of Ardor Smith at his anvil, and lightning was Ardor Wildfire dancing, and the safest place to be in a storm was home by the hearth, protected by Ardor Hearthkeeper.

Thunder cracked above my head and rolled away from us, and I ducked without thinking. Lightning branched across the veil of snow like a white tree, and the sight burned into my vision so that when I closed my eyes I saw the same shape, a green tree against darkness.

The waves no longer marched by ranks, but heaved up in confusion and burst against the ship from all sides in a great froth. Oars were as useless as straws in the heavy seas. Drudges cowered under the benches, crying out at every thunderclap and covering their ears. The ship pitched and wallowed, and sometimes she managed to climb to the peak of a wave, and sometimes dove through an oncoming wall of water, and even sure-footed sailors fell and were swept across the canting deck; a few went overboard.

I clung to the ropes of a baggage chest, willing the ship forward. There were gods in this storm, Ardor in the thunder and lightning, Torrent in the churning waters, and Crux in the snow-filled sky, all of them hurling winds at the fleet. Did they mean to founder us? Or did they contend over whether we should be saved or destroyed?

I feared worse. I feared they took no heed of us, and waged a mock battle for their sport, and all my frail hopes, and the great ambitions of the king and his sister, Queenmother Caelum, and all these ships too, were merely kindling to be broken between sky and water.

I shook in dread, in awe—but something fierce in me was not humbled, it roused in answer to the storm's ruthlessness, so that I nearly laughed in the teeth of the wind. What did our insignificance matter, our brief lives? At that moment no more was required of me than to witness the gods storming, their vast discord. I couldn't regret seeing it, even if it was the last sight I ever saw.

The air crackled and I felt a touch, a hand stroking upward along my spine. My skin prickled everywhere and my hair stood upright. The storm split open with a wedge of light and sound, and a blinding whiteness struck the mast and reached for me.

CHAPTER 1

Thunderstruck

 didn't know where my limbs were. I had no edges between inside and out, I was a heaviness that swayed, plummeted. Was lifted, fell again. Nothing steady anywhere.

I heard shouting, but couldn't disentangle words from the crashing and rumbling and shrieking and roaring that filled everywhere.

Everywhere but here. Here was silence.

Wildfire

The silence. What was wrong about it, what was missing: breath, blood throb, heartbeat.

A buzzing in my ear. *They say you're dead.*

The buzz was intimate, it crawled in the whorl of my ear, so I knew I had an ear. *Buzz, buzz, buzz. Dead, dead, dead.* Left ear or right, within or without, I couldn't tell exactly.

It was the only voice that made sense in all the clamor. It must be true that I was dead, for I no longer understood the speech of the living. I never knew the dead had a language of their own.

The droning persisted. *Your heart forgot to beat,* it said.

I didn't recognize the voice, but I recognized its gleeful malice. It belonged to a man I knew well, though I had somehow mislaid his name. A man I detested. A man I had killed.

His was the only shade to greet me. I would have wept, but to weep takes breath.

Wildfire

If I was dead, I must go. I mustn't tarry.

I willed myself to rise. But my will had come undone from flesh and shade alike, and I couldn't move.

Nevertheless, something stirred within me, a small disturbance. And though this thing seemed weak, it found an opening in my heaviness and forced its way out. Was that my shade? That tiny frail fretful creature? How could it leave *me* behind?

Oh gods, no. It wasn't my shade. It was my last breath departing.

"Sheesdeadintshe?"

"Ithosheedbeburntup."

"Donstanthergawkin! Covererup!"

My friend knelt beside me and I knew her voice, and felt her great bulk near me. She dug her fingers under the corners of my jaw, and by her touch I felt my skin fastened to my skull, I knew the shape of my own face again. She said, "Firethorn! Cmoncmonbreathe! Iswearyorheartsbeatin."

I took in a shallow breath and I wasn't numb anymore. Ropes of pain tightened around my chest. I wanted to hold on to that breath forever, but I had to let it go.

The next breath was a long time coming. And the next.

Wildfire

I awoke. There was no part of me that didn't hurt. I wouldn't open my eyes. I feared what I might see, the confusion of it.

I swallowed. It was a victory to command that least little act.

A cloth settled over me, rough and scratchy. It was outside, I was inside, I was flesh again, and the boundary of skin between me and all else was raw, exquisitely tender.

I lay on my side, drawn up tight from spasms, taking shallow breaths because a deep breath was like tearing something open. I thought my friend was rocking me, rocking me so hard I feared falling from my bed. I heard her saying, "Podeahmydeahomydeahpodeah." As if I were a child. I opened my eyes and saw her broad face looming over me. A crystalline nimbus flared around her head. Words were given shape by her lips: "Poor dear!" Her daughter was there too, and the boy, his hand wrapped in his mother's dress. The sky flashed, too white, too bright. I closed my eyes and saw a green throb. Sound spilled over us and drained away.

The girl dabbed a cloth under my ear. It came away red.

There were men watching, jabbering. I should have been able to understand them. I was no longer dead.

My friend wiped her eyes on her headcloth. She took my hands between hers and began to chafe them, saying, "Yorhandsersocold. Podeah. Ithotardorhadkilledyu." It hurt, it hurt. I pulled my left hand away, but the right hand wouldn't answer to me. The shadows around the edges of everything flickered and closed in.

If I was alive, why did the shade still pester me? I heard him hissing, in a fury that he'd been cheated of my death; I saw him too, and he was nothing but a fly, a manfly, a shade so puny his mightiest shout was a mere *bzzzzz*. He darted about, circling my head. I almost laughed at him.

But when I slept, he was huge and heavy and his rage nearly swallowed me whole. He lay down on me backward, my bones a scaffold for his weight. He braced his knee against my throat and stoppered up my breath while he took his trophy, flesh from the woman's beard at my groin. He sawed away at a flap of skin covered with tightly coiled coppery hairs. He smelt of the sour sweat of a sick man. I choked and coughed and tried to push him off me. This happened again and again.

I awoke. He was still there, droning in my left ear. A sound I couldn't banish. I would have killed him again, if a shade could be killed. I moaned. The sound worked its way out of me, into the tumult of the wind and waves, and was carried away.

Above my friend's head I saw a tall tree with one broken branch. Petals of snow fell from a white sky and I was soothed by their cold touch on my brow. Perhaps I said, "What happened?" She leaned toward me, but when she spoke, I heard a different voice—I thought it was her unborn child. He said, "Wildfire ate you." I was delighted he spoke so clearly.

I awoke. This time it was dark. I was being rocked. A cradle. A ship.

My head was pillowed on Mai's thigh. She was there with me, she'd been there always when I awoke. She rested against a wooden wall with her head tilted back. For a moment I couldn't make sense of her face, seeing it from underneath: the soft swags of flesh under her chin, the darkness within her nostrils and her open mouth, the pale swelling cheeks that hid her eyes. Her breathing was loud, whistling.

I turned onto my back. I could move both legs, but my numb right arm didn't obey me. I picked up my right hand with my left and let it rest, curled up, on my belly. My other limbs ached with a bone-deep ache. I held my left hand before my face. The skin had cracked open between my fingers and along the deep creases of the palm, but the cracks were dry, not bloody.

The sea slapped the hull of the ship.

I looked at the tree. The mast. As the ship rolled, the mast tilted overhead, and the lopsided moon slipped through the net of rigging. Stars shimmied like minnows.

Mai's daughter sat nearby. Her eyes glistened. She leaned toward me and said, "Firethorn, aruthursti?"

Aruthursti. Aru thursti. Thursti. Thirsty.

I slept and slept, I slept so long that I was confused by the twilight I saw on awakening. Was it evening or dawn? The blushing sun hovered by the horizon as if undecided whether to sink or rise, and I, who had always known east from west without giving it a thought, didn't know which way we sailed as we sailed away from her. I was unmoored. I was on the ship, but where was the ship on the sea and when were we in the day?

The sea wasn't a place, it was a terrifying in between, without landmarks, nothing fixed. The waves went rolling away, nothing to them but motion.

The storm had chased the fleet in every direction like wolves among sheep. Suppose the helmsman too was lost?

I drank ale from a curved shell that stood on a silver tail chased with scales. I devoured the flesh of a porpoise, and wheaten pottage dyed gold with saffron, and then five minnows in pastry, one after the other, so many because they were so small. Still I was hungry. And so thirsty.

I sent my left hand under the scratchy blanket to make an exploration. I found smooth skin. I touched, naming throat and breast and nipple and navel and belly and cleft and thighs. Under my fingers the skin was roused to a sensation just shy of an itch. Hard to bear. A teasing pain. The right hand lay useless on my belly, colder than the other flesh. It didn't belong to me.

I was not clad in garments, but there were rags twisted around my legs and shoulders. The edges of the cloth crumbled between my fingers. Why? Charred. Burnt. My fingers sorted the rags into smooth thin and soft thick, which I recognized as kinds of fabric, though I could not at the moment name them. Fire had shredded my clothing. Why wasn't I burned too?

This I'd seen before, how one thing burned while another was spared, one lived while another died.

I found a burn on my left hip. The skin was raw and blistered, and as soon as I touched the wound, it insisted on hurting. I peeked at it under the blanket. The burn was shaped like the blade of a knife.

I remembered the storm. Thunder and lightning and snow and wind and waves and then nothing.

And all these memories of sleeping and waking, waking and dreaming, daylight and darkness and daylight—they were as jumbled as beads in a sack, and I couldn't string one after another. I had no idea of how long.

I loaded ashes in a barrow on a cloudy day, and trundled along the rutted path to the terrace just below the house. I meant to plant herbs there. The crows raised a fuss at me, jeering, *Whah! There she goes, there she goes!* I scattered ashes over the dun hay stubble. I noticed the roof of the house had a slate missing; I needed to see to that. My shoulders ached. I warmed my hands in my sleeves, and watched two crows play chase-the-wagtail. The air smelled of clean cold. Snow was coming.

My forgetfulness was vast, beyond reckoning. I lay awake in the dark, making an inventory of what I could remember.

I made lists of names: Firethorn, Sire Galan. Mai, her daughter Sunup, her son Tobe. Mai's cataphract, Sire Ferocious. The shade, the fly—Sire Rodela.

Wildfire

Ship, mast, sail.

I knew I was aboard a ship. I knew Galan wasn't here. Where was he?

I tried to conjure him beside me, the unruly hair falling over his brow, his eyes giving me a look. His eyelids tilted downward at the outer corners; sometimes this made him seem lazy or amused when he was not. Then there was the proud line of his nose, never yet broken, and the lips indented at the corners; the thin white scar under his jaw and his long neck with the beating pulse; the way he wore the laces of his surcoat loose so that the pleated gauze shirt spilled out at his chest and sleeves. I would untie a green-dyed leather thong and pull it free from the embroidered eyelets of his surcoat, and then untie the white cord of his shirt below the notch at the base of his throat. Under his shirt I would find skin paler than his face.

His strong long fingers, elegant but for the scars, the thickening at the knuckles. A warrior's hands. The hard palms.

I saw him by glimpses, pieced together, mismatched. My summoning didn't quell the longing, it made me restless, shifting against the hard planks under my hip. I touched my hand to my mouth, seeking the taste of his last touch.

It sometimes happens in battle that a soldier doesn't know he's been stabbed, and only later feels a weakness come over him and finds the wound in his side—so I'd been surprised to find I was smitten by Galan, after I lay with him behind a hedge on a festival night. *Easy to find, easy to forget,* we say of such chance meetings during the UpsideDown Days.

Galan refused to be forgotten.

A bird perched in the rigging and sang, *I live, I live, I live!* It was nothing but a small puff of feathers, the possessor of a single song that it offered to the wind with all its might. It was a long way from any shore. Surely it would stay with us until landfall rather than dare to cross so much water again. But it flew off, out of sight. I used to know what sort of bird it was.

The sun climbed behind us, and therefore we were sailing west. She sent a ray of light through a gap in the clouds and struck my eyes.

I remembered. We were sailing west and to war.

Tobe was crying and Sunup was trying to feed him porridge. Tobe and Sunup. Naming people fastened them to me, and fastened me to where I was.

So much noise nearly drowned out the buzzing of Sire Rodela. Everyone and everything talking at once, Tobe wailing and Sunup coaxing and waves mumbling against the hull and wind whispering through the rigging and drudges chattering and sailors shouting. My head hurt.

A man said, "Lukaterwillyu? Thotsheedsleepfrever." He was standing up, looking down on me. He was swaying—the ship was swaying, he was standing still, holding on to ropes. I picked at the noise to separate his voice from the hubbub. I understood the rough tune and tone of his speech: the rise and fall of question and statement, the nasal lilt of mockery, and even the humming undertone of fondness. Then, after a delay, I understood the words: *Look at her, will you? Thought she'd sleep forever.*

I knew that fellow; he was named Trave, and he was one of Mai's varlets, or rather he served her cataphract. But already others were speaking, more than one at once, and the wind roistered about and scattered their words out of reach.

Pinch said, "Didjasee howt jumptoer? Thlightning jumptoerboom!" and he clapped, "En thruerdown, thruercros thedeck. Sheotta bedead," and meanwhile the waves said, "Shushshushshush," and a gull said, "Aship aship plentitoeat," in a long fading caw overhead, and Mai said, "Leaver alone." She elbowed Trave out of the way and leaned toward me. "Canyu situp? Sit up?"

My limbs were feeble and slow to obey. My right arm trembled and refused to help bear my weight. I panted.

Mai said, "Can you hear me? I thought maybe you went deaf onaccounta you were bleeding from anear."

When I concentrated on Mai and watched her lips move, I could understand. Mostly. But it was laborious.

The blanket slipped and Mai pulled it up around my neck and over my shoulders.

I tried to speak. "What, what . . . what upended . . . what opened?" I knew just what I meant to say, yet I couldn't find the right words or the sounds to make them. Words seemed far away, and I had to travel toward them with slow, halting steps. This vexed me. I tried again. "What . . . hammered . . . hampered?"

Mai didn't seem to notice. "Lightning blew you out of your slippers—picked you up enflungu enufetcht up in a heap. You looked deadas dead, your clothes alburntintatters. I've never seen such a sight before and I hope I never do again. Nothing broken, praise the gods. You couldve split open your skull! But yortufasan old root."

Wildfire

I lifted my left hand, my obedient hand, and she pressed it against her cheek.

"I'm glad, Coz," she said. "So glad you're better."

I wanted to be glad. But I was afraid. I'd become a laggard, a simpleton.

I sat on a rower's bench and stared at the sea, the smooth swells that lifted us and passed on, and smaller waves that crossed the swells at an angle. Now and then three large waves would march by, one after another, adorned by whitecaps. Behind us a spreading fantail of ripples broke the surface of the water into blue and gray slivers of light.

After the chaos of the storm, it was soothing to see the distinct and orderly patterns of the waves, which reminded me of designs weavers made from the play of warp and weft, color and interval. Was this what sailors saw when they looked at the sea, did they recognize and name these patterns as weavers named theirs? Though I could not, just now, name one design among the many the Dame had so painstakingly taught me. The names were gone, and all that remained was the memory of the quiet in the weaving room, and the steady growth of order as the shuttle crossed back and forth between the warp threads.

There were ships about us with their sails full of wind. And coming nearer, bobbing in our wake, things that marred the pattern of the waves: drowned men, broken spars, an upturned hull black with pitch.

Mai tried to pull a garment over my head, one of her winter underdresses. I wanted to help, but my right arm was so weak I couldn't raise it above my head. Though I could twitch the fingers of my right hand, which pleased me so much that I wept, saying, "See how the little ones, the . . . the diddles . . . the fidgets—how do you call them?—the things that finger things, see how they fiddle now!"

Sunup and I could have fit inside Mai's dress together and left room for another. Even so, I was grateful to be covered, for it had occurred to me, somewhat too late, to feel shame at my nakedness. Mai hitched up the skirts about my waist so they wouldn't trail on the deck, for she was considerably taller than me, and she pleated the bodice, tying it about me with crisscrossed cords the color of new-minted copper. Such was her skill that it looked as if it were meant to be that way, or so she said with satisfaction, "And not as if you're a foul trust for roasting." She fashioned a headcloth for me from a scrap of the green wool dress I'd been wearing.

Foul trust? I puzzled over that.

Fowl trussed for roasting. Always this gap between sound and sense.

"I've no shoes to fit you," Mai said. She handed me a heavy cloth sack on a long cord.

"What's these things?" I could feel hard disks through the cloth.

Mai laughed. "Why, it's everything of yours I could find. I think I got most of the money you'd stitched into your hem and seams, all but what some light-fingered whoreson sowpricker of a sailor found first. But your girdle and all that you carried in it were destroyed. So you take this." She searched under her skirts and brought out an oilskin packet. "I had saved some for myself, but I shan't be needing it until after the child is born, and maybe by then you'll have found some more. You'll be wanting it yourself soon, I daresay." She winked and I took the packet from her.

I unfolded it and saw two handfuls of white, black-eyed berries. I thought I should know what they were, but I'd misplaced the meaning as well as the word. I looked at Mai.

"You don't know what they are?"

I shrugged. Mai tucked me under her arm and pulled me close. I rested against the great sloping shelf of her bosom. "Ah, Coz, poor dear! You gave me these berries. They're childbane, and you and I sold them all over the Marchfield to whores and dames alike, to keep them from conceiving. You truly don't remember?"

"Truly, truly, Mine . . . Mai, I mean." My throat closed up. "There are, there are . . . it's as if my find is full of halts, you see? My my empery is like my . . . drapes . . . the cloth thing I wore—all charred. It's holey."

She gave me a little shake. "You're upside down and backward now, but you'll get better. It was a gift, you'll see. Once the rumormongers get hold of the tale, everyone will know that Ardor Wildfire gave you a big blessed buss, that you're thunderstruck."

"You call this a . . . blissing? A besting?"

"The god branded your cheek with lightning and left you lopsided. A lopsided face is a sure sign of a cannywoman, and every harlot in the army will seek your advice, and be willing to pay dear for it too."

Mai had called me a canny before, and this time I didn't trouble to deny it; but why did she call me lopsided? I touched my face and discovered my mouth was sagging on the right. I pinched my cheek hard. "My face is just slipping. Sleeping. Surely it will wake!"

She said, "It comes out muddled, doesn't it?" She still had her arm around me. I pulled away, hearing mirth in her voice as well as sympathy. I couldn't bear to be laughed at just now.

Mai was a canny herself, I remembered that much, and she was lopsided too. I wondered I'd never noticed it before. The left side of her face had a smile of plain good humor, from the dimple beside the mouth to the crinkled crow's-feet around the eye; the right had a sneering upper lip and a shrewd gaze.

I stared at her with distrust, and she stopped smiling. Then all at once I saw her whole again, and saw her fondness for me, and no longer doubted it. I tried to tell her how grateful I was for the way she'd cared for me, always there when I awoke, and while I fumbled to speak she waited with a pained, patient expression. But the words were too distant, and I couldn't reach them. When I wept in frustration she kissed the back of my hand. "Never mind, dear heart," she said. "Never mind."

I awoke in the night to find a priestess leaning over me, guarding a candle flame with her hand. A gust of wind made wax drip on my arm. We stared at each other, the priestess and I. She wore a diadem of coiled copper wire over a wimple. She touched my unbound hair, like in color to the burnished wire, and then my left cheek. She muttered a blessing over me and went away.

I sat up gingerly. Mai slept on the deck beside me, her cloak draped about the peaks of her hips and shoulders like the folds of a mountain's skirts. I felt for the pouch I'd kept hidden under my kirtle, and then recalled that Mai had given me a cloth sack. I tugged it out from under my bodice and found the divining compass pouch inside the sack, nestled amidst the coins.

I tipped the bones into my palm, glad I hadn't lost them. I felt the touch of the Dame and Na. One placed her hand on my arm, the other on the crown of my head, so softly I could almost mistake the feeling for the caress of the wind. I wept for gratitude that they had not left me. And I wept for pity that they were dead, and I'd never see them again in this life.

I spread out the divining compass on my lap, and kissed the bones and cast them, and leaned closer to peer at the godsigns, to see which avatars the Dame and Na had singled out. And I discovered I could no longer read. The godsigns around the horizon of the compass were mere marks, no sense attached to them. The Dame had taught me to read, and with that gift she'd honored me and raised me above her other servants. I'd prized the knowledge, and now it was gone.

Sire Rodela's buzz had faded until I almost forgot to hear him. Now he began to whine in delight, louder, nearer, taunting.

It was a clear night. I looked up and searched for the godsigns writ in the stars by the gods, the constellations we copied in ink, making dots large or small according to whether the stars were bright or dim. The skyfield was so much more intricate than I remembered; I could find too many patterns, patterns upon patterns, and all meaningless.

If I couldn't recognize the godsigns, could I remember the gods and their avatars? I counted them on my fingers, starting with Ardor, though I couldn't tell which sign on the painted compass belonged to the god. First Ardor Wildfire. Then Ardor Smith. What was the third avatar, the woman? I couldn't remember, nor could I summon the name of another god. Wildfire had stolen my speech, the godsigns, and knowledge of other gods. Was Ardor so jealous?

I stared at the divining compass. How satisfied I'd been, when I painted those circles and lines, and inscribed each arcant with the name of a god, to think that I was re-creating within this small compass the orderly arrangement of the world. I might as well have tried to draw fixed lines upon the surface of the water. The tiny circle contained a vast deep sea, a place of currents and turbulence. Gods moved within it, nameless to me now, nothing to divide them, nothing to contain them. Uncertainty spilled outward from the compass, and I feared I would wander in this unmapped ignorance forever.

Warriors carried torches and swords and pikes through the streets of a town. The stuccoed buildings were three and four stories high, side by side and face-to-face along a narrow cobbled street so steep that in places it became a stairway. Painted wooden balconies were on fire above me, and flames and smoke and screams billowed through the fretwork shutters. A carved blue door burned and broke away from its top hinge. There were bonfires in the streets, heaps of blazing furniture with bodies discarded upon them. The stink of pyres.

I was little. I knew I wasn't supposed to make a sound, but I was sobbing. A linen chest lay open on its side, white cloth spilling into the mucky gutter. Down the street a woman sprawled on the ground. I couldn't see her face because her skirts had been pulled up over her head. Only her red hair was showing. Her bare legs and belly were smeared with blood. One knee was up, the other down. One arm was bent backward under her, the other stretched out, the palm open and empty.

Sparks and embers ate holes in the linen that used to be kept safe in the chest in the house. I watched a wisp of smoke forming above it. Warriors ran past me, making a joyous uproar that didn't sound human; they wore helmets, and their faces were hidden behind visors shaped like animal snouts. Wildfire loose in the town.

Wildfire

I fled the dream, and woke to find the uproar was real. Soldiers and sailors aboard ship were whooping and bellowing. The glad news spread throughout the fleet by way of shouts and drumbeats; three lanterns were lit on every prow. The men sent ahead had taken the town and secured the port. Lanx was ours.

It was early morning. The sea and sky ahead shone a luminous blue, divided, one from the other, by a dull uneven gray line. Land.

The sun sent low rays across the water, and the land took on color and shape. We sighted the walls and spires of Lanx, and as we drew nearer, their stone turned from gray to gold in the sunlight—a golden city on steep hills, held fast between two branches of a wide river on its way to the sea.

CHAPTER 2

Marked

arsmen rowed us into harbor. The passengers stared and pointed and exclaimed at the wonders of Lanx—the towering lighthouse, the quays lined with two-story arcades, the palatial gilded barges, the squalid hutboats moored side by side so that people strolled across the decks as if they were streets, the massive iron water gates that spanned the murky reaches where the river emptied into the sea—and all that was just the harbor, beyond which was a most marvelous city of bridges and towers, with houses piled so high that one's doorstep was another's rooftop.

Lanx was the first city I ever saw, and I couldn't endure the sight of it—or the smell either, from shoals of debris stinking of shit and tanneries and dead fish. I lay down under my shaggy old cloak and pulled it close around my ears.

To see was to be bewildered, and I was weary to my marrow of bewilderment. Curiosity had plagued and served me all my life. I hardly knew myself without it.

Gulls alighted in the rigging and jested and laughed their harsh, mocking laughs. I swear I could understand them nearly as well as I could understand people—which is to say, not well. As the fleet assembled in the harbor, sailors counted the stragglers to see how many ships had been lost to the storm. Foot soldiers and cataphracts alike wagered on whether the queen-mother's ships or the king's would be first past the water gates, for their precedence would be telling. The long day passed in gossiping and waiting, and I dozed, rocking in my cradle.

The whiphands whistled and oars dipped and rose with sparkling pendants of water drops, and we glided between the open gates. We turned from the broad river into a narrow stone-walled channel, and the hills rose up around us, close enough that a man looking down from his doorstep could spit on us. One man did just that. A boy on a drawbridge threw a handful of stones that skittered across the deck. Women watched us from small square windows, half hidden behind latticework shutters. Someone jeered. I cared for none of it. None of it. Only let me find Galan, let him be alive.

Mai's old dog settled down beside me and gave me a wistful look so I would scratch under his chin. In time we both slept.

Perhaps I was still asleep when we landed, for what I recall is a dream of streets and stairs, daylight and darkness. Pain was the one sure thing, the wedge splitting my left temple, and the rope twisted around my chest so that I labored to breathe. My arms and legs tingled and went numb. The hissing in my left ear went on without pause.

Aboard the ship sleep had been my healer; I'd slept and slept and each time I'd awakened with some small gain. I could move my right hand, and smile somewhat from both sides of my face, and understand speech without puzzling at it word by word. These small victories had misled me into believing that I was meant to live. Now the pains in my head and chest told me I'd taken too much for granted. Wildfire might yet kill me.

Mai said, "Getupgetup, we've found out where Sire Galan is quartered!"

I forgot to be glad he was alive, because I forgot I'd ever doubted it. I was fearful instead. Galan wouldn't want what lightning had made of me. Why would he desire a lopsided sheath, weak and muddled, too backward in mind, too forward in chasing after him?

I don't remember saying good-bye to Mai, but I must have done so. I left a warm room and struggled up steep narrow streets paved with crushed white shells. The ground seemed to tilt as it had on the ship, and I shuffled along afraid of losing my balance. It was dark down between the high walls, but above, the heavens shone the pure lapis blue of twilight. I stopped to catch my breath, and looked up to see doves fly across the ribbon of sky overhead as suddenly as if they'd been flung. I swayed, and a man let me lean on him. That was Tir, Sire Torosus's jack. He was long legged and impatient. They had sent five men to escort me to Sire Galan's quarters. I didn't think to wonder why so many.

Someone lit a lamp behind a high window, a square of yellow brilliance in a dark wall. I saw a woman silhouetted against the light as she closed the shutters. Wind dodged around corners and harried us.

We climbed many stairs in a tower. Sire Galan's room was cold and deserted. Tir and a cantankerous porter with a smoking torch went away and left me alone in the dark. I dropped my cloak in a heap by the door. Thick panes of glass, inset in the fletch-patterned shutters, silvered in the moon's radiance. The room was crowded with furniture, more than could be useful, and the tables and chairs had the delicacy and slender legs of the palfreys they breed for dames to ride; I was used to sturdier stuff. A bed with latticed walls stood on a platform three steps above the floor. Sire Galan's baggage squatted here and there, dark barrels and sacks and baskets. His camp cot had been unfolded in a corner.

I crossed the floor to a niche in the stone wall that served as a hearth. A clay statue of Ardor Hearthkeeper knelt in a smaller niche above it. Her name came to mind so easily now; I marveled that I could have forgotten it. Though her dress was glazed clay, her headcloth was made of real silk. One end of the cloth was draped over her face, concealing one eye and her mouth, for she is a keeper of secrets.

The spark, ever ready, is one of her many gifts to us. I took the flint from the statue's outstretched hands and kindled a small fire using apple wood I found in a basket. I stood unmoving before it, in a state of prayer no less prayer for being wordless, in gratitude for the warmth of Hearthkeeper's embrace, the loving touch of fire tamed and contained. I felt the constriction loosen around my chest, easing the passage of my breath. Fire curved around the logs, a veil of orange and blue, and flames pried their way under bark and licked out through every crack, and I watched as the wood was transmuted to garnets and rubies. Such beauty, I couldn't look away. Hearthkeeper whispered to me: *Burn bright, burn fast. Give what light you can, the rest is ash.*

Much later I heard the door open, and I turned away from the embers. A woman entered, carrying a basket overflowing with white linen. She set it down on Sire Galan's cot, saying, "Who are you?" She spoke in the High, but she rounded and clipped the words oddly. Her gown was thin as a harlot's, showing her nipples and woman's beard like shadows through gauze dyed the yellow-green of willow leaves in spring. Galan had given me a headcloth of that color—the green that signifies beginning—when he and I were new together. Had Sire Galan already taken a whore into his bed, or put another sheath in my place?

"Who are *you*?" I said, using the Low, the language of mudfolk, thinking she was vain to use the High. Did she suppose I'd mistake her for one of the Blood?

"What?" She spoke again in the High. Her face had not been unfriendly before. Now it was.

I tried the High this time: "Who are *you*?"

She pursed her lips and was silent. Her eyes were outlined with black ink and she had yellowing bruises on her face and around her neck.

I saw she wouldn't answer before I did. "I'm, I'm Firetorn. I'm Sire . . . Sire Galleon's grief—" I heard myself and winced. "No, that's the way wrong. I mean to say his his his . . ." I couldn't find the right word—or any word—so I made a lewd gesture that anyone could understand.

"Why don't you just say it—you're Sire Galan's codpiece, aren't you? Are you too proud?" The woman took a candlestick from a ledge above the cot and lit the taper, and came close to me. "You must like the dark," she said. "What's that, a birthmark?"

I touched my face. She was peering at my left cheek, but it was the right side that was lopsided. Perhaps I had a burn there, though it didn't feel sore. "No. I don't know. We were crossing in the swarm, there was riled ire . . . dire and dirdam everywhere and rumble thumping. It was thudder-bright . . . thunderbright, that's what did it!" I made a zigzag gesture and struck myself on the chest, pleased to have come upon the exact word I needed. "You see? Thunderbright!"

"Why do you talk that way? Are you a clack?"

"A what?"

"A clack. A dimwit."

I looked at her closely to see how cruel she meant to be, and saw she did make mock of me, but indifferently. If she'd been jealous, there'd have been more malice in it. Either she was sure of Sire Galan, or she was not his. I said, "So what are *you*? A . . . a horse? Not a horse, no, but one that men ride, any many men—a hole? Whole?"

"I'm not a whore, if that's what you mean." She crimped her lips together and shook her head. She lit another candle, and carried her small bloom of light to golden doves that perched in the branches of a tall bronze tree. She put fire in their open beaks and I saw they were oil lamps. She kept her back to me and her motions were as eloquent as her face.

Now we were both offended, and what did that serve? I said, "Nor am I a a dum . . . dimdolt. What happened to me—the thunderdolt is what's wrong. Blighting, brightening stuck me and killed me dead. But I woke up. Now my speak is tonguesy-turvy."

The woman turned and beckoned me to a chair near the bronze tree hung with lamps. I could see how, with some effort, she put aside her vexation. I sat, and she sat nearby.

"I am called Penna," she said. "I serve Sire Edecon—as his codpiece, I suppose. And his laundress." One eyebrow went up. I admired the bold black strokes of her eyebrows, arched like the wings of a shearwater, and how each could swoop and rise on its own. It was easier to admire her now that I knew she did not belong to Galan.

"Sire Addlecon? Who's that?"

"If you're Sire Galan's tart, how is it you don't know that Sire Edecon is his armiger?"

"But Sire Galant's . . . his man, you know the one, the man who fights besight him, on his shy side, his shield side—his, his . . . halibut, his hatbringer—that man is dead."

She laughed. "That's a fine way to put it. His halibut! His armiger is very much alive and upright, I can attest to it."

"Is it a new harbinger then?"

Penna shrugged as if she didn't understand. I could see she'd not been told of Sire Rodela, the armiger who'd served Sire Galan so badly. To think of Rodela was to hear him buzz, a sound lurking behind every other sound.

No doubt this Sire Edecon had been with the troop of Crux all along, but I couldn't place his name. Had he been armiger to one of the cataphracts who'd died in the Marchfield, and therefore in need of a new master? I was quite ready to dislike him if he was the one who'd injured Penna. I pointed to her bruises and asked, "Is that his?"

Her mouth turned down. She got up and moved away from me. She took a shirt from the basket and gave it a hard snap to shake it out. She draped it over the back of a chair, where it took the shape of a man with dangling arms. Soon the room was full of these pale phantoms.

Noise in the corridor, voices and footsteps.

I stood and braced myself against a table, my breath coming fast. Under my fingers I felt tiny ridges of marquetry on the tabletop, an inlay of ivory and shell. The footsteps stopped outside the room. I could smell the smoke of pitch-pine torches and see a thread of light under the door. The voices went on, two or three men talking at once, saying farewell, and one voice cut through the others, clear laughter on a rising note, unsullied by cares. The door opened and the room filled with men, shadows crossing the light. One of the men had torchlight tangled in the curls that sprang free from under his cap. Golden threads glinted in his surcoat.

The voices stopped abruptly.

Galan took a few more steps into the room. Someone raised a torch and put it in a bracket by the door. There were but four men, though they'd seemed a multitude: Sire Galan, his two jacks, and a man I supposed was Sire Edecon. I couldn't remember the names of his jacks, no matter that I knew the men well.

One straight look from Galan, and there might have been no others in the room. How could I have forgotten this look, this considering look, and how he could transfix me with it? He had a private smile hidden somewhere about his eyes, not worn on the lips for all to see. He seemed to take my measure, not to tally up my faults, but to savor what he held dear. What was his. What he might do. It was the welcome I'd hoped to find, and never counted on. For that moment I believed I was whatever he saw in me.

He said, "I met the Crux's ships. You weren't with them."

Perhaps he'd forgotten that he tried to send me away. I shrugged. I couldn't trust myself to explain.

Now he was grinning. "I thought maybe you'd come, because I know how you are—stubborn. You traveled with Sire Torosus's woman, is that it?"

I shrugged again. But I couldn't help smiling.

"I'll find out," he said, laughing, and crossed the room in a few long paces and pushed the table aside. I saw a new scar, still raw and red, just under the green dots of the clan tattoo on his cheek. He put his arms around my waist and pulled me against him and I felt a shiver and shock pass between us that left the sweat prickling on my skin. I'd felt that before when we touched, and now I knew it for what it was: lightning's caress, Wildfire surging in the blood. I tasted the wine Galan had drunk, his full lower lip, his curving upper lip, and I was a starveling at a feast, my kisses all hunger and gluttony, and his were the same.

Galan released me and took a step back. Now he saw me up close, and there was something more—and less—than gladness on his face. Upright furrows appeared over the bridge of his nose, and his mouth tightened. Such a slight alteration, to make such a difference.

"What's this?" He touched my cheek.

"Thunderbright!" I made the gesture I'd made for Penna, two fingers pointing and zigzagging through the air, striking myself on the chest. "On the way, the waves, the . . . swimming flying thing, the the the—"

"The what?" Galan frowned. It frightened me.

One of the jacks muttered, "She sounds a proper naught-wit, or half-wit, anyway." That was Spiller talking: I knew his name now and that of Galan's other jack, Rowney, just as I knew Spiller was fond of his own wit even when others failed to admire it.

Sire Edecon looked at me over Galan's shoulder. He had straight hair the color of wheat straw and a fair beard. His nose was crooked and flattened, probably broken more than once, giving him the rakish look of a man who likes a good brawl. He said, "Is it a tattoo?"

I covered my cheek. I couldn't imagine what caused such wonderment.

"It's no tattoo," said Galan. "I don't know what it is."

"It was thunderbright, thunderbright!" My voice rose. I was convinced I had the right word, and didn't know why they failed to understand. "In on the . . . float—the boat, the ship, there was a . . . harm, there was flicking everywhere."

"A harm? You mean a shipwreck?"

"No, a *harm*—with clouts and snow and will and terrible, terrible . . ." I gestured, showing the turmoil in the air.

"A storm?"

"Yes, and it licked me, you see?"

Galan flinched. It pained him to hear me speak.

"Perhaps she means lightning, Sire," said Penna, coming up behind Sire Edecon. She wasn't shy, that one. "I think she was struck by lightning."

"You were struck by lightning aboard ship?" He spoke slowly, as if he feared I couldn't understand.

I nodded. My face was numb.

"How can it be lightning? You aren't burned."

I looked down. Did he doubt me? Wildfire had marred me, made my speech foolish and my body feeble. Surely he could see and hear for himself that I'd been wounded.

"And you lived." He pulled at the buckles of his baldric, and Spiller came forward to help him. Galan gestured him away. He dropped the baldric on the table and the hilts of his weapons clattered against the inlaid tabletop: the greater sword, the lesser, the mercy dagger.

"Well, so—here I am," I said, gesturing to myself, trying to smile. "But I think my start stopped . . . I don't know. And and and when I broke up, I was all in a fuddle, a fussle—a muckle." I covered my mouth so he wouldn't see how my smile sagged on one side into a frown. So he wouldn't know how ugly I'd become.

Galan reached for me and I hid my face against his shoulder and neck. His surcoat was thick with embroidery and gold-wrapped threads. I took in the smell of him and began to cry. A judging self observed my wailing and whimpering, remembering how Galan had reckoned me unfit to be his companion in wartime—and now I was. Ardor Wildfire had made me so.

Galan held himself stiffly, as if he were angry. His arms were hard and confining. But one of his hands pressed the small of my back, and the other, under my shoulder blade, began to rub in small circles, as a horsemaster rubs a restive horse. At last I quieted enough to match the rhythm of my breath to his. I wiped my face on the abundant sleeve of Mai's gown.

Galan's voice was muffled against my headcloth. "I'll keep you safe if I can, even from the gods themselves."

The bed's high wooden walls were pierced with a pattern of stars and swallows. We climbed up onto the mattress, which crackled and smelled of some sweet herb, and Galan drew the curtain behind us and we were in a room within the room. He put his sword, unsheathed, on a narrow ledge along the wall of the bed, and hung his mercy dagger from a hook. A lantern inset with amber glass spilled light on white linens and a fur blanket and treasures heaped and scattered about: coins and golden cups and gossamer silk stitched with gems. I sat down cross-legged and picked up a coral box inlaid with a silver boat and silver net. The workmanship was so fine, I wondered if the artisans here were people like myself, or belonged to a race with nimbler fingers and keener eyes.

These luxuries were his plunder from the battle, I supposed. But the luxury I treasured was to be with Galan, and be alone with him. For too long we had slept in a tent with his men, and nothing to hide us from them at night but the bedcovers. Now he knelt with his back to me, his shirt hanging loose about him as he searched for something. I put my hand on the bare skin of his calf and wondered if it was still my privilege to touch him as I pleased.

Galan turned and said, "Here, this is for you." He held a mirror before me, and I misunderstood, thinking it a strange sort of gift to show me to myself.

I'd sometimes peered in the Dame's mirror, but she hadn't cared to be reminded that she was plain, and her bronze mirror had been tarnished and dim. This one had a disk with a flawless sheen. It seemed more a window than a mirror, as if I looked through glass at someone else. The woman looked so strange, so stricken. It was hard to find myself in her.

The right side of the face was a mask, with the mouth turned down and the eye hiding like a shy cunning creature under the drooping eyelid. On the left, the eyebrow and eyelashes were singed away, and there was a glitter of fear and surprise in the tiny black mirror of the pupil.

And on the left cheek, the mark that had caused so much wonderment: jagged lines radiated from a spot near the outward corner of my left eye, branching and branching again into finer lines, like frost feathers, like lightning itself, if lightning could be stilled. I touched my face, following the widest bolt, which went over my jaw and neck. The lines were as ruddy as burns, but they weren't raised proud to the touch like a blister or a welt.

I'd been branded as plainly by Ardor Wildfire as were the Blood of the god's own clan, who had Ardor's godsign tattooed on their cheeks as infants. I'd never seen or heard of such a mark; would it fade, or stay with me for life?

Galan watched me, and I wondered that he looked at me the way he used to do, though I was so much altered. I put the mirror facedown on the bed.

He tugged on the coppery cord Mai had used to bind up the folds of the gown, and the knot came undone at once. She was a clever woman, and I daresay she'd tied the cord just so, thinking of the untying of it. Galan smiled, saying, "Why are you wearing this? Where are your clothes?"

My mouth was dry. "My own was was—" I took off my headcloth, and my hair, released from the wool, crackled and rose around my head like a cloud. I spread out the cloth to show him that it was a scrap of the pine green dress he'd had made for me, and how it was tattered and charred.

"Gods," he said, putting his hands in my hair and pulling me closer, pulling me down onto his plunder. He lifted himself on an elbow and pushed everything aside. I found a dagger with a jeweled sheath under my back and laughed as I threw it away.

"Wait," he said, and he knelt and blew out the lantern, and I saw his prick standing upright under his shirt. But when he lay on his back in the dark he did nothing but hold me and stroke my shoulder. He tucked my head under his chin. The lamplight outside made its way through the pierced wooden walls of the bed, casting wavering stars and swallows with flickering wings over his white shirt and the bedclothes. Someone in the room beyond picked at a dulcet without making a tune.

His prick had softened. I put my hand under his shirt, on his thigh. "Why not?"

He muttered, "You're hurt."

I thought: *he doesn't want me now.* That was my fear, whispering in a voice like Sire Rodela's.

Whores had taught me how to be brazen; I'd heard them bantering about what to do if a man flagged. I would not be shy. With my fist and little nips from my teeth, I showed Galan I didn't want him to be too careful.

Galan gave a choked-off laugh and said, "You thief, you little thief!" and I didn't understand why he said it, nor did I care, for he turned to me, suddenly impatient. If I was bold enough to challenge him, he had an answer for it. I was swimming in the folds of Mai's dress, and he rucked up my skirts and pinned me down. I dug my fingers into his buttocks and felt his muscles harden as he pushed his way in. My quim was slippery and he slid in tight, and the breath went out of me. The bristles on the ridge of his jaw rasped against my tongue.

As he bore down on me, he said again I was a thief, the thief of his peace, and I knew he was angry after all at my disobedience, but it didn't frighten me. For once our moods did not quarrel; he wanted to take and I was of a mind to yield, or perhaps he wanted to give and I was ready to take, it was all the same. I was glad I could speak in the fluent language of touch. I tangled my fingers in the lattice and turned my head and let him ride, and gods, how sweet that was, after misspeaking and misunderstanding and missing him. He breathed into the ear I'd turned to him, his breath coming harsher and faster, and hidden in it the sound of my name.

*　　*　　*

Wildfire

Afterward we laughed that we'd been so hasty. By then the lamps and candles were out in the room beyond the bed, and we saw by hearth glow and moonlight. I slipped out of Mai's dress and pulled the money sack over my head. Galan took off his shirt. He had a bandage on his back—I'd felt it under his shirt—and I asked how bad the wound was, and how he'd come by it. He said it was nothing. Chance had looked out for him in the battle, and so had Sire Edecon, who'd fought commendably well.

Galan was too offhand. I remembered how he used to brag of his deeds in tourneys of courtesy, and wondered if he found something distasteful in boasting now that the killing had started. I didn't ask questions where questions were unwelcome, and so I banished what I didn't care to know. It was easily done.

He had bruises and nicks in plenty, and I could match him, for when the lightning had hurled me across the deck, I'd landed hard. Besides the new knife-shaped burn on my hip, the strike had reopened old wounds, the burns on my back and shoulders I'd gotten when Ardor's men set fire to Galan's tent, and the flayed strip at my crotch where Sire Rodela had taken his trophy of flesh and hair. The scabs had split open, and likewise the pinkish new skin growing under the scabs. Lightning had searched out my raw places. I hadn't felt the old wounds amidst the pains of the new, until Galan made too much of them.

I lay on my stomach with my head pillowed on my arms, aching everywhere, and all my sinews seemed tightly wound around the spindles of my bones. Galan sat beside me and stroked the ridge of my spine, and slowly the tightness eased. His hand stilled, resting on the small of my back. He said, "I shouldn't have tried to send you home."

"Don't again," I said.

"I thought you'd be safer there, without me. I began to believe Chance wanted too much for the luck she gave me, that she meant to take your life in exchange for preserving mine. But I think—"

"What?"

"A gift from a god is never without price, but to refuse a god's gift—that too has a price."

Hazard Chance: I remembered her now, a wooden statue on an altar in the Marchfield, clad in russet paint. She wears a blindfold to dispense good or bad luck, but everyone knows she peeks from time to time, and loves a bold man as much as she despises a cautious one. She's partial to redheads too, that's why Sire Galan had taken me for his sheath after the UpsideDown Days—he thought I was a talisman, a token of her favor. That was an old hurt, one that should have healed long ago. Now it pained me again.

When Galan had left me behind, he left behind his luck. So he had believed.

He crossed his arms, making fists of his hands. I reached for him, but he raised his left hand to stop me. I saw a brief flicker of a mocking smile. "It seems the gods taunt us. You're not Chance's gift after all; Ardor, the god of my enemy, has claimed you—claimed you for all the world to see."

"*I'm* not your empty." I caught his hand and brought it close, for I'd seen a mark in the center of his palm, a russet tattoo about the size of my thumb: .ˑᵛ

"What's this?"

"An offering," Galan said.

"But what is it, what does it say?"

"I thought you could read."

"I could, but now, now no more . . . I know it's a a . . . baudkin, or or knotsign—"

"Godsign?"

"Yes, that's it—godsight—but to me it seems just notsense. So? What does it say?"

"Ah. Before the battle I made a promise to Hazard: I dedicated my left hand to Chance and my right to Fate."

He let me pry open his right fist. I leaned over his palm. Inscribed on his skin were the lines with which he was born, minute and delicate whorls, and the creases and calluses he'd made by his deeds, by years of grasping weapons and reins, taking and letting go. What was this labyrinth in his palm, if not a map of what he was born to do and what he had chosen to do? And at the center of the labyrinth, the godsign of Fate. I recognized it now, recalling how Hazard's stars had always looked to me like a skein of geese in flight. The wavy line underneath meant an elemental avatar: ⸫

I knew there were syllables to go with the signs on his palms. I couldn't recall them; reading was still denied to me. But Ardor Wildfire had been merciful and had restored the god Hazard to my memory.

I looked up to find Galan watching me with one eyebrow cocked. A chill raised gooseflesh on my arms. A dedication, he called it, but it seemed arrogant to me, as if he claimed to deal Fate with one hand, Chance with the other. And besides, it seemed almost a womanish thing to do, marking himself with the indelible sign of another god, the way a dame receives the godsign of her husband on her cheek when she marries outclan. He'd courted Hazard Chance a long time—did he mean to wed her now? She might smile on his presumption. She does love a dare.

I couldn't risk a quarrel, being without the means to speak my mind. Instead I asked—and I meant it to be sharp, though it was blunt by the time

Wildfire

I finished—"Where is the other, the third thing of the god, the third . . . vanity, avanitte? Is the sign on your . . . prink, your prankle there? Hmm?" I pointed to his dangle.

He grinned and reached for his longsword, a new sword and a fine one, with a hilt covered in pebbled hide and ornamented in golden fish. He turned the blade to show me the engraving of Hazard Peril's godsign: ⸪ The upward slash of a male avatar was a deep gouge that marred the otherwise perfect steel.

Galan put the sword back on the ledge beside the mattress and I scowled at him. "So why? Have you become a beast now? No—I mean a prill, a priest. Do you claim to do dog's bidding?"

"It isn't a claim. It's an offering." He looked down at his hands again, as the right one concealed the left. His grin faded. "I offered Hazard my hands and my blade, to use as the god wills."

I said, "How will you know?"

"Know what?"

"What the goad wills?"

I lay listening to Galan sleep; sometimes his breath came quickly, sometimes slowly, so that I held my own breath waiting for it. The wooden cot in the room beyond creaked as Sire Edecon coupled with Penna, and she moaned, a soft helpless sound that could have been distress or pleasure. I doubted it was pleasure.

Later, scurrying thoughts and a fierce cramp in my leg drove me from the bed. I pulled Mai's dress over me and opened a tall shutter and found it was a door leading to a small wooden balcony that clung to the masonry of the tower. The balcony walls were of spindles and lattice painted several shades of green. I looked down into the branches of a cedar that gave off a spicy fragrance. I'd never been in a building taller than a tall tree before; how had they raised the huge stones so high? Far below me were walled courtyards and gardens. Moonlight made quicksilver of water confined in stone channels, the brightness cut by dark bridges.

I held Sire Galan's gift, the mirror. I tilted it this way and that, and caught the reflection of the moon hovering over the city and the sea. The gift was a treasure, valuable for the silver alone, and more precious still for the superbly cast handle, a fox standing on hind legs, holding the polished disk between outstretched forepaws. Na had told me a story about the fox—I remembered it now—she said Crux Moon was jealous of his sister the Sun, and tried to steal her light by making a mirror of his face. He polished his skin, taking off one dull layer after another to get to the bright silver underneath—but he polished too well, until the fox he is inside showed through.

41

And once again the moon was the Moon, Crux Moon, and I saw the fox in the dark smudges on his bright face. It helped to have a story, even a simple one told to children. It put the god Crux back into Sun and Moon, and filled the Heavens with import. Crux was Galan's clan, and Crux the god-sign on his cheek.

Now I had Ardor, Hazard, and Crux, and surely the other gods had not withdrawn from the world, it only seemed to be vacant of them. Soon Ardor might permit me to recollect them all.

This hope was perilous. It must have been the feckless Moon who made me so imprudent as to think I might be healed, and speak again as I used to when thoughts and words had been entwined, when often I discovered what I was going to say in the act of saying it. I wondered at the wealth of words I'd owned before, without counting myself rich. Now I lacked two words to rub together that made sense.

Impoverished in words, impoverished in recollection, but not impoverished in mind, that was one mercy Ardor had shown me. The face in the mirror was not exactly mine, but the self within, however injured, was the same. Was me. A ceaseless river of thought and feeling still flowed within me, even without words to channel it, even though it was dammed up when it came time to speak. But the river was unruly now, a turbulent flood that cast up imaginings and the wreckage of memories and dragged them under again. And I was awash in it, a surge of hope one moment, despair the next. Or fear.

As now, in bed again, I lay rigid alongside Galan, hands fisted, jaw clenched, sinews taut, while dread swelled up huge in me, crowding out my breath. "You are not one of Hazard's," Galan had said. "Ardor, the god of my enemy, has claimed you." Would he keep me now that he no longer believed I was Chance's favorite? He had other reasons to care for me, I knew that, but I saw how he winced when I mangled words. So I must speak less.

I turned away from Galan, and he turned with me in his sleep and put his arm over my waist. I took comfort from his touch. And I thought, what was this terror of mine but a visitation, another god rediscovered, an old acquaintance? Having no body of its own, Rift Dread makes free of ours.

On and on I endured the passage of the night. I was adrift on a river of thought that flowed toward the bountiful ocean of sleep, but I never reached that ocean, and all about me was salty water, and I couldn't slake my thirst.

CHAPTER 3

Oracle

e were in the war now, yet the day dawned very peaceable and ordinary. Spiller and Rowney were up in the twilight before sunrise. I'd waited a long time for someone to stir.

Spiller and I weren't friends, but we were allies of a sort. We'd both hated Sire Rodela. I'd ignored Spiller's little thefts from Sire Galan and he'd treated me tolerably well, considering I was a woman and his master's sheath, and therefore both below him and above him. We had the habit of honing our wits, each on the other's tough hide. But my wit was blunted now. I said a good day to him when he arose, but it came from my mouth as dog day, and when I set out to chaff him for sleeping late, I called him a slayabed instead of a layabout. He bested me easily, and made me laugh against my will.

Today was a Peaceday, the one day of rest in a tennight of labor, but there were some tasks that couldn't be shirked. To prove I could still be useful, I went to fetch water from the courtyard fountain to fill the barrel beside the door. I descended the winding stairway, which had uneven stone steps worn smooth and slick in the middle, only to find that I'd forgotten the leather waterskins. I climbed back up and forgot the chore altogether until Rowney reminded me. He went downstairs with me to see I didn't misplace myself too.

I was ahead of him as we climbed back up, carrying the sloshing waterskins. I stopped to rest, for with every breath came a sharp pain under my ribs. When I turned around I caught Rowney looking at me. He ducked his head and his ears turned pink. "It's too much for you, climbing all these stairs," he said.

"Let me just . . ." I sat down and panted.

"The mark is going away." There was worry and wonderment in his face.

Spiller cooked heavy frycakes of yesterday's porridge, standing close enough to the hearth for the grease to spatter his already filthy jerkin. His hair was the dun color of old thatch, and like old thatch it stood out every

43

which way. He tasted a bit of frycake and wrinkled up his nose. "Faugh! They must feed fish to the pigs, because even the bacon fat tastes of fish. And nothing but stinking fish sauce for seasoning."

Despite Spiller's complaints, the frycakes were delicious, and I ate as though I hadn't eaten for days. I was surprised the smell of the food didn't awaken Sire Galan and his armiger, but they slept on.

I watched the Sun emerge from the sea and climb above the horizon. The city walls turned rosy and streets ran blue with shadows. Spiller told me this tower belonged to the clan of Crux, which was plain enough, now that I noticed the designs customary to the clan: songbirds woven in the borders of tapestries and inlaid on the backs of chairs; fletches and stars in the lattices. The style was different, the patterns familiar.

On other hills there were other towers. One of them was burning, blackened, the top gap-toothed, as if stones had been pried out and cast down. Gray smoke plumed up and a wind from the sea took it inland. I stared at the broken tower, thinking of a room such as this one, but with a dead man and woman in it. That I could see it so clearly didn't make it true.

Pain set upon me, sharp and sudden. The tower swayed like a ship. All I could see were eddying sparks and cinders, all I could hear was Sire Rodela's rising drone. I groped my way to a chair and sat bending over, my head down by my knees.

Rowney said, "Has she fainted?"

Spiller said, "She'd better not spew. I'm not cleaning up after her."

I straightened up. The pain was bearable now. Through the tears, everything looked watery, sparkling.

"What's the matter?" Rowney asked, coming to my side.

"I don't know. A sudden rain here, a pain here in my tempest." I held my forehead and rocked. "It's such a, such a . . . torrididdlement, a torment, torrent weeping."

Spiller laughed, saying, "Pay no mind to what makes no sense."

Rowney said, "Torrent weeping, there's sense in that."

"Maybe," Spiller said, "but it's no more than everyone knows."

I wiped my face on the tail of my headcloth. Penna swam into view in her sheer green shift, and a bluish corona surrounded her. I hadn't heard her get up. She came quietly on bare feet, with her black hair still uncovered. The dark lines painted on her eyelids were smudged. "What are you saying?" she asked in her strange accent. "What is wrong?"

"Such airs she has," Spiller said, "always talking in the High."

Rowney said, "They don't any of them use the Low, hadn't you noticed? I don't believe you speak it, do you, Penna?"

She said, "What?"

44

"See."

"Indeed I do see. Even the drudges here think they're high and mighty," Spiller said.

"What?" Penna knew they were talking about her.

Spiller began to grin. "Look at the tits on her, will you? She's not as scrawny as some I could mention. When Sire Edecon's back is turned, maybe she'll—"

"If you don't lock your tongue behind your teeth, I'll do it for you," Rowney said.

"Oh, you act the prig now," Spiller said, "now that *she's* here. But you'd have been in line if Sire Edecon hadn't come along, don't pretend otherwise."

I sat hunched in the chair, blinking. The pain ebbed and my muscles unlocked. But there was still darkness in the room, or in my eyes. Penna moved away, and in her bright dress she receded like a lantern carried into the distance. She approached again and gave me a cup of water that tasted of brine.

I thanked her in the High. I hadn't understood, until Rowney said so, that the mudfolk here in Incus lacked a language of their own. I pitied them. Where we came from, those of us who worked closest to the Blood, the house drudges and horse soldiers, were apt to slip between tongues when we spoke amongst ourselves, two words in the Low, one in the High, according to what sounded best. The Low was a handy way to hide secrets when masters were in earshot. Though Sire Galan understood it rather too well.

Penna glanced out the window and turned away from it, her face hard and still.

"Who is that?" I asked her, pointing at the tower to show what I meant.

"That's the keep of Torrent," Spiller said in the Low. "Where we had the battle."

"What happened in the fright, in the . . . fray? Sire . . . Sire Gladden wouldn't—he never said. Was anyone cost?"

Spiller said, "We didn't lose one, not one cataphract."

"Two armigers were slain," Rowney said. "One was Sire Fanfarron's and the other Sire Pava's. Also the jacks of Sire Gavilan, Sire Vejamen, and Sire Farol." He didn't name the dead men, but their masters, so that the shades wouldn't be tempted to linger, to overhear what was said about them.

Sire Pava was the Dame's nephew, and he'd been my master after the Dame died; I knew his armiger well, though I couldn't for the moment recall his name—he was the priest in our village before he became Sire Pava's toady and armiger. I wouldn't lament him. As for the other dead, neither their names nor their faces came to me. It was as if the battle had not taken place, and there was no one for whom I need grieve.

45

Yet it had taken place. The wind was from the sea, and carried to us the stench of the burning tower. I asked, "What of them? The ones there?"

Rowney said, "They're gone."

"What, gone? Where?"

Spiller answered me with a gesture, drawing the edge of his hand like a blade across his throat.

"Spilled?" I said.

"You could say that."

Penna scraped a burned frycake onto a wooden plate. She didn't eat with her fingers, as we did, but delicately, with the tip of a small knife. I wondered she didn't cut her tongue. She watched us warily. Sire Rodela was getting louder, shriller; I think he delighted in our meanness in speaking so that Penna wouldn't understand. But wouldn't it have been worse if she knew what we were saying?

Rowney sat down with Galan's helmet in his lap, and buffed the visor with a doeskin. His face was vacant, as if he'd gone into hiding behind it. "It was an old feud, see? Very bitter. It was mostly between the clans of Crux and Torrent, but the city wasn't safe for anyone, especially when other clans started taking sides. So they all raised walls around their keeps, and built these watchtowers—and when one clan made their spire taller, all the others did the same. But one side couldn't get the better of the other, not until we came along. Queenmother Caelum said the only way to make peace in the city was to destroy Torrent's holdings in Lanx, and make sure there was no one left alive to carry a grudge."

"Even the—even the vermin?" I could see by Rowney's puzzlement I didn't have hold of the right word. I pointed to Penna and myself and said, "The . . . wifemen?"

"Women too," he said. Spiller grinned at the muddle I'd made; I would have laughed myself, in disbelief, if not for the look on Rowney's face.

Spiller said, "We left the maids so the queenmother could marry them off as prizes. Divine Hamus had to prick them with his thumb to make sure of their maidenheads. They should have given the task to a man who knew how to enjoy it. Though they're slippery little minnows, not a proper woman among them." His grin wavered. It was a sham anyway. He wasn't as hard a man as he proposed to be, not yet.

"And the dodges of the keep—the . . . grudges, the drudges? Them too?"

"If there was no use for them. *She's* one of the lucky ones. Sire Edecon took a fancy to her." Spiller nodded toward Penna. Perhaps Sire Edecon wasn't to blame for the bruises on her face and neck; maybe he'd saved her from someone else.

Wildfire

Sire Rodela seemed to revel in this talk of killing, and he filled my left ear with a pulsating, needling whine at the thought—which I couldn't help thinking—of some man having his way with Penna while others, maybe Spiller, maybe Rowney too, waited their turn, meaning to kill her after. I cupped my hands over my ears and he was just as loud. I wondered no one else heard him.

Rowney said, "Their enemies did that, the clan of Crux in Lanx. Them and the queenmother's Wolves. It wasn't us."

"I did my part, I don't know about you," Spiller said. "I was after them like a ferret into every little hidey-hole."

Rowney looked at him with disgust. "We did some killing. They did the murdering."

"You should've seen Sire Galan," Spiller said. "He's like a fire when he gets going. They couldn't douse him!"

I rubbed my temples, for there was a circlet of pain around my head. "Aren't you afaird? She said spill them all, so there'd be none left to fardle a a grutch, a grouch. But what of . . . Current?" I wasn't sure what to call the god, but the names of its avatars—the Sailor, Wellspring, and the Waters—came to me unexpectedly, like coins found in the street. "Don't you fear revenys?"

I spoke in the High this time, so Penna too could understand, but it might as well have been a foreign tongue. Spiller twiddled his lower lip, making mock of me. Rowney looked uneasy. He was a brave man in a fight, but wary of me. He'd decided I was a cannywoman after he found out I could see in the dark; what must he think of me now?

Penna stared, her black brows drawn together. I tried again. "I don't see how they darst, our kind, our king and queenmocker . . . Careless . . . Callous—ah, you know her fame, I can't say it. How dared they send our flight across the flat, the wet flat, the Wasters, even as they attacked Torment's clay? No wonder the god sent a, a a . . . snowbone . . . and then it was not flat, the wet—the rivers, the wavers, the deep steep—they highed up," and I showed them with my hands how the waves had risen up all around, tall as hills, and fallen upon us, "and and swept the men who man the . . . soars, swept them underboard, and fathomed many sheep."

Spiller said, "What are you fretting about? I heard there were but five ships lost in the storm. And the battle is won. The gods smile on a victor, they say. Besides, we have Blood of Torrent in our army too, as pure as any here in Incus. Why shouldn't Torrent favor us?"

I couldn't think of how to answer him, for I was puzzled by what I used to take for granted. It was long, long ago that avatars of the twelve gods had walked in human form among the mudfolk of Incus and chosen mates;

from those unions had sprung the twelve clans of the Blood. It was not so long ago, but still a long time as men count it—six generations—that an army of the Blood left Incus to conquer Corymb, the land where I was raised. Now the descendants of that army returned to Incus as invaders. Queenmother Caelum had invited our trespass so she might take back the rule of Incus from her own son, whose name I couldn't at present remember. Prince Craven, was that it? Surely not.

I found it bewildering that one branch of the Blood would fight another, no matter that they were cousins six generations apart. But I was more confounded to learn that the clans of Incus were already at war among themselves, fighting old feuds and contending over whether Queenmother Caelum or her son should rule the kingdom. I daresay I should have known this; had I known it before the lightning, and forgotten?

It struck me now, and perhaps for the first time, that a war between mother and son was unnatural. Surely the gods found it abhorrent. Or were they drawn by this contention—mother against son, kin against kin, neighbor against neighbor—to contend against each other, or even within themselves, avatar against avatar? Perhaps Wellspring would aid one branch of the clan of Torrent, and the Sailor another.

No—the gods didn't fight our battles; we fought theirs. Wasn't that the way of it?

I said to Spiller, "That was no batter, what was done over there, in that burning terror. It was a slatter, a a . . . slayer. Slaughter. Ill begun is ill done, and I don't belie that it, the god—that Portent, I mean—will be appleased by a few bodes, boats. You mark, you mark . . ." I bent over in my chair, gripping my head, in torment now from the headache and the high ceaseless whine in my ear. "A water spite, wife, is a a . . . Blood strife, a Flood strike."

Spiller raised his hands and said, "Enough of this stuttering and muttering. I can't be bothered." He turned his back on me and stalked away. He pulled a side of bacon from a sack, and began to slice it for Sire Galan's breakfast, holding the slab against his chest and pulling his knife toward him so the bacon curled.

Penna asked Rowney, "What is she saying?"

I hardly knew. My mind had snagged on the thread of a notion, and I couldn't let it go, I must follow where it led: Galan entering a room such as this one with his sword drawn, with Sire Edecon at his back, maybe Spiller and Rowney too—and a naked man starting from his sleep in the lattice-walled bed—a round-shouldered woman with bedclothes clutched about her, choking on a scream—Galan striking quickly, once, twice.

I saw this bright as a memory, but it couldn't have happened that way, because in a time of feud no one sleeps without arms at hand. So I imagined it again, another way, with the man reaching for a sword that hung on two pegs attached to the lattice. He wouldn't have died without drawing the blade from its jeweled sheath. And where were his servants? Lying outside the door, where they'd been cut down. Spiller stooped over one, fingering the hem of his tunic, looking for coins.

Shouts and cries should have awakened the couple. Why then was the man so startled? Why did the woman stare in disbelief as her husband was struck down, as Galan turned her way? Surely he wouldn't have killed her.

This much I was sure of: blood on Galan's blade and gauntlet. Blood spattering his silvered visor, a mask made to match Galan's face, but with a blank serenity of countenance most unlike Galan—the visor held in the gaping beak of his helmet, shaped like the head of a gyrfalcon.

In a room like this one he'd picked up a coral box from a table, a round box decorated with a silver boat and net. He'd raised his visor and opened the lid to smell the unguent inside. He'd given it to Rowney to carry in a sack slung over his shoulder. He'd gone on to the next room and the next. I saw him running up the winding stairs of a tower, nearly out of breath. Sweating. He'd left his visor up. On his cheek he had a cut shaped like the sickle Moon.

Sire Galan rose late, and blamed us all for letting him sleep too long, as if we should have known his mind. Before he put on a stitch of clothing, he ate a frycake standing up and washed it down with a swallow of ale. Spiller scraped his jaw with a sharp blade and rubbed his face with a pumice to smooth away the stubble, and then Galan stood on the balcony and splashed himself with water from a basin. He called for Sire Edecon to get out of bed and stripped the covers from him. Sire Edecon groaned and turned over on his stomach. He was a burly man, and the heavy muscles of his back and buttocks were smoothed over by a bit of fat. Sire Galan was lean, with broad shoulders and narrow haunches; the cords of his sinews and threads of his veins stood out under the skin.

Galan demanded a clean shirt and hose, and where were those new boots of his, and the surcoat with the foxtail tippets at the shoulders? Spiller and Rowney rooted about in the baggage, which had arrived by ship the day before, and Spiller cursed the misbegotten sod who'd packed it in his absence. He found a boot here, a prickguard there, one of Galan's leggings missing and the other boot amongst the tent fittings. Rowney found a pair of my slippers in a sack with his saddle, and I smiled to think of Galan's horsemaster tucking them away for me.

The jacks helped Galan dress. They put on his new hauberk, plundered from Torrent, no doubt, for each of its fine steel links had a small crescent of colored enamel, so that the whole shimmered with rainbow scales like a colorful fish.

I sat swaddled in Mai's gown, feeling useless. The swimming dark that had come over my vision had faded, but the world still seemed dim and flat. Except for Galan, giving off brightness.

He came over and stood behind me. Hidden from the others, he teased a lock of hair out from under my headcloth and wrapped it around his finger, and when he tugged on the hair I felt it to my roots. He said, "What shall Firethorn wear? Not this rag." I could tell he was smiling by the sound of his voice. He went to the bed, and turned around with a gown of gauze I'd noticed the night before. It shaded from azure at the shoulder to cobalt at the hem, and tiny gems were stitched to it like stars against an evening sky. The colors were of a brilliance that could only be achieved on silk. I'd never worn silk before.

"Wear this," he said.

"I'm not in that," I said.

"Why not?"

I mustered the only arguments I thought he would hear. "It's . . . blood, bile—it's not, not clean." I meant to say blue and not green.

"Not clean? It's perfectly clean, not a mark on it."

"No—I mean to say it should ought to be *greed*. And besight, I won't be shown through, it's too fin, fine, thin."

"Are you afraid you'll be stared at? It's the custom of the country." He gestured at Penna to show she wore a garment just as thin. "They'll stare more in that sack your friend gave you."

Penna averted her face from him, and from the way she glared at the floor I knew the gown had been looted from Torrent. Sire Edecon began to laugh. He said I was the first sheath he ever met who could still blush.

Sire Galan held out the garment. "I'd like to see you in it. I got it for you."

"How? Whose cut did you thropple for it?" That was an argument I hadn't meant to use.

"So it's not your modesty that's offended after all. You take me for a thief." He dropped the dress into my lap and stood looking down at me. "Do you mean to give up eating and drinking?"

I didn't know what he meant. I shook my head.

"I thought not. Because I never heard you ask where I got the coins to pay for your meat and drink. Where did the coins come from, hmm?" He leaned over, his hands on the back of my chair, his braced arms fencing me in. I thought the delicate carved chair back might give way in his grip. "What do you think a sheath is? What do you think a sheath does? Once my father took me to see a battle, and afterward I saw sheaths thick as crows after a reaper, gleaning every coin they could find. You chose to follow me. You should have left your qualms behind on the other side of the Inward Sea." He pushed himself away and turned his back on me.

I was fairly bested. Even if my tongue had been obedient, I had no answer. In silence and in penance, I went to the bed and drew the curtain behind me. I looked over the cloth for rents and bloodstains and found none. I put on the dress, and my bruises showed dark under it. When I came out my face was burning and the rest of me was cold. I wouldn't look at anyone.

Peace had come to the city of Lanx, so long at war within itself, and King Thyrse and Queenmother Caelum had decreed this a festival day. The victorious army paraded through the city, riding in great galleys rather than on horseback, for the principal streets of Lanx were water, not stone. The king in gilded armor stood with the queenmother on the bow of the first galley, under a canopy of cloth-of-gold. They led the procession from one keep to another, accepting the submission—freely given or not—of the clansmen in the city.

We were aboard the galley of Crux, second in line, the clan having won its place by the notable victory over Torrent. The warriors of our company mingled with warriors from Lanx. Not long ago these distant kinsmen of the Blood of Crux had been unknown to each other; now they were closer than kin, they were battle brothers.

Painted oars flashed in unison. Throngs of people watched from the walls and hills of the city. Spiller and Rowney and I had found a place on deck, near the sterncastle. We leaned on the rail to watch Lanx going by, but my eyes were drawn to Sire Galan on the forecastle, standing with his uncle, the commander of his company.

His uncle's name was Sire Adhara dam Pictor by Falco of Crux, but he went by his title of the Crux, for he was First of his clan in the kingdom of Corymb. It was his duty to lead the clan's Council of Houses and serve as Intercessor with the Council of the Dead. Before I came to Incus, I had thought Sire Adhara was First of his clan in all the world. I'd never considered that clan Crux in Incus might have its own First, and that there could be two men known as the Crux, two living representatives of the god.

The Crux was fond of his nephew. One could see that, seeing them together. One would never guess he had well nigh condemned Galan to death by forbidding him to ride, in punishment for starting the feud with Ardor. He'd offered Galan a choice: fight on foot or walk home from the Marchfield in shame. Galan had chosen to fight, though he knew as well as anyone that a cataphract without a horse draws enemies as a carcass draws flies.

Sire Galan had won back his uncle's esteem, and if their accord was less than perfect, I was the cause. The Crux didn't much like his company to wag a tail of camp followers. He'd permitted Galan to take me for a sheath, because he relied on Galan to be fickle: a few nights, a tennight, and I'd be gone. When Galan didn't tire of me, the Crux had called me a canny, saying I led Sire Galan around by his dangle.

He'd done what he could to rid Galan of me, and nearly gotten his way when Sire Galan tried to send me home. I wondered if the Crux had found out yet that I had followed.

We glided under the arch of a bridge. Jacks from our company were arguing with those from Lanx over which city was richer, this one or Ramus, where our King Thyrse held court. But all agreed that if Lanx was this wealthy, Malleus, the foremost city of Incus, must have treasures beyond imagining. Rowney said we'd all be rich when we took her, even the bagboys, and we'd pick her clean.

"Not so," said a jack named Cockspur. "Not if the She-wolf doesn't let us at it. She means to keep it all for herself. That's why she wanted all of Torrent killed, to put fear into the other clans in Lanx so they'd surrender, which they did. They're too timid to fight, and when there's no fight, there's no sack, see? So all we got was what was in that one keep—and mine is half spent already, for the merchants here are a thievish lot. Haven't you heard the soldiers from other companies grousing because they got nothing?"

Spiller took a swig from a wineskin and passed it on. "You don't think our king will bow down to a woman, do you? He means to help her until it's time to help himself."

Even as the king and the queenmother accepted homage and tribute, they offered it where it was due, halting at the great temples of Lanx to sacrifice to the gods. Many warriors followed them ashore to worship the god of their clan, or one whose favor they sought—a god helpful in battle, perhaps, such as Rift or Hazard. Each temple was under the protection of its clan, but stood outside keep walls, open to other worshippers. As we went from one to the next, I would ask, "Which one is this?" and one of the jacks from Lanx would answer. In this way the names of gods were given back to me. Some sounded familiar, such as Prey and Carnal, while others seemed altogether new, such as Delve. I repeated the names to myself, fearing they might slip away again.

King Thyrse and his sister disembarked to visit the temple of Ardor; before them down the gangway went rhapsodists playing praise songs, and behind them Auspices leading three offerings: a spotted cow, a ram, and a sort of deer with curving horns instead of antlers. In procession they mounted the steep steps from the quay to the temple. I turned my back on the odd sight of a cow climbing stairs, and sat down on a coil of rope. I was tired and my head ached and Sire Rodela buzzed, and it was long past noon and we were not yet halfway through the round of keeps and temples and courteous speeches. I snugged my new cloak about me, glad of the cold wind, else Galan might have made me go outside wearing only the gossamer gown. Instead he'd given me this mantle of thick felted wool, dark green, and threatened to burn my old sheepskin if he caught me wearing it again.

Sire Galan came pushing his way through the crowd of jacks, calling out for me. He had some men with him, Sire Edecon and three other cataphracts and their armigers, and I was relieved that I remembered their faces and reputations, if not their names. One was a bastard son of the king, called Sire Gawk, or perhaps Sire Quack. He had long thin legs and a long thin neck with a big bobble in it, and if he somewhat resembled a heron, he had some of the heron's poise and swiftness too, which he'd acquired in tourneys in the Marchfield. He stooped to look at my face and said, "Remarkable. What did the Crux say? Did you show him?"

"The Crux didn't say, and I didn't show him. But I happen to know his varlet told him all about it," Galan said, rubbing his finger and thumb together to show he'd paid the jack to gossip. He turned to me. "I thought we should go to the temple of Ardor, and give thanks to the god for sparing your life. Shall we?"

"Perhaps we ought better go amorrow, another day?" I said, pointing over the side. A crowd of men had alighted from the galley that flew Ardor's banners, and were walking down the quay toward the temple steps. Mortal tourney had ended the feud between the warriors of Crux and Ardor, by the king's decree, but no decree could abolish hatred. They might no longer be Galan's foes; nor were they his friends.

He grinned in a manner I'd learned to distrust. "It's Peaceday, isn't it? What day could be better?"

We went ashore, Sire Galan and his friends and their varlets and me, and we followed the warriors of Ardor up the steps. I'd forgotten much of what had happened in the day and night just before the lightning struck, but now the god permitted me to recollect a certain vow I'd made after I threw the bones. The Dame and Na had told me to propitiate Wildfire, and I'd misunderstood their warning, thinking it was meant for Galan. Perhaps it was too late for propitiation, but I still had a promise to keep.

I was gasping by the time we reached the temple square. Sire Galan asked me what the matter was, and I said, "Nothing . . . I just need to, to catch my death," and he said I mustn't jest about such things. I showed him my gold coin and told him my errand, though I couldn't think of the word for the dried tears of the amber tree, and kept calling it mercy or merry.

The warriors of Ardor entered the temple, but we lingered outside in the crowded square. The cataphracts and their men watched fire-eaters swallow and spit out flames, while Galan and I visited the peddlers who sat under awnings at one end of the square, selling talismans and offerings. I was triumphant when we came upon a man selling myrrh. "See, merry!" I said, and Galan laughed. The peddler used his scale to measure out a small heap of myrrh equal in weight to the goldenhead. I hadn't thought it would be so costly. Galan made me a present of a tin amulet, stamped with the godsign of Wildfire, to hang about my neck.

We climbed the last few steps to the temple portico, and Sire Galan urged us through the throng standing in the shadows of the great columns, into the doorway. A wedge of sunlight slanted down through the portal, brightness filled with white smoke and interrupted by our shadows. An Auspice of Hearthkeeper stood in our way, a crook-backed ancient with a blue shawl concealing her mouth. She said, "Mud can't come in here; their shrines are around the sides."

Sire Galan dismissed Spiller and Rowney and the other varlets with a gesture.

The priestess said, "Her too."

Galan's hand was behind my back, twisted in my cloak. "Lightning struck my sheath and she lived. We've come to offer thanks to Ardor, and to ask the Auspices of Wildfire the meaning of this omen." He spoke more loudly than was warranted, and his voice, enlarged by the chamber, echoed back at us.

Men crowded into the light from the darkness within. The First of the clan of Ardor in Corymb was among them, the Ardor himself. I'd seen him in the Marchfield, but never so close. His face was a heavy slab of flesh, and he wore his black beard trimmed close to his chin. Sire Galan had killed his son in the tourney, and it was as if I'd done it myself, I remembered so well the slippery feel of the hilt, the blood spraying the visor.

The Ardor stood next to the priestess, straight where she was bent, and he rested his hand on the hilt of his dagger. "Don't let him pass. He profanes the temple."

Sire Guasca—that was the name of Galan's friend, the king's bastard—stepped up beside me. He kept his hands empty at his sides, but his fingers curled.

Galan smiled in the face of the Ardor's scowl. "I mean no sacrilege here, only sacrifice." Sire Edecon put a velvet sack in Sire Galan's hand, and he untied the drawstring and drew out a goblet made from a nautilus shell set in a cage of golden fretwork. Light filled the polished pink throat. Sire Edecon stepped forward and emptied a purse into the goblet, so many goldenheads that they spilled over and rolled across the floor.

"A praise gift, in thanks." Galan offered the goblet to the priestess. She took it, saying, "She may pass."

He started forward, and his hand on my back was insistent and reassuring. Sire Guasca and the others were close behind.

The Ardor would not move out of our way. "Will you sell the god's blessings for gold? I know this man. He's a man of Crux, and no more trustworthy than the Moon."

Sire Galan said, "I swore before the king—as you did—to end our feud on the tourney field. And we ended it, I thought. But if you wish to start a new quarrel by calling me a liar, I'll oblige. Others will bear witness I didn't start it myself."

The priestess of Ardor stepped between them. Her voice quavered, but she spoke roundly. "You will not brawl in the temple."

The Ardor looked over her head at Sire Galan. "I didn't call you a liar. Did anyone hear me say that? But you are Ardor's enemy, and I can't let you mock the god."

"I pray the god doesn't take me for an enemy," Sire Galan said. "And if I offended in any way, I hope my sacrifice will make some small amends."

Onlookers crowded around, giving us less room to advance or retreat. The priestess put her palm on Sire Galan's chest. "It seems you came to make trouble."

"No. I came with an offering and a sign. The offering has been accepted. The sign has yet to be read." He took my jaw and turned my face toward the light from the doorway. His fingers pressed too hard on a painful spot under my ear. "Look at this! This is no trick."

"Let go," I hissed at Galan. "You're hurling me."

The priestess came close to peer at me. Her eyes, half hidden by the fragile pleats of her eyelids, were milky blue and opaque. She said, "You may enter."

Galan turned his hard grip into a caress, a touch that lingered on my throat, before he dropped his hand onto my shoulder.

The Ardor didn't move aside. He said, "I am the First of Ardor, and I say they shouldn't."

The priestess said, "The First of Ardor lives in Malleus. You might claim to be the First in your own land, but here you are second. This man is welcome to worship in Ardor's temple, and to bring his sheath that we might examine the portent. You're not to meddle in this."

Galan pushed in front of me and I followed, with Sire Edecon at my back and Sire Guasca beside me. I thought the Ardor and his men wouldn't give way, but they did, just enough. We passed between them, out of the sunlight.

*   *   *

The temple was built to the measure of gods, not men, and I was awed by it. The other worshippers didn't seem awed; they strolled about, greeting each other with loud cries, noisy as a flock of sparrows in a holm oak. Galan led me down the central aisle, between columns planted like rows of stone trees, their branches upholding the vaulted ceiling far above in the smoky haze. I wouldn't look behind to see if the Ardor followed.

Three fires burned at the far end of the vast room, and they seemed small at first, dwarfed by statues of the Hearthkeeper and the Smith behind them. These colossal statues were not diminished, as we were, by the vastness of the temple; the temple had been made vast to house them. The Smith stood behind his forgefire, and in the ruddy light his bronze shoulders and torso gleamed as if covered in sweat. His burnished arm was upraised, and he seemed about to move, to bring the hammer down on the golden ingot on his anvil. The Hearthkeeper, carved of luminous alabaster, knelt beside him. She was wrapped in a cloak, her forehead hooded and her mouth covered, and the alabaster folds clung to her like fine gauze, revealing a secretive smile and the curves of her body. She cradled a blaze in her outstretched hands. Wildfire, the elemental, which has no human form, was manifest in a lake of fire burning in a stone bowl.

Forgefire, hearthfire, wildfire, breathing out noisy winds turbid with smoke. Their light pulsed and made shadows leap. I could only reckon the true size of these fires—greater than any Midsummer bonfire I'd ever seen—by the tiny figures gathered at the distant altar, King Thyrse and the queenmother, rhapsodists and Auspices and onlookers. The flames towered above them, as the statues above the flames.

We approached the crowd before the altar. Already the ram had been opened, and Auspices searched his liver, bellows, and heart for omens. The cow waited patiently, obedient to the man who held her halter, whereas the wild hart lay bound, trembling, with his neck outstretched and his round dark eye rolling. I'd never been so close to the queenmother; the hem of her crimson and white gown was marked by scarlet drops of blood. The charnel smell was sweetened by burning candlebark.

I knelt before the statue of the Smith and looked up, and the face that looked down was not as I would have imagined him, had I dared imagine: a flattened nose, beard squared off like a spade, twisted ringlets rising from his scalp like flames. No matter, the sculptor had called on the Smith and the avatar had answered, entering the bronze in its passage through fire. I touched my forehead to the floor. I'd been between the Smith's hammer and anvil once, when I ate the poisonous berries of the firethorn tree in the Kingswood; he'd tempered me and let me live. In his honor I'd taken my new name. I heard his hammer now, the thudding between my ears that drowned out Sire Rodela's tiny whine. To do the Smith reverence I cast myself down, my face against the stone tiles, my arms over my head.

I'd come here to fulfill my small promise, the tribute of myrrh, and to give thanks for my life, which for a third time the god had spared instead of taking. Above all I'd come to plead for healing. Now that I was before Ardor in its temple, prayers deserted me. These things I'd carried here—the offering, my gratitude and hope—were unworthy. Ardor would know that my gratitude was hollow, the heart of it all eaten away by a worm of resentment that the god had robbed and afflicted me.

Galan knelt and spoke to me, and all I heard were unintelligible noises. I crawled toward Wildfire. The rim of the bowl was above our heads, and the flames higher still, tinged with green, giving off a plume of black and pungent smoke. I prostrated myself again. The heat was searing, a reminder that to come too close to the god was to be consumed. My cheek was pressed against the tiles and I couldn't raise my head, for there was a great weight on me, the god treading on my back and skull, treading me down. I was emptied of everything but the hammerfall and din of pain, everything but the question. What did Ardor want of me, why had the Smith saved my life so that I could be broken by Wildfire? Was I caught between cross purposes?

But no, surely there could be no contradiction; the three avatars were but forms Ardor took to show itself to us. All fires partake of the one fire. This is a mystery Auspices ponder; it was never for me to try to comprehend. And what use was it to question the god's purposes, when my mind—small, narrow, no longer whole—could not encompass the answers?

And yet understanding seemed so near, so imminent. Ardor's presence was a word on the tip of my tongue, about to be spoken. I felt that if I could only speak that word, I might give voice to the god's utterances, and in the very act of speaking, come to understand. And I trembled and longed for this; I relinquished myself to the god to become an echo for revelations. But thought and word, word and tongue were severed, and I was baffled when I tried to speak.

Yet for a moment I saw. All fires partake of the one fire. I too partook of that fire, it burned in each living being; it was the quick that divided the quick from the dead. I saw my hearthfire, my heartfire, a small tongue of flame wavering and bowing before the winds of happenstance. And when it flickered out, still it would be in the one fire burning. I'd thought the flame belonged to me, but it was only lent.

The weight lifted, the presence withdrew, and I wept. I'd sought mercy and found only the inexorable god. *I do as I will.*

✣   ✣   ✣

I opened my eyes on a glittering orange haze, and found I could raise my head. Strong hands lifted me to my feet. Sire Galan put his arm around my waist to steady me. I had lain a long time unknowing before the god. The cow and hart had been sacrificed, and their entrails examined; the king and queenmother had left the temple.

Now that the burden was lifted and the din silenced, memory was hardening around the shape of that moment in which I'd felt the god's presence. The memory was an empty shell; the moment itself couldn't be contained. What was beyond words proved also to be beyond remembrance. Yet I still felt, within the bony shelter of my ribs, a small flame burning.

Two Auspices of Wildfire stood before us. They had long hair and wore dirty rags and they stank, for hierophants of Wildfire are forbidden to wash. One was an old man and the other a young woman, yet they looked alike.

The priestess thrust a torch toward my face and I shied away. She examined my cheek. "This is your servant? She's been called to serve another now."

The old priest said, "Why else did you bring her, if not to dedicate her to the temple?"

Was this what the god had meant, treading me down? That I should be a temple drudge? I shook my head and opened my mouth, but I was still speechless, and the great *no* inside couldn't get out. Galan tightened his arm around me. He'd gambled, taking me to a stronghold of Ardor, but he hadn't reckoned on this hazard when he'd rolled the bones. He kept his voice light, as he sometimes did when he was at his most dangerous. "She follows me to war. Haven't you heard? Wildfire runs with us."

Sire Edecon laughed, a yap with no humor in it, loud enough to remind the priests that Sire Galan wasn't alone.

The Auspices glanced at each other. In the darkness beyond the colonnades I could see black slits in the walls, windows to darker corridors beyond. I heard murmuring: A crowd pressed to those windows, gazing in. Mudfolk barred from the heart of the sanctuary.

The priest said, "There are signs here. She must be examined."

"Alone," said the priestess.

Galan said, "We'll go now," and pulled me back. I was afraid of the Auspices, so I went with him. But my fists were clenched. Galan had given a wealth of gold to the god, but he'd been stingy with his respect. He'd visited the temple to taunt his enemies, and used the mark on my face for his excuse. Did he think the mark meant nothing? I wished to know the meaning of the omen, even if he didn't care to. I'd been foolish enough to think the god might speak to me directly, and it was no wonder I'd been rebuked.

Wildfire

Ardor spoke through its Auspices. It was their duty to interpret omens, and it might be their privilege to heal as well, if the god permitted it.

We weren't many paces away before I stopped Galan, and opened my hand to show him the lumps of myrrh, and my palm sticky with the amber resin. And words came at last, all jumbled in the rush. I said, "Wait, see? I must go back, I have this cicatrice, scarifice to make. Because I want to wonderstand, to be . . . heeded, readed. Maybe the . . . Aspects . . . the Auspicates of the one who lightnings, maybe they can help, maybe they can anneal me." I could see Galan was reluctant. I touched his sleeve. "You will come if they try to inkeep me?"

"Don't be long," he said.

Behind the great bowl of flames was a low doorway. Wildfire's Auspices stooped to enter, and I followed them into a small room. Daylight through a high window showed gray smoke meandering through the air, a clutter of oddments on a table: a rind of cheese, a clay cup holding a puddle of blue ink, a bone flute.

The priestess poured oil into a bronze basin on a tall tripod, and set the oil alight. It blazed up, bright even in the sunlight. I showed her the myrrh and she nodded, consenting to the sacrifice. It gave off a sweet smell as it burned. She sprinkled salts on the fire and green flames wavered among the orange ones, sending up black smoke to twine with the gray. I sat where she bade me, and the priest sat knee to knee with me. He had a bony face with narrow eyes, and his gray beard was long and waggled as he talked. He leaned forward and rubbed the mark on my left cheek with his thumb. "Were you struck yesterday?"

I tried to put in order my memories of morning and night and day and night and afternoon. But truly I couldn't tell. "I think—one daze behither—be behint that. Or thrice. Have you seen such a mar afore? What is it? Is it some kind of a burnt . . . brunt—a a . . . brand, which I must wear forever?"

"These signs fade quickly; it's well you came here when you did. Were you otherwise burned? Wounded?" He had a gentle voice.

"Some little . . . sparks, here and there, that's all. But my tent, my . . . top hurts, such a terrible terrible hardache. And you can hear how—when . . . Willfire stroked me down, how it clevered, it cleaved my . . . prong from my taughts." I put my two forefingers together to show how tongue and sense had once been yoked like a pair of oxen, and now they were bullish, pulling apart. "So I cannot speak my find. I have offered many plaints, but the god didn't heel me, so I wondered, I hoped you could ask . . . Attar to repent . . . relent."

He poured a few drops of water from a flask into the cup of drying ink and stirred it with his brush. "Sit still."

He began at the center of the lightning mark on my left cheek, drawing the wet brush lightly across my skin. I closed my eyes when he painted over my eyelid, and I kept them closed as he followed the branching bolts to every end, pulling aside my headcloth to lay bare the path through the hairs of my scalp, and down my neck to the slope of my shoulder. Ink cooled on my skin in the wake of his brush. He hummed as he painted, breath and hum and breath, and I followed the thin thread of his song inward, to the place where I was snarled and cut. The path was too tangled and I lost my way, but something loosened in me that had been tightly knotted, something opened that had been closed.

I returned to the outward reaches of myself and opened my eyes. The priest rested his brush on the lip of the cup. I straightened my headcloth and made a gesture of thanks, hand over my heart. The headache was gone. But I knew, even before I opened my mouth and found words as unbiddable as ever: the priest had soothed me, but he hadn't cured me.

"I am grateful," I said. "But . . . but is there aught . . . naught you can do to heal my breach?"

"You speak as Wildfire wills—the better to speak its will."

"But I speak . . . gabbledash!"

"Would you expect Wildfire to speak so that anyone could understand?"

The priestess sat at the table with her own brush, looking at my face and copying the mark into a book of pleated, sized linen. I pointed to the book, saying, "What is the meeting of this skin, this . . . scare that Illfire faced on me? Can you tell me that?"

The old priest said, "You've been called to serve Ardor. To serve in the temple."

I stood up, shaking my head. That wasn't what the sign meant, he couldn't mean that.

"I think you'll find it painful to refuse the god."

"You can't . . . you can't—I go where I'm found, I'm found to go. You can't halter . . . halt me."

The priest said, "Do you think we're trying to take you captive? Not so. But stay awhile. We have questions."

I sat down again and the priest leaned toward me, his face intent, expectant. His head was in front of the shallow basin of burning oil and there were flames rising behind him; he seemed to wear them like a crown. "What do you see? Have you *seen* anything?"

"I see what anywhom would see. I see you."

"Do you see anything in the fire?"

Wildfire

"You mean the crowd, the crown of fire?"

Smoke or shadows flickered and rose around the priest's head, silhouetted against the flames, and I recognized the dark tinge of fear. Surely he was not afraid of me, but there was no doubt he was afraid.

"You see a crown? Who wears it? Queenmother Caelum or King Corvus?"

"Who is that, King Cravas? Oh, the prize—you must mean the prize, the the . . . prince." So that was the queenmother's son, the name I'd forgotten: Prince Corvus. They called him king here—I hadn't realized.

The priestess wrote something down on a folded page of her book, next to the lightning mark.

The Auspex straightened up, moving out of the light, and said, "A crown of fire, yes. But who wears it?"

It was laughable that they'd ask me, as if I possessed secret knowledge. Laughable, yet I couldn't laugh at them. The Auspices and their clan were trapped between warring ambitions, and feared to err by choosing the losing side. I pointed to the flames rollicking around the edge of the bowl. "There is no sanctity for you, no no safety, no matter which sight you choose, the queenmalice or her son. Because the the . . . thing that burns—no, no, the very burning itself, the . . . pyre . . . fire, it glees, it is all gleeful, it lives to burn. It doesn't mean malefice by it, but neverthenaught it sets all ablame, you see? Whoever wears it will be spurned."

"Yes, but who wears it? What else did you see?"

"I saw a shadow in the crow, the . . . crown. A dread."

"Crow. She said the crow, King Corvus." The priest seized on this stray fragment of a word, made it whole. I looked at what the priestess was writing, and the godsigns, upside down, made no more sense than I did.

I shook my head in vexation. "No, no! Don't you hear me muttering, nattering? Utter natter. This is an end."

They asked me other questions, but I refused to say more. I'd misled them already, trying to speak the truth. It made me distrust everything I'd ever heard from Auspices. Why did they need my answers? Didn't they have their own auguries? Or was I just one portent among the many that begged for interpretation?

I was incapable of uttering what the god might say. I knew this, even if the Auspices didn't, for the knowledge had been impressed upon me when I groveled before the altar. If that was what Ardor required of me, then I had failed. Perhaps the fault was in me, because I was mudborn, without a divine lineage to strengthen my clay. A flawed pot will crack in the kiln—perhaps this remnant of me, aching and twitching, halting and slow, was all that was left after the god had fired me and found me an unfit vessel.

Would my speech be fettered to the end of my days? How would I endure it? I resolved to banish hope; it was too bitter when hope was overthrown.

Sire Galan was waiting for me with his friends, standing in the heat of Wild-fire's altar. When he saw the paint on my face he took in a short breath, say-ing, "Did they hurt you?"

I put my hand out to reassure him. "It will wash."

"Don't, though."

"What don't?"

"Don't wash it off."

"Why not? It's just taint. I thought they tainted me to pure me, you know—for a a melody, a meredy. But you can hear how I'm still brangled."

"They wanted something of you—what was it?"

"I think a a . . . orator? Or no—a miracle? No—I mean . . . oracle. An oracle."

"Ha! Indeed?" Galan took my arm above the elbow, and he set such a pace through the temple that I had to hurry to keep up. Many men stood before the door, and among them Ardor's clansmen. Surely they didn't mean to fight on a Peaceday, in a temple sanctuary, but they stared at me, they whispered and hissed. Galan's grip was painful, but when I looked at him sidelong he grinned. He had a font of joy that bubbled up in him when there was danger. It fizzed through my own body as if I'd drunk of the same perilous waters. He didn't slow down. Again they moved aside. Just enough.

He hadn't come here to flaunt himself; he'd come for me, to make sure his enemies would know I'd been touched by the god. To keep me from harm. No wonder he was pleased by the paint on my face.

Galan said, "And were you?"

"What?"

"An oracle?"

I remembered the priest bending toward me in earnest inquiry, and the priestess writing down nonsense, and I began to laugh. "I was, I am an ora-cle!" I said loudly so the men of Ardor would hear. "See what is written on my disgrace? In this taint? Ask the Suspiciouses what it said, I can't say, I have a torn tongue, a thorn tongue, a tongue of fire." I stopped searching for the right words, I laughed and let them all fly out, and how the onlookers gaped! We passed through the portal into daylight and ran down the steps, and Galan was laughing too, and also Sire Edecon at my left shoulder, Sire Guasca on Galan's right, and the others behind. As if I were one of them.

CHAPTER 4

The Black Drink

 hand of days we'd been in Lanx, a hand of nights I'd been without sleep. Last night there had been a great storm over the city. I'd felt it coming from a long way off, by the smell in the night wind and by some other faculty of perception I hadn't known I had—as if a weight pressed on some faraway part of me. An approaching tread.

Then thunder had rumbled around like carts over cobbles, and Wildfire had scrawled across the sky and lit up the slashing rain. I sat in the balcony watching, frightened, unable to look away. There had been strange melodies in the storm. The spire above me hooted with every gust from north-of-west, and when the winds shifted, another spire would answer in its own distinctive voice, for each clan tower had a windcatcher that sounded only when the wind came from the direction ruled by its god. This was how the city sang its ships home in a storm. The windcatchers' sounds had been there all along, crooning with every breeze, but I hadn't heard.

By dawn the storm had passed and I was wearier than the night before. I sat in the balcony trying to do a bit of sewing, while Penna sat across from me working on Sire Edecon's brigandine, replacing tow padding stained with sweat and blood. We worked quietly together, and I found it restful. Sire Rodela buzzed—he always did—but I could ignore him more easily during the day, when I kept busy.

Both my hands did my bidding without weakness, but I noticed a strange thing: my right hand was always cold now, my left always warm. I squinted at the stitches, which didn't march as straight as they should. I'd persuaded Sire Galan I couldn't go about in wintertime clad in a thin shift, no matter if it was the fashion, and he'd given me green wool enough to make two dresses. Penna had helped me cut it, and now I was stitching an overdress with sleeves that laced to the bodice at the shoulders, and slits along the front and back up to my thighs. That way I could show off one of the gauze gowns Galan had bought me as an underdress, without showing too much of myself.

He'd given me other presents: boots that laced about my calves, sturdy enough for many miles; a shiny willow green headcloth with a white cord to wrap around it; a small knife with an ivory handle to replace the one destroyed by Wildfire; a leather girdle with an oilskin wallet. I didn't refuse his gifts. I'd lost that quarrel; by my master's largesse I was reminded of my place.

Mud soldiers were saying the king planned to spend the winter in Lanx and march on Malleus when better weather came in springtime, and I wouldn't have minded. But Sire Galan said we'd be gone inside of the tennight, as soon as the army had provisioned. Today he and his men were off to the market of Carnal to buy horses (to buy whores, Spiller said, trying to make me jealous, for both were ruled by Carnal). The Crux had asked Galan to go, saying he had an eye for horseflesh. I thought it was cruel to send Galan to buy horses he couldn't ride, but Galan seemed flattered to be entrusted with the task. The Crux's horsemaster, Thrasher, would do the dickering, for in Incus the Blood would not soil themselves by buying and selling, and left all such negotiations to the mudborn. The custom had been readily adopted by the cataphracts of our army—and a fine custom it was too, for feathering a drudge's bed.

I tried to thread the needle, but my hands shook and the needle seemed to change size when I stared too long. I held the needle and thread out to Penna, and said, "Can you . . . ?"

Sire Edecon hadn't bought Penna wool or boots. Perhaps he just wanted her for his convenience here in Lanx. I hoped she would march with us, for it would be good to have her company. She never spoke of her plans, nor of what had happened in the keep of Torrent. I allowed her the reticence she seemed to prefer; she allowed me my ignorance.

I said, "I have wood enough for two, for two things you wear on yourself—two like this . . ." I lifted the dress to show her what I meant. "I'll gift you one, if you like. So you can stay warm this cold, this . . . Crone. While we are on camping."

We had a small brazier on the balcony floor between us, and she leaned down to put more sticks on the fire, and didn't answer.

"I'll help you stew it, stetch it," I said.

She looked up with something of a smile. "I've seen the way you sew."

"I know. It's all cracked, all crooked. Like my speak."

We went back to our sewing, and there was silence again.

Someone opened the door to Galan's room and called out, "Is anyone here?"

I dropped my sewing and ran from the balcony into the room, and embraced Mai, so glad to see her I had to blink back tears. She was wheezing hard, and I fetched her the sturdiest chair I could find. "I can't stay long," she said. "And if I'd known there would be so many stairs to climb, I'd not have come at all."

"I'm so pleaded you did," I said. "But did you come all one? Isn't it perilment?"

"I left Trave and Pinch and the others downstairs, so they wouldn't stick their long noses in our business. What happened to your face? Did the bruise turn blue? It looks frightful. But you're not so lopsided, and you sound better. Do you have your strength back?"

"And you? No more seavexness?"

"Thank the gods. I thought I'd die of it. I thought we were all going to die, to tell the truth. When the lightning struck, it brought half the mast down, did you know that? Crushed two men, and almost capsized the ship before they cut it clear. But why the paint on your face? Who did that?"

Penna came to the balcony doorway, and she and Mai eyed each other. I tried to introduce them, but their names came out all wrong, and they laughed and introduced themselves. Soon I had Mai settled by the hearth with a brazier at her feet and a wooden cup of ale in her hand. Penna and I went on stitching, and I told Mai about the Auspices of Ardor, and how they had painted me and I'd called a crown a crow and a fire a pyre, and she was much amused by it. "I told you people would take notice," she said.

I asked after Sire Torosus and Sunup and Tobe, and she said they were all well, but that their lodgings were not so fine as ours. Their company was quartered with their distant cousins, the clan of Delve in Lanx, who'd been impoverished by the feud. They needed both the shipwrights of Crux and the sailors of Torrent to transport their ores; by trying to appease both sides, they had pleased neither. So their welcome to Sire Torosus's company had been cold and stingy, as you might imagine, she said. And she didn't doubt that they would forswear the oaths they'd been obliged to give to the queenmother as soon as our army had marched away. Of course they weren't too fond of her son Prince Corvus either. Mai said, "You can't trust any of these Blood from Incus. They have no idea of loyalty."

I was afraid Penna might take offense, so I got up and made a fuss of returning to Mai the gray dress she'd lent me. And Mai mockingly praised my blue silk dress; she said she wouldn't mind the fashion, come summertime, but Sire Torosus didn't approve.

"You are from Corymb?" Penna said to Mai.

"Indeed," she said.

"And you are from Lambanein?" she said to me.

"Who, me? No. Where is this? I'm for, from . . . Cram, Crom, Corm too."

"I know you came from Corymb. But you were born in Lambanein, weren't you?"

"Why do you say that?" asked Mai.

"Her red hair," Penna said. "Many of those Lambaneish people have red hair, like King Corvus's wife."

I remembered how Sire Galan had once called me Hazard's breed, and I'd disbelieved him. But was there a place ruled by Hazard, a place where red hair was common? I took up my stitching again, and my cold right hand shook more than ever. "Where is this Lamenting, this . . . kindom? I never heard on it before."

"South, isn't it?" said Mai.

Penna nodded.

I said, "I don't know where I was bared, borne. I have had true delves of a place, a . . . lack, lake, and worriers riding over the highs, and and my . . . the man, the man-mother, he pointed to them." Mai looked at Penna, and Penna at Mai, and I saw they hadn't understood me. I'd had two true dreams of my father—I knew they were true because there were scents in them, and ordinary dreams are without smells. I'd dreamed we went riding over a mountain to sell a colt, and my father saw warriors behind us on another mountain, and though I was young, I understood he was afraid. In the second dream he was dressing me in an embroidered felt cap and vest to go to market. From these short dreams I'd learned two things: my father was a mudman who bred and traded horses, and he was fond of me. Impossible to explain all that, with my clumsy tongue. But I didn't like to see Mai and Penna share such glances; were they laughing at me?

I said, "So maybe I came from this—this . . . lake, land, place? What did you call it? But all I have left is dernes—I mean dregs—because I dismember it. I was only little when I was taken capsized, maybe four airs of age, no one knows. And that was about a dozzle—let me think—a dozzin or thirteen ages along ago. I was a caitiff—like you, Pendant—a captif."

Penna bent over Sire Edecon's brigantine without saying another word, and this time it was Mai and I who conferred by glances. Maybe I was wrong to call Penna a captive. She could run, couldn't she? Slip out the gate, disappear in the city—Sire Edecon wouldn't know where to look for her. But where would she go, how would she live? For a moment I imagined looking through her eyes at a world suddenly emptied of every dear and familiar person, and I flinched.

Mai was the first to break the uncomfortable silence that followed my words; she offered up the latest rumor, that the commander of the Wolves had asked the queenmother's hand in marriage—though she was thin and hard as a plank, said Mai, and she doubted the Wolf or anyone could get a child on her, she was so old—she must be forty, at least.

"Not so old, I think," Penna said. "Queenmother Caelum bore her eldest son, Corvus, the same year she was married, and he is twenty—and surely she was less than fifteen years of age when she wed. And what did the queenmother say to this Wolf?"

"She refused him, of course."

Mai was still gossiping when the Crux sent his varlet Boot to fetch me. I put down my sewing and looked at Mai in a panic. The last time I'd been summoned by the Crux, he'd made me face his manhounds in a trial by ordeal, to prove I spoke the truth about Sire Rodela's lies. Likely I'd have died then if Galan hadn't stood beside me in the dog pen. And now Sire Galan was off on one of the Crux's errands, and I doubted it was coincidence.

Mai got up and stood next to Boot. Boot was a big man but she was bigger, and for a moment I thought she might lay hands on him. But she had more sense. She asked me, "Should I send my men to search for Sire Galan?"

"No, don't," I said. "Only tell him if I, if I . . . dispart . . . despair . . . dispeer. So he knows who to shame."

"Hurry up," Boot said, yanking my arm to pull me out of the chair.

Penna looked at me with her black brows pinched together.

Boot led me up the stairs to the Crux's room. It was no bigger or better furnished than Galan's, but it was higher in the tower, as befitted his rank. The Crux sat at a table with two of his priests beside him, Divine Hamus, Auspex of the Sun, and Divine Xyster, Auspex of the Moon.

The Crux was hatless, and his white linen shirt was half unlaced and hanging loose over a pair of leggings. His feet were bare. It was unlike him to rise so late. He was well muscled, and the dainty chair in which he sat creaked when he shifted.

"Stand by the window," Divine Hamus said, and he got up to look at me. It was a north window and the light was bright, though not direct. It made my eyes water. Bright light was painful since I'd been thunderstruck.

"This mark is false," Divine Hamus said to the Crux. "It was painted on."

The Crux said, "So it's a sham? She wasn't struck by lightning?"

The priest answered, "I've heard the tale from too many. It was witnessed by two cataphracts of Delve and a priestess of Copper."

"Wash off the ink," the Crux said, "and see what's under it."

Divine Hamus's nostrils flared delicately in disgust, and he pursed his lips.

I covered my cheek and said to the Crux, "My Sire, Sire . . . Galance, your . . . niece, your—what is the word?—your nephew—he told me to live it on. He will be ired if you do that."

The Crux bade Boot scrub the ink from my face and neck. By the time Boot was done my left cheek was burning, rubbed raw. Both priests came close to look at me, and both agreed: the mark—supposing there had been a mark—was gone.

Divine Hamus's servant handed him a cage that held two sparrows. The priest groped inside the cage and the sparrows fluttered away from his hand, beating their wings against the wooden bars. He caught one and drew it out, pinching its neck between his fingers until it went limp. He laid the bird on a white cloth on the table and slit its belly with a tiny jeweled knife, and peeled away its skin whole, including the head, wings, feet, feathers and all, as if he were taking off a cloak. What was left was a tiny morsel of flesh, which he divided into parts and examined. The Auspices of Crux were skilled in divining by the Sun, Moon, stars, weather, and birds— by anything that moved across the Heavens. To them the sky was a mirror, clear and bright, reflecting events below on earth. When they sought to know of household truths and troubles, they looked within the bodies of dead birds. The gods write omens large and small.

Divine Hamus whispered to the other priest, and the Crux watched them without moving. There was no comfort in his stillness; his wrath remained under his strict command. He might release it whenever he chose, to hunt or harry me.

When Divine Hamus straightened up, the Crux spoke. "I want to know why she followed us. Is this Ardor's doing, to put a foe in our midst?"

"I'm not," I said, "not a . . . fie."

Without looking my way, the Crux made a gesture that silenced me. My mouth was so dry I couldn't swallow.

Divine Hamus said, "There are no signs of corruption in the heart or bellows, nothing that speaks to Ardor's malice. But there's a wen near the eye, which signifies a disorder of Crux. Blindness, maybe, or its opposite."

"Its opposite? Seeing too much—spying? Be plain!"

Divine Hamus, who was short and stout, drew himself up as tall as he could go, saying, "I speak as plainly as the signs permit. To do more would be to misread, and perhaps to mislead."

"Maybe you should kill the other bird then, and tell me something useful." Divine Hamus seemed much offended.

I heard a laugh, a woman's laugh. I turned, but she was hidden behind the lattice screen and gauze curtains of the Crux's bed. "Don't pester the poor priest," the woman said, and a white foot emerged from behind the bedcurtain, followed by a slender ankle and a round calf, and then by the rest of her. She wore a velvet overdress dyed a vivid magenta, and her bare neck and shoulders were smooth and youthful. But her face showed considerable years, and years of merriment, in the hen scratches around her eyes. She wore her hair uncovered, like a maid or a wanton; it was plain she was no maiden.

She had Boot bring her a chair and a cushion so she could sit beside the Crux, and I was amazed at the intimacy this suggested. To my knowledge, the Crux had been abstemious around women, and held Galan to scorn for being too fond of one. He scowled at her, and she smiled back unperturbed. She might smile and smile, but I doubted she meant me well.

She said, "Why don't you ask her if she does Ardor's bidding? Maybe you'd get a plainer answer."

"A plain lie," said the Crux. "Drudges and women never speak a true word when a false serves them better."

"You lack courtesy," the woman said.

"If courtesy is untruth, then I admit the lack."

"It's courteous to remember whom you are addressing."

"I do remember, Divine Lepida," said the Crux. "Indeed I do. I remember you promised to restore my nephew to his good sense. And what did he do? He compounded his folly by bestowing a fine holding on her."

I kept my head bowed, even as I stared at the priestess from under my eyelashes. Magenta was Carnal's color. She must be an Initiate of Carnal, a member of the cult dedicated to the mysteries of Desire. The Crux had paid the Initiates to cure Sire Galan of his fondness for me. I counted her an enemy, though she would probably scorn to call me one, I was so far beneath her. But the Initiates had failed, hadn't they? I kept my triumph at this thought from showing on my face.

"If he gave her a holding, why is she here?" the priestess asked.

"Precisely." Now the Crux looked straight at me, and I kept my gaze on the ground. The tremor in my legs made the floor seem unsteady. "Why *did* you come? If you don't say, my boy here will have to give you a beating. And I'm sure it will be a good beating, for if his fist isn't heavy enough, he'll feel mine."

Boot stepped up beside his master, and I stared at the threadbare hose sagging about his ankles, unwilling to look him in the eye. This was not what Galan had imagined would happen when he'd made sure his uncle heard about the lightning.

"You have my leave to speak," the Crux said. "Why are you still silent?"

"I I I—it was not—it was . . . because—"

The priestess said, "This is the creature who was supposed to have cast a glamour on Sire Galan? She's a simpleton!"

"She speaks well enough when she wishes."

Divine Xyster said, "Sire, there is something that will loosen her tongue and leave her without a bruise to which Galan might object."

"What? Do you propose to get her drunk?"

"In a manner of speaking. We can give her the black drink."

"But it will poison her," Divine Hamus said.

"Not if I give just a little. Just enough. The more lies she tells, the sicker she'll get. It will school her to tell the truth." Divine Xyster, as the carnifex of the company, treated the men's wounds and sickness; his lore differed from mine, for I was a healer of women. He knew his poisons, as every healer must, for they are also our most potent remedies. But there was no healing in the black drink, so far as I knew. It was used in trials by ordeal, for it was supposed to spare a truthteller and kill a liar. In my village they'd given it to a mudwoman who had accused Sire Pava's horsemaster of forcing her. For a day and night she had sickened, writhing and swearing that she spoke the truth, and I was not the only one who believed her. After she died the horsemaster was free to do as he pleased again.

The Crux said, "Try it. But mind you don't kill her."

By then I was shaking so hard in every limb I couldn't conceal it. "No, Sire, plead, I beg! I mean to speech, but but it comes out wrought. The got got my tongue. It's it's—" And I wrung my hands to show him how my words were all twisted. Hadn't he heard what the lightning had done to me? Boot pushed me into a chair by the window.

Divine Xyster left the room, and returned with a clay cup and flask. The drink was dark and gritty and foul. The priest forced it down, pinching my nostrils closed so that I had to swallow in order to breathe. I gagged and spat some of it out, but he poured more down my throat. Before long I was leaning over the windowsill, retching up the drink, but it had already done its work. I was as dizzy as if I'd spun and spun in circles. Something sharp jabbed me in the belly, in the flanks. Sire Rodela buzzed loudly, relishing my pains. I wiped my mouth and asked for water, and Boot gave me some. He looked sheepish when I glared at him.

The Crux stared at me. "Why are you here? Why did you follow us?"

"So as not to be lacking."

"My nephew saw to it that you'd lack nothing if you stayed behind."

"I'd have been a lack-all, a . . . lack-what."

"Lacking what?"

"To go side by side with him." I leaned forward and tapped the shadow that lay on the table next to his arm. "Like that. As nearnigh as that is to you. I'm not to be less or or . . . driven, given away." The Crux shook his head, his impatience growing. He couldn't see I pointed to his shadow, he truly didn't see it, though the sunlight was bright and his shadow therefore dark. It was the unnoticed thing. If I could have gone unnoticed like that, I would not have been here before him.

The Crux looked accusingly at Divine Xyster. "Your black drink has not improved her. She still talks nonsense, but more of it."

But the priestess had understood. "You think to be Sire Galan's shadow? The more fool you. A sheath is not a shadow, she can be *left*. There's nothing between your legs that Sire Galan can't find by any wayside."

The Crux said, "She's trifling with us."

"Maybe," the priestess said. "But I do believe she answered you. She's not the first bitch to dog Galan."

"What does Ardor have to do with this?" the Crux asked me. "Did they send you?"

"Did who what, Sire?"

"Did the Ardor send you after Galan?"

The black drink was a hard lump that kept rising from my belly into my throat, and I swallowed it down again and again. Saliva filled my mouth and I spat out the window. All these foolish questions. I was losing patience. I was losing my fear too, though I was trying to hold on to it lest I forget to be careful. I said, "Sire, pardon your begging, but I know nothing whateven of the the Fist of Altar. The time I saw him close was when he tried to halt us from entering the . . . from visibling the god in its . . . in the thing wherein it keeps. Sire . . . Gall, he was in a fiery about it, that the First would dare try to prevail him from traipsing in the the god's keep, house . . . its ample."

Divine Hamus asked, "What did you tell the priests of Ardor when Galan took you to the temple? What did they want?"

"They pained over what the lightning bode left here." I pointed to my cheek. "It left a a . . . mock, what faded."

Divine Xyster said, "Is that all? They painted your cheek?"

"And then they copied the firebrand down, in a blank. I don't know what for. Then they asked me corruptions."

The Crux looked to Divine Hamus with his eyebrows raised.

Divine Hamus said, "Corruptions?"

"Yes, cryptions."

"Questions," said the priestess of Carnal. "Such as?"

"Oh, flailish ones! Wriggles, writtles. But what I said, they writ down."

"What did they ask about us? About the feud with Ardor?" Divine Hamus said.

"They care naught of it." Sire Rodela was droning loudly, and I shook my head, trying to shake him out of one ear or the other.

The Crux said, "Then what did they ask?"

"They asked how . . . who would wear this . . ." I put my hands around my head to show him the crown.

He shook his head, baffled.

"See, I saw a flare all crazing up around the head of the old past, the priest, and I said I saw a crow of fire and they said who? And they thought I meant one thing, the black blackbird prance, ponce—what's his name? The son-of-a-hoor, of the queanmother, the queenmurder. But I didn't, it was just crone, crow, crown of fire, just so, because I couldn't find the heard." I could still taste the sour ferment of the drink. It had blackened my mouth and loosed this spate of words, and I marveled at how quickly they flowed, almost without effort.

The Crux and his priests leaned toward me, and Divine Hamus said, "The queenmother is the crone, and Corvus the crow. What else besides the crown of fire?"

"Nothing. It was all hornswaggle, tonguewobble. I'm tighted of this." Now I stared brazenly at the Crux, leaning toward him as he leaned toward me. Meddlesome old man. I didn't deserve this, I'd never done harm to Galan, his precious nephew, never. The sunlight fell full on the Crux's face. His beard was grizzled and his eyes were a clear golden brown. He had an old scar on his brow, a white line that crossed his temple, divided and puckered his eyebrow, and narrowed his left eye. The scar made the left side of his face look fierce and unforgiving, but the right side was stern, watchful. The right side reserved judgment, waited for me to condemn myself out of my own mouth, after the black drink made my tongue flap.

In just such a way he'd looked at me before sending me to face his manhounds, dogs bred for war. I'm sure he thought they'd kill me. Sire Rodela had lied, but I'd been the one to stand the ordeal, and for a long time now I'd been forced to carry my rage at this injustice, for what else could be done with it? And it had grown cold and heavy and hard in my belly like a stone child that will never come to birthing. But that heavy rage was dissolving now in the acid of the black drink, and spreading through me like an intoxicant. "Flap flip flop," I said. "I know what you want. You want my taunt, my tongue to swim slippery slick, lickety spit."

"You talk nonsense," the Crux said.

"You too. You four." Him and the priestess and his two priests, his lapdogs.

The Crux said, "When my nephew could have anyone, why does he choose her? Ill spoken, bad tempered, and thin as a mule on the far side of winter—why would he want her if she hadn't done something to capture him? And why keep her? I've told him before, never bring on campaign a woman you're not willing to leave behind."

Wildfire

"He did grieve me," I said.

The priestess of Carnal said, "Sire Galan doesn't strike me as a man who'd fancy a meek mouse."

The Crux said, "Maybe. But this shrew?"

"Ask Sigh Galan, ask and ask again," I said, "you never liked his awkward. What, did you never have a leman who could thaw you, make your sap to rile? Couldn't she do it? I daresay she tried." I nodded at the priestess of Carnal. How easily one word led to another! Though I saw the mask of judgment slip on the right side of the Crux's face, I kept speaking, and before I knew it, I was boasting. "I wanted no glamoury flum tricks of a Profligate of Canny to diddle my sire; I have blaze enough to keep him charmed, and since the lighting I burn even heavier."

I stretched the Crux's patience until it broke, and where was his self-command now? He slapped my left cheek and the tender flesh stung as if a pattern of fire burned across my face. Nausea rose in me again and I clapped my hand over my mouth and swallowed hard. The grit was under my eyelids too.

Divine Xyster said, "See how she sickens when she lies?"

I laughed behind my hand. This black drink of theirs was useless; it made me sick, but no sicker for falsity. I lied outright when I said I had used no tricks on Sire Galan, for I'd bound him to me by a secret rite, burying a womandrake in a muddy riverbank. But the Crux must not hear of it, and Galan must not hear of it, no matter how trippingly words came to me. No matter that the binding had proved so weak that Galan had left me on the wrong side of the Inward Sea.

I rubbed my tongue on the tail of my headcloth. "You give me poise and then accuse me of illing!"

"A liar will sicken."

I pointed at the cup. "What's in that? I want more." Was the thick residue made of ground seeds? I thought it might be clay, mixed in so the poison wouldn't kill. Whatever it was, it made my stomach shrink and my head swell until it was hollow and light and full of billowing smoke.

Divine Xyster feigned not to heed me, but the Crux said, "Why?"

"You've found a clue, a a cure. Give me more, I've a clamor that wants to get out. The blighting stopped up my mouth, why do you suppose? If Allfire loves me so much, why did it make me mute?"

Divine Xyster looked at the Crux, who said, "She's drunk. You've made her drunk!"

Divine Hamus said, "I never heard that anyone craved the black drink."

"Maybe so, but why blither about it?" I grinned, exulting in my rage. "No mother, no brother, no fother to make a bother, that's what they say of a low woman. But, Sire . . . my Sire, your nief, he will be wrath that the ink is gone. And if I tell him Bite did it, he will be wrath with *you*."

"You won't tell him," said the Crux. "It wouldn't be wise."

"Or what? Will you have your prates give me more of the blank drink? You should've given some to Sire Bordello, if it's so true, instead of unleashing a pack of manhunts on me. But you always knew the bondager laid about me—lied—didn't you?" Sire Rodela circled my head with a loud whine, and I tried to snatch him out of the air. I shouted at him, "Sire *Rodela*, Sire *Rodela,* do you hear me? You whoreson lowson! I heard tell your mother was a sprawling woman, so many dipped in her welter that she ran dry. You don't like that, do you? I'm glad if I offense you, because you served me the same. And now you can do nothing but hizz. If you could do else, you'd have done it."

I'd dared to utter a dead man's name. Divine Hamus made the avert sign to keep his shade away, but the shade was nearby, and had been all along, rejoicing that I was sickened by the black drink, that I spoke so carelessly the Crux was bound to kill me. That's what Rodela said, buzzing in my ear. The Crux looked dismayed. He said, "What are you talking about? Who are you talking to?"

"Don't you ear him? I'd swot him, but I can't see him. Even dead, he is a nonsense. Noisense, nuisance," I said. "Can't you hear him whinge? That's Sly Rodomont, my sire's cozen and a man after my own despite. He should have been born all mud, instead of just besmutched by it, for he'd have made a fine stanking tanner. He stitched my pelfry inside his helmet—I found it there, a little bit of skin with my woman's fear."

The fly landed on the back of my head. I waved him off and he whirred away and back, so loud, too loud. I felt the nausea rising again. I was clammy and shaking from chills. I shouted at Divine Xyster, "Fend him away! What kind of shyster are you, can't hear a shame when he's buzying about the room? You know he means to swarm us, he never lived but to do hurt! And he must be wrath with you—I heard you put a gorge on his slying tongue, and he choked on it." No doubt I should not have said that, though it was a thing everyone knew, how Sire Rodela had raved as he lay dying, with his skull split from a blow he'd taken in the tourney, and how the Crux had ordered his carnifex to gag him so he wouldn't disturb the whole encampment. Some said he choked on the gag, and that's what killed him.

Divine Xyster leaned stiffly toward me, bent at the waist, holding his flask of poison. The priestess of Carnal rested one pale foot atop the other under the heavy folds of her dress. She seemed bemused. Whereas Boot, the varlet, had nearly unhinged his jaw with gawking. I could have counted his missing teeth. They all seemed to move so slowly. I'd been a laggard for days, and now I was too quick, words had outpaced sense.

The Crux watched me. He had drawn a deep breath, and I waited for him to let it out, but the silence stretched on and on. His scarred eyebrow was raised, the eye under it half closed. He rubbed his lower lip and waited. Had I condemned myself already? Had I mentioned my own part in Sire Rodela's slow death? Had I spoken of the poison that caused him to rave, that I gave him with my own hand?

"I never was your enmity, don't you see?" I said to him, pleading. "I wouldn't be so much as a shallow, a shadow between you and Sire Gallant, because you are dear to him and because you are his knuckle, his father's brother, and because you're the grindlestone he's honest against. The harder you grim him, the keener he gets. You unhorsed him, you spurned him on, and didn't he prove bitter for it?"

I had a smear in my eyes and I saw the Crux with a shadow glow about him. I turned and spat out the window again, trying to rid myself of that taste, and turned back to him. "You think I'm your animous because Ardaz, Ardux—because Willful afflictened me. Or mayhaps you think the god chose me *because* I am your animous. Is that so? But you are misbroken. The god Arson was never your enemy, no more than I. No, you were what came to hand. Because the clan Arson shewed themselves guilefilled and without honest, honor. So their god turned a wry eye on them and allowed you the vigour in the moral tourney. Did you think it was all your doing? Not so, you were as sharp blames from the Smite's forge, to diminish, admonish them. I know you hated to leave so many alive to glib about, but you may have at them yet, if the Smite isn't sated."

There was a pang in my gut. I clasped my arms over my belly and bent over and heaved and groaned. The taste of the black drink flooded my mouth though there was nothing left to bring up. "You've killed me," I told the Crux, told them all. "What will Sire Glance say?"

Back in Sire Galan's room, I lay on the bed unmoving and waited for him to come home. And when he did I lied and said I'd washed off the mark myself, did he think I could wear it forever? Perhaps there would have been a quarrel if I'd not been so sick. He was afraid for me. He thought I might die, and the color of fear leaked from his skin.

The Crux and I kept the secret; it was ours to keep. There were others who shared it, but they didn't own it as we did. I couldn't tell Galan how I'd squirmed and thrashed on the floor while the Crux and his Auspices knelt beside me, how I'd labored and strained as if in the travail of childbirth, but brought forth nothing but nonsense words and curses. The Crux had told Divine Xyster he'd given me too much, and the carnifex had answered that I'd get over it. But he'd looked grim, his face furrowed with shadows.

I suffered the night long, and could have sworn I never slept, yet in the morning I remembered having dreamed.

It was a cold day, and I was out with my digging stick, tasting dirt. The soil in the garden behind the house was black, it tasted sweet and smelled rich; in years past it had been well fed, kept in good heart, as we say. On the terrace below, where I meant to put lavender and incensier and marjoram, the earth was chalky, and tasted of ashes I had sown there. In the orchard I took a handful of dirt and squeezed and it made a clump in my palm. I tasted it and found it leafy. I knew what I would plant there, under the old trees. But I had a craving for the taste of clay, and wasn't satisfied.

I went downhill, taking the steep stony path from terrace to terrace, and down through the old hazel coppice and hawthorn thickets until I reached the river. Trees leaned over the dark water, trailing bare branches, and I walked along until I found an old fallen willow. Where it had been uprooted it had torn away part of the bank, and I lay on my belly on the turf and reached down for the reddish clay I saw exposed there. And I ate and ate, I crammed clay into my mouth until my belly was soothed by it.

CHAPTER 5

Daughters of Torrent

 miss my horse," Sire Galan said. "Do you think my uncle would mind if I rode a bull?"

Sire Edecon said, "I daresay he would, if he knew." He looked at Sire Galan with a smile to see if he'd take the dare.

Galan was clad only in his hose and Sire Edecon in his long shirt, and they'd been idling at home all the long cold rainy day. They'd dined on greasy redfish, and the smell lingered, making my belly roil. I was still queasy from the black drink I'd been given the day before.

Sire Edecon picked up his dulcet and began to pluck at it. "The Crux is too harsh. Many of us would be willing to plead on your behalf that he rescind this punishment."

"My back itches, Spiller," Galan said, and Spiller took off the bandage and poulticed the wound with foul-smelling liniment, and obligingly scratched up and down his spine. Galan said to his armiger, "You're very kind, I'm sure—but the Crux has said I'll go to war afoot, and so I will, to war and back again, until he sees fit to say otherwise."

Sire Edecon played several strings at once, a sour chord. The dulcet's soundbox was inlaid with a mother-of-pearl crab in a swirl of gold dust, and it had silver pegs to tighten the strings. Its sound was silvery too, despite his clumsiness. "Then I'll play a lament for your lost horses," he said in jest.

Galan reached out and put his hand down hard on the dulcet's strings. "Don't," he said, not jesting at all.

Sire Edecon propped the dulcet against a chair, saying, "Forgive me, Sire. I meant no discourtesy." Sire Rodela would never have done that. Where he overstepped, he kept on trampling.

"Forgiven," Sire Galan said. After a silence, he said in a lighter voice, "Let Rowney play. He can do more with a song than torture it."

Rowney took the dulcet and tuned it. I was surprised he knew how to play, and more surprised by his sweet song, for I'd never before heard him sing anything that wasn't lewd. I knew the ballad, about a girl who pines for the Moon. The tune was melancholy, and when Rowney sang, *The Moon hid his light in a cloak of night,* I added my voice to his. He looked up and smiled. I mirrored him note for note, sometimes higher, sometimes lower, until the song was done, and it was only then I realized that every word had come to me without fail, in its proper place. I'd opened my mouth and out they'd come, just as they used to. Was I healed so suddenly?

Sire Galan said to me, "You shouldn't be so shy of singing. Why have you waited so long?"

I said, "It was a moon I knew. Besides, most of . . . Tawney's are too— they're howl-mouthed—ahh!" I bit back the next words. They were wrong again, still wrong.

"Howl-mouthed. You hear that, Rowney? Your songs offend, they're indelicate." Sire Edecon was teasing, but I feared Rowney was insulted. He had his head down and his palm over the dulcet's strings.

"I didn't mean—I meant . . ."

Rowney looked up. "Soldiers' songs are for soldiers. But how about this one?" I knew the rollicking tune, but Rowney and I had different words for it. We traded verses. Rowney sang in the Low about a widow and a wayward hen, and I sang in the High about a fox and a ferret. Galan joined me, and then Sire Edecon as well, whose voice proved sweeter than his playing. We couldn't finish for laughing. It eased me that my speech was unhindered, if only for the length of a silly song.

Rowney asked me, "Why do you suppose the words come freely when you sing?"

I shrugged. A phrase from an old song came to me and I sang, *I wish I had garlands of words . . .*

And he sang, *With which to wreathe my heart's desire,* and he smiled at his boots.

Sire Edecon said, "I know a good song, but I daresay it will make your sheath blush, she's such a prig. Do you know this one?"

> *A tender bride of twelve*
> *Will heed her husband well.*
> *A bride of thirteen years*
> *Will bring her husband cheer.*
> *If she has turned fourteen,*
> *A bride's no longer green.*

Rowney picked out the tune on the dulcet, and Galan joined in too, and they sang as loudly as they could.

Wildfire

At fifteen and a day,
A groom she won't obey.
A sixteen-year-old bride
Is bound to sulk and chide.
A bride of seventeen,
Will make her husband mean.
If she's eighteen years old,
Her groom she will cuckold.
At nineteen years of age,
She'll make her husband rage.
Wed a bride of twenty,
If her dowry's plenty.
Should maiden prove not maid,
Her house she has betrayed.
To her father send her,
Let him reprimand her.
Find yourself another
With a stricter mother.
If she's no more than twelve,
No doubt she'll please you well.

Galan said to Sire Edecon, "Well, you'll know the truth of that old tune soon enough, won't you?" The men laughed. I didn't know what they were joking about.

Sire Galan wanted me to go to the feast that evening. Everyone was going, the whole army, he said, and we should all be well fed. "Yes, on fish," said Sire Edecon. "I tire of fish. Cod may go disguised as roasted goose, but it stinks all the same."

I said I hadn't the strength, which was true. But it was also true that I didn't wish to go. Sire Galan leaned on my chair. "Is that my hose you're darning? You should let Rowney do it. I swear he has the neater hand."

"It's donething, something I *can* do," I said.

He frowned and looked out of the window. It was the most sober look I'd seen cross his face all day. The breeze made his forelock flop over his brow. He tucked straying hair behind his ear. I knew it wouldn't stay.

I smiled up at him. "I could also snip your hat, I mean your hair."

"I won't let you near it," he said, with a grin that was quickly gone. "You should come. I don't like to leave you here alone."

"Why?"

"You're ailing."

"No, I'm just weaked, peaked. I want a rest."

"I'll leave Spiller with you."

I shook my head. Spiller would make me miserable for it.

Rowney said, "I'll stay."

Sire Galan gave him a considering look, as if wondering whether to be jealous.

I said, "No, I don't need anyhow, anyhim." I touched the back of Galan's hand and he turned his palm toward me and laced his fingers between mine.

"Your hand is as cold as the Crone's," he said, and I knew I'd gotten my way.

They left toward sundown and I was alone. I thought I'd had enough of solitude in the Kingswood, enough for a lifetime. But I craved it now. By night I lay awake among the sleepers—six of us in that room, which was smaller than Sire Galan's tent—and heard them stirring in their separate dreams. Their presences seemed to billow and press upon me, and I envied their forgetfulness. By day I was taxed by the constant struggle to speak and be understood, and troubled by my failures. To be alone was to have the gift of silence.

I climbed the tower stairs as slowly as an old woman. The steps were pinkish stone, smooth as the inside of a shell, but as I climbed I came to rougher steps that had not been polished by so many feet. I sat down and gasped until the pain eased in my side. The rain had moved on, and a square window showed a sky of deep blue with a mare's tail of cloud flaring gold. I got to my feet and started up again, stubbornly wanting to get to the top, to see what could be seen.

Another turn and the stairway ended. A wooden ladder was propped up inside the narrow shaft. Cold air came dropping down. I climbed the ladder and came out on a small platform rimmed by a stone parapet. The gilded spire of the windcatcher rose above me, carved to look like a pair of wings cupped together. The wind was not from the direction of Crux, so it soughed around the wings, but didn't sing.

I leaned on the balustrade and looked out over Lanx. The city was a story told stone by stone. Penna had said that when she was a child, the palaces of the clans faced the streets openly, with great windows and portals, and long arcades that sheltered markets and welcomed idlers. Because of the feud the arcades had been filled in, and walls raised upon them higher than any rooftop. In this way the Blood had walled out their enemies, but also their own mudfolk, the carpenters of Crux, fishermen of Torrent, weavers of Wend, and all the others. Now streets ended abruptly at walls or disappeared under rubble. Many fine bridges had been torn down to prevent passage from one hill to another, while the clans built their towers higher. As each vied to overtop the next, they'd exhausted quarries one by one. Here a stratum of golden stone had been laid, then pale stone, then rosy.

The towers shone as the rest of the city subsided into shadow, and I saw it all plain, how Lanx had battened on the feud, grown taller by way of brawls and ambuscades, duels and murders, as its people busied themselves making and destroying. Already they were dismantling the tower of Torrent. They'd use the stones to build something new, something beautiful. For Lanx was beautiful, despite its scars. I was no part of the city and I wouldn't stay. But I understood for the first time how one might be content to live and die here, one among the many.

I sat down and opened the divining compass on the floor beside me. There was Hazard's godsign, the skein of geese, and there was the sign of Crux across the compass: I'd stared long enough at the tattoo on Sire Galan's cheek to commit it to memory. Crux's direction was north-of-west. I turned the compass around, trying to line it up according to the Sun. Which gods were on either side of Crux? I couldn't remember. But there was Ardor—I had the godsign stamped in tin on the amulet Galan had given me outside Ardor's temple. And I remembered that the Queen of the Dead was next to Chance, and the Warrior next to Peril—they had always seemed to go together well—so Rift was beside Hazard. But on which side of Hazard?

I recollected the names of eight of the twelve gods and mislaid the rest. I pulled the drawstring tight to close the pouch around the finger bones, and the Sun hid her face and I was cold in the sudden night.

Sire Edecon returned from the feast with a new bride.

Forty maidens of Torrent had been spared when their clan was destroyed. Eight and twenty of the maids—all those under twelve years of age, including even babes-in-arms—were betrothed that night and given to be raised in the households of their affianced. Two and ten maids, those twelve years and older, were given outright in marriage. In gratitude for service in the battle of Lanx, the queenmother had offered a bride to any man of Crux who wanted one. Most of the Blood of our company were already married; it was accounted a man's duty to secure an heir before he went to war. But Sire Edecon had older brothers in need of wives themselves. He'd counted on war to make his fortune, and never imagined he'd marry one.

The dowries were generous, for Queenmother Caelum poured away the wealth of clan Torrent without stinting. So she celebrated and completed her victory, and made sure that there would be no heirs to carry the names of the dead houses of Torrent in Lanx.

Sire Edecon's bride was called Dame Vairon, and she was fourteen years old. Penna slipped off the new dame's cloak and led her to a chair by the hearth. Dame Vairon's eyelids were swollen and red, and I couldn't see the color of her eyes because she wouldn't look up. She'd lost her father and mother, her brothers and all, and now she was married to a man who'd helped kill them. She had lain under Sire Edecon before witnesses at the feast, and done her part, which was to bleed in proof that she delivered her honor intact into her husband's keeping.

Bawdy jests are customary after a wedding, but there were no such jests that night. Dame Vairon brought silence into the room with her. Sire Galan and Sire Edecon began to talk about something, anything, but the silence remained, making their speech seem loud and false. They were soused with drink, but Spiller was much the worse for it. He fumbled at the clasps of Sire Galan's enameled hauberk, cursing under his breath. Penna hovered close behind the bride's elbow, like any good handmaid, ready to anticipate her mistress's requests. It seemed to me that Penna knew Dame Vairon, but the dame showed no signs of familiarity.

Sire Galan said, "Take the bed tonight, Edecon, and I'll take the cot."

"No, no," said Sire Edecon.

"Oh, yes," said Sire Galan. "After all, it is your wedding night."

"So it is," said Sire Edecon, none too gladly.

Dame Vairon wore bridal finery of nine gossamer gowns, one over the other. The outermost was pale willow green for Crux, and the innermost of deepest cobalt blue for Torrent, and the rest dyed shades in between. Just today, when Maid Vairon became a dame, she'd added two new gowns. When she had children she would add more. Penna had told me some dames wore as many as seventeen. Mudwomen were forbidden by law to wear more than two.

Penna took the gowns off one by one, save for the last. The new bride climbed into the bed and drew the curtain, and in time Sire Edecon followed. In the middle of the night, as I lay awake, I heard her mewling and hiccupping like a child afraid to wail out loud. Sire Edecon climbed down from the walled bed and went to lie with Penna on her nest of sacks and blankets. I heard her say, "Not now!" I heard him murmur, coaxing her. I heard her give in. When he was done he went back to lie beside his wife again.

Much later I got up to knead a cramp out of my leg and to sit in the balcony. I could hear the mournful moan of a windcatcher. Bats swooped and darted over the gardens.

In the night, when my muscles ached and I skittered from thought to thought, Sire Rodela liked to pester me. I put my head down on the sill and prayed that he would go away. Didn't he suffer too, from tormenting me? To stay so close to the living must remind him constantly of what he'd lost. I wiped my nose on my sleeve and felt tears cooling in the breeze on my face.

"Why do you sit here at night?" Galan asked from behind me, in a low voice. "Why do you leave me?"

Gods, he'd startled me, coming so cat footed. He hadn't bothered to put his shirt on. I reached for his hand.

He took his hand away. "No, tell me why—I want to know."

"I have . . . clamps, crawls in my legs and it hurts and I can't lie stiff and I can't please, sleeve—" I took both his hands this time and wouldn't let go.

He sat on the bench. "You can't sleep. Night after night you can't sleep."

I whispered, "I can't. I don't know—it's the lighting, it must be. I'm so wachid all the time, so wankle . . . so tried! I don't mean to tremble you."

"I thought you were mending. But you're not, are you?"

"I am minding. I will."

"Come here," he said, pulling me toward him. I sat sideways on his lap and leaned on him and put my face against his neck.

"This cannot be commendable," I said.

He laughed. "Not commendable?"

"Cumberable?"

"It's very comfortable," he said. It was not; nevertheless, I counted myself fortunate among women.

I dreamed that down by the river I cut red osiers to make withy fences for raised beds behind the house. I climbed the hill again with a great bundle on my back. The Sun was bright and warm, though the winds were cold. I drove in stakes and plaited the withies around them. I squatted back on my haunches and brushed hair away from my face with my forearm. There was no one about, and I could wear my hair down if it pleased me. A hawk overhead tipped his wings and drifted toward the gray trees of the wood to the west.

When I awoke, the names of the seeds I meant to plant in the raised beds were on the tip of my tongue; I could nearly taste them, though I couldn't utter them. I said to Galan in astonishment, "I slipped!"

Sire Edecon peered out between the curtains of the bed. "Penna? Where is she? Where are they?"

We'd all slept too well, it seemed. Penna and Dame Vairon had left the room and none of us had seen or heard them go. Sire Galan nudged his jacks ungently with his foot. He didn't wait for Spiller to get up, but began to dress himself. He pulled his shirt over his head and said, "Edecon, you talk to the guards at the gate and find out if they saw them. Rowney will search the privies, and Spiller the baths."

"So you think they ran away?" Sire Edecon looked about for his hose.

"Don't you?"

I said to Galan, "What should, what would I do?"

"Wait here. I daresay they'll stroll home soon and make mock of us for searching. I daresay it's nothing, nothing."

Spiller held his nose and muttered, "Stupid fish. Why can't they stay where they belong?"

Penna came back when the morning shadows were still long. She was panting from the climb. She paused with her hand on the door and said, "Where is everyone?"

"Where is *she?*"

Penna came into the room, shaking her head. "She slipped away in the night. I followed, but I lost sight of her." She shrugged and turned away from me, and shook out the quilt that covered the cot and began to fold it.

She'd looked at me too long, and then she wouldn't look at me at all. And her black eyebrows were too straight and still. She'd schooled her face to hide something. "Henna . . . Penna, where did she go?"

"I don't know."

Of course she knew, or she'd be out searching. I said, "Where she begones?"

Penna stopped fussing with the bedclothes, and sat on the cot and bowed her head. There was defiance in her stiffness, but I saw that she was shaking.

I went to her and put my hand under her chin and made her look at me. "Where?"

Penna spat to one side and spittle dripped onto my hand. "Why should I tell you, you muddy slit?"

I held her hard by the chin. "Where? What have you done with the name, the . . . dammed, dame?"

"What have *I* done? What have *I* done? How can you ask after what your precious thieving master and his men have done?" She struck my hand away. "I did my duty, which was to remind Dame Vairon of hers."

84

"Oh, Penant," I said. She and I had worked together a hand of days, hauling water and slops and firewood, sitting by the window sewing. We'd made bread and eaten it together, and I'd believed what it was easiest for me to believe, that we were friends. All the while she'd felt alone among her enemies.

Yet we were friends, that too was true. Perhaps she had found it hard to cleave to hatred every day. She'd expected more of her mistress.

Penna was weeping. She wiped her face on the hem of her kirtle and left black streaks on her cheeks from the outlines inked around her eyes. "How could she give her enemy heirs, how could she *think* to do it? To breed his sons?"

"That poor guilt," I said. "Poor thing."

Penna bent over her lap, and the cries she made sounded like something being torn. I understood what she'd said and what she'd left out, and there was a pattern in it that I saw quite clearly. Two braids, each with three strands: mourning, wedding, drowning; a daughter, a bride, a shade. As a living wife, Dame Vairon had no power. As a shade, she could take vengeance.

In haste I put on my headcloth and started for the door. Penna got up to follow me, and I told her, "Got, get, go, get astray while you can still run!" But when I ran down the winding stairs, she was close behind.

The courtyard reeked of shit and rotting fish, and I covered my nose with the tail of my headcloth. The drains had backed up and spilled slime over the gleaming pavement. Drudges ran here and there to no purpose, while men of the Blood bellowed at them.

In the commotion I found it hard to pluck out words. Sire Galan came toward me with his long strides, saying, "Iseeyoufounder," while Sire Edecon shouted over his shoulder, "Watsrongpenna? Watsrong?"

I said to Galan, "Come close and speak in my hear."

"You found Penna," he said. "Where's the dame?"

I said, "I think she's spilt herself, the pride. She's gone and gone under."

Galan put his hand on my arm. "She's what?"

"She's gone and drought herself, drained!"

"Did Penna tell you something? What did she say?"

"No, I saw it."

Sire Edecon said, "Saw it with your own eyes? Then where is she?"

"Not saw, not with my, with my . . ." I pointed to my eyes. "With my mind's sign, sigh. I think she's in the ill, the . . . will. You must hurry!"

"Ill will?" said Galan. "Whose ill will?"

Penna held her head up. Her eyes, set deep in ink-smudged sockets, stared fixedly at no one. I didn't understand why she stayed.

"No, *will*," I said. "The . . . round down where water comes up. The the . . ." The words were dammed up, as if my very urgency were a barrier. I could think of no better way to set them free than to sing them, and so I shaped them to a tune and sang: *Look to the Waters to find Torrent's daughter. Where Wellspring sleeps, I think you'll find her.*

Sire Edecon said, "Do you know what she's on about?"

Sire Galan told his armiger to find some men and search the cisterns, the drains, even the fountains and laundries—anywhere within the keep a woman might drown herself. We went to the well, and Penna followed us, and by that I knew he'd sent Sire Edecon off in vain.

There was but one well that I knew of, in a small inner courtyard. It was not much used, for there was water from the fountains for drinking, and rainwater in the cisterns for washing. No one drew water from the river and canals, for it was brackish, and filthy besides.

The heavy stone slab that covered the well had been pushed ajar, leaving a crescent-shaped opening. Sire Galan shoved the slab on its pivot, and it grated across the top of the wall. His voice dropped into the well and sounded muffled and hollow. "I don't see anything."

I leaned on the wall. Galan and I were shoulder to shoulder and our two shapes were silhouetted against a wobbling circle of blue brightness a long way down. The shining water rebuffed our gaze, but where we cast a shadow I saw under the surface. A glimmering pale shape moved like a languid fish; perhaps Dame Vairon's bare leg, stirring in the currents of an underground river. A plink! And ripples spread from a tear I dropped into the well.

"Do you see?" I asked.

He shook his head.

"She's there. Lay me down in the buckle, bussock . . . the basket," I said, pointing at the overturned bucket and the windlass, "and I'll fet her."

He said, "You're still weak. You couldn't do it."

Penna said, "I'll fetch her."

I hissed at Galan, "No, not unless you want her to brine too! She'll cull herself, don't you see? I can do it, let me. I'll tie a a . . . hope around her and you shall wing us up."

"No." He put his hand on my shoulder and gripped hard. "If Dame Vairon is down there, it will do no good to have two drowned. I want you to find me a boy who can swim. Find help and don't dally."

It was hard for me to understand. He gave me a shake and repeated himself, and I ran, and as I left the courtyard I looked back over my shoulder and saw Galan had caught Penna by the wrist and was shouting at her. She had her head down, but she didn't try to pull away.

Wildfire

A kitchenboy named Kerf sat on the bucket and Sire Galan lowered him into the well, and by then there was a crowd to see it. Kerf eased himself into the cold water and looped the bucket rope around all four of Dame Vairon's limbs. He shinnied up the rope and Sire Galan and another man turned the crank. The drowned bride swung and thumped against the wall of the well, and slowly she rose. They untied her and laid her down on the pavement in a puddle of water. Her lips were purple and her skin was marbled with blue. I pulled her cobalt blue gown over her limbs, but the cloth was as thin as a second skin and hid nothing. Her hair was unbound and I combed it away from her face.

Penna could not do these services for her mistress, for Sire Galan had tied her with her hands behind her back to the wooden post that held up the stone well cover. The spectators muttered, and their quiet was more ominous than their clamor had been.

Sire Edecon came running, crying out the news that they'd found two of the new brides drowned in the cistern. He stopped short and then took one step and another until he stood looking down at his wife. "Why did they do it? Why? And why is Penna tied?"

Galan said to him, "Do you think your wife pushed the stone cover off the well by herself?"

I said, "I could do it. Anybody could. It lacks but a clever—a a leaven."

Sire Galan turned on me with a frown. "Then who pushed it back?"

Sire Edecon knelt on the pavement. "I don't understand. The marriages were honorable, a beginning, not an end." He touched his dead wife's hand, and the tenderness in his gesture pained and surprised me. A dove landed beside the body and pecked at an invisible seed.

One of the clansmen from Lanx leaned over him and said, "Come, this is no way to act. You've been wed a day, not a lifetime. Better for you that she didn't live to make your days miserable and your nights tedious."

Sire Edecon stood and said, "What should be done with Penna? Am I supposed to kill her?"

Galan shrugged. "It's for you to say."

Sire Edecon advanced on Penna and she crouched and sidled back to put the post between them. He dragged her by her headcloth until her bound arms were stretched out behind her. The cloth came untied and he took instead a handful of her black, abundant hair. He drew his knife, and held it as if he wasn't sure what to do with it.

She looked up at him, and the long curving column of her throat was within his reach. She swallowed.

Some mudfolk chanted, "Kill her! Kill her!" She glared at the crowd, and some stepped back as if she'd pushed them. For a moment our eyes met, and I shivered and was glad when her hating gaze passed to others. She cried out,

> "The daughters of Torrent are become shades.
> Torrent will devour your ships,
> and fish will feed on your merchants.
> Your wells will offer poison
> to quench your thirst.
> Your children will drown in the womb!"

Sire Edecon bade her be silent, and struck her across the mouth with the fist that held the hilt of his dagger. She crouched there, her hair unbound, the ink from her eyelids smeared all over her face, and when she shouted, the voice that came from her did not sound like her own, it was loud and hoarse, not a shriek but a roar. She compelled us to hear her out, for she had given herself over to the gods and was ready to die.

> "I saw my man killed before my eyes.
> I saw my sister Heddle dragged down the stairs.
> I gave myself to a dog
> to save myself from wolves.
> The shades of the brides will linger
> in this well, this cistern.
> They will make of your keep a desert.
> They have avenged their fathers.
> They have avenged their mothers.
> They have avenged their sisters.
> They have avenged their brothers.
> I should have drowned with them,
> but I lived to utter this curse,
> and to claim my share of vengeance."

Sire Edecon's knife trembled in his hand. He stepped back, and the man who'd spoken to him earlier came swiftly forward and slashed Penna's throat with a short sword. I saw she was a fountain with life streaming from her. I covered my eyes and heard the watchers cheer. They cheered louder still when the man cut out Penna's tongue.

A hunt was on in the keep of Crux. Someone had scuttled the ships at dock in the night, slipping underwater with an augur and drilling holes in the planking. Someone had stopped up the drains so that stinking wastes had backed up into privies and courtyards and the laundry. Someone had served blowfish of the wrong sort for breakfast, and a dame and three of her children were sick to death.

Penna had not been the only drudge of Torrent in the keep. There were others, spoils of battle like herself, taken for bedservants or horseboys, a new handmaid perhaps, or a fish cook, a varlet. No one had thought there was harm in it. Now the masters of Crux hunted down their untrustworthy servants, and their mudmen helped, and perforce their guests, the Blood and mudfolk of our company. Our drudges risked being taken for men of Torrent themselves, being strangers, unless they showed themselves fervent in pursuit.

An outcry went up when they found another of Torrent's daughters, one of the betrothed, caught against the grate of a drain that emptied into the canal. She had drowned in filth. She'd been but eleven years old, and slender enough to crawl down the bathhouse drainpipe. Everyone thronged to see her.

Another outcry, "A fight! A fight!" and people went running to the stables where a horseboy held off three attackers with a pitchfork.

Mobs of men dashed about, in each other's way or each other's footsteps, until the Crux and the heads of houses in the keep took the hunt in hand. They sent beaters to work their way inward from the walls and down from the top of the tower; others combed through the dirty warrens underground, where most of the drudges of the keep lived. The beaters drove toward the Blood waiting in the great courtyard between the tower and the gate. Some women joined in, for anger ran high. The rest of us, along with old folks and children, were herded into the walled orchard to keep us out of the way.

I sat under a hazel tree and watched water slide between the straight walls of a watercourse. There were minnows just under the surface. I wished I'd closed my eyes before Penna died, and not just after, so that I would not have seen Sire Edecon stumbling forward, streaked with red, and Penna falling toward him.

They took the dead daughters of Torrent to the charnel grounds outside the city, on the southern bank of the river, and built elaborate pyres for them. The servants of Torrent were burned with less ceremony. They didn't trouble to sort the living drudges from the dead before setting the fires.

The brides had made a pact to kill themselves on their wedding night, and seven of them had done so. Some denounced the brides who had drowned, calling them dishonored, and some denounced those who had refused to kill themselves. It was not for me to judge them or Penna, my friend. Surely it had taken courage to die, yet I wished Penna had found the courage to go on living.

CHAPTER 6

March

 thought I would be walking, since Sire Galan had to walk, but he would have none of that. He'd bought a jenny mule for me, and I straddled her bony back and the two fat sacks she carried. Her name was Frost, and she was white with a rime of gray on her roached mane. She went heavy laden, and I suppose she was more saddle sore than I was, but not by much.

We were five days and less than twenty leagues from Lanx, marching westward to the city of Malleus, and Sire Galan said we would be there in a score of days, more or less—more if we kept dawdling. There was a rumor, so widely believed that most took it for a fact, that Prince Corvus would sit snug in Malleus and make us besiege him, rather than march forth to stop us; though some soldiers claimed he wouldn't fight at all, he'd run away before we got there and deprive us of a battle.

The army on the march was an ungainly armored beast nearly a league long, and we in the baggage were in its swollen belly, flanked on either side by foot soldiers in the fields. Wherever the great beast crawled, it left a wide swath of destruction: orchards pruned to stumps for firewood, yards turned to middens, fields and pastures trampled, hedges and fences breached.

Every company had its place in the order of march, and the clan of Crux was part of the vanguard, far ahead of the baggage. Sire Galan set out every morning before dawn, striding along on foot among his fellow cataphracts on their great warhorses, and I wouldn't see him again until we made camp in the afternoon. He went lightly armored, wearing a padded linen shirt and leggings, and his new hauberk with enameled links, which I thought too delicate for battle. He hung his greater and lesser swords and his mercy dagger from his baldric. His armiger Sire Edecon rode at his side, and Spiller and Rowney took turns riding behind him, carrying his helmet, buckler, and scorpion. His plate armor was packed away in the baggage.

Sire Galan kept the pace, staying close by his uncle's stirrup; in silent rebuke, some said, for an unjust punishment. But Galan never said so, never offered a word of complaint, though he was quick to take offense if he thought he was being slighted for walking. He was more often praised, as most young hotspurs accounted it a great exploit that he went on foot. Of course none saw fit to praise his three foot soldiers, Cinder, Nift, and Digger, who walked just as far every day, carrying heavy burdens, and then labored in gangs to dig ditches, cut wood and fodder, build fences, and haul water when we reached camp.

We were following a fine straight road, paved with crushed stone and wide enough for two carts side by side, across a region of Incus called the Wolds. It was a fertile countryside, full of towns and villages, but a nuisance for travelers heading west, as we were. The land rose in long swells running mostly north to south, so that we had to climb one hill after another. In many of the valleys between these ridges there were lakes to ride around, or rivers to cross.

About midday we came to an unexpected halt. No one knew why. A ford ahead, probably. The slow and ponderous stoppage started in the front of the line and only gradually became known in the rear, so that those of us in the middle were crammed together, or forced off the raised gravel road into muddy ditches and fields. Men and horses and mules lost their tempers. Cook, the Crux's provisioner, swore at Sire Farol's bagboy, who had scraped his oxcart so close to one of the Crux's that if he moved he'd break some spokes.

We in the baggage were in a valley; the head of the army was over the next hill, and the tail over the hill behind. The weather was cold and blustery, and it was raining hard. Spiller grumbled. It was his turn to lead Sire Galan's baggage mules, and he thought it beneath him. He said that Sire Galan should have made Rowney a bagboy, he didn't need two jacks. Or he should get a new bagboy, a horseboy too. Spiller had good cause for complaint, but I was tired of hearing it.

"I'm going to see Fie," I told him.

"Fie? Who's that?"

"You know, my my friend."

"The broad-buttocked sow? Give her a kiss for me, eh?"

Delve's baggage was ahead of us in the line of march, so I rode Frost into the ditch beside the road and up the other side and trotted through a field. Mai's oxcart had a canopy of hides, stretched over wooden arches, that resembled nothing so much as the flanks of a starving cow. I called out to Mai and she waved and gave me a cheery greeting. I tied Frost to the cart and climbed into the back, past Pinch sitting on the driver's seat with a long switch. Mai, Sunup, Tobe, and the piebald hound had a nest back there on sacks of grain and beans.

I took Mai's hand and said, "Have you been eating?" Her nails were chewed to the quick and had white spots. Her belly looked like she'd swallowed a barrel and was just as hard, but the rest of her flesh, what I could see of it, hung in heavy swags. I visited her most days on the road or in camp to see how she was.

She laughed. "Mouse doesn't have a taste for fish, and what else is there? I could dwindle by half and still make twice of you, so stop fretting." There was a powerful stink in the cart from a cask of pickled herring. No wonder she lacked appetite.

Tobe climbed into my lap, and he explained something to me in his own peculiar language that daily came more and more to resemble our own, which only Mai and Sunup could understand. Then he got bored and squirmed to get away, as if he wanted to go and play among the cartwheels and hooves. Sunup took him in hand and they lay down on grain sacks near the dog. She murmured to Tobe, telling him a story.

I told Mai the war was not what I'd expected. "I thought there'd be fighting, big boffles. But it's more like a feastable every night, a feastival."

"Ha, boffles," she said. "Are you bored? We'll go in easy as a greased pig, but I daresay we won't be so quick to come out again. By the time we get where Corvus wants us, we'll be cold and weary and hungry and he'll still be cosy in Malleus."

"We won't go hungry so long as we have . . . stick, stack . . . stackfish." I was trying to make a jest of sorts. We had bales of stockfish, everyone did, and everyone loathed it. It was dried cod, hard as a plank and just as tasty. One had to pound it with a hammer all evening before it was fit to soak and stew.

Sunup was saying to Tobe, "You see, it was because the Moon was hungry. He dressed up like a silver fox and followed the wolves. He said, 'I'm your cub, leave some for me,' and the wolves said, 'You don't smell right.'" Tobe giggled when she pretended to sniff him.

Mai said, "I've got something for you." She fished out her purse from under her tight bodice, and gave me a silver coin, a graybeard.

"What's this for?"

"For talking to Flammakin yesterday."

Mai had invited me to her tent yesterday evening, and I'd arrived to find she had another visitor already, a woman I'd never met, this Flammakin. She was the sheath of a Wolf. The queenmother's Wolves were from the northern borderlands of Incus; they kept themselves aloof from King Thyrse's warriors, and rumor made them out to be fearsome creatures, hardly men at all. But Flammakin seemed ordinary enough, dithering on about two men she was seeing behind her cataphract's back, and which of them she should run off with now that her Wolf was getting tiresome. I thought she was there to consult Mai, who was canny in the arts of Carnal Desire.

I said, "Why so? We didn't have much of a . . . convention . . . consternation." Flammakin spoke the High with the accent peculiar to the northerners, so that I could hardly understand her. And I'd had the usual trouble making myself understood.

When Mai laughed, the whole cart shook. "She was perfectly well satisfied. She's going to take your advice."

"What advise?"

"She's going to take up with Sire Noctambule."

"Which one was he, the rich or the handersome?"

"The rich one," Mai said.

"I never said such. What did I say?"

"It hardly mattered. Flammakin just wanted to be advised to do what she'd already decided to do."

"So for this you took coins on my behand? What was your shave?" The more Mai guffawed, the more indignant I was.

"I don't see the harm," she said when she was done laughing. "Flammakin was delighted, and you're the richer for it."

"Still. I'm not a revelicker, a a revelighter. Don't do it again," I said.

The cart lurched forward as the army started to move. Pinch began to whistle. And Sunup said to Tobe, "The fox said, 'That's because I'm hungry. I've been eating pease pottage and coleworts, I've been eating radishes and onions, no fit food for wolves like us.' So the wolves caught a stag and ate up every scrap of meat. And the fox stared and stared with his tongue hanging out until they took pity on him and let him gnaw on the shin bones . . . ," and she pretended to bite Tobe's leg until he squealed, "and the thighbones and the hip bones and the rib bones and the neck bones and the skull," and every time she named a bone she nibbled on Tobe until he was laughing and shrieking. "And that's how the Moon got full!"

The hungry new Moon was due to show himself tonight, if the clouds would only part so we could see him. The month called Long Nights was beginning and long nights meant short days and short marches. While it was still afternoon, the army made camp near the brow of a hill, beside a steep ravine that offered some protection, firewood, and a good fast stream at the bottom for water.

Rowney and I headed down the wooded slope. It wasn't safe for me to forage alone. I had acquaintances in every clan company, and no longer trembled every time a man looked too long at me or called me a lewd byname, as I used to do when I was a newcomer to the Marchfield. But with so many men roaming in packs, there was reason to be wary.

I collected dead branches, working my way downstream and keeping my eyes open for childbane bushes, which prefer wet feet. I'd been searching for it since we left Lanx, and I was beginning to fear it didn't grow in this kingdom. I'd used the last of the berries Mai had given me. My tides weren't late, not yet.

I knotted my skirt to make a carry sack, and gathered red haws from a thorny tree. They were sweeter than usual; perhaps I could give some to Cook in exchange for an egg. It galled me that I couldn't think of the name of the tree, for it was common in hedges and thickets. The Dame had taught me its song, a riddle and incantation, and now the tune came back to me with but a few words. Something about throat's ease—*It bears the fruit we call throat's ease,* that was all I recalled. I sang it over and over, hoping it would lead me to the rest of the song and the name. Why should it matter what the tree was called, so long as I knew what could be done with it? Yet it did matter.

Something rustled in dried leaves under the briars. Rowney crept forward, and pulled off his leather jerkin and scooped something up with it, saying, "Aha!" He'd caught an unlucky hedgehog that had come nosing out of the thicket to see what kind of evening it was. I heard a muffled thump as Rowney dispatched it with the blunt side of his ax.

"Hawtorn!" I said to Rowney, pleased to have remembered the name. The haws would make a good relish for the winter-fat hedgehog. We'd sup well tonight.

"Hmm?" he said.

We climbed up the banks of the ravine and I stopped to catch my breath and hitch up my bundle of firewood. All day dirty fleeces of cloud had covered the Sun. Now the rain had stopped and the Sun's face showed between the clouds and the horizon. As her orange disk touched the rim of the world, the bristling back of the ridge to the west was edged in fire. It was a fine sight to see the encampment whole, in the ruddy sunset light: a great wheel with King Thryse's large pavilion at the hub, and the rest of the pavilions in orderly lines between the spokes, with bright banners flickering in the wind, and plumes of smoke curling up from campfires. And it was a fine thing to be part of something so much grander than myself. I'd be content to march forever, so long as we never reached a battle.

A dream came to me at the end of a wakeful night. In the dream I wandered the terraces seeking remnants of the old gardens, plants that had survived in sheltered spots, or their offspring, sown by the wind. Even on the near side of winter there were treasures to be found, seeds clinging to dried flowerheads of fennel, dill, and anise, and lousewort with a few seedcases that had failed to split open. I found green crowns of chicory and wintercress. I dug and divided pungent-smelling garlic, and pulled parsnips for my supper. The plants were gifts and their names came to me without fail. I recognized the signs inscribed by the gods in root, stalk, leaf, and flower. When I awoke I savored the names that lingered on my tongue.

Weariness was a burden that every day weighed more heavily on me, for every night was restless. But this morning I was as rested as if I'd slept the night through.

We had yet to encounter enemy warriors. It seemed the gravest danger a hotspur faced these days—and not a slight one, to be sure—was from one of his fellows in a mood to take offense. In the morning a cataphract from Ardor had the audacity to stare at Sire Galan as he marched along. Spiller told this to Rowney and me in the evening, by way of explaining how he—Spiller, that is—came by his broken nose.

He said Sire Galan had spoken up when this cataphract eyed him, saying he wondered why he gazed so discourteously. And this fellow, Sire Lapalissade, said he meant no discourtesy; he merely stared in wonderment to see a man of the Blood riding such a poor nag as Shank's-Mare—meaning Galan on his own two feet. Then Sire Galan made remarks about the cataphract's horse and his horse's lineage. It looked to be a hot quarrel until Sire Guasca reminded Sire Galan of his oath not to feud with Ardor.

Sire Galan said he wasn't feuding, but there was nothing wrong with a bit of sport, was there? They ought to have a cockfight.

Sire Lapalissade said, "With spurs?"

Sire Galan said no spurs, if they drew steel it would break the truce.

So Spiller, Sire Gausca's jack Lich, and Sire Lebrel's horsemaster Weed were put up against three jacks from Ardor, and the betting started.

Spiller said, "One of Ardor's jacks crowed like a rooster and called us a flock of hens, and said he was the cock for us, and we might as well show our tail feathers and get it over with. And I said if I showed my backside it would be to blow him down with a fart, because he was such a light fellow a puff of wind would do for him."

"I wish I'd been there," Rowney said. "I'd rather fight than talk."

"Oh, I fought. How do you think I got this?" Spiller pointed at his face. His nose and brow were red and swollen, and he was already turning purple around one eye. His jerkin was stained. "I think my nose got broken. You should have seen all the blood!"

"You were beaten. Doesn't mean you fought," Rowney said.

"You ask Sire Galan. Sire Meollo clapped me on the back afterward and said I should be called Bloodspiller. So that's my new name. A good one, don't you think?"

"I'll wager three copperheads the only blood you spilled was your own," Rowney said.

Sire Galan had a new tent, and it was better than the old one, larger and more cleverly devised, and envied by fellow cataphracts who hadn't had the luck to lose a pavilion in the Marchfield so they could buy another. Likewise his new folding bed was of fine workmanship from Lanx. It was wider than his old cot, and had four painted posts holding up a canopy and gauze curtains, so we two had a pavilion within the pavilion when we retired to bed. Three mules were required to carry the tent and its fittings, and one for the bed and bedclothes.

Galan was off somewhere with Sire Edecon, gambling. It was long since he'd wagered on a certain maidenhead, but he still courted Chance. He left Spiller and Rowney to guard his baggage and me, for there were thieves about who didn't respect any man's reputation. The jacks were wrapped up in their blankets, sleeping off a quantity of ale.

I sat sewing a second dress from the wool Galan had given me. It made me melancholy, thinking of how Penna had helped me with the one I was wearing. When my eyes began to burn, I shook out the feather quilts and spread them on the folding bed, and lay down and listened to rain on the tent.

A long time later Sire Galan came in alone, and said, "Are you sleeping?" I sat up and he poured coins from a sack onto the quilt: copperheads, silver, gold. I sorted and counted them. I could still count, even if I'd forgotten how to read.

"Did you get these many from the codfight?" I asked.

"Some. Some I won tonight." Chance had been generous to him since he'd tattooed her name on his left palm. The more he offered at hazard, the more she returned, and in gratitude he gave her a tenth of his winnings. When he lost, when Chance blinked instead of winked, it was soon forgotten. Once a man was accounted lucky, it took more than an occasional loss to change his reputation.

I picked up a goldenhead and stared at it: a man in profile, with a humped nose and a beard. "Who's this?" I showed Galan the face on the coin. I thought it might be the queenmother's dead husband, but I couldn't manage his name. "Is it King . . . Mortal . . . Vital, Vitler?"

"It's the princeling, Corvus," Galan said. He tossed me another coin. "This is his father, King Voltur. Take both if you like." He stirred the coins and picked up a third blonde. "Take this too. You're due a share of good luck."

Wildfire

King Voltur's goldenhead depicted him with a heavy brow and a square beard in ringlets. Queenmother Caelum's face was on the third coin. She had reigned eight years as queen regent between her husband's death and her son's majority, so why shouldn't she have her own coins? For a jest, I bit down on the blonde as if it might be gilded lead, but it was gold, solid and sour. I let it drop, and Galan sat down on the bed and kissed me. I was so overstrung that he merely had to touch me to cause a shiver. I was jealous of the sway Chance had over him.

Rowney woke up and tended to his master. He pulled off Sire Galan's boots and folded his surcoat with the exaggerated care of a drunk. Galan had blisters upon blisters on his heels and toes and soles, and he wouldn't be comfortable until they turned to calluses. I scraped off loose white skin with a knife, and put on a greasy salve Divine Xyster had made for him. I could care for small pains such as this; a woman mustn't touch a man's open sores or wounds lest her touch taint his blood, and harm rather than help him. His feet were icy.

I could tell he was cross about something. I didn't think the blisters were enough to account for it; he'd suffered them for days without complaint. We got under the quilt and I pulled the coverlet over our heads. In the dark I could watch him but he couldn't see me. There was a strong scent of sweet balm from the foot salve. I said, "I heard about Sire . . . Lackadaisy, or or Lapscallion—the cockapert who insulted you. Are you still hungry at him?"

He laughed. "Hungry? I could swallow him whole, and still be hungry. He's not worth the trouble."

"What then?" I said. "What is it?"

"I won from Pava tonight. He wagered more coin than he had, and offered me his lesser warhorse in pawn until he had the money. Is he a fool or did he mean to offend me, offering a horse? He doesn't know how close I came . . ."

"He's a nincumfoot, a foot nine times over," I said. "He's too much of a forward to insult you apurpose."

"A forward?"

"No, I mean a a . . . cower, a coward."

"I hate that Pava knows," he said in a low voice. His hand wandered to my waist, and dawdled between my hips and ribs.

"Knows what?"

"Knows you."

"It wasn't the same." I put my forehead against his chest, hiding my face from him even in the dark. "I'm dearth to him . . . dirt. He has forgotten it. It was all a long, a long ago."

A year and a half ago, the Kingswood and Marchfield and Wildfire ago. If I told Galan the truth, that Sire Pava had forced me, would that ease his jealousy? I uncovered our heads and stared at the canopy over the bed. If I told him, it would make more trouble between them, and there was trouble enough already; and if I told him and he did nothing—why then, I'd be disappointed, wouldn't I?

Galan leaned on his elbow and looked at me. "He owes me a cart full of money. Tell me what you want and I'll delight in making him pay it."

"Well?" he said, after a pause.

"I am thanking," I said.

He gave a short, mirthless laugh.

I said, "It's a good warhouse. His side, sire was my old Dame's best stalwart . . . stallion."

"Not the horse."

I could think of nothing to take from Sire Pava that would cost him enough. But he did have something I wanted. I said to Galan, "What I ask, Sire Pawn doesn't want. But I swear he will miss it when it's gone. And it's somewhat you need."

"Is this a riddle?"

I spoke quickly and let the words tumble wherever they'd go. "I want you to take two of his boasts, his boys. Flit is my cousin, he's the fastest rotter in camp, good for errors . . . errants and messages; he'll make your swagboy. Ask for . . . Ef, for for Ev as a horseboy. He does all the work, because Sire Pava's horsemonster is a nasty, lasty sot. Spitter and Tawny— Splitter I mean—your jakes are in need of help. There are too many horses and males to care for, and too much boggle."

Fleetfoot wasn't my cousin—I had no kin. But I'd promised his mother, Az, that I'd look after him, and now I thought to do him a good turn. In the riot after the mortal tourney, a swordsman had lopped off half of Fleetfoot's left hand and part of two fingers from his right. Likely he'd make a poor bagboy.

But I was sure Ev would be a good horseboy. He'd worked in the Dame's stable since he was small; he had the horsemaster's gift, though Sire Pava had never noticed.

Galan said, "This is what you want? I'd rather take something of value, something Pava will miss—such as his gold chain with the emerald and pearl medallion. Wouldn't he turn green to see it around your neck?" He ran his finger down between my breasts, where the pendant would rest if I wore it.

"Sweet," I said. "But I couldn't abide the touch of his cold."

*   *   *

Wildfire

Galan lay sleeping with his arm over me; he had deserted me again. However long the night, it would pass quickly for him.

I thought of remembering and forgetting, how I could do neither one nor the other at will. I couldn't remember ordinary things, such as the name of the hawthorn tree, or where I'd packed the jar with the rising dough for the waybread this morning.

And I couldn't forget, couldn't banish from my mind what Sire Pava said after he had chased me down by the river, or Fleetfoot's wounded hands, or Penna with her neck outstretched. Or how the blood of drudges stained Sire Galan's clothing after the hunt for servants of Torrent, and Spiller said it was a pity we'd lost the laundress, and Rowney laughed.

And Sire Rodela relished the memories, and took joy in denying me sleep. His mocking buzz burrowed into my left ear, and when I tried to dig him out I got an earache for my troubles. I wished to put an end to all vengeance between Sire Rodela and me. I felt his shade was encumbered by malice, a rusted carapace that weighed him down even as he thought himself armored in it. Free him and free myself.

To be tormented by a god—robbed of memory, speech, and strength— was an affliction about which I could do nothing but pray. To be tormented by the dead was another sort of trouble entirely. I would seek Mai's counsel. She would know how to send away an obstinate shade, so that Rodela could no longer keep me from my ease.

Fleetfoot and Ev came to us the next morning, and Spiller right away began to call Fleetfoot Hamfist. It was apt enough, for where the boy's left hand had been cleft through the palm it had healed pink as a ham and just as blunt. And he was clumsy, with only half a thumb on one hand and a thumb and two full fingers on the other. When Spiller found out I'd asked Galan to take Fleetfoot in pawn, he called me a crook-eyed meddling mule-headed old auntie. But truly I think he was glad to have someone new to complain about.

Even Spiller couldn't complain of Ev. The horseboy acquainted himself with the horses and mules, murmuring to them, running his hands over them, learning their strengths and flaws. He had the knack of moving slowly and working quickly, and soon even the most foul-tempered mule nuzzled his head when he leaned down to rub liniment on her sores.

The boys had a war dog with them, a whelp that should have been culled, for she was as maimed as Fleetfoot. She carried her injured right hind leg tucked up under her belly, and went about doing the things pups do: cavorting, nipping, pissing on sacks, and chewing on saddles. She was dun in color, save for her black feet and muzzle, and she was fast for all that she had but three good legs. Her disposition was such that it was impossible to stay vexed with her. Spiller called her Piddle, and the name stuck, though Hamfist didn't.

I didn't like to see Fleetfoot cringe when Spiller raised a hand against him, or the way he spit on the ground when Spiller looked away. Once he'd been a lively boy, quick to laugh, and the fastest boy in the village races, delighting in swiftness like a gazehound. Now he was a sullen foot dragger.

That night when Sire Galan came to bed, he fussed at me that I'd made him take a bagboy who couldn't even tie a knot, but I saw he was only mock angry—just as he'd cursed, then laughed, when Piddle wriggled up to him beside the fire and gnawed on his baldric.

I said, "Flickfleet is fast. Put him against any lack in the army and he'll beat them in a trace, a trice, a race. You'll win twice his keep in waggers."

Sire Galan laughed so hard his eyes watered. He said, "Waggers! Waggers!" and hooted until I poked him in the ribs. It went better than I'd hoped.

I hurried Frost along to catch up with Mai's oxcart. She was sitting on the driver's bench. Pinch walked along beside the ox, flicking his switch and singing in time to the squeaking of a poorly fitted wheel.

> *Oh why the onion in your hand?*
> *I asked of the queenmother.*
> *Why it is for to make me weep*
> *The tears to move my brother.*

I climbed up beside Mai and we jounced along. She wore a magenta sling to support her vast belly, and she eased it from her neck to her shoulders, and told me the latest gossip about the trouble in Lanx. "The fishermen won't fish, they say Torrent is angry. The queenmother ordered some of them gaffed on their own hooks and hung from the walls of Torrent keep, but still they won't go. So it's all aboil there. I heard Queenmother Caelum sacrificed twenty ships to Torrent. She had them rowed out to sea and set ablaze—to placate the god, she said—but I warrant it was to make certain there'd be no easy retreat for us. I'm sure I don't need to tell you that if we lose the port, we'll be pinched between Lanx and Malleus."

Pinch was eavesdropping. "It was those brides," he said, making the avert sign. "There's a curse on us now."

"I heard you prophesied it," Mai said.

"Me?" I said.

"Yes, you, my dear. I heard you said, 'A water wife will bring you strife, a curse to last you all your life.'"

100

I said, "Who told you that? Some . . . thundermonger?"

Mai shook her head. "Poor silly girls, those brides. If they'd lived, I'm sure they'd have found more pleasurable ways to punish their husbands. But they made a fine end, didn't they? Maybe now a man will think twice before he gives a maid cause for vengeance."

I sat leaning against Mai, thinking of the maids of Torrent and others who'd already fallen in this war. Since we left Lanx I'd often caught sight of Penna from the corner of my eye, and turned my head to find it was nothing, or rather something white—a shirt showing between the laces of an oversleeve, or a gull landing in a field. She made use of such things, briefly. And at such times I felt that the dead of Lanx followed us like an invisible swarm, drawn by what they had once possessed, for their intimate belongings had been stolen instead of burned as was proper. I shuddered to think of Galan surrounded by shades as thick as carrion flies. That he was ignorant of their presence did not make him safe.

I said, "So many hates—how will we appease the debt, dead?"

She said, "I shouldn't worry about the dead. Few of them have the strength of will to do harm."

I said, "But if they do? Who can avert their . . . verses?"

Mai patted my arm. "Let the priests worry. It doesn't weigh upon us."

"But but—" I leaned close to her and whispered. "Ever since the frightening struck me, I have a . . . taunt in my ear, a haunt. I can't get rid of it, and I don't want any suspex to know. Do you know of someone who could banish it?"

She gave me a searching look. "Who is it?"

I shook my head.

Mai said, "Don't you trust me, Coz? Ah, never mind, I won't pry. But why don't you catch this shade by the nose, eh? Get it to tell you useful things."

Had she found my finger bones and divining compass when I was thunderstruck? Why else would she say that? I looked at both sides of her face, and couldn't tell what she knew. "Oh gods, Nay, Nai," I said. "Not this one. This shard, this . . . sharp is full of grimace and I must be rid of him. Can you help?"

"It will cost plenty."

I opened the purse I had hanging around my neck. Mai took two of the goldenheads Sire Galan had given me, and a silverhead—the one she'd given me two days ago. "This one's for my trouble," she said.

Long after dark the sounds of men carousing and brawling could be heard through the cloth walls of the tent. Sire Galan was out roaming with his armiger at his elbow and a jack at his heels. It seemed to me he was less eager than he once was to come home to bed. Yet he'd be eager enough to avail himself of me when he did come home—and I to avail myself of him.

Meanwhile the wait. Rowney was outside dicing with a jack named Cockspur, and Fleetfoot was asleep, so it was safe enough to spread out the divining compass on the bed. I'd memorized another godsign—Delve—which had been stamped upon the grain sacks in Mai's cart, and I found it on the compass with some satisfaction.

I recalled all twelve gods now, and all their avatars, though my tongue stumbled over the names when I tried to speak them aloud. After many evenings puzzling over the compass, I had notions about where each god should be in the circle, but without the godsigns to fasten them down, I couldn't hold them in mind all at once. The gods jostled, they traded places.

Our camp was like the divining compass enlarged, a circle divided into twelve equal arcants. Each afternoon surveyors marked the chosen ground and laid out crossing paths, and varlets cleared the land and raised pavilions. But our encampment wasn't as evenly portioned between the clans as the compass was between the gods. Troops under King Thryse's personal command and the queenmother's Wolves took half the camp, and the rest of the companies shared the other half, crowding two or more to an arcant. Several new companies had joined us in Lanx, from clans loyal to the queenmother.

The camp also was divided by circles, like the divining compass. The inner circle held the pavilions of the cataphracts; the second circle the foot soldiers, surrounded by baggage carts; and the outer circle the mounts, pack beasts, and livestock cared for by horseboys and drovers. And all around the horizon of the camp, we were guarded by sentries and dogs.

There was order to it, the same order each night though we moved from place to place. I found my way about by the clan banners raised around the pavilions, for I remembered well which color belonged to each god. If I had a banner from every clan, I could stitch them together to make a new compass.

Banners were hard to come by. I just needed little scraps of cloth. Crux's green was easy, and Mai would give me copper-colored cloth for Delve, and magenta for Carnal. Maybe I could dye cloth—no, easier to buy it. I still had a gold coin. One could buy almost anything in the market that sprang up outside camp every night, full of whores, sutlers selling food and drink (mostly drink), and traders who ventured out from the towns.

I kissed the bones and pulled tight the drawstring of the compass.

* * *

Wildfire

The sky was just lightening to gray in the east, and we were packing to leave, when Sire Erial sent his jack Bean to me, asking if I'd see to his ailing sheath. Bean said a mule had kicked her. I hadn't been called upon as a greenwoman since Wildfire struck me, and I wasn't sure I could heal someone else when I was in need of healing myself. But I couldn't refuse to try.

Sire Erial's sheath Mole had earned her name by the habit of scuttling about with her head hanging low. Though she and I were both followers of the company of Crux, we'd hardly spoken. I used to try to talk to her, but she was too timid to give me a greeting. There was a rumor that Sire Erial let his armiger and jack and bagboy and horsemaster use Mole when he was not inclined.

Sire Erial's tent had already been taken down. Mole was lying on a straw-stuffed pallet on the ground. Her face was tanned by the Sun, but sallow rather than ruddy. Grimy too. She wouldn't look at me.

"You got kicked?" I said. "Can I look?"

Mole nodded. I peeled off the blanket and found her wearing a filmy green shift in the fashion of Incus. She was thin, whittled down by too much work and not enough food. Through the gauze I could see a purple bruise on her left side, near her bottom rib. I put my warm right hand over the bruise and pushed down gently. Her ribs felt solid, no wiggle or give, but she yelped in pain. I'd seen worse bruises on Sire Galan and his men after tourneys, and I wondered if she was pretending to feel poorly to get out of working.

But my hand told me otherwise. She wasn't feverish; her skin was cold and damp from sweat. I pressed on her abdomen and felt some swelling and hardness there, on the left side. She moaned and shrank away from me, her belly muscles tensing. I said, "You don't have a broken thing, a broken jab . . . jib, but—I beg person, I'm sorry—I must see where less, where else it hurts. Here? Here?"

"My shoulder too," she said, with her head turned away from me.

"For why? Did you get kicked there too? No?" That was puzzling: Her shoulder had no bruises or tenderness, and she could move her arm, but she had pain inside. She was shivering now and I covered her again with the blanket, which was dirty and torn. She did laundry for her master and his armiger, no doubt, and neglected her own.

I looked up. Bean and the bagboy Oakhead were busy rolling up the canvas panels of the tent to pack on a mule. Sire Erial sat nearby on a folding camp chair, with his back to me and his feet to the brazier. A mule hadn't done this to her. More likely she was lying on the ground, and a man kicked her. In passing, maybe. A beating would have left more bruises. This thought put me in a fury, which I tried my best to hide. "Which mule . . . fool was it?" I said to Mole.

Her eyelids lowered. She wasn't going to tell me.

Without turning to look at me, Sire Erial asked, "Can she ride?"

"Hasn't she been riding?" I said. The bruise looked several days old.

"She's worse."

I leaned closer, my hands around her wrists. Her pulse flickered rather than throbbed, and her breathing was quick and shallow. Her sweat smelled sour—she was none too clean—but at least there was no scent of corruption.

I could ease her pain with willow bark and soothe-me, and keep her warm with blankets, so she might ride with Sire Erial and his men. But I thought she'd mend sooner if she stayed behind, free of serving them one after the other, free of kicks and blows. I whispered, "Vole, listen. Will you bide or will you ride? Understand? If you cannot, if you haven't the stretch, the strengithe—then I will seek a peace for you, a place—some cram, farm, croft herearounds."

She shook her head. I pulled out the pouch hidden under my bodice, and emptied it of coins: one blonde, and all the rest copperheads. It was all I had left. I put the coins in her hand and closed her fingers around them. "If you want to stay above . . . behind, I mean, I wouldn't leave you all all alost—I'll find somewhere, somewhat for you."

"I must ride," she whispered, and tears slid from her eyes and sideways down her cheeks. "I can't die alone—I'm going to die, I know it. Who would care for me? No one. Don't think worse of me, I beg you."

She tried to give me back the coins, and I pressed them into her hands. "You shan't die," I said. Though in truth I wasn't sure. I tucked the blanket around her and turned to Sire Erial. "She needs to go in a baggage."

"What do you mean, a baggage?"

"She needs a baggage—you know, what wheels along. And a cloud to wrap around her, she's too cold." I held up a corner of the blanket. "Like this, a cloudlet, only stuffed with fur, with furthers?"

Sire Erial shook his head. "I heard you were addled. I didn't believe it until now."

I helped Mole sit up. I took pains to gentle my touch, to straighten her dress and tease out the tangles in her matted hair. At first she shied from me like a skittish horse, and it was a victory to win from her a tremulous smile. I said, "Now, can you stand, do you think?"

I put my arm around her waist to hold her steady. For a moment it seemed as if she might swoon. Sire Erial came over and said, "Where are you going? What's wrong with her?" I'd never noticed how young he was, with spots on his face, and stray hairs on his upper lip and chin that showed he had yet to shave. He was, in my estimation and that of his fellows, a better braggart than fighter.

I said, "I think it best if she rides in a cookstart, an an . . . oxstart, but not astride, Sire. I'll ask the . . . the one who cooks, the Cox's provendiser, if he can take her. And she must not be ridden, because a man's hate, his weight, will do her hurt. You must leave her belone for a month at least, you and your men."

I found I couldn't fear him, not when rage was so much more delightful. I put my warm left hand on Sire Erial's arm, and he tried to shake me off. "So, Sire, are you the one who kicked her? Was it you or one of your villains? It was you, wasn't it?"

"A man may chastise his sheath," he said. "Sire Galan should chastise you, then you'd not be so brazen."

"It's not for you to advise him, Sire Folderol, he does as pleases him. And it pleases him to have me willing, not skulking and sulking like a a . . . moodiwart, a moil, mole. Ah, well, you're green—perhaps you don't know there's more pleasaunce to be found when your . . . if she is pleased too, hmm? Maybe she'd be better pleased if she wasn't shared. Or do you fret that your badboy would mind? Are you afraid of that, Sire? You could buy your men off with a few quims—that is to say with two cobbleheads for a cheat drabble-tail."

"How dare you speak to me this way! I'll pluck out your tongue for it!"

I bared my teeth at him and tried not to laugh. There was nothing to him but bluster. "My tongue was already plucked, Sire Erien. Can I help it if Wildire made me unspeakable? So heed me. Do you want her to mend? Then wait till after this month of loneliest, longest nights, and then—and then let her ride you—let her ride pillion on the pillicock, let her mount the stallion, eh? And maybe in a little while she'll be mare to you again."

I let Sire Erial go, and he rubbed his arm, staring. He caught sight of something over my shoulder and his face changed.

I turned and saw Galan a few paces behind me. He was smiling, but not in a comforting way.

"I, I sent for your sheath," Sire Erial said. "Because Mole is sick."

"I heard," said Galan.

I said, "His sheaf can't ride. I must see if . . . Cook will take her in an oxcart."

Galan took my arm and marched us away, and Mole leaned on me, moaning. She was so slight it was easy to bear her up. I got her settled on sacks in the back of one of Cook's kitchen carts, and gave her my old sheepskin cloak for a coverlet, as Galan wouldn't lend her a featherbed.

By then Sire Galan's belongings were packed and the mules were all standing patiently in line.

Galan asked, "What did you say to Sire Erial?"

"Nothing. Nothing but some good uncle, good counsel." I grinned, thinking of Sire Erial staring at me as goggle-eyed as a frog bemused by a snake that intends to eat him.

He looked at me hard, but there was a trace of mirth in the crinkles at the corners of his eyes. "I'd tell you to govern your tongue, but I know you can't. Or won't. But have a care, my heart. Most men aren't like that rabbit Erial. I don't want you picking quarrels that I will have to fight."

"My hearth," I said. "My heart." I reached out to touch the full curve of his lower lip. He stopped my hand by catching it in his own.

"Will you mind?" he asked.

"I'll try. You start quibbles enough of your own, don't you?"

But I was remorseful, fearing Sire Erial might be harsher to Mole now. Some take correction contrarily, by increasing their faults.

CHAPTER 7

Snowbound

 stood outside the tent looking up at the lopsided Moon, waxing toward the half. It was a clear night, and I was glad to see stars after so much rain, but the faint ring around the Moon promised yet another storm. I counted three stars in the ring; every star meant a day till rain or snow fell. That's what the old Auspex of Crux in our village used to say, and he was known for a shrewd weather priest. It would be snow, I thought. The turf underfoot was brittle and covered with hoarfrost. The cold rains had chilled us through; this was another kind of cold, keen and dry.

I closed my right eye, and the Moon was sharp edged and bright, his silver beginning to turn gold as he descended toward the hills.

I closed my left eye instead, and was afraid. In my right eye the Moon dimmed, turned a dirty yellow, and the shining ring around him was a gossamer web. The sky no longer appeared deep black but rather the color of lead. Many stars had vanished. I looked through each eye again and there was no doubt: a haze had gathered in my right eye.

The sparks and coronas that had troubled my vision after the lightning had faded days ago, along with the hammering headaches. Perhaps this too was but a passing affliction of my sight. It was a slight change after all, so slight I hadn't noticed it when I used both eyes at once.

I heard Sire Rodela humming with pleasure in my ear—gloating. That must mean my vision would get worse.

We entered lands belonging to the clan of Eorõe, which was loyal to Prince Corvus. Still we marched unopposed. Rumors of the slaughter in Lanx traveled before us. Towns and villages supplied the grain, fodder, and meat demanded by the queenmother's requisitioners. Soldiers were forbidden to go marauding for their own enjoyment, but it was impossible to stop light-fingered foraging. Few of the local folk dared protest when sheep, chickens, piglets—or even a son or daughter—vanished into the army's maw. Our warriors found the townsfolk contemptible. "Too much peace makes for a soft belly," Sire Edecon said.

It was true, there had been many years of peace here in the heart of Incus, and the towns weren't fortified and garrisoned for war, though many had ruined towers and breached walls, reminders of less peaceful times. Years and years ago, when King Voltur first came to power, some of the Firsts had been like little kings themselves, each one in his own domain. He'd humbled them, destroying their clan strongholds and putting an end to their petty wars. These days the high-ranking Blood of Incus preferred to play at courtier in Malleus, leaving the care of their people and lands and enterprises to poor country cousins, or even mudfolk—some of whom managed to profit from our passing by selling supplies to the army at steep prices.

It was certain the prices in the market outside our camp were higher than I'd imagined possible. I went there in search of childbane and cloth with which to make a new compass. The trouble was, I'd given my last coins to Mole, and for barter I had nothing but some remnants of cloth left over after making my dresses. I promised Fleetfoot an onion pie if he'd come with me, and Rowney came too, saying he needed a cobbler to mend one of his boots. I found the market bewildering. I could hardly tell who was buying and who was selling in such a crowd. Childbane was nowhere to be found. A rag peddler took my scraps of good green wool in return for two small pieces of linen, gray for Prey and yellow for Eorōe. He easily bested me in the trade. In the hubbub his words became commingled with the words of others, and I couldn't understand him. As if I were thunderstruck again.

The storm came in three days, as promised. A wind from the west hurled snow in our faces. Frost balked and tried to put her tail to the wind. I gave up walloping her with my heels and dismounted and dragged her along by the bridle. By the time we halted, around midday, all was blinding gray confusion.

The wind blew down any stretch of canvas raised against it. We made a shelter by building two walls of grain sacks and baggage and laying tent poles crosswise over them. Then we draped Sire Galan's waxed canvas tent over the poles, anchoring the edges so it wouldn't fly away. We crawled under it, Galan's jacks and Fleetfoot and I, and the dog Piddle. Ev stayed outside to tend to the horses and mules. I worried about how he and the foot soldiers would fare without shelter.

It was good to be out of the wind and snow, but the discomforts of our refuge were soon apparent. We lay side by side like logs, and the air, once it grew warmer, also grew more rank. The canvas flapped alarmingly in the wind, until snow weighed it down so that the roof sagged between the poles, closer and closer to us. We made do without fire. Spiller passed around a skin of ale he'd kept from freezing between his leg and his horse, and I rummaged in my saddlebag for raisins and twice-baked rockbread, so called because you could break your teeth on it if you didn't soak it first. I looked through the slit we'd left open to the storm. Not that there was much to see. It was midafternoon, but it seemed like twilight, ash gray and sunless. Now and then the dark form of a man would stagger past, shrouded against the gale. Already the snow was knee deep.

Spiller said, "What I wouldn't do for a ham hock!"

"Hush," said Rowney.

"Or perhaps a hen stewed up with turnips and onions."

"I'd like a sausage," Fleetfoot said.

"Who asked you?" said Spiller.

I could smell a fire and meat roasting on it. No doubt it was the Crux's provisioner at work. Cook could make a feast appear anyhow, anywhere. The Crux's varlets had raised his tent somehow, but I wouldn't have been surprised if it had blown down around his head, and the heads of Sire Galan and his fellows. I almost wished it on them, out of envy. It was the Crux's duty to feed the Blood of his troop, as it was Sire Galan's duty to feed us, his servants. Sire Galan had purchased food in Lanx that was supposed to last for a month of campaigning, and mules to carry the food. I blamed Spiller, who'd done the haggling, for getting barley that was half chaff, and beans hollowed out by weevils. We were all thoroughly sick of stockfish, sprats in mustard, and herrings in pickle. Still, we ate better than Galan's foot soldiers, for Spiller was stingy with their rations.

I had Rowney to one side and Fleetfoot and Piddle to the other. The boy had fallen asleep with his arm over the dog. Piddle raised her head, sniffing, and when I caught her eye she licked my cheek. Rowney lay on his back. I didn't know how he could stand having his nose so close to the sagging ceiling.

"What *would* you do for a ham hock?" Rowney asked.

Spiller said, "What do you mean?"

"I daresay there are ham hocks and chickens and sausages in the next town. We could go get some."

"Now?"

Rowney laughed. Spiller's voice had gone high. "Of course not now. When the snow eases."

Spiller raised his head and I saw him grin. "Whenever it suits—I'm for it. I'm tired of pease. Pease isn't a man's food."

"Best not wait too late," I said. "Or all those ham hacks and passages will be in the maws, jaws, of the keenmother's Woes."

Sires Galan and Edecon came wading through the drifts. They stamped and brushed snow off their clothes and crawled into the shelter. We all had to shuffle about so that I was next to the wall of baggage and Galan was next to me, and we were even more crowded and stinking—warmer though.

Sire Edecon said there was a powerful stench of mud, and the varlets should sleep outside; it was like sleeping with hogs. Sire Galan said Sire Edecon should not be so delicate with respect to his nose, and it was brutal cold outside and a peril to man and beast.

We drudges said nothing at all.

I dreamed the weather turned warm, the airs soft and misty, and gnats swarmed over the fields. I planted cuttings of gooseberry and honeysuckle and crab apple east of the house. There was a ruin of an old barn or croft farther down the hill, just a corner left of two stone walls, and against the south-facing wall I was amazed to find wallflower still in bloom. I picked some for a tisane to bring on my tides, which were a few days late in coming.

Another gray twilight, dawn this time, and Rowney started a commotion in the shelter by wriggling out of it. Piddle scrambled out next, putting her big paws on whoever was in her way, and I followed. Snow sifted down in gentle flakes, nothing like the fury of the day before. Our shelter was nearly buried under a drift that looked like a frozen wave, with ripples all over the surface and a sharp crest. The wave had broken over Rowney when he burrowed out. He brushed snow off his hair and shoulders. It was so early there were only a few other drudges stirring.

I was surprised to see there was a town quite nearby, in the valley below. Like many of the towns we'd passed on the way to Malleus, it had a paved square lined by houses of two or three stories set close as teeth, and a scattering of crofts on the outskirts. Sometimes the towns were at crossroads; this one had a drawbridge over a navigable river that made its way south along the narrow valley. Smoke rose from the chimneys, but this morning I didn't envy the people snug in their houses. It was the first heavy snow of the winter, and I delighted in it as much as Piddle, who romped about, breaking the smooth crust.

I heard Spiller cursing at Fleetfoot, trying to roust him out to get wood and water. The boy crawled out from under the canvas, scowling. He could barely wield a hatchet, but Spiller didn't care: it was a bagboy's duty to fetch wood, so fetch it he must. I helped Fleetfoot as usual—not that he was grateful.

By the time we got back with brush and wood, Galan's foot soldiers were digging a clearing to put up his tent, and Spiller was melting snow on a small fire. He taunted Fleetfoot for being lazy and clumsy, and the boy wagged a finger as soon as Spiller's back was turned, making the sign for a cowardly dog.

A little while later Spiller knocked Fleetfoot on his buttocks for losing a wooden spoon or a bag of currants, and the boy sprang up and threw a handful of snow in Spiller's face. Spilled howled and swung and Fleetfoot skipped away.

Rowney looked up from shoveling snow and said, "Boy, you better fleet-foot it as fast as you can, because if Bloodspiller gets hold of you, you'll be sorry." But Fleetfoot couldn't run, or it would be said he didn't have the heart to finish a fight he'd started, even if the fight was with a man and he couldn't win it.

I said, "Splitter, leave him be, he's just a boy."

Spiller said, "A boy in need of a whipping," and he rushed at Fleetfoot, who dodged him easily and threw more snow.

The drudges within shouting distance gathered to watch and wager. And to laugh, because the more Fleetfoot dodged, the more Spiller got riled, and the more he looked a blundering fool. Piddle dashed about, barking as if it were a great game. But at length Spiller lunged and caught Fleetfoot by his tunic, and served him with heavy blows. Fleetfoot flailed at him with his right hand, and got in a hit on Spiller's nose, still sore from the cockfight. Piddle caught a mouthful of Spiller's leggings. Neither did the jack much harm.

The lad wasn't going to cry mercy. I dithered, thinking that if I stepped between them, Fleetfoot would never hear the end of jeers about hiding under my skirts. And then he'd have to pick fights with the jokers.

Spiller knocked Fleetfoot to the ground and knelt on his ribs and struck him in the face. Piddle bit Spiller on the arm and hung on, and he shouted, "Call off the dog or I'll wring his neck!" In due time Rowney and Cook pulled Spiller off Fleetfoot and congratulated him on his glorious victory. They said he was a fine fellow and he'd shown it by defeating a ham-fisted boy.

"I didn't defeat him, I gave him a beating," Spiller said indignantly, "which is what he'll get any time he's insolent."

The spectators praised Fleetfoot for his courage in defending himself one-handed, and he wore his bruises like banners, having won the fight even in losing it.

By the next morning the blanket of snow that had shone so clean and white was filthy and tumbled. The cold was unrelenting. We'd sheltered wherever we could during the storm, and afterward dug in where we found ourselves, so the camp had no proper order to it. Drudges had scratched holes in the frozen ground with pickaxes to raise their masters' pavilions; foot soldiers made their own shelters by tunneling into hard-packed drifts. There were heaps and walls of snow all around.

We drudges were cross because Sire Edecon had stayed in the tent all day yesterday with his dulcet, picking out a tune that never came to an end, and he'd started up again today though the Sun had just begun to yawn over the horizon. If Sire Galan hadn't been sleeping soundly, he'd have thrown a boot at his armiger.

Rowney shouldered his ax.

"Are you getting more wool, wood?" I asked him.

"Yes, and ham hocks."

"Shall I go?" I said.

"I wouldn't, if I were you," Spiller said.

Of course that made me want to go. Rowney set out in the lead, puffing clouds of breath, breaking the way through snow up to his waist. I followed Spiller, and Fleetfoot followed me, and Piddle came floundering along beside us, covering twice the ground in her eagerness to be everywhere.

Outside the camp the snow was unsullied. Small winds kicked up plumes of fine grains over the polished faces of the drifts. The road was hidden, so we went through the fields, approaching the town from the south, coming up behind the walled gardens of the larger houses. I saw a few wizened apples with perfect caps of snow, dangling from a bough that reached over the brick wall of a garden. I pointed to them and said, "If you heft me up, I'll get those." Imagine, they had apples enough to leave some on the tree!

Spiller tried the plank door in the wall and found it latched but wobbling on its hinges. He threw his weight against it, and grunted and staggered backward.

"The snow's too deep," Rowney said.

"Come on! Lift me—I can get on there," I said.

"I'll hoist her," Spiller said with a bit of a leer.

"No you don't," said Rowney, and he stood by the wall and laced his hands together like a stirrup to boost me up. I climbed to his shoulders and to the top of the wall, and then to the bough, after shaking it to dislodge its load of snow. I threw apples down at them.

"They have heats of firerough in there," I said.

Rowney said, "Can you get down and clear snow so we can open the gate?"

I let them in, I did. And Sire Rodela's buzz got louder, becoming a sort of prickle or itch behind my eardrum, where I couldn't get at it.

Wildfire

Rowney knocked on the back door, and chickens scolded us from their coop. A streamer of smoke rose from the chimney, so we knew someone was awake. The Sun was just coming up behind the clouds, giving them a pearly sheen.

A woman's voice inside said, "Who is it?"

Rowney found the door unlocked and threw it open. A serving maid was standing in the doorway; her hair was sleeked back and plaited. She wore a thin dress, an apron, a shawl, and a pair of embroidered slippers. She took a step back, saying, "What do you want? What's your business here?" It sounded like the yelping of a little dog. Rowney pushed his way in and she backed up. The rest of us followed.

Inside the house, the light was yellow and lively from candles and a new-made fire in an arched stone niche, but it was cold. The maid clasped her chapped hands together. Her face had gone stark pale except for the ruddy tip of her nose.

Spiller looked in the pot suspended from a pothook over the fire. "Oats," he said with disgust.

"Where are your master and mistress?" Rowney said in the High. "Upstairs?" The maid had her back to the table in the middle of the room, and he was standing too close, leaning over her. She kept her eyes downcast as she nodded, and her shoulders were hunched as if she expected him to hit her. My throat was dry. Rowney was a tried soldier, the only one among us who'd been to war before, for he'd accompanied Sire Alcoba's older brother on a campaign. I knew it, but I'd never seen it till now, when he put menace on like a cloak.

"Having a cuddle, I wager," said Spiller. "Hey? Hey? I wouldn't mind a bit of a cuddle with *her*." He was in a jovial mood. The girl couldn't understand his words, because he spoke in the Low, but she knew what he meant right enough; soon she'd be leaking tears. Sire Rodela sniggered in my ear, even noisier now than when I'd opened the gate to the garden.

Rowney disappeared into the front room, and Fleetfoot down the trapdoor to the root cellar. Spiller climbed on a stool and cut down the half-eaten ham hanging from the roof beam. He sat at the table and sawed the ham with his dagger. He demanded that the maid bring him bread, ale, eggs, and mustard, and she hurried to do as he asked. His bruises from the cockfight were turning from purple to yellow, and his nose was healing askew. He was a fearsome sight.

I went into the front room after Rowney. The ground floor had but two rooms, the kitchen to the rear and a clothier's shop facing the street, with a long table and bench for tailoring. Wide shutters, pierced in a crossweave pattern, could be raised along the front to open the shop to the street. The clothier was prosperous enough to afford sheets of mica in the openings of the shutters. A glazed clay statue of Wend Weaver stood by the door. Rowney was pulling folded cloth from the shelves and shaking it out, looking for money. He emptied baskets of scraps and thread on the floor.

The stair to the sleeping loft was two notched logs set side by side, steeply inclined. I saw descending a pair of bare feet, shins, and knobby knees, and then the tail of a long shirt. "Rolly!" I called in warning.

Rowney was there in an instant, shoving the haft of his ax in the man's belly. The man ducked and saw Rowney, and came the rest of the way down the stairs. "What do you want?" he said. His voice was strong but his looks belied it. He was stooped and nearsighted from his work, but younger than I'd expected after seeing his stringy legs.

"Sausage wouldn't go amiss," Rowney said, smiling. "But we'll take whatever you've got, food, wood, money."

"I'm a poor man, Sire," the clothier said. "I don't have money, I have debts."

The High came out of the mudman's mouth as if he were born haughty. It made him sound insolent—I couldn't tell if that was Sire Rodela's opinion or my own.

"You have money," Rowney said, raising the ax blade to the man's throat.

I put my hand on Rowney's sleeve. The muscles of his arm were hard, though he held the ax loosely. I said, "I thought somewhat, a bit of eat and firewool . . . That's all we need."

Rowney gave me a look.

A thud from upstairs. Someone had shut the trapdoor and was dragging something heavy over it.

Rowney said, "So it's upstairs, your money?" and the man shook his head, but Rowney took his answer from the fear in the man's eye and pushed him aside. He thumped against the trapdoor with the butt of his ax, and a baby began to cry upstairs. "We've got your man down here," Rowney called. "Best for him if you let us up."

No answer. Rowney turned to the clothier again and gripped his shoulder and sat him down forcefully on his bench. The man's weak gray eyes were watering. Rowney leaned down to talk to him. "I want you to sing out, now. Tell them to open the door up there. We just want a look around, we're not going to harm anybody."

Spiller had come in from the kitchen to see what Rowney was shouting about. "I'll make him sing. I'll tickle him with this, see if he sings out then." Spiller waved his smallsword in the clothier's face. "Sing a song and we'll let you go, I promise."

Wildfire

"I can't sing, Sire, I beg your pardon," the man said. "I have a poor voice, I fear."

I heard Sire Rodela's jeering laughter come out of my mouth. I couldn't help being amused by the way the man squeaked—Spiller was laughing too. Meanwhile Rowney had climbed halfway up the ladder and was chopping at the trapdoor with his ax, at an awkward angle, sinking the blade in and wrenching it out again. Splinters rained down and a woman screamed upstairs. The baby was bawling, the kind of cry that goes on and on and stops abruptly until the child catches breath to wail again.

Spiller mimicked the clothier, saying in a high voice, "I can't sing, Sire, I have a poor voice, I fear!" and then, in his own voice, "I don't care if you sound like a goose, you will sing. Don't you know any songs? Sing 'Will ye or nill ye,' or 'The baker's wife.'" Fleetfoot came to the kitchen door and stood there grinning.

"I don't know those songs, begging your pardon, Sire." The man cringed. He avoided Spiller's eyes, wouldn't even sneak a glance at Rowney wielding the ax. He was servile, a coward. He wasn't going to raise a hand to protect his wife and child, but he was obstinate about his money, wasn't he? He should have more sense, give Rowney what he was after.

Spiller was still laughing, but his jest had turned sour. He wanted to make the clothier sing just because he wouldn't. He put the point of his smallsword to his throat and ordered him to sing; he didn't care what song. I'd been sure Spiller wouldn't hurt the man, but now I began to wonder. The clothier opened his mouth and nothing came out, and Spiller leaned closer, pressed harder against his throat. The man sang—though you couldn't call it singing, it was more of a croak—

> *Hush little one, stop your crying.*
> *Your mother can sew and she can spin,*
> *She'll weave a fine cloth to swaddle you in.*

Spiller guffawed and said, "Don't you know any songs fit for men?"

Rowney was vexed that Spiller was wasting time on the clothier. He shouted for him to come and help, and both of them put their shoulders to the trapdoor and they managed to lift it a handspan, only to have an iron-tipped stave jabbed in their faces. But Rowney was quick. He grabbed the stave away from the woman upstairs and they heaved at the trapdoor again.

I crouched by the overturned basket of scraps, looking for pieces of cloth the proper color and size for my compass. I looked up to see the clothier sidling toward the front door. He met my gaze with a pleading look. Sire Rodela hissed with laughter in my ear, but I didn't say a word.

"Wait!" Spiller called, jumping off the ladder, but by then the clothier was out the front door and blundering in his nightshirt through the snowdrifts to the house next door, howling for help.

"She let him go!" Spiller said. "Let him prance right out the door!"

I shoved all the scraps into the basket and stood up. I said, "Guess we'd best hurry now, before he comes back with somebody brawler, braver, like a blacksmite."

Sire Galan's varlets were angry with me, even Fleetfoot, who spoke longingly of the treasures left behind in the root cellar. Spiller said he'd been getting along well with the little maid, he'd have had her bent backward over the kitchen table if I hadn't interfered. Though he did admit it had been a fine sight to see Rowney running along with captive hens in each hand: what a battle they waged against him, how they heaved themselves about and flapped and scolded! And Bloodspiller laughed as he said this, his laugh remarkably like the squawking of an outraged chicken.

Rowney didn't say anything, but his silence was reproachful.

I couldn't pretend I'd been ignorant of what we were about. I'd picked up logs from the woodpile as we ran out through the back garden, warmed myself by the fire made of stolen wood, and helped to eat the chickens. And I had enough cloth now to make myself a new divining compass, for I'd stolen the basket of scraps. I wasn't above looting—or thieving, call it by its rightful name—if I wasn't above enjoying its fruits. As Sire Galan had once made painfully plain to me.

So I went along. And when I saw the serving girl with her lips trembling, hadn't I felt a sweet thrill of contempt? The more I'd seen of myself in her, the more I'd despised her weakness. It still gave me a queasy, slippery excitement in my belly pit to think of it: Rowney digging his ax blade into the tailor's throat. What Bloodspiller might have got up to in the kitchen.

I reproached myself. But I blamed Sire Rodela too. He'd goaded me on, buzzed so loudly I couldn't think, tainted me with his joy. I couldn't wait to be rid of him. Mai had promised me it would be soon, very soon.

CHAPTER 8

The Summoning

e were pent up in camp while gangs of foot soldiers labored to clear the road, and snow drifted down to cover it again. Tomorrow was Longest Night, and there would be a bonfire and a feast. From now on the days would get longer, which was cause for celebration. Cause to mourn too, for now the Crone had us in her bony grip, and it would be months before she would let us go.

Sickness was rife while we were snowbound, especially the squirts and a deep cough we called the rattle. Neither was likely to be fatal, but a woman craves being looked after at such a time of weakness. I brewed up a tisane to ease the rattle, and made up a mash of barley bran to dry up the squirts, and went visiting as a greenwoman once again, accompanied by Fleetfoot and Piddle. By now everyone seemed to know that I'd been struck by lightning, and I do believe some whores sent for me just to marvel at my muddled way of talking.

I stopped by Sire Erial's tent to bring Mole another decoction of willow bark and soothe-me. I'd been seeing her daily and only now was she willing to look straight at me, from time to time. She was sitting on her pallet, wrapped in my old sheepskin cloak—that cloak had served me well, keeping me warm all winter in the Kingswood, but with a sigh I gave up all thought of getting it back.

Today Mole had put on a headcloth. It was a sure sign she was better, that she took the trouble to cover her hair. I sat beside her and spoke quietly so the bagboy wouldn't overhear. "Are they leaving you be?"

She looked sideways at me and nodded. She whispered, "Will you take this back, please?" Her hand darted out from under the cloak to put a goldenhead in my palm—no doubt the same one I'd given her. "One of them will steal it. It makes me too afraid, I can't stop worrying about it."

She didn't seem to be joking. I tucked the coin in my money sack. "If this gilt, glit, glower . . . glowdenhead is keeping you awake at fright, I'll keep it. But you can ask if you need it."

117

"I'll get by," she said, a little sullen. Defiant even.

So she could be something other than meek. Maybe she thought I looked down on her because she'd chosen to stay; and because I had just one man, a generous one who gave me golden coins, while she had Sire Erial and the others. But truly I understood. I'd been foolish to think she might be better off with strangers in a foreign land than among people who knew her. How I must have frightened her with my strange notions and speech, when she'd been so ill and afraid already!

Before I left I managed to make her laugh at something I said, something bungled and backward.

Fleetfoot and Piddle and I wandered a labyrinth of icy trails, between mounds of snow higher than our heads, looking for the copper banners of Delve. We found Sire Torosus's tent, but Mai wasn't in it. She was staying in her oxcart. If she was avoiding men, she must be nearly ready to give birth.

The oxcart was up to its axles in snow, and the small cleared space before it had been much trampled and befouled by the ox confined there. Tobe and Sunup were playing outside, and Tobe came running so I could pick him up. Every time I saw him he was steadier on his feet. Piddle and the piebald dog barked at each other and then made peace.

Mai sat in the cart with her legs stretched out before her.

"Is your travile come so soon?" I said.

"It could be now or in a hand of days," Mai said, "whatever Mouse decides. Remember I told you I lost the last child bearing it? I took to my bed beforehand for a tennight, and when it stopped moving about inside I knew I was in for terrible travail. But Mouse is still thumping. What a bruiser he promises to be! So I don't mind the wait."

I rubbed my hands up and down Mai's legs gently, more gently than I kneaded my own legs when they cramped. "Do your pegs ache?" I asked.

"Oh, indeed. But can you rub my back? That hurts worse. Push right there, push hard. Ah, that's good. You're stronger than Sunup."

"You said you could get help for me soon, May. When will it be? I can't sleep, the haint is always business in my ear."

"The summoner says tomorrow is a most propitious day for it, couldn't be better. At Longest Night the Queen of the Dead hears all petitioners."

"A suddener? I need a vanisher, banisher to rid me of this . . ." I pointed to my ear.

Mai lowered her voice. "Trust me, Coz, as I trust you. Pinch will take you to him tomorrow. Do as the summoner asks, for he's wise in the ways of the dead. Now, what have you got to give him?"

"I already gave you quits—two blands, two goldenheads, remember?"

"But you still need to pay the toll, with something you'd be loath to give away. I never saw you disinclined to part with coins," she said. "Something dearer."

"I believe I've finished my lament," Sire Edecon said that evening. "Would you like to hear it?"

Galan curtly answered, "No," as if speaking to a servant. Sire Edecon put the dulcet down with a thump, and the strings whispered in vexation.

"Oh, never mind," Galan said. "Let's hear it."

Sire Edecon had to be coaxed, but it wasn't long before he played the song through for us without fumbling more than once or twice. A good rumormonger made a song of parts that fit together tightly and rightly, so that even if you'd never heard it before, and couldn't guess how it would go, once it had been played it seemed it could have been made no other way. Perhaps because of Sire Edecon's ignorance of the craft, his song had a haunting strangeness. He'd written it for his dead wife.

He sang of how he offered his bride life and she chose death, saying god and kin called her to do her duty. He asked if she did not bear a greater duty to him, her husband, and she replied she could not be an honorable wife if she were not first an honorable daughter, and she must seek the terrible embrace of death rather than the delightful embrace of her husband. And so forth at length. When Sire Edecon was done there was a long silence, during which he began to blush and fidget.

I felt a chill pinch on the back of my neck. Didn't he fear his wife's shade at all? Did he think he could appease her with flatteries, by calling her graceful and beautiful, which she was not, and by putting eloquent lies in her mouth? Perhaps she could be cheaply bought, but not Penna. I thought of Sire Edecon lying with his sheath on his wedding night. He would never sing of her.

I wondered why, though his song was false, it caused me to weep. Which much amused Sire Rodela.

Sire Galan said, "I wouldn't have believed such a fine song could be patched up from the oddments I've heard from you these past days."

"Then—what do you think of it?"

"You've made me shed tears for her. Isn't that answer enough? It saddens me to think of your wedding night, which should have been joyful. And that terrible morning . . . I believe your song will live a long time—long after us."

"You do?"

"We probably won't outlive the tennight, but I'll wager the song will last a month at least," Galan said, and all the men laughed, even Sire Edecon, and that eased the mood. "Edecon, listen. Give it to a rumormonger—you know the one named Lark?—with a couple of silverheads, and let him polish it up and make the song famous. But keep your name out of it, it's bound to sting the She-wolf like a swarm of hornets."

"Mmm," said Sire Edecon. "I hadn't thought of that."

It was a thing I didn't understand, why the men of the king's army laid the blame for the brides' curse in the lap of Queenmother Caelum—which meant they blamed her for all manner of hardships, from rain and snow to mildew on harnesses. They said the queenmother had demanded the massacre of the clan of Torrent in Lanx from sheer bloodlust. All her lusts were ungovernable, but most especially her desire to rule.

"The king will like it. He's fond of a good song," said Sire Galan. "And it makes the She-wolf look the bitch she is, doesn't it?"

"It's unnatural for a woman to be so ambitious," Sire Edecon said, and quoted the old saying: *If you let a woman wear the spurs, she'll ride you to ruin.*

Sire Galan said, "Have you met my mother?"

"Yes, I had that honor, on the occasion of Sire Destello's wedding to Dame Mollete—my cousin, you know, on my mother's side. Why do you ask?"

"I wondered if you'd noticed the spurs."

There was an uproar in the camp and Spiller went to find out why, and came back excited. There was to be a hanging! Everyone ran to see it, everyone but me. I stayed behind to sew my new compass. I had all the cloth I needed now, with what I'd stolen from the clothier. I hadn't taken much, after all, just scraps he might have used for patches, none of them bigger than my hand. I sorted out the proper colors and cut the scraps into arcants of equal size, and arranged them to make a circle, starting with the gods whose places I knew for certain because I'd memorized their godsigns: Ardor, Crux, Delve, and Hazard. I placed the other gods where I thought they should go, then moved the pieces around, uncertain. It was quiet in the tent, but not so in my mind.

At last I started sewing. I had to trust that the order was right when it felt right. I took large stitches, afraid the men might return. But the hanging was taking a long time, long enough. I warmed my cold hand with my warm one, and mashed some inkberries, and tied a bit of my hair to a stick to make a brush. I painted the three circles one inside the other, and lastly the godsigns around the horizon, each on the proper color, I hoped.

It was done; not so well done as I would have liked, but orderly nevertheless, and I could tell each god at a glance without having to puzzle out its sign. The meaning of this compass seemed to differ slightly from the old one. The colors made each god more distinct, and yet its avatars more unified, three in one. I looked at it with my left eye and then my right; it bothered me that the colors were faded and yellowed seen with my right eye, as if the compass were already ancient.

I was ready to throw the bones, to see if the Dame and Na would still speak to me, but I heard men outside the tent, their voices loud, and I rolled the bones in the new compass and hid it away.

The jacks and Fleetfoot came in. Spiller said it had been quite a spectacle: The queenmother and the king threw money to the crowd, and promised sacrifices and a feast at the bonfire tomorrow night. Five mud soldiers from the clan of Growan swung for looting, and one of the queenmother's men, to show how Queenmother Caelum frowned upon the despoliation of the kingdom she claimed for her own.

Rowney said he wondered that the king took it so meekly, standing beside her with his arms crossed. Was he a man still, or had she taken his sacs for a pair of baubles? Because everyone knew Wolves had been roaming the town in packs. They'd picked the townsfolk clean to the bone, and then cracked the bones and robbed them of marrow. You could tell the cataphracts of Growan were none too pleased to have their men singled out for punishment. Rowney said it was good I'd foreseen that the queenmother would execute pillagers, and saved us from doing the rope jig ourselves.

It was easier to let him think so.

Sire Edecon came back to the tent in the middle of the night without his master, and I waited up for Sire Galan. While his men slept I had time to strengthen the seams of my new compass and thread a cord around the edge for a drawstring. I took pains with the work, but I was distracted by Sire Rodela droning in one ear and the refrain of Sire Edecon's song in the other: *I'll have no more of life, I'll have no more of life.*

With small stitches I whiled away the long night, thinking of how Galan had spoken of his mother to Sire Edecon, and how he never said such things to me. How I'd never asked. I'd tried to wrap myself in ignorance, like a babe in swaddling cloth, telling myself it was not my place to know the whole of his life—that other life he led in Ramus, that he shared with his wife and infant son, that he would resume if he survived. And for a time, such was my jealousy, I thought I'd sooner lose him to war than to that other life.

It was nearly dawn when Galan returned. And when he undressed and lay down beside me, smelling of wine and woodsmoke, I tried to make him forget mother and father, wife and son. I thought of wives immortalized and sheaths forgotten, and worked upon him as deliberately as a whore works on her patron, until he was slick with sweat and breathless. All the while Sire Rodela kept up his mocking buzz, until at last Desire took pity, and kindled her lamp and led me to a narrow instant where all else was forgotten, and the world was as small as the two of us, Galan and me.

Pinch and Sunup came the next afternoon to take me to the summoner. I was surprised to see Sunup, but she told me that Mai had said she ought to come and help. We followed Pinch down a narrow trail trampled in the snow, heading well south of town and the army encampment. As we went, Sire Rodela's buzzing became louder and more frantic in the hollow of my ear. I gritted my teeth and rejoiced that he was frightened.

We reached frozen mudflats along the banks of the river, and Pinch led us into a field of tall, buff-colored reeds. We found the summoner waiting with three of his followers in a circular clearing. The reeds made a wall around us, and their heavy russet tassels swayed above our heads. Underfoot they had been trodden into a mat over the snow and ice.

The summoner was so emaciated that his face revealed the shape of his skull under the scored parchment of skin; his graying hair was long and disheveled. I'd expected his dress would be out of the ordinary, to show his trade, but he wore a plain leather tunic and wrinkled hose. His followers, however, wore long red robes. They stood warming themselves by a brazier on a tripod. I recognized one as a whore I knew by the name of Sweetpea. She was a soft little partridge of a woman, the last one I'd have expected to see there.

The summoner's bloodshot eyes singled me out at once, and when I felt his gaze strike, my heart seemed to lurch to a stop. I stood still. He beckoned me, and my heart thudded again, and slowly I came near him. When I was in reach he clasped my hand and jerked me closer. For a man so thin, his grip was strong. Around his neck was a string of bone beads carved to look like skulls. He smiled, and his stained teeth were chipped, as if he'd been chewing stones. "Have you the toll?" he asked. His voice was guttural and deep.

I opened my old divining compass and held it between us where no one else could see it, thinking I should have found something more valuable to give him—something better than a circle of painted leather, with a few shell beads and an ivory hand on the drawstring. But he accepted the toll.

"Take off your clothes," the summoner said.

"Why?" I was shivering. I'd been shivering since I saw him.

"We have other garments you must wear. Hurry. We've waited too long for you already."

Wildfire

Mai had said to trust him. I didn't, but I trusted her. Two of his followers came forward, and one slipped the cloak from my shoulders. I unwrapped my headcloth and took off my overdress. The other woman—tall and nearly as thin as the summoner—unrolled a length of red sacking with a ragged hole cut in the middle. I was reluctant to part with my gauze underdress, but the summoner was impatient. I shucked it off and the woman pulled the sacking over my head. The summoner smeared chalk on my face and arms, and tied a girdle around my waist to keep the crude garment from flapping open. Clackers dangled from the girdle: wooden skulls with loose-hinged jaws that rattled as I moved.

All the while I was thinking, *Nonsense!* and Sire Rodela was agreeing, *Nonsense, nonsense!* And I was so cold. I didn't see how I could be colder and still live.

The summoner took my arm and led me through the reeds to the river. The hidden Sun, already westering in the short day, cast blue shadows from trees on the opposite bank. The water was under ice and the ice under burnished snow, a flawless smooth surface, save for the black hole in the ice with snow heaped around it. When I saw the hole I pulled away, crying, "No!" and he held on and marched me toward it. He was asking, "Are you willing?" I barely heard him over Sire Rodela's din. He said again, "Are you willing?" and gave me a shake. "You've paid the fee. The shade doesn't want this, but you do."

I think I heard Sunup saying, "What are they doing?" and Sweetpea answering in a soothing murmur.

The summoner pointed to the water showing in the maw of ice. "Go in and come out the other side," he said.

Sire Rodela's whine rose in pitch and drove an awl of pain into my ear. I jumped in. The water came up to my chest and stole the breath right out of me. If I'd been able to imagine what it would feel like, I'd never have done it. The summoner put his hand on my back and when I hesitated he pushed me under the water in a rush of bubbles. My skin tingled as the cold touched me everywhere and I wished I could go numb, but it hurt. *I'm willing*, I thought, but my body was unwilling. I began to thrash and the summoner's hands held me under. Cold burrowed into me, even into the channels that held my marrow, into the rooms of my heart, searching for my hearthfire to snuff it out. It was a trick and he was going to kill me, punishment for something, some offense to his mistress, the Queen of the Dead, and like a fool I'd gone with him. Rodela shrieked in my ear and I felt the dead swarming all around, tugging at my garment with the strong river currents.

The same hands that had pushed me down in the water heaved me out onto the ice. I lay on my stomach, shaking and fighting to take a breath, and water drained from my mouth. I was seized, pulled upright, and I stood there gasping and raising clumsy hands to push hair out of my eyes, and I saw the summoner was gone and Rift Queen of the Dead had taken his place. She sang in a high shrill voice, and Pinch and the summoner's women drummed to drive the song swiftly along. Sunup shook a gourd rattle. They raised a great commotion and I was led stumbling back to the trodden circle of reeds.

It didn't matter that I saw through the summoner's disguise, that the Queen's mask was a black sack painted with a crude white skull, that her hair was made of hanks from the tails of horses, that her red robe was patched and stained, that her hands had the summoner's crooked fingers and dirty nails. She was in him.

Sire Rodela was afraid, and he tried to drown out the drumming, but it came to me through the soles of my feet and the twitching of my shoulders. I stamped one foot, then the other. I was cold as a corpse, even my warm hand was chilled, and my flesh was unwieldy, thick, heavy, and numb. But every time I stamped I jarred pain into my feet, and it was better than no feeling at all.

I raised my hands to my cheeks. The hands felt cold and strange to the face and the face likewise to the hands. I drove my deadened legs against the ground, stamp, stamp, stamp, driving sensation upward, heel, ankle, shin, knee, thigh, cleft. The Queen of the Dead sang one tune after another, I did not know why; her words, in the tongue of the dead, were unintelligible to me. Sire Rodela strove against her with all his might, screeching with desperate dissonance. He no longer lingered in the portal of my ear, but entered deep inside my skull.

Rift Queen fixed on a melody, chanting the same line over and over, and Sire Rodela was snagged by it. His buzzing began to follow hers, entwining the way two threads entwine between the spinner's thumb and finger, until it was one song inside and outside of me. She had found his song, and the music seized me, seized us, Rodela and I. The song demanded a heavy tread with stiff shoulders and elbows jutting out. The song wanted the body to swagger, to trample everything underfoot, and it wanted the mouth to sneer, lopsided, and the belly to jerk, grunting out a song, *Bitch, bitch, bitch!*

I saw Pinch gaping even as he hammered on the drum, and I went and danced before him, staring until he lowered his eyes, while I sang, *Whoreson, whoreson, whoreson!* and fizzed with laughter. The jaws of the wooden skulls clattered as I stamped.

Rodela was full of gloating satisfaction to be so enlarged after his confinement as a fly. His rage was powerful and tireless, and he drove me spinning around the circle. Heavy sacs hung between my thighs, and a stiff prick wagged, and I strutted toward Sunup and made her afraid of me. And I found I had my little knife out of its sheath, and to cool myself and quench an overweening thirst I raked the blade across my scalp until the blood trickled down and I tasted it. *Bitch, bitch, bitch!*

Now I compelled the music, and even the Queen of the Dead herself must follow my song, faster and faster. I was full of strength and in the ecstasy of the dizzying dance I saw the living and the dead gathered around me in the circle. The reeds nodded and rustled like a crowd of stately personages, and in the shadows gathered among them I saw shades taking shape and dissolving, and from the corner of my eye I saw the white hem of Penna's kirtle, and against my breast I felt the Dame and Na, tucked away small in their finger bones in the pouch.

I'd believed that the realm of the Queen of the Dead shared but one border with our world, and that was death, from which the dead set forth to cross her barren lands. But her realm was closer than I'd guessed. It did not lie beyond our world so much as alongside it. What did it take to slip between this world and that one? Dying, that was all. The dead journeyed beside us, not away.

I danced that netherworld closer until there was not even the thinnest gauze between that world and this one. The dead far outnumbered the living. Why did I fear to join them? Why should it matter when I died—a moment, a day, a year or many years from now? For in the realm of the Queen of the Dead can be found eternity.

I danced until Sire Rodela's shade was sated, until I regained dominion of every length and joint of my body. In the nearness of death, green life swelled in me, and I reveled in the sweetness of living. And for the first time I gave thought to how I'd cheated Sire Rodela of his days to come, cheated him of his miserable pleasures, such as tormenting those beneath him, and counting over and over, the way a miser fingers his gold, the slights inflicted by those above him. What else had he savored when he was alive? Maybe the sight of his bay horse with green ribbons braided into the mane, or the scent of spring arriving on a late-winter breeze, maybe even such simple joys. I didn't know. What I'd taken from him was beyond my reckoning, yet I'd measured it, priced it at the cost of a scrap of my flesh and the humiliation I'd suffered over his lies. For that I'd poisoned him and stolen his life.

My dance came to an end. I knelt shaking on the ground, and one of the women wrapped me in my cloak. Sire Rodela's fretful buzz subsided to a drone as faint as the undersong of my coursing blood: something that could be forgotten.

I was grateful to be cured, but the summoner warned me that from time to time the shade might demand the release of a dance; and I might be called upon to join in rites for others afflicted in the same way, to drum until the dead were satisfied. Henceforth, he said, I was to obey the prohibitions of the Queen of the Dead, avoiding the touch of anything dyed violet, and abstaining from the flesh of hedgehogs, which play at being dead. He gave me a red cord to wear around my waist, under my dress, as a reminder of my obligation to her.

That night when I lay naked with Galan, he slipped his fingers under the cord and asked me what it was for. I said to give me courage. The next day I hung my new divining compass from the cord hidden under my skirts.

This red cord was a talisman, like the cheap tin amulet I wore around my neck that was stamped with Wildfire's godsign. With it I divided myself in half. Below the waist I kept my fear of death and desire to live, above the waist I kept the courage to strive against or embrace the inevitable. I'd been split left from right by Wildfire, and top from bottom by Rift; yet this splitting helped to heal me. When first I was thunderstruck, I was nothing but a thin skin around chaos; now I was like the compass, territory partitioned by the gods, by division made more orderly and comprehensible.

CHAPTER 9

Mischief

e marched away from the encampment, setting forth between walls of crusty snow, and as we couldn't spread out beside the road, our line was long and exposed. The outriders' horses were soon exhausted from breasting through the drifts. We halted less than a league down the road, and it hardly seemed worth the trouble to get there. But at least we didn't have to smell the stench of the burned town.

Last night the soldiers had built a bonfire to celebrate Longest Night. Skinny old Growan Crone had eaten well of the sheep and cattle sacrificed with prayers for a mild winter, so all of us in the army had plenty of meat for once, and plenty of drink too. I watched the bonfire and listened to it roar. Drudges dashed up to feed the flames with limbs and trunks of trees from orchards, and shutters torn from houses. Two men shoved a cart full of straw into the fire and it blazed up at once, sending straws and sparks tumbling high in the air. The hot wind buffeted me and I leaned into it, glad of the heat, glad of the flames that called to what was wild in me.

There was another bonfire that night. I heard a great clamor and scrambled up a hill of snow to see what everyone was shouting about. The town in the valley was on fire. Someone had torched it—men from the company of Growan, furious over the hangings, so said the rumor that spread as fast as the flames. Soldiers streamed downhill toward the town to take what plunder they could find before it burned. Sire Rodela would have delighted in this, he would have filled my ear with his shrillness. Without him I felt pure clean dread. I prayed they got away, the clothier and his wife, the baby and the maidservant. I prayed they all got away.

But some townsfolk died in the fire; I felt them as we marched, clinging to us like the reek of smoke. The army of shades that accompanied our army was growing. And today I found no comfort in the knowledge that the dead journeyed beside us rather than leaving us behind.

*   *   *

By evening the weather had changed, and the snow began to thaw. I lay beside Galan, listening to water trickle and drip. Two days ago I'd made a strong decoction of horsetail stalks to bring on my tides, without success. It wasn't the season for them, they were too brown. I must look for a bay tree and use its leaves and berries. If that didn't work, I'd be visiting the miscarrier soon.

This was the second night since Sire Rodela had been banished. How his pestilential shade had whined whenever I was on the verge of sleep!—I'd been sure that once I was rid of him, I would sink into Sleep's ocean every night. Not so. I lay awake with worries swarming about my head. They had been there all along, but Sire Rodela had buzzed louder. Now I knew: It was Wildfire who kept me awake, Wildfire who had altered me, so that no matter how much I needed and craved sleep, I was denied it. I prayed Lynx Sleep would cure me of this affliction, since Ardor had not relented.

I pulled on my overdress and went to sit outside the tent on one of Sire Galan's camp chairs. After so many days of cold, the breeze seemed almost balmy, and there was a provocative scent of sodden earth that promised spring, though spring was far away, another country altogether. In the light of the full Moon I took from my pouch the linen scrip that granted me tenancy of a house on a mountain, and unfolded it on my lap. The linen was stiff, sized to make a smooth surface, and the godsigns marched in neat columns down each lengthwise pleat.

I opened out my compass to compare its godsigns with those on the linen. With the help of the colors, I could tell one sign from another, but I still couldn't read. Each godsign could be written five ways, with one of three avatar marks, with none, or with all; a small sound belonged to each of those ways. Add sounds together to make words, and godsigns could say anything. But my memory was a coarse net, and nothing so small as a piece of a word could be caught in it. I'd remembered many things since the lightning, but in this too Wildfire had not relented.

Yet it seemed to me the scrip could be read in another way, as a chant or a prayer, the names of gods and avatars one after another. I bent over my work, deciphering the signs, murmuring the names. The Dame had told me that a godsign shown with the three avatars together is the god as it appears to us in its manifestations; a godsign shown alone is the whole god, what we know and what passes our understanding.

Someone stirred behind the door flap of the tent, and I hastily balled up the compass and tucked it in my sleeve. Galan ducked out with the feather-stuffed quilt around his shoulders and said, "Aren't you cold? What are you doing?"

I pointed to the white linen unfolded in my lap. "I'm trying to see if I can read these little ink things, the godsings. I have remembered which belongs of which god, but I can't make them—I still can't remember the songs they are supposed to make, when they are march one after the other—so as to make worths, to mean somewhat."

"You'll ruin your eyes trying to read in the dark." He plucked the scrip from my lap and tilted it to catch the moonlight. "You still have this?"

"Of course I do. It's a pleasure to me, a treasure. But I wish I could hear what it says."

"Why? Do you wish you were back in Corymb?"

"Never." I slid my hand up his arm, under the quilt. His skin was warm. "But you were fond of this place, this haunting lodge, so I am fond of it too. Didn't you say you used to hunt there when you were just young, with those birds, you know the kind—beckons . . . felcons? Will you tell it of me?"

"Come back to bed and I'll tell you all about it."

"Best tell me first," I said, laughing.

"My feet are too cold." He'd come out barefoot and he was standing on thawing ice.

"If you promise."

Inside the tent he lit an oil lamp and hung it from a hook under the bed canopy. We sat with the coverlet wrapped around us, and he read to me in a low voice from his gift. "It says, 'Bear witness that I give my sheath Firethorn tenancy, for her lifetime, of my holding that lies on Mount Sair—' "

"Show me my name. Which sights are in it?"

"Here—see?"

"And Mound . . . Mount Fair, how far is that to where I'm from?"

"Mount Sair is five days' ride from Ramus—that's why we stopped going there, father said it was too far from his duties—and from Ramus to Sire Pava's lands is about another tennight, I'd say. So—to go on—'my holding that lies on Mount Sair and is bounded by the Needle Cliffs to the north'—you should see those, they're marvelous, thin spires of golden stone—'and Wend River to the east and south, and to the west the Athlewood; the stone house and byres, the lands, and rights to coppice, pasture, and spring.'"

"Is someone living in the stolen house, the stone house?"

"There used to be a gamekeeper there, years ago. I suppose it's neglected now, but the house has a good slate roof, and I daresay it would still be sound."

"A slant, slate roof? Is there an an ornate, I mean an ornament, a place of trees, of . . . amples, apples, and . . . plumps and paricots and pears, and lazynuts and such, down on a trace belied the house? To the west of it?"

"An orchard? Yes, a small one. It must be all overgrown by now."

"Very," I said. "It lacks pruning."

I should have known the dreams I'd had of gardens and orchard and wood and a slate-roofed house on a mountainside were true dreams, for they were redolent of scents: dirt, smoke, mountain winds, my own sweat. If they were dreams of the land Galan had offered me, did that mean I would live there someday, despite having refused his gift? It frightened me that I'd never dreamed of Galan there; I was always alone.

Now that we had a bagboy to manage the mules, both jacks accompanied Sire Galan on the march. Ev usually rode with them, on Sire Edecon's spare mount, a gelding without much to recommend him except that he was large. Today Ev tarried to ride with his friend Fleetfoot in the baggage. Frost lagged behind them; I watched the boys as they talked, Ev leaning down toward Fleetfoot on the lead mule.

In a little while Ev slowed down to visit with me. He seemed worried. Perhaps he was overworked, and if so it was my fault, as I'd asked Galan for him. Most cataphracts had a horsemaster and a couple of horseboys; Galan had Ev. Sometimes I forgot how small he was. He had to stand on a stump to groom Sire Edecon's warhorse.

"Are you tired?" I asked. "There are too many hornets and mules in your charge—too many horses—aren't there?"

He said, "Fleetfoot is sore troubled. He can feel his hands and fingers—what was cut away—and they pain him terribly. He thinks he's mad or hexed, so he won't seek help."

"He hides it well." I hadn't guessed Fleetfoot was suffering, even when he was silent or sullen, even when I heard him restless in the night as I myself was restless. His hands had healed, by outward appearance, the skin growing pink and shiny over the flesh. This deeper hurt of which Ev spoke—I'd never heard of such a thing.

"Can you help him?"

"Me?" I was surprised to be asked. Fleetfoot had no open wounds that could be tainted by a woman's touch, but even so—even if I knew how to help, which I did not—I doubted he would accept succor from me. Only little boys turned to a woman for healing; it was not for a lad who fancied himself a man.

Ev said, "I just thought . . ."

I waited, but he didn't say more. "I don't see how," I said.

"I thought . . . Everyone says you're touched, you know things. That a god tells you things."

"Oh, I'm touched indeed. You can hark in my babble that the god dumbfounded me. There's no *use* in it. I go on inspired of it, I mean in spite of it. You should ask Divine Shyster, the harmifex. He knows more of such grievous inquiries . . . injuries than I—perhaps he'll know what to do."

Ev started to turn his horse away. I thought of the touch-me-not flower and how it closes up when roughly handled, and reached for the gelding's reins. "Of course I'll help . . . Flicktooth if I can. I'll try."

I didn't dare approach the carnifex directly. Ever since he'd given me the black drink, and I'd said too much, I'd ducked behind tents and carts to keep out of his way; when our paths had crossed, I'd averted my eyes. And sure enough, when I'd pretended not to see him, he had pretended not to see me.

I asked Sire Galan for help that night when we were under the quilt on the folding bed, in that place which belonged to just us two.

"Poor lad," Galan said. "He doesn't complain of it."

"Do you think he's gone mad? Or is he acrossed?"

Galan lifted my hand and flattened it against his cheek. I knew the landscape of his face by touch, by its hollows and ridges, rough and soft. He said, "I've heard of this before. My sister's husband lost a foot in the battle of Rivalis three summers back, and yet the foot pains him still, as if someone was stabbing him in the heel with a mercy dagger."

I moved my hand away from Galan's face. "You have a sitter?"

"A what?"

"A a sister."

"I have three, as it happens. They're long married. I hardly see them."

"I suppose you have . . . fewmets and nieces too?"

He laughed. "Oh yes, plenty of them."

I turned on my side, away from him.

"What's the matter?" He turned too, fitting himself around me with his legs crooked behind mine, and one arm under my neck and the other over my waist. "You'd rather I didn't have nephews and nieces?"

"No, of course not. It's no meddle, no matter." I schooled my breathing to ease the tightness in my chest. Such foolishness, this jealousy. "So this man with the missing hoof—what does he do against the plaint, the pain?"

"He drinks himself into a stupor every night," Galan said, against my neck. "But I don't think that would suit the boy, do you?"

"Will you ask Divinster what to do?"

"He'll say there's not a thing to be done."

"But will you ask?"

"Mmmm," Galan said.

Sire Galan made occasion during the next day's journey to speak with Divine Xyster about Fleetfoot's complaint, and the priest said the lad was neither mad nor cursed by a malicious person; he was afflicted by Rift, and more's the pity. He must ask Rift for aid, for no man could cure him. The boy had run onto the tourney field in the riot, and had his fingers cut off, and it was clear the god was not yet satisfied that his violation of the sacred precinct of the tourney had been requited. When Sire Galan told me this, I asked what his wife's husband had done to Rift that caused him to be afflicted the same way, and he said he'd never heard a word against him.

It gave me no joy to take the carnifex's answer to Fleetfoot. When the lad went walking with Piddle after supper, I accompanied him, saying I had a treat to give Frost. It had taken but a word from Ev for me to see all that I'd failed to see before: how Fleetfoot winced for no reason, or went about with his body stiff and his teeth clamped together. He sometimes reached out with fingers that weren't there, and looked astonished and dismayed when he failed to grasp a bowl or a buckle.

But this evening he seemed untroubled. There was a spring to his step and he watched with a smile as Piddle dashed ahead of us. We followed a path trampled in the snow.

"If told me," I said.

"If what?" Fleetfoot looked at me sideways.

"If, Ev told me about your haunts. About how it hurts." I held up my own hands to show him what I meant.

"I told him not to say." He scowled and plucked a dead branch from the hedge with his three-fingered right hand and flung it for Piddle.

I said, "Garland, Sire Garland, Galan says this same thing happened to his sister's wife. He lost a boot and it still harms him."

Fleetfoot turned toward me with a smirk. "His sister's wife?"

"Oh, you know—her her houseband."

He broke off another branch and swept it before him like a scythe, hacking at dried weeds that stood up above the snow. Piddle tried to drag the branch away from him, and Fleetfoot scowled again.

I said, "You have not gone mad."

He raised his half hand and shook it at me. "No? Why then do I feel my fingers making a fist?" The stump of his thumb pressed against his palm.

"I know," I said. "It's very painful, I know."

Fleetfoot met my gaze with defiance at first. Then he looked away and shrugged. "It can't be helped, can it?"

"Tomorrow we'll make a scarcity, a sanctity, a sacrament to, to . . . Rift, for the Aspect says this foment is sent to you by the god for some transgracious."

"I haven't got two copperheads. How can I make a sacrifice?"

"Gift likes blood," I said.

Wildfire

After the plenty of spring and summer and the harvests of fall, winter seems a stingy season, but dormant plants have much to offer in their sap and bark and twigs, roots and buds and seeds. That evening I made a tisane for Fleetfoot like the one I'd given to Mole, steeping the fissured bark of an old willow with dried leaves of soothe-me. I thought the priest spoke the truth, and Rift needed to be placated, but it would do no harm, meanwhile, to try to ease the boy's pain and help him sleep.

So many mudfolk had trespassed during the mortal tourney between Crux and Ardor, myself among them, one of a mob of spectators pushed pell-mell downhill onto the field. The warriors had turned from their battle to attack us, killing in a god-inspired frenzy. We ran lest we be trampled, then we ran from the killers. We were all to blame or we were all blameless, for how can one drop of water in a flood swim where it wills? Why was I spared while Fleetfoot still suffered Rift's enmity? It is one of the mysteries, why the gods punish some transgressors and let others go untouched.

I never liked to visit Rift's pavilions, though I had a few acquaintances among the sheaths of that company. To judge by women's gossip, the cataphracts and armigers of Rift were much like any other men. The priests were another matter. The clan had more than their share of priests, a whole troop of bald Auspices dedicated to Rift Warrior. It was said these priests liked to keep their enemies close enough to embrace; the more they advanced in the arcana of war, the shorter their blades, until the most adept fought barehanded. They held themselves to be superior to other warriors, and for that—as their superiority was hard to dispute—they'd earned envy. They also held that coupling with women made a man weak; for that they'd earned the scorn of whores.

I took courage from the red cord around my waist, and went with Fleetfoot to sacrifice at Rift's shrine. The altar was a large block of stone they carried from place to place on a red oxcart. An Auspex of the Queen of the Dead sat nearby on an ironwood chair inlaid with ivory skulls. I'd seen her making sacrifices before tourneys in the Marchfield, wearing red robes and a tall red hat with a sharp prow and wings on either side like great sails. This evening she wore a plain red wimple. Her lips made a thin seam between the deep vertical lines bracketing her mouth.

The priestess's handmaid asked us sharply, "What do you want?"

I whispered to Fleetfoot, "You'd best say. I might get it wrong and cause suspense."

He kept his eyes on the ground and mumbled, "I've come to offer sacrifices to the Queen of the Dead and the Warrior."

The priestess's foot twitched under the puddled hem of her long over-dress, which was lined with black marten fur. She must keep warm indeed in such a robe.

The handmaid said, "What do you offer?" and she spoke in the cadence of ceremony.

"Blood," said Fleetfoot.

I opened my purse and fished out a couple of coins—not the largest, the copperheads, nor yet the smallest, the goldenheads, but two silverheads. For a drudge, it was a handsome amount. I held the coins toward the handmaid and the priestess raised her eyebrows and gave a nod of assent. She nibbled on a sweetmeat, a dried apricot.

In the Marchfield we mudfolk had been free to sacrifice at the twelve altars that stood around the king's pavilion at the center of camp, where all directions and roads met. Now it seemed we had to beg for the privilege of worshipping. I wondered if the Auspices would soon turn us away altogether, as was done in the temples of Lanx.

Fleetfoot held out his left arm for the priestess to make the cut, and when she saw the stump she asked for the other hand. That one lacked two fingers, but she found it acceptable. She made a shallow cut and squeezed blood into the bowl. "If it please you, Divine," Fleetfoot said, "make the next one deeper." She looked hard at him then, as if she truly saw him, while he gazed at the brass bowl with the red pool in it. The next cut made his jaw tighten, but as he watched the blood flow, his expression eased. Sometimes one hurt will drive away another.

I offered my own arm and said, "I would be generous too, for I owe thanks to the Queen of the Deed."

In the night I heard Fleetfoot turn and turn again, and once or twice I heard him whimper. His offering had been accepted, but it had not sufficed. I eased from under the covers and pulled on my shift, and squatted beside the lad where he lay wrapped in a blanket he'd stolen from the clothier. Piddle raised her head and thumped her tail. Fleetfoot's eyes glistened with tears he refused to spill.

"It's no use," he said in a whisper. "I'd cut it off myself if it wasn't gone already."

How cruel of Rift to torment the boy!—but of course Rift is cruel, how foolish to wish otherwise.

"What does it feel like?"

"It itches but I can't scratch it. And sometimes it burns and burns. Not as fire burns—more like when you've been working outside in the cold and your hands and feet freeze and when you come inside it hurts worse, it burns. But it doesn't stop burning, it just won't go away."

He sat up and wiped his nose on the blanket. He looked so dejected, I reached out and hugged him. He was too much the man to give way and be comforted like a child, but he allowed my embrace. I wished I could gather him up, tuck him safe in my purse, so he wouldn't suffer further harm. I reached for his left clubbed hand and clasped it between mine. To my warm left hand, his hand was cold; to my cold right hand, it was warm. My left hand felt his hand incomplete, with stretched skin and puckered scar, but my right hand felt his fingers. This was a strange sensation, and for a moment I could make no sense of it. I held my breath and closed my eyes, and let out the breath in a sigh. "Wriggle your finders," I said.

"I have no fingers."

"I know, but still. Are you wiggling them?"

"No."

"Yes, yes you are! I felt it. But only the littlest, the the nice. The niece." There's a children's game everyone knows in which the fingers of the right hand are named grandfather (the thumb), father (the forefinger), brother, son, and nephew; on the left hand, of course, are grandmother, mother, sister, daughter, and niece.

"What am I doing now?" Fleetfoot asked.

I laughed and opened my eyes. "You're wiggling all your elbows!"

He pulled his hand away and put it behind his back.

"I'm sorry. I'm not laughing at you. Let me rub your arms, hands," I said, and I was surprised he let me. "Did the . . . did what I gave you to drink, the thissum, thisan, help? Did you sleep at all?"

Fleetfoot shrugged. "Not much."

I tried to stroke warmth down his arms and into what remained of his hands, to ease the cold burning he felt. His eyelids began to droop, and he leaned against me. All I could give him was the comfort of touch.

The next day we packed before the Sun rose, to be ready to march at dawn. Then the Crux sent his varlets around to tell us we were not leaving that morning, perhaps later in the day. Galan said, "A tennight's march from Malleus and we're supposed to sit twiddling our dangles?" and he went off to find out why.

A tennight from Malleus! I'd begun to think we would march all winter across the Wolds, up and down the rolling hills, and never arrive. This suited me, but the men, most of them, seemed eager for battle and bored without it, and the untried hotspurs boasted of feats not yet accomplished.

When Galan came back I asked why we tarried, and he said with scorn that rumor had it the queenmother was feeling poorly.

By midday we were sure we would stay another night in the camp, but no, we had to move out in haste and march a league or two. As Frost trotted along, I pondered how to help Fleetfoot, and fell into a waking dream. With one eye, my left, I saw the passing road: tall stalks of wandflower standing upright above a patch of snow, and a flock of chiffchaffs stripping the last berries from a rowan tree. With my failing right eye I saw dark loam, and my hands pushing something deep into it, some kind of white seeds that I planted a handsbreadth apart. The earth had a good rich fragrance. It was alive with reddish worms, and little sowbugs trundling over the clods, climbing their tiny mountains. I saw the seeds were finger bones, like the Dame's and Na's, but unpainted.

Frost stumbled and I jerked awake. I knew the smell of that dirt—I had even tasted it. It was loam from the dream garden on Mount Sair.

Despite having the odor of a true dream, this one could not be true: I'd never plant finger bones, it was absurd. Did that mean the other dreams were false too, and I'd never see the house on the mountainside?

Yet there was portent in this reverie, a sign. Na must have sent it. She was Fleetfoot's aunt, and would do her best to guide me. I must throw the bones for him. I'd remade my compass so that by color and godsign I could find my way around it, and for the first time since lightning struck, I could hope to make sense of what the bones might say.

Sire Galan mumbled when I got up in the middle of the night, and I told him my legs had cramped and I needed to walk the stiffness out of them. It was a still night with thick clouds over the Moon and stars, and the darkness suited my purpose. I crouched outside the tent and opened the divining compass. I tried to hold Fleetfoot in mind, to see him as he once was, unmarred and untroubled; as he was now, maimed inside and out; as I hoped he could be, healed of his pain. I cast the bones three times to seek a way toward his healing: first for his nature, second for the nature of his affliction, and third for the gods who governed the remedy and might grant or withhold a cure.

I asked Na and the Dame to point the way, but on the first cast Na, the red-tipped bone, fell outside the circle, saying nothing. Why was she silent? The Dame's blue bone landed on Artifex and crossed the line to Frenzy.

I cast the second time, and Na landed squarely on Mischief, and the Dame on the Sun.

On the third throw, Na fell upon Chance, and the tip crossed into the domain of the Warrior. The Dame landed on Mischief, with the tip of her finger on Desire. I thought it strange that both bones landed askew, touching upon male and female, one god to another.

I cast quickly so as not to be seen, and I pulled tight the drawstring to make the compass into a pouch again with the bones hidden inside, and I went back to bed to think. I'd thrown the bones in pairs and the three casts made a chain of linked signs, but what did they mean?

The bones didn't speak to me—maybe they never had, not the way they'd spoken to Az, conversing so that she could overhear. But they showed me images now as never before, images that were clearest in my cloudy right eye.

When the Dame touched the two avatars of Eorõe, Artifex and Frenzy, I saw Artifex digging clay from the bank of a narrow ravine. She looked like Az, a small bird-boned woman with a crooked back. She shaped a man of clay around an acorn heart—Fleetfoot himself, born of Kingswood clay. Fleetfoot's mother had given him just such a tiny clay man with an acorn heart to wear as a talisman. I wondered if he still had it.

Artifex was the only dead avatar, and required no one's worship, yet I revered her. She'd fashioned the first people—mudfolk—from the clay of many rivers, making them pale, ruddy, or dark, and used her last breath giving life to them.

Fleetfoot's clay, his flesh. The Dame had pointed from Artifex to Frenzy, and I saw Frenzy as a clay jar with strong doublewine in it, and a broken handle: Frenzy for rage or bliss, madness or intoxication. Must Fleetfoot drown his pains in drink, like Galan's kinsman?

The Dame said Sun, the Sun casts shadows—a shadow had to remain true in some manner to the shape that cast it. The clay jar had a broken handle, yet the shadow's handle was whole. Its shadow, its shade. When I'd held Fleetfoot's hand between mine, I'd felt the shape and motion of his missing fingers. The flesh was maimed and the shade was whole, the shade insisted and the flesh denied. Their quarrel caused pain, for one should fill the other, no more and no less. Suppose his shade could be remade to fit the new shape of his flesh?

I was heartened to think that on the last throw Na had pointed to Rift Warrior, by way of Chance. She seemed to say that with Chance's favor I'd find a cure, a way to appease the seemingly implacable Warrior.

But why did she land on Mischief on the second cast? What did he have to do with the nature of Fleetfoot's pains? And the Dame had also touched Mischief, on the third throw, while pointing to Desire—so there was Mischief in Fleetfoot's affliction and in the cure. I saw the avatar clearly, a boy a little younger than Fleetfoot, wearing a merry and malicious smile. Mice swarmed about his feet. He was untrustworthy; he could mean an obstacle or another sign reversed. Yet the Dame said I must ask him for help.

For once I didn't mind my wakefulness. I puzzled over the avatars, their agreements and contradictions. Night became twilight, and the army stirred, and dogs barked and men cursed, and Spiller let cold air into the tent, and still I didn't understand. I feared I might be incapable of understanding the bones now, because I no longer remembered all the attributes of the gods and avatars, knowledge everyone else took for granted. Day by day memories had been given back to me, but how much remained forgotten?

I prayed. I prayed to Wildfire, whose sign had not appeared, and to Chance and the Warrior, Mischief and Desire, calling upon them for a cure.

Usually we halted on Peacedays to repair wagons and harnesses, and forage and rest, but today we marched to make up for the time lost the day before. I dozed on Frost's back, and didn't realize how much we were dawdling until I looked up and saw the baggage train far ahead. I found myself in the rearguard among clansmen of Wend. They passed by on their great horses while I tugged at the reins to persuade Frost to stop eating grass that grew in the ditch by the road. An armiger was singing in a fine voice, and I paused and raised my head, recognizing Sire Edecon's song about that girl of Torrent. It was strange that sadness should have such a honeyed sting.

> *You had one night of me,*
> *I had one night of you.*
> *I will ever be your bride,*
> *But I'll never be your wife.*
> *I'll have no more of life.*
> *I'll have no more of life.*

The Blood of Wend passed, and I turned off the crowded road to ride through the field alongside. Most of the snow had melted. I came to a hedge that divided one field from the next. Foot soldiers had hacked a huge gap in it so they could pass, for the hedges in this country were so thick even a goat couldn't slip through them.

I reined in Frost and slid off her back, amazed by the abundance I saw in the verge between field and hedge. It was as if the finger bones in my dream, planted as seeds in the domain of the gods, had brought forth a harvest of signs; I would have missed them if the Dame and Na had not shown me where to look.

I gathered what was offered: from Artifex, fibrous stalks of hemp, still standing tall; from Frenzy, grains of the bearded darnel grass, which cause drunkenness; pinecones from the Sun; a bundle of maple twigs from Chance, who favors any plant that casts its seeds on the wind; the leathery evergreen leaves of a bear's-foot hellebore from the Warrior; a drake root from Desire, not forked like a man or a woman, as was usual, but clubbed like Fleetfoot's hand.

As for Mischief, I already had an idea about him. I relied on Ev to bring me mice—there were always mice in the grain stores, and cats and boys to catch them.

I had something to do I didn't want the men to see, a painstaking and grisly task. I sat in the back of Mai's cart while she told me the gossip and what she thought of it. I stitched as we bumped along, and pricked my fingers many times. Sunup watched me sew and asked questions I wouldn't answer.

Mai said she'd been talking to a certain rumormonger who traveled with one of the companies from Lanx; he claimed that by his reckoning Prince Corvus's foreign wife Kalos was long overdue to give birth. It should have been a month ago, he said—but she thought he was being paid to say so.

"Why?"

"So people will think the child was stillborn, maybe. Or that Princess Kalos is going to give birth to a giant serpent."

"Will she?" I said.

"Not likely," Mai said with a grin. "Queenmother Caelum must be frightened now that the birth is so close. If Kalos brings forth an unblemished boy, the queenmother will lose many of the troops who have pledged to her."

"I did hear that this Precious Lokas . . . Kalose—that she had green shiny shells all over. Skells, scales, I mean. Like a slitherer, you know, one that slithers."

"I've heard the songs too. But I doubt very much she's a lamia who can change into a serpent. I don't know what the queenmother has against her, but it's not that. Maybe this princess stiffened up Prince Corvus's backbone as well as his prick, eh? That might be enough to make a foe of the queenmother."

Sunup spoke then, saying she'd heard Prince Corvus was a handsome fellow, and Mai said even a humpbacked, one-eyed king was reckoned handsome by the flatterers around him. And whom had she been talking to? Sunup said it was Sire Deruda, and Mai said stay away from him or get a walloping—a man who liked girls so young wouldn't want her when she was grown. Sunup turned sullen and quiet. Her breasts were starting to swell, and I too feared what might become of her if she lost her shyness.

Mai had color in her cheeks, but it was from red paste such as whores like to use. I said, "You'll send for me as well as the bidlife when your time comes, won't you?"

She said I'd be sure to know, for I'd hear her screaming clear from one end of the army to the other. I winced, and Mai patted my hand as if I were the one soon to face the travail. As I was leaving I turned and caught a bleak expression on her face, one she hadn't cared to show me.

I wanted darkness for Fleetfoot's rite, for I wanted him in awe of me. He knew me too well. He'd seen me the day I came out of the Kingswood, in rags and with my hair matted and snarled. I was a beggar then, slow to speak and wary after a year alone, and of her charity Az and her boys had shared what little they had. He esteemed me no more—or less—after I was lightning struck, but rather teased me when I misspoke. There was mischief in him, though little malice.

I arranged it all with Mai and Ev. Mai sent her man Pinch for me late, saying she was feeling poorly and wanted my help. I said I'd take Fleetfoot as a runner, and Pinch could see me safely there and back. Galan grudgingly let me go. But Pinch went one direction with his lantern, and Fleetfoot and I another. Piddle came too, of course. We walked between tents, some brimming with light and others dark, to the meadow where the horses of our company were pastured. The tethered horses raised their heads when we came by, but didn't challenge our passage. I told Fleetfoot I meant to cure him that night, and left my doubts out of it. He followed willingly enough, whether or not he believed me. The clouds were heavy, hiding the half Moon. Fleetfoot stumbled over fallen branches and tussocks of grass that I avoided without thinking; sometimes I forgot that others saw poorly in the dark.

Ev met us with some of his friends, two dogboys, a horseboy, and one of Sire Pava's foot soldiers, a lad named Dag. I hadn't expected so many watchers. In the pit of my belly I felt an uneasy excitement, as if a snake stirred its coils inside me. I would fail and they'd know me for a mountebank, a charlatan. Yet I was eager that it be done and over, that what was pent up in me should find release.

In the pasture there was a small hollow suited to my purpose, which held the sunken ruins of a croft and an ancient guardian tree, a rowan. We sat in a circle with Fleetfoot in the middle. I gave the boys a song to hum, the same melody a bird had given me when I ate the firethorn berries in the Kingswood. The tune was a gift of Ardor and it steadied me. It had no words, and as we hummed I drummed on my thighs to set the pace. The boys took up the rhythm, thudding palms against flesh. I turned my back on them and hunched over and rubbed flour on my face so I would shine in the dark. I smeared charcoal on my eyelids and lips to give the blank white face features. I uncovered my hair and brushed it out with a wool carder so that it crackled and rose in a haze of curls around my head. I didn't want Fleetfoot to see *me* when he looked at me. The summoner had taught me that.

When I turned back toward the circle, someone gasped. I made my voice thin and harsh, through a tight throat, and I invoked the gods to whom the bones had pointed, setting the offerings between Fleetfoot and me: hemp, a flask of doublewine I'd stolen from Sire Galan, pinecones, maple twigs, and bear's-foot leaves. I poured wine into a cup that contained a paste of ground drake root and grains of darnel-grass—a small amount, for both are exceedingly potent. I asked Desire and Frenzy to bless it, and took a mouthful that burned like fire down my throat and up my nose, for it was twice as strong as ordinary wine. I passed the cup to Fleetfoot and with a gesture told him to drink it all down. He gulped and gasped. With a coal from my fireflask, I lit the offerings. The pinecones and frayed hemp stalks caught quickly, and the smoke was sweet and pungent. I spat the doublewine onto the fire, and it made flames leap up all at once, blue and orange. The firelight caught Fleetfoot's face from underneath and left his eye sockets shadowed. His lips were parted and he stared at me. I thumped on my leg to make the boys sing faster.

I didn't feel the presence of the gods, and I feared they'd spurned me. I took the finger bones from my pouch and kissed them, the Dame and Na, and I put Na's bone in Fleetfoot's three-fingered right hand and closed his fist around it. I kept the Dame in my lap. I called their names aloud, and I sang to Na, "As your sister's son is blood of your blood, help him now," and the words came out in perfect order. When I sang their names, I felt a chill descending the ladder of my spine. Piddle made a strange noise, between a whine and a whimper, and her hackles rose. I looked beyond our circle and saw we'd drawn other witnesses. Horses watched, standing still and alert, their eyes shining in the firelight.

There was awe in Fleetfoot's face. I took his left hand, his half hand, between mine again. I felt his missing fingers distinctly, throbbing against my palms. His hand was cold, flesh and shade, and I thought of his shade as some dark form of wax that would soften in heat, and I gave him some of my warmth. My breath rose in a white plume, but I'd long since ceased to feel the cold of that night.

With a loud cry I called on Mischief, and Piddle yelped in startlement. I felt Fleetfoot try to jerk away, and I held him fast so I could pull a glove over his stump: Mischief's glove, which I'd stitched of mouse skins. For where the mouse is, there is Mischief, and where Mischief is, the mouse follows.

Ev had brought me twenty mice, and it had taken every one, for their hides were so thin and delicate they tore easily. The fur was softer in nap than the finest velvet, gray brown on the backs, pale gray on the underbellies. I'd pieced their skins together to fit Fleetfoot's new hand, as best I could remember it, to teach his shade to fit what was, rather than what was gone. A new whole.

He cringed when he saw the glove of pied fur, and the tails that dangled from it, but I wouldn't let him go. "Hold still!" I hissed, for it was hard to put on the glove one-handed. Ev came forward and held Fleetfoot's arm steady, and I forced on the glove, which fit tightly, and squeezed the shade into it, down into the flesh where it belonged. "Wear this at night," I told Fleetfoot, "or when it hurts."

There should be a proper end to a rite, but I hadn't thought so far ahead. The boys stopped singing, first one, then several, until Dag was the only one left. He stopped with an embarrassed laugh, and Piddle got up and shook herself with great shuddering vigor, which caused more laughter, and we were done—though I didn't know what had been done, not for certain. But I thought I'd felt Fleetfoot's shade or shadow change under my fingers, the way the clay took shape in Artifex's hands. I was trembling, strung so taut I must vibrate, and I was cold again too, as if I'd given too much of my warmth. I put away the bones and rubbed my face on my skirt, smearing the charcoal and flour together. I heard a slap, someone hitting the rump of a horse, and looked up to see Galan standing on the other side of the circle, and a stallion sidling out of his way. Galan was wearing his surcoat unlaced. His linen shirt was bright beneath it, spilling out from the sleeves and over his sagging hose. He'd come without his boots.

The boys scattered, even Fleetfoot and Ev. I didn't blame them.

I reached for my headcloth, ashamed that he saw me with my head bare before others. Ashamed and afraid.

"No," he said, his voice thick, and in two strides he was on me, leaning down with his hand on the side of my neck and his thumb pushing up my chin. He'd walked right over the small fire, scattering embers and raising sparks.

I stood up, though his hand pressed me down. He rubbed my face hard with the sleeve of his surcoat, saying, "What is this? What is this?" And all I could think was that he'd sully the fine brocade. A laugh was rising in me and I must not let it out. I must not. I didn't know how I could be so afraid and so mirthful at the same time—unless it was Mischief in me. I'd called Mischief and maybe he hadn't left. He was one to linger where he wasn't wanted.

"You lied," Galan said. "And it makes me wonder how many other times you've lied and I didn't find out. You said you weren't a canny and I believed you. That makes me the fool the Crux said I was."

I opened my mouth to naysay him, but the words wouldn't come. He shook me hard.

I said, "The priest couldn't give Feltfoot sooth, and neither would Rift Barrier, so I did. He was suffering so much, I couldn't bear to see it."

"So you *are* a canny," Galan said.

I shrugged and said something close to the truth. "I am what Ardor made me."

"I saw you. I heard you." He rubbed my cheek with his thumb and showed me the gray smudge. "Would you make a passel of boys follow at your heels now, as Rowney does? I've seen him, don't shake your head, you know it's true." He was almost growling now, his voice had dropped so low, and I held my breath because the sound of him set something humming in my belly. "It makes me wonder . . . ," he said, stepping forward so I stepped back and back again. There was a horse behind me, so I stopped. Galan had one hand on my neck and the other on the horse's withers, so I couldn't move, and the horse turned its head and snorted. "It makes me wonder what you did to *me*."

I'd never tell him about the binding, never. He wouldn't forgive me for it. He wouldn't believe that by the time I'd buried that womandrake by the river, it was too late, we were already bound.

He pressed me and the horse shifted and stepped away, and there was air at my back and nothing holding me up but his hands on me, on my buttocks and under my armpit, hoisting me up face-to-face with him, and I wrapped my legs around his waist and my arms around his neck, and we both staggered. He went down to his knees. I lay back against the ground, but I kept my legs around him. He slid his hands up my thighs, pushing away my dress. I watched him and started to smile. Mischief was in me for certain that night. I dared Galan and he knew it. He leaned over me, bracing himself with one hand against the ground. Some of my hair was caught under his hand, so I couldn't turn my head. His other hand was between my legs, hard fingernails and calluses and knuckles. He shoved three fingers into me while he watched my face, and I saw he wanted to startle me, maybe even hurt me, but I pushed myself against his fingers, taking him farther in.

And Galan took his hand away and yanked at the laces of his hose, and he lowered himself on me and pierced me and scraped me against the ground. I dug my heels into him. I saw the pattern clear as day, how on the last cast the Dame's finger bone had landed in Mischief and pointed to Desire, and Na's had landed in Chance and pointed to the Warrior, and I wondered if this was the necessary end of the rite, the way to the Warrior's unforgiving heart. I hadn't wanted Galan there, but he'd been summoned nonetheless. I felt every pebble and clod and blade of grass under my back, and every wrinkle and fold of linen and brocade against my front, and Galan's weight and hard muscle pressing everything into my skin, and it was all I wanted, to be rubbed tender inside and out, to be given over to the world's touch.

CHAPTER 10

Raiders

all the gods at your peril, for they do not suffer to be dismissed. Now I saw mice wherever we camped. No doubt they'd always been there, but never so many. I saw them from the corners of my eyes, little flickers of darting gray motion, and by the time I turned my head they'd scampered off. Holes in the grain sacks, holes chewed in Galan's linen underarmor, its tow stuffing stolen for nests. Holes chewed in his strongbox and Fleetfoot's blanket. The mice brought fleas and we all itched and scratched.

Fleetfoot slept with his mouse glove on. He said it helped.

I built a neat little house of grapevines on the brazier and set a fire inside it, and sat watching it burn. Most nights gazing at a fire was as close to dreaming as I could get. The bark curled away from the wood in long strands, and I wondered how many lifetimes those vines had been tended in the vineyard we'd sacrificed for our fire.

Spiller poked at the blaze and made the house tumble down. "Sire Galan takes me for a nursemaid. He should have left your sheepdog Rowney to look after you." He was sulking because Sire Galan was off hunting with the Crux, and he'd taken Sire Edecon and Rowney—and even Fleetfoot, to serve as a messenger—and left Spiller behind. They were searching for a party of outriders from the clan of Eorōe, who had been ambushed, and the Blood taken prisoner; their varlets had been killed, all save one horseboy who'd lived to tell of it.

"So go," I said.

"I would have gone and gladly."

"No doubt, Spitter," I said, though I did doubt it, remembering how Galan had been unhorsed once in a tourney, and Spiller had been too cowardly to do his duty and pull him out from under the hooves of the warhorses.

"You never call me by my name," Spiller said, scowling into his cup.

"I can't help that it comes out twitted. I meant Spilter, Spiller, you know."

"I mean Bloodspiller. That's my name now, I earned it."

145

I shrugged.

"Why not call me by my name?"

"Because it's ludiculous."

"Because you think I'm dirt. Who made you my judge? You were always too proud to take my orders, always high-handed. And now that you're godstruck you're even worse." He threw the lees of his cup into the fire and put it out. "It's a waste of breath to talk to you. I'm going to sleep. I shan't sit up and worry till morning."

Spiller lay down with his back to me. It was true that I'd judged him long ago, and never thought much about him since, though we lived side by side. Now he'd taken a new name, and it seemed he wanted to live up to it. Hadn't I done the same once?

The camp quieted. I wrapped myself in the feather quilt and lay down outside the tent, with my feet downhill. I couldn't bear to stay indoors, sleepless, while even now Galan walked and the others rode into the night. The waning Moon was at half, bright enough to light their way. The constellation of Hazard cleared the brow of the hill, arrowing toward the Hub star, and I marveled at how easily I could pick out godsigns again, their patterns bright and clear against the starfield. But that was with my left eye; my right eye saw only the brightest stars, and the rest disappeared into a sparkling mist. From one day to the next, the change in my vision was slight; but after a hand of days, a tennight, there was no doubt it was getting worse.

I hated that Galan and I had parted on a quarrel, a silent quarrel. He'd not spoken to me above three curt words a day since he caught me lying to him. He said nothing at all at night, but coupled with me nevertheless, and there was rage in his desire. It called the same from me, and we met as on a battlefield to test the temper of our bones, the resilience of our flesh, and the reaches of our endurance.

A drudge who doesn't lie to her master is a fool. Did he think I should ask permission for anything and everything? He must grant me leave to shit, even, for I couldn't go alone to the ditches. Galan no longer let Rowney or Fleetfoot escort me when I gathered remedies in hedge and field or visited the sick, it was Bloodspiller all the time now. Bloodspiller could be bribed, but likely he took my payments—copperheads or chores I did that should have been his—and tattled to Sire Galan anyway.

I would have groveled to end the quarrel, but Galan wasn't ready to be mollified. So now I feared he wouldn't come back, just because we hadn't said a proper farewell—which was foolish—as if a kiss from me could keep him safe. I had but to close my eyes to see, with the unreliable eye of the mind, the many ways he might come to harm.

Wildfire

I lacked courage, there was the cause: the courage to wait as I must wait now, for the outcome of Galan's hazards. I wondered how Mai had endured it, battle after battle, campaign after campaign. No wonder Galan thought I was too soft to be his sheath. He had tried to spare me this.

I touched the red cord at my waist. The Queen of the Dead was very close tonight; her realm and ours occupied this same hillside, and her poor subjects, the dead, inhabited our camp. Some were bewildered, some angry. We haunted them more than they haunted us. The shades were hungry to be in our thoughts, craving our sorrow or fear, craving to be acknowledged. I couldn't see or hear them, but I could no longer ignore them, as others did, with the complacency of the living.

Surely they were to be pitied more than feared. Why then did I feel dread? The fear for Galan was my own, but this Dread came from elsewhere; it was the god Rift taking possession of me, making its presence known, so that suddenly I was sweating and short of breath, and my belly was quivering and my heart stuttering. In my throat, a stone that could not be swallowed. And all over my body, a prickling, itching, crawling sensation as if an army of lice marched about on me—or worse, as if the vermin had gotten beneath my skin. I couldn't get at them no matter how I scratched. They were an insistent creeping torment. Rift Dread manifest in the swarm.

I wasn't large enough to encompass this Dread, and yet it found no outlet, so I must enlarge around it until I was monstrously swollen, as vast as the hillside that swallowed me whole: my head the crest, my feet the valley. I seeped into the earth, losing all sense of the edges of my own body, that small leaky sack of skin. Hedges and thickets were my hair, and stones my bones. The earth was a smothering weight, and I couldn't move except to shudder. In the burning pit of my belly was the large fire before the king's pavilion. Waning campfires stung me with small lances of heat.

A dog began to bark.

There, in the crook of my knee where the horses of our clan were tethered, the horsemasters stirred in their sleep, troubled by dreams. One stallion snorted and another whinnied, restless. The sentries with their dogs were pinpricks of alertness around the camp. They stared into the dark, and strained to hear, but by now too many dogs were barking. I felt vermin creeping amongst the roots of the hair on my scalp. A troubling of the hedges. A horrible itch. I couldn't tear my arm free to scratch, for my limbs were rooted in the hillside. Nor could I summon voice and breath to cry, *Danger!*

Then Dread released me, and I heard myself panting and the sound was loud as a roar. And I was wrapped in the quilt again, terrified and shrunken in my own body. I sat up and wailed, and my hands, being freed, began to scratch. I tore at my scalp with my fingernails, and screamed, "Stranglers! Stranglers in the camp!"

Spiller was up and out of the tent, shouting, "What is it? What?"

I pointed east, where my head had lain, where a hedge ran over the brow of the hill, and cried out, "They're cunning!"

"Who's cunning?" asked Spiller. He buckled his sword belt and I put on my overdress and my girdle with the knife in the sheath. And the afflictions of fear, ordinary fear—galloping heart, wheezing breath, dry mouth— were familiar and even welcome.

War dogs howled. They were riled all over the camp, so danger seemed to come from all directions, or none. But I still felt that itch somewhere to the east, somewhere on my forehead and scalp.

Many men slept through the clamor of the dogs, snug in their exhaustion. There had been alarms before, and nothing had come of them. But most of the warriors of our company roused and some went rushing about with swords drawn. They lacked a commander, for Crux was off leading the party of searchers. Someone kicked the cookfire awake and sent up a fountain of sparks. Sire Guasca, in a shirt so well bleached it served as a beacon, scolded the men for flailing about like chickens after the farmwife has wrung their necks.

Divine Xyster asked in a stern voice who had raised the alarm. The sentries carried horns to warn of an attack, and no horns had sounded.

I backed away from the fire and Spiller caught me by the arm. "Go on," he said. "Tell them what the fuss was about."

I shook my head.

"Afraid to tell?" he said.

"I don't know—maybe it's nothing. But I felt a fidget, a flummox . . . over there . . ." I pointed toward the hedges where I'd felt an itch. Perhaps I'd imagined it, but if so, the manhounds had too.

Then shouting started north-of-east, near where I'd pointed. From the sounds of it you'd think an army had fallen upon us, but I was sure it was no more than a score of men, stealthy men on foot. I'd felt them creeping. What could they do against an army? Steal horses, probably. I tried to tell Spiller so, but it came out "Steal houses."

Men thundered past us in the dark, bellowing and brandishing weapons, running toward the sounds of battle. I was more afraid of them than of the enemy. How could they see whom to fight? Spiller dashed after them to find out what was happening.

A mob surged back toward us, broke into individuals who scurried this way and that. Mole went running by me in her thin dress, with a blanket over one shoulder. She didn't see me, she wasn't looking. Just running. She stumbled over something, and got up and ran on, leaving her blanket behind, and that stung me into motion. I was ashamed I hadn't thought of helping her, for she was still recovering from the kick of that mule, her master. I hadn't thought at all, I was standing there like a loaf.

I hurried after her and picked up her blanket. She'd tripped over a bill-hook that some foot soldier had abandoned, so I picked that up too. It was a poor cousin to a scorpion, with a shaft tall as a man and a hooked blade with a spiked tip, and I'd never used one save to prune trees, but it comforted me nevertheless to have it in my hand. I caught up with Mole easily. We went downhill, away from camp, both of us instinctively seeking safety in dark and quiet rather than crowds, and the slope spilled us down across a fallow field. We thrashed through high weeds, and broke the frozen crust of the soil and slid on mud beneath. Both of us were barefoot. Mole stumbled often in the dark. At first she didn't dare look to see who ran beside her. When at last she saw that it was me, she slowed, clutching her side, and I slowed with her.

We crouched by a boulder so she could catch her breath, and I wrapped the blanket around her shoulders. She coughed once, twice, three times. I hoped any listener might mistake it for the coughing bark of a fox. I could tell her injury pained her by the way she gripped my hand. The run downhill had been a blur, but now I had time to notice, and everything was sharp and clear. Three pollarded plane trees rose above us, each with a pair of limbs ending in malformed knobs that looked like many-knuckled fists against the sky. The blade of the billhook was rusty.

Mole looked at me askance, and I realized my face was twisted in a grin. Galan was so eager for battle, he went searching for it with his sword Peril in hand. Had he stayed, he'd have found it without the least effort.

There seemed to be less uproar coming from the camp. Mole whispered, "Let's go back," and I almost agreed. But I saw something uphill from us, a dark splotch. It could have been mistaken for a shrub or a log, but it seemed to undulate. I put one hand over Mole's mouth and pointed with the other one.

I looked from the corner of my eye, the better to see in the dark, and the splotch changed shape and I saw it was a man raising his head. He was on his belly, pushing himself down the hill feet first, and his dark cloak had distorted his shape. He glanced over his shoulder and the sharp wedge of his nose jutted from the shadow of his hood.

I feared he was headed toward the same small shelter we claimed. Was he wounded? Was he one of our men, or an attacker?

"Get up and run!" I said, pulling at Mole. I took the billhook, and we ran down toward the woods and thickets that marked the path of the stream where we got our drinking water. Mole fell and I tugged at her arm. Dread was crawling all over my back and I glanced behind and saw the man was closer than I'd thought possible, only a few strides away and coming fast. I turned and dropped on one knee, as I'd seen Galan do once in the mortal tourney, and I braced the butt of the billhook against the ground and shouted, "Stop! A fend, a friend!" in the High, still in hopes he might be a man of our army.

But when I saw his face under the shadow of the hood, I knew him for an enemy. His skin was smeared with charcoal to hide him in the night.

He was no boar to run onto a blade, even one too rusted to shine by moonlight. He stopped short, going abruptly from headlong motion to stillness, and his long cloak settled about him. His thin lips were pale between a close-cropped black mustache and beard, and I could just see the rim of his bottom teeth, paler still. His expression was strangely bland and untroubled, but I heard him breathing hard.

The cloak was of glossy fur, nearly black, fastened in front by way of two golden brooches linked by four golden chains. Where it hung open, I could see he wore a quilted red tunic and leggings. No hauberk or plate, no weapons in his hands, but I knew by the way he controlled his movements that he was dangerous. He'd judged to a nicety where to stop. If I jabbed at him with the billhook, I might just touch him. There was contempt in that.

"What trumpery are you?" I asked. I heard Mole behind me, crawling away. I willed her to go faster.

He pushed back his hood and his pate was shaven. He hadn't covered it with ashes and patches of his scalp gleamed in the moonlight. I knew then by all the signs—bald head, cloak of bear fur, and linen armor—he was a priest of Rift Warrior. And I knew that if he wanted to kill me, I couldn't stop him. I almost assented to death at that moment. It seemed easier to go assenting, and I thought of Penna with her neck outstretched and understood her better.

I heard a hectoring, shrill voice—the voice of some objecting part of me—saying, *Run! Run!* But I dared not turn my back on him.

His expression gave no warning when he moved. He stepped forward and his cloak swirled over the billhook, and he wrapped the fur around the blade and yanked to pull the haft from my grasp. When he swung his cloak, I saw blood dripping down his right hand; he'd led with his left, and his breath rasped in his throat. He was wounded.

I didn't resist the pull on the billhook, but followed it with all my force, pushing the spike toward the priest's right armpit, lunging from a kneeling position and falling forward as the hook scraped between his body and arm.

Wildfire

I felt a thump when I hit him, and heard tearing sounds, but I lacked the strength to force my blow home through fur and padded underarmor and the shield of his rib cage. I landed on my side, and the haft of the billhook jerked in my grasp and I stubbornly held on with both hands. I caught a glimpse of his face, the muscles strained and knotted over the skull. He grunted but didn't fall. Every moment I thought, *There's the end,* and after every such moment I was surprised to find I was still alive, though I shouldn't be.

Stones clattered about us, then more stones. Mole's aim was poor in the dark, and a stone stung my back. One struck the priest on his brow and started a small freshet of blood. I wished she hadn't been so brave. He'd be obliged to kill us both now for the abomination of our stoning him as if he were vermin.

The priest dropped the billhook and freed his left arm from the cloak and took a swipe at me openhanded, caught me on my shoulder. I rolled away, still clutching the weapon. The billhook had snagged in a rent in the heavy fur. I twisted the blade and tugged until the cloak hung awkwardly from the chains around his neck. I was an arm's length beyond his reach and my only chance was to keep him that far away.

He broke the billhook's haft—though it was seasoned ashwood, thicker than my wrist—by stomping on it too fast for me to see. And I was left with a broken stave in my hands, rolling downhill, getting knees and hands under me, and as I climbed to my feet I saw the priest disentangle the billhook's blade from his cloak and drop it. That he scorned the blade made me dread him more.

I lost my footing on the steep bank of the stream, slid down on my buttocks, and stopped with a jolt at the bottom. I couldn't hear him behind me and I was afraid to look. Just like Mole. As if there was some protection in remaining ignorant. I broke the glistening ice and splashed through the water, and cold bit my feet to the bone. I scrambled up the farther bank. Shale outcroppings gave way underfoot in brittle shards. Surely I'd have heard him if he'd crossed the stream after me. I dared a glance and he wasn't on my heels, wasn't anywhere. He was everywhere, in the shape of every tree and boulder. I crouched under the drooping boughs of a cedar that overhung the bank and tried to quell the sound of my breathing.

Be still, still, still.

I saw the jut of an elbow, the curve of a shoulder under a cloak, down there by the stream. A breeze came and stirred a branch, and I realized I'd cobbled my enemy out of shadows.

Then I saw a too perfect curve, as perfect as the Moon, and a reddish black sheen around it. Gods, he was close! Eight, ten strides away, lying

151

halfway up the near slope. I'd looked too high for him before, man height. The priest's head turned slightly from side to side. His eyes were slits and I could see the faint glimmer of the whites. He didn't know where I was or he'd be on me.

I became afraid he could see the mist from my breath. Cold lanced upward from the ground, through my icy feet, and the need to move was nearly unendurable. To move and put an end to it. But the priest was wounded. The longer he bled, the better.

I too was bleeding. My upper arm burned where he'd clawed me, leaving three neat cuts side by side. The blood welled out hot and turned cold as it soaked into the swaddling wool of my sleeve. He'd swiped at me once with his hand and cut me three times. How had he done that? It was so fast, I never saw the blade.

I thought of the moment I'd lunged at him. Everything I did before and after was clumsy, but for an instant I'd known what to do and done it, and I felt an unexpected pleasure in that sense of rightness. I wobbled as I crouched, feeling the strain in my legs. I put out a hand to steady myself and felt the soft brown duff of decayed needles. Good ground for stealth. In my other hand I held the broken shaft of the billhook, as long as my arm.

I watched darkness swim about the priest. Shadows formed and dissolved, and the only constant was the pale curve of his skull. I was so fixed on him that when a rustling sound came from behind me I nearly pissed myself. I turned and saw a hare nibbling on the bark of a young cedar. The hare was as startled as I was. It looked at me, its eyes flat, shining, and unblinking. When it began to chew, I breathed again.

Then the hare startled, and went dodging uphill through a stand of coppiced willows in great erratic bounds. A red fox streaked after it, and the last I saw of them both was the whitewashed tip of the fox's tail vanishing between the withies. The pursuit was fast and noisy, but I heard something or someone else as well, crashing through the brush on the other bank in reckless haste. I turned back to the priest, and he wasn't there. He was moving along the slope below me, stooping as he went, his left hand outstretched before him to fend off branches. I heard his breath coming in gasps. He was not particular as to quarry. If he lost me, Mole would do as well. He straightened up as he crossed the stream, and took the hill on the other side without troubling to be silent.

I broke from cover and followed him, the hare chasing the fox. Moonlight shone on the ice and I followed shale steps upstream, stepping on stones or fallen logs that breached the water. The priest's quarry turned and bumbled downhill, jumping and sliding. I heard a thud and a grunt and a curse—Mole colliding with a stump. I crouched beside the stream and

Wildfire

Mole ran past without seeing me, her skirts drenched. The priest was just behind her, and I swung the broken billhook haft and landed a two-handed wallop on one of his shins. I heard a crack, and couldn't tell if it was his leg or the wood that broke. He fell forward.

I knew from listening to fighters talk that a blow to the shin could render a leg numb and useless for a time. I'd reckoned that much, but it was mere luck, not cleverness, that put me on his weakened right side and not his left.

I stood and thumped him on the back just as he rolled and struck at me with his left hand. The cloak that protected him from blows slowed him down now that it was wet. He missed me and caught my skirt, shredding it with three cuts at once. I jabbed at his face with the splintered end of the haft, but at the last moment I pulled the blow, too squeamish to grind it into his eyes.

He made a fist and struck at me again, and this time I saw between his fingers three curved blades that had been hidden when he held his hands open. Linked iron rings on all four fingers held the blades in place. A bearclaw, they called it. Only priests of Rift used that weapon. I scrambled backward and screamed as he raked me across the thigh. The priest tried to get to his feet but his leg gave out. He landed hard on his left knee, the other leg stretched out stiffly behind him. His right arm trembled as he propped himself up. He kept his good arm free. Surely he was in pain—his breath sounded rough as an armorer's rasp. But his face was impassive.

Even a shackled bear is dangerous—just ask the bearbaiters. He might be feigning hurt to lure me closer. Or so I'd run and he could catch me by surprise.

Mole had run off downstream, and I thought she was long gone. But she came back, carrying a big stone in her hands. Her eyes looked large in her small pinched face, and her upper lip was shiny from snot.

She heaved the stone at the priest, aiming at his head, her movements awkward. The stone hit him on the hip and came apart in thin jagged pieces. Mole was sobbing. She groped around in the dark and found a broken oak branch still bearing a few tattered leaves. She swung and he caught the branch easily and twisted it out of her hands. He whipped at her with it, his face for the first time showing anger, and I wondered if he was breaking one of his many vows by using such an inferior weapon.

I stood there useless. I saw Mole's rage and wondered why I felt nothing myself. I was chilled clear through, mind and body numb. The priest started to haul himself to his feet, using the branch. He mustn't get up.

I hit him square on the anklebone and heard another crack. A splinter of wood went flying from the broken haft. He began to sway and I swung again for the same spot and hit hard. The oak branch snapped under his weight and he dropped to his hands and knees. Mole had found a better stone, a fist-size lump of granite, and she hammered at his bare round head. I hit his left arm and felt the elbow give way even through the heavy cloak. The ice in me had cracked and underneath there was a deep and fast current of fury at the priest's impassivity. I wanted to break through it, break him. Never once had he spoken to us. We were prey to him, nothing but beasts. I hit him behind the ear and the haft split in my hands, right down the middle, and left me with a sharp stake.

For some reason that stopped me. I'd have had to push the jagged point in under his chin.

Mole went on working doggedly with her stone, trying to break his skull, which proved to be difficult. He fell on his side. Blood leaked from cuts in his scalp and ran over his face. I said, "Stop. He's dying. Let's go."

"I want his cloak," she said. Her hand shook but her voice was steady.

"Why? It's fair bur, it's bear, see?" I didn't understand, because a mud-woman could never wear such fur, she wouldn't be allowed.

She hauled the cloak out from under him and gathered it up in a great sopping armful, dragging the golden chains across his throat. She gave the fur a twist and the chains tightened. She twisted again, strangling him. The priest made choking sounds, and I said, "Halt it!"

He went limp, and Mole stooped to undo the brooches that fastened the chains to the fur. He rolled and clouted her on the side of the head so fast I couldn't believe it, couldn't believe it when she sat down in the stream and fell over. I tugged and tugged at her arm to drag her beyond his reach, but he was no longer moving.

Mole was already dead. The priest had broken her neck and clawed away part of her face and laid bare the jawbone. So it was better that it was quick.

The heat of his life spilled out into the night. I could see it like a dark flame guttering. His eyes were open, but he seemed to look past me. There were long pauses between each breath. Another would come after I was sure he was dead. I wasn't kind or ruthless enough to finish him.

When his hands were cold and would never move again, I stole his bearclaw to keep for a hidden weapon. I understood then why a warrior loves plunder enough to risk the anger of the dead, and how the victor savors his victory twice, first over the living man, then over the shade who must suffer the sight of his weapon in another man's hand. I wanted to take the priest's strength for my own; I hoped by diminishing him to make myself greater.

CHAPTER 11

Shiver-and-Shake

oon it became known to all that we'd suffered a visitation by Auspices of Rift Warrior. The attackers left behind execrations: small clay statues of the king and queenmother, stamped with the sign of Rift and inscribed with curses to bring upon our army plagues, hunger, and discord. To set free the curses, they'd broken the statues and sown shards about the camp, some said even in Queenmother Caelum's bedclothes. Three corpses were found headless, all of them Wolves who'd stood high in her counsel. As for the other dead, two cataphracts and a hand of varlets, most had been mistaken for foes in the darkness, and killed by their fellows.

No dead enemies were found. Sire Erial's men went to fetch Mole and carry her to the pyre, and the priest's body was gone, and all signs of him too.

We left that accursed place without the Crux and his men. Early in the afternoon, my hopes were raised by a party of riders coming up behind us, but it was just men of Eorōe returning empty-handed from the search for their captive kinsmen, having lost the trail in a bog.

That evening foot soldiers dug a wide ditch encircling our new camp and put up a palisade of sharpened stakes behind it. Priests of Rift and Torrent led a procession up and down every path to ask the gods to protect us from the execrations; they sacrificed bullocks and claimed there were signs of victory in their entrails.

But the gossip was about Prince Corvus, and how he had Rift's Blood in his veins by way of his father, King Voltur. He must have an army of pet priests of Rift. His were better than ours. What had our Auspices of Rift done in the raid? Run around like foot soldiers. King Thyrse and his sister Caelum were Blood of Prey, a fine warlike clan—but no clan, no lineage of the Blood, was born to war like Rift. Suddenly this prince seemed more formidable.

*   *   *

Bloodspiller and I raised Galan's tent by ourselves, for the Crux and the others were still missing. Some hotspurs of our company talked of riding out to search for them, but Divine Hamus said the omens were unfavorable, which he always said when it suited him to be cautious.

I made a fire outside the tent and waited for Galan. Waited and worried. Sometimes my worries took wing and became prayers. Bloodspiller went to the market and came back with an amulet, an unglazed clay bead the size of a plum; he already had three just like it that he'd bought from revelators.

I waited until he was snoring to take the priest's bearclaw from my saddlebag and slip it over my fingers. It was made for a large hand, but I could wear it. I made a fist and the claws showed; I opened my hand and the claws were hidden between my fingers. The blades were curved steel, bright and sharp. The iron rings were inlaid with delicate silver filigree. It was a tricky weapon to use, for it was all too easy to cut fingers on the blades.

My wounds hadn't pained me during the fight, but I felt them now. The cuts on my upper arm were shallow; on my thigh the claws had dug deeper. Before we marched that day I'd poulticed and bandaged my wounds, and sewn up the rents in my skirts and sleeve, and washed off the blood.

I wanted to mourn Mole but I was having trouble remembering her face as it was before it was torn open. Likely she'd be alive now if she'd run away instead of staying to throw stones at the priest. I wondered why she'd done it. I wondered why I'd followed the priest instead of running myself when I had the chance—I hadn't thought, hadn't chosen. Was this what bound Sire Galan to his battle companions? I'd seen the bond from outside, and never before felt its tug.

In Mole's honor I cut off a lock of hair and watched it scorch and shrivel on the fire. Then I wrapped the bearclaw in an old sack and put it back in my saddlebag.

Toward dawn the dogs south-of-east of camp began to bark and a sentry blew the alert on his horn. The camp stirred like a kicked anthill. I sat up on the bed and waited, and in a few long moments the sentry sounded three falling notes that meant "No danger."

It was the Crux and Sire Galan and the others returning to camp in rowdy high spirits. But bad news outruns good, and they were sober by the time they reached us, having learned that our camp had been attacked while they were off hunting for the missing outriders.

They'd tracked the outriders and their captors halfway to Malleus before the Crux's dogs lost the trail—and here Chance played a fine prank on Sire Galan, sending him luck of no profit to him personally. The cataphracts separated to search in different directions. In the middle of the night, Galan and

Wildfire

Sire Edecon crept up on a camp of soldiers guarding fifty warhorses, some of excellent breeding, some jades—mounts from Prince Merle's own herds, on the way to Malleus. According to a horseboy Galan had captured, the horses were to be kept in reserve during the battle. Which suggested that Prince Corvus intended to meet us in battle, rather than wait to be beseiged.

It was the first I'd heard of a prince named Merle. Prince Corvus's younger brother, Galan said. The rumormongers and rhapsodists of our army had never seen fit to sing about him.

The Crux and his party returned without the outriders, but with fifty new mounts. Merle's men were even now being questioned. Sire Galan's good fortune in war had won him horses he wasn't allowed to ride, and gilded his already golden reputation. But he told us that he counted himself unlucky, coming back to find the camp had been raided in his absence.

Spiller peeled off Galan's wet hose, which were stuck to his feet with ooze from his blisters. His soles were cracked and rough. Galan waved Spiller away, saying, "You let the fire go out? Get it going."

"Nothing left to burn, Sire."

"Well, find something! Beg or borrow if you have to. And ask Cook for something to eat. We're famished. Get something for the boy too. We've been running for two nights while Sire Edecon and Rowney rode, the lazy bastards."

He'd warm himself with vexation if a fire wasn't handy. Fleetfoot sat on the ground, easing his own sore feet. The boy's lips were purplish and he looked more exhausted than hungry. Piddle lay by his side, too worn out to do more than thump her tail on the ground.

Galan pointed to my dress, which was stained where blood had seeped through the bandage on my thigh. "You were hurt?"

I shrugged.

"Let me see."

"I don't want to uncover them, the scuts. They mend best if they are not pestered."

Galan said, "And where was Bloodspiller when you were hurt?"

"It was in the stark and everyone was running and we got desperated. Separated." I could read the signs of anger in his face. I knew them well. I reached out and dabbed at a streak of mud on Galan's jaw with my sleeve. "You're not wounded yourself, are you?"

"Nothing a warm bed won't cure." But his smile came and went too quickly. Perhaps he was remembering he was angry with me.

Galan and his men didn't have time to rest, not then, for the sky was turning gray and drudges were stirring, and we marched at dawn.

* * *

A boy came late the next night, when everyone but me was asleep, to ask if I would tend a sick woman, and Galan said no. I got up anyway and he grabbed my wrist. I reached for my underdress and he tightened his hold on me. "Who is it? Who's sick?" he asked the runner. The boy might have been five years old or seven; he was small and underfed, clad in a filthy tunic made from a grain sack stamped with a quatrefoil crest, with rags tied around his feet.

The boy didn't answer. Galan said, "Come closer! Tell me who is sick."

He approached, staring at Galan in fear as if he didn't understand. So I asked him in the Low who was sick, and he answered in the same language: "My my mother."

"What clan?" Galan asked, in the Low this time. It always surprised me to hear it from his mouth.

"No clan," said the boy. His torch trembled in his hand.

"No clan? Is she some muddy whore then? Answer me!"

I jerked away from Galan and pulled my shift over my head. "Why do you shout so loud, don't you see the chill is frightened?"

Galan stood up naked behind me and caught me by the scruff of my neck. I felt a jolt from the crown of my head to the root of my spine, and stiffened my back against his grip. "You're not going," he said. "You don't even know the woman, do you? Or is this another false summons?"

I couldn't turn to face him because he held me too tightly. "Please, Sire, she must be very ill, if they sent the tad for me." I had to go, didn't he see that? It was more than duty; I was compelled to it. I needed to help where I was needed. To deny healing opened a chasm in me between what I was and what I ought to be.

But what could I do? I could insist on going and take a beating and still be unable to go. He didn't even have to raise a hand against me—he could quell me with a glance, I was so afraid of losing his favor. A coward. My shoulders slumped. I bowed my head and began to weep, and Galan let go of me. The boy stared, not understanding what had happened.

But Galan amazed me. I could be so sure I knew what he was thinking, and so wrong. He pulled on his hose, laced up his prickguard, put on his shirt, his surcoat, his boots—dressed himself, letting Bloodspiller and Rowney sleep. I looked at him in wonder, and he looked back without giving up one hoarded mite of anger, and said, "I mean to see what you do."

The boy led us through the camp and past sentries, whom Sire Galan appeased with a couple of copperheads, and down a mud-slick trail to a small lake in the valley below. Galan's lantern made me blind to anything outside the swinging circle of its light. It started to rain, and Galan cursed. In a copse of slender willows by the water, the boy knelt before a briar patch, frosted purple wands of raspberry and green coils of dog rose. He rooted under the thicket and disappeared. I crouched and peered after him.

His mother lay on a nest of matted grasses under the briars. Her face looked like a yellow bone. I'd never seen her before, but it was plain she was a laundress; she had but one possession worth stealing, a kettle for boiling linen. Galan cursed again when I crawled in beside her. There was no room for him too. He knelt and handed me the lantern, and I set it down between us. Let him look, if he was so determined. The brambles were propped up with forked sticks, but every time I moved I snagged on thorns.

The woman didn't own a blanket, only a couple of torn sacks, which she'd thrown off. She was burning, hot and dry, as if she'd sweated all she could. Her dress was twisted about her waist, and soiled—she had the squirts and she was too weak to crawl from the nest to relieve herself. I leaned close to smell her breath, but it was hard to tell one stink from another.

The boy squirmed out of the shelter to fetch me water in a clay pot. The laundress's tongue was dry and brown. I dribbled water over her cracked lips and then made a teat out of a rag for her to suck. She roused herself to look at me. "What . . . ?" she said. But she seemed too tired to sustain fear; she turned her head away, as if resigning herself to whatever might come.

I cleaned her with one of the sacks, and Sire Galan watched, his face marked with disgust or queasiness. The boy looked at me with trust I didn't deserve. She was in mortal danger from this fever. If I didn't cure her, Galan would think me the worst kind of canny—a cozener, a cheat. I never took money for healing, surely he knew that! But he only knew I had coin he'd never given me.

If I didn't cure her, the boy would be alone. I must put him out of mind, him and Galan both. I prayed to Ardor, who had given me the gift of drawing fever. I rubbed my hands over the woman's bony face and limbs, her stark ribs and sunken haunches. Her thinness came from long acquaintance with hunger. My icy right hand took her heat without thawing, but the rest of me warmed, and sweat pricked out all over my back. I drew heat from her until her fever broke and she started to cool, and then to shiver.

She grew colder, too cold, so that I was frightened by it. I lay down behind her under my cloak, my chest to her back and my knees bent behind hers, the way two fond sleepers nestle. I put my left hand over her heart, which quaked within her chest. I felt a small flame within her, no bigger than that of a candle wavering in a cold wind. Such a small sensation, a mere flutter in my palm, hard to discern while her body shook. An invisible flame, but if it were to flicker out, she'd be a corpse.

Inside me the hearthfire of life burned strong and steady as a brazier full of coals, and I called on my own warmth now to warm her, and the fire blazed up obedient to my call. I held her in a close embrace, and I overflowed with heat, spilling through my skin, through my burning left hand pressed over her chest and belly. She warmed, stopped shaking. We were so close I could see beads of sweat strung on the fine hairs of her scalp.

I murmured a prayer to Ardor in thanks and wonder for this gift, newly discovered. The lightning had done this, divided my two hands, made one cold, the better to draw fire, and the other warm to give it.

I gave the laundress warmth without stinting, until I was shivering and she was hot, and then she was too hot and I took heat from her, left hand to give, right hand to take. At first this giving and taking was like breathing out and in, but more and more it became labor, and breathing too became labor, and I began to gasp, no longer sure if I was helping her or she was killing me.

One of us moaned. She was cold again, so cold, but she had stopped trembling. I had no heat left to give her. Was she dead? I stilled my own breathing to listen for hers. Cold silence. I saw her ahead of me, naked and bony, her flesh tinged blue. She stepped into a black icy river, and with every step she went deeper until the water closed over her head. I followed.

The other shore of that river is not across, but under. Currents coiled around my legs, trying to hold me back. When I was submerged, I looked up into a dark sky held in a noose of horizon above my head and saw a gull flying. The gull's cry was wordless, full of sorrow and regret, and I knew it was Penna beating her wings endlessly against a contrary wind. The feverish woman had dwindled small, or gotten far ahead, and I was stumbling on a stony shore.

I called out to her, "You mustn't leave your boy! What will become of him?" My heart churned. I tried to follow her through air thick as mud, I tried to run, but it took all my strength to shuffle one foot forward and then the other—all my strength and I wasn't fast enough. She disappeared among the multitude, and I lacked the courage to seek her among so many dead, there in the netherworld.

Whether my eyes were open or closed, I saw the same thing, a world bleaker than the bleakest winter day. There was no color anywhere, nor even the notion or memory of it, as if color had never existed. And everything was too heavy. The shades were of a substance denser than flesh. The only lightness in that place was the wind that pushed against me and hissed, "Go back!" I took a step. The next step was easier, as if I waded through water instead of mud, and I knew I was leaving. No need to turn around when every direction was away.

Wildfire

I abandoned her there. I was running faster and faster. I was lying in shallow water, soaked and clammy, my blood thick with a slurry of ice. Strong hands clasped my wrists and dragged me onto the shore and out of the bramble lair, and Sire Galan leaned over me with his hands on either side of my face, blaspheming and praying.

He made a bonfire, and I warmed myself by it, not realizing that I warmed myself by the laundress's pyre. The fire seemed the most beautiful sight I'd ever witnessed, so alive with color and motion, so light and free and quick. Galan cut branches with his sword and threw them on the fire, and the sparks were dazzling. The boy stood there with his filthy skin and tunic glowing. Tears made shining streaks through the grime on his face, and his open mouth welled with darkness.

I tried to take off my dress because I was too hot. My hands were slow and disobedient, and Galan caught them and held them fast. Riders came to see about the fire, and he spoke to them and they rode away.

Galan hoisted me and dragged me uphill. My legs weren't much use. The laundress's son was just behind us, and Galan turned and looked at him, his mouth set in a severe line. The boy followed nevertheless.

The land of the dead is not for the living. I shivered and shook, as cold as if I were still at the bottom of that river. My skin was covered with bumps like the underbelly of a frog. I couldn't speak for the chattering of my teeth. I lay beside the brazier, wrapped in a feather quilt. Galan sat beside me, heating stones, and when they were warm he wrapped them in cloth and put them under my feet and hands. I couldn't feel my legs. My hands were too far away to answer to my commands, too far even to pain me when the warmth began to scorch.

Galan was furious. It was in his face and movements, the way he picked things up and set them down, hard and quick. All I could do was shake.

There came a time when I couldn't even do that.

It occurred to me that I was dead. Death was easier than I'd thought, easier than life. Less caring. I was wandering in darkness so absolute my night eyes could see nothing. I feared I might wander forever and never find an obstacle or any change in the slope or roughness of what was underfoot. I untied the fireflask from my girdle, and pulled out the coal in its swaddling of mossy firewort. The coal tumbled and rolled away, and I felt for it with my fingers. It was cold to the touch—gone out? I took it in my palm and breathed on it.

I'd called on Ardor to heal the laundress, and Wildfire had answered. But it was Wildfire who made her fever rage, and caused the flames of her hearthfire to escape its bounds. I should have called on Hearthkeeper instead—these gifts of drawing and giving fire, surely they were blessings from Hearthkeeper herself. I'd failed to see this, and failed the laundress, and maybe hastened her death. We'd been locked together and the heat had ebbed and flowed between us, powerful, unstoppable, until it flowed away into the realm of the dead, swallowed like a river that vanishes into sand.

I prayed to Hearthkeeper fervently now, and breathed on the coal again and felt a throb of warmth against my palm, and saw a faint glow, the only light in the world. The heat stung, and I hastily put the coal on the ground and fed it strands of firewort, which flared and were consumed.

The coal couldn't catch without fuel, and what was there to burn in this desolation? My feet were heavy and stiff, they no longer felt a part of me, having turned to wood. I broke off one toe, then another, the little toes that didn't matter so much. They cracked like dried sticks. I fed them to the coal. Flames wrapped around the wooden flesh and it hurt—Gods, it hurt!

Galan put another hot stone by my feet, and crouched beside me. His face was carved of warm wood, with polished curves and hollows, and delicate lines incised around his eyelids and nostrils. I stared at him fixedly because my eyes were frozen. He moved out of my sight, then back in. He held the mirror with the fox handle before my face, and I saw my own empty stare. "You live!" he said, showing me the mist on the mirror.

The hearthfire in me had a ravenous greed, it ate heat from the stones, and when Galan took my hands I stole heat from him too. He gasped and swore, but he held on.

The jacks were taking down the tent. I sat outside and eased up my kirtle to bare my shins to the fire in the brazier. My littlest toes were not broken off after all, but red and spotty and swollen from chilblains. The laundress's son sat nearby, his bony knees drawn up to his chin and his arms clasped around them. He seemed almost a lackwit, but I supposed he had no other shield against fear and sorrow than to refuse to feel. He cringed when the men came near, especially Bloodspiller. The jack had laughed at him and given him a name, Ears, because his ears were big as jug handles, but the name his mother had given him was Wren.

The boy scratched so much he made my head itch. I called him to sit in my lap, and ran a thistle nitcomb through his hair. I had diligently kept us free of lice by preparing lousebane and candling the seams of our clothes. Lice didn't care who was high and who was low, and Wren had brought them to our tent.

A quarrel with Galan was coming—I knew this as surely as I knew when storms were on the way, and perhaps for the same cause: old injuries starting to ache. I wasn't surprised when he stood over me and said, "I hope you don't think I'm keeping the boy. I daresay you're sorry you killed his mother, but you can't keep him."

I squinted at him. "I didn't kill her. Sometimes I can help, sometimes not. Next time I shall do better."

Galan looked at me, his face tight and cold. "There won't be a next time."

I refused to quarrel. If I spoke I'd enrage him further and it would be for naught. So I kept the thought to myself: *You can't forbid me.*

He shook his head and walked away and the boy and I stared after him.

That day Prince Corvus returned the captive outriders whom the Crux had tried to rescue. He sent them with gifts of horses, robes, and spices, and a message that he was ready to settle the terms of battle. We learned this from rumormongers before we'd finished raising the tents in our new camp. Auspices made sacrifices and read the omens, for it was beholden on them to know the time and place of battle most favorable to our army. In the evening a delegation of priests set forth to parley with Prince Corvus's conciliators.

We were to have a properly conducted battle to decide a properly conducted war. There were other sorts of war, such as the campaign of extermination our king had carried out against enemies to the south of Corymb. He'd slaughtered them without mercy for the abomination of using weapons that killed at a distance. He'd razed their muddy villages down to the hearthstones, and resettled the broad grasslands with horses, and men to look after the horses, and women to look after the men.

But this war would be fought by two armies drawn up in ranks and contending at a time and place foretold. The battle would begin with rites and sacrifices and end with one or the other army in possession of the battleground, and therefore the kingdom. It was to be bounded like a mortal tourney, so the war would not spill everywhere to the ruination of Incus.

The conciliators haggled and we waited. Men went off raiding, and the king and queenmother looked the other way. Some of the warriors were trying to get what loot they could now, afraid the conciliators might make peace. Mai claimed the queenmother encouraged plundering to make Prince Corvus more eager to settle, for while he sat in luxury in Malleus, we were encamped on a hillside scoured by winds, freezing one day and mired in mud the next. We were one long march from the city. The battle, which had seemed to recede before us as we crossed Incus, was nearly upon us.

The conciliators dillydallied, and the shiver-and-shake came to camp.

I knew my enemy now. I should have seen it at once, when it killed the laundress. Every winter the shiver-and-shake had raided our village; last winter, when I was hiding in the Kingswood, it took Na. It was deadly fond of the very old and the very young.

The shiver-and-shake crept about at night; if its shadow crossed five sleepers lying side by side in a croft, it might embrace one or two or take them all. It went abroad in daylight too, striking people down with sudden pains. Whether it came with a caress or a blow made no difference. The fever killed within a hand of days, or failed in its purpose; those who lived could expect a second visit in a tennight or so, when it returned to taunt rather than kill.

I was called to a brothel in the afternoon, and I went, since Galan wasn't there to stop me. He'd told Bloodspiller and Rowney not to let me go, and Bloodspiller did try to get in my way, telling me I'd catch a beating from Sire Galan.

Two women and three children had taken ill in the crowded brothel, a striped pavilion that stood proud over the ragtag tents of less prosperous harlots. The queans' pander was nowhere to be found. The skinniest whore, who went by the name of Longbean, spat between the gap in her front teeth and said she hoped he took a good dose of canker away with him when he ran off with the strongbox and his favorite doxy.

The whore Gentian said we were cursed by the maids of Torrent and the priests of Rift with their vile execrations, and it was no use trying to cure anyone the gods had cursed. She wailed that she was doomed, we were all doomed, the army was doomed, until I put a stop to her crying with a strong dose of soothe-me. But Gentian only said aloud what we were all thinking. If five were sick in this one tent, then how many in the army?

There were the harlots Marigold and Jillybell, and Jillybell's little daughter Blushrose, and the twins Snowdrop and Snowflake, whose mother had gone and orphaned them last year; the girls were too young to whore, and worked as servants. So many at once, I was daunted. But I wasn't alone facing down the shiver-and-shake. Most of the harlots were more sensible than Gentian, and they'd been keeping their sick companions clean and offering them nourishment. Tansy, the old woman who did the whores' laundry, was scrubbing linens after sitting up for two nights with Jillybell.

I went from one sufferer to another, looking for signs that I might understand the nature of their malady and their strength to resist it: the color of skin and tongue and the whites of eyes, the pungent smells, the music of the body—heartdrum and pulse, the timbre of breathing. The taste of sweat and spit. Whether they were hot or cold, dry or damp.

When I pressed my palms against the skin of their bellies or breasts, I felt

Wildfire

the strength of their hearthfires and fevers. I'd been mistaken, thinking them one and the same. With my touch I prayed to Ardor Hearthkeeper, and she answered, letting me take heat with my right hand and give it with my left. I was careful to touch each person only for a little while, and only as much as I could endure.

Of all the sufferers, I was most afraid for Jillybell. I knew her as a merry woman, prone to giggling, but now she lay shaking in dread. She'd fallen ill three days ago, after the raid by the priests of Rift. She said she'd seen the shiver-and-shake roaming our camp, a pale phantom. It had taken her by the neck and given her a shake, and made her so stiff she couldn't turn her head, and now it was crushing her skull slowly, as between the jaws of a nutcracker. She moaned and moaned. I brought her fever down, but by evening she was screaming from pain and fear, and crying out that she was falling though she was firmly on the bed. The screaming was a torment to me, for I didn't know how to ease her suffering.

The shiver-and-shake carried a sack full of miseries along with the fever, doling out some to one victim, some to another. It is always so with sickness, that no two people suffer alike, which is why a greenwoman must study the ill person as well as the illness to find the best remedy. I should have been able to think of five or ten plants that might serve Jillybell. The Dame had kept a store of herbs for such occasions, each harvested at the time and season of greatest potency, but that was no use to me now. I had only what I could find in midwinter near our encampment, and my memory was almost as empty as my sack of cures.

I left the stinking tent so I could breathe, so I could think, and the air outside was as cold and clean as a mountain stream. I took a deep draught of it. I was full of heat, and mist fumed from my breath and skin. The tents of the whores were, like the rest of the market, outside the protective circle of ditch and stakes. I walked away from the noise of the camp, and knelt under a tree on the cold ground, under a thin sickle Moon, the last moon of the month. I took out the divining pouch hidden under my skirts, and held the finger bones in my palm, and felt the touch of those dear shades and was comforted.

I threw the bones for Jillybell, once for her character, once for her malady, and once for a remedy. The bones of the Dame and Na landed close together on the last throw. They agreed: Wildfire and the Waters must be beseeched for help.

I threw three times for Jillybell's daughter, and this time it was the Dame alone who pointed to Wildfire and the Waters on the last throw, while Na landed outside the horizon on the godsign of Torrent—the whole god. I read the bones for the other three sufferers, and certain signs

165

appeared again in different places—Hunger was one—but always Wildfire and the Waters were the avatars to be propitiated.

Wildfire for the slow conflagration of fever, Wildfire for the parching relentless thirst. The Waters for the way the fever came in waves like those during a storm at sea, crests of burning, troughs of chills. The Waters for the high tide of delirium and the ebb tide of exhaustion, the most dangerous times for the stricken.

It was easy to see these two elemental avatars—unbounded, tempestuous—as the cause of suffering. But the bones said they were also the cure. Was there some necessity in the burning and the rhythm of fever and chills, something that helped, if it didn't kill? One must balance the other: fire against chills, water against fever and thirst, so the feverfire would scorch rather than devour, and a sufferer might ride the waves without foundering. And of course—said the bones—we must beg Wildfire and the Waters to be merciful.

I went in search of remedies, staying within the circle of the outlying sentries with their dogs. It wasn't safe to wander alone, and at first I was afraid. But I found I couldn't remain afraid, there in the garden of the gods, which is the whole world, and yet for me, that night, was bounded by the compass of our camp. It was most fruitful where gods did the tending; not in the fields, but in the boundaries, the hedges and ditches and thickets. The finger bones had pointed to avatars, and it seemed to me the avatars had sown plants that I might find them now, and harvest what was needed: shiny evergreen leaves of the holm oak, barberries, five-leaf root, bullace branches, and tender feverfew leaves that had lingered into winter.

With each plant, a harvest of memories: the Dame teaching me its riddle song, or showing me how the god had marked the plant with signs when it was created—in the ridges on the bark, the taste of a leaf, or the color of a root—so that we might know its uses and be forewarned of its hazards. And back in the tent, as I prepared what I'd gathered, every task invoked the Dame and Na. I scraped bark from bullace twigs and mashed red barberries with a mortar and pestle, and it was as if we worked side by side, as so often we'd done when they were alive. Memory resided in my hands, which knew what to do.

There were such agreements between signs and plants that I was assured the remedies would be potent. But no healer can cure if the gods are unwilling. I told Gentian that sacrifices needed to be made to Ardor Wildfire and Torrent Waters on behalf of the sick, generous sacrifices, and she collected enough coins from the other whores to make an offering of two sheep.

Late in the night came a quiet time. The old woman Tansy kept vigil with me, her head nodding. I sat watching and listening to the sick, touching them sometimes. There was no longer even a flicker from Jillybell's hearthfire when I gave her warmth. She had fallen into a stupor and was wandering between the realms of the dead and the living, where I didn't dare follow. I wondered if I could have helped had I been called to her earlier.

The Queen of the Dead took Jillybell. Wildfire and the Waters relented and let the children and the other whore live.

I ducked under the tent flap. Spiller was cooking frybread, and Rowney mending a hole in one of Galan's boots. Sire Galan was up early, or perhaps he'd never slept. He sat on the camp bed with his weapons around him. It soothed him at times to give the blades the sharpest edge, and polish and oil them to make sure no rust marred the steel. A clay lamp in the shape of a dove hung from an iron crook next to him, illuminating his unkempt hair, the brown skin of his face and neck, burned from days and days of walking, and the paler skin where his shirt hung open. The cords of his neck were taut. He snicked his longsword into its sheath and propped it at the end of the cot.

Before, facing down his jacks, I'd thought that I might get a thrashing, and that was bad enough. Now I thought I'd been too trusting. I shared his tent and his bed on his sufferance. Did I take it for granted he wouldn't cast me out? I'd been too sure of him and too complacent. I took the measure of my defiance—of which I'd been proud—and found it after all a weak and paltry thing that wouldn't withstand the threat of losing him.

Fleetfoot made haste to leave, taking the slops with him to empty in the ditch. I crossed the tent to Galan but stood out of his reach.

"I hope it was worth it," he said. "I hope you saved some whores. I've already flogged Bloodspiller and Rowney for disobedience, but I can't quite decide what to do with you."

He had his dagger belt in both hands. He wrapped the strap a couple of turns around his right fist, keeping the heavy buckle against his palm. It would be worse if the buckle were free.

"That was injust, for you to punish them on becount of me."

"They needed reminding that they're under my command, not yours. Especially your swain here."

I glanced over at Rowney and saw him watching us, his face tight and angry.

"I did what I must," I told Galan.

"So did I," he said. "I can't abide disobedience."

We'd woken Sire Edecon. He rolled his eyes and pulled the blanket over his head. I saw the boy was still here, curled up in the darkest corner of the tent. His eyes glimmered. He was sucking his thumb.

I said, "If you don't want me to disobey, don't forbid me from my duly, duty."

"I was mistaken, I see, in thinking your duty was to me."

"The sliver-and-scrape is amongst us and folk are dying of it and what little I can do I must, even if it means I don't lie along of you the whole sight long."

Galan raised his voice. "You did not used to *want* to leave my bed, nor did you receive so many summons, nor spend your nights among cankered and flea-bitten whores! You have nearly killed yourself to make others well, and they died anyway. I want you to admit they die anyway—you put yourself at hazard for nothing, you put us all at hazard. Suppose the shiver-and-shake follows you back to this tent? You don't know what you're doing, this is just your ignorance and obstinance, your pride and willfulness to set yourself against me. If you don't wish me for a master, why did you follow? You could have done as you liked. I gave you that and you flung it back in my face, and why? Why?" He stood up with the strap in his hands and I took a step backward. He was so close, but I felt the world between us. I couldn't understand how he could think I'd answered a summons to heal just to defy him. How selfish he was.

He said, "My uncle asked me that and I thought I knew the answer. I thought it was for me you came, not my money or any other cause, but as you have so little regard for me, I have to wonder."

He seemed to become aware that he was shouting. He stopped and took a breath and leaned over me, pulling the strap tight between his hands, and he said in a low voice that was worse than a shout, "I don't know which is worse, a canny or a cozener. I saw with my own eyes what you did to the bagboy—that horrid piebald glove, what was that? And what did you do to me, set a fishhook in me to see me dance? Like you did in the field that night, hmm? My dangle jerking upright at your command, just as my uncle always said."

I caught hold of the strap, my hands between his hands, and though our flesh didn't touch, I felt a spark. There was not the whole world between us after all. We were but a hairsbreadth apart. Had I not just been thinking what he'd said aloud, that I was jerked about wherever he led?

I whispered, "That was mistress, Mischief. I was not myself then."

"If you're not yourself, who are you? Or what?"

"I am what . . . Ardent made me. I think the brightening made a crack in me and I am opened up." I touched the crown of my head. "So I am visioned, visited. You understand?"

"So I suppose you cured the whores tonight?"

"One was lost of the five who had it. I could not . . ." My throat closed up. I was weary of all of it, of sickness and fear and rage and quarreling, of the struggle to speak when he lacked the patience to hear me out. His words and voice were angry, scornful, but in his face I sought contradictory signs. It was not only cannies, as Mai claimed, who had uneven faces. We all had them. And Galan's divided face betrayed a divided mind. On the left side I saw his fury that I'd disobeyed, and his fear of me and what I might be. On the right I saw his vexation that I'd risked myself so recklessly, and his fear I might come to harm over it.

I wanted to reach for Galan, to hold him and be comforted, but I knew he wouldn't tolerate my touch. I said, "Of course I have regret, regard for you, of course. You *know* why I followed. But the god gave me a . . . theft—Illfire did—a a . . . gefthe, a . . . gift to heal the ill. I'm oblieged, I must do what I can, you see? And don't you think I wish I had more . . . witdom? The got, the god stole from me too—the strickening took much of my knowdom, what I used to have of the green . . . the greenlorne, and I am just now recollecting it. I couldn't save . . . Jenny, Jinnybell, but I was able to be of some servant to them, the other whorelets. So I beg you, don't for-beg me, don't punish your japes for what I must do. I'd rather take blights on my own back than suffer them to suffer for me."

Galan threw down the strap and pushed past me and out of the doorway. I sat on the bed, my legs gone weak. I heard Bloodspiller say to Rowney, "I told you he wouldn't do it. You owe me four copperheads."

I didn't get any rest. Not long after Galan left, another summons came, this time to the tent of the Auspices of Hazard. The priestess of Chance was down with the shiver-and-shake, as was the priest of Fate and three of their servants. The carnifex of their clan was a vigorous old mudman who welcomed my arrival. We worked together through the day and evening, he with the men and I with the priestess and her handmaid. He had a store of herbs laid by. We were both puzzled that the shiver-and-shake was striking down people in their prime as well as children and old folk. It seemed fiercer here than in Corymb.

The Auspex of Chance was elderly and frail. When she was a young dedicate she'd offered her eyes, and her eyelids had been stitched shut so she'd be as sightless as her mistress. She greeted me courteously when I came in, and touched my face to see me. She said, "You have the red hair, I hear, so pray to Chance for me. She hasn't always repaid my devotion."

I left the tent so I could throw the bones for the priestess and her maid in secret. By the signs I expected them both to live, and I had what was needed to hand, in bark and roots gathered the night before, and herbs the old carnifex gave me, dried vervain and wormwood and seeds of parsley. I took heat from the Auspex and she slept placidly. But as I made ready to leave, the fever rose again. She stiffened and jerked, and gray spittle foamed at the corners of her mouth, and I feared she was going to die after all. When I put my hands on her, I felt her hearthfire churning and sullied with smoke. I stroked my fingers along her limbs and torso, trying to comb the flames so they would flow like a smooth river instead of roiling like rapids. Her fit stopped, and she eased into sleep again.

I left before she woke, when Rowney came to say I'd been sent for elsewhere. He led me to a lean-to of sticks thatched with rye stalks. A couple of sorry two-copper whores lived there with their pander, who was scarcely more than a lad—the son of the older whore, Dogrose, as the younger whore was her daughter. The daughter was sick, her eyes glazed, and the son was awake and scratching. He said to his mother, "I hope she doesn't charge much," meaning me, and Dogrose said, "She won't ask a copperhead, and suppose she did? What's it to you? You're not the one who has to flip up your skirts to earn it."

Rowney took offense on my behalf—it would be a poor sort of greenwoman who took money for healing, a gift of the gods. I didn't mind. I grinned at Dogrose and bent over her sweaty daughter. She was hardy and her hearthfire burned steadily; even before throwing the bones for her, I felt sure she'd live.

On the way back, a laundress found me and said her friend Sloeberry was sick, and would I look in on her? So I did, and then I visited the priestess of Hazard Chance, and found her sleeping quietly.

I went to the tent of the whores to see how they fared. The sick ones were mending, but Tansy, the old woman who had been so stalwart, had fallen deathly ill. I'd never seen the shiver-and-shake strike so hard and fast. Tears tinged with blood oozed from her swollen eyes, and her nose bled and dark bruises showed where no one had struck her. I threw the bones for her there in the tent, sitting beside her pallet, facing the canvas wall, hardly caring that someone might see. There were certain combinations of signs that frightened me: the Smith again, the same as for Jillybell, and Prey Hunger. The lice were dead on Tansy's head and body, just as on the laundress in the briars; that was a frightening sign too, of her blood turning poisonous, or the fever burning too hot to be endured. I stayed with her, stroking her hands. She shook and shook, cooling too fast, and I gave her what I could, but my own hearthfire was burning low. Before the end her hands turned gray, turned to clay.

By then the Sun was well and truly risen, and another day and night had passed—an endless time, I had thought while I was in it, and yet afterward it seemed to have gone by with unaccountable swiftness.

As I walked back to Galan's tent, I saw priests of Torrent dragging a dogcart around the camp, calling for everyone to give up any loot they had of Torrent's clan, so it could be burned to avert the curse. Cataphracts and drudges and queans and drabs threw armor and coins and seashell trinkets into the cart. The Auspices were solemn and they sang sonorous prayers. Behind the dogcart came an oxcart pulled by two bald priests of Rift, asking for sacrifices, and behind them supplicants slashed themselves in ecstasy.

Dread came over me and darkened my vision, and filled me with the conviction that every effort was futile. A burden of weariness bore me down. I looked each man in the face and thought, *Dead man, dead man.* I saw a gaggle of whores in striped skirts, and I knew it was just my fear that clothed them, one and all, in the drab guise of shades.

CHAPTER 12

Council of the Dead

 sank deep into Sleep's ocean, but instead of rest I caught a terrifying dream. I dreamed I gave birth to a tiny mouse, a small pink thing like a morsel of ham, and I tried to care for it like any other child, but I lost it among tousled and reeking bedclothes.

I sat up, sure I'd dreamed of Mouse, Mai's unborn child, ready at last to be born. It was bright outside, late afternoon by the look of it, and I'd slept most of the day away. I wasn't accustomed to so much sleep and I felt dazed, as if I'd come a long way back from elsewhere in waking. The door flap was open and there was a smell I hated on the wind, pyres burning outside the camp.

The laundress's boy, Wren, was sitting beside Rowney, helping to polish Sire Edecon's greaves. Of course there wasn't a speck of rust to be found on the armor, Rowney had seen to that. I wondered if Sire Galan would keep the boy, no matter what he said. Perhaps the Dame's husband had acquired me the same way—taken me in as a kindness to an orphan—rather than stealing me as a red-haired talisman to bring him luck, as Sire Pava once had claimed.

"Where's Sire Galan?" I asked Rowney.

He shrugged and picked at fraying threads around a hole in the knee of his hose. "Who knows? The camp is buzzing like a hornet's nest after boys have knocked it down. People came asking for you while you were away—asking about the sickness. But I thought you'd best get some sleep, if you could."

I said, "I needs must go to May, Mai. I dreamt her . . . travel . . . travail had started."

The army was not so careless of its defenses as it had been before the raid. The carts of the baggage were lined up around our encampment, to make another barrier behind the wall of sharpened stakes. Some of the carts were occupied, but most were empty. Mai had tied a strip of magenta cloth, the brightest thing to be seen, to a pole above her oxcart. My dream had not lied. She had started her travail and raised Desire's banner of childbirth to warn men to stay away.

Sunup sat on a stool beside the cart, sewing. I asked if all was well with her mother, and she nodded yes, but her lips turned down as if she meant no. The piebald dog was sunning himself, minding his own business, until Tobe began to tease him by hauling on his tail.

I heard Mai call from inside the cart, "Is that you?"

She sat up when I came in. The grain sacks had been replaced with sacks stuffed with dried bracken and heather, and they crackled under us and smelled like autumn. She'd baked the delicate raisin cakes that are given to visitors at a birthing. Rose oil in the lamp gave off a soothing scent. From the arched ribs of the canopy hung clay tablets stamped with prayers, and strings of snail shells to encourage the child to slip out. Mai had given many a woman charms to ease her travail, and now she did all she could to help herself.

I ate a raisin cake and told Mai I'd dreamed of Mouse being born. I didn't tell her about the tiny squirming mouse and how I'd lost it, for fear she'd be as disturbed at the omen as I was.

"Good," she said. "I was beginning to think Mouse would never make up his mind. The pains come and go."

"You have thrice, throes already? I'm sorry I didn't come soonest. I've been hither and tither, because the the . . . shriver, the fever-and-shake is in camp, and—"

"Oh, I know. Pinch has it."

"How is he?"

"Limp as a drowned cat, but he'll mend. How is the king, have you heard?"

I stared at her.

"Coz, if you'd gather your wits instead of wool you might learn something. Don't you know the king has the shiver-and-shake? Seems everybody knows but you," Mai said unkindly. "He's like to die, they say."

I opened and closed my mouth. I'd never known a time without King Thyrse. He'd ruled longer than I'd been alive.

Mai said, "He's not made of stone. He's flesh, same as you and me."

"If he dies, what will happen to us, to the harm?"

"What do you think?"

"We'll lose?"

"You're the one who prophesies, not me. All I know is, lose or win, we'll be buggered. He should have given us a real heir instead of pretending he'd live forever. If he dies, his bastards will come crawling out from under every rock, and each First will vie to be Foremost, and the queenmother will likely claim to rule us too, as she claims to rule Incus."

"I'll pray for him," I said.

"Pray for me too, will you? Ask Desire to make my travail swift and easy." She said this wryly, as if in jest, but I saw the fear she was trying to hide.

"Shall I fetch the bidwife?"

"Oh no. It's much too soon for that. I need a nap," she said. She heaved over on her side and the cart rocked.

I climbed out to the driver's seat and looked down at Sunup. "What are you sewing? Is that a placket, a blunket for the, for . . . for the one in your mother's belly?"

Sunup was so worried she didn't even smile at my mistakes. She showed me the small blanket she was embroidering with a design of silver-gray mice between crisscrossing stalks of wheat. The heavy heads of grain were picked out in gold-wrapped thread. "It's for Lynx Mischief," she said. "It's a sacrifice, so Mischief will look after Mouse."

I stood on the driver's bench and looked at our camp, and saw a crowd before the king's pavilion, quieter than a crowd ought to be. The Sun was in the west and the air about her was brassy and bright. A south wind came rushing up the valley. I heard it on its way, hissing and clapping canvas and leather against poles, and when it arrived it pulled loose the end of my headcloth. Chittering sparrows, which had been pecking for spilled grain next to the cart, took to flight and were hurled away.

I saw Sire Galan before he saw me. I waved and caught his eye, and jumped down from the cart. He greeted Sunup courteously by name. She'd done him a good turn once, helping to nurse his concubine, and he was not too proud to acknowledge her. To me he said, "The Crux wants to see you."

"For why?" I put the spokes of a cartwheel at my back, and felt the elm-wood hub against my spine. It helped me stand upright, for the strength had gone from my legs. I'd learned to dread any summons from the Crux, no matter the messenger who delivered it.

"He has questions," Sire Galan said. He stood with his back to the Sun, two paces from me, and I could hardly see his face.

"Maize needs me. Her trembles have come."

"She can spare you. Else why are you dawdling out here?"

"I can't go! He'll put me to the order, the ordeal."

"Are you afraid he'll make you face the dogs again? He won't, I assure you."

"How do you know?" I cried. "Twice he's questioned me, once by . . .

gods, I mean by dogs, and once by prison. A third time he's likely to get his way and finish me for good."

"Twice?" Galan closed the distance between us and Sunup got out of his way. Her stool fell over. "What do you mean, prison?"

"Not prison—poison. Poison. They gave me the blink, the black drink, and nearly did me in, and what they got of it I don't know. You must ask them."

"Who did this? Who gave you the drink?"

"Your uncle and his prats. And a Carnex of Carnal Design."

Sunup scrambled into the oxcart and I heard her moving behind the canopy. She could hear us and no doubt Mai listened as well. I was shamed by it.

"When?" Galan asked.

"In the city—in Lacks—when I sickened, do you remember? When you were about your uncle's busyness, buying him courses, coursers, horses."

"Ah, I see. And you didn't think to tell me this?"

"I didn't mean—I only wanted—I feared to come betwixt you and the Cracks."

"Too late for that," he said. "I told you before not to keep things from me I ought to know. What did you think I'd do, hmm? Kill my uncle over *you*? It shows a poor opinion of my judgment. And what was the Crux so anxious to know?"

"Why I followed you."

"Yes, and why did you?" He walked a few paces and stood with his back to me, looking toward the bright hills in the west.

He would leave me, I thought. We might go on living side by side and sleeping hip to hip, he might make use of me as he pleased, but I would be reminded always of what I'd lost. Which was just what the Crux wanted, that his nephew would keep his sheath in her proper place, if he insisted on keeping her.

Then I thought of the battle ahead, and how there never was much chance Galan and I could go on together, though I'd lived as if there was. I'd lived as if the battle would never come. We should not be quarreling with so little time left to us. I straightened up and took my hand from a wheel spoke. There was a splinter in my palm. I climbed on the front of the cart and looked in at Mai.

She said, "Don't fret about me. I don't need you now. Go, and tell the Crux what he wants to hear—understand?"

I jumped down from the cart and Sire Galan was gone.

The Crux sat in a carven high-backed chair in his pavilion. His face wore a frown that engraved more deeply the notches above the bridge of his nose and the grooves beside his mouth. One hand gripped the arm of his chair and the other propped up his chin. Galan was speaking to him in a low voice, and he stopped when I came in.

I knelt before the Crux and met his gaze. He detested insolence, yet I offered it by looking him in the eye. Pleading and weeping wouldn't avail with him, and though I might come to do both in the end, I refused to begin that way.

The Crux had brought all his tent furnishings with him from Corymb: figured carpets and folding furniture and bronze lamps on chains. The tapestry of the Sun, Moon, and Heavens hung behind him. I could hardly believe that beyond the waxed canvas walls lay the kingdom of Incus, for it seemed we were still in the Marchfield, had never left, and I might have to go outside and face the manhounds again. I looked down and clasped my hands together in my lap, the cold hand and the warm one. Both were sweating.

"I thought you said she refused to come," the Crux said to Galan.

"She did."

"I was befraid," I said.

Sire Galan said, "Now that she's here, what do you wish to do, Sire? Give her the black drink? Or do you do such things only in secret?"

The Crux canted his head and looked at Galan. "This is no time to argue about your sheath. There are matters of more importance."

"You picked the quarrel. You cannot pick the time to amend it." Galan stood as far from me as he did from his uncle. It was no more than a few paces away, but all the same a distant territory, from which he looked upon us both with a hard expression.

The Crux said, "It's my duty to care for the clan—and you."

"Yes, you care for me. Any more careful and I'd be dead. You took away my horses—perhaps now you'll require me to go to war without a sword. You don't mean me to come home, I think, for fear I might inconvenience your son and heir." When Galan spoke, for a moment I believed him. His distrust made of the Crux's actions such a simple pattern; and the Crux's son—Galan's cousin, to whom I'd never given a thought—was a thread that stitched all through.

The Crux struck the arm of his chair and roared, "Don't snivel to me about going without a horse! You deserved that, and if you want to save your precious life, you have my leave to start walking home tonight. I'll be glad to be rid of you! I have no fear for my son and I don't coddle him—as I refuse to coddle you—and if you weren't so vain you'd know that."

When the Crux spoke he pulled the thread; there was the old design again, not as tidy, not as comprehensible. But truer, I thought, for I did believe the Crux loved Galan well and was willing to kill him if need be, and saw no contradiction. And I did believe Galan too loyal and too fond of his uncle to scheme against his heir. But I could see both patterns at once now, like a throw of the bones that can be read two ways. So I was no longer sure.

There was a long silence, in which I heard Galan breathing harshly. He'd said too much. Even if he believed it, he'd said too much and given the Crux advantage, for advantage lay in being wronged.

Galan looked about and found a chair with taloned feet and a tall back inlaid with ivory plumage, and he placed it carefully where he'd been standing and sat down. "I mean to stay," he said. "I mean to fight, and when the battle is done, if I live, I'll take up riding again, and you shan't stop me—will you, Uncle?—for I will have borne as much as honor requires and more. And now honor requires that I ask what you did to my sheath. For as you once pointed out to Sire Rodela, she's under my protection. Who attacks her, attacks me."

"No harm was done," the Crux said. "See for yourself."

"Oh, I think there was harm," Galan said. "I think there was. For I heard a rumor—I gave it no credence until today, for it was a lying, thieving varlet who told me—that you paid the Initiates of Carnal to make her barren."

"It does you no harm to save you from siring mud bastards."

Galan wouldn't look at me, but he crossed glances with the Crux and didn't look away. They put me in mind of two swordsmen who lock blades near the hilt and strive against each other so that neither can move.

The Initiates had made me barren. They'd cursed me with barrenness and I hadn't known. That was why my tides were almost two tennights late. I thought of that priestess watching me while I writhed with the pains of the black drink, and how smug she'd seemed, and it no longer mattered that I'd taken childbane in secret, and planned to seek out the miscarrier if my tides didn't come soon.

Galan had told me once he wanted a bastard from me, and I'd been surprised—flattered even. But I hadn't understood; it was no desire of mine. Now I understood, I did. I could see a child, a person I'd never before dared to imagine. I wasn't as brave as Mai, to carry an unborn child on campaign and face the travail of birthing. But if I was—if I wanted one of Galan's bastards, a child who sprang from us two, with his eyes and my hair, or his hair and my eyes, it was not for the Crux or the Initiates to deny me.

And now I felt sharp pangs in my belly, as if the hex, which had grown quietly in the womb while I went about unknowing, quickened where a child should have quickened, and kicked and clawed. I leaned forward over my knees, rocking, with my arms crossed over my belly. Trying to hold in the wail that wanted out.

Galan's voice was far away. He said, "And the worst of it is that you were right. She is a canny, and unnatural. But it was ill done to go behind my back."

"Are you just now discovering that she's unnatural? Then you're more besotted than I thought. It wasn't lightning that made her so, as people say. The lightning sought her out *because* of what she is; she called it to her. But you're mistaken if you take her for a mere canny, a dabbler in curses and charms, as I was once mistaken. She's a seer, she speaks with the dead. I questioned her with the black drink so she couldn't lie, and I'm satisfied she doesn't bear malice against you or our clan, though she is Wildfire's creature. We have need of her foresight now, and of counsel the dead can give us. This is a perilous time, and therefore a time of opportunity for those bold enough to take chances—and for those Chance favors, such as yourself. There are matters of more import than whether your sheath is barren. Though if you wish it, I'll have the Initiates lift the hex on her. Is that what you want?"

I didn't want to hear Sire Galan's answer; I was sure he'd say something I couldn't forgive. I felt the hex kick within me, and I said, "You paid the Imitates to make me bane, barren. Why should you expect to harvest anything but slights, slies, lies from me now? And do you truly think it's up to the Imitates, the . . . Intimates of Carnage to decide whether or not I will have a child? Let them try to hoax me. A hoax the guards do not permit will redound upon those who aim it. Carmine . . . Desire has shown me savor in Sire Galan's bed, and she won't turn away from me at their demand." I turned to Galan, but he wouldn't look at me. "And what of Wildfare and Bastard Chance—the ones who overlook . . . look out for us? The atavites—the the . . . avatars consort well together; they are two of like nurtures. Don't you think they might wish to see what offsprig would come of our smiting?"

"She speaks more plainly than she did," the Crux said. "Too plainly. She flatters herself. Cross a warhorse and a she-donkey, and all you get is a misbegotten mule."

Sire Galan glanced at me and away. "We don't know her parentage, or where she came from. She was a foundling."

"If you think she's well bred, you've been deceived," said the Crux.

"I never claimed to be of the Breed, did I? But I had a father fond of me. I may be a fondling, but I'm no flyblow. He was a horse tricker by trade, a trainer, a trader I mean."

"You told me you didn't remember your father," Galan said, as if sourly pleased to catch me in another lie.

"I don't remember him. But I dreamed him twice—I dreamed he was a muckman as good as any. May I go now? Are you done of me? Or are you going to give me the bleak drunk again?"

"You may sit," the Crux said. "Sit down. I don't intend you any harm." He pointed to a footstool, but I would not sit.

"What *do* you intend, Sire?" asked Galan.

"I know," I said. Mai had told me just enough gossip, and I guessed the rest. "He portends to be kinded when the kind dies."

There was a stifled grunt from Galan, then stillness.

The Crux said, "The king will die?" He hunched forward in his chair, eager for revelations.

I said, "He is mortal. A fright told me that."

"When will he die?"

"What did your divides say? They hedged and hawed, I suppose, made such a mudgin of the orphans, the the . . . omens so that no matter what happenchance comes to pass, they can say it was foretold."

I saw by the Crux's face I'd come near the truth. I said, "You are the Transgressor, I mean the Intercessor—why not ask the dead yourself? Call on your Countenance of the Dead for help."

The Crux frowned at me, and the white scar beside his left eye kinked. But the right side of his face looked dismayed rather than fierce.

I said, "Oh, I see. You tried and the fades wouldn't answer."

"Are you afraid to try yourself?" he said.

"Of course I am." Though I was tempted. There was great force restrained in the Crux, and I could free it with a word. The whole world could turn upon a word, a lie. I was swollen with potency, and the hex that twisted in my belly. The Crux had given me a gift—the power to mislead him. A man who desires greatly is easy to fool. But I suspected he would let me mislead him only where he was already determined to go.

"Why do you put yourself in her hands?" Galan asked.

I held my hands out, empty, and turned them upside down. "My hands are vacant. May I go now? The shaker-and-shive is stalking the compass, and there are many in need of my hope. This thing you want—I don't know how. I'm not what you think of me."

"But will you try?" asked the Crux.

Every answer led to Galan despising me. I could assent and offer the Crux nonsensical words like those I'd given the Auspices in the temple of Ardor—let him make of them what he willed.

I could refuse; but that would prove me a knowing cheat who hid behind a mask of flour and charcoal to play tricks on gullible boys, and was too craven to play such tricks on her betters.

But when I invoked Mischief, Mischief came. That wasn't a trick.

Galan knew that. Maybe he didn't think I was a charlatan. I saw that fear in him again, of what I was and what lightning had made of me. He liked me better when he thought me weak. I thought of how he'd cared for me after I was struck, when I was shambling and addled, and I grieved to lose his tenderness.

That was unjust—to think he wanted me weak or meek. If he'd wanted such a sheath, he could have had one. He'd taken me instead, and I did believe—though I'd been boasting when I said it—that I'd spoken some truth: our natures consorted well together, for there was Wildfire in me and Chance in Galan. He didn't seek softness, he wanted the flint that struck sparks.

Yet I saw nothing welcoming in his face. His mouth was grim; he waited to hear what I would say, and his hands were on the arms of his chair, palms against the wood, hiding the signs of Chance and Fate. He was a gambler, and I must gamble too. Because there was a third choice before me, riskier than fakery or refusal: to try to do as the Crux asked, and be an honest seer.

The Crux shifted in his chair. I kept him waiting while my thoughts veered this way and that. But those frantic thoughts were just a distraction; in the darkness of my mind, unbeknownst to me, I had already decided.

I told Galan rather than the Crux. "I think I must try."

The Crux said, "Good."

I said to him, "The shades I know—I doubt you'd want their device. Can you invoke your Conceal? Your Council?"

Galan said, "She laughed at Ardor's priests when they wanted her for an oracle. Now she pretends to be one."

"You may go, if you wish," the Crux said.

"I think I'd rather stay," Galan said, crossing his arms.

The Crux rose and went to the tapestry of the Sun, Moon, and Heavens that hung before one wall of his pavilion. He pushed the tapestry aside and revealed a wooden chest, embellished with the godsign of Crux in gilt on the lid. He unlocked the iron clasp with an ornate key. The masks were wrapped in embroidered cloths: seven gold masks, one for each of the houses of the clan. I'd thought there would be more. The Crux handled them with careful reverence, hanging them from hooks on an iron bar suspended from the pavilion's rafters. The golden faces hung high, as if they belonged to tall men, and they seemed to stare, though their eyes were empty.

I'd seen the old priest at the manor take the impression of the Dame's face after she died, pressing clay over her to make a crude likeness. In my ignorance I'd supposed that was her death mask, but it was merely a mold

Wildfire

for the golden mask through which her shade might speak in the Council of the Dead. But a woman's counsel wasn't wanted here.

These were warriors. Two were old men, with every wrinkle rendered; the rest were in their prime, likely cut down in battle. The masks were true to life, and yet, because the impressions were taken in death, they were also strange and slack. Each mask had a clan tattoo incised into the right cheek, and on the left cheek, in bright enamel, the crest of his house. The beards and hair were sculpted of fine coils of gold wire.

I thought the Crux would summon the shades by some rite. Instead he sat and looked at me expectantly. Was this another ordeal, did he mean to prove I was green and foolish? That was true. I said, "I don't know—what am I proposed to do?"

"I told you she couldn't," Galan said.

Twilight had arrived, leaching colors away, and the air was hazed with smoke from a smoldering brazier. I stood and stamped my feet, and quietly I hummed the round of notes that belonged to Sire Rodela's shade. I had visited the realm of the dead before, and it almost killed me. This time I meant to send Sire Rodela, my tormentor, my go-between.

I couldn't compel him to come, as the Summoner had done. I could only ask. I pleaded with him. I sang that I would do him honor—burn candle-bark for him every Peaceday—praise his bravery—recount the tale of his duel with the armiger—if he would help me now. We'd hated each other. He'd attacked me and I'd killed him; he'd haunted me and I'd banished him. This had woven obligations between us. The deepest notes of his song seemed to call forth a deeper echo, and the highest notes made my head buzz. I stamped and felt the ground shudder.

I was amazed and affrighted by how swiftly Sire Rodela came. He didn't arrive from elsewhere, but burgeoned within me. I stomped, and felt thick with maleness, with wide shoulders and strong arms and heavy hands, and a pendulous weight between my legs that made me swagger. Now that he was here, he didn't want to go. He wouldn't be *sent*. We must go together.

The recently dead were gathering in the tent, though I hadn't summoned them. They animated what was there already, standing and sitting and crouching, made of tent poles and stools, casks and chests, folds of tapestry. They wavered in and out of sight in the corners of my eyes: the laundress, asking what had become of her son; the old woman Tansy and the young whore; and others carried off by the shiver-and-shake whom I'd never met in life. Penna was a shirt tossed over the back of a chair.

Sire Rodela raised my arms and shouted, "I want light!" in a voice so harsh it scraped my throat. The Crux got up and lit oil lamps, shaped like birds with outspread wings, suspended from a bronze tree. Rodela laughed to see the Crux obey him. Lamplight drove the shadows and shades into darker corners. The Crux sat down again. I lifted the bronze tree and carried it behind the masks. It was heavy, but I had Rodela's strength. The lamps dribbled perfumed oil, and when the burning droplets touched my skin I felt a searing pleasure.

I went back to my place and looked at the masks with the fire behind them. They were alive now. Their eyes and tongues flickered. I truly didn't know if it was I who thought of bringing them light or Rodela. From moment to moment I was unsure what I should do, yet did what had to be done.

I was singing Ardor's song now, without words, just nonsensical sounds that ran swift as a river. I began to dance, for Rodela insisted on it. I looked down at my feet and saw a pattern in the carpet, one the weavers hadn't put there: a spiral field such as those in my village, with three strips winding one inside the other, planted, plowed, and fallow. I danced along the spiraling path in smaller and smaller turns, feeling the touch of Galan's stare on my legs, hips, shoulders, breasts, the small of my back, my brow and throat. I knew he saw a woman, but I moved like a man, like Sire Rodela, stamping hard.

When I reached the very center of that spiral, I found it was a snare, Fate's labyrinth. Why should a man want to be king, to walk that terrible winding path until the end of his days? A king is never free of Fate; his every act uncoils consequence. Better to be of no consequence.

Wildfire sparked in the air, making the hair stand up on my neck and arms, making me sweat, making me lightheaded. Now I spun in the center of the spiral, pushing out my song with every burst of breath, faster and faster. The masks flicked past me. My good left eye saw the faces of the Council sharp-edged and golden, stern and motionless, and my dim right eye saw metal softening to jaundiced flesh, saw wagging tongues. Good eye, bad eye, left eye, right eye, until I was dizzy, and speckled darkness covered my sight and I staggered and fell.

When I opened my eyes, the world spun around me but I was still, and seven tall men were with me at the center of the whirlwind, staring down. I could tell they were not pleased to be summoned by the living, and if Rodela, their kin and a shade himself, had not been in possession of me, likely they'd have struck me down for presumption.

They were billowing and formless under their golden faces, as if they'd forgotten the shapes of their bodies. They might have forgotten their faces too if there were no masks to remind them. They should be very wise by now, for they'd been dead a long time. I could only bear to see them from the corner of my left eye. When I tried to look at them straight on, their faces shimmered and smeared; they didn't hold. My failing right eye didn't see them at all. It saw glimpses of elsewhere and elsewhen.

With my right eye I saw the king die. His carnifex was bleeding him. The king had already slipped into that stupor that was living death. His face was pallid, and his blood so dark it looked black. It dripped into a silver vessel shaped like a hare. Dripped, and stopped. The Auspices crowding around him murmured. The stink of a sick man's sweat was in the air, under the fragrance of burning candlebark.

It was a true dream. Whether it had happened or would happen, or was even now unfolding, I didn't know.

I saw the king's golden armor ride to war with no one in it. People spoke to this armor as if it were the king, and the armor wielded a sword as well as the king and rode as well as the king, and went on the battlefield where men most needed to see their king. A horse was killed under it and the armor fought on foot. But after the battle was won, the armor clattered apart on the ground, cuirass here, greaves there, mail hauberk all in a heap. No one in it. Died of wounds, they said. A proper death for a king, better than the shiver-and-shake.

I saw Malleus. I saw a woman lift a small boy onto a low stone parapet around a flat roof and point to the plains below, where armies fought. I understood why Prince Corvus came forth to do battle rather than forcing us to pry him out by siege. The city had no walls, save at its very center, the ancient heart of it. Buildings covered the slopes beyond the wall as if a jar had overturned and spilled them everywhere. Malleus was as beautiful as the songs had promised, with white walls and gilded domes and spires. And she was as lush, ripe, and easy to take as a whore.

The woman brushed a fly from her boy's face. He had rolls of fat at his wrists and neck. His skin was brown and his hair bleached the color of wheat straw. The woman wore red gauze and a wide-brimmed hat. She pointed to the golden armor on the field below and the boy squealed. An incensier shrub, green and fragrant even in winter, grew in a blue pot. The woman's face was pockmarked, but the city, she was fair.

I saw and heard Mai. Sunup was helping her sit on the pisspot. Mai grimaced. When she was done she settled back on her nest of sacks, breathing hard. Tobe whimpered in his sleep.

And in the tent just over there, a sheath I knew was sleeping, and I was almost caught by the fever dreams that flickered around her as she burned.

In a wintry wood a black-haired man was running, pursued by wolves. All this I saw quick as a bird darts from one branch to another.

The dead were impatient, they called me away. They filled me with dread, those councilors. When Sire Rodela and I summoned them, we awakened what should have remained dormant: pride, ambition, jealousy, fear, anger, and longing. Now the shades yearned to be clothed in flesh again and to thrust themselves into other flesh, to couple and fight, for coupling and fighting were two sides of an overweening desire: to see their descendants ascendant. They wanted the Crux to be king. If not him, his kin, their kin, blood of their Blood.

Where I sought wisdom, I found low cunning. Rodela reveled in it, hard and swollen under my skin. He had died childless, and now he wanted to father himself on the world. He pulled me to my feet and shouted.

Kings used to be chosen by the consent of the Firsts of the clans, but for four generations—far too long—the clan of Prey had passed the kingship down in succession. It was time to return to the old ways.

A king should be foremost of the Firsts, the best of them all. But sometimes it was better not to choose the best. A strong man like the Crux had too many enemies, both men and gods; a weak man offended no one. Find such a man, and no one would want him, but everyone would consent to him for fear of worse. Make such a man a king, bend him to your purposes, and when the time came, break him. Such was their counsel, and Rodela was their messenger.

He was strong, but I was stronger. I subdued him without the help of the Summoner, driving him down with his song, dancing him to exhaustion. I scratched my face with my fingernails, and when that didn't quench his thirst, I opened my scalp with a knife.

Yet I feared I would never be rid of Rodela now. He was part of me, not his shade entire, but a revenant of a revenant—the part of him I'd tried to murder—his fearful and fearsome rages, his urge for dominion. By taking these into myself, I paid my debt to him, allowing his shade to journey on unburdened.

We spun and spun until I fell again, and I hammered with my heels and rolled my head against the carpet, and there was a hard bit between my teeth and the taste of iron on my tongue. My eyes were clotted with tears. I stiffened and arched and bucked against the hands that held me down.

"Take her away," the Crux said, and the impassive masks looked down on me.

CHAPTER 13

Travail

ire Rodela lingered, soiling my tongue and buzzing in the small bones of my ears. He filled me with an unaccountable urge to laugh when I should not laugh. Sire Galan wiped drool from my mouth, and held me up as I wobbled like a drunkard. He did this without tenderness or cruelty. It would have been easy to be cruel. Yet I wanted to laugh at his disgust and surely it would have been more fitting to cry. He left me in his tent and I washed the blood from my face. I was glad when the mirth faded—such an ugly thing, delighting in detesting. But with Rodela gone, so was his triumph and his strength.

I remembered what I'd seen. I wasn't sure of everything I'd said and done.

I'd left Mai that afternoon and now the long winter evening had begun. I heard loud talk and laughter as I came near her canopied oxcart, and I wondered if I'd arrived too late and she'd delivered her child without any help from me. But no, visitors had come to speed the time of travail: some whores of our acquaintance, Yarrow, Corona, and Gladwin, were squeezed into the cart with Mai and the children. They'd brought gifts of food and ale, as I should have done. The raisin cakes were all gone, save two for the midwife.

Mai said, "Come in! We can always fit one more straw in the broom." Everyone shifted around so that I could sit next to Mai. Her bodice was unlaced and her breasts sprawled on either side of her belly, showing through the thin gauze of the underdress. When a pang came she barely winced. But her face was flushed and her forehead bedewed with sweat. Her head was bare and tendrils of brown hair clung to her neck. She fanned herself with her headcloth.

Corona passed me a chicken leg and I discovered how hungry I was. I couldn't recall when I'd last eaten. All I remembered of the past few days and nights was the shiver-and-shake and how Galan had set his face against me. And I remembered the dead, who even now thronged around us in the crowded oxcart, trying to warm themselves by the hearthfires of the living: Mole and the laundress and Penna and warriors in masks. My skin prickled and I wanted to weep, but someone had made a jest. Too many people were talking at once and I couldn't disentangle the words.

I crammed bread into my mouth and washed it down with ale, and listened to the women trading stories of difficult travails and rumors about the battle to come. And before long I felt myself more in the company of the living than the dead, and when everyone laughed I laughed too, no matter how lewd the jest. A lantern with small panes of glass bobbed as the oxcart shook in the commotion, and light slid over our faces. Sunup kept her eyes on her embroidery, but I'm sure she was listening. Tobe slept through it all, leaning on her, breathing with his mouth open, making a small whuffling sound.

I was beginning to think Mai had enough company, and I should go where I was needed, amongst those suffering from the shiver-and-shake. I should look in on the priestess of Hazard, and Jillybell's daughter. But then Mai said the throes were nothing much, but her back felt like a harrow was being dragged over it. She made a jape of it, but I could see she was in earnest. I got behind her and rubbed hard with the heel of my cold hand.

Before long the midwife hailed us from outside the cart. She climbed in and Mai greeted her respectfully and kissed her hand. "I didn't expect you yet," Mai said. "I didn't want to bother you—the throes are still far apart. Did Sire Torosus send for you?"

Midwife smiled. "My grandmother's shade tugged on my ear and told me it was time. She never fails to give warning."

The midwife was named Coralbell, and she was the mistress of a brothel. I'd heard it said she became a midwife because too many of her whores had died bearing children or trying to be rid of them. In both her callings she was a servant of Carnal Desire, and Desire had favored her with fortune. She was prosperous enough to have two guards to escort her and wait outside the cart. She wore a quantity of gold, chains and pendants and bangles and a girdle of enameled plaques over a magenta sash. Her skin was tawny, and covered with golden hairs so fine they couldn't be seen until she was close enough to touch. I expected her to make more of a fuss when she arrived, but she seemed content to sit and gossip, and keep a watchful eye on Mai when the throes came.

Mai asked, "Any word of the king's health?"

Midwife said, "He showed himself before his tent, dressed in armor. He leaned on his armiger, but he stood on his own two feet, they say, and the crowd raised such a cheer! I'm surprised you didn't hear it."

Wildfire

"I've been busy," Mai said.

"We march tomorrow," Midwife said. "So don't dally, my dear."

The king alive! It made me feel safe, the battle good as won. Why had I been so foolish as to trust my cloudy right eye and the dreams I'd seen with it? True foretellings are a gift of Foresight; she is the least capricious avatar of the god Lynx, more trustworthy than Sleep and Mischief, but still she may mislead. I prayed I had been misled in dreaming that the king died—let all the visions be false, no matter if Galan and the Crux thought me a charlatan in consequence. All visions but one: I had dreamed we won the battle. That much I prayed was true.

I said, "So—are the pontificators, the contakators done talking? How soon is the baffle?"

Midwife looked at me in surprise, as if I ought to know. "The day after tomorrow."

By and by the midwife let Mai's visitors know it was time to leave—such a gentle hint, they didn't know they were being herded. In the same quiet way, she let me know I was welcome to stay. She took off her bangles and set about arranging things to her liking, taking cloth and string and pots and packets of herbs from a painted goatskin satchel, moving with a precise grace that was soothing to watch. Her hands were small and deft, and on the little finger of her right hand she had a sharp curved nail.

She unwrapped a wooden statue of Carnal Desire, an old crude carving polished by the touch of many hands seeking blessings. This Desire was fat, as always, but she was also heavy with child and heavy with presence. Midwife propped the statue in a corner of the cart and anointed it with lavender oil. Mai reached out to stroke Desire's belly. Her fingertips came away smeared with oil and she rubbed it on her upper lip and inhaled deeply.

"Well, Mai," Midwife said, "I'd like to see you eat something, keep your strength up."

"I'm not hungry."

"Drink this." She handed Mai a wineskin.

"What's in it?"

Midwife laughed. "Something that will do you good, so drink! Have you had the bloody show?"

Mai nodded and took a drink and made a face. "Can't you give me something stronger than raspberry leaf tea?"

"Your water hasn't broken?" the midwife said.

"Mouse is teasing me," Mai said, with her hands on her belly. "I had a few pains yesterday. But whenever I began to think I should send for you, they stopped. Is something wrong?"

"Mouse?"

"The boy."

"It's a boy, is it? Lie down and I'll give you a rub."

"It hurts worse on my back."

"All the same," Midwife said. "I want to see which way the babe lies."

The cart wasn't much longer than Mai was tall, and she took up a good portion of it both length and breadth. I sat cross-legged so she could rest her head on my lap. "Your legs are too bony," she said, smiling at me upside down.

Mai pulled up her skirts to bare her belly. The flesh of her thighs was soft and dimpled, floury smooth like the dough of the Blood's fine bread when it has been set to rise, but the huge dome of her belly was solid and taut, as if Mai had swallowed an enormous egg. She bore a slymark, a dark line down the middle of her belly to her cleft, which curved slightly around her protruding navel as if the unborn child had stretched it out of true. The midwife rubbed Mai's belly in circles with scented oil until it glistened, and I thought: it isn't an egg she has swallowed, it's the Moon!

Sunup watched. She'd set her embroidery aside so Tobe could lay his head in her lap. I wondered if she'd seen her mother in travail before. She sat still, but her hands were restless, winding Tobe's black hair around her fingers.

Midwife sat back on her heels and said to Mai, "The babe lies cross-wise."

"You mean bum first? I should have known Mouse would be backward."

"No, dear. He lies crosswise, like a bar across a door. See? His head is here," and she put Mai's left hand flat on that side of her belly, "and here are his buttocks. Can you feel him? That's why your throes don't march along as they should, but dawdle like a foot soldier." The midwife's voice was calm, but one side of her mouth drooped as if she didn't have full command of her expression.

I put my warm hand next to Mai's, over Mouse's head, and my cold hand over his breech. Mouse stirred under the soft blanket of Mai's flesh. I felt her womb tense and harden, and I looked to her face and saw how her thoughts turned inward and away from us.

The midwife knelt between Mai's legs and said, "I'm going to try to bring his head down now, while your pains are still far apart. Lie still." Pressing through Mai's flesh with her fingers and the heels of her palms, she gently nudged Mouse's head downward and his breech upward. When a throe came Midwife looked at me and said, "Hold him!" She grabbed my cold right hand and placed it under the swell of Mouse's buttocks, showing me how to push firmly. Then she pressed Mouse's head down with both hands, and he squirmed, and his head slipped toward the girdlebone and his buttocks moved up under Mai's heart.

The midwife straightened up and her head brushed the lantern and set it swinging. Her face was bright with sweat and triumph. "Praise be. That might do it," she said.

Mai said, "What do you mean, might?"

Midwife wrapped a magenta sash around Mai, between her belly and her breasts, tying it tightly to discourage Mouse from turning again. She arranged a pile of sacks against the back of the cart, and said, "Sit up here, and we'll see if Mouse will stay where he's supposed to be."

"Oh gods, I told you he was contrary," Mai said.

Sunup left the cart to empty the pisspot, and Tobe woke up and protested his abandonment, wailing, "Sup! Sup!" He crawled toward Mai and she told him, "Go on!" with a little push, which made him cry harder, shaking as if his little body couldn't contain his despair. He pulled himself up using one of Mai's knees. He wore a long shirt and a soiled breechcloth.

"Come," I said, but he didn't want me.

"Go on," Mai said to him, gently this time, and I reached out and coaxed him into the circle of my arm.

Tobe had the shiver-and-shake. I knew as soon as I touched him. His skin was clammy and pale as whey. He'd been too quiet, and none of us had wondered at it, being intent on Mai. If I had spared him a thought, I would have been grateful he wasn't clambering all over the cart and its occupants, or banging any two hard things together for the joy of making noise, or swatting someone just to rile them—all the things he always did, so that all day long he heard *don't, don't, don't*. Mai had named her unborn child Mouse, for the Mischief in him, but surely Tobe had been touched by Lynx Mischief as well: Mischief in a playful mood, not a spiteful one.

"I'll take him outsight," I said, "until he quiets down. Have you a clean clout for him?" How could I tell Mai? I could not.

Half the sky was swaddled in a band of gray clouds, and half was clear and bright with stars. A smiting wind from the north carried the scent of snow. Mai's varlet Trave and the midwife's guards were toasting their feet at the fire. Trave nodded his head toward the oxcart. "It must be almost over, eh?"

"Ha," I said. "Not lucky. Not likely, I mean."

I walked away from them, holding Tobe close to me under my cloak. He held himself stiffly as he squalled, and his small chest worked like a bellows against mine. I wasn't Mai and he was indignant that I was trying to fool him. The poor boy had the squirts, one of the miseries in the shiver-and-shake's sack of afflictions, so I crouched behind a big empty wagon and cleaned his buttocks while he kicked and cried. I made a sling of my cloak to hold him on my hip, and I rubbed his back to give him heat from my hand, to stop him shaking from chills. At last he let himself go limp and quiet, and rested his head against me.

I spread out my divining compass. So many times I'd called on the Dame and Na for counsel these last few days, and I was ashamed to ask so much of them, to tug them back again and again to the realm of the living by a thin thread of longing attached to their finger bones. They should no longer be troubled by what troubled us.

But my need was great. I threw the bones for Tobe, then for Mai, six casts in all. Certain signs were repeated in both readings. They touched twice upon Plenty and three times upon Wildfire. Three times finger bones crossed the line between Fate and Dread.

Hazard Fate and Rift Dread. These twinned signs filled me with foreboding and hope, contrary sensations so forceful that I had no doubt the Dame and Na impressed them upon me in answer to my questions. The dead can see farther than the living, and reckon both danger and opportunity ahead, and how by our actions—or inaction—we might change one into the other. I prayed they meant that Tobe and Mai could be helped.

There was another interpretation. They might mean that the gods would take one and let the other live. But if one was to die, which one, the mother or the son? I dared not ask, as if by asking I might bring about that which I most feared. As if I must choose between them.

The bones had pointed to the gods who must be propitiated. I made a cut in the crook of my arm and gave blood to Dread, and burned a lock of hair for Hazard. I had nothing suitable to give Plenty but promises: seed-cakes and a dove, as soon as I was able. Paltry sacrifices, in return for a great favor.

Oh gods, let them live. Let them both live.

And now I must act as if what I did could matter, act in the hope that the gods would not be implacable. The Dame and Na had said as much as they could say. If their meaning was obscure, no doubt the fault was mine, an unskilled diviner. Signs on the compass, signs written on the suffering bodies of Mai and Tobe: none of the remedies I'd gathered so far seemed fitting.

It was not by worrying over the bones that I would get at the marrow of their meaning; I must go gathering.

190

Wildfire

I passed through the guarded opening in the palisade and crossed the ditch. The market was crowded with warriors and mud soldiers, peddlers and harlots. Bonfires sowed sparks into the wind. It must be true then: the king was mending. We would march tomorrow, and the day after tomorrow the army would fight the battle. One and all seemed glad we'd come to it at last.

Only a whore should walk abroad on such a night, when men were wrought up and eager to prove they weren't afraid. I skirted the market, a shadow among the shadows, and passed through a pasture where horses were tethered and into a fallow field beyond, leaving the clamor behind. It was harder to silence the clamorous fears I carried with me.

Tobe dozed against me, small and heavy. Already his brow was warm, the fever rising in him again. I stood still and listened, and heard Tobe pant as he slept; a breeze rustled through the waist-high grasses.

In the quiet I was at last truly able to pray for him and for his mother—not by word or song, not by pleading or appeasing, but by looking and listening. By paying attention. Here no firelight blinded me. I saw the familiar branch pattern, dark against the night sky, of the elder tree, sacred to Plenty. I took what was given, the buds for Tobe's fever, and berries against the squirts and chills. I walked on, and Plenty sent me butterbur growing in a soggy ditch, and shepherd's purse, which stays green and blooming in all but the coldest winters. Fate offered evergreen rue.

I was grateful to the gods, truly grateful, nothing feigned or begrudged. But some of these gifts made me uneasy, being remedies for afflictions that had not yet come to pass.

The blessed quiet didn't last. Tobe roused and began to cry inconsolably for his mother. I hurried back to the cart, and Mai reproached me for being away so long, and bringing him back red faced and bawling. He sobbed, leaning on his mother, his small potbelly pressed against her much greater one. He squeezed one of her breasts, trying to nurse, and milk dribbled from the nipple. She cupped his face between her hands. "What is it, little man? What's the matter?"

"I hurt!" he said.

"How he burns!" she said, and she looked at me and knew. Her face twisted, lopsided, pain on the right, fear on the left. I'd been foolish to think I could keep his sickness from her.

I told Mai what the Dame used to say—that the gods send no malady without also sending a remedy, though we are not always wise enough to discover it. I told her I'd been led by signs to plants that might serve Tobe. I had to give her hope, even if it proved false; she needed her strength for the travail.

Tobe had a terrible thirst, but he craved mother's milk and nothing else. I gave him elderberry tea and a gruel of barley water and elder buds, and he pushed them away, fretful and peevish. What little I made him swallow he spewed up again. In time he fell asleep in the crook of Mai's arm, twitching like a dreaming dog.

Mai let me take him in my lap, and I felt the fever rising in him like a long swell lifting a boat. I drew heat knowing I couldn't take enough, for beyond that swell was another and another, a boundless ocean.

On and on Mai labored. Her back hurt and she kept shifting about, trying to find a comfortable position. Midwife wouldn't let her lie on her side, for fear Mouse would turn himself crosswise again. Sunup braced herself against the wall of the cart and pushed hard with her feet on the small of Mai's back, digging into her flesh. It seemed to ease her pain. Midwife held Mai's hand, and when Mai squeezed she never flinched; she'd say, "That was a good one." Yet we all knew the throes were not strengthening apace.

Mai dozed between pains. Late at night Sunup curled up and slept, and I yawned with Tobe in my lap, and Midwife sat watchful. My eyelids were heavy and I nodded off, and I was in a bright dream on a windy hillside, watching swallows cut the air with their sharp wings. I smelled freshly mown hay. I jerked awake and saw Mai with her face shining in pain. My eyes closed again, my head dropped, and I saw laundresses kneeling by the stream at the bottom of the meadow, thumping wet twisted cloth against boulders. Tobe played near his mother in the amber waters, chasing the shadows of fish. He lost his footing and sat down with a splash and chortled.

I dreamed Tobe's dream and not one of my own. If he could stay there, I wouldn't fear for him.

The army marched before daybreak. We waited to take our place in the line, with Trave and the midwife's guards as escorts, and Pinch beside the ox with his switch. Pinch was weak from the fever, but he wouldn't sit on the cart, so close to Mai in travail. The ox pulled, and the cart lurched over the rough ground, which had been furrowed by wheels and pocked by hooves, and thawed and frozen hard again. I sat in front with Tobe in my lap, glad to be outside, glad to be moving. The ox tangled a harness strap around one foreleg, and we stopped with a jolt, and Pinch cursed and Midwife poked out her head between the door flaps. She retreated back inside and I heard her say brusquely, "Once we get to the road, it won't be so rough."

Mai said, "I can't, I just can't. It hurts too much."

When next the midwife spoke, her voice was gentler. "We'll catch them later," she said.

Wildfire

I gave Tobe to Sunup, and said, "I'll be back, I promise."

The company of Crux had already marched away with the rest of the vanguard. I ran through the fields beside the road, dodging foot soldiers, and men shouted or laughed at me. When I was out of breath, I walked until I could run again. I reached the brow of the hill and saw warriors riding in orderly splendor down the other side, their caparisons bright in the dim snowlight.

The road curved and I cut straight across the fields, plunging downhill. Near the bottom I came around the shoulder of a knoll and stopped, gasping, doubled over from the stitch in my side. On the road below, riders bore the green banners of Crux and the golden banners of the king on poles strapped to their backs. Galan marched among them, carrying his banners on the shaft of his scorpion, under the blade with the sting and claw. He wore his helm with his visor raised. He said something to his uncle and the Crux leaned in his saddle to reply.

I was afraid for Galan, seeing him on foot among the great horses. And maybe I was just afraid, thinking he wouldn't welcome me, not if he was of the same mind as when he saw me last; if I ran down to him, I'd shame him before his fellows. I let him go by, and the army flowed past me like an iron river.

I trudged back uphill, and in the baggage train I found Fleetfoot riding the lead mule and carrying Wren in the saddle before him. I told him Mai was still in travail, and when she was delivered we'd march all evening, all night if we had to, and catch up with them. Send word to Sire Torosus. See you soon, for certain.

The Sun rose behind a shroud of falling snow. Within the encircling ditch all was quiet. The movable city had moved on, but we weren't the only ones left behind. Here and there were solitary pavilions of cataphracts brought low by the shiver-and-shake, some with horses waiting in full caparison, as if their masters expected to ride to battle. Drudges lay on the ground and men stooped over them, to rob or to help. Stray dogs nosed about. All seemed gray, even the glossy plumage of the crows that strutted about where so many men had lately bustled.

As the day wore on, Mai's throes came and went in an unsteady rhythm. Midwife did all she could to speed the birthing. She gave Mai slippery tea and made her sneeze with a pungent snuff of burnt feathers; she bade us undo our girdles and headcloths, lest the knots obstruct the child's passage. She got Mai up and outside, and made her walk three times around the cart. We bore her up between us while her legs shook from exhaustion.

Mai had been panting so long her lips were dry and cracked, so Sunup soothed them with tallow. And when the throes came we winced with her, and rubbed her back and her legs and dried her brow and kissed her and said she was a brave one, a hard worker. Not much longer now, surely. Soon. Soon.

I daresay we were all impatient, but only Mai dared show it. She cursed Mouse and her own laggard body, she cursed Sire Torosus for getting her with child again. And she begged Desire to have mercy, have pity. Had she done aught to offend her? She would give her a mare in foal when this was all over, if she would only let Tobe live, and let this child be born.

In silence I offered up my own prayers to Dread and Fate, vowing sacrifices I couldn't afford. I didn't tell Mai what the bones had said, for fear she would lose all heart.

Mai sagged against the sacks, Tobe pillowed on her arm. He was too listless to fuss. She looked past him at me. *Help me,* she said without speaking. And then a throe overswept her and she brought her knees up toward her belly and her eyes squeezed shut. I wiped her face with a damp cloth to cleanse her of the stinging salt, and coaxed her to drink a tonic Midwife had made. Such small services I could do for her.

Tobe slept through fever and chills alike, while I took heat from him or gave it, until it seemed to flow between us at need. But every fever peak and trough of chills robbed him of strength. And now the shiver-and-shake became a tempest. He began to scream, just as Jillybell had done, from fear and pain. His head hurt. No one could comfort him, not even Mai. Midwife said I should take him outside, and I did, though Mai protested.

It might have been any time between noon and dusk. Snow whirled through a gray sky, softening and blurring everything. Mai's varlets and the midwife's guards had a blaze going. I was glad the men were with us, because people were roaming the camp—likely villagers out to steal from the army that had stolen so much from them.

The Dame and Na had pointed to many remedies, and I blessed their foresight. I made a wreath of rue for Tobe to wear around his head against his terrors, and bound leaves of shepherd's purse to the soles of his feet against jaundice, for his skin and the whites of his eyes were yellowing. To soothe his headache, and prevent the fever fits I feared would come, I added butterbur root to the gruel of elder buds and barley, and sweetened it generously with honey, and gave it to Tobe on my thumb to suck. After a while he fell quiet, and his heart stopped shuddering like a rabbit's.

Already his face had changed, as fever consumed his plumpness. I could see the shape of the man he might become, with deep eye sockets and a strong jaw. His feathery hair was flattened to his head with sweat; his skull was a crucible of dreams.

Midwife jumped down from the cart. She peered at Tobe in my arms and stroked his soft, sunken cheek.

It comforted me to know she had accompanied many a woman through a dangerous travail, and was undaunted by this one. I wanted to thank her for staying when she could have departed with the army, for her courage and calm, but words wouldn't come. I kissed her hand and she smiled at me. She took a pinch of her foul-smelling snuff and sneezed like thunder.

Sunup left to fill the water jar and empty the pisspot, and shortly she opened the door flap and let in cold twilight. "Your boy is here," she said to me.

"Who?"

"Your boy Fleetfoot."

I climbed down from the cart and there was Fleetfoot on a mule, his shanks dangling, and Frost on a lead beside him bearing my saddlebags. Fleetfoot's ears were nearly the hue of Carnal's magenta flag. He slid off the mule's back. The lame manhound Piddle sniffed Mai's piebald dog and the dog sniffed back.

Fleetfoot gave me a small scrap of linen. "A message," he said, hoarse from panting. "And Sire Galan bade me ask if you would be so kind as to accompany me to camp."

"He said that? In so many worries?"

"It is exact." I saw a smirk; we shared a tiny triumph between us drudges.

By the fletch pattern of the embroidery, I knew the linen had been torn from one of Galan's sleeves. He had painted three godsigns on the cloth. Why had he sent this to me? He knew I'd forgotten which syllable belonged to each godsign.

But suppose the signs referred to avatars rather than sounds? I recognized two, Rift Queen of the Dead and Hazard Chance. The third was a male avatar, in a circle with Rift Queen. Was it Prey Hunter? Of course it was, there were Prey's three stars in a row. Prey was the king's clan, the king was the Hunter, and he stood in a circle with the Queen of the Dead. Within her realm, it must mean. The last godsign was Chance—to stand for Galan himself—a meaning I alone would guess. The king was dead and it was a secret. The king was dead and I had foreseen it, so my prophecy was true. Therefore Galan no longer shunned me. I hoped he was satisfied by this bitter proof.

Fleetfoot said, "Can you come back with me? Or have you a message for Sire Galan?"

"Oh, I would, I would go so quick, but Ma still suffers her trials. Can't you stay with us? Stay, please, and when it's done we'll return."

His mouth made a stubborn line. He knew enough to be afraid, yet still he wanted to measure himself against something as large as this battle and as small as his fellows' opinion of him. I didn't know what use he'd be, a foot soldier with three good fingers, but I could see he was insulted by my suggestion.

I turned over the scrap of cloth and with a burnt twig inscribed on it the godsigns of Desire and Wildfire: Desire for the childbirth that kept me here, Desire for the longing to be with him; Wildfire in place of my name. "Give this to Sire Galan. Then take word to Sire . . . Trossers . . . Torosus, that Mai is all alight, alive. But Mice . . . Mouse is not yet born, and when he is we'll follow."

Fleetfoot rode away and left Frost with me. I stood behind the cart, where no one could see me cry. The king was dead and I couldn't grieve for him. I had more pressing cares. I looked up and saw snowflakes falling toward me, and it was as if I were rushing into the gray sky. There were women I might have saved from the shiver-and-shake. I'd neglected them to stay with Mai and Tobe, and yet I feared my help would be in vain. I thought of Galan and how I'd abandoned him. I should be with him tonight, before the battle; it was my duty and my desire. I'd made a choice and chosen wrong.

No. I had chosen to do what was given me by the gods to do, and now I wished to go anywhere but into the small airless cart that stank of fear.

I should have had no room for joy at all amidst such sorrows; nonetheless I possessed a scrap of it, no larger than a strip of linen torn from a shirtsleeve.

In the middle of the night, Mai's pains slowed and then stopped, and she began to weep, saying, "Mouse won't come out. He won't. What's amiss? It's never taken so long, never, not even with the last one who came stillborn."

Midwife took Mai by the shoulders and said, "This child will be born, I promise you! My grandmother told me so, and she never lies. You should show more courage before your daughter."

That put Mai in a temper. "Sunup ought to see, she ought to know. Take a good look, third-daughter! Soon you'll be twelve, and thinking you're a grown woman. I want you to remember this. This is what comes of letting a man poke you. See? Keep away from them. You'd best keep away!"

Wildfire

And Sunup, who was usually so mild, shouted, "Then so should you!"

Midwife sent Sunup outside to brew a tea of raspberry leaves, and she touched Mai's belly with her clever hands and found that Mouse had wriggled around crosswise again, despite the magenta sash meant to hold him in place.

She knelt between Mai's legs, and I helped her turn Mouse for the second time. With my hands beside the midwife's, I felt him inside, awake. Stubborn, complacent, unwilling to be born. It was harder to turn him now. The very throes meant to push him out had snugged him in the cradle of Mai's girdlebone.

When it was done, Midwife chided Mai, saying, "You've offended the unborn somehow. You must beg his forgiveness so he'll stop dawdling."

Mai stared, affronted. "Beg forgiveness of Mouse? He's going to be the death of me, the misbegotten prick, the contrary bastard. He should beg my forgiveness, he should remember that if he kills me, he'll die too. Is that what you want?" she said, shouting now at the unborn, striking her belly with the flat of her palm. "Are you trying to kill me?"

Her shouts awakened Tobe, in my lap, and he called for Mai and his head lolled as if despair made it too heavy for his thin neck to carry. I held him up and he rested his hot face against my neck.

"Hush," Midwife said to Mai. "No wonder Mouse won't come out. I wouldn't come out either to such a welcome. Why have you taken against him?"

"Do you suppose Mite is jealous?" I asked. "Maybe that's why he likes it where he is, where he is the lonely, the only."

"Jealous of whom?" said Midwife.

"Of little Mote."

"He's jealous, he is!" Mai said, weeping again. "And it's certain he's made Tobe sick with it. I swear, if he kills Tobe he'll have to bear my mother's curse."

That was not what I'd meant. I should never have spoken, or rather misspoken. A chill walked my spine. I felt as though Lynx Mischief had clambered into the cart with us. Surely little Mouse, coiled in the womb, did not have venom enough to harm Tobe. In my dream he'd been a pink thing no larger than the top joint of my finger, small and weak and helpless.

I leaned close and whispered in Mai's ear, "The unbairn is not to blame."

No, the gods were to blame: it is said they are jealous when a child is much beloved. Tobe was dying. I feared they meant to take Mai as well, and maybe Mouse. They were pitiless. Yet we were obliged to praise them as wise and merciful, and beg their protection from the very tribulations they bestowed on us—we must hide from them even in our thoughts.

Might as well blame a river for flooding as blame the gods for causing us suffering. But I was bitter. They'd sent me remedies that failed, and I counted them as enemies, and hardened my heart against them.

I could wish my heart harder still so I wouldn't feel these sharp pangs of tenderness for Tobe and Mai and the unborn, for Sunup and Midwife—for all of us frail mortals. All so dear to me, even the shades who huddled here around the knot of the living, some of them called to us, like Midwife's grandmother and the Dame and Na, some drawn by passion and suffering they could no longer feel. I almost envied them. Better to be unfeeling. I labored for breath. I thought my heart might be riven by it, this tenderness forcing its way out.

Cold drops fell on my face; snow had melted from our heat and seeped through the oxhide canopy. A thread of light gleamed through the slit in the door flap. Dawn at last. The day of the battle.

Mai's pains had returned with great force. She couldn't bear the confinement of her clothes, so she labored naked, squatting face-to-face with the midwife, gripping her arms. Sunup, so small and thin, tried to help bear her mother up as she rocked and swayed. When a throe overtook Mai, she squeezed her eyes shut. Rivulets of sweat and tears ran down her red cheeks. She forced sounds through her throat that were hurtful to hear, not whimpering or keening or grunting, but something that partook of these. Midwife coaxed her, "Come now, Mai, let him down, that's good, let him down," and her words were a chant that ebbed and flowed in time with Mai's own harsh music.

Between pains Mai fell back and wept and said it was impossible, she couldn't bear it, she hadn't the strength. When she said she was going to die, Midwife scolded her. But when the next throe came, Mai crouched and bent to her labor. She wanted to push and Midwife wouldn't let her, said it wasn't time. So the throes moved through her. She was gripped by the birthing and she must go on until she was released, for the travail could not be shirked, and must be endured even beyond the last reaches of endurance.

I couldn't help her. Tobe was in my lap and I knew his time was coming. His eyelids were half open and his eyes rolled, seeming to look in different directions at once, or nowhere at all. He let out a dribble of piss, and I told Mai I should bathe him to cool him down. She let him go. She trusted me.

Outside the cart he stiffened and his limbs began to jerk, and his neck crooked backward so his head almost touched his spine. His hearthfire had become wildfire, it burned through him like lightning, flashes followed by darkness. I drew it to me through my right hand, thinking surely I could contain this inward lightning better than Tobe. But what leapt between us stung me as well. My muscles cramped, and I fell to my knees. I saw branching white bolts against a bright glare, then the dazzle of sunlight on the amber ripples of a stream. Tobe had splashed in this stream before, playing beside his mother in a dream, and now the waters were rising. I hunched over the boy in my lap. I thought as long as Tobe didn't sink he would stay alive, and I held his head above the water as he flailed, and lightning surged between us skin to skin.

But the water was rising too fast, and though I strove to hold him above it, his brow was submerged, then his pearly lids. He bled from the nose, and his tears were tinged red. Bruises surfaced all over his thin skin, as if everywhere I had touched him, trying to soothe him, I'd caused him hurt. And indeed he flinched from me, yet he no longer knew the pains his body suffered. I thanked the gods for showing him that much mercy.

I waded with Tobe. He was all underwater now, the light on the surface flickering over him. The stream came to my chest, shoulders, neck. I saw the Queen of the Dead under a rippling veil of water, but I knew she stood on a dry shore. I was surprised to find her young and fair. Her bodice laced up the front like a mudwoman's and she untied the laces. She took Tobe from me and gave him a breast to suck, and the bloom came back to his cheeks and the milk fat to his flesh. He suckled with his eyes half open, sleepy and content.

Tobe's neck was damp against my forearm. He was such a light burden, yet heavy as a friend's heart, heavy as all the world.

I wrapped Tobe's body in my cloak and climbed into the cart. Mai said, "How is he?"

"Asleep. Let me keep him awhile, he's quiet." I settled myself across from Mai, with Tobe next to me, beyond her reach.

Mai wheezed through many more throes, until she no longer had the strength to squat, but lay propped up against a heap of sacks with her legs akimbo. Her waters gushed forth at last. Midwife praised her and said it was almost time. She oiled her hands and slipped two fingers into Mai's cleft. She glanced at me, and I was dismayed to see her afraid. I crawled over to help, but she shook her head.

"Mai! Mai, look at me!" Midwife said, for Mai's eyes had strayed to Tobe. "Your passage is open at last, but Mouse has turned crosswise again. Since he won't come headfirst, I'm going to see if I can catch him by the feet. Have you ever had a babe feet first, Mai?" While she was talking she slid her whole hand into Mai's quim, all the way in up to the wrist. Her other hand was on Mai's belly, nudging Mouse's buttocks. "Listen, Mai— never fear, I've caught them headfirst, feet first, bum first, and backward."

Mai's face drew up tight as a purse and turned red. Midwife said, "Are you pushing? Don't push! You mustn't push."

Mai ground her teeth and wept and her legs tensed and trembled as Midwife fished inside her, but she made no outcry. She held on to Sunup and me and I saw the others grimacing and realized that my face too wore the mask of pain, all of us caught up in Mai's agony. Midwife brought forth two tiny feet from Mai's cleft, holding the ankles delicately between her fingers. The wrinkled soles faced upward, and the toes looked like a row of pearls. The legs came out to the calf, pale as gray clay against the red engorged lips of Mai's cleft.

"Is he alive?" Mai asked.

The midwife grinned at her. Now that Mouse was on his way to being born, she seemed elated. "That he is."

With each throe Mouse came farther out, and retreated a little afterward, as if he wanted to climb back inside. When the babe's buttocks emerged, Midwife took him by the hips and he slithered out to the nape of his neck. She draped his limp body on her forearm, and at the next throe she commanded Mai to push and not stop pushing, and Mai squinched up her face and strained until veins stood out on her forehead and cords on her neck. Mouse's head was still inside and I feared he was stuck. Midwife slipped a finger into his mouth, and tucked his chin down so his head could come out, and at last he was born.

Mouse lay still and I feared he was dead, though the twisted bluish cord that bound him to his mother was pulsing. Midwife cleaned his nose and mouth and blew on his eyelids. He took a shuddering breath that so surprised him that he whimpered and waved his arms and legs and curled his fingers and toes. His gray skin became suffused with pink and he opened his eyes.

Mai had slumped back against the wall of the cart. She reached for Tobe, saying, "Let me see him."

"Let him sleep," I said, and Midwife gave me a sharp look. She put Mouse into Mai's arms instead, saying it would do them both good if he would suckle. But Mouse didn't know how, and Mai seemed too weary to help him.

Sunup leaned down and took one of Mouse's tiny hands between her fingers, and marveled at his face, wrinkled like an apple stored all winter, and his many small perfections. He cried, *Mnaah? Mnaah? Mnaah?* as if amazed. "Oh, you are born!" Sunup said.

Mouse's companion, the bloodknot that ties the unborn to the mother's womb, had yet to be born. Midwife and I knew that, though Sunup didn't.

200

Wildfire

Mai's afterpains should have pushed it out, but her throes had stopped. And now her blood began to flow in a pulsing red stream, soaking the sacks under her.

"You mustn't give up, Mai," Midwife said. "It's almost over—nearly done."

"I'm done for," Mai said hoarsely.

Midwife hauled on her arms. "You're not dead yet! Get up and help. Get up! I want you to squat and push. Come now, one last push."

Mai strove to pull herself up, clutching my shoulder, the midwife, the cart. She leaned on me and I bore her up as best I could. Blood splashed onto her legs, our skirts. So much blood. Mai's lips turned as white as her pinched nostrils. She was too weak to push. She swore she couldn't do it. Sunup held Mouse, who was still attached to Mai by the cord. She asked in a small voice what was wrong, and got no answer.

Midwife had been patient and steady throughout the birthing, and now her urgency was frightening. She shook black powder from a pouch into her hand, and made Mai lick it up. It was blackbeard, the blight on the rye that makes grains swollen and poisonous: a boon to midwives, but as dangerous as it is potent. It belongs to Frenzy, and can bring madness.

The blackbeard caused throes as fierce as any Mai had yet endured, and soon Mouse's companion was expelled in a torrent of piss and blood and clots. Midwife turned the bloodknot over, making certain all the meat of it was there in the tattered caul, lest any part remain in Mai's womb and make her bleed. It was all there. The flow of blood became a trickle, an ooze.

Midwife tied the cord and cut it. And then, to my amazement, she began to sob, holding Mouse in her lap and rocking, rocking. And I saw she had set aside a great burden. I saw her once again as Coralbell, a tired, frightened, glad woman. As Midwife, priestess of Desire, she had sustained Mai all during the long travail with her conviction that Mai could birth this child. She'd claimed the shade of her grandmother had told her so, and I'd believed her, even when Mouse turned and turned and turned again, refusing to be born. But she'd never said Mai would survive the birthing.

And Mai was still in danger. The pangs given by the blackbeard assailed her, and she writhed and screamed as she had not done during her long travail, for she was not in her proper mind. She weakened. Her skin became pale and mottled, and her lips turned blue. Cold sweat, stumbling heartbeat.

Here at last was something I could do for her. I wrapped us both in blankets, and put my left hand over her heart, her hearthfire, and called upon my own hearthfire to warm her. I was afraid I might not have anything to give, for I burned low from exhaustion. But the fire that blazed up in answer to my call wasn't mine. It came from beyond me, it came through me, a gift of the Hearthkeeper.

After Mai's frenzy from the blackbeard ebbed, and she knew us again, I put Tobe in her arms so she could say her farewells. I told her the Queen of the Dead herself had taken Tobe from me to end his suffering, and surely his death journey would be swift and easy. A young child hasn't time to acquire a burden of many regrets, and Tobe's must have weighed no more than a dandelion seed.

Mai said the Queen of the Dead had taken the wrong child. She wouldn't let Mouse to her breast again. She said he'd poisoned Tobe with his jealousy, and never would she suckle him. She told Coralbell to leave him on the hillside to be killed by stray dogs, for it was quicker than starvation and more merciful than he deserved. A parent, by rights, may decide whether a child is worth the trouble to raise, first the mother, then the father. Still, we tried to convince her to keep Mouse. It would give her reason to live, Coralbell said. He was not to blame, I said. It was the gods who took Tobe.

Sunup wept and wailed for Tobe, and she didn't cease until I asked her help to ready him for the pyre. We washed him; she smoothed his black stand-uppish hair. Mai said nothing more. Hers was a parched grief, quiet and ominous. She held Tobe till midafternoon, and at last relinquished him, and I carried him to the fire that would free his shade of all confinement.

Mai turned her face to the wall of the cart and showed us the marble slab of her back, and was silent.

CHAPTER 14

Lynx

he plain below me looked like cloth, bleached with snow, spread smooth with a light hand that left a few rises and hollows, a few wrinkles. An embroidery of hedges marked off square fields and forests gray as smoke. A broad black river edged with ice meandered southward. In one of the river's coils, two armies had met to do battle, and the snow was speckled with small figures of men and horses.

I urged Frost downhill, toward the battlefield. Mouse was snug and warm against my belly in a sling made from a bloodstained sack. His small fists were clenched beside his face; he had perfect tiny shiny fish-scale fingernails. I was glad he was asleep at last. He'd cried all the way here, such distressing cries I'd longed to stop up my ears against them.

I had found the army's new camp, and a goat tethered to a cart there, bleating because she hadn't been milked. So Mouse had enough milk to content him for a while. But I was still in search of a sheath named Thistle, from the clan of Growan, who'd borne a child the tennight before last. The midwife thought she'd be willing to suckle Mouse. Surely Mai would change her mind and keep the boy after her grief eased.

Most of the tents were empty. I found one of Divine Xyster's servants tending a few wounded men in the priests' pavilion. He told me the warriors had already marched on Malleus to take possession of their prize, leaving bagboys behind to guard their belongings, and most of the varlets had run down to the field to plunder. I asked the man if he'd seen Sire Galan, or heard news of him. "Not a word," he said.

We'd won the battle. We'd won the war.

Sheaths were on the field, gleaning. This is what they do, Galan had told me once. This is what they are. I knew many of these women, counted them as friends, but I hadn't known them like this, with daggers in their hands, crouching by fallen foot soldiers to cut apart their clothes, looking for coins, for anything that glittered, even golden threads. Killing wounded enemies.

Giving them mercy, it was called. I daresay some sheaths, none too particular, did the same to our own soldiers. Many of the bodies had been robbed already. A sheath had to be thorough, like the gleaners allowed into fields after harvest, poor old women who war with mice over scattered grains.

I'd been on a battlefield once before in the Marchfield, after the mortal tourney and the riot that followed it, and seen dead men, dead women too, and I'd done what I could for the wounded. Those struck down that day would have fit in a little corner of this field. This couldn't be understood; it was too much to believe.

I turned away from a man groaning on the ground, calling for water. Water would have done him no good, it would have spilled out again through the gash in his belly. I didn't try to help him. Or anyone. It wasn't that I was afraid; I was numb. I was far away from them, far from the wounded and dying. Far from these sheaths, far from myself. I felt closer, perhaps, to the dead. Why grieve, why struggle, when life is short and death is overlong? To be so far away made the suffering distant and bearable. Yet I hated that it could be borne.

I took the bearclaw from my saddlebag and pulled it on my hand, and kept the claws hidden between my fingers. I searched, but there were too many, some lying one atop the other. In reeds by the river I saw a man sprawled on ice with his head under the water. He wore a hauberk with enameled rings. It wasn't Sire Galan's armor, but very like it. I hauled him out and took his helmet off: Sire Erial. He'd been overlooked by the gangs of drudges who were gathering up the slain cataphracts and armigers. Our dead warriors would ride through Malleus in wagons, so their shades could savor the triumph before departing; the enemy dead were borne to the pyres on the edge of the battlefield. Priests oversaw the work, making sure that the armor of each slain foe went to the man who had killed him. One of a jack's duties, even in the confusion of battle, was to tie his master's banner to a downed man for the tallies later.

Groves and orchards resounded with the rhythmic thunk of axes against wood, trees coming down to feed the fires.

I hailed a sheath from the clan of Growan, calling her by name. She was kneeling by a dead man, and she turned to me with a snarl, with blood on her knife, ready to fight if she had to. Seeing it was me, her face changed, and she got up and came over. She didn't know where Thistle was. "Oh, is that Mai's boy?" she said. "Did Mai die, is that why you need a wet nurse? Praise the gods she's alive! Look at him, such a fine boy; he'll grow up to trouble a doxy's hard heart someday."

Wildfire

Another woman came over; I knew her as a sutler who sold pickles and ale. She cooed at Mouse and fondled him until he woke up and cried; then she praised him for being loud. A boy child should be loud. But she didn't know where Thistle was either. As for Sire Galan, she'd heard he had the shiver-and-shake, and hadn't fought at all—what a pity! The sutler showed the sheath her loot and they began to barter, every great battle being the occasion for a bustling market afterward.

Whores had their own way of getting plunder, by earning it. One harlot knelt over a dead horse with her kirtle tucked up and a soldier kneeling behind her, his buttocks bunching while hers jiggled. Her pander stood nearby, keeping the line of men orderly.

I saw another whore lying on the ground in a bloody skirt, strangled. The mud soldiers' blood was up, yet the conciliators had agreed Malleus would not be sacked. A mudman would get no reward for the long march and the battle won but what he could take on this field.

The dead were everywhere. I do not speak of the discarded bodies, but of the shades. They were shadows as thin and vanishing as the mist we breathe out on a winter's day. They crowded all around the horizon of my vision, flickering in time to the beat of my blood and Mouse's indignant gulping cries. They left me less and less room to see. In the twilight the snow turned blue, and the blood in the snow was black.

Mouse and I took the road to Malleus in the dark. I didn't fear getting lost, for we followed a wide trail trampled by many horses. In time the path led us uphill to a temple, and there I was baffled. There were hoofprints all around the temple and hilltop, but no road down other than the one I'd climbed. Had our army stopped here to worship? The hill was steep, a long way to climb if it wasn't on the way to Malleus. It was quiet, except for Mouse's cries, and a few owls hooting and Frost's hooves crunching in the snow. Not a light to be seen. They must have come and gone again.

It was too much trouble to wonder about it, and I didn't care. I could go no farther, not tonight. Mouse was hungry and I was weary, and here might be food and shelter for us both. I dismounted, and led Frost up the worn marble steps to the temple portico, which had columns as tall as the trunks of ancient firs, and huge bronze-clad doors. There was a smaller door at the side for mudfolk, and I hammered on it. A temple as grand as this would not be without priests, nor the priests without servants.

A porter opened the door a crack and I saw him edged with lantern light. He had a gray beard and fear in his eyes. His sword winked down by my belly.

"Help?" I said in the High. Mouse said it better. His face was red and he opened his mouth wide with every cry, showing his pink gums and flailing tongue.

The porter peered around the door to see who else was with us. Frost cocked her ears toward him and whuffled through her nose. He pulled us in, even the mule, and barred the door behind us.

His pallet was on the floor of the corridor. He wore an undyed tunic that fell short of his knobby knees, and his sword proved to be the sort of everyday long knife any varlet might have. His eyes were watery and kind.

"Did you come for healing?" he said.

It seemed safest to answer yes.

He clucked his tongue. "A fine night to be traveling. Haven't you heard there's a war?"

I jiggled Mouse and said, over his cries, "He's hungry. I have no milce for him, no milk. Have you a wetnoise?"

"He's a stout fellow, isn't he?" The man lifted his lantern and led us down the plastered passage, while Mouse's ceaseless *Mnaah! Mnaah! Mnaah!* bounced off the walls. He pointed to a stairway. "You go along to the kitchens down there, get some milk for the babe, and I'll have a stableboy see to your mule."

I put the saddlebag over my shoulder and gave Frost a pat, saying to the porter, "Mind the boy grooms her now, she's been hard at work," and headed downstairs.

The kitchen was underground in a windowless room. Here was noise and heat and bustle, all hidden from the quiet cold night outside. There were fires in hearths and loaves of bread stacked up high and cooks hard at work, so many I wondered if they were preparing for a festival. A baker with floury arms and a gauze kirtle sticking to her legs with sweat made much of Mouse, and I let her hold him. He stopped crying and began to look about, his round eyes blinking at the people in the kitchens. "Did you bring him for healing?" the baker said, tickling his belly. "What's the matter?"

I said, "For mither's milk. Have you any?"

"Have you dried up? I have a salve for that. Sometimes milk lets down late, so you must keep trying."

"He isn't mine. His bearer wouldn't have him, she refused."

"So you're to be a temple boy, are you?" she asked Mouse, hoisting him up to have a look. He dangled in her strong hands and seemed content, which pricked me with a small needle of vexation.

"What tremble is this? What temple?"

"The temple of Lynx, of course."

I began to laugh. I laughed so hard I felt stabbing pains in my sides, and

Wildfire

I tried to tell her the fine jest that the boy's name was Mouse and all along he had belonged to Lynx Mischief, but I couldn't speak for laughing. I cracked open, and I slid off the bench onto my hands and knees on the floor and hunched my back and wept, my forehead against the tiles, while the baker asked, "What's wrong? What's wrong?" and a curious ginger cat rubbed against my legs. I fell on my side and curled up and howled, not numb, thank the gods, no longer like a shade, but oh, it was unbearable, Tobe lost and Mai so still and stubborn, and she might yet die, despite having won through her travail—and the dead and maimed on the battlefield, and Sire Galan maybe lying dead among them. Mouse and the baker gaped at me, and I rolled on my back and looked up at them and couldn't say a word.

The baker's husband had a cousin who had a friend in the laundry who had just lost a child, and Mouse was taken from me for the night. I was grateful. The baker gave me half a loaf of bread to eat, fine bread of the kind served to Auspices. Better still, she gave me a basin of water to wash myself and my dress. Mai's blood was all over the skirts, and I rinsed off the worst of it, and hung the wet dress by a hearth. I curled up in a corner, in my underdress and cloak, with my saddlebag as a pillow. The ginger cat padded around me and over my chest before she deigned to curl up beside my hip. She purred.

I knew I wouldn't sleep no matter how weary I was and in need of healing, for sleep had long been denied me. But in the temple of Lynx I was not denied. I fell asleep and had a dream.

I lay me down on my pallet stuffed with sweetfern on the porch of my house, the house I thought of as mine. My black cat Gowdylakin sprawled across my belly. It was a cold night, clear as spring water. I could see my breath. I never slept indoors unless I had to. I liked the moving air. I liked to see weather when I awoke. The house was perched high enough that sometimes the weather was below me in the valley over the Wend River, and sometimes above, and sometimes I was in a cloud. I smelled sweetfern and smoke from the brazier. I was tired and it felt good, for I'd done a good day's work between one chore and another, and I'd walked far to get aspen bark to dye wool, down to the stream that flowed to the Wend. I was thinking about which mordant to use to get a bright orange when I fell asleep and had a dream.

On the riverbank, amongst reeds of dull gold, on boggy ground made perilous by round stones and puddles under ice skins, I saw King Thyrse. I knew him by his gilded armor and his helm with the golden antlers of a stag. The king had fought and killed someone. He put his foot on the fallen warrior's cuirass and yanked his scorpion out of the eye slit of the helmet. His blow had gone deep and there was gore, red and gray, on the scorpion's sting. He wiped the blade with a handful of reeds. To judge by the dead warrior's cuirass, which had a belly round as a kettle, he had been a fat man. But his legs were thin.

"Don't take off the helmet," I said, but the king didn't hear me. He unfastened the helmet and pulled it off. The warrior had a bloody socket where the right eye used to be. That eye was squashed and hanging on the cheek. The other eye stared upward, fixed in startlement. The corpse was a boy, nothing but a boy, with a round face and freckled nose. His eyebrows were as orange as the fur of a ginger cat. I couldn't see his hair, for he wore a red padded cap as helmet lining.

It wasn't the warrior's face that interested King Thyrse, but the helmet made to look like the head of a hooded serpent. Gold wire outlined diamond scales inlaid with red and white enamel. He squatted beside the body and turned the helmet in his hands as if admiring the workmanship.

Then I remembered. This wasn't our king, the king was dead. Maybe his shade filled the armor as it had once inhabited flesh. Or maybe the armor was empty, and it would soon fall apart, helm, cuirass, greaves all scattered. But no—a living man wore the king's gilded armor, a living man who pushed up the visor of his helm to wipe sweat from his brow with a rag that had been tucked under his gauntlet: Sire Galan.

Sire Galan tied the rag to the dead warrior's baldric, and it was not a rag at all, but one of the king's golden banners, embroidered with the leaping stag of Thyrse's house, and he was marking the corpse for the tally.

He took a swallow from a steel flask. He had blood seeping here and there between the plates of his armor, on his arm, his calf. There were no sounds of battle, which failed to arouse wonder in me. It was quiet except for some gray wagtails fussing at him from the reeds.

"Give me that helm," Queenmother Caelum said, holding out a slender hand. She rode a white mare in white leather barding, and she wore a long split surcoat stitched from the narrow skins of ermine with the heads left on, showing their pointed teeth and false eyes of onyx; the black-tipped tails hung like so many tassels. Her surcoat marked her as the clan of Prey, but her long gown, which draped over the flanks of her horse, was the scarlet of Rift, the clan of her dead husband.

Sire Galan stood and leaned on the tall ironwood shaft of his scorpion. He leaned with insolent ease, in a way that plainly said he was not under her command.

She had a pack of Wolves with her. The foremost of them had a cloak of

Wildfire

wolfskin with the paws tied around his throat. The helmets of the other Wolves were all alike, iron gray and faceless, and their horses were likewise gray.

"Give it to me," she said, and snapped her fingers.

"I don't think so, Queenmother Caelum," he said.

"You may be in my brother's armor, but you don't command here." Pink spots had risen on her cheeks. Her thin nose was already red from the cold.

There were Wolves behind him too. How they'd gotten there without jingling a bridle, I didn't know. I stood still in the tall reeds, hoping the drumming of my heart wouldn't give me away.

Sire Galan looked behind him and on either side. He smiled. "No, I don't think so. The kill is mine, he's mine." His voice was calm and his hand loose on the scorpion's haft.

The Queenmother laughed. "*He* is yours! Did *he* fight hard, or was he easy? Easy as a trollop, I warrant. This warrior you are so proud of killing is my son's wife, Kalos, and I thank you for ridding me of her and her unborn spawn. I'll give you a purse of gold to compensate you for her armor, if you please. Because I doubt that you, Sire Galan dam Capella by Falco of Crux—you see I know your name—as I say, I doubt that you would like your illustrious name coupled with hers in the songs of rumormongers long after you are dead. And you will be dead if you don't give me the helm."

Sire Galan said, "My king fought here, haven't you heard? He will have the fame of this kill—or the shame of it, if all is as you say." He crouched by the corpse and pulled the quilted cap from its head. The hair he loosed was long and curly and ginger in color, only a little browner than the eyebrows.

"Oh gods," he said. "I didn't know. She fought . . . She fought, not well, but well enough. She even cut me, on my leg I think. I thought she was a portly man, an out-of-breath old man. And when I took off the helmet I thought she was a boy. Gods." He stood and handed the helm to the queenmother. "Take it. Take it. I want no gold for this."

"Where is her horse?" the queenmother asked.

Sire Galan shrugged. "Run off." He backed toward the reeds where I stood hidden. He was near enough that I could smell his sweat and blood.

Queenmother Caelum said, "One of you give me your horse, quick now." A Wolf dismounted and led his warhorse forward. "Put her in the saddle. No, not like a sack of turnips—sit her upright! Tie her on." She was impatient, as if her men should have known what she wanted. The horse sidled and whinnied, displeased to have a dead rider. The Queenmother edged her mare up to the stallion and grabbed the reins. She leaned toward her daughter-in-law, who slumped with her head cocked sideways and the broken eye still stuck to her cheek. Queenmother Caelum jammed the helmet over the corpse's head, and rapped her knuckles on the round-bellied cuirass. "Still alive in there, grandson?" she said.

Sire Galan turned his face away from that sight and I saw him swallow again and again with a sour look, and I knew he swallowed his own rising bile, foul as bilge water.

When Queenmother Caelum told her men to set Kalos on fire, and drive her horse toward the field where Prince Corvus fought, beset by many warriors—for quiet as it was in that bend of the river, the battle was not over—when she ordered this, Sire Galan raised his voice against it, calling it a vile deed that would anger gods and men.

She didn't trouble to answer him. One of her Wolves crept up behind while Sire Galan shouted, and felled him with a heavy blow. Sire Galan didn't hear my warning. He groaned and turned his head so his cheek rested on a stone, and by that I knew he was alive.

The Wolves stuffed reeds and sedges under Kalos's armor and tied bundles of reeds to the saddle and set them alight, and I smelled the smoke. The warhorse screamed in outrage and tried to flee the fire. He bucked and dodged, his hooves digging through the ice and mud of the bog, but no matter where he ran he could not escape what was burning. The corpse flopped on his back. Several Wolves galloped after to herd the horse where they aimed it to go.

Queenmother Caelum watched in silence until they disappeared from view. I couldn't understand the look on her face, which was neither satisfaction nor pleasure. She seemed solemn, as one who watches a holy procession. She rode away with her wolf pack, but not before she'd tossed a sack of coins toward Sire Galan as she'd promised. He wasn't able to naysay her.

I lay down beside him and didn't mind the ice and the hummocks beneath us, or the cold water soaking my clothes. I took off his helmet and padded cap, which no doubt had saved his life, and lifted his head so my arm could be his pillow. His eyes fluttered open. He wasn't surprised to see me, though he should have been. And I remembered I was only dreaming.

I woke up and turned on my pallet. My feet were cold. I'd slept the night through and day was breaking over the valley. I stared at the carved rafters of my porch. Long ago they had been painted blue to ward against malice, and the paint was worn and faded. I heard a rider and sat up. I heard footsteps on the stairs and took the sheathed knife from under my pallet, but the voice that called my name was his. When he came he always came without warning. Had he been riding all night?

Wildfire

He was looking for me indoors, in the cabinet bed. His footsteps were fast and hard striking. I remembered then I was only dreaming. I was unwilling to wake. I called him to me instead.

He banished my cat and stripped and crawled under the blankets, complaining that my pallet was too hard and narrow and my feet were cold, and why did I sleep out of doors when there was a perfectly fine bed inside?

"To hear the Sun come up," I said.

"Why, is she noisy?"

"Oh, very noisy here on top of the world. I can hear her footsteps."

"You're a strange one," he said, surprised. As if he could have forgotten.

He had white scars on his body, and here and there were some I didn't recognize. I rubbed the welts with my fingers. I was fond of his scars because they were the marks of wounds that had failed to kill him. We had to learn each other again after every parting.

His cheek scraped against mine. I said, "Are you growing a beard? Is that the new fashion among the hotspurs?"

"I was in haste," he said.

My quim was tender-skinned and I cried out without meaning to. He grinned down at me and eased out, and I gripped his shoulders to slow him down when he drove into me again, and his eyes narrowed and his breath caught, and I clenched hard against him, and he liked that game and so did I, and it was all pleasure by then.

I didn't want to wake up, and I returned again and again to the dream even after it ceased to be a true dream with the taste of Galan's sweat and the smell of mountain weather on a winter morning, even after Galan became, not his own self, but a creature of my fancy who could no longer surprise me.

I sank deeper, down past the swimming dreams in the shallows toward the fathomless embrace of Sleep's ocean. But a thought swam into my mind, that if these dreams of Galan were true, he was alive, and today I would find him.

I awoke so suffused with desire that the rub of the cloak against my sore nipples and the weight of it against my belly and groin, and the touch of my lips one against the other—all these aroused me, and I was once again the bare, peeled stripling I had been after the lightning struck, without bark to harden me against such exquisitely soft blows.

Temples of Lynx are famous for the dreams that may be granted to supplicants there: healing dreams from Sleep, foretelling dreams from Foresight. Mischief sometimes sends dreams as well, but those are unsought and unwelcome. Though I hadn't slept in the dormitory for worshippers, Foresight had given me true dreams. I knew by the smell of them: mountain air, sweat, blood, smoke. And Sleep had granted me, for a good part of a night, the oblivion so long denied, the respite I'd been craving. I was grateful.

There was a shrine for mudfolk underground, near the kitchen. I gave what I could in sacrifice, some barberry root I'd dug up for the fever, which could also be used in a dye recipe to make the orange hue sacred to Lynx. It was customary to tell dreams granted in the temple, so the omens could be interpreted, so I told mine to the attendant, a young drudge in the service of Sleep. He was in some manner intoxicated, his pupils enlarged, his speech slurred as if his tongue were weighty. I recounted both dreams, the one within the other, but I chose not to say it was Sire Galan who wore the armor of King Thyrse. The god would know already, but it was a secret best kept from men. The drudge as he listened stopped yawning, sat upright on his three-legged stool.

He led me upstairs, and the building was loud with the sounds of many people, but I saw few in the corridor. By then I was impatient to find Mouse and my mule and be on my way. He said, "It won't be long," and shut me in a small room. The plastered walls were painted orange to shoulder height and whitewashed above. A thick wool curtain divided the room down the middle. I peeked behind it and no one was there, in the three chairs carved of cedar with horn inlays. Such chairs were not for me. I sat on my saddlebags and waited.

Air from an open door stirred the hanging, and from the other side I heard the scrape of boot soles against the floor, and the slither of one layer of gauze over another. A woman behind the curtain questioned me. I supposed her to be an Auspex of Lynx Foresight, unwilling to demean herself by speaking to a mudwoman directly, but obliged to listen. Foresight sometimes chooses humble mouthpieces.

I told my dreams again. The Auspex had questions: Did you know the man in the king's armor? Did you see or hear any birds? What kinds? What weapons did the killer carry? What shapes did the clouds make? What were the words, the exact words, uttered by the queenmother? The man? Why did another man wear the king's armor?

I said, "Because King . . . Tryst . . . Thrust died of the shiver-and-shade before the battle. They didn't want his men to know, lest they lose hardness, heart."

Did you dream that too?

"I did, another time."

I told the truth, all but Galan's name, for fear that if I lied, I'd offend Foresight, Lynx's cat-headed avatar.

Wildfire

The woman commanded me to wait, and left me long enough for my belly to begin gnawing on itself. There was a door on the other side of the curtain. When I peered out I saw a warrior sitting on the low wall of a colonnade surrounding a courtyard, the hollow center of the temple. He barked at me to get back inside. I slammed the door, still seeing in my mind's eye the sword in his lap, the fine cuirass in the style of Incus, and the tattoo on his cheek marking him as Blood of Rift. A long red cut on his jaw was crossed with black stitches. Not one of our warriors. The courtyard was full of horses, hundreds of them crowded together. In the kitchens they'd been baking bread all night for an army, not a festival. For our enemies.

Those must have been sentries, pretending to be owls hooting in the dark. They'd let me ride up to the temple, and why not? I was harmless, a woman with a screaming child, seeking sanctuary in a holy place.

Too late now to recall gossip I should have remembered last night, about the clan of Lynx in Incus, and how they were old enemies of Queenmother Caelum. When her husband, King Voltur, was killed twelve years past, she accused the Firsts of Lynx and four other clans of plotting to kill him. She had them executed in a terrible and ingenious fashion, torn limb from limb by carthorses. The clan of Lynx still treasured their grudge against her.

I opened the other door and looked into the windowless corridor. A mud soldier stood outside with a billhook. He winked in an unfriendly way. I retreated, and sat in the corner with my back against two walls. It seemed safer there, though it was nothing but a trap. Mischief up to his pranks again.

When he came in and pushed the curtain aside, I knew him. Hadn't I seen his sharp profile on a golden coin? Hadn't I heard the rumormongers sing of his raven black hair and eyes of sapphire blue? Yet when they had made much of his broad shoulders in their songs, they had broadened the truth. He was narrow and tall. I had a glimpse of his face before I knelt and bowed my head. I saw it divided top from bottom, not left from right. In his eyes, sorrow and fear; in the set of his mouth and jaw, frigid anger.

By the reckoning of the songs, he was little more than twenty years of age. This was the fourth winter since he'd attained his majority, his kingdom, and his wife. The fourth winter since he'd banished his mother to a keep in the barren northlands of Incus. He looked older than twenty. He was neither a boy nor a prince. He was a man and a king. Our rumormongers had lied about that.

He had with him an Auspex of Rift Warrior, as tall as his king but of greater girth, burly as a bear. A man old enough to be the king's father, with heavy jowls and rolls of fat on his nape, and a red rooster tattooed on his bare scalp. I thought of the priest of Rift lying dead in a stream, and his stolen bearclaw, wrapped in a cloth in my saddlebags, and I flushed.

King Corvus came too close to me and I kept my face downturned. He pushed back my headcloth and pulled loose a lock of my hair and rubbed it between his fingers as one might rub cloth to judge of the weave.

He spoke harshly to me in a language I didn't understand. When I failed to answer he tugged on my hair and raised his voice, asking the same question or another, I couldn't tell. He nudged my thigh with his boot. "I know you understand me," he said in the High. His words were roundly shaped, precisely cut. "Did the arkhon send you? Were you there on the field to gather tales of my ignominy?"

He stepped away and I found I'd been holding my breath. I dared the briefest glance at his face. His nose was long and thin and had a hump where it had been broken, and his nostrils were pinched as if he smelled something rank. He spoke again in the unknown language and I shook my head.

He began to pace back and forth. He wore soft leather on his feet, the lining for the steel shoon of his armor. Four paces from door to door, four paces back, and he had to shorten his stride to fit. He bore himself straight. "They tell me," he said in the High, "that you speak with a strange accent and confuse your words, so I know this is not your native tongue. Did her father send you? Did you see her die?"

I shook my head again. My eyes were lowered, but a drudge knows how to see without being seen to look. He had a trimmed black beard along his jaw and stubble on his cheek. He'd washed his face and neglected to wash his neck, which was spattered with mud and blood. Likewise his clothing. He had stripped off his armor and left on the red cloth underarmor. The color was as brilliant as fresh blood, and the quilting was intricate. Everywhere the cloth showed signs of hard use, smears and stains, tears and slits where the tow stuffing poked out, rust marks and wear from the buckles of his plate armor.

"Answer!" he said.

If I said what country I came from, he might have me killed. "No, Sire, I came to this tempest in search of a wet norice to nurse little Noose, for I can't feed him, and Catsight sent me a dream. That's all. I'm nothing, a muckwoman."

The priest opened the door and said to someone, "Find this Noose. She came with someone called Noose."

A woman outside said, "I heard she arrived with a newborn babe, no one else."

214

Wildfire

The priest shut the door and turned to me. "Is Noose your child?"

"Not Noose . . . Mouse, I meant, Divise, Divine, I beg pardon. He isn't mine, the bait. He belongs of my friend. She didn't want him."

The priest watched me, and I felt his impassive gaze as a weight, a threat, and a judgment. Yet it was impossible to tell from his face what judgment he made. He turned to his king. "It's not a true dream. King Thyrse is alive, we all saw him on the field."

King Corvus said, "Why do you pretend Foresight sent you a dream? You were there on the battlefield, else your clothing would not be so stained with blood. You saw my wife's killer. You saw my mother set her corpse afire. I'll take you with me so you can tell your master how his daughter died, and I will tell him to his face how I found her burning and cut my son, his grandson, from her body but it was too late, and maybe then he will rue that the soldiers he promised me never came." In his mouth *mother* was a curse.

He turned away as he spoke, but not before I saw the grief come to his mouth, and how his lower lip weakened.

I wondered why his wife had donned armor and ridden to battle, gravid as she was. The most fearsome thing about her had been her helm. Underneath was a girl in woman's estate, not the Kalos of songs, the shape-shifting serpent woman, the dreadful lamia. In the yellowish haze of my right eye, I could see her last ride, and the king's golden banner tied to her baldric, streaming fire in the wind.

I thought Foresight had sent the dreams to grant me sight of Galan. But that inner dream was never meant for me. It was sent to torment this man, King Corvus, as if he were not tormented enough by what he'd seen for himself: the impaled eye, the burning rider. A terrible dream, and I'd told my questioner the worst of it, how Queenmother Caelum had knocked on the cuirass and taunted the unborn child, the soon-to-be stillborn child. An avatar had used me to tell King Corvus one last poisonous truth. So the gods foment enmity among mortals. But we are apt to enmity, and have no need of help.

"She is cruel, Sight," I said, thinking of Foresight. Thinking of Queenmother Caelum.

He turned toward me, having mastered all signs of his sorrow. He spoke bitterly in that other language. The only word I could pick out was Kalos.

CHAPTER 15

Corvus

The temple smith put his hand around my wrist and I didn't realize he was taking my measure. He shaped an iron band into a small circle, with ends that didn't meet. He bent back the ends and punched holes through them, and by then I knew what he was making, and tried to run. His apprentices seized hold of me, and I struggled and got blows and bruises. I might have been a whinnying horse for all the heed they paid to my pleas and curses. The smith quenched the iron in a barrel of water. The manacle was still warm when he put it around my left wrist and hammered a rivet through the flanges. It was a tight fit, pressing against my wrist bones.

An apprentice led out a sturdy, plump girl, maybe eight or nine years of age, with a broad little face and braided hair the color and sheen of bronze. A temple servant, in a shift of orange wool. She must have been used to fair treatment, for she didn't cringe the way some drudges do, in expectation of blows; she seemed more bewildered than afraid, until the smith put a cuff around her wrist. She started to shriek when he riveted it closed, and he went on unperturbed. He fastened us manacle to manacle by a heavy length of chain.

I could not mistake the sign of Ardor Smith on these doings, the god shackling me to some new purpose.

A horseboy lifted me up on a spirited bay horse, and put the girl in the saddle in front of me. It was a cataphract's saddle, with a high pommel and cantle, and the two of us fit as snugly as an armored man. The horseboy mounted another horse and led ours by a long rope tied to his saddle. I had no blade to cut the rope, they'd taken my knife and the saddlebags with the hidden bearclaw.

They wouldn't let me see Mouse. He was to be a foundling after all. I touched the pouch holding the bones of the Dame and Na, hidden under my skirts, and prayed he would, like me, find those who cherished him.

King Corvus rode in the vanguard and set a hard pace, heading east into the hills before turning south. The roads were narrow tracks churned to slush

216

and mud. The girl and I rode amidst a rabble of jacks and horseboys—men who'd lost their masters in the battle for Malleus, I supposed, and followed the king to save themselves. Warriors of the rear guard drove the stragglers, flogging mounts and riders. I could only guess at the number of the king's men. Galan's company had almost a hundred men on horseback, the greater part mud soldiers. King Corvus had maybe five times that many, maybe more.

The girl had never ridden before and was frightened to be cantering along so far above the ground. She shivered from cold and fear and I wrapped my cloak around both of us. She wore her thin dress and wooden pattens with straps for her feet, unfit for winter. I had warmth to spare, for I could strike heat from my fury. I asked why she was a prisoner. She didn't know; she'd done nothing. Her name was Catena. She worked in the kitchen, and she was scouring pots when a soldier came and dragged her upstairs to the smithy. I didn't want to believe the girl was chained to me for no reason but to keep me from running.

No more than two leagues from the temple, we were set upon by the queenmother's Wolves, who came howling down on us from wooded hills on either side of the road. It was a fine spot for an ambush. All was confusion: the war cries of the Wolves and shouts of the king's men, a roaring in my ears that drowned out the clamor of steel. I tightened my arms around Catena and gripped the pommel with both hands, wishing I had reins and feeling helpless. Men milled around us, a mob without purpose, deaf to orders. Some of them were fighting. Most looked frightened, trying to stay on frightened horses. This aimlessness seemed to last a long moment, then the mob surged uphill toward the trees, running away, and we had no choice but to go with them, after the horseboy with the lead. We rode into the woods, ducking and swerving to avoid branches, and I urged the bay on, trying to keep his head next to the rump of the lead horse, afraid they'd go on opposite sides of a tree and we'd all tumble, brought down by the rope between us.

Fleeing men are easier to cut down. Someone hit the horseboy and he fell from the saddle, and we were following a riderless horse. I was sure I'd be next; I felt it right in my neck, that I was going to be struck there. I leaned over Catena, afraid my bony back would be but a poor shield for her. She was clinging to the saddle, and the pommel must have been hitting her in the chest, driving the breath out of her. If she made a sound, I didn't hear it. An unhorsed mudman managed to snag the reins of the lead horse, and suddenly we were turning, and he had one foot in the stirrup and was hopping up and down and we were going the wrong way, toward the fight. It didn't matter, they were fighting all around us now, bald warrior priests running silently downhill through the trees, taking the Wolves by surprise. And then the Wolves were running, gone almost as suddenly as they'd appeared.

I didn't know then that the king's outriders had spied the Wolves lying in wait, and the king had sent some of his honor guard, priests of Rift Warrior, to outflank them on the heights. That made sense, afterward. As it made a ruthless kind of sense that the king had ridden knowingly into a trap, to trap his pursuers. But what didn't make sense, what never made sense, was why Catena and I lived when so many around us died. No wonder Sire Galan worshipped Chance, and pursued her fickle favor.

Long after dark the king took shelter in a small keep built on a mound. In the Kingswood it would have been thought a fine manor; here in Incus it was a middling poor one. The master and his wife and his seven children and his servants prostrated themselves before the king, and the master bade him welcome, and indeed the king welcomed himself to everything they had, food, drink, beds, and horses. I was so weary I slept as soon as I lay down on the stone floor of the loft. Catena shared my cloak and my warmth. I knew nothing and forgot everything, for the blessing of Sleep had been restored to me in the temple of Lynx.

I came awake all of a sudden, from blissful oblivion to misery. Catena was nestled against me, breathing with her mouth open. How trusting of her to sleep, I thought. How trusting of me.

King Corvus sat in the dark. He had taken the master's chair of stout oak, most unlike the spindle-legged furniture of Lanx. He slouched with his long legs straight out before him, crossed at the ankle, and his head resting against the chair's carved backrest. His eyes glinted, staring up at nothing.

Maybe I made a sound. He turned his head and blinked, and asked a question in that other language. When I didn't answer he asked in the High, "Did you dream?"

"I wish it was a drame, Sire. But I see it wasn't." I lifted my arm and shook the heavy chain that bound me to Catena, and woke her up.

King Corvus drew in his legs and stood abruptly. He stepped over two sleepers to crouch beside Catena and me. She cringed and I put out my hand to keep her quiet. He said, "The Auspex of Foresight believes you told the truth, that you dreamed what you saw. She doesn't think you are Kyphos's creature. If that is so, dream true for me. Dream true."

He straightened up and walked away. His voice had been quiet and cold. I understood that he didn't need a reason to kill me; he needed one to let me live.

*   *   *

Wildfire

The bay had a bone-rattling trot, and the sound of hooves thudded in my ear, every footfall a blow. I began to feel queasy, as if I rode a boat, not a horse. The sky had cleared and the brightness of the snow stabbed into my skull. My eyes rolled in sockets lined in coarse, scratchy wool. I was cold, so why was I sweating? No, I was hot. I tried to take off the cloak, but Catena said to leave it be. I wondered why I swayed in the saddle and why the ground tilted this way and that as we passed over it.

The shiver-and-shake was stealthy, it clouded my mind so I wouldn't recognize it. When at last I did, I was outraged, as if I, of all people, should have been spared. I had cared for the afflicted, and pitied them, but I'd been unable to imagine their torment, and I'd supposed that I wouldn't give way to groaning and screaming as they did. Now I heard a thin noise that coincided with my exhalations, and realized I was whimpering.

Catena turned in the saddle, saying, "What's wrong?"

My teeth chattered as I answered. "I have a feeble. You must hold my arms so I don't fall, and pinch me if I start asleep. Can you do that for me?"

Catena wasn't the fluffy gosling she at first appeared to be, but fierce as a goose. When a mud soldier rode too close and rubbed his hand up my thigh, I was too weak to push him off. She hissed and pecked at him with her fist, until the varlet who led our horse turned around in the saddle and shouted at the soldier to keep his pricking hands off me.

"You just want the sow yourself, you greasy gruntling," the soldier said, crowding next to us. "You think because you lead her you can have her."

"She's the king's fancy. She's not for the likes of you," said the fellow who led us—the same one who'd caught the horse during the battle. A horseboy, but not a boy. A scrawny man, in a quilted linen tunic and leggings that served for armor; by the faded blue-green color of the linen, he was a servant of clan Growan. A cut had laid open his sleeve and arm.

"She's not for you either, Mox," the soldier said. "So what about the other one? She's a plump little thing."

Catena called them both winkly spitboys and said their dangles were all pungled, or some such. She'd been long enough in the kitchens to learn how to curse like a cook. Mox laughed at this, showing a lot of brown teeth, but he reined in so the soldier had to ride around him, and he put his boot on the rump of the soldier's horse and gave a push, sent him trotting away.

We halted after sunset. Catena and I slid off the horse and my legs folded under me. Mox hoisted me up and dragged me into the lee of a tall hedge, where men were making camp, and Catena had to follow on the leash of chain. She sat next to me and began to weep. "Are you dying?" she asked. Though I denied it, I wasn't as sure as I pretended.

*   *   *

Late at night, after everyone had gone to sleep but the sentries, I had to piss. I found I couldn't stand. I didn't even have the strength to sit up. I rolled out from under the cloak we shared, as far as I could get from Catena, and yanked my shift above my hips and let the hot piss come gushing out. I rolled back, cursing the wetness on my legs and buttocks, and pulled the shift down again. The filth shamed me.

I covered myself with the cloak, then I burned and pushed it off, then shivered and tried to tug it away from Catena, resenting the comfort she found in sleep. I wept for self-pity. I had left the cursed army behind, and the curses had followed me. If the king found out I had the shiver-and-shake, he would probably abandon me or kill me out of hand. Abandonment would offer a chance to escape—but suppose he left me chained to Catena, and I was unable to walk? Better to die quickly.

Living meant terrible exertion and suffering. Living meant I must search for Galan, and I didn't have the strength, just then, to hope I might find him. He was far away, and death seductively near.

When dawn was just a promise, the men were roused to break camp. The king sent his body servant to summon me. When he found I couldn't stand, the servant got two men to drag me while Catena walked behind. They dropped me at the king's feet and I slumped sideways. Catena crouched next to me.

"What's wrong with her, Garrio?" the king asked his servant.

Garrio touched my forehead and said, "Fever, Master."

In the dim light the king looked more a shadow than a man, and like a shadow, expressionless. He said, "Put her on the horse."

Garrio was old enough, or worried enough, to have acquired gray hairs in his beard and lines across his brow. He helped Mox hoist me into the saddle, and put Catena up behind me. I drooped over the pommel, clutching the bay's mane. I thought the girth of the saddle was loose, for I was slipping sideways, falling.

Garrio saw I couldn't hold on, so he had a drudge who was clever with his hands, Mano they called him, weave a basketwork of withies and fasten it to the front of the saddle to prop me up. They trussed me so I wouldn't fall. We rode closer to the king now, where Garrio could keep an eye on us. Mox still held the lead rope.

For some time after, I wasn't sure where we went or where we halted. I dreamed all the time, in delirium. Day and night lost their meaning, their orderliness. Sometimes we galloped, and sometimes I was unloaded like baggage. Catena washed me as roughly as she would scrub a pot, and the cold water felt delicious. Garrio crouched at a campfire and gave me barley water. My voice was brittle and cracked, worn out from speaking. He listened, but what was it I said? My right hand was limp and the right side of my face drooped, and the shiver-and-shake burned through me like slow lightning.

I lay on my back, shaking with chills. Catena lay beside me under the cloak, sharing her warmth like a cat or an ember. I was grateful, but I made her cold. I took more than she gave. Move away, I told her, I think I told her. Move away.

We seemed to be on a steep, stony goat track, and the bay's hooves started cascades of pebbles at every footfall. I leaned on the wickerwork prop and panted, staring down at the road. We climbed to a grove of wide-spreading oaks on a hilltop bronze with beaten grass. Rooks were thick as leaves on the leafless branches. The Auspices studied the birds, which are sacred to Rift, and the king's counselors quarreled over the omens. King Corvus heard them out, his face stern and still under a tall hat covered with the glossy wings of ravens. One of his priests was a bear, seen by my right eye; my left eye saw him as a man in a bearskin cloak, brown fur with silver-tipped guard hairs. I'd seen him before, in the temple of Lynx and on the road, always at the king's left side like an armiger. The king's strategos. He said we should go through the town of Saxetum to get horses and provisions, on the way to Owl Pass.

The rooks argued too, *Caw! Caw! Caw!* They contested over which could cast more scorn on the king. Some called him a caitiff coward. Did he think he'd find kindness in another kingdom, cowering at the foot of another king's throne, now that he'd lost his own? Cozened of it by a cunning canny. They shrieked with laughter, making such a din that men paused to listen.

The First of Torrent in Incus said the king should skirt the mountains and march to the Outward Sea, sail from the harbor at Urtica. The First of Delve pleaded with the king to take refuge in his clan's copper mines on Mount Somno—easily defended, he said.

Some rooks cawed at this, said copper couldn't cut steel, said the king couldn't cower behind the clan of Delve, beware of their custody.

I laughed to see the priests attending so prayerfully to the rooks' gibes, and said, "Listen to the rooks mock the cock of crows!" Garrio tried to hush me up.

The quarrel went on, but the king had already decided on his course, heedless of advice from birds or counselors. He refused the hospitality of the First of Delve, who was affronted. The Delve took his men and rode away west.

The king stood in his stirrups and pointed after them, shouting out that any man who lacked heart should follow them, he'd let them go gladly. He didn't need such men, they were already forgotten. He was the better contented with the men who remained with him, knowing they were both brave and loyal, when so many had proved otherwise. In brighter times—for there were bright times to come—he would remember those who stayed beside him in this dark time, he would show how he prized them. His face was flushed, and his voice carried far.

Some score or more of mudmen did canter off after the First of Delve, but the king turned his back on them. The rooks' concourse was done. They rose up in a great thunderclap of wings and flew away south, and we followed.

I lay beside Catena at the bottom of a well, under stars and rags of clouds and doves perching on long poles. The doves cooed and jostled and settled into slumber. The floor we lay upon was plastered with their droppings. This must be a well of Sleep, blue-black Sleep, and I was drowning in it. I could hardly breathe. If I climbed that ladder, could I catch a breath?

I got up, amazed by how easy it was to stand, to climb the notched log ladder and step through a narrow window onto a rickety balcony of poles—but only half of me did this, my right-hand self, for I was divided left from right. The right self was chilled, the skin covered with goose bumps. No manacle.

The left-hand self was lying down at the bottom of the well, burning and sweating, shackled to Catena. Nothing united these half selves but a strand thin as spider silk, no more substantial than a gleam.

Up on the balcony I saw a sentry dozing with his mouth agape. His teeth were stained as if he'd drunk woad. His feet hung over the edge of the balcony and his hand rested protectively over his prickguard. This was a tower, not a well: a ruined watch tower on the border of a kingdom long forgotten. Three tall firs beside the tower swayed in the night wind, and I clung to my perch and shivered, and turned my one-eyed head to look at the ground below.

The right self had the bad eye, and saw everything tinged with yellow, dim and haloed, shimmering with a rank luminescence. Huts of mudfolk were built against the tower walls, fragile as the papery nests of wasps. I spied motion downhill among trees and boulders, one, three, six, many shapes that glimmered when they moved, like pale grubs in a spadeful of dirt. Enemies, Wolves.

Not my enemies; let them come. It was not for me to wake the sentry on the balcony, dreaming of a boy he knew when he was six, the two of them fishing. I could see his dream, a minnow nibbling at his beard.

222

Wildfire

I kept my mouth shut, but my voice made mischief, buzzing in the sentry's ear. "Wake up! Wake up!" Doves flew out of the roofless tower in a sudden clatter of wings. The sentry sat up as if he'd been stung and peered over the edge of the balcony. "To arms!" he bellowed, and howled in imitation of a wolf.

The Wolves howled back and sprinted uphill. They lit torches, and set the thatched huts on fire, and the inhabitants fled. A few were cut down as they ran, but they weren't the real quarry.

A man with a shortsword in a scabbard on his back climbed the ladder to the balcony. He was a young priest of Rift, and the eye tattooed in indigo on his bald scalp was wide open. He clouted the sentry on his ear for failing in his duty, and the sentry groveled. "How many?" the priest asked. I whispered to him, but he never heard, and he never saw me, not even with his tattooed eye. I was afraid of the Wolves; I wasn't sure if they would save or slay us, Catena and me.

Smoke billowed up, and down in the haze my other self, the left one, was choking. The fire in the doorway burned through the portal of my good left eye. Wolves crowded in with their shields locked together, making the turtle's back. Inside the door they burst apart, and King Corvus and his men were waiting.

There was a cow byre inside the ruined tower, with warhorses stabled in it, and a Wolf torched it before he fell. Fire stood up tall in the thatched roof and began to leap and caper. Wildfire was loose, and my left self was wonderstruck. The byre was made of wicker and clay, and the horses inside kicked it apart and went dashing about the tower, screaming in fear. Men shouted.

The fire was loudest of all. The tower became its throat, and its outrushing roar a song of twining winds. Its thunderous fast cadence took possession of me and everything that moved. Fire and shadow kept perfect time, for where one advanced, the other retreated, and never missed a step. I would have joined the dance for the ecstasy of it, but I was crippled and chained and I could only jiggle my leg and strike my thigh with my palm. The rattle of the iron links pleased me. I was moved to sing a firesong, which I made of words given me by the Hearthkeeper, and a melody given by a bird that had perched on a firethorn tree in the Kingswood.

> Burn bright, burn fast.
> Give what light you can,
> The rest is ash.

Catena tugged the chain, saying, "Come on! You must—I can't carry you." Her round face was ruddy in the firelight, and tears glistened on her cheeks. It was hard to move, I was limp and clumsy, only half present. I rolled over and dug in my left knee, my left elbow, and we crawled away from the burning byre. My left self saw chaos in the flames now, instead of the dance that moved the world. I remembered to be afraid. Catena was sobbing and shaking, and I gathered her close to me, and we made ourselves as small as children hiding in a linen chest in a burning house.

My right self was on the balcony, shivering, watching the priest slide down a rope. He unsheathed his dagger and ran into the darkness down the hill. I was mute. I had lost my voice in the labyrinth of his ear, whispering to him of Wolves. Wind seethed through the fir trees and I let it go through me until I was as cold as the night. I wanted to follow the priest down the rope, run away, free my right self from the anchor of the left, the heavy flesh and iron chain.

And I might have gone, but I heard a thin whisper of a song, *Give what light you can*, and my voice was in my throat again, where it belonged. The melody doubled, as I was doubled. *The rest is ash*. I was bound by threads of light and song, stitching me together, left and right, until I was one whole again.

By morning the weather in my mind was clear of mists and storms. The fever had broken. The shiver-and-shake had failed to kill me, and though I knew it would return once more, in a tennight or so, I no longer had to fear it. Yet I was perilously weak. Catena helped me sit, and Mox brought us boiled barley. I ate dutifully, queasy from the stench of pyres and smoking rubble.

It hadn't all been a dream. Catena had saved me last night. If she hadn't roused me, I might have stayed transfixed by Wildfire, singing until I died.

Her face was smudged with soot and streaked with tears. She ate left-handed, awkwardly, because of the chain on her right. Her wrist had swollen around the cuff. I'd been so overwhelmed by my own misery, I hadn't been able to spare a thought for hers.

I asked Mox for water so I could clean Catena's face. "You should see yours," Mox said, and Catena smiled.

It stung the pride of the king and his men, down to the lowliest varlet, that the Wolves had gotten close enough to harm us. They thought they'd outridden all pursuit. The priests of Rift were most humiliated of all, having failed in vigilance. The penance they paid was secret, a matter for Rift Warrior; rumor had it his disciplines were severe.

The sentries who had failed to raise an alarm were executed. Divine Volator, the young priest of Rift with an indigo eye tattooed on his scalp, was given the task of striking off their heads, one, two, three; he was obliged to be executioner because, unlike the other priests, he still used a sword. The first head to fall belonged to the man I'd seen on the balcony dreaming of fishing.

I had lost count of the days of my captivity and now the Moon was at half. I tied knots in the red cord around my waist, guessing it was about seven days since the battle, and my dream in the temple of Lynx.

Queenmother Caelum's Wolves harried us southward through rolling hills. They cut down laggards and attacked the king's outriders and foragers. Soldiers died trying to steal a nap by a hedge or a lamb from a flock. The Wolves winnowed the king's army of stupid and weak men; likewise brave ones, the first to perish when there was fighting to be done. Above all, unlucky ones.

Such a long pursuit of a defeated enemy was unusual, but rumor had it the queenmother was sore offended by her son. He'd failed to die in battle, as he ought to have done, and furthermore he'd failed to surrender himself once defeated, as was agreed when the terms of battle were negotiated.

On the eighth day the bay could carry us no longer, he was so afflicted with saddle sores. Catena and I were given a new horse, a black mare taken from a village somewhere. It was plain good policy for the king's men to steal mounts and leave nothing for the Wolves but jades.

When I dismounted that evening, I didn't fall. The next morning I walked a few steps leaning on Catena's shoulder. The shiver-and-shake had taken most of my strength, but I was obstinate. I persisted.

The ninth night Wolves burned the village in which we were encamped. It pleased them to do this, to drive us from shelter and then take their ease while we rode on in the dark. I hated them as much as King Corvus's men did, for depriving me of rest.

By these measures I tallied the days that took me farther from Galan, each one a new knot in the red cord. That true dream of mine, which had brought me so much trouble, had at least given me reason to believe he was alive. As did the tug of the bond between us, one end of which was so knotted under my ribs that I felt it as a constant ache, a constriction that would ease only in his presence. I'd bound Galan to me in secret, but that binding was only one small strand of the cord we'd made by braiding together our days. I hoped distance could not unravel it. If Galan felt it too, he would know I lived.

I wished I'd kept that scrap of his sleeve on which he'd written the three godsigns. I would have cherished it as a talisman, as I cherished even the thought of it, as a sign of his forgiveness—no, better than that, of his acknowledgment that I didn't need to be forgiven. A sign of his welcome should I make my way back to him.

I wondered if he searched for me. So many ways a woman could disappear, on a road in wartime. He would know that. I thought of Frost's hoofprints in the trampled snow and knew Galan would never find me.

It seemed I was to be the king's dreamer.

On the tenth day of my captivity, I was summoned before dawn to see King Corvus. He had taken shelter in the hovel of a charcoal burner, and the door was so low that even Catena had to stoop to enter. The hut had a few stones for a hearth, and a small fire filled the air with smoke. The king sat on a sheepskin. There was no furniture in the hut, not even a stool, and it was so small I had to kneel close to him. Catena leaned against me under my cloak, and soon she was asleep again. She had a gift for sleeping anywhere and anytime.

He asked what I had dreamed and I hardly knew how to answer. His body servant, Garrio, had instructed me on the proper way to address the king. Mudfolk were not supposed to speak to him at all, but if for some reason they were required to do so, they were obliged to say Corvus Rex Incus, Master of Masters—except for Garrio, who called him Master, for otherwise, he said, nothing would get done.

I was daunted by so many names and titles for one man. Names were the hardest words for me to say; I found it difficult to speak even an ordinary one without bungling it. And the more I feared to misspeak, the more likely I was to do it. I said, "I had no dreams worthy of your novice, Crevice— Crowish?—no, Corpus Wretch Incus, Bastard of, of . . . bastards. Forget me—I have a disexpedient mouth—the warts come jumbling out."

He said, "Sometimes I wonder if you learned our language too badly or too well."

"I beg burden, meaning no offense, Sire . . . Converse Rex Inkle, Mazzard of . . . It is my same touch; I grew up speaking it. I used to speak as well as anyone, and my tooth did my chiding, bidding. But then I was thundershucked, and now I can't speak plaintively to save my strife. It struck me here, the lighting." I pointed to my left cheek, under the eye. "I have not yet found a curse for it."

"When were you struck by lightning?"

"Some while ago, Rovus—"

He made a swift gesture, saying, "Don't speak my name at all if you cannot speak it better! Now go on. When?"

"At the very begging of the war."

"How is it you weren't burned and disfigured?"

He was not the first to want some outward proof. I started to make a truthful answer—to say I didn't know why Wildfire had spared me—but I thought better of it. "I was begared," I said. "On my bark . . ."

"Show me."

I had hoped he wouldn't ask. I pulled off my cloak and turned my back to him, and Catena grumbled in her sleep. The chain drew taut against my left hand. I loosened the laces of my overdress and shrugged it below my wingbones, and bent my neck to show him the burn scars on my back, nape, and shoulders.

It was true Wildfire had given me those wounds, but not by way of lightning. It had happened when men of Ardor set Galan's tent on fire in the Marchfield, and Wildfire nearly ate me. I'd never seen the scars myself, of course, but I had felt them after they healed, small ridges and lumps where burning canvas had fallen on me.

King Corvus held up an oil lamp and I felt the warmth of the flame on my neck. "Did you know that some of these burns have the semblance of the constellation of Ardor? Here, here, here, here, and there." I felt a pressure so light it troubled the fine downy hairs of my nape and shoulder without touching my skin. I feared he would see the flush rising on my neck. I waited, kneeling with my head bowed and my back to him until the heat subsided. He made too much of a scattering of sparks; Galan had never seen a pattern in the burns.

Good. Let the king be credulous. I felt his eyes searching me down to the quick. I tied up my laces and faced him, and found he wasn't looking at me at all. After a long moment he turned his gaze my way. "Were you always a dreamer?"

"No more than anybody else." I pointed to my head. "Wilefire augered a hole in my hat. But the streams, dregs that entered there come from Lynx Forcesight, I suppose."

"So now you dream true."

"Only betimes."

"And tonight?"

I shrugged. "The dream was fault, false, I think. I couldn't smell it."

"Could not what? Spell it? Do you mean find godsigns in it?"

"No, no! *Smell.*" I tapped my nose.

He let out a short, sharp laugh. "So I must inquire of oracles if their dreams stink?"

"I don't know. It's just me, mishaps."

"And the dream of my wife—did it stink?"

"It smelt of fire and flood . . . blood."

It had smelled of other things as well: Galan's sweat, horses, snow, mud, icy bog water, and the queenmother's heavy perfume of muskmallow and lily.

In the long pause I heard mice scrabbling in the thatch overhead. I risked a look at the king's face. He rested his chin on his palm and hid his mouth behind his hand, and I imagined weakness, his lips trembling. But he straightened up and took his hand away, and his mouth was hard, frowning. His eyes were sad.

He said, "The king of Corymb is dead. That much is true. They say he fought bravely and died of his wounds after the battle."

No doubt he had his spies. They must have ridden their horses to death to catch us. I dared ask, "Who is kinged now?"

"Why don't you dream and tell me?"

Despite myself I made acquaintances among the king's followers. I had sores under my manacle to remind me to hate them, but it was hard to bear a grudge against the men who looked after us—a small group among the nameless multitude. Garrio had taken me in charge, another of his many duties, since his king required my services. I dimly remembered him caring for me when I had the shiver-and-shake. Mox had lost his master in the battle, and later his master's spare horse, so it was a bit of good luck for him that he'd ended up leading us. Now he was assured of food when there was food to be had. Lame and Chunner were the king's horseboys (his horsemaster and jack had died of wounds); Lame had one leg shorter than the other, which was no trouble when he was riding, but hampered him on foot. Chunner was a lad about Fleetfoot's age, with bright eyes, a snub nose, and a head of curly hair.

These men and the boy Chunner rode with us by day and shared a fire and food with us at night. I learned their qualities, for when a man is weary, frightened, cold, and hungry, you see him at his worst or at his best, depending on his nature. Catena and I needed our guardians. Yet I couldn't forget they were also our captors.

Catena and I were protected by rumors too, many of them absurd, such as that King Corvus nightly summoned me to his bed; I was a thrush—a spy—from his wife's father; I was a highborn foreigner, and my ransom would pay for the king's next campaign; I was the king's oracle, who would lead them to safety. The soldiers didn't know what to make of me, so they made much of me.

Daily I had reminders of what could happen if we were not so well guarded. Men fell sick, or their wounds festered, or their horses foundered, and if they couldn't keep up, no man tarried to help. There were quarrels, especially among the masterless horse soldiers. I saw a man stabbed because he refused to give up a warm place by a fire. Sickness, wounds, fights—these killed more of the king's men than the Wolves, though they were less feared.

As for women, this army had no sheaths or whores to ease the men, for the king had never reckoned on retreat. Some men took maidens and women from villages we passed through, as they took food, horses, fodder, firewood, anything they fancied. Took them, used them for a night or several, left them alive or left them for dead. I didn't know if King Corvus knew this, or cared.

Most of the townspeople went unharmed if they gave provisions to King Corvus. But when they did, Wolves came along after us and burned them out. Wildfire running south.

I meant to escape when I'd regained my strength, when I saw a good chance. Until then I needed the king's protection. If I was his dreamer, I must give him dreams. True dreams were granted by the gods, and I knew no way to summon them. Very well, I'd give him false dreams that seemed true, and if he was misled by them, so much the better. To that end I applied myself to gossip, listening to rumors, reports of things half overheard, boasts—not that one should trust anything a mud soldier said, but it was all there was to go on.

One night by the fire, I asked Garrio and the horseboys what had happened in the battle for Malleus. They quarreled over the facts until it seemed they had fought different battles entirely, for Mox had been with his master in the right flank, the king's horseboys had been in the center, holding spare mounts for their master, and Garrio had been waiting on a hill, and had seen it from a distance. They all agreed on this: the commander of Corvus's left flank had turned his companies against the center and scythed through it, cutting down many of the king's loyal men straightaway.

The man King Corvus had trusted on his left, his shield side—the man who betrayed him—was his brother Merle. When the king's men spoke of Merle, they called him the Starling. They didn't dare utter his name in the king's presence.

I threw the bones. Catena and I were curled up knee to knee and she was asleep. In the space between us, in the darkness under the cloak, I opened the divining compass with my unchained hand, and smoothed it out. The last time I'd thrown the bones was for Tobe and Mai, and now I sought foretelling rather than healing. I wanted the Dame and Na to show me how I might escape. On the first throw, for my character, they pointed to Iron and Chance, which I took to mean I must be strong and lucky. On the second throw, for time, they spoke of the past and present, Hunger and the Sun; but of the future—which I sought to know—they didn't speak. On the third throw, for the gods, Na told me to look to Hazard Fate, and the Dame rolled outside the compass and said nothing.

I prayed to Fate as Na advised, though I thought it was useless. I found it easier to believe that Chance or Peril, those mighty personages, would yield to my prayers than bodiless, boundless Fate. Fate was a realm for men of consequence, and if I trod a maze within that realm now, it was not by choice.

I thanked the shades and kissed the bones and tucked them away, none the wiser for their advice. But I'd learned to wait for their meaning to come to me. I hoped they would point the way as we rode, and their counsel would become manifest in the unfolding of events.

That night I didn't dream, and hardly slept. In the morning King Corvus summoned me, and I rubbed charcoal on my eyelids before I went to see him, so I might look more like a revelator. Divine Aboleo, his strategos, was with him. I was afraid of the Auspice, afraid that, through divination or some arcane art particular to Rift, he'd find out about the dead priest in the bear cloak, or be able to tell a false dream from a true one.

I almost faltered, but I remembered Chance and how she loves boldness. My voice shook. I wove a tale from the way the bones had fallen the night before, the godsigns one after another. The tale took shape in my mouth, it seemed, and found its way to my hazy right eye, so I saw it as I spoke. As if I'd dreamed it after all. I said, "I dreamed of your bother . . . mother, sitting down to a feat. She pulled an iron dudgeon, no—I mean a dagger—from her sheath and it was covered with rust, Dastard Chance's color. Oh, she was famished, she set to table do-gladly and began devouring everything. What she ate—she had a little blackbard . . . blackbirth, a a startling on her plate, and she carved it up and ate the wings and the plump boast, breast. She had fathers sticking out of her mouth. She sat out-of-sorts, not in a room, and it was white snow she spread the feast upon. The bird was stuffed with reasons and hazenuts. The . . . queenmaster ate alone. She pricked her hand on the rusty daglet, and I saw a drupe of blood, red as a cherry, swell on her pall."

"I cannot understand you," King Corvus said. "You talk such nonsense." Yet he seemed not at all displeased to hear his mother had bled. He wished her ill. I couldn't deny he had cause.

Divine Aboleo too seemed pleased with the dream. I supposed he was there to tell the king what it meant. I might dream of signs, but it was not left to me to interpret them.

Wildfire

Another day as we rode along, I asked Garrio if the king's wife, Princess Kalos, had been a lamia, as the rumormongers sang it. Was she covered with fine scales, and could she turn into a snake? He said he knew one of Queenwife Kalos's handmaids, who claimed the queenwife wasn't scaly at all, but she had a tattoo of a serpent wrapping around her waist, quite a frightful thing.

"Did she wear it in horror of . . . the dreadful one, of of Cleft Dread?"

"She didn't worship Rift," he said.

"Which gaud did she worship?"

"Who knows? They are full of strange notions where she came from. But she made sacrifices to a serpent."

"A torpent!"

"She kept one in her bedchamber and offered it tribute—little frogs and mice and crickets. That's what her handmaid told me."

I asked if the queenwife had married King Corvus in order to curse Incus, and Garrio said of course not, that was slander spread by Caelum to give a reason for war. When everyone knew it was the queenmother who had cursed Queenwife Kalos, causing her to miscarry twice.

"Why did she ride to war, Raggio? Why risk the chide she carried?"

He had no answer.

Sometimes I couldn't help but remember what the king had said when I told him my dream in the temple: how he'd cut their son out of his wife's dead body, and the child too was dead. And I remembered him that night in the stone manor house, sleepless, staring into the dark with his eyes dry as stones.

I threw the bones again, and asked again how I might be free. The next morning I told King Corvus I'd dreamed of a woman who swallowed two stones the size of eggs, and her belly swelled and became egg shaped. She was in turn swallowed by a serpent, and I could see the shape of her under its scaly hide.

"I see," he said. I was afraid he did see, that he guessed it wasn't a dream at all, much less a true one, but rather a lie patched up from godsigns and threadbare gossip. His mouth turned down as if he tasted something bitter.

I had caused King Corvus suffering. I was perhaps a little sorry, not for him, but that I'd misused what the Dame and Na had told me. Yet they seemed to collude in what I did, or at least show me how to do it. In the second cast, for time, the Dame had pointed to Mischief.

I could almost admire the king. He seemed tireless on the march, riding in the vanguard or up and down the line, and his height made him visible at a distance. His seat on a horse was if anything too perfect, too upright and stiff. He spoke to one cataphract or another to give them encouragement, but he had not the ease to make other men easy, as our king did—had done, when he was alive.

I could almost admire him. Yet I couldn't help but hold him in contempt for being fool enough to take me for a seer and my lies for omens.

CHAPTER 16

Boarsback Ridge

 couple of warm days melted the last of the snow. We climbed between two hills, and black and white goats bolted away from us, their bells clanking, chased by a couple of varlets who wanted meat for dinner. The goatboy leaned on his stave and watched, helpless. I looked past him and saw a blue wall of mountains across the southern horizon.

We rode toward them. There was a rumor that the king hoped to claim refuge in the southern kingdom of Lambanein, which was ruled by King Kyphos, his father-in-law. The rumor outraged common sense. To get there the army would have to cross the mountains, and cross them in winter, when its passes were—as everyone knew—impassable.

One of the jacks had grown up hereabouts, and been the butt of mockery for his country ways and his southern accent. He unwillingly bore the nickname Wheezer. Now it pleased him to frighten us with tales of avalanches, killing storms, walls of ice, and cold that could freeze a beard so brittle the whiskers broke off. And there were wolves, real wolves, not like the queenmother's lapdogs who followed us, and mountain lions and cave wights, and also man-eating bandits—they preferred little girls, Wheezer said, poking Catena—but they were hungry enough to eat men, and we would be too, soon enough.

We climbed into foothills, drab and dun. Villages were scarce, and where the land was cultivated it looked likely to bear nothing more than a fine crop of stones. Pastures were grazed down to scurf by sheep and goats, or abandoned to thickets. Trees huddled in copses or steep gullies cut by streams.

Always before us reared the true mountains, fortresses with spires of black granite, fluted turrets of ice, and parapets roofed with snow. Their summits belonged to a realm partly of earth, partly of sky, but altogether hostile to life. They gathered weather around them according to their moods, sometimes appearing as massy bulks, stark black and white, that tore tufts of clouds from the Heavens; sometimes hovering gray and gauzy over mists that hid their heavy earthen foundations. They were called the Ferinus, and after I saw them, the round peaks of the Kingswood were forever diminished in my memory, made small and tame, less deserving of the title of mountains.

The closer we came to that wall, the more it was borne in upon us that the unbelievable rumor was true. The king was not merely running from the Wolves who were nipping at his heels; he was going where all along he had meant to go, to Lambanein. And taking us with him.

I didn't intend to be with the king when he tried to cross the mountains. There were others of the same opinion, even among the warriors of the Blood. Men sent out in foraging parties never came back. Did the Wolves get them, or had they deserted? One cataphract from the clan of Lynx slipped away with his armiger, horseboy, and jack, and when he was caught the king made no more speeches of good riddance. He had priests of Rift execute the mudmen outright. The cataphract and armiger were given more honorable deaths. They fought on foot, armed with scorpions and swords, against a priest with a bearclaw. It was over so quickly that people argued for days about exactly what had happened.

The men were sullen. The king's counselors quarreled, and their disagreements, which should have been secret, were taken up by cataphracts and varlets alike, as every man seemed to think himself wise enough to advise the king, if the king were only wise enough to listen.

I tried to bribe Mox to let the rope slip—there were many such mishaps on the road, he wouldn't be blamed for it. Or he could ride with us, didn't he want to get away? But he was the king's man now, an important fellow, and he refused. I was vexed, but I could hardly blame him for being more afraid of the dangers he knew—the Wolves, the king's priests—than the unknown Ferinus. We were all between one and the other, between sword and wall, as the saying goes. Mox watched us more warily after, and so did Garrio, when he found out.

And then the shiver-and-shake returned for its second visit, bestowing on me three more days of fever and chills, aches in my head and joints, aches everywhere. My strength was at such an ebb that I swayed in the saddle, and Catena had to haul me upright to keep me from toppling. I was near enough to dying that the veil between realms thinned, and I saw companies of the fallen mingling with those still alive. I glimpsed Penna perched on a bare stump of a fir that looked like the mast of a ship. I asked if she could help me and she called the way gulls do, as if laughing or weeping, and flew away southward.

Wildfire

My left eye saw the forelegs of our mare flashing as they struck the ground, one leg black, one with a white stocking, and every step closer to the Ferinus. My right eye saw Tobe, and here was the strange thing: he was walking on the bottom of a transparent lake, its waters turquoise in the shallows, cobalt in the depths, and I could see him clearly with his black hair floating about his face, and his skin blue, a blue boy. The stones of the lake bed seemed to be covered with snow that puffed up in a white cloud at his every footfall. The bright lake was in a round, steep-walled valley on the very peak of a mountain. I smelled and tasted the sharp tang of the vapors smoking up from the lake's surface. I called to Tobe, but he was too deep to hear me, or too intent on his journey.

The next morning the king was alone when he summoned me. I told him about the boy in the blue water, without telling him I'd dreamed it while awake. He asked what it meant. I said, "I don't know. Why don't you ask your prate?" and the king was angry. Afterward Garrio told me I should be more respectful.

My misery eased. The Heavens favored us, stilling the winds and giving us clear skies and the Sun's warmth. The Ferinus seemed near enough to touch, yet they were many leagues away. In another day's ride we came upon a solitary conical mountain rising from a high plateau, its slopes piebald with patches of snow and black scree. A lake was set in the hollow summit like a jewel in a stone clasp. There was no reason to climb the mountain; our way led past it. But the king sent Garrio to ask if it was the lake of which I'd dreamed, and I said yes.

Garrio took me to King Corvus. This time the king was attended by Divine Aboleo. I had to tell what I'd seen all over again, and my voice quavered when I spoke. Catena held my left hand, my fingers burning, hers cold.

The Auspex said the omen was clear as daylight. The lake belonged to the Queen of the Dead, and its color was of the blue that protects against the malefic eye. "We must ascend," Divine Aboleo said to the king, "and you must bathe in that lake and ask protection of the Queen of the Dead. The Wolves are the queenmother's baleful eye upon us, and that eye must be shut. She has cursed our every step so far."

The Auspex could read omens in a horse's entrails or the cawing of a couple of crows, and to him I was of the same order as horses or crows, nothing more than a vessel of signs. The king, however, seemed to see *me*. He looked on me with some distrust.

The four of us climbed the mountainside, and I took some secret amusement from seeing the king and his priest slow their pace to that of Catena.

With every step we slid and started cascades of stones down the slope. At the summit the walls of the lake were of jagged rock, coarse and dark as cinders.

King Corvus looked at the lake and the lake looked back, and it was hard to say which had the bluest stare. Wind ruffled the surface of the water and stirred the vapors, which smelled as they had in my dream of Tobe. I put my hand in the water and it was not merely warm, it was hot.

"Go in," the king said to me. "You enter first and we shall see."

Catena started sobbing. I asked her what the matter was and she wailed, "I can't swim!"

"Never you mind," I said. "You sit here on the sure and I'll go in."

It was awkward to disrobe while manacled. I took off my headcloth, and pulled my dress and underdress over my head and passed them to Catena with the left sleeve around the chain. I gave my pouch into her keeping. The cold air raised gooseflesh all over me. I was bony as the Crone herself, and ashamed to be seen naked by the king and his priest.

The water was clear and the bottom of the lake fell away steeply until it vanished into cobalt blue depths. I stepped onto a boulder, ankle deep, and white silt billowed around my feet. I winced at the heat and the king asked what was wrong. I shook my head and climbed down onto a ledge, and squatted with my left arm outstretched toward Catena. She reached toward me, the chain taut between us. The water was up to my neck and it was blissful. I was warmed through, even my cold right side. I put my face underwater and opened my eyes on a blue world. I took a sip of the lake and it tasted of salt and clay and metal, and was hot as a medicinal tisane. I sank deeper and my hair stirred around my face like sea hay in a rising tide. The water wakened me all over, cleansed me of the rough hide of dead skin and dirt I had lived in so long. I thanked Tobe for showing this lake to me.

Catena tugged on the chain and I lifted my head out of the water. She was crying as if she thought I meant to drown myself and pull her in after me.

"Cat, Cat . . . Catena," I said, "don't fret, it's quite safe." Clothed as I was in water, I dared to glance at the king. He abruptly looked away.

Divine Aboleo said, "Get out, and be quick about it."

I stood, and water ran down my skin and mist rose up from me. I wished I could have stayed in the lake all night. I climbed out and Catena pushed my clothing toward me over the chain. I dressed, first the left arm, then the rest of me, and the cloth stuck to my wet skin.

Divine Aboleo said, "Why do you wear the red cord around your waist?"

Wildfire

I kept my eyes on the ground and said, "To humor the Keen of the Dead. I mean honor her."

The Auspex grunted as if he doubted me. He said to the king, "Come, we must go around the lake. Can't you see the water is sullied here?"

We waited, eyes averted, as the king disrobed and entered the water, and Divine Aboleo followed him in, singing and chanting. In time the sky overhead became as dark as the blue heart of the lake.

Later Catena and I sat by a fire with Mox and Lame and Chunner, and they wanted to know why we had climbed the mountain with the king. Mox made rude guesses, and I told them the truth, seeing no harm in it. Rumor crept from one campfire to the next, and men slipped away to climb the mountain, by ones and twos at first, and then in groups with torches, to seek the lake's protection against the malefic eye of Queenmother Caelum.

The king's men held me in higher regard afterward. Cataphracts who had never spoken to me before greeted me by name; mud soldiers, on the contrary, grew tongue-tied. It was the Auspex who had claimed the lake for Rift Queen of the Dead, and said it would protect them—I knew nothing of that. It seemed to me the healing waters of that lake were sacred to many gods, Torrent and Ardor among them.

In the middle of the night, Garrio came to say the king summoned me. He had to carry Catena, who refused to wake up. King Corvus had a hut to himself. He sat cross-legged on a wool blanket over a pile of rushes. He wore his grimy red silk underarmor, and his long-boned feet were bare. Behind him was an upright loom with a half-finished blanket patterned in undyed wool, from black, white, and brown sheep such as we'd seen pastured in these hills.

Garrio put Catena down and left. I knelt beside her and looked at the floor.

"Did you dream?" the king asked.

It vexed me to be awakened to share his sleeplessness, and I was unready. I'd been too weary to cast the bones that night to fashion a dream that might please him. "I was just having a fish when Gabbery came to wake us. Now it's swimming off, I can hardly recollect it."

"Tell me what you remember."

I told him my real dream as best I could, though I protested it wasn't a true dream, as there were no odors in it. "I dreamt a whitewashed place, an inside place, a . . . room, all the color of skinned milk except for a row of four blue collars—pillars—that seemed to float in all the witness. Something was missing from that room, something red and tall that should have stood behind the blue uprights."

I watched the king's face from the corner of my left eye, seeing shadows cast there by the fire. He tried to be impassive, but the shadows made visible the smallest twitch of an expression.

"Is that all?" he said.

"I think—I think what was missing was a staring of a god. About so high, of wood or stone, and painted dread."

"You've been there, in that temple," he said in accusation.

I shook my head. "No, I never. Where is it?"

He spoke harshly in the language I now knew was that of Lambanein. I couldn't understand the words, but I understood the threat in them.

I bowed until my forehead touched the ground. "I swear I've never seen that white temper before. If you punish me for dreaming, I will dream no more."

"If I punish you, it will be for lying."

"I'm an honest seek, I can't always say what you wish to hear."

"Do you call yourself honest?"

"I told what I saw, but I don't see so well. I'm going blunt in one eye." I raised my head and pointed to my right eye. "My sight is dimming, but now and then I catch visitors, visions there."

The king came close and peered at my eye, and I stared over his shoulder. He said, "The webeye. How did you come by it so young?"

I'd been afraid it was webeye. I knew a woman once with webeye in both eyes, her blind irises like milky moonstones. "It came after the lightening."

"Look at me," he said. "Look at me and be an honest oracle, and without fear tell me what you see."

Unwillingly I looked him in the face. "Nothing."

"Nothing? That's honest enough."

"No—I meant—I mean I see with plain slight, no divisions. I see a king."

I saw what I had seen before, a face made of bone and flesh and shadow. I saw a man who had lost his wife and unborn son and been betrayed by his mother and brother. A man whose great dominion had dwindled to rule over rabble. He sought guidance from the same counselors who had misled him to defeat, and from signs and omens easily misread. He looked for wisdom even from me and I told him lies. He had no claim to my loyalty, therefore I couldn't betray him. I looked away and rubbed my wrist above and below the shackle. The flesh was hardening under the cuff, and the itch was terrible, worse than the pain of the raw sores. I refused to pity him.

"I see a man," I said.

*   *   *

Wildfire

The Wolves trailed King Corvus the way a pack trails a wounded stag. They thought they had him at bay before the wall of mountains. They captured one of his outriders and returned him with a message asking for a parley, and the king agreed to hear them out. He arrayed his men around an outcropping with a long view, and sat himself down on a boulder and ate a dinner of cold sausage and journey bread. Garrio heard the parley, which meant we heard about it later.

The leader in the wolfskin cloak rode up with another man in attendance. He said to the king that Queenmother Caelum sent him fond greetings; that she abhorred their estrangement and the necessity for war, and had the most fervent desire to bring reconciliation and peace now that the war was won. The prince (he called him prince) should have his throne back; it was his, after all. She wished for the good of the kingdom to be queen regent until Prince Corvus attained the wisdom to govern. She would grant him the northern keep as the seat of his throne, and he would no doubt find it as comfortable as she herself had found it during her years of exile. And with an elaborate bow (Garrio said, demonstrating), the Wolf offered King Corvus a glove of crimson velvet for his right hand.

Then he drew from his belt a mailed gauntlet, made for the left hand. If the prince refused the most generous offer of the right-hand glove, he must accept the gauntlet. The Wolves were ordered to take the prince alive so he could be executed in a manner befitting a coward. His corpse would be left unburned so his shade would have a long time to regret the folly of refusal.

The king seemed to be thinking it over, said Garrio. He said to the Wolf, "What of my men? Does she offer clemency?" And the Wolf just flapped his hand as if to say it was no great matter. So the king brushed a few crumbs from his beard and leaned back, propping himself on one hand and holding out the other, like so.

"Which hand?"

"If you can't guess," Garrio said to Mox, "you're more of a foolhead than I took you for."

Garrio made Mox and the other drudges laugh, and it surprised me how they were cheered by the king's refusal to surrender. They'd rather follow a reckless king than a craven one.

King Corvus chose his ground and turned on his pursuers. He set his warriors and mud soldiers on foot along the sharp spine of a ridge with their backs to the south and the low winter Sun. For the first time since the retreat began, the men bore the king's indigo banners on poles strapped to their backs. The Wolves would have to dismount and climb the ridge to

239

fight them, on a narrow trail with treacherous footing of loose rock and brittle slate.

The king offered Rift Warrior a gelding in sacrifice, and his Auspices pulled the entrails through a slit in the hide and pronounced the omens favorable for battle. A vulture descended in a spiral and landed on the dead horse, and burrowed its head into the belly. It was an ugly, ungainly thing on the ground, bald as a priest of Rift; all its grace was in flight. King Corvus pointed to the bird and called out to his men, "See how my father is with us today, and our sacrifice is accepted." The men raised a cheer, and some cataphracts hammered the hilts of their swords against their bucklers.

Catena and I sat on the ground, waiting for the battle on the curving backside of the ridge. Winds pushed heavy clouds toward us, and jacks wagered on whether the rain or the Wolves would get here first.

King Corvus stood not far uphill, speaking in private with his strategos. He didn't seem to mind that we might overhear, no more than he minded the horses grazing nearby. Yet I felt watched: two eyes stared at us from the back of his helmet, inlaid in lapis and mother-of-pearl.

The king said, "It's true I feel my father close—he sometimes speaks to me, saying fire begets ashes. Or he wonders if his son is his son. Did you know even a shade cannot be sure if his wife cuckolded him? I ask him for counsel and he reminds me he won his first battle at the age of fifteen. I tell him I lost my first at twenty. I fear he comes to mock, not to help."

Divine Aboleo's bald scalp was bare, displaying his red rooster tattoo. He turned toward the king. "I hope he mocks you out of your melancholy, for I tire of it."

Our chance was coming, I was sure of it, and oh, I was impatient. But the hillside was naked, and we were as easy to spot as a mole on Mai's broad back. No cover until we got to the bottom of the ridge, among the trees and boulders. And we'd have to go on foot. The saddled horses were well guarded by horseboys.

So we waited. Catena yawned and leaned against my shoulder and in time she fell asleep, which much amazed me. The clouds moved toward us, letting down their long hanks of rain. And soon we were inside the storm and it was twilight gray and cold and pitiless. The horses hung their heads and turned their rumps to the wind.

Someone caught sight of Wolves on the next hill over and a cheer went up that woke Catena. We stood and held hands, the same hands already linked by a chain. The Wolves carried the queenmother's banners of crimson edged with white, the colors darkened by the rain. The sight awakened the memory of the first true dream I'd ever had, of riding with my father when I was a small child through bare and rocky mountains. In the dream we had turned to see a line of soldiers with black banners on a mountain behind us.

I shivered and knew that gods were gathering here. Nothing interests them so much as war.

The king and his men stood outlined against the sky, offering battle. The Wolves howled as they approached, and the king's warriors hammered on their shields. Catena and I began to creep down the ridge without a word said between us. I was afraid if we ran, a horseboy would take notice.

Some Wolves reached the top of the hill, and the king's men crowded around the head of the trail until priests of Rift, bellowing and pushing, made them get back in line along the crest and await their turns. I saw men fighting, caught in a net of rain. The ground was so stony that the water ran over it in small rivulets. Some of the rivulets turned red. A man screamed for his mother until someone silenced him.

A Wolf broke through the line and came hurtling down the hill toward us so fast it seemed he might outrun his own legs. He carried an ax and his banner swayed above his head. A horseboy shouted "Hoy!" and ran after him with sword drawn, and I saw the horseboy was Mox, in a boiled leather cuirass molded in the shape of a man's muscular torso, which made his thin arms and legs look like spindles.

Mox and the Wolf collided and horses whinnied and shied away from them. Mox sat down abruptly with his feet straight out in front of him, and clutched his groin; the Wolf fell in a heap as if his garments had just been emptied.

Catena tugged at the chain, hurrying downhill.

I tugged back. "We must see if Mock needs help."

"But the Wolf might be alive!"

I made Catena follow. Mox had a slash in his groin, along the crease between his right leg and abdomen. He held his hand over the cut and blood oozed between his fingers. I pulled the queenmother's banner from the pole on the Wolf's back and told Mox to press it hard over his wound. I cursed the chain, the king, and even Catena, who gawked and hindered me.

The Wolf—who was not a warrior of the Blood, but a mere varlet—had a hole in his chest. Pink foam bubbled from the wound and air whistled in and out. His lips were turning purple and his chest heaved. He was awake and aware, and helpless to do anything but try to breathe. I took his dagger and cut a small strip of cloth from my hem, and wadded it up and tamped it into his wound. The whistling and bubbling stopped. His eyes rolled in his head. His mouth was wide open, but no air went in or out, only a spill of frothy blood. He began to thrash. Mox was shouting, "Let him alone!" I ought not to have touched the varlet, I knew that, but I acted in desperation. I treated him as I would have treated a woman, and it seemed I'd done it all wrong.

I pulled out the cloth and the man gasped and foam gushed from the hole. The next time I waited until he had exhaled before covering the wound, and he kept breathing. Then I stole his leather wallet, cutting the straps that fastened it to his belt.

Mox must have thought I was trying to kill the man. He said, "I'll finish him. I thought I'd done for him already."

I was amazed to see the man struggle to sit up and speak. His voice was hoarse and wheezy. "A pox on you, you sowpricking pizzle. Come and get me, if you think you can."

"I will too," Mox said. He got up and swung his sword at the varlet seated on the ground, and the man parried with the haft of his ax, and there was a dull thunk when steel met ironwood. Mox was just a horseboy, he'd never been trained like the warriors of the Blood to guard and attack and counter. Nor had Rift Warrior blessed him with a killing frenzy. He seemed as frightened by the blows he struck as the ones aimed at him. He had a look of disgust on his face. But he went on striking at the man. He warmed to it.

Catena needed no urging to run for it. The shackle forced us to match strides, though my legs were much longer than hers. She tripped once and pulled me down after her. Her wooden pattens were ill suited to running or climbing or winter. We put two steep hills between us and the battle, resting when we had to, while somewhere behind the clouds, behind the mountains, the Sun descended to her rest. The cold rain turned to sleet, and Catena said she could go no farther. We sought shelter under an outcropping, but the wind that came blustering down the narrow valley flung sleet in our faces. Soon the trees were sheathed in ice. All around us in the dark, tree limbs cracked and came crashing down.

We didn't dare light a fire, but my hearthfire blazed up when I called on it, so I no longer felt the cold. I burned fever hot, and I poured this heat lavishly into Catena as she lay shivering in my arms.

The clouds moved away and took the sleet with them, and the sky lightened. The Sun climbed over the mountains and showed us a white and shiny world. Needles and twigs sparkled. Branches of fir and pine hung low, weighed down by ice, and the trunks had pale gashes where limbs had been torn away. The ground was strewn with storm wrack. Uprooted trees leaned on neighbors, or lay on the ground in a welter of broken branches.

Wildfire

I shook Catena awake, saying we should be going.

"Let's go back," she said. "Please, the battle must be over by now."

"Go back? What if the Worms won, what then?"

"They didn't win."

"How do you know?"

Catena pinched her lips together and wouldn't explain.

We'd never spoken of escape. I thought there was no need. Surely she hated the shackle and chain as much as I did. Was she loyal to the king? His cruelty toward her was more terrible because it sprang from indifference to whether she suffered or no, lived or no.

"Come on, we've got to scurry. We'll freeze otherwise." I stood and Catena remained sitting.

"Can't we build a fire? I'm cold."

Stupid, stubborn girl. I sat down again and emptied out the wallet I'd stolen from Mox's opponent. The varlet had carried four dice, eleven copperheads, half a loaf of bread, a shred of dried beef, and a flint. I gave Catena the bread and meat and tucked the flint into the pouch I hid under my skirts. "Eat a bittle," I said. "Then we must be going."

"Going back?"

I had the varlet's dagger. The head of the rivet that fastened my manacle had been hammered flat, and I tried to get the blade under it to see if I could pry it out.

Catena held the bread in her lap and stared. "What are you doing?"

"What do you think? Once these mankles are off, you can do as you like, go back or sit here and roast your tots by a fire, I don't care. We left a trial a plowboy could follow, let alone a Howl or a pride of Rift, and I'm not about to wait for anyone to come and catch us."

I sawed at the shank of the rivet, enraged by the thousand petty annoyances of the shackle, how it baffled and balked me at every move, how it chafed our thin skins and left us raw. I succeeded in dulling the blade, nothing more. It was a poor man's dagger, of poor steel.

Catena clutched her knees and watched me sideways. She shivered and a tear ran down her cheek. I bit my lower lip and turned my attention to the chain. I found a link with a large gap and tried to lever the ends apart with the dagger. The link bit the blade and spat out the point, which struck me above the eye. I turned to Catena and shouted, "What's the natter with you? Don't you want to be free?"

She looked at me as if I'd betrayed her, as indeed I had. What had I been thinking, threatening to abandon her in the woods? I shouldn't wonder at her reluctance. She'd been stolen from the kitchens and thrust into the midst of strangers, but the strange had become familiar, even comforting. Garrio had saved her morsels from his master's dinner, and Mox had given her a stolen doll made of rags, and Chunner had teased her and made her laugh. She thought she was safe with them.

I put down the dagger and clasped both her hands between mine. "Contenta, I think we must seek a tillage, village, don't you think? We don't know who *won*, sweethearth. We must go forthwith, not back. And you'll feel warmer walking."

She didn't agree. We sat on the cold ground and quarreled, a dispute of few words and many silences. In the end she gave in, though I hadn't convinced her. She was frightened into it, more like, afraid of my anger. I hated to bully her, but it had to be done.

We turned east, and it was strange, after journeying so long southward, to head resolutely in another direction. I saw no paths, but there were signs of men: hazel coppices and stumps of trees felled by axes; a place where pigs had rooted for acorns. Catena slithered in her pattens on the icy banks and fell often, jerking the chain and galling us both. I scraped resin from a pine tree and smeared it on her wooden soles to make them sticky. She sulked and wouldn't speak.

We walked a long way before I dared climb to the top of a hill. The only smoke I saw was behind us, roiling up in a black column. They must have been burning the dead of the battle. To the south, the mountains glared white, glazed in ice. Already the day was half gone, and we were closer to the battlefield and the mountains than I expected to be. No village in sight, no village anywhere.

By the time the Sun descended toward a notch between two peaks, Catena had tired. I tried carrying her on my back; she was lighter than when she'd left the temple kitchens, but by the gods she was still too heavy.

We halted on the edge of a steep bluff. The valley below held twilight, and a shining silver river edged with a lace of ice and fringed with golden reeds. I'd hoped to get farther east before turning north, and it would be good to put that river between us and any pursuers. But how could we ford it chained together?

I looked up and down the valley, and saw gray dots of sheep on a distant slope. Ice turned rosy in the last sunlight. I prayed to Ardor as I had prayed all day, and this time with more hope: *Ardor, guide us to a smith.*

We descended the bluff, slipping sideways down the path of an old landslide. Down by the river night had fallen, and I stood on a marshy shore, wet up to my shins where I'd crunched through the ice. My feet burned from the cold. I heard rustling in the bracken, and turned to see a lynx slouching out on the rim of ice to drink. It looked our way and its eyes flashed gold. We stared at each other, more curious than frightened. It had a fine white ruff around its neck, and jaunty black topknots on its ears. The lynx turned to the water and lapped, and blinked at me again, and then crept into the river and swam. The current carried it sideways, but I saw its head bobbing until it reached the other shore.

Lynx offered to guide me, but to what destination? Lynx Foresight had made me captive in the first place; Lynx Mischief might lead me astray for a prank. But one couldn't ask for a clearer sign. We'd seek a crossing tomorrow, when the Sun could warm us and dry our clothes.

I used my stolen flint to cajole a flame from shredded bark, and soon had a fire going, and put stones in it to heat. Catena wrapped herself in my cloak and fell asleep. I fanned the fire so no sharp-eyed pursuer would see a dark smear of smoke across the stars, but in truth I'd already made up my mind we were not followed. Perhaps the king had lost the battle—perhaps he was dead.

There was an unwelcome thought in my mind. It had been there ever since I'd broken the point of the dagger on the iron link: how much more easily the blade would cut flesh and even bone. Poachers say a badger will gnaw off its own foot to free itself from a snare. To sacrifice one hand would free us both—though the wound would be grievous, it would bleed and bleed and it might mortify. It might kill. I held the edge of the blade to the back of my wrist, to see what it would feel like. I pressed hard and drew a red line.

I feared I didn't have the strength to cut off my own hand; it would have to be Catena's. The knife was dull and I would have to saw back and forth. I doubted I could saw through the bone. I'd have to get the knife between the knobs of the joints, like a carver taking apart a goose. She wouldn't sleep through it. She would fight.

If there came a time when I must, when she would die or I would die if I didn't—then I would.

But by then I might not have the strength. I should do it now. How could I swim across the river with one arm bound and Catena on my back? I'd seen her when we forded rivers, clinging in terror to the saddle. Likely she'd choke me.

Even my thoughts were shackled, every one brought up short by the chain.

I put the dagger down and draped the chain over a flat rock and took up the heaviest stone in reach and pounded on a link with all my strength. Once, twice, thrice. The chain jumped and twisted under the blows. Catena started awake and asked what I was doing, and I kept pounding, praying to Ardor Smith, asking if ever he favored me to make the iron brittle. The stone cracked and split in my hand and I took up another one, ignoring how my palm stung with every blow. The sound of the hammering carried across the hills, each clang with its diminishing echoes, and it was too loud but I. Would. Not. Stop.

I was weeping. No use, no use, no use, the hammering said, until at last I was defeated. Catena sat with her shoulders hunched, as if she feared I'd strike her next.

I looked up and saw a man standing between birch trees. He had a shaven head and a black cloak, and for a moment I thought he was the shade of the priest Mole and I had fought. But he was truly there, a living man and not a shade, I could tell by the orange fire reflected in his black pupils, which flickered as his eyes glanced from Catena to me. I recognized him by his unmoving, ever-open eye, the one tattooed on his scalp: Divine Volator, the young priest who had executed the king's sentries when they failed in their duties. He moved forward and squatted by the fire, and held out his empty hands to warm them. A peaceable gesture. He wasn't planning to kill us.

I let out the breath I'd been holding. "So the king won," I said.

It wasn't a question, and he made no answer. He never spoke to us, not once on the long way back.

I was ashamed before the priest, as if he could tell by looking at me that I had contemplated severing Catena's hand. I was ashamed also to feel relief that he had found us. He had spared me the decision and the act, and was it so much easier to be told what to do? I was a coward twice over, once for being willing to maim Catena to save my skin, and again for lacking the boldness to do it. Twice shamed, twice craven, and captive once again.

CHAPTER 17

Lost

y the time Divine Volator led us back to the army, the dead had been tallied and praised and burned and the Battle of Boarsback Ridge had become a storied victory. Each man told his friends what he'd seen and boasted of what he'd done. Though their accounts didn't agree in every particular, all swore that the king had slain many Wolves himself, three or four at least. The enemy broke, and there was a fine chase, and the Wolves were hunted down like the stray dogs they were. They'd harry us no more.

I made my own tallies of who was missing, and I learned roundabout, for it went unspoken, that the king had lost more men after the battle than in it. Many had frozen to death during the sleet storm, weakened by wounds, fatigue, and sickness. I should have rejoiced that the king had lost so many followers. But I saw the shade of a horseboy named Lino, who'd stolen grain from his master for our mare, and his eyes were rimed with frost, staring at nothing. I saw Mano with his clever hands turned to marble, cold and hard and veined with gray. I was sorry I'd learned their names. As for the nameless dead, the smudges of shadow I saw in my right eye—I refused to look.

Catena and I had run in the wrong direction. Not a league west-of-south was a village with a smithy. We stopped there so the farrier could make calked sandals with spikes for the horses to wear on the icy roads of the mountains. Garrio was sorry about it, but he conveyed the king's orders to the farrier, who shortened the chain between Catena and me until it measured the length from my elbow to my wrist. Awkward, impossible, a torment to us both. Catena wept that night with her head on my shoulder. She blamed me, but she took what comfort I could give.

We were never going to get away. We were going to die in the mountains. Or if we lived to see the other side, I'd be a world away from Galan.

I decided never to tell the king a dream again, and I waited to see if he would kill me or let me go.

247

King Corvus summoned me. The victory had cheered his men, but he looked at me with a familiar bleak expression. He had a split lip and bruises on the bony prominences of his face, and bandages on one leg and both arms. A wolfskin cloak covered his back, with the forelegs tied loosely around his throat. He asked what I had dreamed, and I told him I couldn't remember. He didn't dismiss us, but turned his eyes away, and Catena and I stood leaning upon each other, waiting, while cold climbed from the ground into our feet and up our legs, until Garrio hissed at us to leave.

I told King Corvus the same thing the next morning, and by then he must have known I was lying. He didn't threaten, but all the same it frightened me to defy him.

For two days the king didn't send for me, and I began to hope he would forget about us, so we could fall behind, slip away. A couple of jacks sought me out to say that now I'd lost the king's favor, they'd be having sport with me, and Catena too. Nothing like a virgin to whet a man's prick, they said, being the kind of men who enjoyed a girl's fright. Garrio and Mox saw them off, but I was reminded that even the king's indifference was dangerous.

We followed the road to Owl Pass, and rumpled foothills became the skirts of the mountains, and peaks glowered down on us from all sides. The road dwindled to a goat track, and the track forked and the forks branched, and many small trails climbed over naked shoulders of rock, leading to nowhere but high pastures, windswept or buried under snow.

We were lost. Not a man in what was left of the king's army knew the way.

After two days of wandering, we came to a village walled around by thornbushes, in a long and narrow valley. I was amazed anyone could live in such a stony place. The thatched roofs of the huts swept nearly to the ground, reminding me of the conical straw hats of reapers. The men of the village prostrated themselves before the king. All the women had fled.

Wheezer said around here they didn't care much for kings. He'd been born in a village like this, and knew every trick they used to hide what they had from tax collectors. He took pleasure in searching out beets and turnips and baskets of grain buried under the dirt floors, and bacon in the rafters. But they were poor folk, and there wasn't much to go around, not for hundreds of men.

The king's men took carved spoons, blankets, furs, hay, firewood, sheep, goats, and shaggy mountain ponies from the village. Some cataphracts stole a few women too, or rather girls no older than Sunup, whom they found hiding in a cave farther up the valley. To be sure a maid is fit to bed, the saying goes, pluck one too young to wed. When the girls screamed and wept they were beaten.

The king commanded the village headman to guide us, and for three days he led us on trails marked with high cairns of stones. Often we had to dig passage from one cairn to the next through snowdrifts. The guide spoke in such a rough accent that it was hard to tell he was speaking the High, and sometimes Wheezer had to translate his assurances: Yes, this was the path to Owl Pass, didn't he know every path in these mountains? Of course it was impossible, this was not the season for it—we should try next summer; nevertheless it was the way to Owl Pass.

The headman led us to the burrow of an old mine, in a canyon with no way out but the same dangerous way we'd come in. Then he had the audacity to taunt the king, and boast he'd led him into a trap in revenge for his daughter, who had been among the girls taken. She'd died of her injuries. He was stoned to death like vermin, and his body left for wolves, the real wolves that sang nightly from ridge to ridge. We doubled back for two days, treading in our own footprints, until we found another route. Rumor had it the king sent priests all the way back to the village to burn it to the ground.

I'd tried to save the headman's daughter, but I hadn't been able to stop her bleeding. In truth, I'd wanted to shun her and the other girls as if their plight was a pestilence. As if it might happen to me. There was little enough I could do for them: give them bandages or poultices or the warmth of my hand. I never asked their names. A few days of hard use smothered the spark of life in their eyes, and they stared back at me as distant as shades. And then they were gone—set free or abandoned, it amounted to the same thing. I wondered how many found their way home, and what welcome they got there.

The king and I were both stubborn. He went on summoning me, and I went on saying I hadn't dreamed, or couldn't remember. Some days he was alone; sometimes Divine Aboleo was at his side. Often Garrio waited in attendance, ignored by the king as if he were a chair or a dog. Garrio would plead with me afterward to tell the king something, anything—to avoid the king's wrath, he said. But I knew Garrio thought I could help, and refused for spite.

In truth I dreamed vividly, plentifully—of tables piled with food and beds piled with quilts, dreams that left me neither full nor warm. But some were more nourishing. I dreamed of the house on Mount Sair, where it was spring. I worked in the garden, dividing and transplanting roots, sowing seeds, planting slips of red osier to make a living fence, for willow is quick to root. I ate ramps and spinach and pintle shoots and fiddleheads, everything green and full of life. Dreams of no use to the king, even if I'd recounted them.

By then many of King Corvus's men believed I was a dreamer blessed by Lynx Foresight. One day a cataphract sent his jack, Voro by name, with a question: Has my wife taken a lover? I told Voro I would fish for a dream, and the next morning he returned for an answer.

I had dreamed of the king. He visited a keep in company with its owner, and the owner's dogs, shaggy, dun-colored hounds, greeted the king with gladness, fawning and groveling and licking his hands. Days later he returned to the keep alone, and the dogs attacked him. I told this dream to Voro without mentioning the king. And I believe I said something like *dog-collared horneds* instead of dun-colored hounds, along with a few other mishaps of the tongue. Voro smirked and gave me a gift from his master, a hood lined with squirrel fur and adorned with tippets of squirrel tail, which I gave to Catena.

The dream lacked the lucidity or odor of a true dream, but I thought there might be truth in it nevertheless, and a warning I refused to deliver, about the welcome the king might expect, arriving uninvited at the home of his wife's father in Lambanein.

The king summoned me and I told him I hadn't dreamed. I suffered the same belly-clenching fear I felt every day that I refused him, but this morning I felt satisfaction besides. Garrio was right, I was spiteful.

If I could have dreamed a true dream by command, surely I would have dreamed a way to escape. At night I threw the bones and searched for patterns, hoping the Dame and Na would offer guidance. By day we climbed and climbed and our road seemed that much steeper to me because every step led away from Galan.

We camped about noontime near a forest of stunted trees, mostly oak and pine—I'd seen this in the Kingswood, how the higher one climbed, the shorter the trees became, and the more twisted by the wind. The king ordered his men to gather firewood, for soon we must cross stony heights where there would be nothing to burn but what we carried with us.

We'd used up the flour, turnips, and coleworts taken from the last village we'd passed, days before. Catena complained of hunger. She hadn't gone a day without eating in her life and thought she might die of it. Hard work in the kitchens had toughened her, but she was used to kitchen comforts too, plentiful scraps and warm ovens. She wasn't the only one going hungry. By now, besides Mox and Lame and Chunner, five or six lads shared a fire and food with us at night, masterless horseboys or those with cruel masters, who came to us after being turned away from other campfires.

Wildfire

I saw no reason we should go hungry, when the gods offered gifts of food even in these austere wintry mountains. Usually I was forced to pass them by, and it irked me that I couldn't forage, hampered as I was by the chain, watched always to see I didn't stray.

Tonight we would dine well, I told the horseboys, if they would help. Mox scoffed at this, asking if I expected to feast on snow soup.

I said, "I wager we can make some snow sop that even you will find eatable."

"Out of what?"

"Out of haycorns, of course."

Mox said only swine ate acorns. He came from Malleus, and distrusted any crop that didn't need the help of man to thrive. But in the Dame's village, people ate acorns in lean years, and I'd always found them tasty. Mox let us go gathering, and came along to keep an eye on us. It was late in the year to be harvesting, but we filled several sacks with acorns, and then sat by the fire, discarding worm-eaten ones, hulling good ones, and pounding the kernels with stones to make a coarse meal. Catena and the boys talked and laughed, and with so many hands the work went fast. We boiled some of the meal to leach out the bitterness, and the rest we tied in sacks and left to leach in a swift-flowing stream, under the ice.

The acorn soup was bland and sweet, and Mox liked it well enough once he was persuaded to try it. We also roasted pine cones so the scales would open, and shook out the seeds and cracked them between our teeth. Garrio came to our fire late in the evening, after tending to the king's comfort, and he brought us mutton bones and an onion; we started a new soup, having eaten the other all up. A jack came by and stood watching us, not begging, not saying anything. Lame went to shoo him away, and I said, "Let him sit. There's enough to go about." His name was Marestail, and he took a dead snow hare from his pack and shared it with us.

The next morning I made heavy cakes of roasted acorn meal, mixing it with dried currants and lard Garrio gave me—cakes to eat and cakes to carry. And we loaded sacks of acorns and pine cones on our horses, though men laughed at us.

We entered the domain of ice and stone. It was so cold it hurt to breathe. Snow did not fall there, it flew, and scoured skin from our faces even as the wind tried to pry flesh from our bones. When we were not blinded by snow, we were blinded by the Sun, which made our eyes water so that our eyelashes froze. Men grew icicles from their mustaches and beards. I tore strips from a stolen blanket to wrap Catena's head and hands and feet, and she wore what was left like a cloak. We covered our faces with gauze, and

251

soon the cloth was frozen hard. The iron manacles stuck to our wrists and pulled off scabs and skin.

Many horses were lost, and men had to walk, and our pace slowed. The mounted men in the forefront of the line sometimes were able to stay on top of the snow crust, but more often had to advance through the drifts. It was no easier for those behind, tramping through slush, or breaking through the crust only to be caught by the pocked ice beneath. Ice balled up under the horses' hooves, and they couldn't stay on their feet.

Sometimes the king's outriders found promising routes—false promises, wasting days, wasting lives. We were all disheartened by it. The king was no longer searching for Owl Pass. He wanted to go south, so we went south, and when we couldn't we went east or west or turned north until we could go south again. He was as implacable as the weather.

Lame's horse died, and it was hard for him on foot, with one leg shorter than the other. We came upon him sitting in the snow, and he said he was giving up, he couldn't go any farther.

I slid down from the black mare, and told him to climb up behind Catena. Lame shook his head in mute denial. He had such a look in his eyes, as if he were already dead and long departed on his journey, too far away to care about the living. I couldn't lean over to shake him, because of the chain, so I kicked snow at him and yelled, "Are you weaker than a little glad, a little girl? Look at Taken . . . Caten, she isn't complaining."

"I can't feel my feet," he said.

"Then you shouldn't walk on them for a while. Come on, up you go."

Mox was ashamed then, and offered his horse to Lame, and all afternoon we took turns riding, the horseboys and me. Walking was so hard, I didn't wonder Lame had wanted to give up.

In camp that night I looked at his feet. The tips of his toes and toenails had turned white and hard and wooden from frostbite. I wrapped his toes in gauze torn from my underdress, and tucked one foot under my arm and held the other in my left hand, and gave him heat. When the flesh thawed the pain was so bad that Lame wept.

Garrio asked me to warm his hands, which had turned red and speckled from chilblains, and what Garrio knew, others were sure to find out. Some I couldn't help; it was too late to stop their fingers or toes from the blackening. A certain jack who had pestered me before came by to tell me his dangle was frostbitten and stiff, and asked if I would thaw it. I warmed his hands, and said he must do the rest himself, as I was sure he knew how. The horseboys drove him away with their laughter.

Frostbite was painful and disfiguring, but the mountains sent more deadly afflictions too. Sometimes the afflictions killed outright, sometimes by making a man daft, so he made foolish mistakes that killed him. I could help with the chills that caused a man to shake and turn white and suffer confusions; I gave him heat, and steadied his hearthfire with my warm hand over his heart. But I didn't know what to do about the drowning, which caused a man to suffocate on bloody froth from his bellows.

Sometimes men came to me for help when I was exhausted and low in spirits, and every ember of my hearthfire was smothered under a heap of ash. I had to reach deep inside me for something that could burn, and it was painful, as if I scraped marrow from my bones. But I couldn't refuse. It made no difference whether I liked a man or disliked him, I was given the gift that I might share it. And there were times—rare and blessed—when the Hearthkeeper opened a way through me to hearthfire, forgefire, and wildfire, all of these at once: allfire, I called it. I blazed then, and never felt the cold, and by Ardor's grace I was a hearthfire to others.

We made camp on a steep ice field, surrounded by stone spires crowded along a curved ridge like too many teeth in a jaw. The summit of the mountain rose high above the ridge. All day we'd climbed toward those stone teeth, hoping we were crossing the shoulder of the last mountain before the southern foothills, for we could see nothing higher than the peak we labored under. But when we reached the top of the ridge, we saw another mountain before us, and others ranked behind it.

From above, the ice field had looked like a wrinkled gray tongue, but as we descended to it we found the wrinkles were deep fissures. We walked a narrow path between turquoise boulders and pinnacles and crevasses. In places wind had polished the ice until it was slick and shiny; elsewhere it was littered with gravel and broken stones. The king sent scouts to find a way down, for it was too dangerous to go on.

The ice turned gold and orange as the Sun descended behind the peak that barred our way south. The sky was blue glass. Wind swooped down on us from the ridge above. Auspices sacrificed a lame horse, looking within it for a map to get us through the mountains, but the entrails were as twisted and coiled as the path we had traveled to get to that slope.

We had run out of wood. For days we had gone without campfires: no heat to guard against the devouring cold, and no light to shelter us from the immensity of night. We mudfolk warmed ourselves by the carcass of the dead horse, and ate its flesh raw—tough and chewy, but better food than none, which was what the Blood got, being forbidden to eat horse meat. And I was grateful to the horse, which had been sacrificed so we might have guidance and warmth and sustenance, but it frightened me to see us that way, mouths and chins bloody. How close we were, after all, to beasts; Artifex made us, but it was Ardor's blessing, fire, that made us mankind.

Men heaped ice in rough walls to make a shelter against the wind. Catena and I were in the lee of the wall, Lame on one side and Chunner on the other, in the midst of a crowd of varlets. We shared warmth and cloaks and blankets, and also lice and stink and coughs. I made sure the youngest boys stayed in the middle of the pack, and the others took turns on the outside. A man could freeze to death with his back unprotected.

I sucked on a lump of snow, and my thirst was not quenched. I heard water running in the depths below, and wondered if it flowed south out of the mountains, or if it was trapped, as we were. This ice field was a frozen torrent, and horses might die of thirst tonight for lack of the water locked in it.

The ice field rumbled and grated and creaked, and made sudden cracks that sounded like tree limbs breaking; worst of all, it moaned, long and sonorous moans that came from everywhere and nowhere. Wind keened between the stone teeth and roared down the mountainside. I heard eerie harmonies in the din, and thought of the mountains resounding night after night to this song, a song not meant for our ears.

Catena curled up beside me with her head in my lap and panted. The higher we climbed, the harder she fought for breath. Every time I dozed, I woke up afraid she might have died. I warmed her hands and feet with care, and looked for red streaks or signs of the blackening around the iron cuff on her wrist. It made me flush hot with shame to think I'd wanted to cut off her hand. I hugged her and rocked a little, praying that the gods who'd seen fit to protect her so far would keep her safe through what was to come.

I thought Catena had fallen asleep, so I was surprised when she asked me to sing. Sometimes she wanted a song, sometimes a story to comfort her. That night I said it was her turn. Didn't the cooks sing as they worked? She must give me one of those songs.

She sat up and said she would teach me a chain.

"What's that?"

"I sing first and then you start, and we sing the same thing round and round, making links in the chain. You see? It goes like this:

> *Who made the bread to rise?*
> *I did with my leaven*
> *Who made the bread to bake?*
> *I put it in your oven.*"

254

Wildfire

She had a thin voice, and I could hardly hear her over the noise of the ice and wind. She said, "I sing, *Who made the bread to rise?* Then you begin while I keep going."

"It's a silthy song," I said, and Catena giggled.

She began and I sang next, and I stumbled at first, but soon we were going round and round, her voice climbing in a question while mine was descending in an answer, and then mine rising while hers was falling. Chunner joined Catena, and Marestail sang with me, and before long others were singing as well, a small knot of us making a clamor in defiance of the frightful sounds of the mountain.

Mox sang a drinking song. He said his dead father, the old sot, had taught it to him in a dream. The song went:

> *I, even I, must die,*
> *So why should I bother to try?*
> *It is better to die drinking,*
> *Than to lie thinking,*
> *That I, even I, must die.*

A very fine song, it was agreed. Too bad there was no ale to go with it. We bellowed it over and over and I saw cataphracts and armigers singing too.

I said I had a song to keep them warm. I said each of them had a hearthfire inside that they must tend carefully so it would not go out. When they had need of warmth, they could sing this song Ardor gave me, and when they did, they must think about adding wood to their hearthfires to make them blaze up. I was daunted by their sudden silence, but I sang out anyway:

> *Burn bright, burn fast.*
> *Give what light you can,*
> *The rest is ash.*

I sang it three times alone, time enough to conclude it was a poor song after all. But when Catena took it up she made a chain of it, and the links fit together as if they were meant to be sung that way. For a few more rounds it was just the two of us, her clear voice and my lower one. I faltered, and a deep voice joined in and gave me strength, and another and another. The mountain seemed to take notice. Ice cornices cracked and fell from the ridge, and snow slid like waterfalls down rock faces, and plumes of crystals rose glittering in the moonlight.

I looked at the faces of the men, their heads thrown back or bobbing, mouths stretching wide, singing out to keep from fear. Some of them had done cruel things, I'd seen this for myself—they'd taken food from the mouths of poor folk, burned houses, forced themselves on women and girls, robbed from each other. There were some among them who'd let another man die rather than suffer the inconvenience of helping. At times I'd thought it would be for the best if the Ferinus swallowed all the king's men.

But now I saw them flickering in the wind like candle flames. How could I wish any of them dead, when we burn for such a short time and are so easily snuffed out?

I threw the bones in the darkness under my cloak, while Catena was sleeping, and asked the Dame and Na for help, as I had asked many times. I went to sleep thinking of the godsigns they'd shown me, and some of them—the Sun, the Stallion, the Warrior—were woven into my dreams that night. I had a true dream of my father, the third I'd had of him, and it began the way the first dream had ended.

We were going home after selling the colt, riding over a saddle between two mountains. Before us was a narrow lake in a valley far below; behind us, on another mountain, was a line of horsemen bearing black banners. The line stretched around the mountain's flanks and we couldn't see the end of it. There was snow on the mountain peaks, but the sunlight was hot and glaring. I smelled dust. My father had a pointed reddish brown beard and a hat of embroidered blue felt. He shaded his eyes, looking back at the horsemen. "Come now," he said. "You must get on the horse with me."

I said, "But, Fedan, I'm not a baby. I can ride by myself." Fedan was not his name, it was a word meaning father in a language I'd forgotten. I'm not sure what language we spoke in the dream, but we understood each other.

I was on my sorrel pony. Her hair was like my own in color, and she was as sure on the mountain trails as my father's roan gelding, and I said so. Fedan leaned from his saddle to untie the lead from the pack mule's halter. He flicked the mule on the rump with the rope, and she took a few steps and stood bewildered. My father was frowning, and he spoke in the voice he used when he was vexed with me. "Come here! Hurry now!"

I was frightened by his anger and did as he asked. I slid off my pony's back and handed the reins up to my father, but he wouldn't take them. He said, "Take off the bridle. She'll find her own way home."

My father dismounted to lift me into his saddle and he got up behind me. He'd let me ride his horse Ganos before, so I wasn't afraid for myself, but I was sure wolves would eat my pony. I let the tears fall, but I didn't sob; I didn't want him to know I was crying. We went at a gallop over the bare turf of the pass and down through the forest of stunted trees and down until we reached a precipice. When we halted, Ganos had dark patches of sweat on his withers. I could smell the horse's sweat, and my father's.

We stood on the cliff's edge looking down past flocks of clouds to the floor of the valley, where our town was one of many nestling in folds of the mountains by the lakeshore. Ancient pine trees grew in crevices on the rock face below our feet, some upright, some leaning or twisted, but all lopsided, with branches on one side only, growing toward the void. No man would dare cut those pines. I knew that without being told, the way one knows things in dreams—just as I knew there was a trail down the precipice.

Yet when I awoke, I was doubtful. There were things in the dream that made no sense. Surely I was too young to be riding to market over the mountains—in the dream I was too small to reach my father's stirrup. I remembered that in the second true dream I'd had of him, he had teased me, saying he needed me to do the haggling or he'd sell the colt too cheap. I wondered why I'd been so favored. Had I no brothers?

I wondered also why I'd never seen my mother in a dream, the mother who must have embroidered the red and yellow checks on my little felt cap. I shied away from thinking of her. Better to think of my father, his strong weathered hands, and the familiar scent of him, hard work and leather and horses. But his sweat had been pungent with fear.

The king summoned me in the morning. He sat on a seat hacked from ice and covered with a wolfskin, and he had a red silk cloth wrapped around his face against the cold, so that only his eyes were showing. He was a man of tawny complexion, but the cold had pinched away his color. His skin looked waxen, and his black eyelashes and brows were stark against it. The silk fluttered when he spoke. He asked the question he always asked.

I'd made up my mind to help him, but I didn't want him to know it. I lifted my left hand and Catena's swollen right hand rose with it. She whimpered when I pulled on the chain. "I did dream," I said, "but why should I tell you?"

The king's eyes were slits above the red cloth. "Why should I let you live?"

Catena knelt down and hid her face against my side and whispered, "Don't, please don't. He'll kill us."

I'd made up my mind he wouldn't kill us—no, certainly he didn't intend to kill us—no more than he meant to kill all the men who'd died in his service. I shook the chain and said, "If you find me a way out of these mangles, I might find you a way out of the mountains."

Garrio, standing behind his master, made a warning face at me.

The king said, "Earn your freedom. Dream ten true dreams for me, and I'll strike the shackles."

"Five."

"Are you trying to bargain with me?"

I shook my head and raised my manacled hand again. "Not bargain—beg, I'm begging. Do you see how Catna's hand is sullen? If it festers, she might lose her life to the tarnishing, and then I'd be handfast to a curse, a corpse. How would that serve you?" Catena pulled on the chain, trying to make me lower my hand, saying truly her hand didn't hurt. She could bear it.

The king said, "You'll run."

I gestured at the mountains. "Where? I too wish to find a way out. Five gleams should be enough."

He said, "No. Ixa."

I refused, showing him the five fingers of my right hand and saying, "Dene." Then I realized we had both spoken in a foreign tongue. It had been a long time since he'd spoken that language to me—the language of Lambanein.

"Ha!" he said, striking his hand against his knee. "I knew you came from Lambanein, you have the look of it." He asked me a question in the other language, and when I shook my head, he raised his voice and I could tell he was berating me.

I felt as I had after the lightning struck me, that his words were just the wrong side of meaning. I twitched the fingers of my left hand, remembering *kave peta cato yane ixa,* six seven eight nine ten; and then the right hand, *nea avo eta setra dene,* one two three four five. My hands made fists and I bent down and covered my eyes. There was a lump in my gullet hard enough to choke on, and I swallowed it down. I said, "I dreamed of black penance, banners. Whose color is black?"

"No one's."

"Black banners carried by whoresons riding through a path, a pass."

"In winter? Now?"

"No. It was hot."

"Are you sure the banners weren't indigo, like mine?" King Corvus said.

"Maybe. They were dark, they could have been. I dreamed these horsemen rode through mountings."

King Corvus said, "What mountains?"

"They had snow taps in summer. How many are so high? Do you know them?"

"I should," he said. "We are lost in them now. Tell me the rest."

I told him I'd dreamed of a valley with a long lake, and around the lake a bright necklace of towns. I said there was a hidden path, too steep for horses, down the precipice at the head of the lake. The king asked if the lake bent in the middle like a crooked finger, like so, and if the hills were terraced where the land fell steeply to the shore, and I said yes. He said the lake was called Sapheiros, and his father, King Voltur, had taken that valley in a war with Lambanein, having long coveted it. He supposed I had dreamed of his father's army.

So it was true then, and Penna had guessed aright: I was Lambaneish born, from this valley with a crooked lake—though the word *Sapheiros* was unfamiliar to me, unlike *ixa*, unlike *fedan*. And it could be, it must be, that the warriors my father feared were King Voltur's men.

I'd heard rumormongers sing of King Voltur's last war, and how after his victory he was killed by the Firsts of five rebel clans, and the queenmother had punished them for their treachery. That was some twelve years ago. About that many years ago, I had arrived at the Dame's household, a small child, part of her dead husband's baggage. Perhaps her husband had sold his sword to King Voltur for the campaign to win the Lake of Sapheiros—a warrior might travel far to a war that offered rich plunder. Or there had been an alliance between Incus and Corymb. Our kingdoms weren't always enemies.

King Corvus said, "Your so-called dream is useless. By any reckoning we're leagues and leagues to the west of the Lake of Sapheiros and the pass that leads to it. Did the arkhon instruct you to lead us astray?"

"We are astray through no fate of mine; it's not I who led us here. And I don't know what this arcant is."

"So you still pretend you are not Lambaneish."

"I think maybe I was born there, in that victory with the lake I dreamed of last night. But I have no remedy of it, I was too young when I left. I didn't even know that I knew those little ones." I held up my hands, showing him my fingers. "Those little counting words, the . . . mumbles."

"Then answer me truthfully: where do you come from? It's plain you're a foreigner, though you're learning our language quickly. Day by day you sound more like someone born to it."

"I told you before," I said. "Where I come from, this is the language we speak. It was because . . . Addled Wildfire struck me—because of the lightning that I can't speak prosperously." I was surprised to hear the king say I was speaking more clearly, when I must struggle to make myself understood, which was wearisome to both of us. And yet it was true—I stumbled over one word now, instead of three or four, before finding the one I sought. I'd always supposed a cure—if there was one—would come all at once, like the lightning. I'd failed to recognize this slow and arduous healing.

"You still haven't said where you come from. Where is your home?"

I said, "I am a sheath, so home is wherever my shade, my blade is."

"Your blade's name?"

"Sire Galan dam Capella by . . . Falchion . . . Flacon—by Falco of Crux, I mean."

"Ah. From one of the bastard houses of Corymb. Why didn't you say so?"

"Because we are venomous, enemies. I feared you'd kill me."

"I think it's time you told me how a Lambaneish woman became the sheath of a warrior from Corymb. And how you came to be at the temple of Lynx at Mount Quaer, dreaming a dream of my wife."

The next day, on the way down the ice field, Mox rode his gelding across an ice bridge that many had crossed safely before him, and the bridge gave way. He fell into a crevasse and his horse landed on top of him. Divine Volator climbed down a rope and found Mox was dead, his neck broken. The priest finished the horse, as there was no way to get him out. They left Mox's body down there; no wood for a pyre.

Death was so commonplace. I thought it had lost the power to surprise me.

We were safe from the queenmother's malice now, but so long as we wandered in the mountains we were not safe from the malevolence of the Ferinus. When a cornice of snow gave way underfoot and spilled men and horses down a precipice, or a stone fell from the heights and crushed a man's skull, or an avalanche swept away the ponies carrying the last of our barley, or for the third time in a day we had to retrace our steps on paths that led nowhere—men blamed the mountains, and I too felt the cruel antipathy of the Ferinus. We trespassed where we were unwelcome.

King Corvus had led us there. I thought to myself, *Blame the king.* But if they lost faith in him, what was left?

I had at last convinced the king I was a true dreamer and not a thrush sent by his father-in-law, the arkhon. And now he looked to me as if I could guide us out of the Ferinus, and yet I wasn't a true dreamer. False dreams wouldn't serve now. I didn't want to lie, I wanted to live. But true dreams didn't come at my bidding; they were gifts of the gods. I threw the bones, asking what to do. As always, the Dame and Na spoke most clearly of the gods to be feared and appeased. They both pointed to the Queen of the Dead.

For two days we were blinded by a blizzard, unable to march. Catena and I lay among varlets in a hollow in a snowbank and overnight more snow covered us with a thick blanket. I had my arms around Catena and I felt the rising and falling of her chest as she breathed through her mouth. She had coughed a long time before she slept. I was afraid to sleep, convinced that if I succumbed, my hearthfire would go out; my body would stiffen and my shade would rise, and I—the remnant of me—would go forth in that other land. I wouldn't be hungry or weary or cold or half blind or tongue-tied anymore; I would no longer suffer pains and weariness. But it was lonely among the dead.

I began to shiver. I clamped my jaws together so my teeth wouldn't chatter. A shrill whine approached my ear—a buzz.

Sire Rodela. He was pleased I was dying.

I'm glad you can take pleasure in something, I told him.

He laughed his hissing laugh, and showed me the corpses: Catena and I lying under snow until the thaw. The thaw comes late in the heights, in the month of Midsummer. In the warmth our flesh softened and began to stink. A bear found us and took us apart limb from limb, and other creatures came, vultures and crows, a fox, a stoat, a few voles, and scattered our remains. These bones with shreds of flesh engendered maggots and swarms of flies. Sire Rodela made me look. This is why corpses must burn, he said.

It was hideous to look upon, until I saw that when I was eaten I became part of other creatures and other lives. I partook of a fly that buzzed above a fast creek and perched on a bending stem of horsetail rush and preened its glossy wings. I partook of many flies, or they partook of me; I saw through many eyes, and each eye was faceted, so that everything I saw was fragmented and multiplied. I flew everywhere and saw the terrain in darting glimpses as I zigged and zagged. The flies were short-lived, but each bred other flies, and some followed the goats and the boys who herded them up into the high pastures, and some stung the rumps of chamois that leapt from boulder to boulder, and some pestered the horses of traders who rode through a pass, and some buzzed around the heads of men who climbed down a precipice toward a long lake in a valley, carrying burdens on their backs. It was confusing to be so many and see so much at once, but I began to make sense of it, to bring together what had been divided.

When I understood what I was seeing, I saw the way out.

I told this to King Corvus and his priest—calling it a dream—and the king insisted we were nowhere near Sapheiros. He asked me about the shapes of mountains and routes of roads to see if he might recognize landmarks. I had my doubts too, for why should I trust Sire Rodela? But I kept them to myself, and arranged the folds of my green cloak to show the ranks of mountains we still must overcome.

Divine Aboleo said the dream was a true omen, that Rift Dread, manifest in the swarm of flies, had shown us the way. The king believed him, though he didn't believe me.

CHAPTER 18

Sapheiros

t cost us four arduous days and many men and horses to crawl across the handful of leagues I had flown over in my dream. I pretended to know where we were going, even when I was uncertain, for the snow smoothed and altered the shapes of summits and valleys. When the men burdened me with their hope—their blame too, when things went wrong—I understood, a little better, the strength of the king's will. He had clung to his persistence, all else being doubtful.

On the forty-sixth day of my captivity, we stood on a ridge below a grim pinnacle and looked down on the Lake of Sapheiros. It was not as I'd dreamed it, the lake with bright blue waters, the mountains in their summer greens; but it was like enough. Here the Ferinus stretched out two low arms of mountains into the plains of Lambanein, embracing a long, narrow, crooked lake that shone silver under a gray sky. I was surprised to see the water wasn't frozen. The sight of the lake—like the sound of its name in a tongue I didn't remember—filled me with inexplicable dread. I might have been born there, but I knew nothing of how to live there, among strange people with strange customs.

The stone bones of the mountains around the lake were fleshed with dun meadows. There were gray orchards and stands of evergreens so dark they looked almost black, and here and there a dusting of snow on the summits. Terraced vineyards ascended the steep slopes from the lakeshore.

Our footing was precarious. We were buffeted by the same wind that had carved the snow on the ridge into a frozen wave and polished it to a hard gloss. We looked down at treetops. Lopsided pines and firs grew from the rock face, driving their roots like wedges into the smallest cracks. Impossible for anything but an ibex, King Corvus said, but I denied it. I crawled over the crest of snow to point out a ladder hidden among the trees—just as I'd promised, when I'd warned him we would have to climb down on foot and leave the horses behind.

The king called for his best climbers, saying there appeared to be a way down, and the men sent up a cheer. Three men set out that afternoon, and by midmorning the next day, we thought they were lost. By dusk the climbers returned with guides and food and fodder and, best of all, southern wine. There was such a huzzah when the wine and food were handed out that the noise started a snowslide, which rumbled and roared past our camp, sweeping away Sire Molobus's jack and horseboy, an armiger, and three ponies. Even that was greeted as a good omen because it missed the rest of us.

Catena said the wine made my nose red and my teeth blue. We had eaten well, and I would have been content were it not for the chain and manacles. I'd found a pass and still the king hadn't released us.

He saw our suffering and refused us freedom. But he had led his men over the mountains and all of them had suffered to serve his will, and half of them, I reckoned, had died. Why should he be more merciful to us? Never was a king who did not require others to die for him, never was a king who did not make war. But war had been foisted upon this king. He had lost ingloriously—but defeated the Wolves gloriously—crossed the Ferinus in winter gloriously. No one knew it could be done. And by doing so he had perhaps gained sufficient coin of glory to raise himself a new army and march back again to Malleus in the coming summer. Tonight his warriors and his mud soldiers loved him. Rumormongers would sing of what they had accomplished.

I wondered what the king would do with Catena and me when he was safe in Lambanein. Would he still summon me every morning to hear my dreams? He might be ashamed to recall he'd relied on the fancies of a mud-woman. He might discard us, leave us to fend for ourselves in an unknown country where they spoke an unknown tongue. It was strange to think, when I'd chafed so long at my captivity, that the best I could hope for now was to remain in King Corvus's service, so I might accompany him when he returned to Malleus. How else could I get back across the Ferinus?

But this was foolish. It was unwise to lift my eyes to look so far ahead—we were not out of the mountains yet.

The next morning we were summoned before sunrise to see the king, and wordlessly I held out my left hand with the manacle and chain.

The king smiled broadly enough to show his teeth. "For today you will be unchained from the girl," he said. "We are going down the mountain and they say they can't carry two at once."

"And foremorrow?"

"Tomorrow we'll see."

The king summoned a brawny mudman named Rile who did what I'd been unable to do; he opened a link by hammering an iron wedge with a lump of granite. When he first severed the chain, I was still hampered by it. Catena and I had been harnessed so long that I had a habit of curbing every gesture, and it seemed strange not to have to be mindful of her at every moment. We were glad to move freely again, but I didn't count us free so long as we wore the manacles with their short tails of chain.

The king had decided to descend the mountain by way of the ladders with about three score men, a little more than a fifth of those who had survived the crossing. And Catena and me. The rest of his men would go on horseback, taking a longer route that led into the same valley. It was thought impassible from early fall to late spring, but the king's men were not daunted, having come so far already. And now they had trustworthy guides, food, and fodder for the horses.

The Sun began to climb up as we readied ourselves to climb down. On the narrow windy ridge above the first ladder, Garrio had a blindfold ready for me, and he tried to persuade me to get into a basket on a porter's back. He said it was the way it was done: all summer these fellows carried travelers and goods up and down the mountainside. Blindfolds prevented the passengers from screaming or fainting with fear.

I said, "I'd rather climb. I don't want to be a bungle."

The porter spoke to me in Lambaneish, and when he saw I didn't understand, he spoke in the High, in a thick mountain accent. He said it was nothing to carry a skinny wretch like me—he'd carried a colt down on his back once, which had made less of a fuss than I was making. "If you climb yourself, you'll likely balk halfway down like a stubborn hinny, and we'll have to carry you after all. Or you'll fall and take others with you."

Still I refused. I couldn't imagine being blindfolded and carried. Garrio said he'd rather ride, if he had the choice. He didn't know that I dreaded confinement far more than heights. Catena sat down in the snow and began to whimper, and I saw my fright had made her more afraid. I crouched beside her and whispered, "Never mind, never mind. Look at those panters—they look very sturdy, don't they? You shall ride and I'll stay close to you." I pointed out that Sire Refulgo, who had a broken arm, and the horseboy Quirt, who was afflicted by the shiver-and-shake, had been hoisted up in their baskets onto the backs of porters and waited their turn to descend.

Catena climbed into the basket and suffered herself to be blindfolded. I heard her crying quietly. The porter squatted and put his arms through the leather straps of the basket and rose with Catena on his back. I kept my hand on her head and tried to soothe her as I would a skittish horse.

It was a cunning trail. When danger threatened from the north, the people of the valley took the ladders down and forced invaders to go by way of a farther pass. The path was hidden under overhangs and down chimneys of rock; here and there the path makers had carved a few steps or widened a ledge to make a resting place, or tunneled through a buttress of stone. All those contrivances would have meant nothing without the ladders that stitched the trail together. We climbed two to a ladder, no more, lest a rung break or a climber falter, and I descended just below the man carrying Catena. At first I talked to her, saying it was not so hard, it would soon be over, until I couldn't spare the breath.

I'd gotten my way, and I had cause to be sorry for it. Wind from the south hit the mountain like waves against a sea cliff, shaking the ladders as if to shake us off, and it made a sound like waves too, roaring and hissing against the stone. The ladders were made of fir poles lashed and pegged together. The bark was rough and sticky with resin. My hands were numb, and I feared I'd lose my grip. Stones came hurtling down on us, dislodged by climbers above. Sometimes rungs that seemed sure twisted or broke underfoot and I had to catch myself with a jolt. My belly cramped with fear.

We halted, waiting for men below to cross a sheer rock face by wedging their feet into a narrow sloping crack, while clinging to a rope strung through iron rings. Catena's bearer and I shared a small pinnacle with a crooked pine tree. At first I faced the wall, clinging to nubbins of rock. My legs trembled and burned from exhaustion. Then I turned and pressed my back against the cliff and slid down until I was sitting, and I hung my legs over the edge of the precipice. Catena asked if we'd arrived, and I told her, "Not yet."

It began to snow, and the flakes swarmed hither and thither like mayflies. The porter passed me a waterskin—I thought it was a waterskin, until I took a drink. It was strong, fiery doublewine, and I coughed and spewed some out through my nose. The porter laughed to see the look on my face and the tears caught in my eyelashes. We were not halfway down and I thought I couldn't go much farther. Perhaps I would die on this cliff, having led the king to it. Perhaps the gods required no more of me. Well, hadn't I lived to see more than ever I'd expected? In my lifetime were very few dull days. A dull day takes longer to pass and leaves fewer memories. If memories were coins, I'd die a rich woman. I smiled back at the porter and took another swallow, and the doublewine warmed me all down into the bowl of my belly.

There must have been courage in the bottom of that drink, for I found the strength to keep going, down the ladder and along the crack in the wall, and farther still. I saw my grimy hands with skin stretched tight over the knuckles, clasping the rungs of a ladder, and behind the ladder rough granite seamed with white quartz and splotched with lichens. I looked below to see where to put my feet, the next step and two thereafter, but I tried not to see all the way down. I climbed until I forgot everything else, forgot myself even, because I was merely movement, and I no longer felt the burning in my arms and legs, or the ache of stretched sinews, the tremors in my limbs, the cold.

The last ladder was the worst. It was made of rope, a sort of net stretched over a bulge in the cliff wall. I crawled halfway over the bulge and there was nothing under my feet. Others had gone before me; it must be possible. Yet I froze there with my belly against the rock and my feet hanging over the valley floor. The porter tired of waiting and clambered past me. Once he was below he put his hand on my ankle and guided my foot to a loop in the net, and so, slowly, I left the solidity of rock and entrusted myself to the quivering rope web.

I dangled over the ground and climbed into the shadow under the jutting brow of rock. There, nestled in a notch at the base of the cliff, I saw the slate roofs of a village. Hands reached up and lifted me down to a ledge. A steep stair, carved from the living rock of the mountain, led down to the long portico of a stuccoed house the color of an apricot. I sat on the tiled floor of the portico and shook. Catena crawled out of her basket and leaned against me. We looked up at the net stretched over the looming cliff, the mountain blocking half the sky, and I couldn't believe we'd climbed down safely. Impossible that it could be done. Yet we had done it. I had done it.

The smith had hair almost as orange as the flames in his forge. He chiseled the head from the rivet that fastened my manacles, and forced apart the iron band, and some of my skin came with it, leaving a bracelet of raw flesh. When it was Catena's turn, she cried from the pain.

The smith said something to me in Lambaneish. His voice was loud and gruff, so that he sounded fierce—all the Lambaneish men seemed to talk that way—but his face was amiable enough. I turned up my palms to show him I didn't understand. Garrio was no help; he knew only a few words in that tongue. The porter who had taken us to the smith said, "He asks where you come from, what town."

"Tell him over the mountains, that way." I pointed up toward the cliff above the town.

The smith stopped smiling, and turned his broad back on us to hone his chisel on a grinding stone. I said to the porter, "Ask him if he knows a horse trader, a man with a thin face and a reddish braid, beard. He takes horses to basket in the mountains."

The porter translated and the smith turned back and replied. The porter said, "He says many traders."

"The man was my fond, my fedan," I said. *"Fedan,"* I repeated to the smith.

The smith shrugged and said something. "Many traders, many bastards," the porter said.

I knew now why the king had disbelieved me when I denied being Lambaneish. There were more redheads in this village than copper coins in a peddler's purse. It wasn't just the hair, it was the stamp of the faces, wide at the brow, narrow at the jaw, familiar as looking in a mirror. Some of the townsfolk looked like they could be my kin; maybe they were.

My kin. I always thought I knew what had happened to my parents, because of what had happened to me. My father would not have let soldiers steal me—therefore he must be dead. I hadn't wanted to wonder who killed him and how. Better that my mind's eye stay shut than open to such a sight.

Now I questioned that certainty; now I dared to hope.

We walked from the village under the precipice to another village by the lakeshore. When the fishermen came back with their catch in the afternoon, the king ordered them to take us south in their small blue boats. The mountains were so steep along the north end of the lake that one had to go by boat to get from town to town. The rowers labored against a strong wind that kicked up froth on the waters. It had been snowing up on the precipice, but in the valley it was raining. Even the chill winter rain felt warm to me, and the south wind balmy. There was no ice on the lake, no ice anywhere in sight. We had arrived in a milder kind of winter.

The towns along the shore glimmered in the gray light, against the dun brown mountains. The houses were clustered on steep streets, with facades stuccoed in ivory or ochre. Stone watchtowers stood on the heights above.

Catena sat on my right, which seemed unnatural, for when we'd been chained together she was on my left. We shared my wool cloak, and I put my arm around her and hugged her tightly. "I'm so glad," I said, and gave her a kiss on the forehead.

She said, "Is there any cheese left?" which made me laugh. I gave her cheese, flat bread, and wizened black olives, food I'd saved when the villagers fed us, for I did not yet trust our hungry days were over.

It was dusk when we disembarked on a rocky promontory halfway down the western shore of the lake, and climbed stairs to a palace built upon the steep outcropping. We had arrived in winter at King Corvus's summer palace, in the only part of his kingdom his mother had not yet taken from him. The king had outpaced the news of his defeat, and arrived unannounced, and his steward rousted the servants out of their winter sloth and made them bustle. And soon there were fires and more food and drink, and best of all pallets and blankets, and the best sleep I'd had for a long long time.

But by the dawn twilight I was up and wandering unfettered and alone in the terraced gardens. I marveled to see green again, and unfamiliar kinds of trees with foliage like ferns, or topknots that reminded me of plumes on a cataphract's helmet. The myrtle shrubs were full of noisy birds.

I walked along a colonnade that encircled three sides of the outcropping, first looking north to the snow-capped Ferinus, then south toward the plains at the end of the lake. There I stayed, leaning on a balustrade as the Sun rose above the mountains, and mists smoked from the still surface of the water. I could see why the king's father had stolen this jewel of a sapphire lake from the kingdom of Lambanein. Why men had died for it.

But that war was long over, and the other war, the new one, far behind us. We had reached a haven, yet I found its beauty disquieting. It filled me with a sweet wintry melancholy.

I missed Galan, of course. That thought was sharp, it made longing well up in me like fresh sap. I wondered at how swiftly and easily the pain could be provoked, because in truth there had been days, many days in the mountains, I hadn't thought of him at all. I'd thought of the next step and the next, for every step had been a mortal choice between another moment of life or a long fall. Now I was glad of the painful assurance that I was still bound to Galan despite the distance. I hoped, selfishly, he was pained by it too.

I heard someone approaching, and when I saw it was the king, I ducked my head and sidled past him, for fear I'd trespassed. He made a gesture that said I might stay. And he too leaned on the balustrade, gazing south.

"I see you're without your shadow," he said, and for a moment I didn't understand he meant Catena, and I looked down to see if my shadow lay at my feet.

"My shadow is sleeping," I said.

"But you rose early. Were you troubled by dreams?"

"No deeps."

I watched him from the corner of my eye. His beard was neatly trimmed, his hair was glossy, and he wore a surcoat of red wool covered with arabesques of golden cord. I wondered why he wasn't glad, why worry showed on his brow and melancholy on his mouth, even now that we'd attained the refuge so long desired, so costly to reach.

"So you leave again?" I said.

A sharp glance at me. "Soon. We head south as soon as we can get horses."

But we're tired, your men are tired, I wanted to say. "It's beautiful here," I said instead.

Wildfire

King Corvus propped his hip on the balustrade and leaned against a column. "Do you recognize it?"

"I never dreamed this. I only saw the lake from above, from the past. I don't think I was ever here in this parlous, this palace."

"I have been here twice," he said. "On the way to Allaxios to meet my betrothed, and on the way back home with her."

He turned toward the water again, and I bowed and slipped away. I clasped my right hand around my left wrist, and the pain of my sores banished all pity.

The king was generous to the Blood who had followed him over the mountains, promising that each would receive a horse befitting his rank; less generous to his subjects in Sapheiros, from whom the horses were to be taken. He sent out a party of men to collect mounts, escorted by four priests of Rift, one bearing a sword and the others, more dangerous, armed only with daggers. A fellow named Pasco was horsemaster at the palace, and he was in charge of the requisitioning with the help of Lame and Chunner and some other horseboys.

I asked Garrio if Catena and I could go along on the expedition to get horses. I didn't expect him to say yes, but he shrugged and said he didn't see any harm in it. Catena didn't want to go; she was tired of going places, she said. And truly she was tired, she couldn't sleep enough.

We took a flat-bottomed ferry across the lake. Pasco was one of King Voltur's soldiers who'd settled in the valley after the conquest a dozen years ago. He got to gossiping on the boat with Lame and Chunner, saying, "We'd best hurry or all we'll see will be the backsides of horses on their way up the mountain. Once they get up in those ravines and woods, we'll never find them. You have to watch these Lambaneish bastards, they're naught but cozeners and thieves—they can steal your shirt without taking off your coat."

He had a pair of Lambaneish horseboys with him who heard every word, but he didn't seem bothered by it.

I said, "Beg pardon, but have you ever come across a sharp-feigned man with a ruddish-brown beard, a man who sells horses?"

Pasco looked astonished that I could speak at all, let alone in the High. He answered to Lame, as if he'd asked the question. "Could be anyone—there are more redbeards here than not."

"He had a roam, a roan named Ganos," I said.

"Huh. A horse named Ganos. Does she think I know every useless jade hereabouts?"

"She's looking for her father," Lame said, having heard the gossip.

"Don't know him," Pasco said, and spat over the side of the ferry.

269

We landed below the Town of One Hundred Mares, and went past a fish market along the quay crowded with several sorts of customers, to judge by the clothing: women wearing short vests over their dresses, and felt caps stitched with bright embroidery—mountain folk such as we'd seen even in the villages on the other side of the Ferinus; other women were clad in yellow or orange dresses and shawls; still others in fur-trimmed cloaks in the fashion of Incus. There were also men and women with shawls covering their faces, which I thought peculiar. I wondered if they were disfigured, and ashamed of it.

We climbed cobbled stairs and streets between three-story buildings. The town looked prosperous, save for a few rubble-strewn gaps in the rows of houses. We met a herd of sheep coming down, and I stood in a doorway to let them go by. Above me I saw a woman in a saffron shawl reach out to close the shutters of a painted balcony against the Sun. Her face was turned away from me, but the curve of her arm, bared to the elbow, was redolent of a memory I couldn't quite recall. And I had the same sensation when I saw a woman turn to chide a dawdling child, a little girl in a green felt cap; the woman had a high reedy voice, and she spoke with such a lilt and so many rising notes that she seemed always to be asking questions, even as she scolded the girl. The sound was naggingly familiar, like a lullaby with a remembered melody and forgotten words.

We started above the town and worked our way down. Pasco had the king's warrant and a list from the steward, and he bullied his way into one stable or farmyard or pasture after another, taking one horse from a small-holder who had only two, and five horses from a landowner who had thirty. We were unwelcome everywhere. Unwelcome also the tidings we carried of King Corvus's defeat—his disgrace, for losing his kingdom to his own mother. Most were amazed, even disbelieving, that he'd crossed the Ferinus unseasonably. Amazed, uneasy—what would it mean for Sapheiros, this war in Incus, the king's exile? Maybe some of the Lambaneish felt a secret glee at the news; if so it was well hidden under sullen resentment.

It was useless to ask questions. I watched instead, searching each man's face for signs of likeness to a father I'd seen only in dreams. He'd be twelve years older now, if he lived. Would I recognize him? And this was just one town on a lake more than ten leagues long—I saw how foolish I'd been to hope.

We drove about thirty of the horses up to a pasture on the mountain behind the king's summer palace, and I sat on a boulder with Lame, tired and out of breath. A redheaded Lambaneish horseboy came over and squatted beside us. He looked about my age, maybe a little older. He said in the High, "Who is this man you search for? Your father?"

I nodded.

"But you don't know his name. How will you find him?"

"I won't," I said. "I disremember too much, I was too young when I was taken."

"Taken?"

"In the war."

"What do you remember?"

"He had a horse named Ganos." I laughed a sour laugh and pitched a pebble down the hill. "We were riding back from market over the pass, and he saw soldiers coming, and we left the horse and my sorry pony—I mean the pony was sorry in color, she had hide like my eyebrows, this color, see?—and we climbed down that big foot at the head of the lake. And I had a pretty red vest, and a little felt cat . . . cap that came down around my ears and tied with strings under my chin, like the children wear here. That's all I know."

"Was there embroidery on the cap? What was the pattern?"

"It was red and yellow chicks, checks."

The boy shrugged. "So many died then. I expect he's dead."

"I expect so," I said.

That night Catena and I slept curled up together, and it was a comfort to us both. But I awoke suddenly, disturbed by a forgotten dream, and found my left side was damp with sweat and my right side had gooseflesh. I couldn't go back to sleep.

We were a hand of days on the lakeshore, while the king collected mounts and provisions. Some he sent up the pass above the Town of One Hundred Mares, to aid his men coming down, but he didn't wait for the rest of his army to arrive. We set out on a winding road that clung to the folds of the mountains, riding south to Allaxios to find out what hospitality Arkhon Kyphos, the king's father-in-law, would offer him. Behind us stretched a mule train laden with treasures, for the king had plundered his palace of silver platters, golden ewers, hangings, robes, bales of wool from coveted breeds of mountain sheep, and casks of doublewine from his vineyards; gifts for the arkhon, Garrio said, to sweeten his disposition.

We had a long ride ahead of us, long days to cover many leagues. Catena and I shared one of the sturdy, shaggy mountain horses. I didn't regret leaving the Lake of Sapheiros behind, for our stay there had awakened a sleeping sorrow. When we reached the plains at the southern end of the lake, I turned in the saddle for a last look at the valley. The peaks of the Ferinus, all ice and stone, were a rampart stretching from horizon to horizon, and Galan was on one side of that wall and I was on the other. My manacles had been struck off, but I was still imprisoned.

CHAPTER 19

The Manufactory

t was a journey of eight days from Sapheiros to the eastern-most gate of Allaxios, home of Arkhon Kyphos, the ruler of Lambanein. The city was built on a steeply terraced mount that stood solitary among the gentle swells of the lowlands. Mount Allaxios wasn't much of a mountain compared to those of the Ferinus, but we saw it shimmering from a long way off, for it had a shining crown, the golden rooftops of the Inner Palace where the arkhon dwelled. Solid gold tiles, Garrio claimed, each one worth a fortune. He didn't mind reminding us he'd been here before.

Mount Allaxios showed a forbidding face to travelers approaching from the north or west, craggy precipices rising above a river that bent around the mount like an elbow. But we arrived from north-of-east, and saw welcoming terraces covered with buildings and gardens. A broad canal seemed to issue from the very summit of the mount—though surely that was impossible—and it flowed down the great stairway of terraces and straight across the fertile plains like a shining road.

This much we saw from outside the high walls of the city. I expected that the gates would be flung open for King Corvus, that he would be greeted with the pomp and courtesy befitting the arrival of a king, no matter that he came as a beggar, having lost his wife, her dowry, and his kingdom. But no one was permitted to enter Allaxios without being clean, and the Lambaneish had a strict notion of cleanliness. We followed attendants into a magnificent building that delved into the ground instead of rising above it, with five stories of colonnades around a central atrium. Catena and I descended the slippery marble stairs together, as close as if we were still shackled, and we seemed to climb down toward a wavering oblong of silver sky, for the lowest level of the building was half submerged in water. Shining ripples doubled the stacked colonnades.

I took the building to be a temple of Torrent Wellspring, though I didn't see her statue among the limestone carvings softened by time and water. And in its way it was sacred, but it was also a crowded bathhouse that echoed with voices and laughter, and the music of water flowing from spouts into basins, from basins into pools and channels, and from channels into the atrium, in shimmering veils between the columns. Men and women and children bathed naked in the chill winter air, rinsing under stone spouts and sitting in small pools that smoked with steam. They seemed to have no notion of modesty, and yet our male attendants, clothed only in loincloths, covered their heads with brown shawls as if ashamed to show their faces.

We descended to the third level, and the attendants bade us with gestures to take off our clothing. The king undressed first, saying he was sick of his own stink and the stench from the rest of us, and then his men couldn't refuse. A bowlegged man carried our garments away. I turned my back, for it was a pitiful sight, all of us stripped naked of everything but our amulets, the king and about fifty of his men and Catena and I. A poorer lot of clapped-out mules you never saw, ribs and girdlebones and wingbones sticking out, skin cracked, fingers and toes blackened from frostbite, open sores.

Catena and I washed under a spout carved like a ram's head, with a beard of moss hanging from its chin. I scrubbed hard with a small sack of sand, ridding myself of grime and ashy skin, and I found it a pleasure to be clean. Catena shivered under the water, saying she'd never bathed in her life and saw no reason to start now.

The attendants had razors of black obsidian, long shards keener than knives, with which they offered to shave us. The king told his warriors that the noblewomen of Lambanein would refuse to couple with them if they had hairy bodies—which gave much cause for banter and gibes. He lay down on a marble bench and permitted his body to be shaved, even the hair around his dangle. The barber trimmed his beard and the hair of his head, and combed out his nits with a fine tortoiseshell comb. Then most of his warriors were willing to allow the same liberties; the priests of Rift were downright eager. They had their heads shaved too, and their scalps and jaws burnished with pumice.

Then it was the turn of the mudfolk, and suddenly it was plain why our attendants were burly men with fists like small boulders. They meant to take all our hair, make us bald naked as priests of Rift, and they were not as courteous as they had been with the Blood. Lame hit his barber, and the barber hit him back, and there would have been a brawl if one of the king's Auspices hadn't struck Lame down with a heavy blow, and threatened the same to anyone else who made a fuss.

A woman barbered Catena and me. Her face was concealed under a yellow shawl with a brown stripe, but she showed her disgust by picking a louse from my scalp and crushing it between her fingernails. She hissed. She scraped me with the obsidian razor all over my body and between my legs, and I trembled in shame and smarted in all my tender places. She cut away my long hair and did not even leave me eyebrows.

We never saw our clothes again. Catena and I were each given two unequal lengths of yellow cloth, a wooden disk, and a cord. With these we were expected to clothe ourselves. We were so puzzled by this that another woman—whose face wasn't hidden—helped us dress with the patience afforded to simpletons or young children. She wrapped the longest cloth around me twice, pleating it in front to leave room to walk, and brought two ends of the cloth over my shoulders and fastened them to the front with the disk and cord. In this way, without sewing a stitch, she made me a garment. The shorter cloth served as a shawl. After she dressed us, she dusted our arms with yellow powder, from the backs of our hands to our elbows.

I leaned over the railing of the colonnade and saw myself in the pool two stories below. Dried marigold petals floated over my reflection, and below it a long white carp waved its tail. I looked strange without the red hair that made me familiar to myself. My head seemed so vulnerable in its nakedness. I twisted the shawl around my bald scalp like a headcloth, to protect myself from gazes.

This day, by the tally of knots on my red cord, I had been two months captive: six tennights, each represented by a double-knot.

There was one last indignity before we could enter the city. We were each given a paste of herbs formed into a ball the size of a cherry. Among other flavors I recognized bindweed, which might as well be called the unbinding weed. We stayed outside the city walls in a long hostel full of tiny rooms, while we got over the squirts brought on by the purgative. It was a hive of women; where the men lodged I never knew. We rested and ate, and healers gave us salves for our sores, and by the end of the three days Catena and I had stubble on our scalps.

It was the spring Equinox, and the tenth day since Catena and I had entered the gates of Allaxios. We'd been taken straightaway to the palace of Arthygater Katharos, one of the arkhon's many daughters, and put to work as textrices in her manufactory, Catena as a spinner, and I as a weaver. We hadn't seen the king or any of his men. No one told us why we were bondservants, or how long we'd be obliged to serve, and we quickly found questions were considered impertinent, especially if asked in a foreign tongue.

The manufactory was two stories high, with arcades on both floors overlooking the inner courtyard. This court had paved paths, a fountain with a hollow bronze woman ceaselessly pouring water into a stone basin from her water jar, a tiled watercourse, and an old pear tree, and it was pleasant enough. But all I'd seen of the sky for ten days was the small rectangle above the green-tiled manufactory roof. There were no windows in the outer walls, and but one door, and that was locked and guarded.

The Equinox wasn't a Lambaneish festival, but Catena and I were celebrating it nevertheless with bondwomen from Incus: Dulcis, Dame Abeo, Nitida, and Migra. Shortly after we came, they had invited us into their small circle, glad of the company of others who spoke the High, and now we sat under the vaulted roof of the arcade, chatting and spinning like old friends. It was a chilly evening, but one couldn't welcome Growan Maid indoors. The sky above the courtyard was streaked with drizzling rain, and silver drops clung to the black twigs and buds of the pear tree. We sang a few prayers to honor the coming of the Maid, and Dame Abeo treated us to sesame and honey fritters bought from a peddler. She was the only one of us High speakers born of the Blood, but on this side of the mountains she was just another bondwoman.

I gave Catena a present I'd made for her, a little doll of straw wrapped around with thread, and she thanked me prettily and tucked it away. Perhaps she thought it too childish—though she could be childish too, I was delighted to find out. Sometimes she played with other young girls, running around the courtyard or dormitory at night until tired women scolded them and made them stop. But tonight she seemed content to ply her spindle with the rest of us. When she came she hadn't known how to spin, and her taskmistress had covered her arms with pinches from sharpened fingernails.

We worked all day for Arthygater Katharos, but in the evening we spun for ourselves to earn a few coins. One could always sell thread. A single weaver might require thread from as many as ten spinners to keep her busy; the finer the weave, the more spinners. The woman who oversaw the dormitory lent us wool and flax, and we spun it, and she paid us a few coins and advanced us more fiber, and so on. No doubt the arthygater profited from this trade somehow, as she profited from the few peddlers allowed into the manufactory, who sold us sweets, needles, fuel for small fires, lamp oil, songbirds, and such.

Lambaneish coins were cylindrical beads stamped with figures; the least valuable were of pewter. The women wore these beadcoins strung on the cord fringes of the net caps they wore in place of headcloths. I'd been shocked at first to see women going about with their hair showing under these caps as if they still had maidenheads, but I had my own net cap now, and a couple of beadcoins to hang on it. Someday I hoped to have many coins, enough to get me home.

Dulcis was prattling on, and likely I was the only one listening to her, for she told the same stories over and over. Her conversation was still new to me, and perplexing enough to be interesting. She was saying, "Diakonan was smitten with me, poor fellow, but he hadn't a coin to call his own. Instead of buying wax figurines, he'd make them out of clay himself, clumsy things, most unflattering, and mark them with his teeth and nails to show how he meant to mark me—if I gave him a chance, which I wouldn't."

"Was he the girdsman?" I asked. It was difficult to tell Dulcis's many suitors apart. She boasted endlessly of men who desired her, but I never saw a one. She boasted of her beauty, and I confess I never saw that either. It was true she had a double chin—which Lambaneish men found delectable, she said—and her skin was hardly wrinkled at all, considering her age. She'd been in the manufactory twenty years.

"Oh no, Diakonan was the porter," Dulcis said. "The guardsman, oh my dear, I was content to let him mark me as he wished. You should have seen me after our couplings, all covered with bites and scratches! I think he gave me as many scars as he had himself. He was a bold fellow, very passionate, adept in the twenty-five Postures—a rod like oak! I swear when we did the vine and column, he could hold me up without using his hands."

"However did he get in to see you?"

"He used the needle peddler as a go-between, and bribed the porter," Dulcis said. "Only one key fits every lock, don't you know that?"

"The same portal . . . porter? Diakoman?"

"Oh yes. It used to make him wild with jealousy."

"This key you speak of—"

"Money."

"Yes, money. Can it unlock the dorter so we can get out?"

Nitida said, "You could never lay hands on enough coin for that. The arthygater doesn't mind if men sneak in from time to time to beget more bondservants, but any porter who let a woman run away—well, I daresay he'd lose his life in an unpleasant fashion. She'd probably have her tormentors skin him alive."

The timekeepers rattled wooden clappers to mark the seven passages of the day and the three passages of the night, that we might rise, work, eat, and sleep at the proper times. Every day I sat weaving from daybreak to sunset. The loom was upright rather than level, and the warp was kept taut with weights, but aside from such peculiarities I was reminded of the Dame's workshop: the same rhythmic thump of beaters and swish of shuttles between warp threads, and the sound of women's voices. There were a dozen weavers in the room, and many such rooms around the manufactory courtyard.

Wildfire

I wove yellow cloth with a broad brown stripe down the middle: *tharais*, it was called. Every day I was supposed to weave a cloth twice the length of my outstretched arms, of which a third was used for a shawl and the rest for a wrapper. We were able to weave quickly because somewhere, in another room, textrices warped our looms and wove starting bands of black and white checks.

These tharais garments were coarse as sacking, of lumpy nettle thread dyed with onionskins and walnut hulls. Dulcis said they were for the lowliest servants of Arthygater Katharos, the kind who went about hidden under the shawl, like the woman who had shaved us in the bathhouse. Textrices wore tharais cloths only during their tides, when they were obliged to cover their faces and eat and sleep in seclusion. The rest of the time we wore finer *tharos* cloth, wool dyed yellow with weld, with the same checked starting bands that marked all the arthygater's servants.

Our taskmistress scolded and slapped us if we were too slow, and spit the word *tharais* at us as if it were a curse. I came to think the word meant something poorly made, or rather something not worth the trouble of making well, since she never punished us for slovenly work.

I'd always heard it said that Artifex traveled around the world and made people from the clay of different riverbanks, so that each kind of folk was a different color. In that weaving room was proof. There were bondwomen from kingdoms I'd never heard of; some had wan skin, others were red cheeked, and some ruddy brown. Most of the Lambaneish women were buff in color and tended to freckle, like me, and at first I was taken for one of them, newly arrived from the provinces. They greeted me and spoke in a friendly way, but as soon as I opened my mouth, they knew I was a foreigner. After that only a few bothered to try talking to me, but they conversed freely among themselves, and their talk was a river in which I fished for meaning. I learned words for nettle, hemp, linen, wool, shuttle, warp, loom, barley, chickpeas, olives. Things I could point to or touch: sky, tree, fountain, roof, floor, column, hair, hand, foot, garment, bead, lash. The music of the language came more easily to me than the words, or rather came back to me—the high, singing intonations of the women's speech, so different from the rough growl affected by the men.

One weaver had a small boy too young to be taken from her and sent to the men's quarters. The boy pulled bobbins of thread out of his mother's basket and tangled them up, and she yanked his hair for it. He wailed, *"Emmin! Emmin!"* Mother! Mother! I recognized the word by the pain it gave me the first time I heard it. *Fedan, emmin*; father, mother.

Now and then I fished up such little words, words I didn't know I knew, minnows caught in a net dragged through dark waters.

٭   ٭   ٭

In the underground dormitory we High speakers claimed our usual place by a certain stout, whitewashed pillar, and spread our thin blankets over a heap of straw, and used our wool wrappers and shawls as coverlets. Catena and I lay side by side to share warmth, as many women did, and I told her one of Na's old stories about the hunter and the hare-woman. Now that we were safe from the wild Ferinus, she enjoyed being frightened. Her hair had grown from fuzz to fur; I ran my hand through the soft bristles and wondered if she would want to leave with me, to cross the mountains again.

Catena slept. The only light in the dormitory seeped from two shuttered lanterns, one near the door and the other across the room by the privy bench, and their faint flicker made the ceiling loom even closer. A woman was coughing somewhere in the room, a dry hoarse cough, a sound as hard for me to ignore as the cry of a baby. I had a quarrel with myself, thinking I had no herbs, and couldn't speak her language, and it wasn't my place to care for her—I had no place here, I didn't belong. But I found it impossible to do nothing. I stepped carefully between the sleepers to the water jar to fetch the woman a cup of water. She lay curled up on her side in the busiest and foulest corner of the dormitory, near the long bench with holes where we relieved ourselves all in a row, sitting over hidden night-soil jars. Newcomers slept here if they were unable to claim a better place on the crowded dormitory floor.

I crouched beside the woman. Perhaps she thought I was going to reprimand her for making noise, for she cringed away from me. "Water?" I said in Lambaneish. She sat up and gave a timid smile, and took the cup I offered. She too had been recently shorn. I put my hand on her bony back and forehead, and found her hearthfire was burning steadily. Just a cold, nothing more, but her throat was so raw from coughing that every breath scratched and made her cough some more. She squeezed my hand in thanks, which shamed me, for I hadn't helped.

I went back to bed and listened to her cough.

When at last I fell asleep, I dreamed of walking on the steep slopes above the stone house on Mount Sair. The Maid had come to the high meadows and the Athlewood, bringing a wild sweet fragrance. I gathered mint and mustard and nettles, and went down to my herb garden on the terrace below the house to pick horehound and hyssop. Everything I needed to ease a cough.

Maybe I smelled the musk of horehound and the bracing scent of mint in my sleep, for in the morning I awoke to find those herbs in the straw around our blankets, mixed with poppies and cornflower and other weeds

278

that had grown unwelcomed amidst wheat and barley. I knew a gift when I saw one, but after the bounty of the dream it seemed a chastening, the gods obliging me to be grateful for small favors. I murmured a prayer, but my heart was grudging.

I raked up a heap of straw and began to sort through it, setting aside useful plants—those I'd found in my dream and more—and Catena helped me bundle them and hang them from the low rafters with twists of thread. Some of the goodness had faded from the herbs, but even so they carried the scent of other places and other seasons.

I made a tisane of horehound and hyssop the next night, when I heard the woman coughing, and in this way I took up my duties as a greenwoman again. I was amazed by how quickly this became known, and how many came to me. Many textrices had been hoarding small complaints for lack of any remedy. A few were quite ill, and they'd hidden their misery lest they be sent to a temple to die, for the arthygater had no tolerance for bondwomen who couldn't work.

There were certain peculiar Lambaneish illnesses caused by angry spirits they called *meneidon*. Most of these meneidon were water wights dwelling in streams, fountains, cisterns, and drains; others dwelt in stone or wood. Our courtyard fountain had a meneidon, and there were said to be several others lurking in the manufactory who were quick to take offense and hard to placate. They sometimes afflicted people with fits or staggers or palsies for transgressions such as emptying a bucket of foul water in the wrong place. The only true cure for such illnesses was to appease the irate meneidon, but at times I was able to ease a woman's suffering.

I learned new words in Lambaneish, belly, womb, tooth, pain. Nitida or Migra would translate when gestures failed. I used what I could find: sage or meadowsweet in the bedstraw, germander and thyme growing between the stones of the courtyard. Sometimes I was deprived of any hope of helping, for what I needed grew outside the manufactory walls. Then I was sore resentful to be barred from the realm of all that was green and growing, and from the coming of spring out in the wide world.

Often I turned to the Dame and Na, throwing the bones in the dark dormitory, surrounded by sleepers. It was such a comfort that they tarried with me. Comfort too is a healing gift. Perhaps I had to be humbled to learn that; I had to be reminded to accept with grace those times when nothing could be done but to let the sufferer know she wasn't alone.

Every evening Dulcis burned wisps of wool before her little clay figure of Wend Ram, but she also gave obeisance to the gods of Lambanein, especially the goddess Katabaton. Of true gods the Lambaneish acknowledged only three: the husband-father Posison, the wife-mother Katabaton, and the son Peranon. Such was my ignorance at the time that I was amazed to learn people worshipped other gods than ours. I asked Dulcis how there could be room for them, when our twelve gods divided creation between them, the visible and invisible realms.

"They live in the overworld," Dulcis said.

"And where is that?"

"Where they hold court. It's day there when it's night here, and night when day, and their summer is our winter, and so forth."

"So they are backward?"

"No, it's said we are the backward ones, here in the underworld— backward like a reflection in a mirror."

Nitida, who had bright black eyes, a deep laugh, and the most amiable nature of all the women from Incus, was not in the least devout, and she found my incredulity amusing. "They think our avatars are meneidon, you see—though of course very high-ranking ones. They have meneidon from many kingdoms in their service, just as the arkhon has his Ebanakan guards and diviners from Bivium."

"But what of the Sun and the . . . Fool, I mean Moon?"

"What of them?" said Nitida.

"Well, anyone can see they are goods. The Sun—we see her every day, and she gives us life . . . light to see by—how could anyone deny her worship? It doesn't make sense."

Nitida laughed. "Who says the Lambaneish are sensible? They think the Sun is a wheeled cart driven by Posison, and the Moon is a ship in which Katabaton sails across the night."

"You believe in Crutch Moon, don't you, Dulcis?" I asked.

"Of course."

"Then how can you believe in this Kata—Katabatabon sailing him about?"

Dulcis shrugged. She seemed to have no difficulty believing contradictions.

I found these Lambaneish notions absurd, and most absurd of all their belief that three deities could encompass the greatness of the world and govern its myriad parts. And I was affronted that they took our avatars for mere meneidon, no greater than the capricious spirit in the courtyard fountain. I knew the gods were gods. Hadn't I felt the power of Ardor Wildfire impressed upon my body, and seen signs of the twelve gods manifest here in Lambanein, as everywhere?

*　　*　　*

Wildfire

In the Dame's service I'd never been more than a fair weaver, for my mind was forever wandering outside and wishing the rest of me could follow—but it seemed a waste of time to do things downright badly, as the other weavers of tharais cloth were content to do. And the Dame did not approve of shoddy work. She was with me in the weaving room—in memory always, and in the skill of my hands. I wove to please her, not the arthygater.

When I proved both neat and quick, the taskmistress sent me to another weaving room, where we made tharos wrappers and shawls such as we textrices wore, only of finer quality. The cloth was sold in Allaxios or shipped elsewhere. It was the custom in Lambanein for women to wear yellow, with perhaps a patterned or striped border as decoration (respectable women wore stripes here, not just whores). But the Lambaneish didn't have a single word for yellow, they had eleven, for all the colors they saw between yellow and orange. They could reckon a woman's wealth to a nicety by the dye and thread used in her wrapper, the very finest being of silk colored with saffron.

In this weaving room I came under the flail of a short and short-tempered redhead named Zostra, who stalked about like a hen, thrusting her head forward. The loose wattle of flesh under her chin shook when she upbraided me, which she often did. If my attention flagged and I pulled the weft too tight, or if I stared at a thrush singing in the pear tree outside the windows, she'd strike my back with her lash of stout cords tipped with wooden beads. Or she would pinch me with her fingernails, which she kept long and sharp to prove she never had to weave or spin like the rest of us. I learned Lambaneish insults meaning slattern, sloven, idler, lackwit. Once I pulled down my woolen sock, which was all I had for shoes, to scratch the bottom of my foot, and Zostra flailed at me and shouted, "Tharais! Tharais!" In this way I learned the sole of the foot should be hidden.

The Lambaneish found foreigners such as myself very rude and contemptible; even their word for us was an accusation, meaning strange-ignorant person. But I'd learned a few words and enough Lambaneish manners to avoid offending; I no longer showed my teeth when I smiled and laughed, or touched anyone with my left hand. Some of the women talked to me, such as red-haired Agminhatin, the best weaver in the room. She used to imitate Zostra's mincing, pecking walk behind her back, and make us laugh.

It took me a long time to patch together a question in Lambaneish—and once I'd asked, the answer usually baffled me. The words came too fast, so I watched people closely when they spoke, reckoning what they meant from expressions and gestures, inflections and pauses, just as I had after being struck by Wildfire. Then I'd puzzle out their words—only to find, often as not, they didn't mean what they said. Everyone hated Zostra, and showed it plainly; but as their contempt wore the guise of servility, and their taunts took the form of flatteries, she didn't appear to notice.

Days that are all the same pass slowly. By twilight there were tight bands of pain across my neck and shoulders, cramps in my legs, and aches from my fingers to my forearms. Usually hard work inured me to more hard work, but the aches worsened. My thoughts seemed as bound to one task as my body, and suffered as much from repetition, back and forth like the shuttle, but with no cloth to show for it at the end of the day: Galan and King Corvus, longing and bitterness, two ply of a thread so twisted that sometimes I confused the one I desired with the one who had abandoned me.

During dark-of-the-Moon the Lambaneish women were full of dread, and they began each night by marching around the dormitory hallooing and clapping to drive away malicious thoughts and spirits. Tomorrow was the New Moon festival, and they would greet the Moon's appearance with fervent celebration, as proof Katabaton's ship had not foundered in the seas of night. It would be the first day of rest since we'd come to the manufactory—the only such day each month, for the Lambaneish didn't have a Peaceday at the end of every tennight.

When the dormitory was quiet at last, I sat up and cleared a space in the straw to spread out the cloth compass. I did this almost every night now, after the other women had gone to sleep, hunching naked under a shawl with the divining compass hidden between my knees, casting the bones. When I was not seeking remedies for someone else, I had my own reasons to call on the Dame and Na, asking what had become of Galan and Mai and all my other friends. What of Mouse? What of Garrio and the horseboys, how did they fare?

I asked the bones about King Corvus, and they answered in riddles. I'd served him unwillingly but well—he couldn't deny I'd served him well, and daily I had expected he would send for me. Didn't he need a seer in this strange country? But after more than two tennights in the manufactory, I no longer believed a summons would come. I began to think he'd sold us to Arthygater Katharos. Many bondwomen here had been taken captive in wars or raids, like us, or sold by their families, like Migra, whose wastrel husband used her to pay a gambling debt.

It wasn't that I was loyal to the king. But I was sure he would try to retake Incus, and when he crossed the Ferinus this summer, I wanted to go with him. Dame Abeo told me the passes through the mountains opened about Midsummer Day; when the Maid ripens into summer elsewhere, it's still spring among the peaks. I'd asked Dame Abeo many questions about

Wildfire

Sapheiros, for her family had settled there after King Voltur's conquest, taking possession of one of the fine estates the Lambaneish nobles had lost. She'd been captured in a raid across the border, and seen her father killed—had things done to her of which she wouldn't speak. One learned not to ask. There were many terrible stories, and worse fates than mine. I found this truth to be a poor consolation.

I lay down to sleep, and the straw I'd heaped up under the blanket rustled as I turned and turned again. It smelled of summer fields and a dusty harvest, and oh, how could I wait that long? When the pear tree bloomed in the courtyard, I would leave, I told myself, though the bones warned me not to be ruled by my impatience.

I dreamed false dreams of the king. Bad dreams, lost and freezing and starving again in the Ferinus, and the king asking something of me with a hope I found more painful than his despair, because I had nothing to give.

I dreamed fragrant true dreams of the house on Mount Sair, but Galan never visited these dreams as he had in the temple of Lynx. I dreamed I worked harder than in the weaving room, hauling rocks and water and hay, digging, planting, and pruning. I awoke rested, my limbs warm and stretched and relaxed after those exertions, eased of the cramps I felt after a day at the loom.

More and more I was afraid I would never live to see that house on the mountain. I'd taken these true dreams as a promise of what would be, when perhaps they merely promised what might have been.

How lucky I was those days I forgot to miss Galan. Because it couldn't be borne every day.

I sat with the women from Incus in the courtyard arcade. The winter rains had stopped over a tennight ago, and it wouldn't rain again for half a year—so they said, though I found it hard to believe. Above the green-tiled roof, the sky was a pure deep blue. A few stars glittered like beads between the fretwork branches of the pear tree. Catena was playing with friends, as she did most evenings; already she could make herself understood in Lambaneish better than Migra, who had been here eight years.

For several nights Dame Abeo had been teaching me to read again, and for text we had the scrip Sire Galan had given me. At first I could pick out only my name. But Ardor had been merciful to me of late. I still hesitated and misspoke from time to time, but it was no hindrance to being understood, and my friends from Incus hardly seemed to notice. It was the same with reading. Sign and sound and sense had once seemed walled off from one another, a maze in which I was baffled at every turn. Now the walls tumbled down, and I was free to learn and remember. The godsigns made sounds, the sounds made words, and the words made sense: *Bear witness that I give my sheath Firethorn tenancy, for her lifetime, of my holding that lies on Mount Sair and is bounded by the Needle Cliffs to the north, Wend River to the east and south, and to the west the Athlewood; the stone house and byres, the lands, and rights to coppice, pasture, and spring.*

Dame Abeo praised me for learning quickly, and Nitida wanted to know all about this Sire Galan, what he looked like and why I hadn't gone to the house he'd given me. I'd been reticent to speak of him before, and now perhaps I spoke too freely and made too much of his handsomeness and bravery. Nitida teased me for it, and it was sweet, I must admit, to let the other women know such a man had been fond of me.

Dulcis boasted about the bravery of some nobleman who had adored her many years ago, turning the conversation toward the more interesting subject of herself. By now I too had learned to ignore her tales while pretending to listen.

In my third tennight in the manufactory, as I lay sleeping, someone cut the drawstring of the divining compass that hung from the red cord around my waist, and took the pouch and everything in it, my tin amulet of Wildfire, the folded linen scrip from Galan, and the finger bones of the Dame and Na. The thief also cut pewter beadcoins from my net cap.

I discovered this in the morning, and Catena and Dulcis and the others helped me search, sifting through the straw around our sleeping place. I raised an outcry, asking everyone I knew if they had noticed a thief. Agminhatin, the redheaded weaver from Zostra's weaving room, took offense as if I'd accused her; others shrugged, indifferent. I risked a beating to stay behind in the dormitory and shake out every one of the blankets folded on shelves along the wall. I prayed the thief would take the coins and leave the rest, but I couldn't find a scrap of cloth or a bone.

That night Dulcis said a dung beetle must have taken it. She said everyone knew they trained their children as thieves, and sent them to climb up through the holes in privy benches to steal from respectable people. Migra agreed, saying the *koprophagais* were up to all kinds of mischief: thefts, ravishments, causing maladies by pollutions, and spying at bathers through peepholes. I didn't know who or what these dung beetles might be, but I was sure one of the other bondwomen had stolen my pouch. I suspected everyone except Catena. I was furious to think of Galan's promise and the precious bones, worthless to anyone else, tossed into a shit jar—or worse yet, to think of the Dame and Na bound unwillingly to a thief who fancied a new talisman. I had been careless; someone must have seen me late at night, casting the bones for myself or for a healing.

It was hard to lose that pleated, knotted strip of linen on which was written Galan's bequest. But it was worse to lose the bones and their counsel. When a weaver came to me with a mysterious malady—red lumps on her legs, shortness of breath, a feeling of oppression in her chest, frailty—I was unable to help. I still had the gift in my hands and the knowledge of greenlore restored to me, but without the bones to show me which avatars governed the matter, and where to look for a remedy, I was at a loss. I yearned for the divination and interpretation, the way the signs sometimes formed lock and key, and questions unlocked answers, or pointed to patterns altogether unexpected in which I sensed the mysterious motives of the gods themselves.

But most of all I was bereft of the ones who cared for me, their presence, their touch. I grieved for the Dame and Na as if they were newly dead.

CHAPTER 20

Tharais

t was my own fault I became tharais. I thought tharais and tharos referred to kinds of cloth, but they are entire domains, which are unknown in Incus and Corymb, and have no names in the High or the Low. Unclean and clean, impure and pure, valuable and worthless make a beginning. Yet many useful parts, things, and people are tharais, such as the left hand, the soles of one's feet, uncooked meat, and dyers—useful, but tharais, therefore tainted.

Before the bones were stolen, the Dame had sustained me through many a tedious day at the loom. Sometimes I had felt her nearby, and heard her humming a song to Wend Weaver, whom she'd loved best of all avatars, and I was granted a morning or an afternoon when the shuttle flew back and forth and the threads were laid down like lines of light, never too taut or too loose. On such days Zostra had paused to watch, and moved on without using her flail.

Zostra trusted me with finer thread now, made of molted wool from gelded sheep, almost as costly as silk. But weaving was a dull duty without the presence of the Dame. I was tempted to commit small ruinations, to tangle the weft into knots and break warp threads—but it wouldn't have satisfied, and Zostra would have struck me and made me pick it out again.

One morning I was working to match a striped border on an old scrap of cloth, and I ran out of a color and asked Zostra for more. She gave me thread dyed with madder, when I had been weaving thread dyed with kermes, a more expensive dye and a richer crimson. They had seven names for shades of red and I knew them all, and I insisted the color was inferior, using gestures when I ran out of words. Had she sold the kermes thread and bought madder and kept the difference? By small cheats small fortunes could be made in the manufactory.

Zostra struck me on the top of my head with her flail, shouting at me for making such a foolish mistake. When she raised the whip to hit me again, I caught the cords in my hand. She tugged and I tugged back, and I yanked the flail away from her and threw it down and ground it under my heel—I took my shoe-stocking off to do so, using the sole of my foot to taint the whip so she wouldn't dare pick it up. To do this was a sweet balm for everything that galled me. I knew I'd get a beating, maybe a bad one, and for the moment I didn't care.

She flew at me, shrieking that I was a filthy filthy stinking tharais! She pulled off my net cap and yanked at my hair, and struck me about the face and head. There was such a fine furious hatred singing all through me that I hit her back, slapped her cheek so hard it stung my palm. She went for my eyes with her sharpened fingernails, and I hit her again, with my fists this time. I tried to knock her down so I could trample her as I'd trampled her whip. She fled from me, out the door and down the hall.

I touched my brow and found that Zostra had drawn blood. The other weavers gawped. Agminhatin was always quick with a jest; she clucked like a frantic hen and flapped her elbows, imitating Zostra running away. No one laughed but Agminhatin herself.

Now that it was too late, I was sick with misgivings. I'd heard too many tales of the arthygater's tormentors and how they marked bondservants who disobeyed, to serve as living examples of the cost of her disfavor.

Zostra returned with two male guards and they marched me out of the manufactory and across a courtyard into another building, where I was presented for judgment to a stout woman named Gnathin, who had an air of fuss and bustle. She was swathed in a wrapper of saffron silk, and the long cords on her net cap were strung end to end with gold and carnelian bead-coins.

Though Zostra was a great power in her own tiny realm, she answered to greater powers. She made her complaint to the stout woman in a shrill voice, speaking of kermes and madder, and gesturing to show how I'd struck at her. Gnathin seemed peeved to be taken from more important duties; she reprimanded Zostra for letting an inferior get the better of her. Then she uttered a few words, and raised a few fingers on her left hand.

Zostra turned to me with a look of malicious satisfaction. She spat on the ground and said, "Tharais!"

In the kitchen court of the arthygater's palace Zostra made me undress. My new garments were the kind I'd woven when I first arrived: coarse nettle cloth, dyed onionskin yellow with a brown stripe. The wrapper went about me once instead of twice, and opened a little in back as I walked. I draped the shawl over my head, for I was forbidden hereafter to show my face to tharos people. The dark stripe made it easier to see through the cloth.

I wasn't permitted to say farewell to Catena. I feared I'd never see her again, or find my stolen bones and the deed to the house on the mountain, for I was barred from the manufactory.

I was tharais now.

It was, perhaps, Gnathin's little jest to send me to work in a dyehouse where they used the madder dye of which I had complained. The sole product of the dyehouse was scarlet wool, which was sold by Arthygater Katharos to the arkhon so that his Ebanakan guardsmen could go clad in identical tunics and breeches.

Dyeing cloth was a stinking business, and therefore tharais. I was banished to the tharais district of Allaxios, where the impure lived and worked: besides the dyers, there were butchers, tanners, and fullers who cleaned and felted wool. There were embalmers—a profession unknown to me before— who buried the dead in quicklime to strip away the flesh, and made plaster statues with the bones inside that were kept in crypts under the city.

And then there were dung beetles, the koprophagais, who scuttled about in gooseshit brown shawls and were despised even by other tharais. The koprophagais trafficked in excrement. They sold dung of all kinds to be spread on the fields; they sold urine to dyers for use as mordants, according to complicated recipes, such as the one that called for the piss of drunkards during a full Moon. Which explained why, in the dormitory, we had been obliged to piss through one row of holes in the bench and shit through another; the arthygater profited even from our wastes. I learned these things and more.

I didn't know enough of Lambanein then to understand the severity of my punishment. And I'd gained something by my exile: a larger portion of the Heavens, a greater share in the coming of spring. Glad Growan Maid came earlier to Allaxios than to the Kingswood, and already she unfurled her bright green banners in every garden. Our dyehouse was in a walled compound on a terrace just above the river, and if I climbed to the third limb of the candlebark tree, I could see over the wall. A green haze was spreading all along the Ouraios River and west across the plains to a solitary snow-covered peak. I'd never seen a candlebark tree before coming to Lambanein, but I recognized it at once from the fragrance of its rusty bark, which we burned at night to keep away the stenches.

Nasthai was my new taskmaster, and he was a lean, stooped, sallow man, who shouted when he spoke to me as if that would improve my understanding. He'd worked in the dyehouse his whole life and his father before him. He and his wife and two sons lived in a loft above the workshop, beside the locked room where bales of cloth and casks of madder were stored. The rest of us—the woman Knotais, Kenoabantapas, and I—slept downstairs among the vats, or in the courtyard if it was warm enough.

I found the dyers unfriendly at first. They thought me too proud. I might have been tharos once, and a textrix living in the arthygater's palace, but I was tharais now, like themselves and no better, even if I'd not been born that way. People did not climb back up once they'd been cast down. I repeatedly made the mistake of using the tharos word for *I*, instead of saying "this one" or "it," as tharais were obliged to do. Nasthai's wife, Mazais, pinched my lips shut with her sharp fingernails to teach me not to do that again. She said, "A little child knows better than you."

In the Dame's household I had preferred the art of dyeing to weaving. I had a knack for the greenlore, and for bringing pure colors out of muddy dyebaths. I never imagined it could be as tedious as it was in the dyehouse. A new shipment of madder root had just come in, a wagon full of it, and day after long day we sorted and pounded the roots, making pastes we spread upon planks to dry and then ground into a fine powder. We used only powder from the bright inner core of the best roots, and the rest was resold. I was wrong about the inferiority of madder: they had a way of preparing the wool over many days with various baths before they dyed it, to produce a red brighter and more colorfast than we had achieved in the Dame's household. Nasthai kept some of the steps secret, and I never learned the whole recipe.

The dyers had lived all their lives in the tharais district of Allaxios, save Kenoabantapas, a man with skin the color of a walnut and just as wrinkled. He'd been a long time in Lambanein, but he spoke the language with peculiar intonations. He was Ebanakan, from the same kingdom as the men of Arkhon Kyphos's personal guard, for whom we dyed cloth. He'd been a sailor—a pirate, Knotais whispered—before he was taken captive. He kept a caged bird, some sort of starling, which spoke in proverbs. "Kiss a thief and count teeth," it would say. Kenoabantapas had lost a good many teeth, and I asked him if he had kissed many thieves. He said, "Only one thief, but many kisses," and laughed heartily, showing his gums, and I joined in. The sound of my own laughter startled me, and when tears welled up I blinked them back.

Spring was too sweet, it made me melancholy, it troubled me with the balmy airs of evening, and fat buds opening fans of silver-green leaves on the candlebark tree. Even the sound of a woman sweeping in another compound could pierce me with longing, knock a small chink in the wall I'd built between this present life, which did not belong to me and yet must be endured, and the life I hoped to take up again as if I'd never left it.

I had promised myself I would leave Allaxios when the pear tree bloomed in the manufactory courtyard, and surely the first blossoms were open. But it was not yet spring in the Ferinus. I must wait for the thaw, bide my time until the passes opened in midsummer. Suppose I succeeded in crossing the mountains, and reached Malleus to find the army of Corymb had already returned home? Then I'd have to make my way alone across Incus and the Inward Sea, across Corymb to the city of Ramus or to the keep of Galan's father. To what welcome? To learn that Galan had taken another sheath, thinking I had died or run away?

I must forbid myself such thoughts; I must think of how it could be done rather than how it was impossible.

Nasthai began to entrust me with chores that took me outside the compound, such as fetching mountain water from the fountain of Nephron, a duty I shared with the bondwoman Knotais. We carried the water in clay vessels, which were heavy even when empty. Each jar had a narrow waist and round hips and a small foot, and two handles like arms akimbo. A full jar was carried upright on the head, and looked to me like a little clay woman standing atop a real woman. I tried my best to imitate the gliding walk and straight backs of the women of Lambanein, but I hadn't their knack of balancing the jar without using hands.

It took many trips to the fountain to fill the huge vat for the mordant bath that readied the wool to take and hold color. There was water close at hand—rainwater in cisterns under the courtyard, or the spring in the fountain house we used for drinking water, or the river itself—but for mordanting Nasthai insisted on the pure mountain water that flowed all the way from the Ferinus on a stone causeway. Upstream from the dyehouse, the aqueduct crossed the river on stone arches, bringing the water to the Inner Palace itself, high on the precipice. The arkhon permitted this bounty to flow lavishly to the rest of the city, down from his gates and past the palaces of his nobles to the fine residences of the upper town and the crowded streets of the lower town. Even the tharais district received a share, by way of the enormous bronze sow named Nephron, whose teats spurted mountain water into a pool. She stood near the upper tharais gate, two terraces above the dyehouse.

One day Knotais and I hoisted the empty water jars on to our shoulders to go to the fountain. We climbed steep stairs in the crumbling wall of a terrace, looking up always toward the marble walls and golden roofs of the Inner Palace, on the summit of the mount. I was delighted to be let out of the dyehouse, but our task was hard on Knotais. At least when we went uphill to the fountain, the jars were empty. She limped because one leg couldn't straighten at the knee—an accident of birth, she said. And she was carrying the burden of a child in her belly, at least six months along. I knew who had given her the big belly, everyone did. It was Chelai, the taskmaster's son, who ignored Knotais these days, when he wasn't rude to her. I'd made her an ointment to ease the ache from her limp, and sometimes at night I rubbed her legs with my warm hand so she could fall asleep. In a mostly wordless way we had become companionable.

At the fountain we stole time from our duties, sitting on the broad rim of Nephron's pool to watch people come and go. I breathed deeply. The air was fresher up here, above the tanneries and dyehouses. I tossed dried maythen blossoms into the water. Nephron was benevolent, unless you offended her by spitting in her vicinity, but she expected tribute.

Now that I could no longer retreat in the evenings to the comfort of a known tongue, I spoke Lambaneish all the time, and perforce I learned faster. There were even times I found myself thinking in that language. But my understanding still outpaced my command of words. I took a palmful of water and let it run through my fingers, and said to Knotais, "Do you go to Ferinus, to Kerastes, where this water comes at?"

She shook her head. No. That gesture was the same wherever I had been.

I rumpled up my skirts in my lap and walked my fingers over the folds. "I, it, this one, walks on Kerastes this winter." I hugged myself and pretended to shiver. "It makes cold."

"You came from Incus in the winter?" She looked sidelong at me, no doubt wondering whether I was a liar.

I nodded.

"Why?" she asked.

"Why what?"

"Why from Incus in the winter?"

"Oh—a big fight." I made two fists and butted them together. "King Corvus and his mother, they fight, and King Corvus runs." The fingers of my right hand crossed the folds of cloth again.

"A big fight—you mean a war, ein?"

"A war, yes." But I could see that war in Incus was too far away to matter. Knotais was silent, her head averted; she wrapped her arms over her belly and rocked a little. Was she weeping?

I put my arm around her. "What?" I asked. "What trouble?"

She leaned into me and sobbed. "Chelai is going to marry, they say—Hamadrai's daughter, have you heard? No one but a koprophagais will ever marry this one!"

"Because your leg?"

"Because they say this one's father was a koprophagais. He wasn't though. It's a lie!" The words seemed to spray out of her. "And Chelai says when his wife comes to stay, if this one offends her they'll marry it to a shit-eating dung beetle. But it won't marry one, it won't!"

I held Knotais's hand with my cold right hand, and thought: at least you'll have your child. And felt the sting of tears again.

I swear something pinched my earlobe hard, just for a moment, the way Na used to do when she was vexed with me, and my hair stood on end. And someone hissed in my ear that I shouldn't be such a miser, keeping all my pity for myself. I was properly chastised—and glad too, so that I smiled even as the tears spilled over, to think Na had come all this way just to chide me. She could be such a scold.

During the long and complicated processes of dyeing the wool, there were sometimes unexpected gifts of a morning or an afternoon when I wasn't required at the dyehouse. Then Mazais might send me to the tharais market on an errand, and not scold too much when I tarried. At first I marveled that I was given such liberty, remembering the tharos bondwomen pent up in the manufactory with but a single scrap of sky. But soon I got used to it, and took liberties I had not been granted, making my way to the riverbank below the terrace walls to harvest wild plants in the marshes and water meadows, mudflats and thickets. I seldom saw another person there, except in boats. The inhabitants of the city turned their backs on the river, and even those whose livelihoods depended on its free-flowing waters did not wander the banks by choice. The Ouraios River had a powerful meneidon, and furthermore, Mazais said, it was the path the dead took away from the city. She said that sometimes shades wandered back upstream, and climbed through drains to emerge in the streets. If so they did not trouble me, the Lambaneish dead.

I found fat pintle shoots poking through dead leaves, fiddleheads in bracken beds, and lily bulbs. I sold these delicacies in the little market square next to the street of the fullers, or shared them with the other dyers. I made Knotais special dishes and tonics: dandelion and chicory salads, infusions of feverfew to raise her spirits.

I also gathered silk grass, hemp, and yellow osier bark to twine and plait myself a carry sack, decorating it with red thread Mazais gave me after I made a lotion of marsh mallow roots to soothe her sore hands. A woman at the market admired this sack, so I made others to sell, staying up late in the courtyard, sitting with my back against the trunk of the candlebark tree.

The beadcoins I earned this way were all my own, money for my journey. I counted and recounted them and hung them on the cord fringe of my net cap so they would click and swish as I walked. They were pewter beads mostly, with a couple made of copper, and not worth much. It seemed odd to walk around the city with my coins showing in this way, instead of hidden in a purse, and indeed, Knotais told me to beware of thieves, especially little children.

I was still a bondwoman, but it seemed I'd find it easy enough to slip away when it was time. That wasn't why I waited. The king had forgotten me; I'd get no help from him. And I was unwilling—afraid—to wander Lambanein and the mountains by myself, living on what I could scavenge or steal from farmers. I must have a guide and provisions. Perhaps I could join some traders, and make myself useful as a forager and cook.

I couldn't hoard food from our allotments. Mazais boiled the barley and beans into pottages with onions, uncounted onions; a woman got three ladles of pottage for every five that went to a man. The tharos wouldn't eat onions, saying they gave a body an unclean smell, and they insulted tharais by calling them onion-eaters. Now I understood why.

But here in the tharais district we hardly ever saw a tharos person; all the insults were aimed at each other. Onion-eater had less of a sting. Though Chelai could make Knotais cry whenever he wished by calling her a dung beetle.

I counted myself better off here than in the manufactory, and I wouldn't have minded my banishment if not for Catena. But I comforted myself with the thought that Nitida and the others would look after her. She probably didn't miss me at all.

I'd been in the dyehouse sixteen days when Garrio came to the gate. It was late morning, and we were in the bright sunlight in the courtyard, culling withered and rotten madder roots so they could be sold to dyers who didn't have to satisfy the exacting requirements of Arthygater Katharos's factor. We were without shawls, and the dyers held their hands before their faces so as not to pollute the gaze of a tharos. I sprang to my feet and ran to Garrio, and we embraced, and he gave me a kiss of peace on my forehead such as a father might give a daughter. We grinned at each other foolishly.

He wore a long tunic and leggings woven of indigo thread shot with peacock blue, iridescent in the light. His face had lost its gauntness, but he seemed older than I remembered him, an old man with a grizzled beard trimmed in two neat points.

Nasthai approached him bowing and bobbing. Mazais had a sour look on her face, and I was secretly pleased I'd scandalized her by being so forward with a tharos.

Garrio and Nasthai exchanged a few words, and likewise some quittance passed from hand to hand, and Garrio said in the High, "Bring your belongings."

I slung the strap of the gather sack over my shoulder, and draped the tharais shawl over my arm. I was already wearing the rest of my belongings, the woolen shoe-stockings and the net cap. "Where are we going?"

Garrio took me by the elbow and said, "Back to the palace." And I'm ashamed to say I didn't once look behind me, or say farewell to Knotais and Kenoabantapas and the others.

"And then home?" I said, meaning Incus. It was a pleasure to speak and understand so easily after the daily struggle with Lambaneish.

"That spiteful old sow didn't want to say what she'd done to you, sending you here. Gods, this place is foul. What a stench! How could you stand it?"

I shrugged. I was used to it. "Have you seen Catena? Is she well?"

"They aren't about to let me into that hen coop," Garrio said.

I looked sideways at him. Garrio was watching his feet to make sure he didn't step in filth. The narrow streets of the tharais district were not clean. "What does Kind Corvus want of me?"

Garrio made a jest about calling the king Kind Corvus, which was no sort of answer. And he pinched my upper arm and told me I was filling out well.

Before I could enter the tharos district, I had to strip naked and scrub myself with sand in a trough fed by Nephron's fountain. Garrio rinsed his feet and hands. The guard at the gate shouted at me when I forgot to drape the shawl over my head. In the palace district I walked in Garrio's wake, as close as a shadow, up steep stairs and through alleys, between high plastered walls topped with spiny tiles, the blank backsides of palaces.

It pleased my vanity to suppose King Corvus had sent Garrio, at some expense of time and trouble, to seek me out. He offered me a way back over the mountains, and if the price was to dream a few dreams, it was cheap enough. Yet I would not forget he had forgotten me. My hands were damp and sweat trickled down the small of my back. I was aware of my own smell under the shawl, and afraid I carried with me the stench of urine and onions. I would be glad to be rid of the tharais taint.

CHAPTER 21

The Bathing Room

ack to the palace," Garrio had said, and I thought he meant the court where the king resided. But he took me to the hindgate of Arthygater Katharos's palace, which I recognized by the blossoming pear tree I saw above the green-tiled roof. I asked why he was returning me to the manufactory, and he said farewell, he'd see me soon. He patted my arm and told me my services hadn't been forgotten. He gave me no time to quarrel with him. And besides, I thought I would see Catena again, and maybe find the bones. I truly thought the king had found a way to make me tharos again.

Garrio left me with the porter, who delivered me in turn to the stout and capable woman who ran Arthygater Katharos's affairs: her factotum, Gnathin. I couldn't tell if she realized that under the shawl I was the same person she had lately banished from the manufactory.

Gnathin let me understand that the arthygater had no use for another tharais servant, especially a strange-ignorant one. She'd taken me as a favor, but I shouldn't expect favoritism. I must never speak to the arthygater—did I know the language of gesture? No?—shit on the gods, how was one supposed to work with such a filthy stupid object?

She spoke rapidly, but by now I understood Lambaneish well enough to follow. I understood also her expression of disgust and her jabbing gestures. She reminded me of Sire Pava's steward, who'd aimed to teach me manners after the Dame died, and would strike me if he saw an insolent look on my face. At least here I was not obliged to smile as I groveled. I bowed my head, hunched my shoulders, and stooped, until I was no taller than the factotum.

She began my education with the same sort of flail Zostra had used, laying the cords across my buttocks. No, no, it was not correct. I must stand like a statue when spoken to, and hold my head upright as if I carried a water jar. If I didn't understand a command, I must brush my tharais ear with my hand, my tharais hand. If my hands were holding something, I must tilt my head to the left. See? There was no sign to show a command was understood, so I stood still. Behind the shawl I made a face at her and mouthed, "Koprophagais!"

Despite that Gnathin swore they had no use for me, a use was quickly found. She sent me to serve as the arthygater's depilator, to remove the tharais hair of her body. Of course I would not serve the arthygater only, but all the noblewomen who visited her bathing room.

The bathmistress, Mermera, didn't deign to speak to me. She was a large woman with a prominent bosom, and she preceded me to the arthygater's living quarters at a pace so stately I had to shorten my stride. The arthygater's court was, in form, much like the manufactory, a two-story building with arcades and rooms around a courtyard, but in every respect more grand and splendid. The walls were adorned with painted scenes, and the floors, ceilings, and columns of the arcades covered with bright mosaics.

The bathing room took up one floor of the southern end of the building, and its walls depicted a garden much like the one in the courtyard. Mermera opened a low door hidden in the painted scene and a bad smell came out. She prodded me with her flail. I stooped to enter the room and when I straightened up, I found the ceiling was but a finger length above my head. If I'd been taller I'd have struck it. Mermera shut the door and went away.

The room was a plastered box no more than two paces to a side. It had no furnishings but a clay brazier and a pisspot, and no light but what came through the cracks around the doors. A niche in the wall held grain baskets and clay dishes and pots; a net bag full of sprouting onions hung on a peg. The stink came from a woman lying curled up on soiled straw and rushes against one wall. Her clothing and bedstraw were stained by the squirts: runny clay-colored shit. I knelt beside her and asked her name. She cleared her throat and said, "This one is Meninx."

I uncovered my head and told her my name, and that I was to serve as depilator. She hid her face behind a hand. I knew then I was to take Meninx's place, since she was no longer useful.

I took her hand so I could see her face, which had been so harrowed and hollowed by sickness that it was hard to imagine how she might have looked when she was well. There was beauty still in her large gray eyes, which she hid under half-closed eyelids. She seemed ashamed, as the ill often are. I told her I was a greenwoman, and she submitted to my gaze and touch without a word.

No fever. Her skin was sallow and clammy, and her breath had a sulfurous taint. I'd never felt a hearthfire like hers, with flames twisted and entangled and knotted just below her ribs, rather than flowing throughout: she was divided, emaciated above this knot, and below swelling with dammed and befouled waters that threatened a chill inundation. Her belly was taut as an oxhide wineskin and made gurgling sounds, and her thighs were soft and puffy.

"How long are you ill?"

Under her eyelids she gave me a furtive look. "This one was low for a long time, years, but this winter the tides came three months long, and this one bled all the time, and could no longer do the work."

I asked what ailed her, and she said, "It offended a meneidon."

"Which?"

"It doesn't know."

"Then how do you know you offend?"

"It is ill, ein?" she said, and closed her eyes, showing me she was too weary to speak anymore, especially with a person who asked such ignorant questions.

She had offended a meneidon, therefore she was ill; she was ill, therefore she must have offended a meneidon . . . The reason chased its own tail. I wished I had the bones and compass to help me understand her strange affliction. But I needed no divination to see that she needed to be bathed, and given clean bedding and garments, and bandages for her bedsores—so many things I could do, and I was impatient to do them. But I thought just then she was more in need of tenderness. I sat with her, smoothing matted hair away from her brow with my cool right hand. Thinking how she must have suffered, lying alone in this small stinking room.

Not all alone. A damp shawl hung from a peg; someone had done the washing she was too weak to do for herself.

In the bathing room I drew water from the large pool tiled with blue waves and golden fish. A bronze heron stood on one leg in the pool, ceaselessly poised over its gilded prey, and its beak was a waterspout. Meninx groaned as I undressed and bathed her. I gentled my hands and moved with great care. She had a terrible sore on her buttocks, as big across as my fist, and smaller sores on her left side, the side she lay upon. I asked why she lay on that side if it hurt, and she said it was worse any other way.

I wrapped her in my shawl and settled her on the cleanest straw I could find. Then I scrubbed her wrapper and hung it on the pegs to dry, and borrowed the damp shawl.

Our small room had three doors. The one to the bathing room was still ajar. Another led to a privy with a mosaic floor and a two-hole bench covered in blue and green tiles—and, I swear, tiles of gold as well. The walls were painted to look like a garden with espaliered fruit trees, showing the plum heavy with fruit even as the quince bloomed.

I lifted the latch on the last door and found a brick stairway at my feet, leading down into darkness. I descended, my shoulders brushing the wall on either side. I was truly blind when I reached the bottom. Even my shadow sight failed, for not a single star cast shadows by which I could see. There is no darkness so dark as that under the earth. I climbed back up to the little room and lit a tallow lamp, and went down again.

A narrow tunnel stretched away to my left; to my right it turned a corner, just past a niche holding a pair of squat jars that no doubt received wastes from the arthygater's privy above. The plaster on the walls was stained and crumbling, revealing stacked stones underneath, or the rough-hewn rock of the mountain itself. I heard gurgling from a fat clay pipe half hidden in the wall. Torch smoke had blackened the low ceiling. These must be the tunnels of the dung beetles, the stinking bowels of the palace that allowed the koprophagais to perform their duties without besmirching the eyes of the tharos. The earthen floor was rutted from the wheels of their barrows.

I chose to go left—east, I supposed, under the south wall of the palace. Outside I knew my directions without effort, no matter how many turns in the path, but inside and underground, I had to think about it. I walked quite a long way before I found other niches with rows of waste jars, and after that a wooden door. Someone had scratched a lewd picture of a winged prick in the plaster beside the door. I rattled the latch and found it locked, and went on.

I heard a woman's voice hailing me, and I turned and saw a woman had opened the door and was peering into the tunnel. "You startled this one, ein? What do you want?" The woman held an infant in one arm. The baby had been nursing, and the woman pulled up her tharais wrapper to cover her breast.

I gave the baby my finger to grip in a tiny fist, and the child yawned and showed toothless gums, and the woman and I smiled at each other, sharing our admiration of these small accomplishments. Of course I asked the baby's name, and found she was called Melimelais; the mother and I traded names, and by then we were on our way to being friends. Nephelais had a broad smile that was apt to dawn at the slightest excuse, such as the way my short hair stuck through the holes in my net cap.

I tried to explain in my halting Lambaneish how I'd just come to serve in Arthygater Katharos's bathing room and found Meninx ill, dying maybe, and how she needed clean rushes for her bed, and honey for a wound plaster, and there wasn't but a handful of barley to eat in the grain baskets. I begged pardon for my ignorance, but did she know where I might find such necessities?

"You must be rich, ein? This one can show you where to find food—but honey? You must seek elsewhere for that." She made a sling from one end of her shawl to carry Melimelais, and led me farther down the tunnel to the larder. The keeper of the larder gave me a ration of barley and broad beans and lard, grumbling that I mustn't expect to get provisions any time I liked. To sweeten her, I gave back some beans; Nephelais had said she could be bribed.

We climbed a stairway to the kitchen yard, and it was startling to enter daylight again. Nephelais introduced me to the day porter, who sat between the tharais and tharos hindgates with a wolfhound at his feet. I let the dog sniff my hand; the man, I supposed, would have to recognize me by my voice.

Back in the tunnel Nephelais told me he was a good fellow, but the night porter was greedy—I should give him two pewter coins when I wanted to go in or out, or he'd demand a grope instead.

"This one can leave? Doesn't the arthygater be afraid her tharais servants run off?"

"Where would we go?" The baby fussed and Nephelais shifted her to the other hip. "What else do you need, ein?" she asked.

"Bedstraw." We set off though the tunnel toward the stables, and I said it was most kind of her to show me these things. Didn't she have tasks she should be doing instead of whiling away the afternoon with me?

She laughed and said her duties were in the evening. "This one is a napkin."

"A napkin?"

"An attendant at banquets, ein? This one washes the guests' feet, it offers the basin and gives purges and cleans them up, and serves as a receptacle."

She used a word for receptacles that could be applied to pisspots and shit jars and drains, or anything that received wastes. "Receptacle?"

"Some guests prefer tharais, they don't like to see a face." She must have seen I was still puzzled. She said, "For copulation, ein? Or the Abasements."

"You mean a whore?" In Lambaneish the word for whore was the same as the word for celebrant, meaning one who attends a festival or maybe presides over it. When Dulcis had called someone a whore, she'd said it with admiration.

"Of course not! Don't you know what is proper? Tharais cannot be whore-celebrants."

Again I asked her pardon, saying I was a strange-ignorant person, and furthermore I used to be tharos before they banished me from the manufactory for striking the taskmistress.

Nephelais hooted and clapped her hand over her mouth. "She must have been surprised, ein? Still, what a pity! She could have just given you a thrashing or had you branded instead of making you tharais. So you used to work in the manufactory? It is just above here."

We turned a corner and passed a long row of waste jars for the manufactory dormitory. There were no doors into the dormitory—lest dung beetles creep into the weavers' bedstraw, no doubt. I was disappointed, for I'd hoped to find some secret way in from the tunnels to see Catena and search for the bones.

We kept straight on, passing the dark maws of tunnels that led to other palaces, and I reckoned we were walking north now, under the eastern wall. I was beginning to get an idea of the enormous size of the palace. We came to a stairway leading up to the stables, where a tharais dungboy gave me as much straw as I could carry bundled in my shawl, for it was one thing the arthygater did not scant or measure.

On the way back Nephelais said the stables were in the forequarters of the palace, where the men lived: the arthygater's husband, Ostrakan; their three sons, two married and one unmarried; and various lesser kin and servants and guards. Ostrakan was a wealthy nobleman, an Exactor in the Ministry of Bounty, but he was titled a Consort, for Arthygater Katharos had the royal blood and rank. Her share of the palace, which included the noblewomen's living quarters, dining court, kitchens, and manufactory, had the undignified name of hindquarters.

I was surprised to hear that the noblemen and noblewomen slept in separate courts. I asked Nephelais if it wasn't inconvenient when they wished to couple, and this made her laugh. "A man of refinement doesn't want to see a woman in the morning, when her breath is sour and her hair is all mussed, ein?"

Nephelais was amiable enough to answer my many questions, and more amused than affronted by my ignorance. I understood most of her answers, though I had to make a good many conjectures when she spoke faster than I could follow. Could she really have meant that a nobleman couldn't couple with his wife whenever he pleased, but was obliged to pay court to her with gifts and poems and messages in order to make an assignation?

Outside the door to the napkin's quarters, Nephelais said, "This one thinks you should come to the next banquet to serve as a napkin. There's coin to be made when the guests are generous. Our taskmistress has to hire extras for big banquets anyway, and if you give her a few beadcoins at the end of the night, she'll be glad to let you serve."

"But this one doesn't wish to be a—how do you call it?—waste receptacle."

"Then if a man beckons, summon another napkin, ein? He doesn't care what's under the shawl, and there are plenty who would change places—because a man gives a little something to one who has done him this service. Ein? What do you say?"

I shook my head. "You're kind. But it thinks—it knows nothing of duties yet, from the bathing room. But it is grateful, ein?"

Wildfire

When we parted, I tried to give her a gift in thanks, three pewter bead-coins from my net cap. She refused.

That night I learned I was to share the little room behind the painted door with another woman as well as Meninx. Her name was Lychnais, and her duty was to wash, dye, and dress the hair of the arthygater and her women. She had a severe look, with the skin stretched over the bones of her face as if she'd pulled her hair too tight when she made the elaborate braids and coils of her coiffure. She didn't seem pleased to find I had moved in, especially when she learned I knew nothing of the art of depilating.

We stretched out that night in fresh bedstraw. My head was against one wall and my feet another, and I was between two women, one sick and the other disgruntled. The room closed on me like a fist. I tried to lie still as long as I could stand it; I turned and thought of Meninx lying always on her left side, suffering, and how my restlessness must be adding to her torment. Long before dawn a servant began to clatter about in the next room, lighting a fire to heat bathwater in the large tank. Our room became very warm, too warm.

In the morning Lychnais squatted beside the brazier, fanning smoke toward the open door to the tunnel with her left hand and stirring a pot with her right. She was melting honeycombs with their honey into a thick golden paste.

She said, "This one thought you would never stop kicking," and gave a half smile, which I was glad to see. I was beginning to fear she might always be cross.

"This one begs pardon," I said. I went to open the bathing room door for air and she gestured to stop me. Already the tharos servants were in there, preparing for the bath.

I pointed to the pot and whispered. "Is that honey to Meninx?"

"No, surely not. It's for taking hair from the skin. You should be doing this, but the bathmistress told this one you were strange-ignorant, so it will do your tasks today, and you'll watch and learn, ein?—so as not to discommode the arthygater with your clumsiness." The honey mixture had melted, and Lychnais poured it into an elegant golden basin suspended on a bronze tripod over a smaller basin full of burning olive oil. The tripod's legs were cast in the shape of tharais servingwomen.

"It is grateful. It is still more grateful if it has, if you give me a little honey, just a little little honey, to put on Meninx's sores. Honey to stop stink and rot."

"This isn't just honey. There is also wax and lemon."

I had learned of lemons in Lambanein; I tried to eat one, but I didn't like the sour taste. "What for?"

"You'll see—you spread it on the skin while hot, and let it cool and peel it off, zup! And the hair comes out."

"Does it hurt?"

"What do you think, ein?"

"Can you give honey for Meninx?"

She nodded toward a clay jar near her feet. "It needs to get more today. If there's any left, you can have it."

I washed copious pus from Meninx's sores, and she covered her face and bit back her cries. There wasn't enough honey to pour into the open sores, so I tore strips from Meninx's shawl to make bandages, and soaked them in honey warmed with a little water. I covered these bandages with others made greasy with lard, just as the Dame used to do.

Meninx said, "There would be enough honey if Lychnais didn't sell it."

Lychnais said, "How was this one to know, ein?" Now she was vexed again.

She told me to fetch more water for our ablutions, and I took up the jar and opened the door to the bathing room. "Not there! Down there," she said, pointing to the tunnel door. "Down and right."

Past the waste jar niches under the arthygater's privy and around the corner, I found a boar's-head spout in the wall. Water trickled from the jaws into a stone basin and from there overspilled into a drain.

Lychnais said my hands were filthy, even after I scrubbed and scrubbed with handfuls of straw and sand. The stain from the dye was deep in every crack in my skin, and darkest in the bed of my fingernails.

Her own hands were ruddy from the henna she used to dye hair. She kept her nails pared short except for those of the thumb and first finger of her right hand, which were long and pointed. I saw she was uneasy. She washed, put on her shoe-stockings and tied the drawstrings around her ankles, and rewrapped her gown to make the folds drape more perfectly down the front. She took off her net cap so the coins wouldn't disturb the noblewomen by jingling. Lastly she arranged the shawl over her head. She told me to hurry, for the first bathers would be arriving soon.

I was surprised. "You want this one there—in there? It doesn't know how."

"Stand still and they won't see you, ein? Keep the hands hidden under the shawl, like this." She stooped and peered through a peephole in the bathing room door. The hole had a small wooden cover, hanging loosely from a nail, which she pushed aside in order to look. She turned and swiftly picked up the tripod with the wax and honey mixture. I followed her into the bathing room.

* * *

Wildfire

On one side of the door with the peephole, Meninx lay on bedstraw already befouled. On the other side, I stood against the wall in the painted garden as still as I could be, while a breeze through the high windows stirred my shawl. Female musicians in the corner played an air as soft as the breeze itself. One made a skittering sound on a small drum, another blew a bird-bone flute, and a third strummed an instrument that looked like a small loom. A tharos servant knelt at a mortar, grinding cloves and anise to scent the air. Another servant reverently set out on a tray tortoiseshell combs, twigs dipped in honey and pepper paste to clean teeth, and a golden casket containing a sack of yellow powder to dust on forearms. Also in attendance were the factotum, the bathmistress, the keeper of jewelry, the keeper of garments, a masseuse, a painter of cosmetics, two women to tend the fire and make sure the bathwater was neither too hot nor too cold, and three to serve refreshments and carry messages. A koprophagais woman, who had crept up the tunnel stairs, waited in the privy room to cleanse the arthygater's buttocks.

The first to visit the bathing room, just after dawn, was the arthygater's mother-in-law. She was accompanied by an elderly kinswoman who dutifully listened to the mother-in-law's complaints on the subjects of constipation and the ingratitude of those who ought to know better. Every noble household was supplied with a number of such inferiors, related or otherwise, who offered flatteries in exchange for patronage. The Lambaneish called them limpets, for the way they clung to their betters and could not be pried off.

After the mother-in-law left, Arthygater Katharos arrived with a following of guests and limpets. It was the first time I'd seen the arthygater, and I was somewhat disappointed to find that she looked unremarkable. I suppose I'd expected her to be beautiful. Not Katharos. She had a face square from forehead to jaw, a small nose, and two chins. Her expression was hard, or shrewd, rather. But when she disrobed and lay down on the marble bench to be shaved by Lychnais, I almost gasped aloud. She bore a tattoo of a blue serpent, which encircled her waist like a girdle and looped around her navel. The tail went between her legs and emerged again at her tailbone; the red forked tongue touched the bony notch at the base of her throat, visible even when she was clothed, if one knew where to look. This must be the same sort of tattoo that King Corvus's wife, Kalos, had borne. No wonder they'd called her a lamia.

The arthygater's skin was smooth and unwrinkled, though she was old enough to have sons who were grown men. No sign of scales.

With a blade made of a shard of black obsidian, Lychnais shaved the hair high on the nape of the arthygater's neck. It was a mark of beauty in Lambanein to have what they called an egret's neck; the arthygater didn't possess one, so she exaggerated it by other means. Then Lychnais shaved her mistress's armpits and groin, and removed the hair on her limbs with the mixture of hot wax and honey, until she was smooth as a girlchild. Highborn women in Lambanein had the hair of their bodies removed every fifth day, and also before festivals, banquets, fasts, and assignations. They showed a positive disgust toward this hair, considering it filthy, ugly (one word for both in Lambaneish), while they devoted much of the day to adorning the hair of their heads, though it was also tharais.

While Lychnais worked on her, the arthygater spoke to one of her honored guests about the purchase of some bales of wool from a certain kind of sheep, and might there be lambs too, at a fair price, in time for the next New Moon banquet? Then she gave lengthy instructions to her factotum, Gnathin—mostly having to do with cloth, to judge from the words I recognized. Gnathin must tell such-and-so not to make any more of some sort of gauzes, for likely they wouldn't sell in Incus this year, and Gnathin must find out if the new bondwomen from Loxos could embroider, and so forth. The factotum counted beads on a cord, one for each command, each bead different.

After her tharais hair was removed, the arthygater was washed and rinsed by her tharos bath servants. Only then was she clean enough to lie in the tepid water of the bathing pool. The arthygater finished her soak, was dried and oiled and massaged and painted, and then it was Lychnais's turn to attend her again by oiling and tidying her hair, which was burgundy, almost the color of a plum leaf. This was no simple matter, as the hair was affixed to an elaborate wickerwork shape, and inevitably it was disarranged during sleep. And of course the guests and limpets also had to be depilated, washed, and have their hair dressed in an order dictated by protocol.

When they left, I thought surely the work was done. But other noblewomen followed, and lastly the arthygater's two indolent daughters-in-law and several of their friends. They had slept late into the afternoon and we had all been obliged to wait for them.

Afterward Mermera watched Lychnais and me to make sure we swept up every single hair and nail paring and burned them in the beehive hearth, so that no particle would remain that could be used in a curse.

That evening I asked Lychnais about the arthygater's tattoo. She said the tattoos were given to adepts of the Serpent Cult, which was dedicated to the worship of Katabaton.

"Are men in the cult?" I asked.

"Of course not!"

"What do they do? Can the arthygater turn into a serpent?"

"This one knows nothing about it, nor does it wish to know, ein? These things are tharos matters, and besides, Katabaton punishes profaners who spy on the cult's mysteries. She takes the form of a huge pale-bellied serpent and swallows them up, swallows them whole." Lychnais shuddered. "This one can't abide snakes, may Katabaton forgive it."

Lychnais wouldn't go near the one that lived in a cage in the bathing room, a slender grass snake with a back bright as green enamel. I'd have thought a creature that slithered on its belly on the ground would be tharais. Not so.

I practiced shaving myself first, until I no longer nicked my arms and legs with the perilously sharp obsidian blade. Lychnais allowed me to practice on her. Sometimes Meninx would rouse herself to tell me how she had performed such duties. They taught me to understand the language of gesture, the left hand speaking to the tharais servants, the right hand to the tharos. We were all afraid of the arthygater's wrath should I prove clumsy or slow to do her bidding.

It was three days before I served as a depilator in the bathing room, on the old limpet who attended the arthygater's querulous mother-in-law. My hand shook and Mermera the bathmistress watched me like an owl. She waited till after the bath to strike me with her flail for allowing the wax to cool so that it didn't spread properly. It would have been unseemly to disturb the harmony of the bathing room by reminding anyone of the invisible tharais servants.

Some of my ministrations were painful, no doubt: plucking long hairs around the nipple, and scraping the razor against the most tender of all flesh. But the noblewomen wouldn't complain. To mention to the bathmistress that I was less skilled than the one who had served before would be to imply that one tharais was not just the same as another.

And now I learned, as I had not in the dyehouse, what it truly meant to be tharais—to be so despised that my face must go unseen, and my voice unheard. I was a mudwoman, and had long borne the contempt of my betters, but never had I suffered a disregard so thorough that I vanished under it. Surely the abhorrence of the tharos was a sort of curse; it caused a malaise, a dreariness that weighed upon me even when my duties were done and I bared my face and spoke to Meninx and Lychnais. And I could see they felt it too.

The tharos were not troubled by the abhorrence they felt, far from it. They were tranquil so long as we tharais were merely pairs of hands that performed necessary but vile services.

I wanted to turn the blade ever so slightly, to cut something other than hairs, to make someone flinch. But I wasn't such a fool as that.

CHAPTER 22

White Petals

eninx's sores showed signs of healing, but there was no denying she was getting worse. She had begun to retch up a greenish and bitter spew, and her skin turned the color of old ivory.

Arthygater Katharos had no use for bondservants with wasting illnesses. If Meninx were to remind the arthygater of her presence behind the painted door by troubling the air with foul smells or cries of pain, she would be sent away to the temple of Peranon. There she would have been one of many, hundreds even, lying in their own filth on straw. It was no place to linger. Those who didn't mend fast, died fast.

For many months before I came, Lychnais had cared for Meninx so she wouldn't be banished to a temple sickroom. She'd covered her stink with fragrances of candlebark and spices, and performed the depilator's tasks in addition to her own. Lychnais had an impatient manner and ungentle hands, and little ways of showing Meninx that tending her was a bother. Yet she'd taken up the burden of her own will; I admired her for it, though I couldn't warm to her.

I was glad to take some of this burden from Lychnais—I found it impossible to begrudge Meninx anything, for she was a most uncomplaining and humble person, so grateful for any small service that it wrung my heart.

A wise healer knows better than to torment a dying patient with useless remedies, but I wasn't convinced a cure was hopeless. And if I couldn't cure Meninx of her baffling Lambaneish illness, I hoped at least to ease her suffering.

When Lychnais was away on an errand, I drew the compass on the tiled floor of our room with charcoal. I scratched the godsign for Wend Weaver onto both sides of a flat fava bean to represent the Dame, and inscribed the sign of Growan Crone on another bean for Na, and cast the beans instead of their bones.

Then I rubbed out the charcoal markings and covered the smudges with straw, and sat there crying, because the Dame and Na were no longer with me, and the signs meant nothing.

Meninx touched my back, saying, "What's the matter?" I hadn't realized she was awake.

I turned to her and took her hand. "Homesick, that's all," I said.

That night I lay restless, worrying about Meninx and praying for her to all the gods, even Lambaneish ones. I knew of herbs that could be used against her various afflictions, but as frail as she was, the wrong remedy could kill her.

I was a greenwoman before I learned how to use the compass for healing, but in those days, before the lightning, my memory could be trusted. And even then I'd been ignorant, I'd taken perilous chances.

I remembered going into the fields after casting the bones for those struck down by the shiver-and-shake, and how the Dame and Na had pointed to what the avatars provided. I had such a sense of surety then, with those sure guides. They saw the pattern entire that I glimpsed by way of signs: the person—never merely a sufferer, but a whole self on whom suffering was inscribed; the gods who worked their wills upon the crisis; the malady and remedy fitting without a chink between them.

Even when the remedies didn't suffice—even when the gods took Tobe despite all I could do—at least I knew I had not erred, had not caused harm to those I aimed to help.

This surety had been stolen from me. I mourned the Dame and Na still, but there was such fury commingled with my sorrow that I could get no ease from weeping. I wondered if the thief who'd stolen their bones had dared show them openly after I left the manufactory.

I must get back in there to find out.

But the textrices would scorn me for a tharais, and drive me out. Zostra would have told them, so everyone would know the price of defying her.

I could brazen it out, say the arthygater had sold me instead. Why shouldn't I be tharos? It was easy to tell Blood from mud by the tattoos on the Blood's cheeks, but there was no such indelible mark to distinguish tharos from tharais. I could pretend to be a peddler and bribe my way in. I could be a real peddler; if I had something to sell I could make money for the journey home. All I needed was tharos clothing.

I fell asleep, and I was on the mountain looking down on the Athlewood, where a strong wind set the bright new leaves to shimmering. Cloud shadows prowled the valley. On sunny days like this, the mountainside was like the flank of a great warm beast with a rough coat of turf and thickets, giving off a green and mineral fragrance of meadow and stone.

I raked soil in the herb garden and sowed seeds of milk thistle. When I went back to my house, I saw swallows building a nest of mud and grass under the eaves, and I greeted them and made them welcome. Oh, I was glad of their company!

Galan had sent me here to wait for him, that he might visit when he wished. I could not live on waiting, waiting and not knowing when he'd appear. Stale bread between feasts was a slow way to starve. I had to find nourishment in making and doing and looking.

Crux Sun had blessed me with this dream, sending signs of swallows and thistles, shining brightly to show me where to look. I thanked her for it, though the dream had given me pain too, touching upon the absence of Sire Galan, who had inherited some of her brightness. I wished I could dream of him.

I climbed the stairs to the kitchen court and covered my face with the shawl. The porter was snoring in his niche, but his dog challenged me. It was fortunate Nephelais had introduced us. I left by the tharais hindgate, fearing that at any moment I might be caught and punished for wandering at will, for I still found it hard to believe the arthygater gave her tharais bondservants such license, while keeping her textrices locked up.

Blossoms from the pear tree had drifted into the alley. I walked along the two-story wall of the manufactory, which abutted the kitchens, and turned the corner; no doors into the alley, no windows. Once I found tharos clothing, I would have to get into the manufactory through the guarded door in the kitchen court or not at all.

I meant to go down to the river through the tharais district, supposing it would be easy to find by heading downhill and south. But I was thwarted. The palace district was full of narrow twisting alleys and stairways, which offered misleading views of rooftops and trees and sky and led to blank walls.

I descended cobbled stairs and found yet another wall, but this one had in it a small wooden door without a latch. Rather than climb the weary way back up again, treading in my own footsteps, I pushed the door open. Another stairway, enclosed this time, and dark and daunting as the palace tunnels. I felt my way down with my hands on the walls. I told myself I'd go ten steps, then another ten, and another, counting in Lambaneish at first, then in the High when I ran out of names for numbers. At the fortieth step the walls changed from alternating courses of brick and stone to solid rock scored with chisel marks. This bedrock too was layered, with slanting seams of different textures, but gods had laid these courses, not men. At the two hundred and eighty-first step, there was another door. I pushed it open and the hinges whined.

I stood on a ledge halfway down a sheer cliff, looking out upon a cleft riven into the body of Mount Allaxios. Swallows darted across the narrow chasm. A long way below, the floor of the cleft was choked with boulders and thickets. To my right, to the west, the Sun sprinkled flakes of gold on the river, and lit the striated stones of the crags, and made every new leaf glow like green embers. I had to shade my eyes.

The stairway continued at my feet, hacked into the living stone of the cliff. I pressed close to the mountain flank as I descended, until I reached the bottom stair, a wide ledge more than a man-height above the floor of the cleft. And there I found a cave nearly hidden by hanging bluebind vines, a waterfall of sky blue flowers. On the rough hollow inside the cave's throat, someone had depicted the wife-mother Katabaton in simple strokes of white paint, now almost worn away. Roots had forced their way through the rock above her head.

The cleft and shrine seemed secret and forgotten, as if I were the first person to visit for years, but there were garlands of browning daffydowndillies on the floor of the cave. I'd lost my way to the tharais gate and found my way to this holy place, and surely my errant steps had not erred after all. I made a garland of bluebind to lay at Katabaton's feet, and prayed she would bless Meninx.

I reached the floor of the cleft by sliding down a slope of scree. Crux Sun lit my path and I jumped from one boulder to another like a goat. From the stony ground, milk thistles stood up tall, already blooming, each tufted purple flower wearing a collar of prickly leaves. It was too early in the year for the potent seeds, but all parts of the plant were beneficial; I harvested several whole thistles, roots and all, and blooms to boil up as a spring tonic.

I went on down to the riverbank, where the Sun sparked on the small yellow flowers of a swallowwort almost engulfed by grapevines. I wouldn't have thought to pluck it if not for the swallows in my dream. I dug the plant up by the roots with a stick, staining my hands with its bright saffron-colored sap, for the stems were easily crushed and broken.

The Dame had taught me a song for the swallowwort, so I could remember its nature and usefulness and thank Crux, who gave it to us. I hummed the tune, but the words eluded me. Yet I recalled very well the Dame steeping the herb in white wine with a sprinkling of aniseeds, and giving it to a woman in the village whose skin had yellowed from jaundice—I could get aniseeds easily, they were used here to sweeten the air and the breath. And the Dame had dabbed the yellow-orange sap on her arms to rid herself of freckles.

I had the Sun's blessed light all the way up the stairs to the door into the mountain. Each day was longer than the day before, and I took heart from it. When Midsummer was here, I would go.

That night I served Meninx the boiled flowers and stalks of the thistle, and her appetite being small, she ate but a little, and Lychnais and I shared the rest. I also gave Meninx a weak infusion of swallowwort leaves and thistle root, and it seemed to do her some good. She was too weak to endure a drastic purgative. If she mended at all, she would mend slowly.

Today was the New Moon, the third since I'd come to Lambanein. Arthygater Katharos was offering a banquet this evening, a special one, for the New Moon coincided with the blooming of a certain famous apple tree. Now Lychnais was preparing the arthygater's hair for the festivities, mixing a paste of henna and indigo. The smell was rank and fertile, like a bog or a woman during her tides.

I served the arthygater's niece, a favorite among her companions. This niece stretched out on her back upon a cold marble bench and closed her eyes. I began to shave her with my slender blade. The hair of her head was red-gold, and of her body so pale as to be almost white. Her quim was like that of a girl, the parts hidden within a smooth cleft. She turned over so I could remove the hair between her buttocks, and I saw her fist ball up on the linen coverlet. I had done this service for other women, young and old, but this time I felt a small, exquisite, painful tremor at the sound of the blade scraping her flawless skin.

I touched the woman's shoulder. She sat up and chatted with the bathmistress, who was neither bondwoman nor noble but something in between. Mermera called the niece Keros; she wondered if Keros might want her nails cut in the style of the raven's beak, ein? So she would be ready when the Crow came courting? The girl blushed, which was taken for assent.

Arthygater Katharos said, "A crow is ill omened, such a tharais carrion-eater. People should not call him that."

I covered Keros's limbs with the wax mixture, which had to be painfully hot or it wouldn't spread. While the wax cooled and hardened, I cut the nails on the thumb and two fingers of her left hand in the raven's beak, with two sharp points close together; the rest I trimmed in the usual half-moon style. So she announced herself ready for amorous combat—and if she didn't wish to reveal it, she could wear golden fingercaps, like thimbles, inset with bejeweled nails.

Keros said, "Suppose he is hairy, ein?"

One of the arthygater's guests laughed and said, "Send a maidservant to him one night and she'll tell you whatever you want to know. She'll tally the hairs on his chest and measure the length of his manhood too, ein?" This guest was the one who had sold the arthygater wool and lambs, Phleibin by name.

310

Wildfire

I peeled wax from Keros's arm and felt her shudder slightly.

Arthygater Katharos said, "His ears are of an excellent shape, did you notice? Long lobes, set close to the head." Lychnais had rinsed the henna from the arthygater's hair, and now she was plaiting it through a wicker cap with horns like a ram. She used silk strands of the same burgundy color to make the hair look more abundant, and ribbons and pearls for adornment.

Keros said, "I wonder if he knows the twenty-five Postures?"

Arthygater Katharos said dryly, "I'm sure my sister taught him all that was necessary. Kalos never was shy."

I tried to quell the sound of my breath, to move shrouded in silence. I peeled wax from Keros's thigh. She was made like a filly, with delicate legs and narrow hocks. Behind the knee I touched a ticklish spot and Keros drew back.

They spoke of King Corvus and Kalos, his dead wife. So she was Katharos's sister—I should have seen that long ago, though Katharos seemed old enough to be the mother of the woman in my dream.

I went down the tunnel to the napkin's dormitory to see Nephelais, as I did whenever I could. She had introduced me to some of the other napkins, and I'd spent pleasant afternoons there, when my work was done, listening to the gossip and joining in from time to time. I seemed to be able to make myself understood now even when I got the words wrong. Nephelais said she could hardly believe I came all the way from Incus, for I knew how to sing when I spoke, instead of mumbling like most strange-ignorant people.

Today I visited her with a purpose, to ask if I might be able to serve as a napkin that evening. Oh indeed, she said, the taskmistress was short of hands and making everyone miserable.

Then I lowered my voice to a whisper, and confided the idea I'd had about wearing tharos clothes to get into the manufactory. I had seven pewter beadcoins and two of coiled copper. Was that enough to buy a wrapper and shawl?

"Don't you know what happens if they catch you in tharos clothing?"

I shrugged. "Give this one a beating?"

"If you're lucky. More likely the mistress would have you maimed, ein? She would be very angry. It's a nuisance, the purges and the rites of purification when a tharais has caused pollution. Expensive too."

"How do you mean, maimed?"

"Cut you. That's what she did to Polukhaitais." She leaned closer. "The arthygater's tormentors cut off her nose, ein? So she can't pretend to be tharos."

It was hard to look at Polukhaitais, for she had two long dark holes in her face where a nose ought to be. I'd supposed she was born that way. She was shy of her disfigurement, and sometimes wore her shawl over her face even in the dormitory, and always ducked her head when she spoke. I said, "But they won't catch this one. It goes out the tharais gate, comes back in the tharos gate, ein?"

"They'll catch you by the stink of onions," Nephelais said.

"But if this one wants to try—what do you think? Does it, can it buy cloths with this?" I jingled the beadcoins strung on the cords of my cap.

"Those pewters aren't enough to buy a rag. Maybe you can make money at the banquet, ein? If a man is generous. Or there are soiled garments sometimes. When people eat or drink too much and spew on themselves, the arthygater has clean clothing brought to them, and this one takes the dirty ones to the tharais launderers to be washed. No one would notice if a pair of cloths went missing for a day or so."

"Have you any now?"

"The last banquet was all old aunties, ein? But tonight Arthygater Katharos entertains many noblemen, they say. It will be a long evening, and as some of them are strange-ignorant ones, they probably can't hold their drink—begging pardon, no offense, ein?"

"The clothes of men do not help."

"Well, you're tall, and the hair is short. In a tunic you'd look a handsome fellow. How are your legs? Do you have fine round calves?" She pinched my cheek.

I batted away her hand and laughed, hiding my teeth behind my hand. "The legs are bony. And besides, a man in the manufactory is a fox among hens, ein?" I didn't know where I'd learned the word for fox in Lambaneish, but *alopexan* came to my tongue as if I'd always known it.

"No, a rooster," she said. "They'll be plucking at the tunic to see what you've got."

"Then this one disappoints," I said. The baby Melimelais was lying on her mother's lap, waving her arms and legs. I rubbed her stomach and she grinned. She had no teeth yet to show or hide.

The taskmistress of the napkins was a woman of eminence among tharais, and she wanted me to know it. She feigned reluctance to let me serve until I gave her four pewter beadcoins. I asked if I might attend Arkhyios Corvus, and she said I couldn't have my pick of guests, who did I think I was? I had to humble myself until she was mollified.

Nephelais and I climbed the stairs to the dining court, a one-story building between the kitchens and the arthygater's living quarters. It was a balmy spring evening, a fine night to dine outside and honor the blooming of the apple tree that was the guardian of the dining court and its greatest ornament. The tree's crooked trunk bore the scars of many years, and the bark was splotched with lichens. The blossoms were a scented white cloud above the roof, and the boughs were hung with lanterns of colored glass and cages of songbirds.

Nephelais and I unrolled patterned carpets over scented herbs in the courtyard arcades. Behind us came tharos servants, carrying large wooden platforms that served as both chairs and tables. They looked to me like wide beds with scrolled backrests, and when the servants arranged silk cushions on them, I wondered if the guests planned to sleep there too.

Nephelais lifted a brass latch in the shape of an onion, and opened a door so cunningly hidden in a wall painting of dancing girls that I hadn't noticed it. We peeked inside. I took the room for a privy, which was indeed one of its purposes. It had a bench with holes for guests to relieve themselves, and straw on the floor like a stable. But Nephelais told me guests took napkins here to use as receptacles. She said there were several such rooms, all decorated with lewd paintings framed to look like windows. In this room the painter had depicted those Postures—seven of the twenty-five—in which a woman turns her back to a man, for tharos men never prick tharais women face-to-face. The women were naked except for shawls over their heads, and the men more or less clothed.

Nephelais giggled at my prudish shock, and hurried me away. No time to look at the paintings, or gape at the tower over the entry, where musicians were tuning their instruments behind marble lattices. No time to wander in the enormous pleasure garden that divided the male and female halves of the palace—had I been permitted there.

The guests were already arriving. In a tiled pavilion just outside the dining court, I knelt with other tharais women to wash their feet. We gave the guests soft shoe-stockings to wear when treading on the precious carpets.

Divine Aboleo sat down before me, and from long habit I kept my head down and my gaze averted from his face, even though I wore the shawl. I drew off his heavy boots, and saw the tips of several of his toes were shriveled, and as black as if they'd been dipped in ink. The blackening from frostbite. It took a long time, months, for the dead parts to slough off.

I hoped he wouldn't notice the scars around my wrist, or the way my hands shook as I poured water from the ewer over his feet. He raised his right foot so I could dry it with a cloth. I put on the shoe-stockings and tightened the laces around his ankles. He stood, scraping the chair across the tiles, and went away. Another guest sat down, no one I recognized.

And I found I was exhilarated. Through the shawl, I could watch and not be watched, touch and yet remain untouched.

* * *

I served four guests seated on a dining platform, and my duties were simple. Between each course I offered guests a silver basin of water sprinkled with apple blossoms to rinse their hands, and cloths of bleached tow to dry themselves. Should they find it necessary to spit, I brought them a deep brass vessel, and feathers if they wanted to purge. A tharos woman served their food and drink.

One of the guests I served was Phleibin, whom I'd seen in the arthygater's bathing room. There she had seemed an intimate—and a trading partner—of Arthygater Katharos; here in the dining court, her importance could be better judged. She was more than halfway down one of the long colonnades, far from the platform the arthygater shared with her husband, Consort Ostrakan, and two honored guests: her niece Keros and King Corvus.

I watched the king. We all did. Even at such a distance from the arthygater's dining platform, the language of comportment could be interpreted. He sat cross-legged on the platform, inclining toward Keros, who faced him. He seemed attentive. He wore a crown, a guest wreath of red flowers.

Phleibin and her husband and another couple gossiped about him as anyone gossips—for the pleasure of a tale, the pleasure of finding things out, and the pleasure of speaking badly about others behind their backs. The shrill voices of the women were easier to understand than the low rumble of the men. I understood this much: Keros was not the first noblewoman paraded before Arkhyios Corvus—here they called him arkhyios, oe prince, for there could be only one arkhon—to lure him into marriage. There had been five such feasts already, and he had failed to show an interest in the marriageable women beyond offering them the obligatory praise poems.

He had failed to show an interest in any women whomsoever, Phleibin said.

"What about boys?"

"No boys either."

"The praise poems were not too bad. Better than I expected from a strange-ignorant person."

"Surely he had a poet do them up beforehand."

"None will admit to it."

"He must pay a lot for silence. When poets have done something well, they want everyone to know."

But Keros was a granddaughter of the arkhon—therefore an arthygater by title—and a prettier prize than any offered before.

Poor girl, they said. A man of no prospects.

Wildfire

I edged sideways to see King Corvus between the columns. He smiled at Keros, his teeth white in his dark beard. But my nearsighted right eye saw him otherwise, saw pictures woven of strands of lamplight and the dark threads of my shawl. I saw the king turn in his saddle to squint at a line of men behind him, on one of those strange days in the mountains when the Sun shone even as winds drove storm clouds across the peaks. There was snow in the raven feathers of his tall hat and the fur of his wolfskin cloak, and snow in his beard and mustache. He bent over, coughing, and straightened up and wiped his face, and spurred his horse to breast the frozen waves and fathoms of snow.

I rubbed my wrist. The higher the master, the more boastful the servant, it is said. How desperate he must have been to listen to me in the mountains—a tharais—a mudwoman. How I'd flattered myself, thinking I might be important to him even now. Because all that, the ice and rock and winds of the Ferinus, seemed a dire dream, and here and now was another sort of dream in which I observed but did not act.

I leaned against a wall painted with dancers. Reflected lanterns shimmered in the waters of the circular pool in the courtyard. Soft breezes carrying scents of apple blossoms and spices pressed my shawl against my face. And now the musicians played a new tune, loud and joyful. *The bride is coming, make her welcome!* Some of the guests sang and clapped in time to the drum, rejoicing: *The bride is coming!*

I wondered who was to be wed tonight. The bride came dancing in from the outer garden. She was much taller than her female attendants, and it took me a moment to realize she must be wearing tall pattens or stilts under her robes. She wore a red wig, and her silver moon mask, twice the size of an ordinary face, seemed astonished; the eyes and mouth were round holes, and the eyebrows curved like sickles.

Her betrothed too was a giant accompanied by a retinue of dancers. His huge mask was of gold, and likewise of gold his cuirass in the shape of a muscular torso. Bride and bridegroom crossed arching bridges to meet on a stone island in the pool, and their dance was wedding and consummation.

No use now to retell the story they enacted that night—for it was a story, and not a real wedding between nobles, as I had first supposed. I couldn't understand all the words, but there were other languages intelligible to the senses: the lover strutting like a stallion, a defiant gesture from a wife who had seemed all submission, her husband's wrath, the frightening stench of oil set ablaze on the surface of the pool, and above all the music, which entered by the portals of my ears and found the quickest corridor to my heart.

The stone island was in turn marriage bed, garden, and battlefield, and lastly a wasteland where the bride—the wife—the adulteress—lay shivering in the cold. She sang a lament unaccompanied, in a voice of such purity she won silence from the jaded spectators, and as she sang, a gust sent a blizzard of apple blossoms swirling over the courtyard, snow falling on a desolate land. The singer's voice thinned to a fine thread, a whisper. When it broke, she died.

I was glad of the shawl that hid my tears. I knew she hadn't truly died. I knew boys in the apple tree had shaken the branches to make petals fall like snow. But it was no mere artifice. It was an enchantment, and I had willingly believed it.

I missed the summoning gesture of Phleibin's husband until he made it so emphatic it caught my eye. I hurried forward to offer the basin and cloth. He was vexed with me and wiped his sticky hand on my skirt, rubbing hard from buttock to knee. He did it again, digging his fingers into my thigh, while he spoke to his wife and the others, saying Aeidin had been in fine voice but Ripan should never have attempted the lover. Did you hear his voice shake?

I was shaking myself, in a fury at his touch and the way he'd tried to ruin the enchantment with his sour whine. If Phleibin's husband wanted a receptacle, let him have one. It would not be me. I slipped away along the wall, and whispered to the first tharais woman I passed, "Do you trade with this one? It thinks he, that man, wants a receptacle." She shook her head and said nothing. The second napkin hissed, "Go back! Hurry!" By the time I reached the third, I'd taken two pewter beadcoins from my net cap. When I pressed the coins into her hand, she nodded. I took her place against the wall, and dried my palms on the wrapper and thought of the man's hands on me.

I was closer now to Arthygater Katharos and King Corvus. One of the guests seated before me was a cataphract named Sire Vafra, a follower of King Corvus. He'd taken the longer route out of the Ferinus, by horseback—so the rest of the king's army must have arrived in Allaxios. A tharos servant poured doublewine in Sire Vafra's glass goblet, and he emptied it quickly. She gave him more, and he drank again. His brown beard was trimmed like a hedge all along his lower jaw, and his bobble moved up and down under the shaven skin of his throat as he gulped.

Sire Vafra wielded what little Lambaneish he knew with a clumsy tongue, in conversation with a plump, white-haired man and his plump, black-haired wife who shared the same dining platform. The wife seemed half the age of her husband, and yet well past her fruitful years. Perhaps her hair was dyed.

A young man arose from one of the platforms and stepped in front of a column. He raised his arms, and spoke loudly over the hubbub, saying something about the breeze and white petals.

Arthygater Katharos raised her voice, saying, "Hush! Let's hear it again." This time everyone quieted, and he declaimed so that I understood every word.

> "You beckon and the breeze
> brings to you white petals.
> I would serve you as faithfully."

He returned to his seat, and a murmur came from the crowd, followed by a surprisingly long, expectant silence.

A woman stepped forward and in a clear high voice she said,

> "Who leans upon a breeze,
> will fall upon hard ground,
> not a bed of soft, white petals."

"Oh, well done!" said the arthygater, laughing, and women applauded in the Lambaneish way, snapping their fingers.

A briefer silence. The black-haired woman nudged her husband, and he stood quickly, as if afraid another would get there before him. He said,

> "To remember this night,
> I gather white petals.
> Longing grows even in hard ground."

He sat down and his wife praised him lavishly. Sire Vafra raised his glass to him and the tharos servant filled it again.

The same woman who had spoken before came forward and said,

> "Night hides under her shawl.
> She passes swiftly by,
> a breeze scattering white petals."

The guests applauded with enthusiasm, and the white-haired man admired the way she'd neatly stitched in the breeze as well as the night.

King Corvus stood and I held my breath. He said,

> "White petals of snow drift.
> They are caught in your shawl,
> immolate on your burning skin."

Silence after this, the highest praise of all, and I wondered if the storm of petals had made the king recall the Ferinus too. Then everyone snapped their fingers and cried Ah! and Oh!

Arthygater Katharos rose for the first time since the feast had begun, and her husband stood with her. She took his hand and said, "This night too must pass in her shawl."

Surely the feast was over. But no, it was merely time for the female guests to take their leave, which they did at leisure, parading around the courtyard to greet one another and say farewell in the next breath. I thought the night would never pass, in a shawl or otherwise, for after they left, whores strolled into the dining court. Rather than saffron garments, they wore silks dyed magenta or cerulean blue or apple green, with bright striped bands at the ends.

The old man beckoned one of the whores, and he must have spoken to her with some gesture, for she sat beside Sire Vafra and twined her arm around his. She had the ruddy brown skin and thick black hair of an Ebanakan, but she spoke Lambaneish as if born to it. Her sandals were of glove-thin leather laced with silken cords. The tops of her feet were bare and the pale hollows of her arches revealed, and by now I knew that was obscene. But drink had made Sire Vafra too sleepy to appreciate her provocative feet. He rested his head on the scrolled arm of the platform, with his eyes shut and his mouth open. She raised her eyebrows and the white-haired man patted the seat beside him.

The banquet commenced all over again: eating, drinking, and improvisations. By then they had tired of white petals.

The first one to recite after King Corvus said,
> "I crave immolation.
> She shows me her cold back,
> smooth as snow on a winter field."

The next said,
> "Why talk of winter fields?
> In spring she'll thaw and yield.
> She will be plowed, if not by you."

The white-haired man stood again, saying,
> "Young men speak of plowing
> as if they knew something.
> Their hands are without calluses."

A young man stood up and said,
> "Show me your calluses,
> old poet! Your fingers
> are as soft as . . ."

He paused, and shouted, "White petals!"

The young man sat down as guests hooted and laughed and hissed. I heard a woman's shrill voice above the clamor. "That's only seven!"

The young man stood up again, and bellowed, "Are as tender as white petals!"

"Oh better, much better," the woman shouted back.

They tired of that game, and turned to others. When the whores had arrived, I'd been scandalized to think the banquet hall would be turned into a brothel—and curious, I admit, to see the twenty-five Postures and more besides. Wondering what King Corvus might do to prove or disprove the rumors of his abstinence.

But there was a reason the word *whore* in Lambaneish had its double meaning of whore-celebrant. Their trade was not the simple exchange of coin for coupling. I watched the whore lean against the white-haired poet, her head on his shoulder. Her affection for the old man did not seem feigned, nor his for her. Affection, familiarity, maybe even an old passion transmuted to friendship.

Three men taking a turn about the courtyard stopped to greet them, and at her invitation they sat down. Two squeezed onto the platform and the last sat on the ground. She dangled her foot next to him and he stared at it while the others talked and Sire Vafra snored.

I'd never heard a woman converse so freely with men, caught up in the pleasure of making her thoughts known. They spoke of the masque that night, and one man dispraised it with cutting phrases that seemed unanswerable. But she answered that every time she saw the masque performed, she saw something new in the old tale, and this time she had been moved by how much Pachys loved the friend he had betrayed. She marveled at how Ripan had shown this with a gesture and a glance, like so, and her praise made the clever man's wit seem sour rather than sharp. Sire Vafra closed his mouth and raised his head and blinked at her.

I was thirsty, and I'd been standing since sundown, and before long the birds would sing up the Sun, yet I didn't tire of watching her. The game afoot was which of them she would take home—the old one, the simpering one, the one with the acid wit, or the one who stared. Or perhaps she'd disappoint them all. Consummation was one art, anticipation another, one she practiced with apparent artlessness.

I almost missed her summoning gesture. I held out my silver basin and she dipped her palms into the water. The yellow powder on her dark forearms looked like gold dust. She belonged to Desire and I could smell her desire in the aromatic musk that clung to her garments. When she left before first light, the white-haired man and his friends left with her. I never knew which one she chose.

Sire Vafra stayed behind. He had been refreshed by his nap, perhaps, or he waited for his king, who sat long in converse with Consort Ostrakan, Divine Aboleo, and several other men. No whores. Perhaps the rumor was true. Sire Vafra called for more doublewine, and when the tharos servant leaned toward him, he put a hand on her waist and pulled her closer. She drew back, murmuring, and beckoned me. I came forward with the basin. Sire Vafra opened his purse and showed me a few beadcoins, and the tharos servant hissed in outrage, "Not here!" Sire Vafra stood and took me by the wrist and pulled me after him. He was too drunk to see the door hidden in the painted scene of dancers. I lifted the onion-shaped latch and we went into the tharais room.

He dropped my wrist and showed me the coins in his palm. Two pewters; even a two-copper whore was worth more than that. He was drunk, unsteady, and I thought I could push him over with one hand if I had to. I shook my head and he took out two more beadcoins, and when I refused again he put his hand on my belly and shoved me against the wall. He leaned on me and put his mouth on mine. Even through the shawl I tasted doublewine, mixed with aniseeds he'd chewed between courses. He reached for his laces with both hands and I gave him a push. He staggered, and I clawed the cloth from my mouth and pulled off my shawl and glared.

I said in the High, "If you offer so little, you'll pay it little mind when I refuse, eh?"

I was too furious to find the look on his face comical, or the looks, rather, as one chased another at a pace hampered by drink: outrage at the insolence of my refusal—puzzlement that I spoke a language he understood—recognition. He stepped back and began to laugh. As he was no longer pressing me against the wall, I put two paces between us, the whole width of the room.

"The king's dreamer!" Sire Vafra said. "So you're a whore now? What's your price then? Let me see what I have." He squatted down, brushed away straw, and emptied his purse on the floor. He had coins and beads of various sorts and sizes, a bronze amulet, pieces of string, and several walnuts. He swayed and sat down, saying, "Oof!" and laughing some more. He looked like a silly boy, snickering to himself. He held up two walnuts. "What do you say?"

"You are filthy as the sole in this one's foot," I said in Lambaneish. In the High I added, "I doubt you can stand upright, you or your prickle."

"Then I'll lie down," he said, and did so, sprawling on his back. "Come over here, and you can have it all, the whole purse."

I walked up to him and put my left foot, clad in the woolen shoe-stocking, on his belly. He didn't seem to know or care it was an insult to be trod on. He reached for my leg and I stepped away, and said, "Tell your king I've been dreaming about him. Can you remember that?" I stooped to pick up his copper coins. As an afterthought, I took a long carnelian bead. "I'll go hire a planking, a palanquin to carry you home."

"Don't go."

I smiled and pulled the shawl over my head. I kept his coins and didn't trouble to seek litter bearers. Someone would soon find him asleep in the straw, and see him home with or without his purse.

Day was dawning when I gave the copper beadcoins to Nephelais's taskmistress and told her I would like to serve again.

"This one thinks a use can be found for you, ein?" she said. I saw from the way she looked at me that it had been too large a bribe.

"It wants to serve Arkhyios Corvus," I said.

"He is not often a guest."

"When he is, ein?"

She laughed. "Got the eyes on the Crow, have you? Good luck. This one heard his taproot got frostbite and turned black and fell off."

"This one hears it didn't," I said.

I hurried back with two soiled tharos cloths bundled in my shawl. Lychnais was busy with the morning preparations. She said, "Meninx fretted. If you have a man, why didn't you say so? So as not to cause worry, ein?"

I crouched by Meninx without answering. I was troubled by the watery sound of her breath, and the way her mouth was pinched in pain as she slept. Her eyelids were satiny and delicate: white petals, not apple blossom but iris, threaded with blue veins.

CHAPTER 23

The Dowser

he cloths Nephelais had lent me were mismatched and soiled with vomit. The shawl, dyed with weld, was from a tharos servingwoman, and the silk wrapper belonged to a guest and was of the bright orange-yellow color from expensive saffron dye. I washed them in the tunnel below our room, and spread them in a patch of sunlight in a quiet alley, and when they were still damp I put them on. I covered my hair with the servant's shawl; I didn't have the beadcoins a woman in such a fine wrapper should display on her net cap.

I came blinking out of a narrow alley into a wide avenue lined with the high walls of palaces, and in the middle of this avenue, a glittering canal between two rows of tall slender palm trees. I retreated into the shade of the alley, overawed. Not only by the splendor of the watercourse as it descended the terraces, with its jets and chutes and statues, but by the guards peering down from towers over the grand foregates of the palaces, and the pavement crowded with litters carried by barebacked trotting men, laden donkeys, riders, and servants on foot.

I ventured into the street again and was at once part of the bustle, another hurrying figure. I tried to walk as gracefully as if I bore a water jar on my head, but fear made me awkward. Something about me—my gait or clothing or smell—surely something would give me away as tharais. And my face was so naked without the shawl. I could be seen.

The avenue led straight down to the tharos gate into the lower city—not the tharais district, where the dyehouse was, but the part reserved for ordinary tharos folk. I nodded at the guards and went through. It proved quite easy to leave the palace precincts.

I was in search of the cloth market, but I dawdled, unwilling to ask a stranger where it could be found. I turned off the canal avenue into narrow streets, following my feet, or perhaps my nose; I found myself in the crowded fragrance market, a narrow street of narrow buildings, each with a counter under a raised shutter. At one counter a little boy ground nuts that released an intoxicating smell. A gray cat jumped up on the counter, and when the boy stopped to nuzzle it, a woman scolded him from inside the shop.

I bought one nut with a pewter coin, to sweeten up the boy's mother, and walked on smiling, even with my face bared for all to see. I need not have worried that I'd be found out. I knew better than to look a man in the eye, but I looked at the women, and they at me as we passed one another, and no harm in it, just ordinary curiosity. So many kinds of people, so many faces, each bearing signs of the life lived. All unknown to me, as I was unknown to them.

I tried to fathom it, how all these folk lived in one city in one kingdom of the wide world. And how each of us in this multitude carried within us another multitude, our ancestors and descendants throughout the ages. And all of us mortal, even kings and cities and kingdoms, and all of us in time forgotten by the living. Some days that would have been a sad thought. Today I was unreasonably exalted by it.

I wandered on until I came to the cloth market, not a single street but a warren of them. I stayed away from the merchants in fine buildings and visited a square where women sat on the ground under awnings, with their cloths neatly folded before them. In Lambanein, cloth was woman's business, and I knew from eavesdropping what a bale of fine gauzes would fetch in Malleus, but Arthygater Katharos didn't trifle with small transactions; I was unsure what I could buy with the carnelian bead I'd stolen from Sire Vafra. I showed it to one clothier after another, and bargained with a seller of used clothing, who took the bead and all my coins in exchange for a linen shawl and wrapper that had been overdyed with weld after the saffron had faded.

I washed my hands and feet at the gate before entering the palace district. In the dusk I changed my clothes in an alley and became tharais again. The only witness was a scrawny brown dog that trotted past me with his head low and tail high. When I got back to our room, I realized I'd forgotten to put on the yellow powder that tharos women wore on their arms. Lucky no one had noticed.

The next afternoon I used the last of the swallowwort and milk thistle root to make the infusion for Meninx. She had taken it four days in succession, and there had been encouraging signs, especially an end to the vomiting. But these small gains could easily be lost. With my warm left hand, I stroked Meninx's thin arms and back, and her swollen legs and belly, trying—as I did every day—to unravel the flames of her hearthfire so they could flow freely throughout her body. Wishing I were deft enough to undo whatever had been done to her.

She said, "Last autumn, when this one was so sick, it gave jasmine garlands to the meneidon in the bathing pool. Where else has it been, ein? Who else could it have offended?"

Lychnais looked up from her bowl of barley cooked with beans and onions. "Maybe one of them took a fancy to you, wants a wife."

I'd heard the tales of meneidon inflicting lovesickness, but I thought it unkind of Lychnais to mention it. I grimaced at her over Meninx's head. She shrugged and scraped the wooden bowl with her spoon.

Meninx said, "This one wishes . . ." I leaned closer to hear her. "It wishes a dowser could come. It has coins saved—take them, take them all."

Lychnais shook her head. We both knew Meninx had no money, all her beadcoins spent long ago on necessities.

I wiped tears from Meninx's face with a damp rag, and she turned her head toward the wall.

In Lambanein the dead walked the river road to the overworld, tharos stepping lightly on the river's skin, tharais trudging underwater—for even in death the tharais way was harder. But the shades of people who died due to offending meneidon remained, aimless and desolate, in the vicinity of the living. Some took up residence in a cistern or waste receptacle and became meneidon themselves, easy to vex and quick to hex. Meninx dreaded this fate. Unless she could find out which meneidon she had riled, she could neither live nor die in peace. My dreams and herbs and all the warmth in my left hand couldn't cure her of this.

Meninx slept, and I asked Lychnais how much it cost to fetch a dowser, and if we could afford one. Where I came from, healers didn't work for coins, though of course they were glad to accept gifts.

"How much money do you have?" she said. "The coin is not just for the dowser. There is the feast, the sacrifice."

I confessed I had no money.

"This one saw coins on your cap yesterday. Where did they go?" I didn't choose to answer, and she said sharply, "So you are asking if this one can afford a dowser, ein? Since you spent your money."

Lychnais had beadcoins on her cap, and I knew how she came by them: she took it as her privilege to steal from the bathing room, selling or bartering honey, wax, henna, unguents, and such, in quantities Mermera wouldn't miss. "This one pays you back," I said.

I set out in my tharais clothing, and this time I found my way easily to the gate of the tharais district, and from the gate to the river, avoiding the street of dyers. I collected swallowwort and milk thistle for Meninx, greens for cooking, fibers for making net bags, and other herbs I came upon. My gather sack was nearly full when I saw drifts of sweetrush growing in the marshes, still young, knee high. I gave a prayer of thanks to Growan, for the sweetrush root belonged to the Crone, the shoot and leaves to the Maid, and the fat spathe and yellow flower to Wortweal, and all parts of it were useful.

I hitched up my wrapper and waded into the muck. The long roots grew sideways in tangled floating mats, and I used the bathing-room knife to harvest a section about as big around as my embrace. Men were out on the river in shallow drafted boats, cutting the rushes with billhooks; they shouted "Hoy" at me, but didn't interfere. I cleaned the roots of mud, and bundled the rushes with twists of bluebind to carry on my back.

I remembered gathering the rushes in our village, when in spring the river flooded the low meadow. In my webeye I saw Cook sorting rushes on the shore, looking for the tender centers of the sheaves to serve at dinner; and there was Na, laughing at the ducks waggling their tails in the air as they dove. All of us singing in the Low: *The rushes do grow green, all agreen-oh.*

I spread the outer leaves of the rushes on the floor of our room, for the smell, so pleasant to us, was loathsome to fleas. I bathed Meninx. Once I could have fit my palm into the sore on her buttocks, and now it was shallow and pink.

I scraped and sliced the sweetrush roots, and boiled them in four changes of water to take away some of their bitterness and pungency. The third water I used to make thin barley gruel for Meninx. She had no appetite, but she exerted herself to oblige me. Even this small effort made her weary. I settled her down on the fresh rushes, and she seemed to sleep.

With stolen honey I made syrup for the fourth boiling of the roots, and I stirred while they simmered. Lychnais was off on some errand, and it was quiet in the room until Meninx moaned. I saw she had been crying, and asked what troubled her.

"Nothing, nothing," she said. "This one is just remembering the bird, the day Father took this one to market, and its speedeedee in a cage, and sold these both. So long ago. It's not important."

"Why does the father sell you?"

"It was this one's own fault, ein? It took up the spindle in the left hand always, and couldn't be taught to do otherwise. It was only little, so little. He was ashamed to have a tharais daughter, and he said it wasn't his. He hit the mother. She said she needed peace in the household, and there'd be none so long as it lived with them." She wept even now at the disgrace of it.

I moved the pot off the brazier and sat beside Meninx and pillowed her head on my thighs. She said, "This one cursed the left hand, but what was the use, to curse a curse, ein?"

I stroked her forehead with my left hand and was shocked to feel how cold she was. As I warmed her, I sang, *The rushes do grow green, all agreen-oh.* I'd forgotten everything but the refrain, so I made up words in Lambaneish to go with those in the Low, singing,

> *In spring flies south the speedeedee,*
> *The rushes grow agreen-oh.*
> *Bring my sweetheart home to me,*
> *Oh, oh, the rushes grow,*

and other such nonsense—I knew not what.

The next morning a whore visited the arthygater in the bathing room. This amazed me, for in Corymb women of the Blood do not mingle with whores, much less converse with them in the manner of friends of long acquaintance. There was no mistaking her profession, for she wore a magenta wrapper with narrow stripes of saffron, embroidered with corona flowers in gold thread. Her shawl was gossamer silk. I'd learned the Lambaneish way of estimating a woman's wealth and good taste by the thread, weave, and dyes of her clothing, and the quality and number of beadcoins strung on the long fringe of her net cap. By those measures she was wealthy indeed.

Arthygater Katharos gave her a shawl embroidered with white apple blossoms on a bough splotched with silver lichens; in thanks, she said, for embodying Eikenain with such grace, such passion; she had brought tears to the arthygater's eyes; everyone was talking about the night of the white petals, and would be talking about it for years. After this pretty speech the whore, Aeidin by name, made one of her own, thanking the arthygater gracefully, eloquently, and without fawning like a limpet.

When she undressed I saw she bore a tattooed serpent like Arthygater Katharos; but her serpent girdled the hips, and its tail wrapped around one thigh, and its triangular head rested on the smooth mound where her womansbeard would be if it hadn't been shaved off. I'd thought the tattoos and the Serpent Cult were only for princesses, for royalty.

I wondered what they would converse about, these two adepts of the cult. Perhaps they would speak of their rites and powers, here where no men could eavesdrop. But while I shaved the arthygater and Aeidin, they sifted gossip. Aeidin knew a man with gambling debts, who could be bought—but could he be trusted? The arthygater didn't like his connections, but with debts so great surely he would be grateful. Aeidin had spoken to so-and-so, a Contender in the Ministry of Order, who wished to lease the arthygater's grazing lands on the slopes of Lachesos for the sum of twelve hundred weight in silver a year; and such-and-such a man, an Exorcisor in the Ministry of Purity, had pledged a loan of a hundred thousand weight in gold coins.

A hundred thousand weight in gold. I couldn't conceive of it.

Aeidin said, "What news from Malleus?"

The arthygater smiled. "Trust you to hear when there's something to be heard. A thrush arrived from Incus. He had to beat his way against the trade winds all down the coast, but he made it. This man says King Thyrse is dead. He was wounded in the battle and died soon after."

My left hand shook as I cut the arthygater's nails. She'd told Aeidin she wanted two of them cut in the beak style, with two prongs, saying it would awaken her husband's jealousy, which would arouse him and please her. They had laughed.

"Who is his heir?" Aeidin said.

"He left many bastards, but no heir," the arthygater said. "The Firsts met in council and chose the First of Lynx, this thrush says. Nobody that anybody has heard of. I daresay he won't be king long."

Could that be the same First of Lynx from the Marchfield? I remembered him riding out to meet the Crux on the tourney field with his head bare, showing his white hair and gray beard. He had been respected, but was not among King Thyrse's close advisors, not like the First of Crux. Maybe the Crux had taken the advice of his Council of the Dead to put forward a weak man, a man without enemies, and rule the clans by ruling him.

Aeidin said, "So the clans will fight each other?"

"At present they are too busy squabbling with the queenmother. The clans of Corymb are agreed on one thing, and that is hatred of her Wolves. But it hasn't come to outright battle yet, the man says, so everyone pretends it's only hotspurs clashing in the streets."

I took Aeidin's foot by the heel, to rub her sole with a pumice stone. The skin was already soft, as if she didn't tread the same hard ground as the rest of us. She said, "The war is won. Why don't they take their plunder and go home?"

"Would you go back to Corymb if you could have Incus? If you could have both?"

"I wouldn't have either," Aeidin said. "They are full of strange-ignorant people, and the winters are too long."

The syrup had crystallized on the slices of sweetrush root. I tasted a slice and it was sweet and a little bitter, and spicy enough to make my eyes water. I wrapped them in leaves tied with twine, five slices to a packet, and put them in my gather sack. I left the palace by the tharais gate, and in a deserted alley I donned my tharos wrapper and shawl and hid the tharais cloths in the maw of a drainpipe. I had brought with me a large bunch of fresh-picked swallow-wort. I crushed the green stems and smeared the bright saffron sap on my forearms and the backs of my hands. The color was mottled, but the sap was the best substitute I could find for the yellow powder tharos women wore. Every day a servant carried some of this powder to the bathing room in a gem-studded box, but she took it away again as soon as the bathing was done.

I returned to the palace barefaced. The kind day porter was still at the gate with his dog. The wolfhound knew me, though the man did not. I told the porter I was a peddler, and he let me in the tharos hindgate for a promise of two pewter beadcoins on the way out.

There was another porter to pass, the one at the manufactory door. I'd expected a formidable guard, an Ebanakan perhaps, like the warriors employed by the arkhon, but he was a reed-thin lad, and his price was even lower than that of the gate porter. I gave him a packet of candied root, and he winked as if we shared a secret, probably supposing I was a go-between with a message for one of the weavers. His key was the size and shape of a hand, and the lock ornate and heavy. But what did a strong lock matter if the man with the key was weak?

Inside the manufactory I stood under the vaulted roof of an arcade and watched textrices strolling the courtyard and sitting on the rim of the fountain. The last banners of evening flew high above the pear tree, lemon yellow clouds over the green roofs. I thought of the napkin Polukhaitais, and how her nose had been struck off in punishment for the offense of pretending to be tharos—an offense I was even now committing—and I shivered and stepped out of the darkness under the arcade, and walked the courtyard paths as if I still belonged there.

There were waves of sound from peepers in the pool, and women's voices rising and falling, and I heard Catena laugh before I saw her. She was sitting on the ground with several girls her own age, giggling and playing a game of fast and loose with a spindle and a length of twine. She looked younger than I remembered. Maybe I expected her to look older because I'd lived two lifetimes among the tharais since I'd seen her last. Her bronze-colored hair wasn't as unruly as mine, and it had grown out in fleecy little curls. She was as plump now as when I'd first met her. Arthygater Katharos measured judiciously, so much work for so much sustenance. Her textrices did not starve.

I stood before Catena, who stared at me openmouthed, and I said, "Why so shy? Did you forget me?" I held out both hands to her and she stood and embraced me, tucking easily under my arm. "Well, well," I said, squeezing her tightly, and I couldn't stop smiling.

A woman called out in Lambaneish, and she knew me by name, though I'd forgotten hers. "Look, Feirthonin! She has hair now!"

Red-haired Agminhatin, whom I recalled from the weaving room, said, "How did you get in here? I thought you'd been made tharais and sent to the dyers, ein?"

I held out my arms to show her the skin was tinted yellow. It was fortunate that after a tennight in the bathing room my hands were at last free of the red dyestains. "Who says so? Zostra? She says that to scare you, ein? So you'll do how she says. As you see, I'm no dyer. The arthygater sells me as tharos, more coins for her that way."

"Good," she said, and grinned. "And what did you do to Zostra, ein?"

"What do you mean?"

Agminhatin gave me a little push on my shoulder. "I don't mind. She deserved it."

"Deserved what?"

"She had a bad dream of a viper underfoot, and she withered up and died."

Catena and I made the avert sign, and Agminhatin laughed. I said, "I swear I do not send a dream. Zostra offends of a meneidon—or the mistress, maybe, by stealing too much, ein?" I almost said, *This one swears.*

Agminhatin raised her eyebrows. "It's not that I blame you—I'd have done the same if I knew how. But the new taskmistress is even worse. Perhaps you can send her a nightmare too, ein? She's made my life a misery, telling me to unravel a day's work for nothing, just to show she can."

I said, "I can't help you. I'm not a—" I couldn't think of a word for hex just then in Lambaneish. The closest I could come was throws-filth-in-cleanwater, but that could not be the best way to say it.

I walked away from Agminhatin so she would ask no more questions, but she followed. Catena and I strolled arm in arm to the fountain, where many women were sitting on the rim of the pool, gossiping, Dulcis and Nitida among them. They greeted me with warmth, and soon Dulcis began to chatter like a chiffchaff about a new suitor, and I was wholeheartedly grateful that she was more interested in herself than me. By now I knew Lambaneish well enough to realize that she spoke it wretchedly, though she'd lived here so many years.

We sat under the pear tree on a soft turf of sweet-smelling maythen. The sky was already speckled with stars, and it was almost time for everyone to retire upstairs to the sleeping porch. Catena asked me in the High if I had come back to stay, and I answered the same way.

Agminhatin said, "What are you saying?"

I said in Lambaneish, "That I do not stay, I only visit."

"Who do you serve now?"

Many of the women who had gathered at the fountain had drifted after us, and sat down nearby on the railings between columns, or the turf between paved paths. Novelty was welcome in the manufactory, where days were as like to one another as throws of a shuttle. The women waited for my answer, and the silence lingered.

I said, "I'm a peddler, ein?"

"What are you peddling?" Nitida asked.

"Sometimes one thing, sometimes another. Tonight I have sweetroot for sweet dreams. Delicious, ein? Each for a beadcoin or a skein of thread." I opened several packets of candied root and passed them around. "If you eat five pieces you dream of coupling with one you desire." This was a lie—sweetrush was potent in many ways, but I'd never heard that was one of them. I got the idea from Mai, who used to sell a charm for the same purpose; she never would tell me what was in it.

Every peddler should have a song, so I made one using remnants of melody from some other tune. I sang,

> *From sweet root grows sweetrush.*
> *Grows a dream, dream a dream.*
> *The one you desire, desires you.*

A weaver leaned forward and passed me a pewter beadcoin, saying, "I'll buy some. All my dreams are dull. Last night I dreamed of an orange tree with oranges hanging down like beads, and the night before I dreamed of an orange-painted wall. A friend showed me this wall and said she didn't want her husband to see it."

I said, "These are not dull dreams, these are fruitful—oranges hanging like beadcoins on a cap. Also a secret hidden to a husband behind a wall of women. The higher a woman's rank, the more orange her wrapper, ein? The color of saffron on silk. So you dream of a woman of high rank, maybe the arthygater, she does somewhat behind her husband's back and prospers by it. Perhaps you have a third orange dream—orange is also the color of the meneidon Lynx, Lynx Foresight we call her in Incus, because she gives true foretellings, ein? Perhaps she reveals the woman and her secret. But don't trust any dream with a little boy, or mice or rats, ein? Beware of those."

By the time I stopped talking, everyone was listening as if what I said was profound. I didn't see why; no doubt most of the high-ranking women of Lambanein kept secrets from their husbands, and profited behind their backs.

Dulcis reached for more slices of sweetrush root. "I know you want a dream of your bow-legged rider," someone shouted, and Dulcis giggled, covering her mouth.

Wildfire

Someone said, "Dulcis doesn't care who rides her, so long as she can be a night mare."

A woman clapped and sang out, *Ai, ai, ai, I ride a fine stallion. Ai, ai, ai, no geldings for me.* She stood and swayed, and another woman got up and they entwined arms. The second woman sang, *Ai, ai, ai, Old Zostra tried to hit me, ai, ai, ai, I trod on her flail,* and the first sang, *Ai, ai, ai, Old Klothin tried to hit me, ai, ai, ai, I emptied her pail.* They went on mocking their taskmistresses in verse after verse, and soon others joined them.

Catena sat smiling and clapping, a little apart from me, with her knee touching a friend's knee. Perhaps I reminded her of an ordeal best forgotten. She led the life she had been given, and I should be glad she'd found some contentment in it. Was it any wonder she preferred eating to going hungry, and warmth to frostbite, and a roof and walls to the terrifying immensity of the mountains? Yet I did wonder. How could she be content to stay in the manufactory, working day after day, year upon year until she had spun all the thread of her life?

I clapped too, and sang along. But all the while I was searching the faces of the women for signs. One of them had stolen from me. I distrusted them all, all save Catena.

In the dark room I spread my shawl over the rushes and counted beadcoins and skeins of thread.

Lychnais sat up and said, "Is that Feirthonin?"

"Who else?"

"Where have you been? You promised to say when you would be out late."

"This one tells Meninx instead."

Lychnais must have heard the clinking of the beadcoins, for she said, "What is there?"

"Money. How much is needed for a dowser?"

She edged closer. The room was small, she didn't have far to go. She said, "Perhaps fifteen pewter beadcoins as thanks for the dowser, and five for the dancers. Ten for the feast."

"Food must be bought?"

"Sweets and nuts, and a hen, of course. It wouldn't do to be thrifty-stingy, it would displease the meneidon." Thrifty and stingy were one and the same word in Lambaneish.

"This one can get good food for free, as good as can be bought. If you get the hen, ein? So then is needed twenty-five of the pewter. Here are eighteen, and two skeins of blue wool and one white and one green skein of linen."

"Where did you get all that? Did you steal it?"

I opened my last packet of sweetrush root and said, "It sells this. Take a taste. Good, ein?"

"The honey is all gone," she said. "If they catch you, they'll blame us both, and cut off our fingers."

"It is for Meninx. So she does not be haunted—be a haunt. This Lambaneish illness, this one doesn't know how to cure it. So if it gives you all this, you find a dowser and dancers and a hen, ein? If more money is needed, you give the rest. This one gets food."

She made a face, thinking I couldn't see her in the dark, and I'm sure it was because I was behaving like a taskmistress, when she ought to be telling me what to do, for she'd been here longer. Still, she took what I gave her; I suspected a few coins might stick to her fingers, but I didn't doubt she would arrange it for Meninx's sake.

That night I dreamed of the Dame. I descended the steep stairs in the chasm down to the shrine, and found her sitting on the floor of the cave, in front of the painted Katabaton. She held a long stem of swallowwort in her hand. The small yellow flowers shone against the dark green of her gown. She said, "How could you forget what I taught you? The hatchling is born blind, but the fledgling sees both far and small." She sang a riddle and its answer:

> *What hones the swallow's sight*
> *Before it takes to flight?*
> *It blooms when the swallow is nigh,*
> *And dies when the swallow flies.*

The melody belonged to the swallowwort. I knelt before the Dame, and we gazed at each other eye to eye. She seemed younger than when she died, but careworn. The hem of her gown was muddy. "Perhaps I forgot to teach you that verse," she said, looking away. "It has so many."

When I awoke, I remembered the Dame had told me a tale hidden in the song: she said swallows dropped the yellow-orange sap of swallowwort into their hatchlings' eyes to give them keen eyesight, day after day until they fledged. Had I misinterpreted the omens that led me to the plant? Swallowwort had many uses, and though it seemed to have done Meninx some good, perhaps the cure had been meant for me. To hone my sight, to remove the web in my right eye.

Lying in the dark, I tried to dream my way back into the dream, to ask the Dame questions. I found the shrine again, but she had left. There was Katabaton on the wall in white paint, and as I drifted toward the surface of Sleep, too buoyant to stay under, I remembered what must be mixed with the swallowwort sap to protect the eye from the rasp that sharpened sight: mother's milk.

In the morning I looked at my right eye in the reflection in a basin of water. The web used to look like a faint haze of light on the surface of the iris; now it was nearly opaque. I feared that soon the eye would be useless as a pebble. I begged Nephelais for a small cup of milk from her breasts, and she was generous enough to give it to me when I told her why I wanted it. I bathed my eye with a mixture of milk and orange swallowwort sap. It didn't sting. I thought perhaps it should, to prove it was working, so I added more sap.

It was certain the world looked yellower than usual through my right eye. Perhaps a little sharper, perhaps not. I must keep trying.

The dowser came in the evening three days later. She was an old woman with webeye in both eyes, and despite her blindness, she didn't need to be led. Indeed, she led us, down the stairs and along the tharais tunnels and back again, in search of the meneidon who was killing Meninx. She held a hazel rod split down most of its length, the forked ends in her outstretched hands and the joined end upright as she walked. We followed the dowser like so many goslings after a goose. Her four dancers were as old as she was, and they shuffled along with their hands tucked under their shawls. Long after sundown we returned to our room, where Meninx lay on a bed of sweetrush, for she was much too weak to search with us.

"Did you find . . . ?" she asked, and Lychnais shook her head.

We entered the bathing room, which was safe enough, as the room wasn't used so late in the evening. I was uneasy nevertheless. We used no lamp lest a light be seen through the high windows.

By the pool with the tiled goldfish and the heron fountain, the dowsing rod wavered, but did not dip. The dowser followed the water over the lip of the pool into an open channel, and across the room through a passage in the wall to the courtyard. But the rod no longer quivered. She circled the room, and when she got to the corner that held the drain, the cleft rod shook as if it were trying to wriggle away. She held on tightly, and the rod twisted in her hands to point downward, and we all said, "Ah!" The hazel split at the join with a loud crack, and the dowser held two sticks instead of one. She cast them on the ground.

"Bring Meninx here," she said. We spread rushes near the drain, and Lychnais and I carried Meninx to the bathing room and laid her down. She was weeping quietly, from relief or grief or some mingling of the two.

"How did this one offend the meneidon, ein?" Meninx asked. "It tried to be so careful. Did it not beg pardon when pouring water? When scrubbing the floor? Did this one not give you flowers?" One of the dowser's dancers knelt beside her with a bowl of water in which floated tiny white blossoms of wood-rover. No one plants wood-rover, it springs up where it likes, in shady places, but it is not despised for all that it's a wanton grower. Meninx tried to toss a handful of blossoms into the drain, but she was too weak. The drain was merely a hole, a throat that had to swallow whatever we gave it. How could it be a vessel for anything, how could it contain even a meneidon? I crouched and brushed the wet flowers into it. For a moment I felt dizzy, as if the drain were going to swallow me, and I stood up and backed away.

"Has the meneidon a name?" the dowser asked. No doubt it did, but none of us knew it. "This one will find it out," she said. She crept on hands and knees and leaned down and mumbled into the drain. I couldn't hear what she was saying. She put her ear over the drain hole and listened. When the answer came, we all heard it. To me it sounded like a stomach growling, but to the dowser it spoke a name, Poton.

The dowser stood up and began to dance, bobbing and swaying over the drain. The four old women joined her, scuffing their feet across the tiles, back and forth. The dowser sang, she flattered Poton and called him mighty, and asked pardon on behalf of Meninx, saying she'd brought gifts of flowers and a hen—which was even now stewing with salsify crowns and roots on the brazier in the other room. I hadn't eaten meat for some time, aside from my ration of lard, and my stomach growled as loudly as the meneidon in his lair.

Lychnais joined the dancers, lifting her feet higher than the old women, and setting them down with a slap of her soles on the tiles. She beckoned me, and I shook my head in refusal. She gestured more sharply, and I got up. The steps were easy, back and forth, yet I was awkward, an instant ahead or behind. Afraid to be ensnared by it. Easier to stand outside, thinking I had wasted my money on a cozener. I stamped, stamp stamp stamp, and just like that, I gave way to the rhythm of it.

The high windows of the bathing room were shapes carved out of the purest midnight blue. The room was full of darkness. But I saw the dowser pull something from under her shawl and drop it down the drain—no, she didn't drop it. She shook one end of a cord strung with fist-size beads of clay or wood or metal, and the beads struck against the clay walls of the drainpipe. If I'd not seen her, I'd have believed the banging issued from the drain itself.

The dowser had pleaded with Poton at first, but now she threatened and insulted him. *This one is coming down to you,* she sang in her quavering voice. *This one is climbing down, ai, ai, ai. Leave Meninx be, old misery. Leave the woman be, ai, ai, ai.* The drain rumbled and the sound seemed to come from deep, deep.

Wildfire

The dowser began to spin and sing faster. Lychnais turned too, stamping her feet and holding her arms outstretched. Her eyes were closed and she trod near Meninx, and stepped on the basin of water and flowers, and tipped it over. Water flowed toward the corner, and tiny white petals of wood-rover swirled and spilled over the lip into the dark maw of the drain.

The swallow sees both small and far, so the swallowwort song goes. My ordinary eye saw the dowser spinning. My webeye saw white speckles on blackness, near enough to skim the watery surface of my eyeball and also far away, moving swiftly down. There was no light in the room to cast a shadow, yet I saw my shadow stretching toward the drain, a dark iridescence pouring with the water, and I fell, following the lure of the petals, past the dowser's ladder of cord and beads, down which she was climbing to confront the meneidon.

I fell, I flowed with the waters down the clay pipe into the great drain under the street, which was a street itself, with a narrow raised path beside the water channel for the koprophagais. The drain branched, it went everywhere under the palace district, and the water was divided. The wood-rover petals scattered. I had thought the mountain was solid, but its stone was folded like so many layers of cloth, and water found the voids between the layers, and as it seeped downward it was cleansed.

I recognized her now; it was Penna who lured me on, Penna in the torrent that divided and divided again, and as I chased the petals I too was divided into rivulets of shadow. I'd lost my voice and couldn't beg her not to lead me to a drowning. Some petals were trapped in crevices and deep underground pools; some surfaced in a spring that dripped into a stone trough in an olive grove. One solitary petal found its way into the fountain house near the street of dyers. Others were carried by water seeping through a crack in a half-ruined room, part of the rubble foundation of a palace; faded paintings on the wall depicted women in a hilly landscape, gathering stamens of crocus for saffron. Other petals were swept along in waterfalls that plunged from cliffs below the Inner Palace and into the river.

The river moved swiftly southward, but underneath the surface, rushing waters churned over rocks, and currents writhed, and the flowers were caught in this tumult and so was I. The river was a meneidon, strong as a god, for wasn't it part of the Waters, just as the meneidon of the fountains and wells were manifestations of Wellspring? The Lambaneish did not acknowledge Torrent as a god, but everywhere they worshipped it.

A few petals surfaced in an eddy near the shore and floated among sweetrush. An ibis on orange stilt legs bent its long neck and cocked its head to look at the reflection of the half Moon.

Someone emptied a jug of water over my head and shook me, saying, "Feirthonin, what is wrong?"

My head was sore. I sat up and groaned, and found a hen's egg of a bump on the back of my skull.

"You fell over," Lychnais said.

White speckles bedazzled both my eyes when I tried to stand, so I sat by Meninx and held her hands. Now the dowser roared wordlessly, her voice as gruff as a man's, and she moved like a young man, staggering and twisting and leaping as she grappled with something I couldn't see, neither with my left eye or my right. I swear there were deep booms and thuds from under our feet that could not have been caused by the cord and beads she shook in the drain. Poton was riled, and I felt his anger in the clammy draft that stirred our hair. Meninx's hands trembled like moths between mine.

The dowser stomped and shouted, bidding Poton begone, and then she fell to her knees and slumped over, panting. Lank hair clung to her face, and her wrapper and shawl were drenched with sweat. She straightened her back and held up one hand, clasping something invisible between her finger and thumb. She crawled to Meninx on her knees to show her this invisible thing, which caught the thinnest streak of moonlight. A single long brown hair. The dowser stared at Meninx with her blind white eyes, and Meninx stared back, and for a time all was quiet, until the dowser could speak without gasping.

She said,

"Oh, you were full of respect and care.
The floor was swept and scrubbed.
The nails were burned, the hair was burned.
But one day a strand of your hair fell unseen.
You didn't sweep it up, you didn't burn it.
The hair went down the drain,
down to Poton, the meneidon.
Yes with your long hair he was enchanted,
and he enchanted you in turn.
He wrapped the hair around the liver,
he wrapped it once, twice, thrice.
The liver is the throne of fortitude in a woman,
the throne of boldness in a man.
He strangled the liver and made the flesh fear to die.
He lured your shade with promises
to dwell with him in this place forever.
But the dowser Temnais stole the hair from him.
Temnais unwrapped the thread from your liver,
unwrapped it once, twice, thrice.

Wildfire

Poton followed to steal it back.
Temnais defeated him and threw him down.
It is Temnais who set free your courage,
the fortitude to take the river road,
and not be bound to this place forever."

The dowser stood up slowly and her bones creaked, for she had become an old woman again. She cast the hair into the embers in the beehive hearth, and I could smell it, that one thin hair filling the room with an acrid reek as it burned.

Afterward we feasted, crowded together in our sleeping room, and the dancers and Lychnais celebrated with songs and jests as at a festival. The dowser Temnais was quiet after all her boasting. She ate stewed hen, greens dressed with stolen olive oil, and wild strawberries and honey. I propped Meninx against me and she drank some barley water, four swallows. She was present with us, smiling and even laughing once or twice, but oh, she was frail. The dowser looked my way over her bowl.

"This one saw a woman going past me," she said.

"This one sees you too. It sees you rattle the ladder."

She smiled, not at all perturbed that I'd seen her trick.

I said, "You dowse for what is missing, ein? This one has something stolen, and wants it back."

"This one is tired," Temnais said. "Maybe later. Though with such eyes as yours, perhaps you could find this stolen thing yourself, ein?"

"How?"

"To find something stolen, use a forked stick of alder or willow, but willow is not as good."

"You do this better. Will you help?"

"Where was this thing stolen?"

"In the manufactory, ein? This one is once a weaver. Someone steals something precious from me, from it, while it sleeps in the dormitory."

She hunched her shoulders. "Then it's lost, woman. This is no tharais matter. This one can't help you dowse for it. And don't you try either, ein?"

The dowser never claimed she could make Meninx well. The cure she offered was of another sort, and indeed I think she hastened Meninx's death by easing her fear of it. And there was vanity in Meninx I hadn't suspected. The long strand of her hair, so thin, so weak, had been strong enough to snare a meneidon. She seemed to feel some pride at this. Perhaps she had never been desired before.

For two nights and days after the dowser's visit, Lychnais and I stayed by Meninx's side when we were not needed in the bathing room. We could see her time was near. Her suffering seemed a creature in itself, like a monstrous gutworm that fed on her last hoarded strength. Even when she slept I could see the deep scratches scored by pain down her cheeks and across her brow. I gave her tisanes brewed from marsh nettle and sweet violet to soothe the gnawing in her belly, and to soothe my own need to be useful.

Meninx spoke again of her past, returning to the story of the day her father took her to market with the speedeedee in the cage. She said, "They tied the left hand behind the back when this one got here, so it could learn to do without, ein? This one hated it." She paused. It was difficult for her to find wind to talk. Her breathing was slow and unsteady in its rhythm. "Hated the hand."

I said, "What work is done with one hand, ein?"

"Scrubbing floors."

I took her left hand in mine and looked at her palm, at the fine web of lines. It was not fair, not just, for her poor hand to be so despised. Even scrubbing floors one hand needs the other. One hand scrubs while the other props up the body that leans over the floor. Or both hands push the rag together, scouring back and forth. Both hands wring the rag between them. What madness, to divide right hand from left, call one tharos and the other tharais, favor one and despise the other when both are necessary. Because the wrong hand had been more apt, Meninx had worn out her days in the bathing room and her nights in this small box.

"How long ago? How many years are you here?" I asked.

She didn't answer. Lychnais sat with her knees drawn up and her head resting on her arms. I saw her wet cheek and her ear with hair tucked behind it. She said, "What use to count, ein?"

"No use," I said. "No use, it's true." The Dame's old priest used to call the year a wheel with twelve spokes for months, and as it turned it carried us through our lives. But with my right eye I saw that the wheel of Meninx's year was a millstone, grinding her days into smaller and smaller moments. Turning more slowly now as her breathing slowed. Stopped.

In Lambanein they say the dead travel through the navel of the earth to the realm where the gods dwell, of which our living realm is an imperfect reflection, this world the netherworld to that one. For Meninx's sake, I prayed it was true. And though her shade would carry heavy regrets on the long journey, I was glad she would not go burdened by her fragile, pain-racked body.

CHAPTER 24

Thrush

ychnais was even more afraid of the arthygater's pet snake than of the meneidon of the drain, Poton. The arthygater herself fed the snake milk every day, but it was our duty to give the creature a more substantial meal every two ten-nights or so. The snake disdained carrion, and would accept only living prey. She had last eaten before I came to the bathing room, and now it was time to feed her again, according to Lychnais.

I said, "Snakes eat frogs, don't they? This one catches one and sees."

I'd heard frogs trilling at night in the courtyard, but was afraid to hunt them there. For all I knew Gnathin kept count even of the humble frogs, like the songbirds in cages or the carp in the pool. So I went down to catch a frog by the river, taking the stairs in the cliff to my secret place—for so I thought of it, though it was not my secret alone: another wreath had been laid on the floor of Katabaton's shrine.

I crouched by the cage, which was covered with fine gold mesh, and opened the small door to put the frog inside. The snake ignored it. "Is the serpent ill?" I asked Lychnais. "Her eyes are milky and her skin is dull."

But Lychnais wouldn't look.

It was a hand of days before the festival of the Quickening, which commemorated the godchild Peranon's first kick inside Katabaton's womb, and tonight Arthygater Katharos was offering the first of four banquets in celebration. The arthygater's mother-in-law came to the bathing room at dawn, grumbling to her companion as usual. She had nothing to wear, she said. Arthygater Katharos did not care if she went to the banquet in rags, and neither did her son, and it was disgraceful. Yet they made demands, ein? They expected her to give her best cloth for Keros's dowry, and Keros was no kin of hers, not by blood.

I was a trifle clumsy, distracted. I hadn't realized the walls between the bathing room and the arcade could be removed. Servants had taken them away at dawn, and now only two rows of columns separated us from the courtyard. The painted birds and butterflies in the room, which I'd thought implausibly bright, were not as vivid as the real ones held captive by a fine, nearly invisible net over the courtyard. A doe and two dappled fauns of a miniature kind nibbled on the incensier hedges of their enclosure.

Already a few lilies were in flower. The Dame had coddled white lilies in a sunny sheltered corner of the inner courtyard, and they'd never bloomed for her before Midsummer's eve—still more than a month away, as I reckoned it. But here their great trumpets were already open, and the heavy scent was borne into the room on the first rays of sunlight. The warmth of that light on my skin was balm, a salve on a hidden wound. The Maid had lost her maidenhead and become a wanton, and soon Midsummer would arrive and the passes would open through the Ferinus.

The mother-in-law scurried off when the bathmistress announced that the arthygater was on her way. She arrived early, with two guests. One was her niece Keros. The other, Arthygater Klados, was Keros's mother—and the arthygater's sister, or half sister perhaps.

The arthygater leaned over her snake's cage and I was afraid she'd blame us for the creature's illness. But she cooed, saying, "Look, a good omen! Ankaton is ready to shed its skin." She draped the snake over her arm, but forgot to latch the door. The frog hopped out. I stood still, afraid I'd be blamed. Were frogs tharais or tharos? Was it my responsibility to catch it? I looked at Lychnais and she waggled one finger, so I watched the keeper of the garments and two handmaids chase the frog around the room until they caught it. I bit my lower lip to stifle my laughter.

The arthygater had occupied many mornings already with preparations for the Quickening banquets. Now, as Lychnais wove her hair into a wicker tower, she deliberated with Gnathin over a few last details, such as the flowers in the guest wreaths, and whether such-and-such a whore had lost her looks and should be disinvited.

It took so long to prepare the coiffures of the three arthygaters that they had their noon repast in the bathing room. We stood against the wall and I stared at Keros as she delicately pierced her food with a small silver trident and brought it to her mouth. She concealed her chewing behind her left hand; a noblewoman didn't show her teeth at all, it was immodest.

Arthygater Katharos said to her, "Your mother and I were thinking it was time you had your instruction in the twenty-five Postures, and Aeidin has graciously agreed to undertake it."

"Aeidin?"

"The very best," Klados said.

"So I am to be married?" Keros laid down her trident with great care on her tray. "But I didn't please the arkhyios."

"But you did," Arthygater Katharos said. "You pleased him greatly. He wants you for his brother Merle, ein? We will send him your likeness."

Keros became stiff and still. I saw her in profile, golden beads heavy on the black cords hanging next to her cheek. Only her mouth moved, saying, "The traitor?"

Her mother and aunt regarded each other past Keros's bent head. Klados said, "Arkhyios Merle, yes. The Starling. There's something to be said for knowing a man's price."

"Corvus needs him," Arthygater Katharos said, "and what's more, he needs Corvus. The queenmother tried to have Merle imprisoned on the very night of their victory feast, saying she could never trust a traitor—and it saved her paying him too, ein? He fled east to Lanx, and my thrushes tell me his army is growing. Caelum is taking revenge on those who advised Arkhyios Corvus to exile her—and even those who failed to object—and many Blood are fleeing Malleus. If Merle holds Lanx—we need him, ein?"

"We?" said Keros, looking at her mother.

Klados ignored her disrespectful stare, and turned to her sister, saying, "Which painter should we commission, Nektan or Ichnosan? What do you say to a likeness in glass, ein? Cobalt blue around her saffron robe would set her off like a jewel, would it not?"

"Nektan. I fear glass wouldn't ship well." Katharos turned and touched Keros on the knee. "And if Merle doesn't keep Lanx, he'll never see the likeness, ein? If I had an unmarried daughter, I would be proud for her to have this duty, if she were clever enough. You, my dearest niece, are clever enough. Who else can we trust, ein? Who else could be so intimate, to sway Merle if he can be swayed, to warn us if he cannot? A son proves his worth by the three attainments: wealth, wisdom, and the fame of his valor. A daughter shows her worth by the three excellences: to bear herself above reproach, to bear children fruitfully, and to bear suffering with fortitude. It is infamous for a married woman to seek fame; yet we'll know what you have done in secret and honor you for it."

Keros turned her head and I saw her full face. She looked leagues past me, through the painted garden at my back. She must have heard of the three attainments and three excellences a thousand times, to judge by the expression—almost imperceptible, except around her nostrils—of scorn.

The arthygaters talked thereafter of trivial matters. I ceased to listen, wondering instead how King Corvus could reconcile with the brother who had stolen his chance of victory, and nearly stolen his life. They could bribe

Merle with a dowry worthy of a princess, and still he couldn't be trusted; in that I agreed with the queenmother. The king despised his brother, the Starling. He must hate his mother more, if he meant to make this bargain.

Arthygater Katharos had said "we." We need Merle.

Daily in the bathing room I had watched the arthygater doing business with women; I had dismissed it, too easily, as women's business. A woman couldn't own land, but she could own the use of it, and I'd heard the arthygater offer one friend the lease of good barley fields, and another the right to graze her sheep on certain mountain pastures, and I couldn't tell if she had Consort Ostrakan's approval for such transactions, or went behind his back. She traded favors: a word to a magistrate about a case, a position for a nephew among the arkhon's scribes, an appointment with the arkhon's all-powerful factotum. And the whore Aeidin, who moved freely among men and had the opportunity to speak to them in private, had been about the same work on the arthygater's behalf: gathering gold, gathering loyalty, a currency as valuable as coin. This was how to weave a war in Lambanein.

I went to the tharais taskmistress of the dining court to ask if I might serve that night. I'd spent everything I had on Meninx, and couldn't offer the taskmistress a gift, but I said I'd give her half of what I earned, expecting it to suffice. She pulled me aside, out of the bustling corridors under the dining hall and into her own curtained alcove. We uncovered our faces to speak. The taskmistress was plump, for a tharais, with soft, sagging jowls, and I didn't expect the fierceness I found in her expression. Fierce greed. She leaned close. "Do you think this one a newborn kitten, ein? That it has yet to open the eyes to see what's plain to see?"

I tried not to intercept her glare. I ducked my head and said in a small voice, "This one doesn't mean to offend, taskmistress. It begs pardon."

"This one is offended that a dung beetle like you thinks it a lackwit."

"It doesn't, it swears."

Her mother finger and grandmother thumb were cut in the beak style, and she drew blood as she pinched my forearm. "It knows you're a thrush—very well, it doesn't care. But you can't expect this one to keep quiet for a couple of pewter beadcoins at the end of the night. So tell your master or mistress—the one so anxious to know what Arkhyios Corvus is saying—that this one needs gold. If it doesn't get gold, it will tell Gnathin. And don't think about disappearing without paying up. The arthygater wouldn't be happy to hear her depilator is an eavesdropper, ein? Do you know what she does to little thrushes? She gives them to her tormentor, and he cuts out the tongues so they can't sing, and pulls off the wings so they can't fly."

"This one has no gold. How will it get gold?"

Wildfire

"It cares not how. Get some, get three beadcoins weighing at least twenty grains each. Get it by tomorrow night, or by the day after tomorrow you'll be in the gentle hands of the arthygater's tormentor."

I promised, of course. And I went away smearing the blood from my arm. Na had five or ten sayings about the perils of curiosity and I wished I'd heeded them.

Why was I still in Lambanein, still a tharais captive? I should go now, tomorrow, tonight even—why wait? The arthygater's thrushes were flying south in ships; could I make my way north by sea, without waiting for the thaw in the Ferinus? I joined the other napkins polishing silver basins, and I worked until I stopped shaking, until I could think.

I sought out the taskmistress again in her alcove, and said, "If it please you, put this one to serve where Arkhyios Corvus sits tonight, and it will get you gold. Otherwise it cannot get a message to the mistress."

This puzzled her. If I spied on Corvus and the arthygater, then who was to be the recipient of this message? Perhaps I served the arthygater's husband, why not? What better way for Consort Ostrakan to spy on his wife than to put a thrush in her bathing room, where so many intimacies were shared? I swear I saw those thoughts on her face as clearly as if they'd been inked godsigns on her slack cheeks. I hadn't thought of trying to cast suspicion on Arthygater Katharos's husband. That was luck, Chance giving me a wink.

It seemed the taskmistress's estimation of me rose. Certainly her price did. "Best make it five beadcoins," she said.

Now she wanted to be my ally, my confidante. Now she wanted to help me—help me get her gold, even if it meant betraying her mistress. She saw to it that when the guests arrived, I was the one sent to bathe King Corvus's feet.

His boots were of soft leather fastened with ribbons looped around ruby studs. His kidskin leggings were dyed red in honor of Rift, a color almost as bright as the red wool of the Ebanakan guards. I pushed them up above his shins so they would not get wet. He had sharp ankles and narrow feet with high arches. He'd lost the smallest toe on his right foot to frostbite. There was not a man who'd survived the crossing of the mountains without some scar to remind him of it.

I had my scar too, and this time I didn't try to hide it. The shawl covered my face, but I bared my arm so King Corvus could see the white weal around my wrist. I poured water from a golden ewer over his feet and into the basin, and scattered rose petals in the water for the scent. He did not see the scar. Nor me.

King Corvus was seated in the colonnade between the vast, moonlit pleasure garden and the illuminated jewel of the dining court. He shared a platform with Arthygater Katharos, Consort Ostrakan, and Ostrakan's mother, and I wondered if they had tired at last of parading young women before him. It was a tennight after the New Moon dinner and all the apple blossoms had fallen.

I was no sort of thrush, but even if I had been, I would have learned nothing. Musicians played overhead in the open tower astride the entrance, and it was impossible to eavesdrop.

During the long meal tharos servants offered the diners glorious edifices prepared by the cooks, such as a peacock stuffed with songbirds, brooding over painted eggs on a nest of sugar straw. Once the cooks' artistry had been sufficiently admired, the servants dismantled the dishes and cut the food into morsels suitable to be picked up between finger and thumb or speared with a gol len trident.

Again and again I offered the basin so the guests could cleanse their tharos hands between courses, taking care that the cloth draped over my left arm didn't hide my wrist. But I was unworthy of notice. I bargained with myself: next time I came forward, I would tip water into the king's lap. I told myself I'd wait for the arthygater and the other female guests to leave. But then the whores arrived, and two of the most beautiful joined King Corvus and Consort Ostrakan for an interminable game of guessing fragrances. Afterward there were sweetmeats, and more drinking. I took the basin to King Corvus without waiting for a summons, and sloshed a little water onto his knee. He seemed to take no notice, not even to make the gesture of reprimand with two fingers. I moved away again.

The arthygater's husband fondled the whore next to him. King Corvus unfolded his crossed legs and stood, and with a few low words took his leave. He gestured as he passed me by and I followed, and he led me to a tharais room and closed the door behind us. The walls had paintings of the twelve Abasements, performed by tharos upon tharais; Nephelais had told me men usually gave a napkin a larger gift for submitting to such acts. The king sat down in the only chair and looked at me with his head tilted, one eye quizzical and the other unwelcoming.

I knelt and showed him the scar on my wrist.

"The dreamer, is it? Let me see you," he said in Lambaneish.

I was stifling under the shawl, awash with heat, my brow and neck wet, but I wished I could have kept my face hidden. It was better when I could see him and he couldn't see me. I leaned forward until my forehead touched the ground, and when I spoke, the sound was muffled. "This one served you well once. I, it would do so again, Corvus Rex Ixa—" I stopped when I saw the fingers of his right hand twitch. The king didn't use the Lambaneish language of gesture, but his impatience was plain nevertheless.

"You complained of being in my service, I recall."

I straightened up and spread my fingers over my thighs so my hands would not become fists, and said in the High, "If you don't want my service, why did you send Garrilus for me?"

"Send who? Garrio?"

"To fetch me from the dyers."

He raised one eyebrow.

"I want to go home, back across the mountains. When the passes open this summer, when you cross the mountains with your army—I will be your dreamer if you like, or mend your clothing, only please let me accompany you."

"What makes you think I'm returning to Incus with an army? Did you dream it? Sire Vafra said you have been dreaming."

I touched my forehead to the ground again and stretched out my arms in supplication. "I hear things in the bathing room. I'll gladly tell all I know for ten gold pieces."

He laughed out loud. I wondered if I'd ever heard him laugh before, then remembered how just that evening he'd laughed at some witticism while they were dining; but I'd never heard him like this, so unfettered. "Now I know for certain you aren't a thrush," he said. "If you were, surely you'd be better at your trade. For one thing, you are misinformed. I will not return this summer, but the next. For another, spying doesn't pay as well as you suppose. For ten gold pieces I could hire twenty thrushes, and hear something more than gossip from a cattery."

Not this summer, but the next. Too long, too long. Sire Galan would be back in Corymb by then and I'd have to traverse two kingdoms to find him. And when I did, he'd have his wife at his side, and likely another sheath for those nights when he tired of his wife.

I kept my face to the ground so the king wouldn't see how this news dismayed me. "Sire, I don't need ten golden coins, only I beg you, please give me five to save my life. The taskmistress here in the dining court says she'll have me killed for a thrush if I don't give her five golden beadcoins. For myself, I don't ask for coins, only a little favor that will cost you nothing. Since you don't mean to return to Inkle yourself this summer, perhaps you could persuade Arthygater Katharos to give me to Keros as a maidservant, so I could accompany her by land or sea to Lanx when she goes to wed your bother Merle—I mean the Startling, the Starling, begging your pardon. In Incus I can find my warrior, or follow him home to Corymb if he has already sailed." I was out of breath. I dried my palms on the shawl.

He made a dismissive gesture, but I noticed some slight stiffening of his posture when I spoke of Keros and Merle. The arthygater had told Keros the king favored the match, but maybe he fancied her for himself after all. Or he planned to send his brother a deflowered bride; a petty sort of revenge, if true. I said, "Arthygater Keros, she—"

"Yes?"

"She doesn't wish to marry a traitor. I saw her in the bathing room. She did this." I showed him in profile how her nostrils had flared and she'd looked off into the distance.

"And how did Katharos persuade her?"

"She said it was Keros's duty to make sure the Starling would be loyal to you, now that he'd quarreled with your mother. She said if Merle, if the Starling, could hold Lynx, Lanx, this would be a great help to you. To them." I looked at my lap and discovered my right hand encircling my left wrist, grasping it hard. "Sire, I could get a message to her, perhaps."

"To whom?"

"To Arthygater Keros."

The smallest finger of his right hand stirred. I had guessed wrong. He wasn't interested in Keros, but in something else I'd said. I wished I knew what it was. I said, "The bathing room is where the arthygater makes begins, bargains—for wool, for captives, for loyalty. Have I not heard her raising hundreds of thousands in gold for your army? And gathering wealth for Keros's dowry to bribe the Starling? I know the arthygater is your ally, but I daresay it would be worth something to you to know if she does what she promises."

King Corvus stood and took a golden beadcoin from the purse hanging from his belt. "Here, give this to the wretched taskmistress and tell her she's lucky to get it. Tell her you have powerful friends, and if she asks for more—or if you disappear—the arthygater will learn she's been taking bribes from thrushes. And this is for you." He put three silver beadcoins on my palm. "You can tell her you earned it the usual way." He jerked his thumb over his shoulder. I don't think he knew he was pointing at a painting of an Abasement in which a tharos man stood astraddle a prone tharais woman, who was naked except for the shawl over her head, and pissed on her belly. The man's prick was the size of a stallion's unsheathed.

I covered my face with the shawl so he wouldn't see the red creeping up my neck. Spit soured in my mouth. He said nothing of the favor I'd asked, to serve Keros when she crossed the Ferinus.

The king was at the door, his back to me, before I understood. He hadn't known: the betrothal of Keros and Merle was Katharos's scheme and none of his. This made sense, as it had not made sense that King Corvus would ever trust his brother again. I said, "Don't you want to hear how much Arthygater Katharos has raised for the duty, the dowry? How much gold and jewelry, how many bales of silk she is sending with Keros? The Starling will be able to buy many soldiers with all that wealth."

I saw with my right eye as if I flew higher than a hawk, high enough to see the arthygater's ships stitching up and down the Inward Sea from Lambanein to Incus, and still more ships on the Outward Sea, sailing to kingdoms beyond my ken. I saw mule trains carrying bales of wool south to Allaxios through the mountain passes, and bearing bales of gauze dyed in clan colors north. Katharos was too wise to place all her goods on one ship that might be capsized by a contrary wind. She would help King Corvus raise an army, and behind his back send a dowry worthy of a king to his brother Merle.

"She wants Lanx," I said. "I suppose she wants the whole coast—safe harbors for her shipping, and all the other merchants will have to beg for her by-your-leave to trade in Incus. What did you promise the husband? Whatever it was, she wants more. No doubt she's paying for an army to cross the mountains next summon—but are you certain she means for you to lead it?"

King Corvus turned to face me and leaned against the door. "Women's gossip. I shall never scorn it again. My wife always said that in Lambanein the women do the work and the men are ornaments. I see now it wasn't a jest."

I do believe the taskmistress of the napkins was pleased when I gave her the gold coin, though she had a queer way of showing it. She struck me about the head with the flat of her hand, and demanded more. The blows were no worse than being battered by a pigeon's wing, but they irked me, and I called her a greedy sow. She crowded me into a corner and said, "Give over the rest."

"The rest of what?"

"There is more, ein? More coins. Do you want this one to tell Gnathin what you did with the king?" She fingered my wrapper and shawl, and I pushed her away.

"Wait. Just wait." I plucked out the silver beadcoins from the knot I'd tied in my shawl, and put them in her hands.

She knew there were more coins to be had, because she'd seen the king give them to me—suddenly I was sure of it. In my webeye I envisioned her pressed against a wall, watching us through a peephole into the tharais room. We had spoken in the High, mostly in the High, so she wouldn't know what we'd said—but that we'd spoken at all, and that I'd bared my face to him—this tale could be sold to someone.

The taskmistress could have taken the coins and sold my secret to a real thrush, without letting me guess she had peeped. But Hazard Chance was evenhanded with me. It was my bad luck the taskmistress was greedy, and my good luck she was none too clever.

Her eyes were like little chips of veined quartz embedded in the clay of her face, and I wanted to slap her hard and leave the imprint of my hand on her cheek. But I said, "A cow gives milk every day, ein? She's worth more as cow than beef, especially a skinny cow like this." I showed her my thin arms. "But you feed her, can't starve her. Leave her a little something, ein? A couple of pewter beadcoins so she doesn't starve."

She didn't see why she should. She didn't see that an arrangement that profited us both was more likely to endure. She thought one of us had to have it all and the other nothing.

It was harder than I expected to be a good thrush. I had the advantage of going unnoticed where Arthygater Katharos conducted her business, but I had this disadvantage: I couldn't trust my memory. I wasn't sure which of the arthygather's dealings would be of importance to King Corvus, and felt obliged to remember them all. To this end I made use of my fingers and, when those proved too few, my knuckles, wrists, elbows, and so forth. I wished I had a string of different kinds of beads such as Gnathin the factotum used to remember her mistress's innumerable instructions. Instead, my grandmother thumb became attached as if by a cord to an embroidered tapestry that was overdue for presentation to the temple of Peranon; my left elbow was supposed to bring to mind a debt owed by a certain Ornis for some wool, and the two large guards Katharos told Gnathin to send round if the woman dithered about paying. My right ear was dedicated to the shipment of five bales of orange gauze to the house of Tricari in Malleus; if the intended purchaser had fallen in the war, the gauzes were to be redyed in the colors of Hazard or Delve.

I needed no thumbs or elbows to remember the gossip about King Corvus. Consort Ostrakan had told the arthygater—and she recounted it to others—that Arkhyios Corvus had taken a napkin to the retiring room, and he left first and she came out later, stumbling. "Bowlegged," said one of the ever-present and ever-flattering limpets, and everyone laughed. The arthygater was pleased. She'd begun to think him lacking, and wonder if he'd been to blame for her sister's long barren spell. Of course using a tharais waste receptacle was not coupling, but it allowed at least for the unobstructed flow of his seed; damming it up was so unhealthy—very bad for the liver, likely to bring on constipation and melancholia.

The bathmistress noticed that I wasn't perfectly attentive to my tasks that morning, and when the bathers had all gone she gave me a beating, saying she knew I was daydreaming over some koprophagais, and if I didn't take care I'd end up a filthy koprophagais myself, living in the middens outside the city with a passel of koprophagais brats.

I hardly cared. What a wonderful possession a secret can be.

We scrubbed the bathing room and chased the last of the dirty water down the drain where the chastened Poton lurked. Lychnais took a nap and I took my leave. I was burdened by so much to remember, and had to write it down. Having no linen to write on, I used potsherds instead, which could be found in heaps around the kitchen gates of palaces ruled by less thrifty factotums than Gnathin. I collected shards from cheap unglazed pots of the sort used for shipping olives and fish paste, and carried them in my shawl through the door in the wall and down the stairs in the steep-walled canyon. The place was nameless, as far as I knew; I called it the Cleft of Katabaton.

I sat on the stairs above her shrine. Swags of bluebind hung from the cliff at my back, noisy with bickering birds and droning bees. In a spill of sunlight I laid out the potsherds, and one by one took them up and scratched a few words in godsigns. The act of inscribing was a prayer, one godsign after another, no matter how trivial the words I made with them. I gave thanks to Wildfire with a libation of blood from the crook of my arm, for the gift of reading and writing again.

By the fifth day of the festival of the Quickening of Peranon, I had a collection of these inscriptions, such as:

Lynx, King: I'd forgotten to tell King Corvus of the rumor that arrived on the wings of a thrush from Incus, that the First of Lynx now commanded the army of Corymb. Surely that would interest him.

House Tricari, five: five bales of gauze, dyed the orange of Lynx.

Outward Sea, four: the arthygater and her friend Phleibin commiserating on the loss of cargoes on four ships vanished in the Outward Sea. "Pirates?" Phleibin said; "Intolerable," said Katharos. "The arkhon must do something."

Back, years: a verse recited in the dining court after the noblewomen had left for the evening.

> A strong man's back will bend
> beneath a weight of years.
> Heavy the years of an arkhon!

The other guests were scandalized.

Husband, quarrel: Plain to see, at the banquet on the fourth night of the Quickening, that Arthygater Katharos had quarreled with Consort

Ostrakan. They conversed and laughed, but she didn't touch his knee, or look to him when she'd said something witty to see if he admired it; nor did he, stretching and leaning against the backrest, brush her shoulder or thigh as if by chance.

I'd found the arthygater's feckless daughters-in-law most fruitful for a certain kind of gossip about King Corvus himself, and the regard—or lack of it—in which he was held by the Lambaneish nobles. It amused everyone that the king waited daily upon Arkhon Kyphos, and daily the arkhon refused a private audience by way of his factotum. The factotum would accept King Corvus's bribes and make excuses: I fear it is an inauspicious day, the arkhon can see no one; the arkhon must meet with ambassadors (from one trifling kingdom or another); or, quite often, the arkhon is taking a purge, he is indisposed. Come back tomorrow and I'll give you an appointment, the factotum would say.

Of course the arkhon kept everyone waiting, or his factotum did. Even his sons and grandsons, the other princes of the kingdom, the arkhyios, were rarely permitted to speak to the arkhon in private. People laughed at Corvus's plight, but they were as quick to ridicule each other. The last one to have an audience with Arkhon Kyphos was the only one safe from mockery. The arkhon was the sun on which their harvests depended. When he smiled on one courtier, bounty. When he frowned at another, drought. He was more fickle than the real Sun, who smiles on us all.

Rumor had it that the arkhon refused to see King Corvus for fear he'd ask for the loan of an army. He had given the king sanctuary, and that was enough. If Arthygater Katharos and her sister supplied Corvus with troops, their father might well be grateful that they'd spared him the awkwardness of refusing any other aid.

But there was a simpler and more certain way to rid Arkhon Kyphos of this embarrassing son-in-law. No doubt the same notion had already occurred to one of his sons or daughters, or some less distinguished courtier who even now might be scheming to kill King Corvus.

I shied away from such reasoning, and the ugly conclusions to which it led. That was a failing, Mai would have said. She had little patience for innocence, and none for willful ignorance, and had chided me often for supposing that what our rulers did was beyond our reckoning, as if they were gods.

They were not gods; they were mortals. Strange to think King Corvus might fight his way through the harsh Ferinus only to be strangled by a silken cord of malice in the court of Arkhon Kyphos. Once I'd dreamed of the king returning to a friend's keep when his friend wasn't there, and the hounds that once had fawned on the king attacked him. In the mountains

Wildfire

I'd kept the dream from King Corvus and given it instead to the jack Voro to pass on to his master. The warning had been misdelivered.

But the king didn't need me to warn him of treachery or assassination plots. He had grown up in a court, probably no better or worse than this one. He would not have dawdled, as I had, on the way to concluding someone might try to kill him. His mother would try, for one, if she could reach so far. The fruitful question was, who else?

These rumors, suppositions, verses, questions—gathered diligently by day in the bathing room, and by night in the dining court, so I went sleepless save for a catnap in the afternoon—what could be made of them? If I took these broken pieces to the king, I was more likely to be paid in mockery than gold. And yet it was not my place to know which shard was valuable and which was rubbish. Maybe King Corvus would be able to arrange them into a useful pattern.

Tonight was the fifth and final night of the Quickening, and Arkhon Kyphos was giving a banquet for the notables of the kingdom. The arthygater and her household were to attend, of course, with the necessary retinue of servants. Lychnais was required in case a wisp of the arthygater's hair strayed from its place in the wickerwork tower upon her head, but my services weren't needed.

I had somewhere else to go, and something I was afraid to do. Since I saw the dowser's hazel rod come alive in her hands, it had been in my mind to dowse for my stolen bones in the manufactory. The dowser wouldn't help, so I must try it myself. I borrowed what I needed from the bathing room—knife, pot with embers, mortar and pestle, a jar of lard—and returned to the Cleft of Katabaton in search of something to sell to the weavers.

There were stout white lilies growing wild on the floor of the cleft, like those in the arthygater's garden, with a heavy scent. I collected their long stamens. In the Dame's garden I'd often stained my clothing with their powder, which looked brown but smeared saffron yellow, and Na had used to scold me for it. This powder proved better than swallowwort sap to color my forearms in the tharos manner. The color was perfect, and it didn't fade when it was wet.

I harvested petals of lilies past their peak, faintly tinged with brown, and mashed them with lard to make an ointment to supple the skin and cure blotches. I found water lilies in the still water of a pond abandoned by the river when it changed course, and added their blooms to the ointment, for they were useful against freckles. The petals were fleshy and soft to the touch, with a waxy sheen, and even as I crushed this beauty between pestle and mortar, they offered up their fragrance.

351

I made a small fire before Katabaton's altar and seethed the water lily roots in water. Mai had taught me this—she sold this decoction to quiet lust. Usually a customer planned to give it to some man or other, but sometimes a woman wanted it for herself, when Desire had pestered her too long. Some of the women in the manufactory might be grateful for such a way to ease their minds.

Time passed in which I didn't think of anything but these simple and soothing tasks. The Sun went down. Indigo darkness came quickly in that deep gorge, but the river shone silver under the Moon. The Quickening always falls on a full Moon, Nephelais had told me. I wished it otherwise, for Crux Moon is strongest when full; he might trifle with me by spoiling the aim of the dowsing rod. But I might not get a better chance.

I made my way along the narrow verge between the cliff and the river, from boulders to sandbanks to mudflats, until I found a forked alder sucker, new growth sprouting from the rootstock of an old giant, and cut it down. I peeled the rod and the wood was bone white.

I knelt before the painting of Katabaton and laid down the rod, and also the gift I'd made for her, a crown woven of perfect lily blossoms. I drizzled a mixture of mother's milk and orange swallowwort juice into my right eye until it stung. The Dame told me in a dream it would help me see small and far, and at last I understood what she meant. It would not cure my webeye; I was doomed to go blind in that eye, but the swallowwort might help me see visions caught in the web. With the burnt tip of a stick, I blackened my upper lids with charcoal, as Az had done when she read the bones for me.

The painting of Katabaton was marred by dark stains and pale salts left by water leaching through the rocks of the cave. She had smudges where once she'd had eyes; nevertheless I felt her watching all I did. By lighting the fire before her altar I had summoned Hearthkeeper, and by making the ointment and tincture I had invoked Desire, and it was as if they too looked through Katabaton's eyes. I bowed my head and asked all three to bless my endeavors.

When I looked up again at Katabaton's face, the pallid brush strokes and dark stains and shadows had been rearranged into the semblance of a skull. Roots hanging from the roof of the cave had become hanks of hair. I shuddered and my nape prickled. I was reminded that Katabaton ruled the shades of Lambanein, as the Queen of the Dead ruled the fallen of Corymb and Incus. Or they were one and the same, called by different names.

Her gaze no longer seemed benign. I prostrated myself and pressed my cheek against the stone. I'd used the bones of the Dame and Na despite that it was forbidden to all but Auspices of Rift to keep remnants of the departed. The Queen of the Dead had not hindered me. Sometimes I thought she had helped. But now I saw how much I'd presumed on her indulgence, casting the bones day after day, forcing the Dame and Na to journey a long way to answer foolish questions, or no questions—just so I could feel their presence, and arrange the colors, the signs, and the avatars in pleasing patterns.

I begged the Queen of the Dead's forgiveness for my offenses, knowing there were many, and prayed she would guide my dowsing stick to point to the bones of the Dame and Na. They should not be forced to answer to a stranger and a thief. And I'd never misuse their shades again, summoning them as if they were servants; they were dear to me, I never meant to treat them badly.

If I must, if she asked it of me, I would burn those finger bones and set them free.

I raised my head. In the wavering firelight, her stare never wavered.

CHAPTER 25

The Quickening

lad in my tharos garments, I hurried to the palace through the alleys, afraid of meeting masquers. Tonight two demiurges, the Fortune and Misfortune of the City, appeared in effigy under the full Moon, and in two processions roamed Allaxios from the palace district down into the town. The Fortune of the City came to the foregate of every palace, where he was welcomed joyously and given gifts to persuade him to tarry for a year; the Misfortune came to the hindgate and demanded tribute for the favor of staying away. The masquers who escorted them were paid off in food and drink, though their bellies were already bloated from the feasts beforehand.

Lychnais had said the masquers were up to no good, and besides, all sorts of shades and meneidon were restless during the Quickening, and apt to wander about and take possession of unwary people. She wished she could stay in the bathing room with me, instead of accompanying the arthygater to the Inner Palace. But when she described the splendor of the masquers, their costumes and processions, I thought she was trying to make me envious.

Two guards in boiled leather cuirasses played at horses-and-houses with the porter at the arthygater's hindgate. Nephelais had warned me about the greed of the night porter, and I gave him two pewter beadcoins. The other men demanded something too, leering and gesturing to show me what they wanted. The porter was jealous of his prerogatives, and said it was his place, not theirs, to collect a toll, and so I got by.

The lad at the manufactory door was bored, teasing a cat with a ball of thread. I bought him off with a garland of bluebind and a kiss. He was such a stripling I didn't mind.

The textrices celebrated the Quickening in the courtyard. In honor of the child god Peranon, long banners of violet silk had been draped from the second-story railings. Lamps hung in the pear tree, small birds pinched out of clay. The women were feasting and dancing, telling tales and chasing children. But a few sat quietly apart, melancholy perhaps, the festival putting them in mind of days before they were bondwomen.

How could I have thought to find one thief among so many? The divining rod was a mere stick. I would have broken it and left its pieces on the ground had I not made a vow to the Queen of the Dead that night. Dowsing for the bones was no longer a selfish notion, but a duty laid upon me.

Easier to jump into a cold pond than to enter one toe at a time, Na used to say. I strode into the crowded courtyard. Word went round that Feirthonin the peddler had returned, and Catena came breathless from dancing to greet me. Other friends came forward as well, the High speakers Dulcis and Abeo, and Agminhatin and Menin from the weaving room. I took a seat on one of the straw mats spread out under the pear tree, and arranged my wares before me: dollops of ointment wrapped in lily pads and tied with the stringy stems of bluebind, and the water lily tincture in a ram's horn made of glass. Glass was so commonplace in Lambanein that one could sometimes find a whole vessel in the rubbish. Beside these I laid down the dowsing rod.

Three women swore the sweetrush root had given them the promised dreams, and wanted more; I sold them lily ointment instead. I found buyers also for the water lily tincture, those who wanted to be quit of unrequited lust, Desire's favorite pestilence.

Soon enough someone asked why I carried a dowsing rod.

I stood and picked up the alder switch. "I know you are all honest women. But now and then something gets missing, ein?—an amulet or beadcoin or something you don't wish to lose. Sometimes these little things wander into someone else's belongings. This rod wags at what is lost."

One woman felt obliged to make a lewd remark about another's lost virginity, and many laughed.

"If you want me to look for her maidenhead, I will," I said, holding the forked ends of the rod and swinging the tip back and forth. "But wouldn't you rather I find the one who steals it? Wouldn't he be more useful, ein?" I swaggered about, pretending to look for a hidden man, prodding women's skirts with the rod, and all the while I was watching the faces of those who did not laugh. A woman I didn't recognize was impolitely showing her teeth as she sidled backward, putting other women between us, and her smile looked like a dog's grin of fear. I followed her through the crowd and the tip of the rod jiggled.

Agminhatin said to her, "Where are you going so fast, Phalin?"

"Nowhere," she said, laughing as if Agminhatin had been jesting.

Agminhatin looked at me with her eyebrows raised. Gods, she was quick to suspect and quick to act. While I puzzled over the pliant peeled branch and how it twisted, smooth and sinewy, against my sweating palms, she rested her arm like an ox yoke across Phalin's shoulders.

I looked at Phalin with my left eye, and her grin looked convincing on her lips, but her eyes were fearful. Among so many women in the manufactory were many I'd never met—but if she'd gotten close enough to steal from me, surely she should be familiar. Her face, if not her name.

I closed my left eye. In the haze of my webeye, tinged yellow by the swallowwort sap, I saw a bird's nest that held colored pebbles. Were there bones in the nest too? I couldn't tell.

I lowered the dowsing rod so the tip pointed harmlessly at the ground. "Ah well, since no one misses anything—except maidenheads—and you don't find those again, my dears—though I know a canny once who makes a new one for a price—since, as I say, no one appears to have lost anything, then perhaps no one minds a magpie in your midst, ein?"

"She's trembling," Agminhatin said.

Abeo said, "I used to have a special bead, amber, about so long." She held up her finger and thumb, and the space between was the length of a finger bone.

"Someone took my eye paste," a spinner said. A weaver spoke up, and another, and now no one laughed. Each had missed some small treasure: a tin amulet of Katabaton, a necklace of glass eyebeads to ward off malice, pewter beadcoins clipped from a net cap during the night. Catena had lost a thumb-size doll of straw wrapped in thread. A woman stepped forward and spat on Phalin's foot. Phalin wouldn't look at her or anyone else. She gazed sideways, her breathing shallow and fast.

I had not done this. The dowsing rod had done it, pointed at a thief and made her tremble. I could have spat on her myself, for I was in a fury to think she might have stolen the bones and prisoned them with worthless trinkets. I pointed the rod at Phalin again. "Every magpie has a nest somewhere, ein? I wonder where it is."

Agminhatin said to Phalin, "It will go better for you if you tell us quickly. Otherwise we'll beat it out of you."

Phalin said, "I haven't stolen anything. I swear it!"

I turned in a circle, and the dowsing rod turned with me, and I slowed when the dowsing rod pointed to the stairs to the second-story arcade. I squinted at Phalin with my webeye, and saw her face spangled by lamplight and dappled by leaf shadows, and the shadows were tinged with the color of fear.

"Bring her," I said to Agminhatin. Phalin didn't struggle, she went where Agminhatin drove her, and we climbed the stone stairs, followed by the throng of women chattering like birds at dawn. Dulcis pushed to the front of the crowd, saying, "She sleeps over there," and I turned the dowsing rod where she pointed. The rod felt quiescent in my hands. Phalin's quick eyes slid back and forth, but she seemed less afraid; I saw it by the color of her shadows and the way her hands loosened. I moved the dowsing rod slowly, left and right, watching for a flare of fear, easier to see in the darkness of the sleeping porch. Dulcis leaned over the railing to pluck a bird lamp from the branches of the pear tree, and she held the lamp high so the light fell on Phalin's face. "Put it out!" I said. She obeyed me.

Phalin was more afraid when the dowsing rod turned left, so I went where she wished I wouldn't go. Agminhatin pushed and pulled her to keep her at my side. I heard myself muttering in the Low, the one language no one else spoke here. The words crowded together in my throat and came out pell-mell. I let myself pray. "Ardor help me, for you put the cloud in my eye and bade me see through it. Crux bless my sight, bless the far-seeing swallow and the swallowwort, let me see far and small, let me see all. Wend, bless me, Wend the finder. Lose the needle, the Weaver will find it; lose the lamb, Ram will find it. Wend Plenty is the patron of merchants and thieves, lock and key, and how can Wend bless them both? Bless me, Wend, the Dame was dear to you—help me find her. Bless me, Dame, bless me, Na. Forgive my offense. Are you lost and wandering because of me? I should never have accepted the gift and Az should never have given it. I was too vain, I showed what should have been concealed, and now the Queen of the Dead is vexed with me." And it didn't seem strange to pray to the Dame and Na as if they were divinities, like lesser godlings of Lambanein, ranking below the gods and above me. Even Na, a mudwoman when she lived, was a sort of little god to me now.

Phalin was afraid when I pointed up. So up and up, unwinding a pale tracery from the tip of the alder rod. There, under the eaves between two columns, were three or four abandoned swallows' nests made of clay and straw. I poked them with my dowsing rod and turned to look at Phalin. I could hardly see her face for the shadow oozing from it. She opened her mouth and a flare of fear came out.

Agminhatin climbed up on the stone railing. With one hand she held on to a slender column wrapped with a stone vine, and with the other she made a fist and smashed the nests. Out tumbled broken eggshells, glass, tiles, polished pebbles, beadcoins, needles, twists of thread, a tortoiseshell comb, and even a golden fingercap with a nail studded with rubies. These things were scattered on the floor of the sleeping porch and the courtyard below, and women ran after them and crawled about searching for small treasures. Phalin stood there with her lips parted and I wondered why she didn't run. But of course there was nowhere to go.

I was on my knees, scooping objects in a heap, and Catena helped me. I straightened up and shouted, "Bring what you find up here, and we sort together so each gets what is hers."

Agminhatin jumped down from the railing, and gripped Phalin's garment with her left hand and began to shake. She opened her right hand under Phalin's nose and showed her a muddy beadcoin of coiled copper with a feather sticking to it. "You! You *thief!*" she screeched, as if it were the worst word she could find.

"I never stole." Phalin pointed at me. "She did it. That's why she could find it so easily, ein?" Having but half her wits about her, she'd forgotten that some of those things had been stolen after I left the manufactory, as someone was quick to say. Her cries that she was innocent, that she'd been wronged, only enraged everyone.

Agminhatin slapped her and put a muddy print on her cheek. Other women shoved Phalin, and Dulcis kicked her in the shins. I wiped the bead-coins and other small objects clean on Phalin's skirts to show my contempt for her, and laid them in rows on the tiled floor of the sleeping porch, looking for bones. It was pitiful—though I felt no pity—to gaze at the treasures arranged before me. Phalin truly was a magpie; she seemed to prize a shard of green glass with bubbles trapped inside, or a chip of glazed tile, above dull pewter beadcoins. Though she'd stolen those too.

I looked up at Phalin. "Where are my bones? I tell you, I lay a hex on you if you don't give them back. I make you tremble the rest of your days and your days will be few." I didn't know how to curse, but at that moment I was sure I could accomplish it.

But whether I looked at her with my left eye or right, she seemed less fearful. My curse didn't perturb her. We'd discovered her hoard; perhaps that was the worst thing she could imagine.

Perhaps she hadn't stolen the bones after all. They were not shiny or pretty or valuable. I looked around the crowd, one woman after another becoming individual to me again, strangers, acquaintances, and friends. I shouted, "Where are my bones? Who stole my bones?"

For the merest moment, faster than a blink, I saw a sly expression on Dulcis's face. Then it was gone, as if it had never been, and she looked just as she had before: indignant at Phalin, yet avid too, gleeful to have an event worthy of gossip for months to come. I stood up. "Dulcis?" She looked at me without alarm, and I wondered if I'd been mistaken about that look. Sly, malicious, smug. I'd seen it so briefly.

It was a cold night, and Dulcis had her shawl wrapped closely around her shoulders. I put my hands on either side of her neck and rubbed my thumbs over her collarbone. I felt a cord roll under her shawl, something tied around her neck.

"What's the matter, Feirthonin?" she said in the High. "What bones?"

I answered in Lambaneish. "One is blue all over, that's the Dame. The other with a red tip, that one is Na. You see me, ein? You see me use them."

I tightened my grip and felt her shudder. She said, "I know nothing about your bones. Bones draw shades like carrion draws flies. Why would you keep such things and bring meneidon among us?" She spoke half in the High, half in Lambaneish. In either language she was a liar.

"Then why do you steal them?" I cried. "They're not yours. They don't answer to you!" I pushed her shawl aside and saw a green cord around her neck. I tugged at the cord and pulled a patchwork cloth pouch from under her wrapper—my compass—and I didn't care that she was trying to pummel me with the flat of her hands, or that Catena stared with dismay. I yanked the cord over her head and emptied the pouch. Three silver beadcoins fell out, and Galan's scrip tied in a flat knot. I roared at Dulcis, "Where are my bones?"

She said, "I burned them."

She had a look on her face I couldn't put a name to. I realized I'd never understood her. She had talked and talked to me because I would listen, and all the while she'd cherished a secret enmity before she stole from me, and afterward a secret triumph. Rift Queen of the Dead, ruler of gutworms—what worm had she set to wriggling in Dulcis's belly, to make her so envious and greedy?

The Queen of the Dead had made me promise to set free the Dame and Na, knowing they were already free. Knowing I could not have done it. So she took them and left me sorrowing again. They were lost to me, the Dame and Na, and I grieved for them and for the hope I'd carried in place of their bones.

I sat on the floor of the sleeping porch, clutching the pleated rectangle of linen on which was written that Galan had once been foolish and fond enough to give me a stone house on a mountainside. I was glad to have it back, but I would have traded it for the bones, I would have.

Phalin and Dulcis went elsewhere and I never noticed. Catena took her familiar place on my left, close enough to touch, as if we were sharing warmth in the mountains; she offered the solace of her presence without a word.

It didn't take long for the women to claim their stolen beads and trinkets. They didn't quarrel, except for a small spat about the silver beadcoins, which looked more or less alike. When they were done, there was nothing left but broken glass and tiles and tangles of thread. Some women unrolled their blankets over the bedstraw and settled down to sleep, but most gathered in the courtyard, and their voices rose to us, sounds of laughter and song, for after all it was the last night of the Quickening.

I took the forks of the divining rod in my hands and tore it down the middle and cast the halves down. Agminhatin, who sat on the stairs watching, said, "Give me those."

"Why?"

"One for each thief," she said. "You ought to do it, but I see you won't, crying over those precious bones of yours. So I'll do it."

I picked up one of the halves of my divining rod, and laid the switch across my lap. My fingers itched. With the eyesight of a swallow, my right eye saw clear and faraway an image of Dulcis with her wrapper down around her waist; I saw myself striping her bare back with neat rows of red weals, while Agminhatin did the same to Phalin. I felt a shock of heat at the thought of seeing Dulcis half naked and shamed. This same lust to hurt was what Sire Pava's steward must have felt when he whipped my bare legs with the thorny green briar of a rose. It had moved Sire Rodela to take his trophy from me, and now his shade stirred in his sleep, and emitted a faint hum. I dropped the alder switch as if it scorched my fingers.

Catena had shifted away so our hips were barely touching. She wouldn't catch my eye. "Are you going to curse Dulcis the way you cursed Zostra? Curse her dead?"

I glared at Agminhatin, who had spread that tale, and answered Catena. "Dulcis is commanded to burn those bones by the Queen of the Dead. How do I curse her for something a god makes her do? Let her be punished for a thief, but I am denied revenge."

"Then punish her for a thief," Agminhatin said. "Give them both a whipping, they deserve it."

"It doesn't stop them from stealing."

"What would you do then?"

"Bell them at night." I put my hand around my neck. "Like a goat, so they don't creep about to steal while everyone is sleeping. Shun them."

Agminhatin picked up the split divining rod. "You are far too cruel," she said, and she went downstairs to find Phalin and Dulcis.

I knocked so the stripling porter would let me out of the manufactory; I knocked and knocked, but he didn't answer. I put my left eye to the peephole and saw no one. I sat on the cold tiles of the corridor, listening to the merriment in the courtyard. Waited.

It was late. Suppose dawn arrived before the porter, and some

Wildfire

taskmistress caught me in tharos garb in the manufactory, and took me to Gnathin?

Back in the crowded courtyard, I looked up at the pear tree, wondering if the limb that hung over the roof would bear my weight. I tied my shawl around my waist and tucked up my skirts, and climbed up the trunk and out along the bough. But it was too high above the roof, I feared to jump. I shinned along until my weight bent the branch, and I was able to dangle down and touch the green tiles with my toes. When I let go the branch sprang up out of reach. My legs were shaking.

I scrambled up to the roof ridge. The slope wasn't too steep, but still I walked carefully along, keeping one hand on the ridge tiles, until I came to one of the warriors that stood guard on the four corners of the roof. He was made of glazed clay, and nearly my height; he had a fierce scowl, but his iron sword was rusted and pitted. I straddled the ridge beside him. From this corner I overlooked on one side the alley that ran along the southern edge of the palace, and on the other the kitchen courtyard with its sheds and fountains and herb garden. Behind me was the courtyard of the manufactory.

Now that I was up here, I couldn't see how to get down. I was dizzy, clinging to the skirts of the clay guardian as the roof swayed under me, and I felt as though I were bestride a great beast, which had carried me to a strange new place full of strange inhabitants. For here came the Misfortune of the City, riding down the alley on a large wooden horse on wheels, pulled by koprophagais. Torchlight billowed on the Misfortune's huge mask, which was painted dull white. I'd have expected him to scowl like a roof guardian, but he seemed sly; his eyes and mouth were slits cut in the wood. He was surrounded by a horde of lesser misfortunes, some of them wearing masks made of yellowing horse skulls, and stomping along on stilts so they were head and shoulders above the rest of the throng. The masquers roared songs and played iron drums that clanged and boomed like war. In answer the women in the manufactory courtyard began a cicada shrilling that made me shiver.

The Misfortune of the City hammered with his long staff on the hindgate of the palace. On his tall horse he could almost look over the one-story wall of the kitchen court. His voice was a strange warbling roar; a man carrying a white banner interpreted. The Misfortune said he'd break down the gate or climb over the walls, and enter the palace with his herd to bring a year's worth of bad luck.

The night porter on the other side of the wall called out that the walls were high and the locks were stout, and no misfortune could get past him. The banter went back and forth, each knowing what to say. But the masquers were impatient. Misfortunes galloped up and down the alleys, pushing through the crowd, knocking men over and whinnying like angry stallions. Men drummed on the wall with clubs and called out, "The Misfortune of the City is starving, feed him! The Misfortune is thirsty, give him to drink!"

The Misfortune of the City was not a god I worshipped. I feared him nonetheless, and the misfortunes at his heels who began to chant, "Mares, bring us mares!" In Lambanein they had a saying: one misfortune sires others. I'd heard it without understanding.

Tharos maidservants came out of the kitchen sheds bearing the Misfortune's tribute. The porter opened the gate for them and guards pushed back the crowd. The servers unrolled a long rug in the alley and set out platters of cakes, jars of wine, glass drinking horns, and folded cloths, the dyes brilliant in the torchlight. A pair of women carried out a long tray on which was balanced a mound of gleaming eggs. Masquers crowded about the offerings, snatching at the cloths, spattering wine.

The tharos women ran back through the gate, and I heard some shrieking with giddy laughter. And now a line of tharais napkins came out, each carrying a basin and ewer so the masquers could cleanse themselves. I might have been among them, had the arthygater held a feast of her own tonight. The guards locked them outside, and jeered when the women pounded on the gate and begged to be let back in. A man in a horse skull mask was the first to take a napkin by the arm and drag her into the crowd. I couldn't see her face under the shawl, but I saw her try to twist away.

A man shouted, "We asked for mares, you gave us donkeys. Mares, we want mares! Send us the fillies in the manufactory and we'll go away." Hard loud laughter, and other men began to chant with him, "We want mares!" Someone picked up an egg from a tray and threw it, and to my surprise it broke against the wall with a splash of scarlet powder. Now they were hurling eggs over the wall and at each other, splotching their white robes with orange, crimson, and plum.

I crawled to the guardian at the southeast corner, scratching my hands and knees on the sharp edges of the curved tiles. I must get down somehow, run through the alleys to that door in the wall and down the stairs to take refuge in Katabaton's shrine until this night was over. But there were masquers in the eastern alley too, a small group of men without torches. They talked in whispers, except for a drunken misfortune who raised his voice to call his fellows mollycoddled lolly-pots and pricklickers. They weren't insulted, for he was speaking in the High. One of the king's men.

Two servants approached at a trot, carrying a long pole. They hoisted it up and leaned it against the manufactory roof, and I saw it was a ladder with notches for footholds. The men stood in the middle of the alley looking up. I recognized some of them from banquets: there was the arthygater's unmarried son, Arkhyios Kyanos, and her nephew, princes of the kingdom behaving like common marauders. And one man was a jack from the king's army, Hebes; so the drunken man was probably his master, Sire Cunctor.

The nephew—Kydos was his name—started up the ladder, and other men clustered around the base, ready to follow, and soon they'd be on the roof and what would I do then? Someone told Sire Cunctor in Lambaneish that he was too drunk to climb. I bumped down the tiled slope on my buttocks and gave the pole a shove with my foot. It clattered to the street and took the nephew with it. I'd have been glad to break his legs, but he was unharmed.

The men in the alley bellowed at me to come down and fight. They raised the ladder again and I shouted, "I kick it down faster than you climb!"

Someone said, "It's a woman!"

I did kick it down again, and I laughed, because they couldn't touch me, not even if one man climbed on another's shoulders, and another man on his. Even if they reached the top of the wall they'd find it hard to get around the deep eaves. I crouched on the edge and the masquers taunted me. One fellow went around the corner and came back with as many eggs as he could carry. The men hurled them at me, and everyone missed but Hebes. He hit me on the hip with an egg full of vermilion powder, which stained my tharos wrapper and bared legs.

"Hebes," I called down, "get your drunken horse home while he can still trot, ein?" I spoke in Lambaneish so he wouldn't know me, and he gawped so wide a fly could have landed on his tongue. Ah, this reckless elation, this prickling on my neck—I recognized the touch of Hazard Chance. No wonder she was abroad, on a night when the Fortune of the City and its Misfortune rode the streets on wooden horses.

I quite forgot Hazard Chance was as apt to lead people astray as to lead them home, for she made me sure-footed on the tiles and took away my fear. I ran back along the roof and called down to the guards in the kitchen courtyard. I made my voice sharp to cut through the noise, telling them of the misfortunes trying to climb into the manufactory from the next alley.

On the other side of the hindgate, the tharais napkins had been pulled into the crowd among knots of masquers. One woman stood bent over on the opposite side of the alley, bracing herself against the wall with her skinny bare arms, while a man in a horse skull mounted her from behind. He bucked and pretended to whinny, and men laughed as they waited their turn with her. I prayed she was not my friend Nephelais, but was that not the same as praying down the misfortune on some other woman? My elation soured to a queasy ferment in my belly, and I clenched my teeth as Sire Rodela began to buzz.

I couldn't linger to see if the guards heeded my warning. I ran back and arrived in time to push down the ladder just as the crown of a man's head was rising over the edge of the roof. It was a long fall, and I heard him cursing after he hit the ground. Someone said they should wait for the other ladders, and another man—probably the arthygater's son—said, "You'll never see those sluggards of yours again, let alone another ladder."

"Then let's enter by the foregate." That was the nephew speaking. "If we take off our cloaks the guards will let us in; they won't know we've come as misfortunes. We can take the hindquarters guards from behind, and get the key to the manufactory."

Arkhyios Kyanos said, "We mustn't do that. They'll know we did it."

Arkyhios Kydos laughed. "Oh, I see, I see. You thought your mother wouldn't find out. The women will tell her, you dolt!"

"I have a mask."

"If you're so afraid of your mother, you should go on back to your rooms and play with your dung beetle nursemaid instead, let her twiddle your diddle."

I cupped my hands around my mouth and shrieked, "Are you a man, Arkhyios Kyanos? Are you a man, ein? Because you let yourself be insulted like a boy." I hoped to taunt him into a fight with the nephew, but he turned his wrath on me instead, threatening to use me like a rag and toss me off the roof. I hissed at him, and scrambled over the roof ridge and down the inward side to peer into the manufactory courtyard. Many textrices were still gathered by the fountain, singing and clapping and making so much noise they couldn't hear my shouts.

I could see women on the sleeping porch, on the opposite side of the courtyard, so I ran around the roof again until I was over them. I lay downslope with my head hanging over the edge of the roof and shouted at the sleepers. A woman screamed that there were men on the roof, and she roused others and there was such a hubbub I couldn't make myself understood.

Someone called out to me from under the eaves. "Who is it? What do you want?"

"What do you think he wants, ein?" The mocking voice came from Agminhatin.

"It's not a man, it's me."

"A pity," Agminhatin said. She came to the railing a few columns away and craned to look up at me. I waved and she came closer.

I said, "Are you hoping misfortunes will get in here tonight? Perhaps you expect a suitor, ein?"

"Every year they hammer at the gate and make a commotion. But they're only pretending to be fierce, ein? Once they are stuffed with wine and eggs and aniseed cakes, they go away content."

"Not this year. The arthygater's son and her nephew are outside in the alley with a ladder. You can wait for them if you want, but wake up Catena for me, ein? Because they come soon, by roof or by door, and I want to get her out of here."

"Wake her up? You think she's asleep in all this uproar?"

"I wager she is," I said.

"Done—I'll put two pewter beadcoins on it," she said. Soon she came toward me with Catena by the hand. "I owe you for the wager," Agminhatin said, and dashed off down the stairs.

I said in the High, "Catena, can you see me? There are malfortunes trying to get in here—you understand?"

Catena wrapped a cloth around herself deftly, as if she'd worn Lambaneish clothing all her life. I asked her to see if the door to the outside was open. Before she was halfway down the stairs, she met Agminhatin coming up, who had tried the door and found it still locked. On the other side was such a din she was sure the porter hadn't heard her pounding and shouting.

I said to them, "Maybe—maybe I climb down into the kitchen courtyard and tell the guards to let us out, and we hide in the dining court."

"How can you climb down, ein?" Agminhatin said.

I pointed to one of the long violet cloths hanging from the second-story railing in honor of Peranon's Quickening. "Tie one end of this around a stone or tile or something. That way you toss it up to me. If we tie three or four hangings together maybe I get down. Oh, but hurry, hurry!" I said, for as I spoke I saw with my right eye small and far, as if I flew like a swallow above the roof: I saw men battering at the hindgate with the blunt end of a tree trunk, and the door straining at its hinges. Soon the misfortunes would be inside, boiling around the door of the manufactory, and we'd lose our chance to get out that way.

Agminhatin flung the weighted end of a hanging up to me, and I scrambled to catch it. But already we were too late. There were two men, three, walking toward me in white cloaks across the roof, and these I saw with my good left eye, so there was no need to wonder if they were real. Another pair of misfortunes followed them over the roof ridge, carrying the pole ladder, treading with care down the inner slope. They came from the side of the manufactory that abutted the pleasure garden.

I saw with my right eye a way to make our escape—a single chance—but I couldn't see all the way down that path, for it ended in a dark tunnel, the tunnels under the palace. I called down to Catena, "Misfortunes are already on the roof. Gather your friends and take them to the winter dormitory. And wait there." I urged her to make haste, and after she left I realized she had not once spoken.

I threw the silk hanging over the bough of the pear tree to pull it down within reach. I hooked a foot over the branch to haul myself up, and descended, scraping the tender skin of my inner thighs on the bark.

Agminhatin stood under the tree with some women I knew from the weaving room, and also the bondwomen from Incus, Nitida, Migra, Dame Abeo—even Dulcis.

I said, "They come in the kitchen court too, so we can't get out that way. Look—they're trying to climb down!"

We rushed across the courtyard. One man was halfway down the ladder and another above him. We put our shoulders to the pole and heaved, and it went skidding across the pavement. The topmost man scrambled up and hung over the edge of the roof, and the ladder toppled and brought the other man down with it. He lay flat on his back in the courtyard, the breath knocked out of him. His robe was unbleached muslin, and the clothing underneath was worn; probably an impoverished limpet, trying to impress the arkhyios with his daring. I thought maybe he'd never breathe again, but he gasped at last and I turned away.

Men on the roof shouted at us. The sky was lighter behind them, the stars fading as the Sun's brightness seeped up from the horizon. A misfortune dangled like a spider from a rope attached to a ram's head drainpipe. Nitida and Migra staggered about with the heavy pole, trying to knock him down.

A woman wailed, praying for Katabaton to protect us from the misfortunes, and the year of bad luck they brought us.

Agminhatin said, "Nine months of bad luck, to be sure." She stood with her hands on her hips, baring her teeth.

I said, "We are overrun soon. We should go down to the winter dormitory."

"That's no place to hide," Agminhatin said.

There was no place to hide. Once the men got in we'd be on the wrong side of every locked door.

"We can get away through the tunnels," I said.

"And how do you propose to get into the tunnels? Climb through the shitholes?"

More or less. There was no time to explain or argue. I took the stairs down to the underground dormitory. I looked over my shoulder to see who was carrying the lantern that lit my way, and there was Nitida, with some other bondwomen behind her.

Was the Quickening how the Lambaneish celebrated the UpsideDown

Days, such as we had in Corymb? In those five licentious days many things are permitted that are forbidden the rest of the year—but in our village one could stay home without fear someone uninvited would break down a barred door. I'd met Galan during the UpsideDown Days, and truth be told I was looking to get pricked. Perhaps some of the weavers welcomed the misfortunes, who were merely men, after all, under their masks and robes. But the ones who followed me were afraid—of being taken by force, or a year of bad luck, I wasn't sure which.

The dormitory door had a lock on the outside, not inside where it would have been useful. Sometimes we'd all been locked into the dormitory at night to punish one transgression or another. I slid the oaken crossbar out of its brackets.

"It will make a good club," someone said.

"A good lever," I said.

Catena opened the door and exclaimed, "You're wounded!" I'd forgotten all about the splash of red powder on my legs from the egg Hebes had thrown, and I hastily reassured her and let down the skirts I'd hitched up. Catena was with her friends, a hand of girls who worked as spinners, and they'd gathered up a few of the younger children as well. The light from Nitida's lantern and Catena's oil lamp illuminated a few stout pillars. We huddled together, no more than a dozen of us.

I asked three women to guard the door, and carried the crossbar lever to the privy bench against the far wall. The dormitory hadn't been used since the weather turned warm, so the smell was not too bad. But women complained of the stink and wondered aloud what I was doing.

The bench top was a long plank with a row of holes. I hammered loose the pegs that secured it, and put my lever into a hole at one end and strained to budge the plank, to uncover the niche that opened to the tunnel on the other side of the wall. Bondwomen gathered around to watch; they didn't move to help or hinder. They seemed to have given themselves over to Fate, as if there was nothing further to be done and no effort they could make on their own behalf. This made me furious, and I pressed with all my might on the lever and raised the end of the plank, and Nitida wrapped her hands in her shawl and pulled, and Catena added her lesser strength to ours, and we rocked and slid the plank forward on one end, uncovering the waste jars in the niche.

I heard a Lambaneish woman mutter that we were letting dung beetles into the manufactory, and I turned on her and all the others who had done nothing, and said, "Stay here if you want, and await the misfortunes. But I go. I know a way through the tunnels to the arthygater's quarters, and they don't attack there—they don't dare."

The weaver said, "But it is *tharais*!"

"I'm a dowser," I said. "I go where the rod tells me, even into the hidden ways, then I purify myself. You do the same."

"Your rod is broken," she said.

"This one does as well," I said, and pointed the oak crossbar at the hole.

"The arthygater will punish us," Menin said. Little Neinan in her arms wanted to get down, and he kicked his arms and legs when she held on tightly.

The hole we'd opened was a dark triangle. Nitida held up her lantern and I saw the large waste jars shoulder to shoulder down below. I shoved one over and it crashed from the niche to the floor of the tunnel a step below, and rolled and stopped with a thump. To my amazement it didn't break.

I asked Catena if she would climb down first, and she looked at me with fear and faith and nodded.

I hugged her. "There is no girl in all of Lambanein and all of Incus as brave as you. In you go. Here, take your lamp. Now I'll lower the children, and you make sure they don't stray, ein?"

Some of the children were claimed by their mothers, who would not let them go, but I didn't quarrel. No time, no time. No time to attend to the weaver muttering that I must be a dung beetle since I knew dung beetle ways. Someone said in a loud, spiteful voice, "You see? Zostra did make her a filthy tharais, and she's fooled you all, but not me." That was Dulcis.

I turned my back on her and climbed down through the hole and into the tunnel behind the dormitory. I carried the crossbar, and Catena and Migra ran beside me, and Nitida herded the spinners and the smaller children. Dame Abeo balked, refusing to follow, but Menin came with her son in her arms.

"Hurry!" I called to them, and hurry we did. The flame of Catena's oil lamp was a frail fluttering thing, always about to go out, but I didn't need light to see the faraway visions trapped in my right eye. I could see it all, tunnel and streets and palace, above and below at once. We were under the eastern wall; we turned the corner and soon we had passed the stairs that led up to the kitchen gate, and my right eye saw that above us men were fighting in courtyard and alley. Someone knocked over the Misfortune's horse and a pair of men picked up his effigy and carried it aloft on their shoulders; his large face was awry, and his eye slits full of malice.

We heard men shouting over the din from the street above. They'd followed us into the tunnel, and I'd been so sure they wouldn't dare, lest they be polluted. But it was all upside down now. We ran past the room where the tharais napkins slept, but their door was locked, and all the napkins were in the alley to appease the Misfortune and his herd, to take upon themselves a year's worth of bad luck so the rest of the arthygater's household would be spared.

I told Catena and Migra where they would find the stairway to the arthygater's bathing room, and gave them the crossbar. Carrying it had made me feel brave, but they had more need of it. "The door has a latch, but not a very strong one. You break it with this, ein? I know of no safer hiding place. Now go, go!" I stood against the wall and watched the women pass, and there were more than I'd expected, nearly a score of them, not counting the children. Nitida was at the rear with the lantern, herding stragglers. I was surprised to see Agminhatin at her side, carrying a child under one arm. A look passed between us and I waved her on.

I was in the dark. The lanterns of our pursuers bobbed as they ran toward me. I'd halted by the waste jars for the tharais dormitory, just where the smell was rankest. I didn't want to breathe if it meant taking that smell into my nose and throat, and yet I had to. I gagged as I wrestled a heavy jar out of the niche above the tunnel floor. It broke when it fell, and flooded the floor of the tunnel with piss. I cast down another pot and another, and lastly a jar full of shit, making a barrier no tharos would willingly cross: a large puddle of filth, full of broken crockery.

The man with the lantern was too intent on me to notice what was on the ground between us. He splashed in the puddle and cursed, and I crowed with delight to see him dance backward, his legs jerking as if he wished to abandon the soles of his feet. "Koprophagais bitch!" he shouted. "I'm going to kill you!"

The three men behind him stopped short of getting their feet wet, but they didn't dare laugh at him, for he was the arthygater's nephew, Kydos. Runnels of slime oozed toward them.

I stood on the other side of the barrier with my feet and garments splattered and reeking. Only a tharais, a filthy tharais, would have done such a filthy thing. So I must be tharais then, foul all the way through, inside and out, and though it should have shamed me, I wasn't ashamed just then. I was proud of it.

Arkhyios Kydos wanted to twist my neck, but he would not cross the moat, though it was as shallow as a puddle. I laughed at the revulsion and rage on his face. He couldn't bear to be thwarted. Why else bother to chase a small band of women through the tunnels, when there were so many left in the manufactory to amuse him?

Someone asked, "Who is she?" Another bent over and retched, then backed away, still clutching his belly. I turned and ran into the dark. I'd been like a vaunting hotspur, staying to savor victory, but all I tasted now was bitter rue. I heard Sire Rodela's hammering laughter in my ear, and before me in the dark a scrap of white, which I knew was Penna, always just vanishing ahead. I was left with those two restless and malcontented shades, when all I'd wanted was to find the Dame and Na again so I should not go alone and friendless through this strange land.

I climbed the stairs to the little room I shared with Lychnais. My shoulders brushed the walls as I ascended. I followed the glimmer of Penna's gauze kirtle, and when she vanished all light was gone and both my eyes were blind as a mole's. I sat down on the stairs. Tonight, as soon as one way closed I'd seen another, seen it all at once in my mind's eye, even to the door with the bar I could use as a lever, and the casting down of the waste jars. I'd dreamed it before I did it, but I'd hadn't forseen the look Agminhatin would give me as she passed in the tunnel.

She knew I was tharais. What she knew, others would know. They would not be fooled by my claim that I knew the tunnels because I was a dowser. No tharos dowser would willingly enter there. The textrices would guess I worked in the bath as an attendant, and bar me from the refuge I'd found for them. Even if they let me in, someone would betray me tonight or tomorrow. Dulcis would, and gladly. I couldn't risk being delivered to the arthygater's tormentors to be branded or maimed.

I rubbed my wrist, thinking of Catena. Silently saying farewell to her, and begging the gods we both worshipped to look after her. She would be well, I told myself. It wasn't her own fate that brought her here; she'd been shackled to my fate, and for that I was truly sorry, though it was none of my doing.

I refused to pray on my own behalf. The gods had misled me to this place, pulling me this way and that. Now their opposing wills were knotted so tightly around me that I couldn't find one end or another of their purposes to untie myself. Yet I had no will of my own, I was sullen and heavy as clay.

I sat a long time unmoving in the dark, and my mind's eye was dark as well. I couldn't see two paces ahead, let alone a day or a year ahead, for I'd lost all foresight, not only the true foreknowledge sometimes granted by the gods, but mere imagination. And I lacked the courage to do the unimaginable.

I stood. Keeping one hand on the wall, I took a step down into the blankness and then another—surprising myself, for I hadn't realized I'd decided to move. At the bottom of the stairs, I turned right and right again, venturing for the first time past the boar's-head waterspout in the tunnel under the western side of the palace.

I sang under my breath the song Ardor had given me: the melody from the Smith, the words from Hearthkeeper.

Wildfire

Burn bright, burn fast.
Give what light you can,
the rest is ash.

Louder then, for the song itself gave me courage: *Burn bright, burn fast.* I saw the faintest glimmers from streaks and patches of salts left behind when the walls wept. *Give what light you can.* In my mouth, the taste of something bitter, something burnt: *The rest is ash.*

The tunnel turned and branched, and I went right and left, forward and back, up and down stairs and slopes, and soon I lost all sense of where I was under the city. The bespeckled dark made me think of how I'd chased the wood-rover petals, and indeed I often followed the sound of water, water running beneath my feet or in clay pipes embedded in the walls. A long way underground I entered a drain tunnel with a raised path on one side. The drain was made to carry rainwater from the streets during the storms of winter; now it held a sluggish stream fed by water oozing from the rocks. I bathed my legs and scrubbed my wrapper, and afterward I was cold but smelled less vile. I followed the drain upstream, stooping so as not to scrape the roof.

Thin gray veils of light hung in the darkness before me, and I quickened my steps. I halted under a stone grate, and light touched my face like the softest silk. The grate was too heavy to lift, but I walked on until I found one made of iron, and I emerged into the street like a meneidon of the drain made restless by the drumming of masquers.

I looked down a deserted alley and saw where the hidden Sun dyed the Heavens with the fugitive colors of dawn, and once again I knew east from west. I hurried downhill toward the dawn, going where? Where Chance led me. Here in Lambanein they thought Fortune and Misfortune were two, but they were one in her, and Allaxios was hers until the end of twilight. I went toward what she would give me, or take from me.

Chance gave me a drunk, one of the Misfortune's herd. At first I thought he was dead, because he lay crumpled against a wall with his head downhill. I leaned over him and heard him snort and snore under his horse skull mask.

I stripped him, rolling him out of the cloak twisted about him. The stilts were the height of my knee, carved of wood like pattens, and painted with red and white stripes. One stilt was loose, askew, so the leg looked broken. His mask was fastened to a reed helmet that buckled under the chin. The teeth and lower jaw of the horse skull had been removed, and the inside was padded to rest against a human face.

371

I donned the mask and stilts and cloak and struggled to stand by propping myself against the wall. My feet were too far away and the mask too heavy, and it was difficult to see through eye sockets that didn't align with my own. I tottered along with one hand on the wall, thumping the stilts against the pavement emphatically. I was not a woman; I was a misfortune, a drunken misfortune returning home at the end of a long festival night. In my deepest, roughest voice, I sang the drinking song Mox had taught us in the mountains:

> *I, even I, must die,*
> *So why should I bother to try?*
> *It is better to die drinking,*
> *Than to lie thinking,*
> *That I, even I, must die.*

CHAPTER 26

Court of Tranquil Waters

he king slept all morning and half the afternoon. They brought me to him after his bath. He was dressed in a loose robe of red wool patterned with gold thread, and his beard and hair shone with scented oil.

I prostrated myself on the tiled floor before him. I said I'd had to flee Arthygater Katharos's palace, because the taskmistress of the napkins threatened to betray me despite the gold I'd given her. The Misfortune of the City had assaulted the palace, and in the uproar I'd escaped, and followed some masquers who spoke the High into the Inner Palace to the king's door. I could not return to the arthygater's palace ever again, or she'd put me to the question under torture and then take my head. I begged the king to have mercy, not to give me back to the arthygater or turn me out.

He said, "What am I to do with you?"

A woman doesn't reside in men's quarters in Lambanein, yet I did, for a hand of days, live in the Court of Tranquil Waters with what was left of the king's army. Stagnant Waters, they should have called it, for the long pool in the courtyard was covered with green scum. The arkhon had granted King Corvus a most dilapidated residence, a two-story building about the size of the manufactory, with stables at one end of the courtyard and baths and kitchens at the other. On the two longest sides, behind colonnades, were rows of small rooms furnished with heaps of straw, broken chairs, and beds with torn cushions. The wall paintings had been splendid once.

It was strange to live among soldiers again, and to live barefaced after so long under the shawl. Everywhere I went, I was watched. I remembered how the gazes of men had burdened me when I'd first come to the Marchfield, but I was not the green girl I used to be. And the men didn't see me as a mere skinsheath. They looked at me and saw the king's dreamer. More than one varlet made plain his opinion that King Corvus had wronged me by sending me away.

I was fearful I would lose their regard if they learned I was tharais. Three

373

men had seen me in tharais garb: the king, Garrio, and Sire Vafra. What if Sire Vafra boasted that he'd seen me serving as a napkin, and had taken me to a retiring room? I need not have worried. Living together as they did in a hive of strange-ignorant ones, the king's men had not learned how much it mattered. Blood and mud they understood, not tharos and tharais.

There were no proper women's quarters, though there were women about; the arkhon had supplied his guest with bondwomen to cook and clean and launder, and there were women who visited of their own accord to ply a different trade. I approached a cook to buy a small sack of yellow powder for my arms, and prayed she wouldn't smell the tharais taint, or notice how I shook at my own temerity.

I'd given myself to Hazard Chance in the last passage of the last night of the Quickening, and she had delivered me to the king as surely as if she'd clasped my hand and dragged me here herself. Now I was listless, without even a whim to give me reason to stir.

I passed the time sleeping, by night in the second-story colonnade, and by day in the courtyard on a bed of lemon-scented thyme. I covered myself in a blanket of shadow under a pomegranate tree. In the afternoon the shade would move away from me and I would lie in the Sun awhile, torpid as a snake, before creeping around the tree to another shadow. The shimmer of light through the leaves lulled me. I didn't remember my dreams.

I ought to have been glad I'd left the arthygater's palace. So many times I'd promised myself escape, envisioning a shining day in which I would break the dry husk of my bondwoman's life to return home to Galan. I would traverse mountains to reach him; I would find my way, come summertime.

If I couldn't go this year, it was no use trying.

How many days and nights of my exile had I tormented myself with jealousy, imagining Galan with a new sheath, a mudwoman like me, or a captive woman of the Blood, someone who could be an ornament to his rank? There was pain in it, and pleasure too; I tugged on the bond to make sure it was still taut between us, and that time and distance and the Initiates of Carnal had failed to sever it.

To think of Galan lying with another woman was to think of him alive. I couldn't permit myself to consider that he might be dead.

Garrio thought I must be ill. He squatted beside me and put his hand on my forehead. "I don't have a fever," I said.

"No, you're cold. What's the matter?"

I sat up and put my arms around my legs and rested my chin on my kneecaps, though it was improper in Lambanein for a woman to sit that way. "What will the king do with me, do you think?"

Garrio shrugged.

I said, "I don't understand why he sent you to fetch me from the dyers when he had no use for me at all."

Garrio raised his eyebrows, and all his worry lines were transformed. He looked mischievous. "I did that," he said.

"You?"

He laughed, delighting in my surprise. "I sent a message to you in the manufactory, just to see if you were well, and they said you'd been sent away. I found out where you went, with a copper beadcoin here and a few pewter ones there and a golden bead to Gnathin to take you back into the palace. So you owe me," he said, poking me with his finger.

"The king never sent for me?" Garrio was, perhaps, disappointed that I was disappointed. I put my hand on his sleeve. "I'm grateful to you."

"Well, I did my best. I couldn't make you tharos again, but I see you did that for yourself." He pinched my shawl between two fingers. "At least you don't reek like a dye vat anymore. Though I can smell the onions."

I should have been flattered that Garrio had fetched me of his own will, out of friendship, out of gratitude—when the king had none.

Divine Aboleo, Auspex of Rift Warrior, summoned me one evening. His room was better furnished than most in the Court of Tranquil Waters, having two wooden platforms inlaid with mother-of-pearl. One held a striped mattress, rolled up. He sat upon the other, cross-legged and upright, without availing himself of the cushions.

I knelt doubled over, resting my forehead on clasped hands; only a king deserved a full prostration. The floor depicted the sea in brilliant squares of blue and green glass. I saw the saffron hem of a tharos servingwoman who came to take away a platter of food.

I had glanced at Divine Aboleo when I entered the room, a furtive swift peek to judge the mood of a master. He'd regained the flesh he'd lost in the Ferinus, the folds of fat on his neck and padded jowls. The rooster tattoo was bright red on his gleaming pate. He looked as though it wouldn't matter to him one way or another if he had to kill me.

I felt him stare. I remained with my face a handsbreadth from the ground while he asked questions.

"You offered yourself to the king as a thrush," Divine Aboleo said.

"I did, yes." I tried to recall the inscriptions on the broken crockery, and what the inscriptions meant: House Tricari, five; back, years; quarrel.

But that wasn't what he wanted to know. "You are from Corymb."
"Yes."
"The sheath to Sire Galan dam Capella by Falco of Crux."
"Yes."
"Who is the First of Crux in Corymb?"
Surely he knew that. "Sire Adhara dam Pictor by Falco."
"What kin is he to your master?"
"His uncle."
"How many cataphracts in his company?"
"Their strength was seventeen when they set out on campaign. But four died in the Harshfield and one was wounded and left behind."
"Why so many in the Marchfield?"
"Sickness. Tourneys."
"Tell me about the tourneys," he said. I told him about the time Sire Galan had cut off a man's ear and returned it to him, but he had many questions I couldn't answer. He wanted to know the tallies, the notable fighters and their feats, the quality of their weapons and armor, and the lineages of their mounts.

When I told him about the mortal tourney, his silence urged me on, and I said more than perhaps was wise: how Sire Galan had been forbidden to ride, and how he'd made a fortress of dead horses. How the clans of Ardor and Crux had made an enforced peace, but there was still enmity between them.

My knees were sore and my back ached, and I stared at the floor until the mosaic blurred. He asked: How many ships had been lost in the storm? Who had fought in the treacherous assault on Lanx? Who had massacred the clan of Torrent?

His voice was heavy and uninflected, and his questions thudded on and on. How many bakers in the army of Corymb, how many whores, how much grain did the horses eat, how many leagues did we march each day?

Why did he want to know these trivial things? And why question me, a sheath? What little I knew was stale as old bread, tales of varlets who rebelled when their master fed them salt cod, and baggage carts drowning in mud. He must have learned more from the Wolves captured during the king's retreat. Once a Wolf had howled all night as the Auspices scrutinized him, and in the morning on his pyre we saw the meat and sinews of his arms and legs where they'd peeled him question by question.

For a moment my webeye opened wide and I peered through Divine Aboleo's eyes just as he endeavored to look through mine. He saw too much. He saw the army of Corymb as a tapestry laid over a landscape; he saw it whole and he wished to see it now in every particular, to know which dyes would fade and which were true and which would in time eat away the fabric, and which strands were strong and which might break. With every question he tugged upon a single thread.

The army of Corymb was but one of the armies warring over Incus, and as the king's strategos he was obliged to know them all. But even his formidable mind could not encompass everything. Surely much would forever remain unknown. Pull a thread and something somewhere else unravels.

I trembled with weariness. The questions of the Auspex had plumbed me. I thought back over my answers, praying I'd said nothing that could harm Galan. I should have said less, or made Divine Aboleo pay for my answers with assurances of favor. Instead I'd knelt there wagging my tail in the air like a hound eager to be useful. He wasn't finished. But it was too late now to stop answering.

He gestured to the cushion on the other side of the brazier and said to me in Lambaneish, "Come, sit here and tell me: who visits the arthygater in her bathing room, and what do they say?"

I arose from kneeling in one smooth motion, as was proper, but my knees creaked. I perched on the edge of the platform with my benumbed feet on the floor. With a flicker of a gesture he indicated I should pour doublewine from the flask on the tray before him. I gave him a bowlful and he gestured again, so I poured one for myself. I took the clay bowl in both hands, and waited for him to drink. Only whores drink with men in Lambanein, but I couldn't refuse. The doublewine scorched its way down my throat and up my nose, and nearly made me sneeze.

When my lips stopped trembling, I set the bowl down with a click on the gilded tray. One by one I laid before Divine Aboleo the gossip and guesses I'd collected and inscribed on my memory.

I kept my gaze averted, but I watched him nevertheless. The right and left sides of his countenance were equally impassive, without the contradictory expressions that wandered over less well-governed faces. Yet when he was intent, his left hand plucked feathers from a small hole in a cushion. He wore on his right hand a gold ring that spanned four fingers and was set with fat garnets.

I told Divine Aboleo about Arthygater Katharos's many dealings as she went about selling, bartering, and borrowing to raise money for an army. But his questions showed that he believed Consort Ostrakan planned everything. The priest thought moving a few more bales of gauze to Incus and a few more fleeces back to Lambanein was too paltry a matter to concern a nobleman such as Ostrakan. What was he after?

All by myself, it seemed, I had planted distrust of their most trusted ally.

I said, "Truly I am a strange-ignorant one, privy only to the gossip of women. How do I guess what a great man such as Consort Ostrakan means to do?"

Divine Aboleo said, "Faugh. You're forward enough; don't pretend to be backward."

I was stretched out under the pomegranate tree, swatting mosquitoes, when Garrio sent Lame for me. The horseboy led me up the stairs of the tower over the entrance. Guards and musicians had long since abandoned it to doves. The walls of the fourth story were of marble lattice, open to breezes. Garrio squatted in the patterned shade.

"What's the bother?" I asked him when Lame went away. I peered through the lattice. From here I could survey the grounds and buildings of the Inner Palace, the home of the arkhon and his sons, which covered the summit of Mount Allaxios. The golden roofs of the central dome and the many courts shone as if the Sun had taken up residence there. Even the Court of Tranquil Waters, so long neglected, had gilded tiles.

A large city could have been crammed within the Inner Palace, so great was the space encompassed, and indeed a multitude of people lived there. But there were also streams and ponds, fields, meadows, orchards, and walled pleasure gardens, and even a forest. His realm was re-created there as a small tidy world, a miniature perfection.

"The king has decided what to do with you," Garrio said.

I turned from the view and crouched beside him. I went quiet inside, waiting as one waits between the throw of dice and the fall when too much has been wagered. I could tell Garrio was unhappy; that must mean I was to be tharais again.

He said, "There is this prancing go-between, a musicmaster—he tells the king how to act like a poetry-spouting Lambaneish do-nothing fop." All this he said in the High, except for the word go-between: *kynamolgos*. There was no word quite like it in the High, nothing that carried the same derision.

"Yes?"

"Well, he—and Divine Aboleo, he never favored you, you know—they've convinced the king to send you to a brothel."

"A brothel?" My head was ringing like an empty kettle after a blow, and all I could do was echo him.

"They called it something else, but I heard them right enough."

"To do what? To be a tharais bathservant again? Or a tharos maid, or—or a laundress?"

Garrio scratched at dove droppings on the tiled floor with the tip of his dagger. "Divine Aboleo said you were bold and clever, and you'd be good at it. I don't think he meant a laundress."

"So King Clever is going to be a pander now, eh?" It was a dire insult, but Garrio didn't reprimand me. "What exactly did he say?"

"Very little."

"But what?"

"He said, 'Find one of good repute, so she can be trained properly.' Then the kynamolgos started talking about which one entertained which men of the court, and which had the most influence, and which was invited to the best parties. And they settled on a foreign one; the musicmaster said that would be most suitable."

"A foreign brothel?"

"A foreign whore, some Ebanakan. So the go-between says that as the whore is foreign herself, she'll be more patient with you, and then the king asks how a foreigner can teach you to behave properly. The go-between says she is an adept in all the arts, better than most who are born here. And besides, you are in her pay, says Divine Aboleo to the go-between, and he says, indeed, I have the honor of serving as musicmaster for her young sisters. How else could I have observed at close hand that she is quite the best choice, for she knows everyone and everyone knows her?"

I thought of the Ebanakan whore I'd watched on the famous evening of the white petals, and how I'd admired her grace and her artful ways. In the Lambaneish way of thinking she was a respectable woman. But I'd been raised in Corymb by the Dame, who had a stricter notion of respectability. I had friends among the whores in the army and yet I'd fancied—hoping I kept it well hidden—that I was better than they were. Because I coupled with one man instead of many.

But I was a mudwoman and a sheath, and plainly the king and his priest judged me no better than a harlot. What did it matter if I had to whore to be a thrush? What mattered was that I should attend the best parties. Perhaps I should be flattered they had such aspirations for me.

Garrio said, "I don't see why, if he wants you for himself, he doesn't just keep you instead of packing you off to a brothel."

"If who wants me?"

Garrio raised his eyebrows.

"The king? He doesn't want me. He has a *use* for me. He wants me to pry—to spy."

"Maybe. I suppose no one ever told you that you look a bit like his wife, or maybe one of her cousins, a skinny runt of a coz. You have her coloring."

I'd seen Kalos in a dream, and I didn't resemble her at all. Her hair was the color of a ginger cat's fur, and she had a round face where mine was sharp. Rumor proposed a likeness where there was none, for it made a better tale.

We were silent awhile. Garrio asked, "What will you do?"

I picked up a straw fallen from a dove's nest and folded it between my fingers. "I don't know."

Garrio opened the leather wallet he wore on his belt, and pulled out a pouch stitched from a remnant of embroidered satin. "Some of us—some of us think it isn't so fair, and we have a small—a few coins, that's all. Sorry there isn't more. Just so you can refuse. Here. Take it, take it!"

"Oh, Garrio. Oh my friend." I could tell from the weight it wasn't much money, but I was moved and pained by the gift. How could he know he made it harder for me? Now I'd have to choose. Betrayed by Chance again, that seductress. She was so fickle, vanishing just when one had surrendered to her.

I stayed behind when Garrio left. Doves walked on the railing above me, their feet making a scritching sound, and coos bubbled up from their throats. Face-to-face with the necessity of leaving, I saw that once again I'd mistaken hoping for striving. I'd lulled myself into thinking the king would provide for me. And he had, very neatly too. He'd disposed of me again.

I wondered why I was unsure of what to do. For it was simple: I couldn't be a whore.

I sat cross-legged and emptied the satin purse in my lap. Garrio had strung the beadcoins on a red cord, in the Lambaneish way: three of silver, twenty-six of pewter, two of amber, and one of blue glass against the evil eye.

Thirty-one beadcoins, not counting the glass one. It was dear of Garrio and the others, but all the same I doubted they had scraped the lint from their purses for me. Add those to the coins hanging from the cords of my cap, and the sum was altogether paltry.

It had taken nearly a tennight to journey from Sapheiros to Allaxios, and we'd been given fresh horses at every post town. How long would it take to return on foot? The money wouldn't last, and I'd be living like a stray goat eating roadside weeds—and if I strayed from the road, I'd be stealing. On the plains of Lambanein, every handspan was owned and worked.

I dreaded the solitude more than the hunger. I had known both in the Kingswood, and knew which was worse. And I'd rather face the wolves and bears of the Kingswood again than the men who would prey on a woman traveling alone.

I could stay in Allaxios, become a dowser, and live by my wits and such tricks as my wits proposed. And I'd be stealing from poor folk such as Meninx, for I was not a true dowser who could cure them of Lambaneish afflictions. Or I could sell sweetrush root and woven sacks and the like, and with diligence I might make enough to eat, maybe even enough for shelter, but nothing to set aside to cross the mountains.

Or I could be a whore and the king's thrush.

But to think of any man—even a man such as Divine Aboleo, who had summoned me to sit and drink with him—paying for me. I'd as soon couple with a bear as Divine Aboleo; I should have to make myself into a she-bear with metal claws, golden fingercaps with jeweled nails like the ones belonging to Arthygater Katharos, and prick him as we grappled. Had I not pictured this when I sat beside him and felt the weight of his stare and saw, from the corner of my eye, the strange delicacy with which he plucked feathers from the pillow? I had feared that despite his vows he was thinking of how to devour me, a heavy man like that. Any man who had the money. Carnal Desire was pleased I should think this way and she touched me on my cleft.

Gods, what playthings we are. For a moment my right eye was filled with the divining compass and I saw a single die spinning and coming to rest on Desire. I saw a hand pick up the die to cast again. I used to be so sure I was in Ardor's keeping, and now I was passed from one god to the next, as cheap as any little carved cube of bone: the means of the game and never its purpose.

I dreamed my spade clunked and jarred against rocks as I dug a new planting bed on a terrace below my house on Mount Sair. Another clunk, a different sound. I crouched and put my hands in the earth, breaking up clods, tossing stones into the hedge. I found a rotted leather strap, then a tarnished cheekplate, an iron bit jointed in the middle, and a buckle. Pieces of a bridle too fine for a farmer's nag. Probably used for hunting rather than war, because the reins were not protected by iron scales.

I rubbed the cheekplate on my kirtle. The disk was as big as my palm, and had an embossed design of a fox chasing its tail, in a simple and lively style. It was made of silver under all that tarnish, and it smelled of dirt. I couldn't find its twin, but I did uncover two horse teeth, and planted them again with their long forked roots down.

When I awoke I arranged and rearranged the signs, as if I were reading the bones. The fox in the bridle's silver disk was Crux Moon, of course; the fox showing under his skin meant trickery and deception. But the fox chased his tail—fooled himself?

The dead horse had been used for hunting—Prey Hunter, a seeker and devourer. But why would they have buried a horse, bridle and all, on the second terrace? To dream of a horse meant a journey—that was to be expected, I must leave soon. But the horse was also a sign of Carnal Stallion, meaning lust, potency, generation.

Yet they say a dream of teeth is a warning of sorrow to come. I always thought that was the safest of all predictions.

These were gods of Corymb, and the dream of a place in Corymb. Why then, when I awoke, was the word that tarried in my mind Lambaneish? Alopexan, the fox.

I asked Garrio to ask the king if I could be permitted to speak to him. The king sent word I might speak with Divine Aboleo instead. Garrio wondered why I didn't take the thirty-one beadcoins and the one glass bead and leave while I could. Moreover he feared I'd reveal to the priest that I knew about the brothel, and Garrio was the only one who could have told me.

I swore I wouldn't let on, and then shilly-shallied a day and a night, too afraid of Divine Aboleo to approach him. The next morning I spoke to the priest's manservant when he came to the courtyard fountain to draw water, and in a while he came back to say I'd been granted an audience.

The strategos was in the antechamber of the bathing room, wearing his hose and a thin shirt. His body servant scraped the priest's scalp with a blade like the one I'd used; no tharais barbers here.

I pointed to my webeye and told the priest I'd had a vision. I'd seen myself as a tharos servant at a banquet, and my mistress was an Ebanakan whore. I said I might do well as a thrush, if I were handmaid to a whore, for she would be much in the company of men who would speak unguardedly in her presence, and I might easily overhear them. Did he think I might be of use to Corvus Rex Incus, Master of Masters, in this way?

"Tell me how the whore looked," Divine Aboleo said.

I clamped my arms against my sides to hide the sweat that darkened my wrapper. I'd only seen one Ebanakan whore, and likely they had a different one in mind. "Well—like an Enakanaban, an Ekanaban, of course, with reddish brown skin, and rather short. She had a small nose and a large mouth, and huge dark eyes. Her hair was in a long coif down her back, as thick as your arm."

"She had a name, I suppose."

I pointed again to my eye. "I saw, I didn't hear." I thought, fool, fool, fool. He never believed I was a true dreamer, he'll see through the ruse—he'll know Garrio told—and Garrio will get a beating, never mind what they'll do to me.

"This might be arranged," he said.

"If I had something to tell, how would I get word to the king?"

"That won't be difficult. The whore will have patrons from amongst our men. They'll be sure to seek you out."

"If I am the king's thrush, will it be appreciated?" I brushed the coins hanging from my net cap so they clinked together.

"That depends on how sweetly you sing."

Garrio claimed that Divine Aboleo had called me bold and clever. For a man to be called bold is praise, and to be called clever is backward praise, meaning be wary of him; but for a woman to be called bold and clever is no sort of praise at all. Yet I'd been flattered—and gullible enough to believe it.

The next day Garrio escorted me to the Ebanakan's house. I carried a gift for her, a woolen hanging embroidered with a scene of a peacock hunt. Garrio's stride was long and his steps quick, and I had to dash to keep up.

"Are you angry?" I asked.

He hurried along the paved banks of the canal. I stopped and crossed my arms and waited. He was quite far away before he noticed I wasn't following and turned back.

"Why are you so vexed?" I said.

"You don't have to go."

"Garrio, I thank you, I thank all my friends—but how long would your gift last on the road to Incus? Likely I'd end up a whore, and a hedge-whore at that, working on my back in a stony field."

"So you'd rather be in a prickery," he said.

"I told Divide Aboleo I could be a maidservant to a whore, and spy just as well."

Garrio lifted his tunic and showed me the wallet hanging from his belt. He hefted it and said, "They're paying for you to go there. They called this a dowry—what is that but an apprentice fee? They're going to make a whore of you."

Where I came from, women were sold to brothels, they didn't pay to be in them. What need for an apprenticeship when the task was easy? "How much is it?"

"How should I know?"

"You could count, eh?"

We squatted down on the pavement beside the canal, and he emptied the purse. I caught one of the beadcoins just before it rolled into the water. Garrio didn't have a scale, which was the only proper way to measure the value of beadcoins, for they came in many shapes and sizes. But there were fifteen gold coins, seventeen of silver. We reckoned it a fortune.

Garrio scooped up the coins. The backs of his hands were crisscrossed with kinked veins, and his knuckles were swollen like an old man's.

I said, "Give me that purse and I'll be on my way. Say you were robbed and I ran off."

He looked away and frowned.

"Then suppose you just give me one golden beadcoin, or a handful of silver ones? Enough to be able to leave the city."

He shook his head and his cheeks reddened above his beard.

I threw a chip of stone into the canal and watched it sink. "What's the matter with whores? Don't you like them?"

"Of course I do," he said, without meeting my eyes.

I didn't doubt Garrio bought a woman from time to time, and if I became a whore he could buy me—if he had the coins for it. The thought discomfited us both.

For so long Galan had been my shield from other men. Though we had parted, I'd kept my shield raised high, and on it was written, *I belong to another.* Some men saw this right away; some men never did, or didn't care. But it was mere mist, wasn't it? There was no shield.

CHAPTER 27

House of Aghazal

t wasn't a brothel, never say that. The whores of the March-field had their kinds and degrees, from the throngs of two-copper slags at the bottom to a quean with her own pavilion at the top; so too the ranks of the whore-celebrants of Lam-banein. At the pinnacle were those they called the gifted. Meaning one who receives gifts, and one who bestows herself as a gift, but above all one who is gifted in the arts. Aghazal was one of these, and the house was her home.

I'd watched her at the first banquet where I'd served as a tharais napkin, watched her in fascination as she arched her foot and leaned forward to speak passionately of the masque, and brushed a man's arm to make him tremble.

Aghazal was the Lambaneish word for the small leaping deer we called gazelle in the High, and indeed she bore some resemblance to her name-sake, with her long neck, lustrous eyes, and graceful movements. But she was Ebanakan, and her true name, the one her mother called her, was Yamimarek.

Her house was a tall narrow house on a street of similar houses in a wealthy part of the city, up near the walls of the palace district. The house was full of people, Aghazal's kin and servants. She seemed to be the only whore among them.

Her mother sat at the loom all day, as did her two unmarried sisters. Her aunt cooked, her grandmother herded the little children, and the older girls—cousins, nieces, who-knows-who—helped in the kitchen, spun, and washed clothing. Her father was dead, but her uncle (married to the cook) and his three sons farmed a plot of good land she rented beyond the city gates; at night they came home weary, and then dressed in finery and escorted Aghazal to banquets. At home they guarded her from thieves and from guests who were drunk or importunate. Her young brother served as her messenger; he was the only Ebanakan there who was taller than me. They were not all the same ruddy brown as Aghazal; some were lighter,

385

some darker. A few of the children were almost the same ivory color as a person of Lambanein. But there was a strong stamp of kinship on them all: they were smallish people, with fine bones and large dark eyes that gave a misleading appearance of delicacy.

Aghazal received the purse from Garrio and the cloth from me, with a pretty speech of thanks that I translated for Garrio, for he still knew very little Lambaneish. After Garrio took his leave, she asked me, "Do you sing?"

"I suppose. Like anyone, ein?"

"What songs do you know? What instruments can you play?"

I shrugged and showed her my empty palms.

"Dance? No? Can you recite? Do you know the Odes and Epics, can you recite the Fragments, have you heard of the One Hundred Sage Poets? Do you even know poems exist, can you read, ein? Oh, no doubt it's an accomplishment to read your godsigns, but no poem of any worth was ever written in that strange-ignorant tongue; it's only good for ciphering. You can cipher, I hope, add and subtract and so forth, divide by twos and fives. Do you know the twenty-five Postures? Ah, I can see by your blush you know two or three, but can you name them? Have you practiced?"

She dug deep but couldn't find the bottom of my ignorance. Every other word she corrected me; I had no idea I still spoke Lambaneish so badly.

Could I concoct scents and cosmetics, cook leaf pastry, make lace, play horses-and-houses, play at Spices? Did I know how to sit, how to rise, could I read the messages in beads or flowers, did I know the proper garlands for various occasions, could I answer a poem with a poem if called to do so? Well then, what *can* you do?

By then I was indignant. "I am a true dreamer, and I lead a king's army through the Ferinus, the Kerastes, in winter. Do you do as much?"

I could have devised no better test of what sort of mistress she was to be. She drew herself up—the crown of her head came to my eyebrows—and I thought she might slap me for my insolence. She smiled instead, a smile wide as daybreak, and full of slightly crowded, slightly crooked, brilliant white teeth. She didn't bother to hide the smile behind her hand, as I was not a man.

"Feirthonin, is it?"

"Firethorn."

"That's too awkward. How about Alopexin? You have the coloring for it."

Alopexin was vixen, she-fox in Lambaneish. Aghazal must have seen dismay on my face. "Well, if you like it, ein?"

If I liked it. Had I a choice?

✻   ✻   ✻

Wildfire

Aghazal dismissed me to the bath, and sent a girl named Tasatyala to see I washed thoroughly. The bathing room was small compared to the arthygater's, but furnished elegantly, as Aghazal sometimes entertained her patrons there. The wall painting was unusual. Instead of a tidy garden, it showed a wild marsh where tall reeds, adorned with fan-shaped plumes, curved before an imaginary wind; there were painted birds everywhere, egrets in the pools and songbirds in the sky.

Tasatyala was disgusted that I'd allowed hair to grow under my arms and at my crotch, and she let me know it as soon as I'd stripped off my clothing. She clucked like a hen, though she was a mere chick herself, barely old enough to have hair to remove in those places. She was also shocked to see the swath cut through my womansbeard by Sire Rodela. No hair grew where the scar had healed.

I lay on my back on a cold marble bench while the tharais depilator shaved me. She was skillful, but the blade scraping my skin made me cringe. It amazed me that Arthygater Katharos and her women had lain so complacently under my blade, when I'd been clumsy and ignorant.

I wondered what the depilator looked like, and what she thought—her silence and her shawl could mask anything. I wondered if she would be amused or appalled to find out I was tharais.

They must not find out. At the thought I began to sweat, and I very much feared that my sweat smelled of onions.

The depilator drew a drop of blood. It was my fault for moving, but Tasatyala slapped her for it. Then the hot honey wax, perfumed with cloves, to remove the hair from my arms and legs. The servant had little burns from tending the pot; her fingernails were rimmed with dark stains, so I guessed she dyed and dressed Aghazal's hair as well.

Tasatyala poured ewers of cold water over my head and burnished me with a sack full of sand, and only then was I clean enough for the bath. The pool was lined with turquoise tiles, and in it was moored a white boat, wide enough for two, with a prow carved and painted like a swan's head. I heard water splashing and buckets clattering on the other side of the wall as a servant filled a tank. I lay down in the boat and Tasatyala pulled a stopper from the mouth of a leaping bronze carp, and warm water gushed down on me. The boat steadied in the pool and sank until the rim was just above water, cool water without, warm within.

There in the painted marshland I drifted, under a painted sky showing a flight of geese. The water was as warm as my skin, and I could have lingered all day. But Tasatyala was impatient.

Aghazal came in to look me over, drenched as I was, with my wet hair clinging like seaweed and goose bumps on my skin. "What a pity," she said when she saw the scar Sire Rodela had given me and the burns scattered on my back. "And you have the webeye too. Well, you won't suit those who insist on perfection. You shall have to be artful, if you can. Art can supply a deficiency of beauty better than beauty a deficiency of art."

I asked Aghazal why I was there. Was I her apprentice? Was I her bond-woman, handmaid, guest, pupil? She said I was to be her younger sister. She had a thousand graceful ways to evade a question; it was one of her arts, but by innuendo she let me know it was doubtful I'd make a whore-celebrant. She wasn't rude enough to say so, but she thought I'd fail.

Be Glad! It was a rule of Aghazal's household, written on a wall of her din-ing court. Aghazal taught it to me that afternoon after she rose from a nap.

Aghazal's dining court was small, with arcades on three sides; the fourth side was the wall of a neighboring house, cleverly painted to look like a colonnade on a high terrace, with a view over the rooftops of Allaxios and the plains of Lambanein. The cloudless sky was lapis blue, and the rules were painted on it in red. The writing of Lambanein reminded me of the tracks of a wayward chicken. Aghazal said each sign meant a sound, just as in Incus, but to my mind these chicken footprints were hard to tell apart. She said our godsigns were harder, nothing but scattered dots with the three avatar marks. "But they are written of the sky," I said, "so we don't forget them."

She said, "Written *on* the sky. But our sky is different," and I wondered at this, because the stars were the same everywhere. She didn't want to talk about it; she had something to teach me. She gave me a stylus and a wooden tablet covered with damp clay so I could practice. "The first rule is 'Be Glad!' Ein? 'Be Glad.' Copy it just as you see it."

While I wrote she yawned without covering her mouth, and draped her-self over the scrolled backrest of a dining platform, looking weary rather than languorous. "Let me see—no, that one's wrong. Look." She thumbed out the signs in the clay and scratched new ones. "The foot goes thataway. They are like little dancers in procession, ein? That's it. Now the second rule of my house is 'No Dice But Mine.' See? The single lines divide one statement from the next. The third rule is 'No Fighting.' The fourth is 'She May Refuse.' The last one is 'Be Generous.' I keep it simple for the dullards and drunks, ein? Copy all those down, until you can write it out without looking."

The five rules were for guests of the household. For its residents, there were other rules, not so few, not so simple, and never written down.

I took the name Alopexin, but in the house I was addressed as Fourth, mean-ing Fourth Sister; Sister was a title Aghazal's sisters by blood didn't share. Aghazal was First Sister, of course. Tasatyala was Second; she was Aghazal's niece, and became a Sister when, as a young child, she showed unusual grace and studiousness. She was now thirteen years old. Adalana was Third. She was only six, and had been sent all the way from Ebanaka to study with Aghazal because of her gift for music. Already she could play all the Odes and two of the Epics on reed pipe, lyre, and drums, and sing them in her high unwavering voice without leaving out a single phrase. Tasatyala had been pampered before Adalana came, and had gotten spoiled. Now she sulked. With all her diligence she couldn't master the Odes as quickly as Adalana, who seemed to learn as a bird learns the songs of its kind, by plucking them from the air. So it was that I had three elder Sisters, and two of them were younger than I was, and all of them were more accomplished.

My own music lessons did not go well. The musicmaster, Skolian, told me I was much too old to learn anything, and my voice was rough as a cat's tongue. The only instrument he allowed me to touch was the simplest one, a crescent strung with thin silver leaves that made a wind sound when I shook it. He rapped my knuckles with a brass rod when I made a mistake. I doubted he dared do the same to King Corvus when he gave him lessons in poetry and protocol and deportment—for surely he was the same kynamolgos go-between who had suggested to the king that I be trained by Aghazal.

Skolian said it was hopeless, hopeless, to expect a strange-ignorant one such as myself to parrot correctly, let alone understand, the Odes and Epics. He'd rather teach a parrot—he had taught parrots successfully—indeed, he'd trained one to recite the Fragments and finish any quotation—but he despaired of me. He said to Aghazal, "No money in the world would convince me; it's only as a favor to you, my dear, that I even attempt it."

The kitchen was small, considering the number of people in the house, and it was smoky and crowded. I stood at the door looking in from the private back courtyard, where they grew herbs and vegetables and fruit for the household. Aghazal had sent for me, but she was busy quarreling in Ebanakan with the cook, her aunt Angadataqebay.

When Aghazal noticed me, she said, "I want you to write down what we need for the banquet tomorrow."

I hauled up the jar full of damp clay from the cistern, and prepared a writing tablet. I sat on a bench outside the kitchen door. With the heel of my hand, I smoothed the clay over the board in the wooden frame. I liked the earthy smell of it.

Aghazal came out of the kitchen and sat on the bench beside me. She gathered up her thick black hair and held it on top of her head, and called on Adalana to fan her. We were not wearing our shawls, and our bare forearms touched. Her arm was soft, her wrist plump. She had slender pointed fingers, and her nails were trimmed simply in crescent style, which surprised me. Under the yellow powder, my skin looked pallid next to hers. Aghazal took up the tablet and said, "I'll write first. You copy it, so you'll learn, ein? The banquet will be served in courses of the five kinds of sustenance. Do you know the five kinds? No, don't say, Third. Let her tell us."

"Well—bread, I suppose. And fish and fowl and meat?" Surely there were many more kinds of food than five. What of cheese? Or barley?

Adalana hid a smile behind her hand.

"How long have you lived in Lambanein?" Aghazal said. "By now you ought to know something. The first sustenance is the scented. We're going to begin with civet musk, then oil of juniper to rub on the upper lip, and lastly incense. I'll ask Pikros what ingredients to use. He has the best fragrances, the freshest; buy only from him."

Angadataqebay stood in the doorway and said, "You ought to know that oil of juniper and incense, no matter what sort, will never blend with civet."

Aghazal said to her aunt, "Too much harmony is dull, don't you think?"

Angadataqebay said, "Why ask me? If you're not going to listen." She disappeared inside the kitchen and clattered crockery.

Aghazal had written three signs, three dancers side by side. I asked, "Do those signs say all that?"

"It says scented. Here, copy it. And remember the rest, ein? The musk and so forth."

I noted them in godsigns anyway: civet musk, oil of juniper, Pikros, incense?

She took the tablet back and wrote another word. "Now, as for the second course, we have the licked. The licked arouses the tongue the way the scented awakens the nose, ein? So first there will be fish-pepper paste to sting the lips and tongue. Next, to cool them, snow from the Kerastes sprinkled with honey crystals and gold flakes—one must have something expensive, people expect it. Lastly opos powder to inspire lust."

I copied her word, and wrote fish-pepper, snow? opos?

"The third sustenance should truly be the first, for it's the first known to all of us, ein? That which is sucked. We'll have pickled snails, and of course Aunt Cook must make her famous almond puddings in sacks, mother's milk. Wait till you see grown men suckling like calves at an udder, you'll be amused, ein? And then pomegranates—the last until the next harvest. For the main presentation, the bitten, we'll have ten dishes, each with small accompaniments."

Angadataqebay came to the door again, with a cleaver in one hand and a plucked quail in the other. "You know I can't get everything with what you gave me. Krinean gave you a heap of coins to sponsor this feast, and you'll disgrace him, make him look a cheeseparer."

Aghazal said, "No one will notice if the eels come from the River Ouraios instead of Lake Sapheiros, believe me, not once they're bathed in sauce and buried under sheaves of pastry."

"Krinean will be able to tell. He can taste a rat dropping in a peck of pepper."

Krinean was sponsoring the feast at the house of Aghazal in order to show himself a man of perfect taste, and the sort of man who would lavish riches on his friends—riches of the best kind, the ephemeral. So that those who attended the banquet would reminisce afterward about the food, the scents, the entertainments, and those who hadn't been invited would be envious.

"Stop fretting," Aghazal said to Aunt Cook. "Buy eels from Sapheiros for Krinean and give the other guests river eels—except Aeidin's table, make sure they have the Sapheiros eels. Fifty in gold ought to be enough. You're too flamboyant—if I let you have your way, it would all be too too much, we would seem to overreach. And besides, last time you bought and didn't pay, and I found out afterward when smelly fishmongers and rabbit poachers came to my door to collect."

"It was just one fishmonger," said Angadataqebay. "And you must admit I astonished everyone with the stuffed porpoise. It's so hard to astonish these days, ein?"

But Aghazal was no longer willing to waste time quarreling with Aunt Cook. She had to see to everything herself, she complained, and she hurried off to bother someone else about the preparations.

She had written these words on the tablet in Lambaneish: scented, licked, sucked, bitten. She'd written the word for the fifth kind of sustenance too, but rushed away before telling me what it was. By now I thought I could guess. I wrote in godsigns beside her word: drunk.

Fifty in gold for the food. To think I'd been vain enough to suppose the king had parted with a great sum when he gave fifteen golden beadcoins to Aghazal on my behalf. I was worth less than an evening's banquet—that much I could cipher.

I lined up the little dancers: Be Glad, Be Generous, Be Bitten, Be Drunk. Then I scraped the clay into the lidded jar, and lowered the jar into the cool cistern. When I'd copied the rules of the house, I'd let the clay dry in the frame, supposing I was meant to keep the tablet, and Tasatyala had chided me. The clay was to be reused again and again, and the inscriptions preserved only in memory.

*   *   *

A flower-seller came calling with his donkey, and Aghazal and we Sisters went outside to meet him. Aghazal rarely visited the markets in the lower town, as the best peddlers came to her, offering her first choice of their best wares. She didn't think it beneath her dignity to chaffer. *As soon try to cheat an Ebanakan,* the saying went.

She waved her hand at the peddler's lilies, as if shooing flies. "I don't see what I want here. Have you roses, dawn roses, the yellow ones with the rosy blush? And I'll need thirty jasmine garlands and twelve wreaths."

She fingered the petals of a crimson peony, one of many heaped in a basket, heavy blossoms without stems. "These were picked yesterday, ein? Don't expect me to buy old flowers. But I'll take this many tomorrow, if you pick them and bring them straightaway. I want them to be in bud, all in buds just about to split, so you see the petals showing." She turned to me. "What do I say with these flowers? Do you know?"

Tasatyala spoke up, eager to show her knowledge. "The roses mean *if you love me,* the jasmine is *I entwine,* and the peony is *bashful in the bud, shameless in flower.*"

Aghazal said, "If you are generous, I entwine—any whore-celebrant might make that promise, ein?"

Adalana said, "The peonies—they are taken from one of Kylocides's Fragments, from the First Age of the World."

"That is so," said Aghazal, giving her a kiss on the forehead. "Sing it for us, ein?"

Adalana sang,

> *In the tight bud—soft folds.*
> *The one who tempts the peony to open,*
> *Departs before the petals fall.*

I said, "So your rich man Krinian, has he found another friend? Is this his last feast?" I thought I was clever to guess so much.

"He's not the one I reproach," Aghazal replied.

In the afternoon I stole a few moments for myself, and likewise stole a handful of clay from the jar in the cistern. I crouched by the south wall of the back courtyard. Here was a little corner of Ebanaka, where Grandmother Lagas kept her indigo dyepot; in Ebanaka dying was a sacred art, not a despised tharais task. No one would bother me there, for they feared the meneidon of the dyepot, who tolerated only Lagas's presence. I apologized to the meneidon and asked permission. I had always gotten along with indigo, and thought I could risk it.

Wildfire

I worked quickly, shaping a crude figure of Desire no bigger than my palm, with wide hips, a fat belly, and round breasts. With my thumbnail I gave her a cleft between her legs—or a fig or cowrie, oyster or peach, all names the Lambaneish used for a quim. I lacked the skill to make the statue seem alive, but she would serve as a messenger for my prayers. Carnal Desire had looked fondly on Galan and me. Did she mean to test my fidelity now, or did she—as I suspected—care not a fig, cowrie, or peach for fidelity? I'd thought it an accomplishment to spurn any man but Galan, when perhaps it was merely cowardice. Just the day before, Aghazal had teased me for being a prude, saying, "You think you have a treasure in your strongbox, ein? And every time you unlock your legs you spend some of it. Not so. You unlock to gain treasure, not spend it." Or perhaps she meant to gain pleasure; there was a slippery word in Lambaneish that seemed to mean both.

I begged Desire to illuminate my way with her lamp.

I'd been at Aghazal's house only a hand of days. I couldn't play or sing the Odes and Epics or quote the Fragments; I couldn't sit properly, I didn't know how to address people according to their rank, or when to look and when to look away, or how to eat with a trident, or too many other things to mention. Aghazal's mother Yafeqer said I'd disgrace the house. Nevertheless Aghazal wanted me to share a dining platform with guests. She said she could find servingwomen anywhere; she needed her Sisters to entertain. Second would dance, and Third would play the cithara and sing.

And what could I do, who knew nothing? I said I wouldn't do more than converse, I couldn't. That's when Aghazal called me a prude. But she also pointed to the fourth rule written on the wall of the dining court, the one that said: She May Refuse.

"They'll think I'm a simpleton," I said.

"A man doesn't look to a woman for wit, ein? He wants you to acknowledge that he is witty. If you smile and gaze at him like this, you won't go far wrong." Aghazal pretended to make ewe's eyes at me, and I couldn't help laughing. "Cover your mouth," she said.

I remembered perfectly well how she'd behaved the night of the white petals banquet. She hadn't simpered like a mooncalf. She'd let her wit shine forth, to make her beauty more brilliant.

The tharais servant depilated us. She cut our nails; I had only one, the mother finger of my left hand, long enough to sharpen. Tharos maidservants, Horamin and Palin, bathed us, oiled our skin, dyed our lips, and painted ground malachite on our eyelids. The tharais servingwoman dressed our hair. She wrapped Aghazal's hair around two wicker horns, and held it in place with pins topped with pearls and shells. Over that Aghazal wore a wreath of moonflowers.

Yafeqer attended us in the bathing room and made free with her opinions. Why was my hair so short? Lambaneish women took great pride in the length of their hair; the arthygater's hair, when wet, hung down to her knees. I explained that mine used to be past my waist when I pulled a strand taut, but it had been shaved off when I came to Allaxios.

"You should have bought false hair in her color," Yafeqer said to Aghazal.

"Stop fussing, Mother. I'm sure we can think of something."

The tharais servant tried to wrap my hair around a small wicker cone, she tried this way and that, unspeaking, while I wondered if she was the only tharais servant in the household. How lonely she must be. Yafeqer said, "No, no, no. That won't do!"

The servant tugged hard on a lock of my hair, and I had the urge to strike her, for she too seemed to think I wasn't worthy of so much trouble.

Aghazal pulled the cone from my head abruptly, and I lifted my hands to my smarting scalp. She said, "Don't bother with the wickerwork. Just twine the hair into a wreath of jasmine, marigolds, and pearls. And if stray locks tumble down in the course of the evening, I'm sure it will look charming. No proper garden is complete without an allusion to wilderness, ein?"

The farther down one dwelled on the eastern slope of Mount Allaxios, the earlier the Sun set behind the peak. In Aghazal's dining court, surrounded by buildings three stories high, twilight came while the sky was still bright overhead. Servants lit lamps on bronze lamp trees.

I sat in one of the three proper poses allowed to women, with my weight on my left hip and my knees bent. I leaned toward King Corvus without touching him. The scar on my left wrist was covered with wide golden bangles. Instead of making ewe's eyes at the king, I avoided looking at him at all.

Aghazal hadn't warned me that Arkhyios Corvus would be a guest that night, or that I would be seated next to him, sharing the platform with First Sister and her patron Krinean.

"This is Alopexin," Aghazal said. "She is but lately arrived in the city. She comes from the borderlands near the Lake of Sapheiros, and a dear friend sent her to me as a pupil."

"Alopexin?" said Krinean. "She seems too shy to be an alopexin."

"One doesn't catch a vixen without a chase, ein? Otherwise there'd be no sport to it," Aghazal said.

The king said nothing: so we were to pretend we'd never met. I was short of breath and trying not to quake, and ashamed of my own fright. There was no peril here compared to the Ferinus, yet I felt in jeopardy.

Wildfire

The tharos servants—Aghazal's kin, dressed in saffron cloths with magenta and blue bands—came forward to present the scented course of civet musk, oil of juniper, and incense. But I was already overwhelmed by fragrances. There was no wind that night, but there were balmy airs, stirred perhaps by the wings of insects, bats, and swallows, that carried the scents of the guests' garlands and perfumes.

Among the guests was Arthygater Keros, chaperoned by Aeidin, her instructor in the arts of the marriage bed. Their platform was next to ours, close enough for conversation. The other guests were noblemen and whores—the women accompanying their patrons, or rented by Aghazal for the occasion. They all seemed to be discussing the fragrances served, praising them with words such as bright, dark, elegant, and impudent. I couldn't imagine how they found so many words to say about the unsayable.

Aghazal's sister Dasasana served us the licked course, and I did as Aghazal had taught me: I held my left hand in front of my face, and with my right brought the mussel shell to my parted lips and let my tongue dart out to lick the fish-pepper paste. It burned my mouth, as it was meant to. The guests marveled at the snow from the Kerastes, and praised its coolness. I had eaten too much snow of necessity to think it pleasurable; it made my teeth ache, and gave me a chill, so I had to pull my shawl up over my shoulders. Still I refused to look at the king, but I saw him in my mind's eye, his hand shaking, trying to bring a wooden cup of water to his lips without spilling it, from snow that Garrio had melted with the last of the firewood.

Did he look my way when he ate the snow? He should have. He should have. But I think he looked at Aghazal. Without saying a word about the king crossing the mountains, she had paid him a compliment and reminded her other guests of his great feat.

As the first course was cleared away, Aghazal said, "Will you attend the arkhon's Hunt? People talk of nothing else, ein?"

Rented tharais servants came forward with water so the guests could rinse their hands. Peonies in bud floated in all the silver basins. Aghazal's message was displayed where everyone could see it, yet she spoke to just one person in the room. I very much wanted to know if it was the king.

King Corvus said, "The arkhon was kind enough to invite me. I didn't know there was game worth hunting on the summit of Allaxios."

I peered at the king, who was watching Aghazal, who had turned to ask Krinian something, who was, I discovered, looking at me. I smiled at him and quickly covered my mouth and looked down as if embarrassed. Krinian had brown eyes a little too close together, and a long elegant nose with arched nostrils. His pride seemed touched by King Corvus's remark. "You've never seen such splendid sport, I daresay, not even in the Kerastes.

There will be bears and wolves, boars, lynx, aurochs, stags, chamois, ibex, and ermine."

"No fox?" Aghazal said.

This made me blush. Krinian laughed and said, "Fox, to be sure." He nudged my leg with his knee and I didn't move away.

"It's a marvel so many beasts dwell in the forest of the Inner Palace," King Corvus said.

"Arkhon Kyphos has game brought in, of course," Krinian said. "He has his huntsmen scour the Kerastes for the best specimens."

"I see."

The only one I dared glance at was Aghazal. We had been served the next course, and behind a shielding hand she sucked a pickled snail from its shell. When she caught me looking, the corners of her eyes crinkled with a smile, and I felt a pulse of heat, sweat pearling on the nape of my neck.

"You enjoy the hunt," Krinian said, making a statement of a question in the way of Lambaneish men.

"I'm not accustomed to hunting captive game."

I looked up and saw the king in profile. Had he just insulted his host, Arkhon Kyphos? That was not how we did things in Corymb either, I wanted to say, but could not speak. There the wilderness is outside walls, not within them. King Thyrse had claimed the Kingswood for his own, but he'd flattered himself, for it was many separate kingdoms ruled by royal beasts, and to take a bear or boar or wolf one had to seek him in his keep and lands. How was it hunting to kill a captive beast? Call it butchery, and call a tharais butcher to do it.

Aghazal said, "Ah, here is the mother's milk. I know you're fond of it, Krinian, ein?"

"I wish you'd have your cook teach mine how to make it."

"Never," said Aghazal, "for you'd have no reason to visit me then."

"Oh, but I would," said Krinian, scooting forward slightly. His knee was bony and pressed too hard. I moved my leg so we were no longer touching.

Aghazal, by raising her eyebrows, invited me to share her delight at how Krinian looked sucking the so-called mother's milk through the nipple of a cloth sack. She suckled also, and when she was done she dabbed white cream from the corner of her mouth with her little finger, all behind the modest and inadequate cover of her left hand. Perhaps it was one of her arts to be silly from time to time. The mother's milk was delicious, ground almonds mixed with clotted cream and flecked with sweet spices.

And suddenly the mood was merrier, and people talked faster and louder, and every sally of wit won more laughter than it deserved. King Corvus did not unbend. He wouldn't touch his sack, or suffer jests about refusing. But he sucked pulp through a slit in the hard skin of a pomegranate, and crimson juice ran down his chin. He took a cloth from the tharais servant and wiped his face.

He was attentive to Aghazal, and she spoke softly so he would have to lean closer. They hadn't touched, but I watched for it. I was jealous of how they seemed to charm each other, and how well they looked together, and if my imagination had needed a spur, which it did not, there were the paintings on the walls of the dining court. Usually these paintings were behind closed shutters to protect them from the Sun. Tonight the shutters were open, and the paintings were lit by alabaster sconces, so Aghazal's guests might better admire the artistry of the renowned painter.

In the arthygater's bathing room they had gossiped that the king knew the twenty-five Postures, like a civilized person. No doubt Aghazal knew twenty-five Postures and twenty-five more when those were exhausted. I admired her in the warm, breathing glow of many lamps. Delicate creases encircled her plump neck like thin necklaces, and her skin had a sheen as if she'd dusted herself with gold. She would taste of cloves and salt. If I were the king, I'd want to take her first standing up and face-to-face. I entwine, she had promised. Aghazal would have to hoist herself up to kiss him, he was tall. She would cling.

I wanted to be the one clinging. Arms around his neck, cheek pressed against his chest, legs around his hips—my back scraping against something hard, the column, the wall.

Both my eyes were open wide, and my vision was doubled. With my right hand I twisted the bracelets over the scar on my left wrist, and I shivered in a chill wind from the Ferinus. When had I truly been made captive? Not when the smith put on the manacle. There was no single moment. Unless it was this moment, now, when I saw revealed a new pattern, or rather a pattern already embedded in events, that altered everything—not only what might come, but what had gone before. Memories changed when their meaning changed, and how could I trust them when they were so faithless?

Dasasana carried forth the famous eels from the Lake of Sapheiros for our delectation: a pair of them coiled together, decorated with their long ribbons of fins, adrift in a green sauce. She showed us the dish and Krinian said, "Ah!" and she took them again so they could be delicately removed from the bone, cut into morsels, and reassembled.

I speared a bite with my trident and chewed. The flesh was delicious, but my gorge rose. Self-disgust. I had begged Desire to light my way, but I didn't like what I saw when she unshuttered her lantern. I'd waited so long in Lambanein, in the manufactory, the dyehouse, the bathing room—not for a way back across the Ferinus—for a gesture, for acknowledgment. That he should admit I was necessary to him. I'd cozened myself. I'd been a nuisance, and he'd found a way to rid himself of me and make use of me at the same time.

Krinian seemed in ecstasy over the eels; he smacked his lips and closed his eyes, and he stretched out his leg on the outside of the dining platform, fencing me in. His rude foot touched my ankle, but I was nothing but a whore after all.

I sat perfectly still while my thoughts scrabbled about like mice trapped in the bottom of a kettle. Surely the king had not come here to see me. Perhaps he wanted to meet Krinian, who was, of course, enormously rich. He might wish to borrow money from him.

Under Aghazal's instruction, we Sisters had made wreaths for each guest, messages in the language of flowers. The king's wreath was of roses, deep red, which meant endeavors rewarded—but entwined as they were with scarlet poppies, meaning consolation, the promise was ambiguous.

The moonflowers in Aghazal's wreath had unfurled, for they are night bloomers. Each flower was made of a single flared petal, ribbed, pure white except for violet bruises deep in the throat. Aghazal had moonflowers in plenty growing in her garden, and those too were opening, and their scent was womanly, fleshy and sweet, slightly tainted with the scent of something overripe. Aghazal saw me staring at her and she plucked a blossom from her wreath and tore it with her teeth, and swallowed a small piece without chewing. She didn't bother to hide behind her hand.

She handed the bloom to me, smiling, and I touched it with my tongue. Aghazal dared me, she did, without saying a word, and I ate a shred of the flower. I was about to give it back to her, or to Krinian perhaps, but she forestalled me with a subtle gesture I took to mean: It is yours. Moonflowers were never on the list of delicacies to be served at the feast. It was for the two of us alone, I thought she said with those dark speaking eyes. So I ate the rest of the bloom.

Before long I was like a swimmer who has expelled her last breath and given herself over to sinking. How slowly I sank, as if in honey, and the moment thick and heavy and golden and translucent, and there were bubbles of laughter trapped in it. This descending made me dizzy and I leaned against the backrest, and Krinian tilted toward me. I drew my legs away, and his foot followed and pressed harder. I looked at King Corvus as if I'd been given permission to stare. Sight was sustenance. His hair was black as raven's plumage—so the ballads said, and it was true. His beard was trimmed close, the hair of it not straight but coiled. He wore his red crown of roses and poppies without appearing to notice it. Aghazal had told me to strip away all the thorns on the roses but two. I looked for a scratch on the king's brow, a ruby bead to be licked off. I wanted to pierce my tongue with a thorn, I had such a thirst. My throat was so dry I couldn't swallow. Mad cravings.

But the king's brow was untroubled, no trickle of blood from a thorn, no furrows, and he caught me up in his glance, inviting me, inviting us all to laugh. What was the jest? Just that he was not accomplished. It had to be acknowledged, he said, that he wasn't born a poet, but a warrior. His wit was not his sharpest weapon; he begged to be excused from versifying, to be spared humiliation.

"You're too modest," said Aghazal. "You're a poet and a warrior. Perhaps it takes a man from another country to remind us of days when men excelled in both art and deed, like Oxys and Pachys from the First Age of the World, and Balanos from this our Second Age."

"I've wondered," Krinian said, "who composed the poem you gave at the arthygater's New Moon banquet this month. The one that says—how does it go?—something about white petals of snow burning on your skin."

"No," I said. "'White petals of snow drift. They are caught in your shawl, immolate on your burning skin.'"

It had taken a great effort to speak. I had to strain against my muteness, and my face went red and my heart beat too fast. I forgot to use the high Lambaneish lilt; instead my voice plunged lower and lower until I was whispering. I kept my eyes down, sure the king watched me, but when I glanced up he was staring at Krinian instead.

"I did. I composed it," said King Corvus in answer to Krinian. "I was obliged to say something. And might I ask how one can pay for a verse in advance, when the subject isn't known?"

Krinian speared a piece of eel and popped it in his mouth. After he swallowed, he said, "It would be no discredit to you if you'd had the help of a poet. After all, you can't be expected to know all our ways, as you say. Many a man born here has had some thrush find out the theme for an evening's joust, and paid a poet to work up something beforehand."

"Then I suppose one must be first to recite," the king said. "Because I don't see how one would know what other words one might have to include from the person who spoke just before—breezes or shawls or the night. Or do the versifiers conspire?"

"What shall the motif be tonight, ein?" Aghazal asked. "Would you like to pick one, Krinian? So long as it isn't eels, my dear."

Apparently this was a great jape, or at least Krinian thought so. He laughed boisterously and said, "It should be eels! Eels it is!"

Aghazal said, "It isn't that sort of evening."

The king said, "Just so we're all on the same footing, so to speak—if there are any guests who might have winkled out this evening's motif already—

perhaps we should ask someone else to suggest one. Suppose we ask Alopexin."

"Why not?" said Aghazal, and Krinian, who should have been insulted by the suggestion he would cheat, as the king had been insulted, waved as if he didn't much care. They all looked at me.

I said, "Well, if I might be so bold . . . Perhaps the Fragment by Kylocides, the one about the bud of the peony? The one that goes,

> In the tight bud—soft folds.
> The one who tempts the peony to open,
> Departs before the petals fall."

Aghazal said, "That would be most suitable." She shielded her mouth to cover a smile, but was she amused? Her irises had gone from brown to black, and to look into her eyes was like looking into wells that reflected pin-pricks of distant lamplight. She clapped her hands to call for silence, and told her guests the drinking game after dinner would be on the theme of the peony bud, in the form of six, eleven, and eight, and the winner would be the last man or woman who could still stand and recite. To me she said quietly, "You shall go first, Alopexin, since it was your idea." That was her revenge.

They say I acquitted myself well, but I don't remember. The rest of the banquet is gone, swallowed down the long throat of a moonflower.

I remember a street I didn't recognize in an unfamiliar city that had terraces arranged like petals, concentric and perfect. The thinning Moon was high above the dark bulk of the mountain. I began to walk, unsteady on my feet. Someone hurried after me, calling my name, but as it was the wrong name I didn't answer to it. I wanted to catch up with Penna, who turned the corner always just ahead, and I tried to grasp her gauze skirt, but my hand tore through it as if it were cobwebs. She had black ribbons around her throat and they fluttered in the winds tumbling down the alley. She was a mudwoman like me. Who had taught her to be so proud and implacable? I asked her forgiveness that I was not like her, that I was so weak I preferred captivity to death, that I had been unable to despise my captor. She ran away down the street, an egret on thin legs, running and beating her wings, clumsy until she took flight.

Aghazal swore I never left her house, that she wouldn't have let me go wandering after eating a moonflower. So it cannot be true about the man I met by the bathhouse outside the eastgate. I leaned over a waist-high railing and all the blood rushed to my face. I was tharais again with a shawl over my head. He gave me two beadcoins when he was done, but he cheated me. They were made of bread, not pewter. I ate them dry and the crumbs stuck in my throat.

But I think it might be true that I stood in Aghazal's bedchamber and watched Krinian mount her. It was nearly dawn and the other guests had left, seen home by hired torchboys. Second and Third and I attended our mistress during the ceremony, for this was how we were to learn the twenty-five Postures and the other arts that made twenty-five seem a thousand: the appropriate utterances, bites, scratches, kisses, and embraces to be given and received.

But I thought Rowney was in the room as well, standing at the other end of the bed. I greeted him gladly and asked after Galan and his men and all their doings. They were well, praise the gods, he said, though he himself had taken a lance thrust in the chest; he pulled up his jerkin to show me, and the wound was black with blood and glittering with flies. But he was better now, truly he was.

Maybe we were not in Aghazal's bedchamber, watching her. Maybe she was alone there with Krinian, to serve as an officiant at a secret rite. As for him, I had the strange vain notion he was thinking of me as he rutted, but my quim was dry and I was unmoved. He could never move me.

The next afternoon Aghazal sent for me when she awoke. I sat beside her on the bed as she lay amidst rumpled bedclothes. She said she was proud of me. "You were splendid, much better than I expected—reciting Arkhyios Corvus's poem! Flattering him and making Krinian bristle—he was smitten, as I'm sure you could tell. He has already sent you a gift, and two others did as well, but of course it's too soon to contemplate taking a patron. You were a scoundrel about the peonies, ein? Trying to find me out."

"Do I find out? I don't remember."

"*Did* I find out, you must say."

"You poison me." I squinted down at Aghazal. My eyes smarted from daylight, even in her shuttered bedchamber. My pupils must be enlarged, as hers were. It took great effort to move; I felt I had to heave my limbs about, maneuver this body that was not quite myself.

Aghazal got up and draped a shawl over her shoulders without bothering with a wrapper. It didn't shame her a whit to be seen naked. "You *poisoned* me."

"I poisoned you?"

"No, no, that's how to say it: You poisoned me. Why are you fretting, ein? You didn't take enough to be harmed. And besides—the way you savored the flower—I thought you knew."

"I think you eat, ate the flower to look beautiful. The way you tear the flesh between your teeth, the petal on your tongue—I thought I am to do the same." I'd eaten the rest of the bloom bite by bite, hoping the king would look at me and not Aghazal.

"And by Katabaton, you did it well," she said. "But I'm sorry you didn't know, it would have been better if you'd been prepared. It baffles me that you can be so ignorant and yet appear to have knowledge. Who among the patrons last night would have guessed that yesterday morning you'd never heard of Kylocides? What a surprise, ein? When you began to utter poetry all of a sudden." She laughed and went through the door to her bathing room.

I lay down on her bed, which smelled of cloves and jasmine and the musk and ferment of coupling, and pulled a cloth over me, the silk wrapper she'd worn the night before: magenta, Desire's color.

In a little while Aghazal came back and said, "Move over, ein? I'm still sleepy."

I moved, but not too much, so our hips were touching. I felt full up with sap, my lips burning and swollen, so also my coxscomb quim, and my nipples like hard brown buds on the verge of opening, and what flower would bloom from my breasts? It must have been a last moonflower vision that showed me jasmine and bryony growing all over the bed, *I entwine*.

CHAPTER 28

Taxonomies

 I did so well at Aghazal's dinner party that she said I was not to spin or weave or weed the gardens anymore; I was to learn my lists.

First I had to learn the Lambaneish chicken scratches by heart. Aghazal was far too busy to teach me, so she gave the task to Second. Third and I were both her pupils, and I was humbled to be as ignorant as a six-year-old girl. Ardor had unshackled my tongue so I could learn to speak Lambaneish, and permitted me to relearn the godsigns. Every morning I burned a shred of candlebark at the kitchen hearth and asked the god to permit this as well.

We started with a poem, "Proper Conduct of Children Toward Parents," in which each of the forty-nine lines began with a character of the syllabary. I learned to write *fedan* and *emmin,* father and mother. I learned that a child must never say no to his or her father, and forty-eight other rules as well.

I made a clay tablet with the forty-nine dancers of Lambaneish next to the sixty variants of the godsigns, trying to match the two syllabaries, though Lambaneish had some odd sounds that were like nothing in the High. Making this tablet was a labor of two days, and it taught me how to break words in both languages into small parts.

We learned about Time, from its smallest measures, heartbeat and breath, to its largest, the ages of the world. In Lambanein they had two kinds of months and years, lunar and solar. The years were not exactly of the same length, so they were like wheels turning side by side, one a little faster than the other, and from time to time priests had to regulate them to make sure they didn't get too far apart. The festivals of Katabaton and Peranon were on the lunar year, and Posison's were on the solar, and priests chose auspicious times for celebrations depending on conjunctions of the months and Celestial Objects.

So I was amazed to learn one morning that I was in the forenoon passage of the twelfth day of the Crane Month (lunar), and the Iron day of the

Third Month (solar), in the year 415 of the Third Dynasty, in the year 1006 of the Second Age of the World. Everyone in Lambanein agreed on it; there were no disputes, as there often were in our village, when someone would say, "That was the year the Herders died," and another would say, "No, that was the year the snow was up to the eaves of the Dame's manor."

I'd never kept an inventory of my time before. I'd cared only for the seasons of the year and the plants of the season, what was sprouting or ripening or dying, what was potent and when to seek it.

The Lambaneish have such a penchant for naming, classifying, and ranking that they have created a list of lists, the Taxonomies. Day after day we copied lists, such as:

> The denizens of the Overworld: the gods, demiurges, and greater
>   meneidon, and their gifts and afflictions;
> The peoples of Lambanein, their kinds and arts;
> The strange-ignorant kingdoms, even those on the other side of the
>   Outward Sea: the appearance, dwellings, and manufactures of
>   their peoples;
> The tree of the royal family, of which the arkhon was the trunk, his
>   ancestors the roots, and his wives and descendants the limbs and
>   branches;
> The trees of the five Exalted Families;
> The dynasties of the First and Second Ages;
> The nineteen temperaments of men and fifty-one temperaments of
>   women;
> The thirteen forms of love and the signs by which they can be
>   recognized;
> The twenty-five Postures and twelve Abasements;
> The amorous kisses, caresses, embraces, pinches, scratches, bites,
>   and blows;
> The amorous utterances;
> The flirtations, flatteries, and mockeries;
> The sixteen games and how to cheat at them;
> The languages of colors, flowers, fragrances, birds, spices, gems,
>   and metals;
> The languages of glances and gestures;
> The poets of the First Age and Second Age;
> The Fragments, Odes, and Epics;
> The Conundrums.

Wildfire

Every afternoon when Aghazal woke up she would read what we'd written that day. Sometimes Tasatyala taught us incorrectly, and we had to do the work again. The genealogies were hardest, because the names sounded all alike. Aghazal chalked the arkhon's tree on the wall of the back courtyard. The limbs were his five wives, four of whom he'd worn out in succession with childbearing. The fifth was bearing still. The branches were his eighteen living sons and eleven daughters. There were many twigs too—grandchildren and great-grandchildren—and there would have been more if not for a Lambaneish custom that denied the arkhon's sons the right to marry until their father died. Of course the sons had concubines and bastards in plenty; fortunately we didn't have to learn them.

We found we could memorize the begats if we sang them. I made up silly and scurrilous verses about Arthygater Katharos and some others on the lists, and Adalana made tunes for them. I wrote the verses in clay and squashed them up again.

Tasatyala had started with more knowledge, but I was quicker to master the family trees. There was pleasure in knowing, when I met a Lambaneish noble, where he or she belonged in the ranks of names; I'd taken much the same satisfaction in being able to name every tree in a forest by its leaf and bark and twig pattern, in summer or in winter. But it no longer sufficed to merely hear the names. I needed the words to flow from ear to eye to hand and back again, to hear, see, and feel them, so they might be remembered by my right hand as by my mind.

Day by day I sounded out words and inscribed them. I was diligent, for Aghazal had promised that if I learned my syllabary quickly, she would give me the Odes and Epics to read. Second and Third already knew them by heart. I should never amount to anything if I didn't learn them.

It had become my ambition to amount to something.

Aghazal had many invitations, and I accompanied her from one event to the next. In one evening she might sing and dance at a spectacle in a palace, dine in the mansion of a wealthy townsman, join a party of Moon-gazers in the gardens of the Temple of Katabaton, and then tryst with a patron. I was excused from attendance on her trysts; she would send me home in the cart drawn by her uncle and three nephews. Often she returned home the next morning and slept all afternoon while I studied. Another New Moon came and went, my fourth in Lambanein, but in Aghazal's house the festival didn't mark a day of rest, but a night of work even busier than most.

I was always tired. Aghazal was in a hurry with me and I didn't know enough to question it. But Second asked why: why did Aghazal take me to dine in men's quarters and leave her behind, when she knew more than me, and had better manners, and was accomplished in singing and dancing? She was of an age, thirteen already, and Aghazal had promised her last year that soon she could have patrons of her own. At first I found Tasatyala's eagerness to go whoring hard to understand; of late, much easier. After every visit Aghazal made, she received gifts the next day from her patrons, and they sent tokens for me as well—a praise poem, a cord with bead messages, an enameled bangle, or an ivory amulet of Katabaton. All this, and I did not have to say yes.

I added beadcoins to the fringe of my cap, and hoarded other gifts in a locked casket in a locked cabinet. But Aghazal let me know I was obliged to share—not only with her, my First Sister, but with Second and Third, the uncle and nephews who escorted us, and Aunt Cook, and I mustn't forget the messenger who brought the gifts, and servants in the houses of patrons. I was grateful, wasn't I, to be so well cared for?

Aghazal knew to a nicety how to calculate the worth of gifts. Was the patron generous or had he slighted her? She also knew how much to give, so servants would treat her well without taking advantage.

She sent most of her earnings to Ebanaka, to help her kinfolk, and also to pay for building a house on a lakeshore—like a palace, she said, with vineyards and orchards of fig, apricot, and almond. She planned to move there when she lost her beauty. "Beauty doesn't last like gold," she said.

"I can't lose what I don't have."

She rolled a fat amber bead toward me. "Pakhus gave you this for a glimpse of your teeth. So he might disagree, ein?"

Tasatyala lacked suitors and gifts because Aghazal wouldn't let her accompany us. She swore Tasatyala wasn't quite ready, it was too soon. It was plainly too soon for me as well. Which led back to the question of why.

King Corvus sent a limner to capture a likeness of me. Aghazal dressed me in saffron silks, and the tharais servant wrapped my hair—along with plentiful silk hair, dyed to match to my own—around a spiral wickerwork, and I was laden with golden bangles and armlets and a necklace of gold, pearls, and emeralds. Arthygater Katharos herself did not dress more splendidly. I sat for several long afternoons while Tasatyala and Adalana took turns singing the Odes, and I had altogether too much time to ponder and to wonder.

The likeness was as big as my outstretched hand, no bigger. Why did the king want it? I flattered myself that he might want to gaze at my portrait, for he couldn't gaze at me. What use would I be to him as a thrush if everyone knew I was his servant?

His bride had enchanted him with a painted portrait, so sang the rumormongers and rhapsodists of our army. The ballads said the portrait had spoken to Prince Corvus in his dreams, and he was so ardent he insisted on marrying Kalos against his mother's wise counsel. Had it been the limner's uncanny art that snared him, or a charm Kalos had learned as a devotee of the Serpent Cult, or her beauty? In the dream I had of her, she was not as beautiful as the songs had led me to expect.

Once I believed every ballad I heard was true, before I knew rumormongers could be paid to sing what-you-will. Perhaps Corvus had admired Kalos's dowry, not her person. Perhaps he'd quarreled with his mother for other reasons. I longed to know these things, but there was no one to ask.

I watched the limner, a small man with a long beard that he braided and tucked under his surcoat to keep out of the way. He dipped his tiny brushes into pastes of egg yolk mixed with brilliant pigments, and made tiny strokes. He bent close over his work and bobbed up again to gaze at me. No one had ever looked at me so hard, not even Galan. I asked the limner if I was still lopsided, if the right side of my face drooped more than the left. He said I didn't droop, but of course I was lopsided, everyone was. I asked what expressions he saw on my left and right visages, and he said thoughts chased across my face like the shadows of clouds over the fields.

"Are you a poet too?" I asked.

"Just a painter."

I didn't understand how my face could be changing when my cheeks hurt from the strain of staying motionless. "If there are so many expressions, what will you show?"

He said, "What I've been asked to show."

"What is that?"

"Beauty. Pride. You will look demure, except your right eye is to have a tiny glint of ardency."

"You won't show my webeye?"

"Of course not."

So this wasn't to be a portrait of me at all, not as I was, flawed from my lopsided face to the tough soles of my feet. Divine Aboleo had called me bold and clever, and I'd tried on the words and found them a poor fit, yet I was not so ill fitted to them as I was to the words *beautiful, proud, demure*.

Aghazal ate moonflower from time to time in small amounts. She said it helped keep her awake, and dried up her quim, which many patrons preferred. It made her eyes black and brilliant, and I noticed she became giddy, talkative, and forgetful after eating it. But that might have happened anyway, because of all the doublewine she drank.

I'd refused moonflower when it was offered. What I remembered of it frightened me—dreams that seemed as real as waking, and no way to tell what was there from what wasn't. Much of what I'd dreamed that night had proved false. Surely moonflower was under the dominion of Crux Moon, and shared his lustful and inconstant nature.

But the flower had shown me Rowney, and Rowney had told me Galan was alive. And that, I hoped, was true. That I myself had proved lustful and inconstant couldn't take away my gladness at this thought.

It wasn't my fault, was it, that I was no longer steadfast, that I saw King Corvus's face when I wished to envision Galan's, that I picked over every word the king had said to me as if looking for a precious stone in a bowl of dried lentils? It was the fault of the Initiates of Carnal; first they'd made me barren, and now they'd severed the binding between Galan and me. They must have done it or I'd not be so befuddled, one hope warring upon another—the hope of leaving, the hope of staying.

I'd rather desire Galan than a king who looked on me with such disdain he tried to make a whore of me. Let me long where I was longed for—if I was longed for. If I could see Galan once, if I could speak to him as I'd spoken to Rowney, then I would know if he still wanted me.

I asked Aghazal if I could trust a moonflower dream.

She said, "She's capricious, ein? Once I lost some jade beadcoins and Moonflower showed me where they had rolled into a corner, but many a time she's led me a long chase and stolen my recollection of it."

"Is there a sign that shows which of her dreams are true and which are false? A smell or something?"

Aghazal laughed. "A smell? Not that I know of. Leave her be, ein?"

"But you eat moonflower."

She raised an eyebrow and a shoulder in a most delicate shrug, which I took to mean she was more experienced, more capable than I, and had less to fear from moonflower. Which was indisputable. But I had more need of it. I'd gone without true dreams—even dreams of Mount Sair, which, lonely as they were, had comforted me—since I stayed in the Court of Tranquil Waters. Unless the dream of Rowney had been a true one.

I made a libation of doublewine before the biggest moonflower plant in Aghazal's dining court, and pricked the vein inside my elbow and sprinkled blood around its roots. I prayed to moonflower, and through her to Crux Moon, begging their indulgence. Show me Galan, and I would trade three golden beadcoins for a silver ingot, and have an image made of the full Moon to wear around my neck until I returned to Incus; as soon as I came upon a shrine of Crux, I would give the image in offering. Only let me see Galan, let me bespeak him. Let him be alive. Watch over him.

I vowed I would eat moonflower the next time it was offered. I begged her, if she opposed this, to send me a vision of a dog after I partook; if she welcomed my inquiries, to send a fox. That way I'd know if I dared venture further.

She was as good as her reputation. She sent me a cat.

Aghazal was invited to entertain at a banquet offered by Arthygater Klados, Katharos's sister. We sat with the other whore-celebrants in an upstairs arcade, while the guests ate and drank interminably in the dining court below, entertained by rhapsodists competing for the honor of presenting an ode to Arkhon Kyphos on the subject of his defeat of pirates some years past. No one seemed to be listening to the recitations, not even the historian who was to choose the winning ode.

We were fed many fewer dishes than the noble guests. For the licked course we were offered a paste of sesame and figs. Aghazal tasted it and told me she was certain it contained ground moonflower seeds. When I licked up my portion anyway, she smiled and shrugged.

I crept over to the railing so I could watch King Corvus. He sat beside Arthygater Klados, her husband, and their daughter Keros, the very same daughter intended for his brother Merle. King Corvus inclined his head politely toward Keros. I remembered her red-gold hair was down past her waist when unbound, and the hair on her arms was blond.

Aghazal whispered, "Come back here. You'll be seen."

After the noblewomen departed for the evening, Aghazal and I promenaded through the crowd. An old patron greeted her, and I walked on alone. It was not the first time this had happened, but it still disconcerted me. As long as I was with Aghazal, I was not required to be charming, for she had charm enough for both. Nor did I need to be wary, for she would watch out for me.

My steps tended toward King Corvus, but a man—a youth—caught my shawl as I passed by and said, "If you please, come sit with us awhile." He had bright red hair and pale eyes and eyelashes, and he was most polite, not at all as I'd seen him last, in the tunnel under the manufactory, vowing to kill me—our hostess's son, Arkhyios Kydos. He was sitting with his cousin Kyanos and two whores I'd seen in passing once or twice.

My heart rattled along faster and faster, and I felt a flush bloom on my cheeks. I was just afraid enough to find the fear thrilling. They'd never recognize me, for I was as well hidden as if I wore a tharais veil, dressed as I was in turquoise silks, with my lips dyed red, my eyes outlined with malachite, and my hair woven into a tower. I smiled a false, flirtatious smile, hiding it behind my hand as if I were the sort of woman who could be modest. But it wasn't an entirely false smile, for I was enjoying their ignorance.

Maybe this was moonflower's doing, this gift of fine careless daring, but if so it was an intoxication better by far than drunkenness, for it sharpened rather than blunted the senses.

Kydos moved over on the platform, forcing one of the women to make room for me so as not to seem ungracious. I sat beside him with one foot on the ground. I was unsure of the whores' names; I should ask Aghazal for a list of the principal whores in Allaxios, to study as I studied the tree of the arkhon.

My throat was dry, moonflower thirst. Kydos gestured, and a tharos servant poured doublewine into a blue glass goblet and I drank it down. Whores must drink to keep their patrons company. The servant filled my glass again, and again I drank, and felt the heat flare up. I ate a confection sticky with honey, and when the tharais napkin came forward with the basin, my senses were so acute that I was disgusted by the whiff of onion and sweat rising from her; disgusted also by her chapped fingers and the way she breathed through her nose.

Kydos put a hand on my knee. Again I covered my mouth and smiled. I had yet to speak, and the two whores, Mixin and Perdik, resumed their conversation without my help. Mixin said she liked nothing more than to hear doves coo at dawn while she lay abed, knowing she didn't have to rise. Perdik asked if anyone had heard the nightingales sing in the cypresses behind the shrine of Peranon. She swore they sang in harmony and in chorus, and wondered if they sang to comfort the Weeping Star. I knew—as I wouldn't have known a tennight ago—that she referred to a Fragment about a nightingale who adored a wandering star, and climbed the night sky to bring her his song, climbed until his heart burst and he fell to his death; the star mourns him still. And I knew now that every mention of a bird carried a message. A bird was never just a bird.

I hadn't mastered the language of birds, and might easily go amiss, but I couldn't stop thinking about the one who had adored unsuitably and climbed too high and fallen so far. I said, "How far is it to the stars, ein? Can a hawk reach them, I wonder? Does an eagle flying above the highest peak of the Kerastes, as high above the peak as the peaks are above the plains, say—does that eagle fly high enough? If one were to walk to the very edge of the horizon, surely the stars are close there? This nightingale should go far, not high, ein?"

The whores tittered behind their hands, but Arkhyios Kydos seemed to find my ignorance charming. He said, "You could walk and walk forever and never come to the edge of the horizon."

"Is the world so big then?"

He picked up an orange from a dish of fruit and nuts. "No, look. It's round." He walked his fingers over it. "We're under the sky. It never touches us."

"What's in between, holding up the Heavens, ein?"

"The winds uphold the sky," he said.

"No, the gods do," said Arkhyios Kyanos.

I took the orange from Arkhyios Kydos. "Then where is the Overworld where the gods dwell, ein? I thought one could descend to it through a hole, if there was a hole deep enough. Is it on the other side? Could I walk around the orange to find it?" They were all laughing at me now, and I was sure Kydos was telling me a foolish tale just to prove I was fool enough to believe it, but the notion tickled me, and moonflower was blooming inside me, and I laughed until I got the hiccups.

Arkhyios Kyanos said, "You're forgetting the seas—you'd have to swim too."

"I'd rather fly," I said. "I'd be a gyrfalcon if I could choose, ein? What kind of bird would you be?" I grinned at Arkhyios Kydos without bothering to cover my mouth, thinking of him hopping in the tunnel with shit on his shoe-stockings. He reminded me of a bandy-legged cock, vain enough to think he could chase a fox.

He said, "I'd be an eagle; I'd stoop and take a dove in my talons," and he pretended to swoop down on Mixin, digging his sharpened fingernails into her plump upper arms. She shrieked in the manner called Stung by a Bee.

I was not supposed to be a gyrfalcon; I was supposed to be a thrush. And here was my chance to find out something useful, something more about— about anything. I must tether myself to a purpose or soar away.

Arkhyios Kydos was telling me about his parrot. "I trained him to make the cry of a woman receiving a blow at the moment of ecstasy. He's a marvel, he can do sixteen of the amorous utterances and Mixin is helping me with the rest. I'll take you to the aviary so you can hear him."

The five of us strolled through the dining court and entered the pleasure garden that rose toward the men's quarters, which backed against a cliff. We ascended mossy stairs from one terrace to the next, and beside us a waterfall sang as it rushed down convoluted chutes of stone. Perdik panted convincingly and leaned on Arkhyios Kyanos's arm, and Mixin clung to Arkhyios Kydos. I paused on the stairs to look over Allaxios, and motioned for the tharos servants with the lanterns to pass by. I could see farther without their lights. The coral honeysuckle draped over the pepon bushes smelled so sweet.

In company with Aghazal I'd seen many gardens, large and small, in the saffron light of evening or blue twilight or black night. Of all Lambaneish arts, gardening was the one I most admired. I should have become a gardener, not a whore. A gardener, or a wealthy woman. Imagine owning all of this, calling it mine.

Kydos called to me and I started climbing, suddenly heavy again, my steps going thump, thump, thump, and my heart at a faster pace, going thumpthumpthumpthump. It wasn't the exertion.

We sat on a cushioned platform within the aviary, a tall building with carved pillars and gilded rafters. Its walls were of black silk netting, invisible. Most of the birds were sleeping in cages or roosting in the potted trees. As Arkhyios Kydos coaxed his green parrot to make the cry known as the Agitated Quail, I feared the others would hear the uproar of my heart.

Arkhyios Kydos sent a servant for more doublewine, stuffed figs, and a flute player. The two couples reclined against the backrests with their legs outstretched, and I was glad to be extra. The parrot walked up and down Mixin's bare arm, and she fed it pellets of almond paste she'd rolled between her fingers. She was trying to teach the bird to cry, "Mercy, no!"

"I wonder if Keros has taught her starling to talk," said Arkhyios Kyanos.

Mixin said, "I hate starlings. Nasty, noisy things, and without beauty."

"Clever though, I've heard," said Perdik.

"He hasn't answered yet," Arkhyios Kydos said. "My sister doesn't mind. She doesn't care much for talking birds. She prefers singing ones."

They laughed while I tried to puzzle out the jest. The Starling was Merle, but who was the singing bird?

"Maybe she'll fly away with him," Perdik said.

"I doubt it. My mother has the key to that cage."

Perdik said, "A musician! By Posison's shit, however did she meet a musician? I'm surprised your father hasn't unstrung him yet, cut his throat and the cords that hold his sacs, ein?"

"If your father doesn't do it, maybe you should," Arkhyios Kyanos said. "I'll gladly help."

Arkhyios Kydos made a gesture of dismissal, as if their teasing annoyed him. "I don't begrudge her a little pleasure. Indeed, I pity her. I hope she takes the singer along, so he can turn the Starling into a cuckoo."

Mixin said, "A strange-ignorant one—I suppose he has hair on his chest like an ape. It makes me shudder to think of her under him; she's so delicate, a true beauty, your sister."

Arkhyios Kydos, pretending to be a hairy strange-ignorant man, growled and pressed Mixin down. The startled parrot flew up with a squawk and landed on the construction of wicker, silk, and blossoms affixed to my head. Hilarity filled me and I giggled. Cicadas zinged in the feathery acacia trees, and birds chirped and trilled in the aviary, and water splashed in the tiled fountain, and winds flew by and made off with the flute song. These sounds seemed to fall into the rhythm dictated by the drumming of my heart—even the conversation, which became a wordless music of tones, syllables, and the patter of laughter.

It was too exquisite. The parrot plucked a jasmine flower from my hair and dropped it in my lap. I reached up and he stepped onto my fingers. I looked him in the eye and he tilted his head and said, "No, I beg you!" in a shrill voice, and I laughed so heartily he took offense and flew away.

Two golden eyes reflected the lamplight, there beyond the silken walls of the aviary. A gray cat crouched patiently, hoping for a bird. I had fancied myself a gyrfalcon or a fox, a hunter, when I was just an insignificant brown bird, a wren in borrowed plumage. No wonder the cat was watching me.

Kydos untied the cord that fastened Mixin's garment and began to unwrap her. She lay across his lap and as he tugged, she turned, once, twice, and she was naked. She made small sounds, which were, as far as I could tell, an artful combination of the Seeping Sigh and the Choked Gasp. I stood to leave, and Kydos reached for my hand and said, "Stay." I evaded him and ducked through the door flap in the netting.

The half-Moon was bright. It made the shadows of the cypresses seem to be holes in the ground, holes deep enough, perhaps, to reach the Overworld. I stumbled into one such shadow-hole and lay on my back looking at the stars and the three black trees—for cypresses were always planted in threes—that went up and up like pillars upholding the Heavens. Where was Galan? I prayed to the Moon, which was perhaps unwise.

A tharos servant crouched in the moonlight, waiting for me to order her to do something. She had wide eyes and a small nose and mouth. How invisible servants had become to me of late! But now I wondered what she was thinking. I fumbled to untie a cord on my headdress, so I could pull off a golden beadcoin. I beckoned and gave it to her. She knelt and touched her head to the ground and waited.

"It's not a message. It's for you," I said.

She crawled closer and kissed the hem of my dress. I would never have done such a thing myself. "Oh, go away!" I said, but she didn't go far. I saw her hiding behind a tree. Was she spying now, or hoping I'd fall asleep so she could cut my cords with a little knife and steal all my beadcoins? Snip snip. Such things happened to drunks. I didn't care. She wasn't a person, she was a patient watching cat.

I began to sing Mox's drinking song, the one his dead father had taught him in a dream. In Lambaneish it sounded more poignant. My heart pounded along. *It is better to die drinking, than to lie thinking, that I, even I, must die.* I sat up so I could sing better. The long tree shadow in which I sat stretched out before me, pointed like the prow of a boat. In it I navigated the night, singing to embolden myself on the journey.

A man came up the stairs carrying a silver lamp with a flame the size of my thumb. He sat beside me in the boat. I hailed him, and asked in the High, "Where are we going, Corvus Rex Incus, Master of Bastards?"

He said, "What do you mean?"

"In our boat, in our boat."

"You're drunk." He put his hand on my arm above the scarred wrist, and his touch went lightning quick all through me, head to toe.

"Drunk as I should be, as you ought to be. Wherefore I sing this drunken song. Do you remember it? We sang and snow came roaring down from the rocks."

"You're reckless."

"Would it be any use to be otherwise, Master of Masters? I'll sing a new song for you now, a thrush song. Arthygater Keros has already betrayed her betrothed, betrayed her betrothed." (I liked the sound of that.) "With a little singer, some no one. That's why her parents and aunt are giving her away. I thought it was because she was fatuous, I mean fair and virtuous, didn't you? But no, it's a banishment, a punishment—married off to a strange-ignorant carrion-eater."

"Keep your voice down," King Corvus said. My voice was a dog, leaping up and pawing her master, licking his face. Poor bitch. Very well, I would be silent. "What else?" he asked.

I shook my head. I wasn't much of a thrush, my song not much of a song. He took his hand away and I wished he hadn't.

"You should watch out for those princes," King Corvus said. "They get up to all sorts of mischief, with no one to naysay them."

I stared at him. "At least they have something to get up." Had I said that, or was it the Moon talking?

The king looked away, fury on his brow. "Just be careful."

"I'm doing as you bade me."

"You can't keep your wits about you if you're drunk."

"They aren't my wits anymore, I gave them to Alopexin. Besides, you're the one who ought to be careful. No one is trying to kill *me*."

He said, "Your eyes look strange tonight. One has turned black and the other is white. Is someone trying to kill me?"

Wildfire

"Of course. Some hunter. There's a cat watching you."

"A cat?"

"She's over there somewhere." But the cat-servant was gone, and so was the beadcoin. What a wastrel I was, giving gold to a cat. Aghazal would scold me if she found out.

I looked at the king with my left eye. In the moonshadow of the cypress, lamplight touched his cheeks and brow. He was crowned with a flowerless wreath of greenthorn and juniper, meaning solace in adversity, offering protection. His hosts lied. They should have given him a garland of the speckled leaves and stems of oxtongue, for falsehood. I put my hand on the sleeve of his surcoat to see if he was real or a moonflower dream. Pomegranates were appliquéd on his cuff in red kidskin. My forefinger stirred, stroking the garnets stitched in rows to look like pomegranate seeds, but he felt nothing.

"Sorrowful king," I said. "I'd give you solace if I could."

The cicadas' song diminished, then came on again like a wave approaching the shore. The king gazed bleakly at Allaxios fanned out below us, descending step by step to the plains. He said, "I don't want solace."

"How about forgetfulness?"

"Nor that."

Of course he didn't wish to be comforted, offered a poor semblance of what he'd found in the arms of his wife. As for memory, he would not pull out that thorn even if he could, lest by forgetting he become too complacent in exile.

Desire Repulsed by Scorn is one of the thirteen kinds of love enumerated in the Taxonomies; likewise Desire Met with Indifference. But the list didn't include desire confronted with obdurate grief and willed anger.

When Tasatyala first taught me the list, I'd searched for the name of what lay between Galan and me, exhilarated to lay claim to love in any form. I had found Lightning Passion, and Lust for a Contemptible Inferior, and Adoration of a Superior, and none exactly to the purpose. How could love be named when it was first one thing then another, as mutable as fire and shadow?

Maybe the flame was all that mattered. Maybe what we called love was as promiscuous as the Sun, shining everywhere—yet we stood in each other's light, jealous of it; we tried to name its forms by the distorted shadows we cast, which altered the appearance of anything they touched.

For a moment and one moment only I was a clear bright vessel, a glass lamp, and I felt that love could shine through me to illuminate the beloved. I saw I wasn't fickle, for there was no contradiction in loving more than one, nothing to hoard or parcel out.

Then I was muscle and bone again, an obstruction to the light, casting a shadow: desirous, jealous, and sad. Tears rose to my eyes and I let them fall. King Corvus had immured himself—we all immured ourselves—and the walls were high and solid.

"Why did you have a limner capture my likeness?" I asked the king.

"To send to Merle. So he'll think you are Princess Keros."

"I don't understand. You want *me* to marry the Starling? But he would never believe I'm Keros. He knew your wife—surely he'd see I'm not like her, not born to it . . ."

He let out his breath all at once in a gust of a laugh. "You need not dazzle him with your charms—the gold in your dowry will do that. You need only be admitted to his presence."

"And then?"

"Your guards will do the rest."

"Kill him, you mean." I wiped my tears away with the palm of my hand.

"Are you squeamish? You wanted a way across the Ferinus and here it is. You may even find your Sire Galan in Lanx, laying siege to it—for when the army of Corymb sets sail for home this summer, Merle will be in their way. You'll be doing them a service to get rid of him."

I shook my head.

"You'd prefer to be a whore?"

No no of course not. "But he's your brother—"

"Don't call him that. He is my mother's son; my father's too—I never heard a rumor to the contrary—and indeed he favors my father in looks, and had my father's favor. But he is no longer my brother."

"He was obliged to choose between his mother and you—surely that would try any son's loyalty?"

"Nonsense. He chose himself, as ever."

"But you trusted him?"

"I didn't think he'd be fool enough to believe our mother's promises. But she outwitted us both, didn't she? Listen," he said, turning his bleak gaze on me. "If you wish to give me solace, as you were saying . . . Matricide is forbidden me. As for Merle—it would comfort me to know he was dead."

I started at the hollow between her toes, and drew my sharpened fingernail along the top of her foot, crossing the join at the ankle, up the shin, over the round knee and soft thigh. I picked up wetness between the lips of her cleft and left a shining trail across the small mound where her womansbeard ought to be. She awoke, but kept her eyes closed. She began to smile. Up over her belly, past the folds that hid her navel, leaving a light scratch, and between her breasts and up her neck and over her chin and into her mouth.

Wildfire

She sucked on my finger, then opened her eyes, widened them. She must have thought I was Arkhyios Kydos, though how that could be when she lay half over him and he was sleeping, I didn't know.

"Mixin," I said. "You're on my shawl."

She had wide hips and narrow sloping shoulders, and her bones were everywhere submerged in soft flesh. Even her knees were dimpled. She put her foot on my thigh: an insulting and intimate gesture. "You can have the shawl for a kiss," she said.

I put one hand on the backrest and the other between her legs, and leaned closer. She pushed me with her foot and pulled me with one hand behind my neck. I took her lower lip between mine. Her mouth was small, the lips dyed crimson as pomegranate seeds. Her breath smelled of anise.

Arkhyios Kydos woke up and said, "Oh, there you are. I thought you didn't want to."

"Why not, ein?" Why not. It was what the Moon and moonflower seemed to require of me in completion of their little jape. Though the Moon was behind Mount Allaxios now and couldn't see.

This man, with his smooth cheeks and smooth muscles, so sated with easy delights he had to go rutting amongst the frightened women of the manufactory—I had a mind to astonish him—I who had tried only a few of the twenty-five Postures with Galan, before I knew anyone had bothered to name them. I pointed to his dangle, naked without a nest of hairs. "You don't get far with that," I said. "I might as well have a maidenhead—you'll have to be sharp to prick me." As I pointed his dangle began to stir and stiffen, and I smiled to see him obedient.

Mixin dug her toes into my leg so I wouldn't neglect her, and I slipped three fingers into her quim, as Galan had done to me—my right hand, my cold hand. Her eyelids fluttered and I pushed deeper into the slippery softness. I took warmth from her, drawing the hearthfire of her body toward me through that portal. She moaned in a way that seemed artless, or I was taken in by a whore feigning pleasure, the oldest cheat in the world. She made room for me between her legs and I knelt there, leaning over her with my weight on my left hand, the right still inside her. I felt for her pearl with my thumb. She undid the cord and tugged down my clothing to bare me to the waist. I dragged my nipples over her.

Kydos unwound my wrapper and knelt behind me and bullied his way in, and my quim tore a little, being so dry, and I scratched Mixin inside with my fingernail to make her cry out. My tongue rasped her eyelids.

I supposed Kydos was taking me from the backside because he'd found out I was tharais. While he labored at it, I was thinking of the tharais napkins locked out of the palace to appease Misfortune and his herd, and how

417

the woman had braced herself against the wall of the alley, and I was thinking of the king and his contempt for his brother, to send him a tharais whore, a waste receptacle, in place of a bride—his contempt for both of us—and I might have wept had I not been dry as a desert.

Then Kydos coupled with me face-to-face, which proved I was tharos after all: I'd fooled them. When Kyanos took his place, I brought my knees up to my chest and crossed my ankles in the Locked Casket, wanting to pose a conundrum, which was solved when Perdik added her weight to his. I stole heat from all of them and my skin was scorching, and everything on it dried quickly, their sweat, the men's white blood, and the cream of the women, leaving a rime of musk and salt. I smelled of moonflower, and I was so full of its sweet poison I exuded it from my lips, my quim, my skin, in the form of a powdery bloom, scintillant and dark. I thought it would harm them to kiss me. Which was what I wanted, to intoxicate them, to taint them, to make their hearts clamor as mine did, and burn them with my left hand and make them shiver with my right. They partook of the moon-flower through me, and she was potent.

Aghazal hadn't told me Moonflower was a sacred plant; maybe she assumed I knew. Moonflower told me herself, inflicting her sacrament upon me so that I would understand her in my body, the only way she could be understood, and I was truly her whore and celebrant.

CHAPTER 29

Whore-Celebrant

dreamed I did this, and some of it turned out to be true. I'm not sure how I got home. There were crisscrossing scratches on my back and bruises on my thighs from pinches. My quim was sore. If there had been no marks, I would have known by the gifts messengers had left at the house: princely gifts, from princes. Arkhyios Kyanos sent a shawl embroidered with the pendulous blossoms of a laburnum tree, each petal a sequin of hammered gold; Arkhyios Kydos sent two golden fingercaps that fit snugly down to the middle joints. Aghazal examined them closely and found a secret well behind one of the tortoiseshell fingernails, for opos and the like, she said. She judged from the style that the goldsmith Galakt, ten years dead, had made them; his work was treasured—she reckoned the cost at about forty-five gold beadcoins. Kyanos had sent a poem, and Kydos had sent a message of beads on a cord, which meant—according to Aghazal, for I'd not learned enough to read it—*devastated by the gift of your virginity.* He also returned my shawl, which I'd forgotten.

"You're a virgin?" Aghazal said. "You should have told me. These are fine gifts, but you could have gotten even more for your first time."

"Of course not. I bleed a little, that's all. It was the Moonflower."

"I bled, you should say."

We sat side by side in the dining court breakfasting on boiled eggs, though soon it would be time to go visiting. Sometimes we had two dinners of an evening. I had neglected my study of the Taxonomies and slept until late afternoon.

"I don't understand why you chose those callow boys," Aghazal said, "when you could have had more knowledgeable-pleasurable men."

"They were handy."

"Suddenly you were in a hurry, ein?"

"Suddenly I was."

"Yet you regret it?"

It wasn't hard to guess, I suppose. My eyelids were swollen and I couldn't hold her gaze for long.

"Don't think I'm scolding. On the contrary, I commend you: two grandsons of the arkhon in one night."

"Don't forget Mixin and Perdik," I said dryly. "What do I do, give a fingercap to Mixin and half the shawl to Perdik?"

Aghazal laughed. "I'll invite them to my next party and put them in the way of some wealthy men. Those gifts are yours, you earned them." She peeled an egg and ate half of it at once, biting through the pale yellow mealy yolk. I sat stiff and upright, remembering how I'd touched Mixin, wondering how it would feel to touch Aghazal.

"King Corvus tells me to stay away from them," I said.

"*Told,* he told you. So of course you did the opposite, ein? It wouldn't do to heed your benefactor."

Benefactor—that's what they called a patron who kept a whore-celebrant for his personal use. I shrugged. "It was the moonflower in me."

"Ah, the moonflower. When did he give you this warning?"

"Last night. He came upstairs in the garden—following me, maybe, I suppose. No, he would not. Is he there?"

"Where? When? Now you've confused me."

"In the garden, on the hill, last night."

"I don't think so," said Aghazal. "He sat in the same place all evening. What was he wearing?"

"He wears, he wore a long surcoat with a pomegranate design, and a wreath of juniper and greenthorn and oxtongue."

"Oxtongue? Unlikely. I spoke with him last evening—he asked after you, by the way—and he was wearing a surcoat with golden oak leaves, and around the hem leaping gazelles. I noticed it particularly." Gazelles were the sign of Aghazal's house; she had two life-size bronze gazelles in the dining court, one poised with head up, as if considering whether to leap away, and the other seeming to drink from the pool.

"So it was Moonflower," I said. Was I glad? At first I couldn't tell, cushioned as I was by a sort of smothering numbness. "Then it's all a lie, everything he says, ein?"

"Maybe. Maybe not. What did he say?" she asked, but I wouldn't tell her.

One was never alone in Aghazal's house, nor did one venture out of it alone, and not only because it was safer in company. It was a companionable place. So when I told Aghazal I wished to go alone to visit a shrine of

Wildfire

Katabaton, she was perplexed. But it was not her way to be a strict mistress with me, so she didn't forbid it.

I put on a saffron wrapper and shawl with starting bands of magenta and turquoise stripes, the everyday wear of the women of her house. I threaded beadcoins on the cords of my net cap, including three made of amber and one of carnelian; over the cap I wore a broad-brimmed hat, so Aghazal wouldn't scold me about being too much in the Sun. I put most of my valuables in a big market basket, hiding them under skeins of indigo thread. On top of the thread, I carried thick stalks of moonflower, bearing both the tightly closed flowers and the fruit called thornapples, spiky green seedcases the size of pursenuts.

I talked my way into the palace district, past the guards at the eastern entrance, using the argument of a few beadcoins, and climbed the wide paved street by the canal. Soon I hurried through narrow alleys between high-walled palaces. I had never been so rich or so afraid of thieves.

I found the door in the wall and descended the steep dark stairs until I came out into daylight again in the narrow canyon above the shrine of Katabaton. Katabaton had a grand temple on a high terrace just outside the palace district, with a statue as high as a cypress tree, covered in gold. But she was too high, too grand. She didn't look me in the eye like the Katabaton painted in milky white on the fissured wall of the cave.

I bound the moonflower stalks into a garland for her. The aroma of the blossoms, even closed, was ripe and strong. No one had made an offering since I visited on the last day of the Quickening. I swept the floor with a bundle of gorse, and laid before Katabaton the skeins of indigo thread that Aghazal's grandmother had been generous enough to give to me. It was Katabaton who taught the art of dyeing to tharais, they say in Lambanein. I gave her also a golden bracelet, the one I used to cover the scar on my left hand, and prayed for her to smile on Aghazal and her household.

I found a good hiding place in the cliff wall for my treasures, behind the curtain of bluebind vines. I pulled out crumbling sheets of shale until I made a niche big enough for a glazed pot with a lid, which held my treasures: two golden fingercaps, a golden needle and spindle, a pair of silver dice, an enameled goblet, an alabaster container holding a bag of yellow powder for my arms, the laburnum shawl, and some beadcoins. I hoped it wouldn't be too damp. I closed up the niche with shale. It would be easy to find if you were looking, but who would look?

I was determined to pay more attention to money. Coins had never stuck to my fingers, but no longer. Money was the house Aghazal was building by a lake in Ebanaka; money was food and clothing and shelter;

money was saying yes when you felt like yes, no when you felt like no. Without owning money I didn't even own myself, I could be bought and sold as a bondwoman, or given away as the king had given me away. At least as a whore-celebrant, I was merely rented.

Should I despise myself because I'd exacted pleasure as well as these treasures from my patrons? All those months of longing for Galan's touch, and now the king's, and both denied me, when everywhere else I looked, the gods—Desire or the Moon or Katabaton—held out that gift. That I despised myself for enjoying—and that I had enjoyed—both were undeniable. Enjoyment without joy, hunger that devoured without tasting: I had savored only the first bite, and taken the rest in haste. Even now, thinking about it, I felt the craving. I had subdued that craving by gluttony until I was crammed full, until I sprawled with Kyanos rooting between my legs and my head on Mixin's belly, and the platform became a boat drifting down a canal under trees full of caged birds, toward the oblivion of Sleep.

The Dame was just a memory to me now that I no longer possessed her finger bone, but even as a memory she had the power to reproach. She grew cold, disapproving of my wanton ways. She didn't understand what I'd done, as I hadn't understood why, when Sire Galan already had me, he'd wagered on a maidenhead. Why wasn't I enough?

He'd desired the seduction, not the maid, and once he had her, he no longer wanted her. I'd always thought that was a man's sport, until now. Just that morning Arkhyios Kydos had sent me an invitation with a gift. I'd accepted the gift and declined the invitation. I was done with him.

Gods—I blushed and burned when I thought of what Galan would have done if he'd seen me with those princelings and whores. He might toy all he liked, but he'd spurn me for doing the same. He must never know. But what was one more secret to keep from him, when I'd kept so many?

He would suspect, he would guess something. A captive of the king, riding with the king's men, and never a man touching me? Who would believe that?

I suppose I'd thought if I were blameless, I would not be blamed. But Galan was a jealous man; how well I knew it, though I'd never before given him cause.

I sat on the stairs outside the shrine and pressed the brittle spikes of a thornapple into my palm. Moonflower had to be interrogated; she dodged the truth otherwise. Was it true my portrait had been painted to send to Merle? The limner had made me appear beautiful, modest, prideful, with ardency in one eye. The better to fool a traitor. Unlikely as it was, it was more likely than the explanation I'd been vain enough to imagine, that King Corvus desired to look upon me when I wasn't there. And if that part of my dream was true, then so was the rest of it, and someday soon the king would offer me a way back across the mountains to Galan. How could I think of refusing?

Perhaps we tested each other, Moonflower and I. She was looking for an acolyte and I was looking for dreams I could believe. But I was afraid of her. Two days after eating the paste my eyes still smarted from too much daylight, and my heart wobbled in my chest like a spinning top about to fall. I split open the dried thornapple and offered the brown seeds to a breeze that whistled down the gorge, so Moonflower might take root where it suited her, in the muck by the river or the cracks between boulders.

I asked Aghazal if she could have us invited to a banquet attended by some of King Corvus's cataphracts. She said, "You wish to annoy your benefactor, ein?"

I said, "He doesn't want me for himself. Why does he care what I do?"

"I see," she said. By the next day we had an invitation to dine at the house of a nobleman who had cultivated acquaintances among the king's men. Sire Vafra was one of his guests, and also Sire Quislibet and his armiger, Sire Stria. I was afraid when I saw Sire Vafra. Suppose he made some jest about seeing me as a napkin? He could endanger me with a heedless word, without knowing or caring what he'd done. It was fortunate we were not seated together. I hid behind my painted face, and kept my voice high and lilting, and he didn't appear to know me.

Sire Quislibet had never spoken to me when I was with the king's army—when I was Firethorn, a captive mudwoman. For that alone I chose him: because I could. I culled him from the others with simple Flirtations. We sat on different platforms, and I stared at him until he caught me looking. I quickly looked away, and hid a smile behind my hand. And I turned to the man next to me and touched his arm and laughed in such a way that Sire Quislibet knew I was thinking of him instead. I used to watch the girls in our village when the lads came courting—they seemed to know how to simper and flirt, when I had no notion, and no one seemed to want me. But it proved easy to be coy, after all. Not much sport in it. I discovered I could even blush at will, by sending a wave of heat to my face.

I got up to stroll in the garden, and he followed. I led him a chase, quickening my steps, and running and glancing backward, until I let him catch me in a wisteria arbor. It was furnished with a marble bed, which had a mattress of earth under a smooth coverlet of moss. The nobleman must have had diligent gardeners, to keep moss flourishing in the rainless summers of Allaxios.

While we coupled I uttered Broken Coos and put rows of scratches down his back. I did this with the help of doublewine, not Moonflower.

Later Sire Quislibet reclined against the backrest with his arms behind his head, and I measured his thighs, which I couldn't encompass with my hands. I told him he was strong as an oak, hard as ironwood. I was drunk enough to think myself witty, and he was drunk enough for cheap flattery to be pleasing.

"Ah, you speak my language!" he said.

"You don't recognize me?" I straddled him and leaned close, with my hands on the buttresses of muscle at the base of his thick neck. I smeared him with dirt; I'd scuffed and torn the moss, pushing up against him, and my palms and heels were soiled. I was naked except for the red cord around my waist. He slipped his fingers between the cord and my skin.

"Have we met? I can't even see you," Sire Quislibet said in a complaining tone.

I could see him perfectly well with my left eye. I put my mother finger against the bare patch under his jaw and dug in my sharpened nail to tilt his head back. "Tell your king you met a whore named Alopexin, hmm? Tell him she was good. Wasn't I good?" I moved over his dangle until he began to stiffen again.

He leaned his head on the backrest and closed his eyes. "You won't get anywhere with him. He's made a vow to Rift Warrior not to ease himself with a woman until he retakes Incus."

"That's a pity," I said. "But I won't perturb his vow. Tell him I can sing to him, I know many Lambaneish songs. Surely the god wouldn't object if he enjoyed the memory, the melody of a thrush."

Sire Quislibet was knocking at my door again and I let him in. He wasn't the sort of man who thought it proper for a woman to be on top, and before long he turned me over.

I'd sent the king a message, and I could only hope it had been delivered. I feared Sire Quislibet was too full of his own importance to serve as anyone's go-between.

He failed to send me a gift the next morning. "I could tell he was a boor," Aghazal said. "People will think you're not discriminating. Let them come to you, ein? Make them wait and suffer. So much of desire is anticipation."

Sometimes I thought there was nothing left of me but wanting what I did not have, and I was weary of it. Wasn't it better than useless longing to dizzy myself against someone real and solid and heavy and greasy with sweat? But I had rocked on my round heels and driven myself against the man without getting my fill. I hadn't even managed to forget the gardeners, and the destruction of their perfect moss.

Wildfire

Sire Vafra had recognized me after all. He sent me a letter written in god-signs on Lambaneish silk, rolled inside a golden ring. The musicians who carried the message played outside the door all evening. The letter said he had nine more such rings, one for each of my toes, and he would delight to put them on me and lie down and accept my tread, if I would permit him to call. I asked Aghazal what he meant by that, and she said, "He must like the Abasements."

"I think the Abasements are for tharos men to do at tharais women, as in the paintings. Anyway, he's of Incus. They don't do Abasements there, ein?"

"Nevertheless," she said, after she corrected my speech.

I feared Sire Vafra was making an elegant threat. If I didn't acquiesce, he might tell someone, maybe Aghazal, that I'd been tharais—that I was still tharais, for it's a taint that won't wash, they say in Lambanein. She might be Ebanakan, but she couldn't abide tharais; I'd seen her beat the bath servant for stinking, because she swore the dung beetle had eaten onions despite that she forbade her to indulge.

I sent a message back to Sire Vafra, a bouquet of the kind of geranium that means *I await your visit*. He visited the next afternoon while Aghazal was still asleep, and I received him in the dining court under the shade of a portico. Second and Third sang and played for us, and Aunt Cook sent a niece bearing a plate of stuffed mice.

Sire Vafra was too polite to get precipitously to the point, as he'd done when I was tharais. He sat cross-legged on the platform and took my right foot onto his lap to peel off my shoe-stocking. He put gold rings on my toes, one by one, and scratched my tender arch as if he were a Lambaneish-schooled man. I pressed my sole against his groin and felt his answer.

"Your musicians were very—"

"Did you enjoy them?"

"Loud, I was going to say." I waggled my toes, admiring the rings, and he breathed harder. I took my foot away.

Sire Vafra began to stammer, asking if I would consent to his visits, and be his alone—if I would agree not to go out—he hated to think of me . . .

I said, "Tell the king to come himself next time, eh?" Suddenly sure, quite sure, he was on his sovereign's business. And pleased by it.

"He can't visit here."

"Of course he can, and it's time he did. All Allaxios thinks him a eunuch."

Sire Vafra encircled my ankle with his hand. "Dreamer, I've had such dreams of you. These rings are mine, from me—do you think you could—"

I pulled off my shoe-stocking and offered my left foot. "The rings are yours? I thought they were mine."

I took his rings and sent him away unsatisfied, and he returned the next day and the next, asking how I could refuse him when I'd let Sire Quislibet prick me twice, and the man boasted incessantly of how he'd gotten under the dreamer's skirts for free. As far as I could tell, Sire Vafra's infatuation wasn't feigned. Nevertheless, I liked to think the king sent him to report on my doings, or to serve as a witting or unwitting go-between.

Sire Vafra gave me a new wrapper of sky blue silk shot with indigo, and I taunted him by saying it matched the king's eyes, and he should thank his master for such a thoughtful gift, for I would gladly wear his colors. Sire Vafra protested it was his gift and his alone, and I professed not to believe him. I told him I dreamed often of the king, which was another message I hoped he would carry. These small torments seemed to be the kind of Abasements Sire Vafra sought, though they weren't on the list.

Aghazal praised me for acquiring such a persistent and generous admirer, but in the next breath she reprimanded me for neglecting the Taxonomies and the poets; no doubt Second had complained. I said they put me to sleep, because I was always so tired. She said, "Do you think I'm not weary? A younger Sister shouldn't be idle when her older Sister is working so hard to fill fifty open mouths." She did indeed have many mouths to feed, though perhaps not so many as fifty.

I said, "Why should I master the Taxonomies? It's easy to get pricked, ein? These men don't care what lists I know."

It was the first time I'd seen Aghazal angry with me. She said our art was harder than I thought—every fool made that mistake, because any fool can couple, ein?

She said that after long practice a painter may have sublime moments—maybe even a whole day—when every stroke of the brush is flawless; a musician may discover a song in the act of playing it for the first time, and its every note will be inevitable and exact. So too a whore-celebrant may achieve, for herself and her patron, moments of perfection. It was for such moments that the arts—all arts—were sacred.

But mastery must be learned, even by the gifted. There comes a period of great difficulty when too much learning seems to get in the way. One understands what one can't yet do. That was why I liked moonflower and patrons without discernment, she said. So I didn't have to notice my shortcomings. So they wouldn't.

I offered her five more golden toe rings—I'd already given her three. She wasn't mollified. I understood how I'd insulted her, so I groveled, flinging myself on her bed on my belly and stroking her shin. I begged her pardon so elaborately that I teased a laugh out of her.

I said I would study hard, and be guided by her wisdom, and try to emulate her, and she said, "Let me make arrangements for you to enjoy a few knowledgeable-pleasurable men. If you find that you prefer brutes and youths after all, well, that is your taste. At least you'll know the difference."

The first was her patron Krinean, who claimed to find me delectable, and gave me a necklace of bites and another of gold with citrines and blue sapphires; a second man she chose for his endurance, to teach me patience; a third for his elegance, to teach me delicacy. They were all most kind, but without moonflower I couldn't forget myself, or cease worrying that they'd think me a poor artisan compared to other whore-celebrants they'd enjoyed.

Six men in less than a tennight, after a lifetime in which I'd had only two, and one of them against my will. I was embarked. And the moonflower dream was just a dream, and King Corvus wasn't going to visit. He probably counted the fifteen golden beadcoins and the seventeen of silver a small price to be rid of my importunities, my presumption that he owed me something. By now I knew what my fee was worth, and the only surprise was that Aghazal had agreed to take me for such a small amount. But she was a shrewd judge of odds; already she'd gotten more from me than the king had paid.

I visited Aghazal in her bedchamber when she woke up in the afternoon, to show her my new gift. The last man had sent a poem comparing me to morning dew, along with a shawl of the gauze called morning dew, so thin and fine it could be drawn through the narrow compass of a finger ring. I asked Aghazal if this meant he found me cold and wet, which made her roll about on the bed laughing.

Often we talked and laughed this way, in the morning when she came home too tired to sleep, or in the afternoon when she liked to linger in bed awhile before she had to bustle. Now she sighed and got up, and I stayed there surrounded by her bedclothes. The day was still and hot. Her windows were shuttered. I could hear bees droning and smell the incensier shrub planted in a pot outside her window. I hitched my wrapper above my knees and spread my arms to cool off. Hair stuck to the back of my neck. Aghazal was in her bath, where I should go. I fell asleep instead.

Adalana woke me, tugging my wrapper to cover my legs. "Get up! He's here!" she said.

I sat up, groggy, and combed my hair with my fingers. "Sire Vafra?"

"Your benefactor," Adalana said in a loud whisper. She knew it was important, but she was too young to know why.

"Run and tell him I'll attend shortly, ein? And see what Aunt Cook can give him."

But King Corvus had followed her into the room. He stood looking at the furnishings: the paintings on the wall, the carvings on the legs and backrests of Aghazal's bed, all beautifully made, all on the usual subject. There were no chairs; he sat on the bed and it took strength of will for me not to jump out of it. I knelt instead and touched my forehead to the mattress, and then sat as gracefully as I could manage in the pose they called the Chaste, with my feet hidden. I regretted that I was wearing a shabby, rumpled wrapper, when his surcoat of indigo linen was so stiff and crisp.

"So," he said.

I loved to see him cast about for something to say.

"This is where you sleep?"

As he spoke in the High, I did too. "It's Aghazal's room. The other Sisters and I, we stay in the room of Aghazal's mother. I just lay down for a rest." Only a whore would sleep in the afternoon—I thought I saw him thinking that.

"You'll need your own room if I'm to visit you."

"Are you to visit me?"

"My spies tell me there are rumors I'm a eunuch."

"I have heard that. Also the rumor of a secret vow. That one I believed."

"I shall disprove both rumors." He wasn't looking at me as he said so. His hands were still. In Lambanein people gestured when they spoke. It was disconcerting that he did not.

"Even the true one?"

He looked at me with a bland expression.

I called out, "Second, will you see what has become of the refreshments for our guest?" That fetched Tasatyala out of hiding outside the door. I didn't worry about her overhearing our conversation. No one in the house was fluent in the High, though Aghazal knew a few words of it.

"I look frightful." I smoothed my hair, trying to make it lie flat. A man ought not to see a whore in disarray until after he beds her; he likes to think he is the cause of it.

"Would you care to go to the dining court? There might be a breeze."

He declined.

Tasatyala returned with a table-tray, which she put on the bed between us. Aunt Cook had sent us a licked course of mint and lemon. Something more elaborate was no doubt on its way. Food must be served to guests, no matter how inconvenient their arrival. Tasatyala called Zarfatta to take away the plates when we were done, and went on watching. Aghazal had abandoned the guest to her younger Sisters.

"Would you care to hear a song?" I asked the king. "My Sisters can play for us."

"I had in mind the song of a thrush," he said.

I sent Tasatyala for wine. "And then leave us alone!" I added in Ebanakan. I'd learned a few words in that language, mostly suitable for quarreling.

At last we had wine on the table-tray and were alone in the room. It seemed the king had gotten at least one of my messages. He was here at my bidding, but I wasn't sure what to do with him.

I'd boasted of my usefulness as a thrush, but the last time I'd told the king something useful, I was dreaming and he never heard it; now I told it all again. "Have you heard about Arthygater Keros and her singer? She took one as a lover; it is a scandal. That's why her mother is offering her to the Starling. Though he hasn't answered yet. Perhaps she'll run away with the musician."

"Do you know the name of this singer?"

"Arkhyios Kydos didn't say. But I can find out. There was some talk of cutting the poor fellow's throat or cutting off his sacs. But it seems they're leaving him alone for now, letting him amuse Keros. As the damage is done."

"What damage? Lambaneish have no honor to be damaged. The men duel over poems while the women accommodate anyone they fancy."

I flushed and looked away from him. One would think he'd sent me to Aghazal's to test my virtue. "You dishonor your wife, saying such things about Lambaneish women." Even if they are true.

"Don't speak of her," he said.

I sipped from my goblet of green glass, and tried to breathe. I put the glass down and hid my mouth behind a hand, saying, "Please forgive me."

He made a small gesture: Say no more about it. And after a pause, he said, "Is that all?"

"All of what?"

"You've been here two tennights, and that's all you have to tell me? That Princess Keros lost her maidenhead—supposing she still had it—to some sort of rumormonger, some singer?"

"I heard this from her brother, from a prince of the kingdom, a grandson of the arkhon," I said, and was dismayed that my voice shook.

He said nothing, and in the silence I had time to hear how foolish I sounded. I released the breath I'd been holding. I couldn't lose what I never had, therefore I couldn't lose his good opinion. Once I'd thought I had it, but I must have been mistaken. I said, "I had a dream, a true dream, I think."

"Indeed?"

"I dreamed your—I dreamed the Starling received a likeness of me, the very same one the limner painted. And he thought I was Princess Careless, Keros, and desired to marry me. I crossed the Kerastes, the Ferinus, with a

429

great dower treasure, and an escort of Ebanakan guardsmen clad in red, and when we arrived in Lanx, the Starling welcomed me with a kiss of peace."

The king stared at me, and I knew she hadn't lied. Moonflower hadn't lied.

"And then?" he said. He drank from his goblet and put it down on the table-tray, and I refilled it with wine from the glass ewer, pouring without splashing, as I'd been taught; it pleased me to make him wait.

"I woke up. Is that what the portrait was for? Why didn't you tell me?"

"We saw no reason you should fret about something that might never happen. We sent a messenger, but the embassy is chancy—all Incus is in an uproar, and armed men are roving everywhere." He leaned forward. "But now we know: the messenger will get through and you'll stand before Merle with red-clad guards at your back. I'd hardly dared hope for it."

I hadn't meant to mislead when I told the dream that way; I thought it made a better tale. It never occurred to me that he might take such comfort from it. I raised the same objection I had in my dream. "Suppose he marries me, what then? The Starling knew a real princess of Lambanein once, and he won't be fooled by me."

This time the king didn't admit there would be no need for me to charm his brother, because his brother was to die. He said, "You think not? I think you'll do very well. You're already so accomplished that princes of the kingdom dote on you. I daresay Merle will not be difficult."

I trusted Moonflower more than I trusted the king. Of course he concealed his intentions from me; it was a vile thing to kill a brother.

The day was hot, but I was cold, goosefleshed. The king took off his surcoat so as not to wrinkle it, but left on his hose and thin muslin shirt. I said, "Servants are everywhere, hmm? They see what you do, or don't do. Without servants, nothing can be said to have occurred. I think you should bite me here, along my forearm, where it will show." I held my left arm in front of his face, so he had to look; I showed him my palm and inner arm, powdered yellow from wrist to elbow. "Five stings: here here here here and there."

I was the whore-celebrant Alopexin; that was why I could speak to him that way. And my whorish heart was tried when he took the thin skin of the crook of my elbow between his teeth, and nipped the scarred skin at my wrist and three places in between. He knew the trick of biting hard enough to leave a mark without drawing blood. I groaned. My hands were in fists and I drove my nails into my palms.

When he looked up his eyes were despairing, and his mouth and the black hairs of his beard and mustache were smudged with yellow powder. He said, "I'd forgotten how it tasted."

CHAPTER 30

The Hunt

asps crawled on the rind of the melon we'd eaten for breakfast. In the shade of the portico, Adalana and I copied a list of Permissible Causes of Duels, including the Insulting Poem and Insolent Staring. I knew better than to ask Tasatyala questions, such as how long does it take for a look to become a stare? It was an accomplishment that she'd memorized so many of the Taxonomies at her age; understanding them would take years.

My stylus seemed to be writing without any effort on my part, going swiftly along. I never felt awe toward the Lambaneish syllabary as I did for the godsigns of Incus; yet they were beautiful in their way, the little dancers.

I smelled the clay and the sweet decaying melon and the flowers under the Sun in the courtyard, and felt a surge of love, of Fellow Feeling for my Sisters. I heard Aunt Cook Angadataqebay swearing in the kitchen, as she often did, first in Lambaneish at a tharos servant, and then in Ebanakan, "Shit on you, grandmother!"—a curse addressed to the squat wooden protector of the kitchen, a goddess brought all the way from Ebanaka. Aunt Cook gave offerings to the statue daily, but she also screamed at her whenever food burned or a pot cracked on the fire. My Fellow Feeling swelled to encompass the tharos servant and Aunt Cook and the wooden goddess too, who surely did bless the kitchen, for the food was always good.

When we were done copying, I asked Second, "May we practice now?" We three younger Sisters were trying to master a difficult song in the middle of the Epic of Oxys and Pachys, where the bride Eikenain sings of her Lightning Passion for a man whose name she doesn't know, while he—Pachys—hides in the garden, trying to catch a glimpse of her. He is equally smitten; mischievous Peranon has seen to that. I'd understood none of this, of course, when I saw the epic enacted on the night of the White Petals banquet.

Tasatyala danced Eikenain, wearing bells around her wrists and ankles, and I was Pachys, while Adalana played and sang the part of the nightingale, who is Peranon disguised. I didn't take offense when Second and Third

431

laughed at my mistakes, but began to mock myself, turning the Lover into an oaf and his yearning song into bluster. I strutted and stumbled, pretending to be drunk, and the clowning awakened Sire Rodela, who hummed with pleasure and stretched my legs. Adalana played faster and faster, and I demonstrated prowess—mine and Sire Rodela's—by jumping back and forth across the narrow pool that divided the courtyard, over the carp and the sleepy, tolerant meneidon, between the two bronze gazelles. How long could I leap without stumbling, and how fast? That was the joy of it. Adalana took up her flute made from the wingbone of a swan, and played a high whistling nightingale song. Wasps followed me as I danced, as though I were sweet as honey, and I thought I'd never fall.

On the morning of the arkhon's Hunt, a cat jumped through the open window and woke us up by walking across the bed I shared with Second, Third, and Mother Yafeqer. It was still dark, but time to rise, and Tasatyala dutifully got up, and rousted Adalana, and I turned over onto my belly and pulled a shawl over my head. I'd stayed late at a banquet and earned a chance to sleep. But the cat sat on the small of my back and kneaded me with his claws. He felt heavy and hot, a purring brazier. I told him to go away and he did, leaping to the windowsill and down into the courtyard. But soon I felt him treading about my head, and I lifted the shawl to see him carrying a large dead crow in his mouth. The cat placed his offering on the bed with pride. The bird was still warm.

I went to wake up Aghazal's brother Kabara, who slept in the entrance hall. "I need you to take a message now," I told him. "And if anyone tries to catch you, smash it up before they can read it, ein?" I gave him a writing tablet with the message scratched in godsigns on the clay: They will try to kill him today. "Take this to the Court of Tranquil Waters, to the king's servant Garrio. Do you remember him? He came with me the day Aghazal took me in. He has a beard, grizzled, with more white on the chin than on the sides, but his eyebrows are black. He has furrows across his forehead. Ask for him, everyone knows him there. Tell him this comes from the king's dreamer. No, never mind. Just say Garrio. Garrio, ein?" I wrote on the clay the four signs that made Firethorn. As an afterthought I cut a lock of my hair and wrapped it around the quill of a crow's feather, and pressed them into the clay. The boy couldn't speak the High; Garrio knew little Lambaneish.

Kabara ran off and I worried. Perhaps I should have gone myself. But no, the boy could run faster. The king received so many messages daily, I feared he might ignore mine, and furthermore I doubted Kabara would be admitted quickly to his presence. Therefore Garrio. But Garrio would be fussing over his master's garments—useless fripperies for a man going hunting.

Wildfire

Likely they'd try during the Hunt, in the arkhon's tame forest, among the captive animals. I knelt before a moonflower in the dining court and made a libation of blood and doublewine, and I prayed to Moonflower—though I was forewarned that she had a strange way of answering prayers. I'd prayed for a true dream of Galan, and she'd shown me King Corvus sitting on a high terrace in a surcoat embroidered with pomegranates: a dream false in most particulars, but true in every way that mattered.

I begged her now to send another true dream of the king, that I might give him a clearer warning than the one the cat had given me. I swore that if she helped me, I'd submit to her instruction whenever she was offered, no matter how foolishly she made me behave.

I plucked from the moonflower a dried thornapple that had split into four neat sections, and shook nine dark seeds into my palm. I ground them up and steeped them in hot water and drank the brew down.

All this I did while Aghazal slept. By the time she awoke I was dressed and ready for the Hunt. The tharais servant had arranged my hair on wicker ram's horns that curved around my ears, and added white orchids for gaiety, so that it looked as if butterflies had landed there. I sat on the marble bench and watched Aghazal bathe. Happiness burned in her like oil in a lamp, and I didn't know why. Though I sat still, I felt I was rushing with wind in my ears. My throat was parched. Aghazal stood before me, asking some question, with water in silver beads all over her skin and hair. In my webeye she looked far away.

Aghazal and I sat in a pavilion in the royal hunting park, in the dappled shadow of marble lattices and oak trees. The pavilion was in the treetops, raised high on eight carved pillars. From time to time the trees would be shaken by a passing wind, and the stiff oak leaves would shiver like brass cymbals. We surely had climbed a ladder to get up there, though I couldn't remember it.

There were servants, two tharos women and a napkin. But no men as yet; they were hunting, and if they desired refreshment or repose they could find it at our pavilion or another. We would see nothing of the chase here, but we weren't required as witnesses. The noblewomen, sitting in arcades around a large pen in the park, would watch the culmination of the hunt. Beaters would drive the game into this pen so hunters could slay the beasts and not a one would escape.

But now was the time for stalking and the chase, for testing the cunning, courage, endurance, and strength of man and beast, man against beast. That's how they would kill him. No one to blame for it.

The ceiling of the pavilion was tiled blue, and we sat on a platform on cushions of saffron silk. "You're quiet," Aghazal said. She knew I had moonflower in me; she had only to look at my squinting eyes, each huge pupil ringed with the thin colored band of iris. She sighed, and an attentive servant saw her tiny gesture, and set before us a platter with apricots and sugared almonds. "I forgot it was boring," she said, and I felt as if she'd jabbed me with a thorn. But it didn't hurt.

Today Aghazal smelled nourishing, like baking bread, though she was wreathed and garlanded in honeysuckle. She nibbled on an almond, and I wanted to lick the salt from her lips, which were stained plum purple. She couldn't mistake how I stared at her, and she grinned without hiding her mouth, and went to the door to call a nephew who waited below. "See if you can find Kabara, ein?" She had been vexed with me, perhaps, for sending Kabara with a message of my own, but I had an important patron, I could do such things.

By the time the nephew came back with Kabara, I'd forgotten he was ever sent. Aghazal wrapped one of her rings in an oak leaf and tied it with a magenta thread pulled from her shawl, and sent Kabara off with it, who knows where. On another day I would have tried to find out what they whispered about; it was a game I played with Aghazal, to try to guess the object of her love. Now I didn't care. Kabara had given me a glance and a nod before he left. He had delivered my message.

Mox led me through the tiny Kerastes, steep mossy crags only twice my height, with rivulets instead of rivers. He held me by a leash around my left wrist. Mox was dead, fallen into an icy crevasse, but I'd forgotten that.

We crouched on a boulder and a chamois stood on a peak above us, balanced on delicate hooves, trembling, listening. He leapt away. I held my breath and heard what the chamois had heard, something running through the woods in haste. It was the king in red hunting leathers, wearing a crown of antlers with velvety tines. The antlers looked an awkward burden, but he ran with the swift grace of a stag, dodging trees and ducking to avoid branches, so I saw he was used to the heft and breadth of his crown. His leathers were spotted with sweat. *Prey, protect him.* He was Prey on his mother's side. Why did Prey Hunter have the body of a man and the head and antlers of a stag? Why didn't the avatar appear as a wolf, a hunter rather than one who runs from hunters? I thought I almost understood. Because man is both.

The king ran on, out of my sight. I looked for his hunters, that I might know whom to blame when he was killed. They came on horseback, three men armed with leaf-bladed spears bound to their wrists with long cords. In Lambanein too the gods forbid weapons that leave the hand. But Mox spoke up scornfully, saying the leash was a cowardly cheat. Sire Rodela took a grass stem from between his teeth and agreed, saying in Corymb they'd be ashamed to use a spear taller than a man for hunting. And soon they were talking about why it was better to hunt with dogs than pards, such an odd Lambaneish custom.

The first rider was one of the arkhon's sons, Arkhyios Kyparisos, whose name I'd seen written on the wall in Aghazal's house. The second rider was an Ebanakan guard, and the third a royal huntsman, and behind him on a special saddle sat the beast he served, a pard, a great lanky golden cat with black spots, wearing a red collar, a chain, and a cap to blind him. The riders' horses were spotted too, all of them dappled gray.

So swiftly they followed the king-stag that they vanished while Sire Rodela was still talking about his favorite gazehound bitch. I begged Mox to let go of the leash and he ignored me. The forest gave me a gift: there by my right hand, in a crevice in the boulder, a swallowwort grew with bright yellow flowers and leaves of fresh green. I rubbed yellow sap in my eyes until they began to smart.

Moonflower gives permission to fly. I hadn't known that before. I could swoop and soar, but I couldn't get away from the thin red cord around my wrist. The Sun was a bronze gong, her light so loud and shivering my sharp left eye was blinded by it. I landed on a tree limb, hunkered down in the leaf shadow, and my webeye saw a panther under a thicket. He was dappled black on black with rosettes having five petals. His eyes were veiled, but his head turned as he sniffed the air. From time to time his servant let him lick butter from his hand. The riders drove the king-stag down the narrow deer track toward the waiting panther. He jumped downhill from crag to boulder, running now without reckoning where, his breath hawing in his throat. Kyparisos's horse slid down a scree slope on his haunches and staggered back to his feet.

The keeper took the veil from the panther's eyes and showed him the prey. The panther surged from hiding, so fast, and in three leaping strides took the stag down. The beast was trained to obey his keeper, to earn his food rather than take it by right, and he let the men rob him of his due.

They hung the king-stag from a tree, from the same bough I perched upon. They took the tongue and testicles first, and set them aside as an offering to Prey Hunter. They slit the belly to spill the guts, and I felt a gust of warmth. Dogs lapped at the blood and beggars fought over the offal. The hunters cut down their prey when the blood had drained, and divided the body on its hide. The panther was rewarded with the liver and bellows. Arkhyios Kyparisos claimed one forequarter and Prince Merle the other. The First of Ardor took five ribs, and the First of Lynx five more. A pack of

Wolves received the right hindquarters, and the left went to Sire Galan. Queenmother Caelum took the heart and head and crown of thirteen tines for herself, but she left the crow—that was me—the eyes.

Up on the roof of Agazhal's house was a porch with a shallow slope, where Aunt Cook Angadataqebay and Grandmother Lagas sometimes spread plants to dry, or retired from the hubbub below to shell beans. Now I sat there alone. It was dawn, and the light was green-gold. I turned my arms this way and that, and uncovered my legs. I found bruises on my arms, my throat, and scratches on my belly and thighs. My wicker horns were missing. There were limp orchids in the snarls of my hair. My quim throbbed and ached.

Aghazal had told me the king was alive and I'd come up here to savor it. I was the last to hear the story of how Arkhyios Corvus, creeping through the undergrowth in pursuit of a bear, was mistaken for a deer by a huntsman who unleashed a panther on him. The panther tried to rip out the king's throat and rake his belly with his claws, but the king was wearing a steel gorget around his neck and a cuirass under his hunting leathers. And to everyone's amazement, said Aghazal, the king too had claws, steel claws worn on each fist. He jabbed the panther under the chin and pierced the jugular vein. Arkhyios Kyparisos speared the panther's keeper at once for being so careless.

Arkhyios Corvus was unharmed, and insisted on continuing the Hunt. Of black game he took a bear, two wolves, and the panther that had attacked him; of red game two stags, nine roe deer, an ibex, three foxes, and a lynx. The bear and two of the roe deer were killed during the chase; the rest he vanquished in the pen, in the final slaughter. Arkhon Kyphos rode out first, they said, and killed until he was tired. Then his sons and grandsons had their turn, and then his sons-in-law, including Arkhyios Corvus, and lastly the other guests. I was glad I didn't see it, or remember seeing it.

But there was a foul taste in my mouth and I hadn't enough spit to spit it out. I rinsed my mouth with doublewine, and poured a libation on the green roof tiles for Moonflower. I'd begged her for a sight of Sire Galan, and she had granted it. Now I'd have to fulfill all the vows I'd made, to give Crux Moon a silver moon when I returned to Incus, and to take moonflower whenever it was offered. But gods, she was a harsh teacher; she asked a high fee. I lay down with my back to the Sun and covered my eyes with my arm and trembled.

I'd seen Sire Galan from above, foreshortened, while he waited under the branch for his share of the king-stag. He wore old hunting leathers stamped with a green fletch pattern, and a velvet hat with a golden gyrfalcon broach.

Wildfire

The gyrfalcon held in its talons the quill of a peacock feather showing a brilliant eye, the blind eye of Chance. Galan's hair needed cutting. I remembered exactly how it felt to put my hands in his hair: the smooth curves of his skull, and springing curls between my fingers.

When Rowney had told me in my first moonflower dream that Galan lived, I had wondered, but I had not *known*. Now I knew. He was alive. Alive.

I received no gifts that morning from admirers, so I didn't learn who had marked me. That was insulting. But it was worse that King Corvus gave me nothing. I waited all day before an invitation came to dine with him in his quarters, which was more recompense than I expected. I chose to wear a magenta wrapper, in honor of Desire, and my morning dew shawl, tinted lavender like the inside of a mussel shell. My net cap was threaded in beads of turquoise and gold, and I wore a garland of moonflowers.

Uncle Zubana and Marasa pulled me in the blue cart up to the foregate of the Court of Tranquil Waters. "Tomorrow?" Uncle Zubana asked in Ebanakan with a knowing look.

"Maybe maybe," I said in his language, and turned up my palms to show him I didn't know.

I recalled very well how I'd first entered the king's residence, tottering on stilts and wearing a heavy horse mask. This time I was more graceful. Garrio hurried me along the colonnade, and I was struck again by the shabbiness of the courtyard, the trampled weeds and the pool full of dead leaves and green scum. I took Garrio's arm to make him slow down. My breath came quick as if I'd climbed the terraces myself instead of riding in a cart.

"I can hardly tell it's you," Garrio said.

He took me to the king's bedchamber, and I was dismayed to find Divine Aboleo sitting beside King Corvus on the platform. I sat across from them. I refrained from celebrant tricks, and kept my head down, looking at how perfectly the pleats of my wrapper fanned out across my lap.

King Corvus said, "You had a warning. Who told you?"

"A cat killed a crow and brought it to my bed yesterday morning."

"But you knew where and when," Divine Aboleo said.

"It doesn't take a priest to read a sign as plain as that."

"You have my thanks." The king touched the hollow at the base of his throat, where his gorget had protected him from the panther's teeth. There was such grace in the gesture that it gave me a chill.

I said, "Arkhyios Kyparisos planned it."

"But he speared the panther, and then the panther's keeper," the king said.

I said, "I heard you dispatched the panther all by yourself, with bearclaws."

"You mustn't believe everything you hear," the king said. "Aboleo had the bearclaws; he never hunts with anything else. I had a smallsword, but the panther was on me before I had time to draw it."

The priest said, "The beast was already dead when Kyparisos put a spear into him."

I said, "He had to kill the keeper, you see? So the man couldn't be questioned."

Divine Aboleo said, "Why do you think it was Kyparisos?"

"I saw him in a dream. I saw the arkhyios and his men chase the king, drive him down a trail to where a partner, a panther lay in wait. You ran, Corvus Rex Incus, and you wore the antlers of Prey Hunter himself. The panther brought you down and killed you, and the men divided you. Like a stag. Praise the gods that my dream was only half true."

The Auspex wanted to know all I had seen, and I told it as clearly as I could. King Corvus didn't flinch when I described how they'd cut off his tongue and sacs and head before they flayed him. When it came to Sire Galan, I lied, saying that a man of Corymb, someone I didn't recognize, had been apportioned the left hindquarter of the king-stag.

"What happened after the dream?" Divine Aboleo said.

"Then? Why nothing, nothing further."

"You learned nothing from the men who visited your pavilion?"

"I don't know. What men?"

Divine Aboleo gave an ugly little laugh. "I heard you were drunk, and refused no one. Didn't you keep a tally of how many you bagged during the hunt?"

Oh it was worse, far worse, than I had imagined. I had wondered who, and failed to wonder how many. My belly clenched and I tasted bile. Surely Aghazal would not have let me do such a thing—unless she had deserted me for a tryst with her beloved, the cause of her latest Lightning Passion. I felt betrayed by both of them, Moonflower and Aghazal.

Suppose the priest was lying. Such tales as this were often told of whores; they were not always true.

The king turned away. Should I be glad the king was furious with me, that he could be shocked? He commanded his expressions too well to show it crudely; his face was still, but there were two fine vertical lines between his eyebrows. I found bitter sport in leaning toward him over the table-tray, as if eager to persuade, thereby forcing him to lean away. I said, "Moon-flower showed me your enemy. She demanded a price—I'm sure you don't think the price too high, since you think me cheap. Yet I paid dearly for it. I hope it's of some use to you."

"I have so many enemies," he said.

I could have spat at him for saying that, and for the way he said it, but my mouth was dry and my throat hurt as if I'd swallowed a pin. I was gratified when Divine Aboleo addressed him with impatience, as a teacher speaks to a sulky pupil. "Yes, and it behooves you to know who your enemies are. Don't you see this vision is of Incus, and the armies that will rend your king-dom apart? The Wolves took their own portion, which means they have turned on your mother already, or soon will. That's no great surprise, I grant you, and neither is Merle. But I didn't foresee this man Kyparisos." He turned to me, saying, "What do you know of him?"

The Auspex knew his trade; he had read the signs and discovered the true meaning of my dream, when I had not. Now I must speak of Arkhyios Kyparisos, and speak of him at such length that they'd forget questions I didn't want them to ask. I recalled the arkhyios's position on the tree of the arkhon, and wisps of gossip, things I'd heard once and thought forgotten. "His age is—let me see—he's at least six hands old, I believe. He's the third son of the arkhon's third wife—which means Arthygater Katharos is his full sister. I myself have never seen this Kyparisos, except in the dream, but I've heard he has a voice like a bullfrog, and puffed-up pride to match. He is a Second Exegete in the Ministry of the Outside, in charge of the protocols for Ebanakans. It's rumored he went so far as to learn their language—that shows ambition, doesn't it? He might have cultivated friendships with some of the arkhon's Ebanakan guard, hmm? In my dream, a guardsman rode behind him."

The priest said to the king, "I wonder if Kyparisos attempted your life with his father's approval."

I said, "To win his father's approval, perhaps? People have reason to think the arkhon finds King Corvus troublesome."

Divine Aboleo shook his head. "I suspect Kyparisos of greater ambitions. He may have decided it's better to rule in a foreign land than to wait for his father's chosen son to ascend to the throne and garrote him."

"It's a quaint custom, killing one's brothers," said King Corvus. "I should have done the same when I became king."

I asked, "If the king-stag was Incus, then why didn't Consort Ostrakan and Arthygater Katharos come forward to claim a portion?"

"No doubt they'll partake of Merle's," said the priest.

I said, "The sons have no money of their own, no lands, no men. If Kyparisos is ambitious, he'll need gold and soldiers—who better to turn to than his sister Katharos?"

"Ostrakan cannot support us all," said the king. "He offered me half a million in gold to raise an army, and perhaps as much as fifty thousand to Merle for a dowry."

"It costs nothing to promise," I said. "And what did you promise in return?"

He would not answer that question.

"I only wonder," I said. "The arthygater uses many shuttles in her loom, each with thread of a different color. It could be that Kyparisos wanted to pluck one of these threads from his sister's weave, knowing that so long as King Corvus is alive, he has a rival for gold enough to buy an army."

"It should be easy for you to make the acquaintance of Kyparisos," Divine Aboleo said. "Try to find out."

It was not as easy as he thought. I had never attended a banquet in the Court of the Sons. Their entertainments were not to Aghazal's taste, and she was too respectable—too staid—to be popular with the arkhon's sons. But I too was acquiring something of a reputation, and it must be admitted it was not respectable at all.

I may have flinched. Divine Aboleo said, "Well? Have you some objection?"

"If I might suggest—should we give him more cause for curiosity? About the king's patronage. If he should think the king confides in me—"

King Corvus said to me, "I haven't forgotten the man from Corymb who received the left hindquarter of the stag. I find it strange that you didn't recognize him. He wasn't one of the Firsts from the army of Corymb?"

"Not one I knew."

"How old was he? What was his clan?"

I tried to mince the truth with a few lies. "He was beardless, as is the fashion among the young warriors of Corymb. I couldn't see the tattoo on his cheek. Perhaps he was one of King Thyrse's bastards; he had so many, I didn't know them all."

"What color was his hat?"

"It was dark." How I wished they had served food. A woman could hide behind the business of eating, holding a hand before her mouth to conceal her chewing, to hide the trembling of her lips.

"So the dream took place at night?" said the king.

"No. I mean the hat was dark."

"Black?"

"I couldn't tell exactly."

"There, you see she's lying," said the king to his strategos.

"That's of no consequence, since we know what she's lying about: someone she knew, a young man to whom she is loyal. Is it so hard to name him?"

"Sire Galan dam Capella by Falco of Crux," said the king, and Galan's name on his lips made me shiver.

"A harlot should be a better liar," the priest said, and he allowed himself to show amusement by raising an eyebrow.

"You didn't say your blade was a man of such importance," King Corvus said to me.

"I didn't think he was."

Garrio seemed to think that if I was going to be a whore, it was fine so long as I was his king's whore. Or at least that's what I thought he was trying to say, sometime in the third passage of the night, after I'd left the silence of the king's bedchamber—after I'd pulled pins from my hair, and smeared the yellow powder on my arms, and walked into the courtyard with my sandals in one hand and a flask of doublewine in the other.

Garrio and I woke up the horseboys Lame and Chunner, and we all sat in the open door of the stable loft, with the comforting smell of hay and horses prickling our noses. It was easy to guess what the men needed to hear about their king. "I thought he deserved some sleep," I said, and we all laughed. I made them take an oath of secrecy, knowing it for the surest way to spread a tale.

The talk was bawdy, and I thought I heard a resonant doubling of my voice, a rough buzz beneath my shrillness, when I spoke of Sire Vafra and how I wouldn't let him, and of Sire Quislibet, the big boar-bore, and how he'd grunted. I mocked and boasted and they laughed as if I were a man. Was it all the same to them, Firethorn or Alopexin?

There in the Lambaneish night, Mount Allaxios sighed after a hot day, a scented exhalation rising from gardens and watercourses and baked earth. In summer it was hard to believe in winter, and in the existence of the Ferinus. But we believed. We poured out doublewine for the shades of Mox and Lino and Mano and even Chunner's favorite mule, all dead and left behind in the mountains. We got to talking about Wolves, and how the king had sent them scurrying back to the queenmother with their tails tucked between their bony buttocks. I told them about Mox's fight with the Wolf on Boarsback Ridge, and how they ran at each other and collided, and each man claimed the other as prisoner. I got up and used an old ax haft for a sword and a pile of hay for the enemy to show them how Mox fought—

how he gave the man a tap and dodged away, so dainty with his blows. This roused the braggart, Sire Rodela, to show how it should have been done, and we capered all around the hayloft, slaying shadows until the haft broke on a post.

Lame finished the flask of doublewine and we raided the storerooms for another. I drank until I no longer cared, which was exactly what I craved. But it couldn't last.

Garrio and the horseboys chose a gelding for me to ride. The dark streets were empty except for the koprophagais pulling their stinking barrows and wains. As we passed they shuttered their lanterns and stood still, vanishing under the cover of their shawls so as not to offend us with their presence.

Garrio put his hand on a stirrup. "I hate to see you go back to that whorehouse. You deserve better. Didn't you just save the king's life? He'd never have put on the gorget without your message. Divine Aboleo didn't warn him—what good are his auguries if he can't foretell a thing like that?"

"Oh, the Auspex is a fine oracle," I said. "He predicted I'd make a whore, didn't he? I never had a middenhead that I know of, so don't mourn for my lost virtue."

Garrio looked up, smiling. "I won't then."

"Me neither," Lame said stoutly. Chunner, hanging on to the gelding's tail and stumbling after us, was too drunk to say anything.

The king sent a handsome gift the next day: a short cape of black panther fur trimmed with brighter pard fur, tawny with black spots. He didn't send a poem with it.

Aghazal said, "Oh, it's splendid! Tasteful too, with the solid black and the spotted trim." She had the cape over her arm. She'd sought me out in the back courtyard, where I sat in the shade plucking weeds. I had a foul headache. I squinted up at her and said nothing. I wondered that she couldn't see the black fur was spotted too, black rosettes on black.

She went on talking. "A pity it's too hot to wear it; you'll have to wait until winter. Love Concealed, of course. Though if he supposes people don't know already, he's more of a fool than I took him for."

That was one message in the gift, to be sure: the one intended for others. Let them think he'd lost his head or his heart to a celebrant, and broken a vow for a heedless heartless trull who squandered her favors on others. That was an ancient, revered game in Lambanein; whether or not he proved the loser, it would win him sympathy.

Then there was another message, to me. Only the Blood were permitted to wear such furs in Incus; even in Lambanein, they were more suited to royalty than a whore-celebrant. I took the cape as a promise and a reminder that he meant to make of me a counterfeit Keros and send me across the cold Ferinus.

Yet I hoped the gift bespoke real gratitude. There had been one moment when the king had thanked me and touched his throat, and all the bitterness thereafter had not sullied the gesture.

Aghazal hung the cape over the latticework fence and crouched next to me. "Aunt Cook said she sent you for marjoram and mint back in the First Age of the World, and you never returned. What's the matter?"

I shook my head.

Earlier that day I'd squatted beside Moonflower, by the big plant I'd watered with my own blood, and reviled her as Aunt Cook Angadataqebay reviled her kitchen goddess when a pot broke. I called her a false friend, a bitch, and a traitor for having abandoned me when I needed her in the hunting pavilion. I might have said as much to Aghazal, had I been speaking to her.

I'd pissed on the moonflower too. I still didn't know what I'd done or what had been done to me, but I had a strong urge to put a knife up my quim and scrape it clean.

"Ein?" Aghazal sat in the bed of chives and pulled off a round purple flower head and ate it.

I threw a weed at a pile of its fellows, so many dead green soldiers. Grandmother Lagas's eyes were dim these days, or she'd have seen that creeping stinkwort had invaded the marjoram. "I hear, I heard a vile rumor," I said.

"Mmm? About me?"

"About myself. About the day of the hunt. Were you with me in the pavilion?"

"I went to meet a patron elsewhere. You don't remember?"

I shook my head.

"What is this rumor?"

I told her. I didn't look at her as I spoke.

"Ah, I hadn't heard that. Do you trust the one who told you? No? Then why do you believe it?"

"I don't know. I have scratches here, bruises . . . There was at least one. I wish . . . I wish you'd left your uncle with me, or someone. Something to stop it."

"I warned you about Moonflower. She's not trustworthy. Yet you chose her as your mistress instead of me. Or she chose you."

I glared at her. How dare she chastise me when I was the one betrayed?

But she didn't sound vexed; she spoke as one who states a fact, and looked at me with pity. She said, "Ours is a difficult art, with many ways to seek mastery. Your path is not mine, but it seemed to me I had to let you take it, even if you suffered for it."

"I want to know who they are, the man, the men," I said. "I want to piss on them as I pissed on Moonflower."

She laughed. "I see it's tempting to take revenge, but there are more elegant ways to accomplish it—supposing you want to waste your time that way, ein?"

No doubt she meant well, but it was impossible to hear good advice with Sire Rodela's whine boring into my ears like twin augers. I gritted my teeth.

"It's a hazard of the trade," Aghazal said. "Something like this happened to Aeidin once, and she was so outraged she left Allaxios with her go-between on a mule behind her. She came back of course, for her art was wasted on provincials, and now she's more famous than ever. I'll try to find out what happened, what really happened, but if anyone speaks to you of this, you must just say you were doing Moonflower's bidding. Which is the truth. Everyone knows how she is. At least you'll stay away from her from now on, ein?"

"I can't. I need her." Else I was not a seer at all. Else I was blind and useless.

"You'd better apologize then," Aghazal said with a wry smile. "She can't be too pleased you pissed on her."

I didn't think it possible I would laugh, but I did.

CHAPTER 31

Alopexin

 knelt before the moonflower plant in the dining court and asked forgiveness. In my mind's eye I saw Moonflower as a woman with blue-tinged skin and dragonfly wings, dressed in cloth of morning dew. She hovered in the embrace of the plant and her tiny face had an enigmatic expression. I sprinkled dirt on my head and promised not to abuse her again. I had been a servant most of my days, and I knew how to grovel and beg pardon when not at fault, and how to hide my resentment. I buried two golden beadcoins at her feet, and took three more to a jeweler to fulfill my promise to have a silver pendant made for Crux Moon—the fox in the Moon, like the bridle cheekplate I'd seen in a dream.

Moonflower accepted my sacrifice, but exacted a penance: at night she made me restless, and sent me dreams so full of desire I coursed with sweat and moaned, muttered, rolled, and twisted, and awoke rank with the smell of my own secretions and male seed—they called white blood seed in Lambanein. Mother Yafeqer said I couldn't sleep with them anymore, I was keeping them all awake.

Zarfatta took my place in the bed, and I unrolled a thin straw pallet by the long pool in the dining court. Moonflower opened huge white flowers and sent me her fragrance, and I thought it must mean she forgave me, but I didn't forgive her.

In a house full of women, it is well known that many will be called to have their tides at about the same time. In Lambanein that was the cause of some inconvenience, for a tharos woman during her tides was, for five days or so, in a state of being tharais. She had to abstain from coupling, cooking, visiting, and eating from the same dish as the tharos. She had to use a special waste receptacle. She couldn't weave or spin lest she tangle the thread. She wore the tharais shawl.

Tasatyala had her first tides at the same time the blood flowed for

445

Aghazal, her true sister Dasasana, Mother Yafeqer, and Aunt Cook's daughters Waqesa and Zarfatta. It was our good fortune that Aunt Cook was too old to have tides anymore, or there would have been chaos in the kitchen.

Aghazal said that when Tasatyala's tides had ebbed, she would be permitted to attend banquets; she could have patrons and gifts, and dazzle everyone with the grace of her dancing. Aunt Cook made Tasatyala's favorite dishes, and we had a feast in the back courtyard for the women, amidst bright banners of laundry hung out to dry.

In the cool of the evening, the polluted women sat apart, eating from one dish, while the rest of us ate from another. Most of the women in my circle were too old for tides or too young. One was pregnant—Aunt Cook's third daughter, Gazuf, who was fat and stately, and inclined to be morose since her lover had ceased to visit.

Aunt Cook asked me why I never had tides. "Are you with child?"

My hand was halfway to my mouth with a morsel of peppery fish. I put the food down. "No."

Grandmother Lagas said something in Ebanakan. Aunt Cook said, "Ah, I see."

"What? What does she say?"

"She says you have a knot tied around the neck of your gourd, your womb."

Grandmother spoke directly to me, in Lambaneish. "I thought maybe you did it of yourself. So you won't catch a . . ." She gestured as if plucking a feather from the air. "Catch a *fenetari*, a spirit; catch a babe, ein? Like this one did." She patted Gazuf on the belly.

Adalana watched and listened. Her great brown eyes, her upright posture, reminded me of a fawn, wary because her dam has raised her head to seek danger on the wind.

Aunt Cook said, "It's a good trick to close the womb that way; handy for a celebrant, ein?"

To my astonishment I began to cry. I pulled my shawl over my face as I sobbed. Did they all know the shameful thing that had happened to me? I should be glad the Initiates had cursed me, or I might have caught a babe during the Hunt without knowing who had fathered it; I might have returned to Galan carrying another man's bastard.

But I would never have a child growing under my heart.

Grandmother Lagas patted my knee, and Aunt Cook rubbed my back, saying, "Oh what sorrow! Poor thing. I didn't know you couldn't."

Gazuf said, "At least you don't have to bear a child and give it up," and she began to cry as well.

Adalana asked Aunt Cook in a whisper, "Is Gazuf giving away her child?"

446

She whispered back, "If it's a boy, she'll send him to live with Aghazal's sons in Ebanaka. He must grow up properly, ein? Or he'll be a rascal like Kabara."

I dried my face on the shawl, embarrassed now that the rainstorm had passed. "Aghazal has children?"

"Of course. Two boys."

"She doesn't speak of them."

Aunt Cook shrugged.

I said, "When Aghazal is as big like Gazuf, when she showed, what did you do? She couldn't work then, ein?"

"That was when Ostrakan was her benefactor," Aunt Cook said, "We lived well then, not like now with all this debt, all this coin pinching. He used to visit and play with his sons, until he got sick with jealousy. Aghazal swears she didn't give him reason, but you know her, ein? Always the Lightning Passion, and she's blind to anything else while it lasts."

"Ostrakan—the consort of Arthygater Katharos?"

Grandmother Lagas squeezed my knee and leaned close to me. She was tiny but stout, and had smooth skin for her age. Her gray hair, under a net cap, was the only sign she was old enough to be a great-grandmother. "I can help," she said. "I can untie the knot. If you want."

She was a canny old woman to see that I didn't know what I wanted. I hated the barrenness laid upon me by the Initiates of Carnal, but without it I would not have dared follow Moonflower wherever she led.

I was the king's dreamer; if I was not, I was nothing but a whore. The bones were burned, and I could no longer ask the Dame and Na for signs. Moonflower taught me how to summon true dreams instead of waiting for them. But her gift was poisonous. I had submitted myself to her tutelage, but I couldn't risk the life of an unborn child.

If I had behaved scandalously at the Hunt, it was a petty scandal, for Aghazal heard nothing of it from her acquaintances. They gossiped of Arkhyios Corvus's lucky escape, and soon he gave them something new to talk about: his petition to see Arkhon Kyphos was granted at last—for shame, some said, that one of the arkhon's tame beasts had been so discourteous as to attack a guest.

During the audience the arkhon lavished upon Arkhyios Corvus gifts of spices, cloth of gold, and rubies.

The arkhon ceded him lands.

The arkhon offered to adopt him as a son.

The arkhon promised him an army.

The arkhon promised him a wife.

The arkhon promised him nothing, as usual, but implied everything.

In short, no one knew what Arkhon Kyphos had given or promised the king, but these extravagant rumors passed from one courtier to another, and he was praised and flattered by those who had formerly scorned him. And he was envied. The arkhon was stingy with his favors, and what he gave to one, another went without.

Days and nights passed, four, five, six, and the king did not invite me to attend him. I wished he would send a token to show I wasn't forgotten: a poem, a ruby the size of a teardrop, a cowrie shell, a peach, anything. But I had proven myself too vile. He couldn't bear to see me, even to maintain the pretence that he was my patron. I couldn't distinguish the king's contempt from that I bore for myself. It was no consolation to know that the Taxonomies had a name for what I suffered, that famous poets had already described every particular agony of Desire Repulsed by Scorn.

I had long since stopped tying knots in my red cord to tally the days and tennights, but reckoning by the Moon it was more than four months since I'd stood on the precipice and seen Lambanein for the first time, four lifetimes. The passes must be open again. Yet Midsummer came and went unremarked by the Lambaneish and their festivals.

We were preparing for a different celebration, a feast in honor of Tasatyala's coming of age, to be held on the next New Moon. Second Sister was about to enter the second stage of her apprenticeship, which only reminded me of how hurried and inadequate had been my own education. I gave up my daily lessons in favor of sleeping, and no one seemed to notice. I had suitors in plenty, even if they were the sort of men who mistook a few quotes from the Fragments for knowledge of the classics.

It didn't help that Aghazal was joyous these days; it seemed her Lightning Passion was shared. Yet she was discreet, and kept to herself the name of her beloved.

In the late afternoons we Sisters bathed together. While Tasatyala and Adalana chattered like finches, I remained passive under the ministrations of the bath servants: fingers and combs in my hair, hands rubbing oil on my breasts and buttocks or scraping me with the obsidian blade. Firethorn lay slack, adrift in unbearable melancholy; as Alopexin I arose to go forth, moonflowers in my hair, my lips plum and plump, my eyes outlined in green malachite, my face powdered with mica and my arms with saffron-colored dust. Alopexin was busy. I worked.

I had impressed the arkhon's grandsons, Kydos and Kyanos, who were younger and wilder than the patrons of Aghazal. I was invited to banquets where the entertainments tended to be vulgar: cockfights, quail fights, dog

448

fights, drinking contests, and gambling; the poems were lewder; the singers and dancers performed Antics rather than Epics.

In such company I discovered I was a wit, in my way. My Lambaneish improved between the third glass of doublewine and the tenth, and I was mistress of the list of Mockeries, from the Jolly Scoff to the Dry Taunt. I made gibes sharp as the golden fingercaps I'd taken to wearing everywhere, and some bore repeating, and came back to me as poems or aphorisms. But they earned me enemies.

In Incus or Corymb such words between men would have led to duels, but in Lambanein duels were a rarity, and brutal pleasantries the fashion among the young folk. Sometimes I thought, quite smugly, that Sire Galan would have cut a swath through these coxcombs, with his wit and his sword. His honor couldn't be bought with a cheap apologia written by a hired poet.

My own wit was sharpened by contempt. How easily my companions were taken in! No one knew, no one guessed. Sometimes I myself forgot. And sometimes, when I remembered, I felt a thrill of fear—just enough fear to give me pleasure in my own daring. In one man's bed I draped my morning-dew shawl over my head and swore to him I was a hairdresser; the game delighted him. I suspected it would. He told others who had the same tastes.

It amused me to imagine how horrified my patrons would be if they found out my secret; how they would scurry to the priests and spend lavishly to cleanse themselves of the pollution left by my touch. But they would never guess. How could they? For I wasn't tharais, I never had been. I was born tharos, in the valley of Sapheiros, and no one could take my birthright from me for a whim and a trifle, not Zostra or Gnathin or anyone else.

I wouldn't go home with the same man twice. I wouldn't go home with a man at all unless he paid suit properly, sending servants with garlands and gifts and poems written in my honor, and musicians to sing outside the house at night; I liked a man to be eloquent, with words and speaking looks and gestures—or else his tongue should be hobbled in my presence, as if he were overawed. He might sleep on the doorstep as Sire Vafra did, or hammer on the door and wake up Uncle Zubana. Whether a patron was content to conquer for a night, or wanted to conquer my heart, he had to give lavishly or I'd ridicule him for being thrifty-stingy. A man shouldn't trouble his head about money, such a womanish trait.

I collected marks as well as presents: necklaces of bites, neat parallel lines of scratches from sharpened fingernails. The Lambaneish have a single word for the twinned sensation of pain and pleasure: *erotakhos*. They prize it highly. The marks were soon lost, overwritten by new ones, but most of the gifts I kept. Twice I made the journey down to Katabaton's cave, carrying valuables. I also hid my useless divining compass pouch there, and in it the scrip I treasured from Sire Galan, fearing that otherwise I might lose it when I was lost myself in a Moonflower maze. I gave Katabaton garlands of roses and libations of goat's milk. It seemed no one else visited the shrine anymore.

My reputation rose higher among men; not so among women. At Tasatyala's banquet, certain celebrants, supposed friends of Aghazal, wouldn't even speak to me. They thought one could lay claim to a patron by bedding him a few times, and the rest of us should respect such claims. They praised Tasatyala's grace, learning, and respectful demeanor, and her shyness, so appropriate to a maiden, though she was not to be a maid much longer. They mocked my low voice, my ugly webeye, my ignorance of the Odes, and my clumsiness in the dance. They supposed Aghazal must have been in great need of patronage to take such a rude bumpkin as myself as a Sister.

I'd labored hard to prepare for Tasatyala's banquet; I'd given gold too, and plenty of it, to pay for the celebration in honor of my Sister. But I said nothing to contradict Aghazal's guests.

As for Moonflower, my treacherous teacher—in her realm every sense was more sensitive, and every perception entered me more forcefully. It was easy to believe her domain was the true world, and dull day the inferior copy. In those Moonflower nights, I forgot Firethorn. So it wasn't a great hardship that the next day Firethorn forgot much of what Alopexin had said and done.

But after Moonflower dreams it was as if I wore the tharais shawl again; what I saw was dimmed, what I heard muffled. Moonflower leached strength from my limbs and memories from my mind. Once I broke my vow and refused her when she was offered, thinking to spare myself the painful aftermath.

I didn't try again. I couldn't be Alopexin without her. Firethorn wasn't fit for the task.

I saw Moonflower sometimes, with her delicate skin the color of the veins at my wrists, just barely blue. She had a fly at her heels like a dog: Sire Rodela. She'd roused him from his long drowse and he liked to make me jealous. His shade lolled on the bed while I coupled with a patron, and he hissed that Sire Galan had done things I didn't know about when we were in the Marchfield—did I remember Dame Hartura, Sire Farol's wife? Did I remember how she used to shriek during tourneys until her cheeks were scarlet as an apple? It was all for Sire Galan, a proper man, not like some. "I knew all about it," Sire Rodela said, grinning in his lopsided way.

I supposed the shade was lying, but I put my foot to my patron's face and made him bite my instep. I was wonderfully limber when Moonflower was in my blood, I could turn every which way and stay impaled. I was all dry friction and heat, nothing slippery; a man had to stay hard. I said to Sire Rodela, "If you know so much, why don't you say what happened to me at the Hunt?" He only laughed, pleased to keep it secret from me.

But he buzzed other people's secrets in my ears, how this man had cheated his mother of the profits of her dower lands, and that man's wife had been lightened five times by a miscarrier, for she'd sworn at her wedding she'd never give the old goat an heir. Arthygater Katharos would have known how to profit from such tales with a judicious use of threats and promises, gathering more threads for the great pattern she was weaving. To me this petty gossip was useless—nothing of import to tell the king, no secrets worth the coin I spent for them: my health, my pride, my arduous nights.

After Tasatyala's festivity, the musicmaster Skolian came daily to torment us. Aghazal had been honored with an invitation to present an Ode at a banquet to be given by Arthygater Klados, and all four of us Sisters were to perform the enactment. It was to be Tasatyala's first time dancing a role at a palace banquet, and Aghazal had chosen Akantha's Ode to Nephelin to show Second Sister's gifts to best advantage. Skolian was a bully, and I was amazed Aghazal endured him; but it had to be admitted, he sang well enough to make a stone cry. When he rapped me on the knuckles, I threatened to break his brass baton over his head.

I sowed quarrels all around the house. The servants got the worst of my short temper, for they couldn't argue with me, unlike Aghazal's relatives. I accused the tharais bath servant of making an owl's nest of my hair, and pinched her arm hard enough to leave bruises. It irked me when she reminded me of her presence by being clumsy.

It had been more than a tennight since I visited the king in his quarters. I'd seen him only three times since at banquets, always at a distance. "People must be saying he discarded me," I said to Aghazal.

"No, they say he's at war with his vows, or his better judgment. They are wagering on the outcome, and the odds favor you, Sister. He's a Hero, ein? No one wants a Hero with good sense."

"Then someone should tell him so."

*   *   *

Aghazal and I were invited to a banquet in the Court of the Sons by a certain Arkhyios Kenoun, the Exarchos of Granaries in the Ministry of Bounty. He was an older and rather important arkhyios, being the only son of the arkhon's second wife. Aghazal declined to go. The invitation was meant for me, she said. Alopexin's wanton repute had wandered far if it had reached the Inner Palace, but after all, it had been my aim to put myself in a position to learn something useful.

I'd hoped to meet Arkhyios Kyparisos at the banquet, but I was disappointed. Despite a public proclamation of his bravery in slaying the treacherous panther, it was thought his father was displeased with him. No one dared invite him anywhere.

Arkhyios Kenoun did me the honor of inviting me to share his platform, with his younger half brother Arkhyios Kyprinos and a celebrant named Pantalops, a beautiful creature. As we dined we watched an obscene antic performed by three tharos men in goat masks, a tharais woman, and a donkey, but the guests paid little attention to it. The brothers gossiped about Arkhyios Kyparisos. They wondered what he would die of. If one of the arkhon's sons challenged him outright, the arkhon executed him outright by sending him a basket of asps; but one who defied him secretly died by secret means. His priests wielded curses that could strike at any distance. A wound from one of their invisible poisoned arrows caused a slow and miserable demise from festering boils, convulsions, or itches so severe they made a man flay himself.

I was an outsider, newly arrived in an inner circle of the Inner Palace, and I knew how to be curious, be credulous, be amazed by whatever small secrets the men chose to share with me. Pantalops, elegant as she was, was a jaded jade. She yawned and covered her mouth when I asked my host why the arkhon would want to curse his son Kyparisos, who had saved Arkhyios Corvus from the panther.

Before I left Aghazal's house that evening, I had eaten five moonflower seeds, and in the scented course we had been offered smoke from her leaves. Yet Moonflower had not embraced me. I was dull and the world was dull. I felt as though I were swaddled in gauze. Sire Rodela snickered in my ear, saying that this Prince Kenoun had no use for women, so why had he invited me? He was impotent, save when a tharais boy subjected him to the fifth and seventh Abasements.

Meanwhile Arkhyios Kenoun was saying that Kyparisos hadn't saved King Corvus, he'd tried to kill him; I pretended amazement. He said Kyparisos had asked the oracles at the temple of Posison if the arkhon would be pleased to see the Crow dead, and they said yes. And no wonder, crows were tharais carrion-eaters, and Arkhyios Corvus was polluted with misfortune.

Arkhyios Kyprinos said, "The arkhon doesn't want to kill Corvus. That would only comfort Queenmother Caelum. Kyparisos should have consulted his common sense instead of priests whose interpretations have been paid for by Fifth Wife. She laid a neat snare for anyone fool enough to step into it. I never use those priests myself—I send to the shrine at Mount Omphalos, where one can be sure the oracles are above bribery."

"What of the king's men, Arkhyios?" I asked. "What would have happened to them if the king had been killed?"

Kenoun had a snorting whuffling laugh that issued from his nose, the way a horse might laugh if horses laughed. "I heard you had a yen for strange-ignorant ones," he said. "No fear, they're safe now. But I heard Kyparisos had Ebanakan guardsmen ready to descend on them after he killed Corvus. He had friends in the Orange Banner, and one in every ten guardsmen in that banner was executed three days ago."

"He meant to kill the king's men?"

"There's more profit in their lives than their deaths. The Blood would have been held for ransom and the servants sold as bondmen. You could have visited your friends in the cage, and comforted them in their imprisonment."

I leaned forward and rested an elbow on the table-tray. Arkhyios Kenoun sat across from me and I let him see me rudely slip two fingers of my tharais hand between my sandal and foot to scratch my instep. "I'd have the whip hand of them then, wouldn't I, Arkhyios? They'd have to do exactly as I pleased, ein?" The fifth Abasement was cleaning feet with a tongue and the seventh was performed with a whip. It was so easy to make Kenoun think of them. I smiled.

I could make him want me, but I didn't want him. I didn't want any of them, these sons of the arkhon. The Court of the Sons was a tomb in which living shades were confined. The vision of my right eye was obscured by a dingy pall, and with that eye I saw Arkhyios Kenoun and his brother with yellowing skin and bruised eye sockets, and tarnished eyes. As if they were already dead.

All the arkhyios were as good as dead, all save the one who would inherit the rule when his father died, and kill his brothers. But the arkhon was seventy-five years old and dwelled in the Court of Longevity, and he was going to live forever. He had already outlasted four wives, and for proof of his vigor one need only look at his fifth, who had a belly out to here. In Lambanein they were rather proud that their arkhon sired children so large that their mothers died trying to bear them.

His sons couldn't leave the Court of the Sons unless upon official business. They couldn't leave the Inner Palace at all. Their servants were the arkhon's thrushes, and likewise most of their visitors. Their rooms had peepholes, and I wondered if their skulls had peepholes too, so the arkhon could spy on their very thoughts. Every word Arkhyios Kenoun had spoken to me was spoken in the knowledge that it would be repeated to the arkhon. And to King Corvus—that was why I was there. To be a tattletale. But was there any truth in the tale he told me? In the warning?

I took a certain pleasure in stitching together facts and surmises, and arranging small signs into large patterns. King Corvus was a man with an army, albeit a weak remnant of the great army he'd once led. Here among the sons, without warriors of their own, he was a power, a threat, and the possessor of an enviable prize. If the king had died, his soldiers would have been masterless—an army for hire—and the arkhon would have had to send his Ebanakan guards to massacre them. But the king had survived, and the arkhon had granted him an audience. He was safer now, by a hairsbreadth, than he'd been before.

It was unbearable to sit still any longer. I rose, though it was forward of me to be the first, and walked the paths of the courtyard. If I could find Moonflower in the garden, I meant to eat more of her, that she might cure me of numbness and the absence of desire. Cure my boredom. The courtyard held roses and jasmine, but I found no moonflowers, not until I sat on the rim of the pool and saw, mirrored in the dark water, moonflowers affixed to the wicker spire on my head. I plucked two flowers and ate them both, and set the rest of the blooms afloat beside the reflection of the crescent Moon. They reminded me of ships, of King Thyrse's fleet on the Inward Sea and the lightning so long ago, and I remembered my struggle to speak, Galan's tenderness, and Mai's friendship. It was a blessing I was healed, and yet I'd never properly thanked the gods for the gift of speech restored to me. And look what I used their gift for now: lies, mockeries, blandishments, telling or ferreting out secrets. For a moment I was pierced by shame—just a small prick, as from a thorn or a needle.

I moved my hand through the water to send Moonflower's fleet sailing across the pool. A man sat next to me, took a little ship from the water and ate it. We had been introduced, but I had forgotten which branch he was on the arkhon's tree. I leaned toward him and whispered, "I'm drowning. Save me." But when I tried to grasp his shoulder, my hand passed through him.

"I'm over here," he said.

I said, "No wonder I can't touch you. You're dead too." Or perhaps I didn't say it.

My throat was dry and I dipped up water in my cupped hands and

caught a squiggling reflection of the nail-paring Moon. It hurt to swallow.
The man moved closer to me until our thighs were touching. He told me he
was thirsty and I let him drink from my hands. His tongue lapped my
palms. He smiled up at me; he was a sardonical corpse, a doomed arkhyios.
I grinned back and told him I knew how to raise the dead.

Just after dawn I found myself lying on the paving stones of a steep street in
a familiar but unknown city. Familiar because it was like Allaxios, but
reversed. The mountain rose above me to the east, a bulk between me and
the rising Sun. Her red light gleamed on the gilded roofs of a palace that covered the heights, but below we were still in shadow. The wooden shutters of
the shops were already propped open. I sat up and waited for my queasiness
to subside, and tried to straighten my wrapper. I'd lost my shawl of morning
dew. Someone had pulled the wicker spire from my hair and my scalp hurt.
My hair was tangled; the netting and beadcoins were missing.

A woman lit a lantern hanging from one corner of a raised shutter, and I
thought it an odd thing to do when day was coming. I stood and asked her
the name of the city, and she answered in a strange-ignorant tongue. She had
a foreign look about her, as if her people had been made from chalky clay.

I leaned on the counter of her shop, which had rows of stoppered clay
jars, each with a fish painted in two simple strokes of red glaze. Before me
were mounds of grayish crystals on wooden platters: salt. Gods, I was
thirsty. If my veins had held seawater instead of blood, it would all be dry
by now, leaving behind just such clots of dirty crystals. I asked for water in
Lambaneish, in the High, the Low, and Ebanakan, but the shopkeeper
refused to understand me. I raised my voice and she scolded me. All I
wanted was water—was that so much to ask? I reached across the counter
to pinch her ear, but I couldn't hurt her. My golden fingercaps had been
stolen too. I backed away, and turned and stumbled downhill, past shops
where men stood at counters eating fish soup full of billowy dumplings.

Oh I was lost, lost, and everything had been stolen and I was in a
strange city and how would I get home again?

And all at once the world reversed, and left became right and east
became west, and I knew the Sun was setting behind Mount Allaxios, not
rising, and it was evening and I was running through the lower town, in one
of the enclaves of strange-ignorant ones within the body of the city, and I
couldn't remember what happened after I'd launched Moonflower's fleet.

I began the long trudge uphill. The steep streets and stairs, the terraces
towering above me—even the sight of them made me weary. I seemed to
have no sinews left in my thighs. My heart stuttered. I drank at a fountain
and begged its meneidon to grant me strength.

At home Mother Yafeqer chided me. Where had I been? Had I forgotten we were supposed to entertain at the palace of Arthygater Klados? Aghazal and Second and Third had been obliged to go without me, but there was still time if I hurried. I told her that I'd gotten lost, and been robbed too, and that I was exhausted. Besides, I wouldn't be missed, my part was small because my art was small. Without pity she marched me to the bathing room where the servants repaired me: glue and paint to hide a cracked jar.

Moonflower had swallowed a night and a day and I wasn't prepared for the enactment, though we'd practiced for so long. Kabara escorted me to Arthygater Klados's palace, carrying my costume, a surcoat with padded shoulders, a helm covered in iridescent green feathers, and a long red wig. My part was indeed important, but I thought anyone stuffed into that stuffed surcoat could have done as well or better than I. Kabara, for one. And I was afraid King Corvus would be there and he would shun me for all to see. I slowed my pace. Nevertheless we arrived.

My Sisters were one and all furious, but there was no time for them to scold. I donned the costume and the helmet, in which I could hardly breathe, and strutted like a dunghill cock onto the arched bridge in the center of the courtyard. But I kept my steps too small, as if my legs remembered the confinement of a woman's wrapper. I was pretending to be the poet Akantha pretending to be a man, so she could win the love of the beautiful maid Nephelin.

Akantha was a famous poet of the First Age, but her eloquence was useless in the pursuit of Nephelin, for she couldn't speak to her beloved lest a high voice betray her. She hoped to win her by showing a fine figure, even if that figure was a sham that Nephelin would surely discover at their first tryst, as soon as she found the stuffed leather phallus beneath Akantha's surcoat. I let this show from time to time; we were supposed to make the spectators laugh before we made them cry.

Aghazal played the cithara and sang all the lovely longing thoughts Akantha dared not speak aloud, and Adalana, with her flute, was an impertinent skylark who served as a go-between. Tasatyala sang and danced the part of Nephelin, a guileful girl who was still innocent of the many ways a heart can be wounded. The Ode had been chosen so Tasatyala could shine, and shine she did. I was so proud of Second. It could all be forgotten now—the endless practice, the maddening repetition, the musicmaster's blows and cruel words—as her gifts flowered before our eyes.

Sire Rodela had adored the braggadocio of Akantha in her padded surcoat, and roused every time we practiced, but tonight he slumbered. I had to do it by myself, with my limbs heavy and grit in my eyes and mouth.

Wildfire

Halfway through I glimpsed King Corvus sitting with Arthygater Keros, and at once I became more awkward, jerking along like a puppet propelled by sticks and strings.

In every good Lambaneish tale at least one of the agonists dies, so of course Akantha died before she gained her heart's desire, fighting like a man to defend her beloved. It was said the real Akantha lived to be at least sixty. No matter, the spectacle required her death, and required Nephelin to cradle Akantha in her lap, and take off the helmet so she might see at last the face of the man she loved. The long hair of my wig tumbled out, and Tasatyala sang a lament, and I swear I heard sobs as I pretended to be dead.

I began to cry too, silently, with tears leaking from my closed eyes and collecting in the whorls of my ears. I cursed my thoughtlessness. I should have warned Aghazal, I should have dissuaded her from choosing this Ode, of all Odes the one we should not have performed. All along it had been as plain as the nose on my face and as easily overlooked. King Corvus's wife had died the way Akantha died in the Ode, in the guise of a man. In my dream I'd seen Sire Galan take off Kalos's helmet and reveal her long hair.

I feared they would think Aghazal had alluded to Kalos's death on purpose. She might even be punished for it, yet I was sure she didn't know Queenwife Kalos had been slain. A rumor had been put about that Kalos and her child had died in travail, which was easily believed. But I knew.

The king must have suffered, watching me prance about like a buffoon as if mocking her shade.

I felt Tasatyala's legs trembling under my head, as we waited out the long silence after her last note, before the applause.

The noblewomen retired and the celebrants entered the dining court. Aghazal and Second were surrounded by a throng of admirers, and Second basked in their praises. I greeted acquaintances, but I wasn't in the mood to converse. I strolled past King Corvus on my way to the pleasure garden. He wore a surcoat with a design of golden leaves and pomegranates. He withheld any sign of recognition.

A celebrant walking alone is an invitation. Someone would follow, but it would not be the king.

It was high summer now and the days were long, and even so the Sun's last light faded from the sky. I climbed the stairs beside the waterfall that cascaded from terrace to terrace. Somewhere in this garden was the aviary where I had lain with Kydos and Kyanos, and the celebrants Perdik and Mixin. The stairs were slippery from spray, and my legs ached and I was out of breath.

I sat on a stone step and listened. The masons had been clever when they

457

made this waterfall, for the rushing water was tuneful, it sounded like bells and cymbals. I took off my shoe-stockings and cooled my sore feet in the water. I could see down into the dining court. How delicious, how succulent were the colors of the celebrants' bright wrappers and shawls. The small flames of lamps and lanterns illuminated the courtyard with a glow that trembled and fluttered like moths' wings, and made the reverse, the shadows, seem quick and alive.

My hair was tangled and flyaway, for I'd taken off the wig. I picked rue and wormwood and bound them together with bluebind, and made a wreath to crown myself with regret, loss, and affectation.

I scraped tears from my cheeks with the palm of my hand. How much Moonflower had I eaten last night? Too much. For Moonflower was still in me, still strong. She'd peeled me bare, made me into a dowser's quivering forked rod. Without skin between the world and me, every wanton wind stroked me as it pleased.

I consulted my heart, as the Auspices of Crux examined the organs of birds for signs. I found myself baffling. In my webeye I saw my heart, the size and shape of a clenched fist. I wondered why it was more troublesome to give away my fist-heart than keep it. Perhaps I should sell it instead of trying to give it away. Buy it, take it, leave me heartless. I decided I'd sell it to the man climbing the stairs, for the price of two copperheads, which was all a two-copper whore's heart was worth. I knew that man, but I'd misplaced his name and couldn't find it no matter how I rummaged. He was one of the king's men, an armiger; in the Ferinus he'd proven himself an excellent climber.

He stood below looking up. "Hey ho," he said. "They say you won't tumble a man twice—unless he's a king—but I came to see if my luck was still good." He held out his hand to display the two dice on his palm, each showing a single dot: snake eyes.

"Did we?" I said.

"You don't remember?"

I shrugged. No doubt I offended his pride, but I didn't care. He closed his fist around the dice and his smile was something of a sneer. "I suppose I'll have to do something more memorable this time."

"I may be cheap but I'm not free. My pride is two copperheads."

"I've spent all my copperheads. Will these do?" He put the dice in my right hand, and took my left wrist to pull me to my feet. He went past me up the stairs and didn't let go.

It's no boast to say I gave the armiger his money's worth. When we parted we both had marks to show for it. I'd bitten him hard enough to break the skin and he, not understanding the amorous contests of Lambanein, had grabbed my throat in his large hand and left a necklace of bruises. Of course the Lambaneish had a name for that caress too.

I lay on the turf with the dice in one hand. The other hand stroked the earth and caught tresses of grass between its fingers. The stripling Moon cast a faint light. Three cypresses towered over me, the same trees that had, so many nights ago, made a shadow boat in which the king and I had sailed. He'd said he planned to make a princess of me, and I'd been flattered. But a convincing counterfeit could never be struck from me, no matter how I was gilded. A scratch, and the worthless metal would show.

Between the Moon and the cypresses were clouds patterned like ripples in sand. I pretended the clouds were standing still as Mount Allaxios slid under them, carrying me somewhere. I parted my lips in the hopes of catching some moisture to quench my thirst, but the air was too dry, the clouds too far away. I said aloud, "You truly are a two-copper whore."

King Corvus, standing over me, looked tall as a cypress. "Cover yourself," he said, and threw my shawl at me.

I sat up. The shawl was too thin to conceal anything, and I groped for my wrapper, over there somewhere. The king dropped it in my lap. I draped the cloth over my shoulders and legs. I feared his reproach for the part I'd enacted that night in the spectacle. I didn't expect the reprimand he gave instead.

He said, "Don't meddle with my men."

"Your man, Sire Whatshisname—he followed me. Besides, everyone knows you jilted me."

"I couldn't go on pretending. It makes me look a dupe when you take up with them."

I shook my head, bewildered. "In Lambanein no one expects a celebrant to be faithful, not unless she has a benefactor, one patron only. And even then . . ."

"I'm not Lambaneish," he said, walking back and forth in front of me, four paces one way, four paces another. We were near the edge of the terrace and the land dropped away behind him. He was silhouetted against the rippled clouds.

"What do you care? I served the purpose; everyone knows now you're not a eunuch. And if they think you tired of me quickly—well, people do tire of me quickly. Meanwhile I have not waited in idleness."

"I can see that," he said. He'd wear a furrow in the turf, pacing like that.

"I dined in the Court of the Sons and learned why Kyparisos wanted an army, and it was not to invade Incus. They care nothing here for foreign lands; indeed, they care nothing for Lambanein, which might as well be a tail to the dog Allaxios. They care only that their father will die soon, and one arkhyios will become arkhon and the rest shades, and every last one of them would kill you if they thought they could lay hands on your greatest treasure, your army."

"Do you think I don't know that?" King Corvus said. And I, who had fancied myself clever, was abashed. "This kingdom rests on the shoulders of a frail, hunchbacked wanderwit—an old man who lets other men impregnate his wife so as to seem virile. My presence here has set all teetering, so I step with care, I can tell you. But if I cannot get men and gold from Lambanein, I cannot get them at all—and none will be forthcoming if there is a war here for succession. I said as much to the arkhon—or rather, to his factotum, the only one worth speaking to in this city—and the factotum made me a handsome offer. Firstly, my life. Secondly, an arthygater to be my wife, and a dowry consisting of a palace in the district and a handsome income in wool and rents. Lastly, in five years or so, when the time is deemed ripe, an army to retake my kingdom. All I have to do in return is give him something I no longer truly possess, the Lake of Sapheiros. And do nothing . . . nothing to harm the arkhon and his successor, whoever that may be."

I propped my chin on my knees so I wouldn't gape at him. King Corvus stopped pacing and looked away from me, down over the slopes of Mount Allaxios, which rose like an island from the ocean of night. All around us stirred currents of air.

I said, "Did you accept?"

He turned his head toward me, quick as a bird. "Of course. I paid dear for the offer, didn't I? I sold horses, armor, weapons—some of mine, some of my men's—and the Auspices of Rift hired themselves out to teach these popinjays to prance about as if they knew how to fight—all to bribe the factotum and buy a robe worthy to present to the arkhon at my audience. One must have a gift for the arkhon. When we first came here, I gave him many gifts, and he didn't appreciate them. I've been advised as to his taste now, and this one was better received."

"What of your betrothed?"

"What of her?"

"I just wondered if I know her, if she is one of the arkhon's granddaughters." Alopexin must be jealous of someone.

At this he laughed a true laugh, and said, "I doubt you attend the same banquets. She is a girl of seven years, the arkhon's youngest daughter. I won't settle for a grandchild when there are still daughters to be had."

"I think if you wait for the arkhon's permission, you'll never return; five years will be ten, will be never. You'll forget who you are."

"Did a dream tell you that?" he asked, mocking me.

Why was he here? Why had he sought me out to tell me I was useless, that all I'd done for him was not worth doing? I must be dreaming you now, I thought. Perhaps I said it aloud. He sat down beside me on my right, and stretched out his long legs. For a time there was silence.

He said, "This Sire Galan of yours, to whom you are so unfaithful—do you still wish to return to him?"

I looked at him from the corner of my cloudy eye. His wreath was of greenthorn and juniper, and the pomegranates on his cuffs had garnet seeds, just as I'd dreamed once. When I didn't answer he said, "I have word from Incus. My men were able to overtake Consort Ostrakan's messenger to Merle, and bribe him to substitute your likeness for that of Arthygater Keros. Merle—thinking himself cunning—questioned the messenger closely about Keros, her looks, her demeanor, and her temperament. Above all he wished to know if she was a lamia, if she bore the serpent tattoo. He doesn't know that even a whore can be a member of the Serpent Cult. He thinks—as we all thought—that the tattoo is a mark of royalty. My wife never said otherwise; she was forbidden to speak of anything to do with the cult."

"Arthygater Keros doesn't have a tattoo. I've seen her in the bath."

"Nevertheless, the messenger swore up and down she did, seeing it was expected. So you must have the mark if you're to be Keros."

"If—when—I go, what happens to the real arthygater?"

"We let Ostrakan's messenger return with the Starling's acceptance and demands. Arthygater Keros must set forth with her dowry—so we can steal it. How else can we afford yours? We live here on moonlight and promises, and I've already borrowed all I can against my prospects."

"That was a great risk, letting the messenger live. Aren't you afraid he'll betray you to Arthygater Katharos?"

"We took precautions. But the plan is risky, I never said otherwise."

I sat folded tight, my arms clasped around my knees and my shoulders hunched about my ears like a child afraid of a beating. But the blows were steady; they came from within and there was no avoiding them, since I'd failed to rid myself of my heart.

He couldn't understand why I was silent. He said with scorn, "Perhaps you prefer to be a whore. You seem to enjoy it."

"No no of course not."

"We've made inquiries about this tattoo, and we cannot find an artisan willing to undertake it—they are all too frightened of the sacrilege. So you'll have to become an initiate; it's part of the rites, they say, and no doubt the tattoo will be painful. But it costs money, a large tithe paid to the temple of Katabaton at Mount Omphalos. The initiation takes place at the Festival of

461

Katabaton's Navel, and it's our good fortune it is only a tennight away. You'll need a patron, one besotted enough to spend five thousand in gold to raise a hoyden to the highest rank of whores."

"There is no one like that, no one I could ask."

"There is one," said the king. "I'll be your patron, and a jealous one. I'll dote on you openly, and lavish gifts upon you, and indulge your every whim—such as the desire to join the Serpent Cult—and in return I'll insist on being the only one, you understand? I shall be the man who tamed the vixen, and you shall be the woman who made a king break his vow, and together we'll enact a spectacle to entertain the gossips of Allaxios."

I was too weak to stand without the king's help, and once on my feet I was unsteady. I wound the wrapper twice about me and fussed with the pleats.

Don't bother," said the king, handing me my shawl. "You look just as you ought, well ravished."

I'd lost my weedy wreath somewhere, and he gave me his own, of green-thorn and juniper, meaning I was his solace in adversity, and he was my protection. But that was too severe a message to please a Lambaneish crowd. I pulled tasseled cords of coral honeysuckle from the shrubs near the waterfall, and twined them into garlands to wear around our necks, declaring one to the other the nature of our fate.

The stairs seemed steeper on the way down, and the steps too far apart. I clung to the king's arm. Probably he thought I was drunk. I wished I were. He spoke to me, but I wasn't listening. I was watching his changeable face. He had set aside his somber expression for smiles and glances of various kinds. It appalled me that he could surpass a whore at shamming what he did not feel.

How I must have looked to the other guests as I entered the dining court on his arm! Wobbling, stunned—turning to him in disbelief—weeds in my hair, stains on my garments—while he seemed unspeakably tidy in his stiff surcoat, and unspeakably pleased with himself. Wild Alopexin, caught at last.

Under the arched ceiling of the colonnade, I beckoned a tharais napkin and washed my face and hands in her silver basin. With gestures I bade her fetch a comb for my hair. After a long while she reappeared with a hairdresser. We went to a tharais room off the dining court, where the hairdresser did the best she could. I had no coins, so I gave her the dice. All without a word between us.

I took my place beside King Corvus, leaning against him, exerting myself to perform Flirtations, the ewe's gaze, the feather touch on his arm, the smiles just for him, hidden from others behind my hand. I fed him peppery pickled radishes and his teeth nipped my fingers. I improvised an Ode to a Radish, to her red blush and pale flesh, so shapely, so tasty, such a bite to her. I was flushed and dizzy and my skin burned with dry fever. The king whispered in my ear, asking if all was well.

Very well, oh very well indeed.

But I seemed to have gotten too far away from myself, the thread all unwound from the shuttle, and I couldn't find my way back. I was a spectator who watched the agonists with a critical eye. One could almost believe she was the kind of woman a man like him would desire, though she was not. And he did not.

CHAPTER 32

Moonflower

was ready to forswear my oath to Moonflower, but she wasn't ready to let me go. I had eaten too much of her, day after day for almost two tennights, and now in turn she consumed me. I fainted in the cart on the way back to Aghazal's house, and she couldn't rouse me. Grandmother Lagas made a pallet for me between two Ebanakan shrubs with healing fragrances in the back courtyard. They hung an awning to protect me from the Sun, just showing over the walls of the house. I lay in a swoon all day and night.

I remembered now. Night after night I had made Moonflower my guide, and she had led me and hidden my memories of it. Now those memories opened to me, and I walked through the nights, each one a chamber thronged with strangers, and Alopexin a stranger among them.

In one room we stood in a garden admiring apparitions we saw in the clouds by moonlight, and everything I uttered came out as a poem in the pattern of four, five, six:

> Plum blossoms crowd
> a crooked black bough
> of night starred with lichens.

Other guests tried to match me poem for poem, but no one could do it as effortlessly, for I was not trying.

Another night I watched a cockfight and took offense when a man stepped on my foot. He was a servile scholar, and perhaps that's why I dared to strike him, or I didn't care—Moonflower made me quick to kindle to lust or rage. The man hit me back, and we went blow for blow, and I felt such glee, such fury, screaming with all my might, impervious to pain. We made a better spectacle than the cocks. When I woke up with bruises, I took them to be signs of an especially vigorous patron.

There was the night a nobleman confided in me that he'd borrowed ten thousand in gold from Arthygater Katharos to pay off a debt, and had gambled the money away instead. And now she'd made of him a mere kynamolgos, a go-between, and he couldn't deny her any sort of favor she required. What sort of favors? I'd asked. He was known as a swordsman (the nobleman said, boasting a little); he'd picked quarrels with certain men on her behalf, and killed them. He named the men. No doubt the king and Divine Aboleo might have made good use of his secret, if I'd remembered to tell them.

Among those many nights was one bright day, the day of the Hunt. I squatted beneath the pillars that held up the high pavilion in the oak grove, dicing. A crowd of hunters waited their turn to dice snakes and hawks with me.

Alopexin won more than she lost. She was afire like brush on the mountains after a dry summer. She drank doublewine to quench the flames, but it only fed them. She was giddy and frivolous; her voice was shrill and she laughed easily, above all at her own wit. No wonder the rumor had been quick to reach Divine Aboleo and slow to reach the gossips of the town. The men who gambled with me were followers of the king, and I was giving them a chance at the king's dreamer, the king's whore.

They say Chance cheats, but she didn't, she let the dice fall. When a man won, he followed Chance up the ladder to the pavilion, but it was Desire who turned to embrace him when he reached the top. Desire could have taken a hundred men as soon as three or five, because she suffered a craving deeper than any man could reach. I knew the winners, all five: three cataphracts, an armiger, and an Auspex of Rift, Divine Volator. Probably the young priest was the one who told Divine Aboleo about what had happened during the hunt, how he'd broken his vow and spent his strength on a woman.

I wondered if he'd told his superior everything—how I wrapped my legs around him, and how he raised himself above me on stiff arms and labored in my grip. The look in his eyes was startled, awed. Sweat ran from him in rivulets, as if he were a smith at a forge. He seemed to strain away from me with the upper part of his body even as he hammered into me below.

I could tell my gaze frightened him. One of my eyes had a black pupil with a blue flame in the center and the other was full of smoke. I knew this because I hovered over the platform in a sky of celestial blue tiles, and witnessed everything. Maybe his third eye, the one tattooed on top of his brow, saw me looking. Maybe he saw my iridescent moonflower shadow, how it flowed from my skin and enveloped him, until his arms trembled and he lowered himself down and gave way to my embrace.

I'd wanted revenge on those who possessed me the day of the Hunt, when I was not in possession of myself. But how could I avenge myself on the gods?

*   *   *

I dreamed of falling from a height, and this frightened me so that I woke up. I was on the porch of my house on Mount Sair. Inside me was a huge hunger. I'd been ill, I knew that; I must have been ill for some time, because when I got up I was dizzy and my legs were weak.

I shaded my eyes and went down the stairs to the herb garden on the sunny slope, and fragrance rose around me as I trod the thyme and maythen. But I was hungry for clay and only clay, and it had to be clay from the bank of the Wend River, so I descended all the long way down from terrace to terrace to the Athlewood, shaking as I went, pausing many times to get my breath. I didn't know how I'd climb back up again, I only knew I must have clay to save me from the poison. I dug a handful from the bank, under the roots of a fallen tree, and the clay was reddish and slippery. I pressed it between my palms into the shape of a flatbread, and inscribed on it with my fingernail: She may refuse.

Much as I craved the clay, I was frightened by how the mouthful was heavy on my tongue and slid thick and smooth into my throat and lodged there so I couldn't breathe. I knelt on a pebbled strand to drink from the river and in my throat the clay dissolved into silt in spring floodwaters, and I was the delta that received it. I leaned over the river to drink again and as I touched my lips to the water, the reflection of the Sun smote me and I was thrown down. I lay on the strand and my hot left side convulsed while my cold right side could not move.

I was startled awake from a dream of falling to find I was on a pallet in the back courtyard under a saffron canopy ablaze in the Sun. I was too hot. I pulled off the cloth that covered me, so there was nothing between my skin and the breeze. An old woman and a young girl sat nearby playing a song. The old woman's brown skin had an ashy bloom, and the girl's was like burnished clay. The girl played a skylark trill on her flute; the old woman played a long-necked wooden bird, strung with one string of gut and three of wire, which shivered in metallic harmony whenever she plucked the gut string. She sang through her nose with a quavering voice, and though the words baffled me I understood the melody.

I couldn't sit up. My limbs were willing but too weak. I turned on my side and groaned, and saw four women sitting in a row and spinning in the shade of a portico. One of them hurried over and knelt to give me a drink of water. She wore an orange wrapper, and her skin was warm and sticky and she smelled of myrrh. She poured water in my mouth, and some dripped down my scorching skin like a cool blessing, and some ran down inside me into my big empty belly that was hollow like the clay-lined cistern under the courtyard.

The woman wiped my cheeks and chin with the palm of her hand. I was afraid she would scold me, sure I'd done something unpardonable, though I didn't know what it was. But she leaned over me with a tender look and said, "You've come back to us, ein?"

"What's wrong with me?" I said. "I've turned, returned insight out."

I dreamed I climbed a sand cliff, on the shore of a sea too bright blue-green to be the Inward Sea. Sand crumbled underfoot, and as I fell I screamed and awoke on a pallet stuffed with straw under a canopy.

I lifted my head from the pallet, craning to look at Grandmother Lagas, who sat beside me with her legs straight before her, shelling fat brown beans from pods about the length of my palm. I'd seen those pods on a vine with purple flowers that twined around a column in the dining court; on either side of it grew moonflower plants.

Grandmother Lagas swept the beans from her lap into a bowl. Her arms were stronger than they looked. I used them to pull myself up to sit. I hung my head and panted, hnh, hnh, hnh. Moonflower was going to kill me.

I'd been dry as salt before and now sweat oozed from me everywhere. Grandmother Lagas touched the back of my neck and licked my salt from her fingers. She considered the taste the way Aunt Cook Angadataqebay savored a dish to see if it needed a pinch more of this or that. Grandmother spoke to me in Ebanakan, and I didn't understand her. She sang Adalana's name, and Third came to sit beside us. Adalana said, "Grandmother says your heart is a lame runaway horse, and you must try to slow it down. She has something to help."

Grandmother Lagas had hands with swollen joints and crooked fingers, but they were nimble enough to split a brown bean lengthwise with her sharp little knife, and then quarter the half. She took an eighth of the bean and crushed it in a small granite mortar. She added water and I drank it.

I leaned on Adalana, and watched between my fingers as Grandmother Lagas poured sand on the pavement beside the fountain and leveled it with a broom. She drew a circle in the sand with her digging stick, and crossed it with two lines right to left, and two top to bottom, dividing the circle into nine parts. She sprinkled seeds from nine clay bowls into divisions of her circle, muttering as she worked. Adalana said, "Grandmother Lagas is asking the birds about you."

By the short shadows on the ground, I could tell it was near noon, but the Sun had dimmed, or my eyes had dimmed. My heart was slowing. What

I'd swallowed was coming up again and there was no way to stop it. I spewed up brown flecks of bean and silt and gasped, hnh, hnh, hnh, and there was a pain in my side as if I'd been running. I was afraid.

Grandmother Lagas fetched Old King Rooster from his little palace and set him on the fountain's rim, above her sand circle. The rooster squawked and preened, and while he was bragging a little wren flew down and landed on the circle. She scurried about gleaning like a quick brown mouse. Rooster jumped down to chase her away, thrusting his head at her, and when the wren fluttered off, he strutted back and forth, pecking at seeds.

I fell back on the pallet and Adalana wiped my face with linen dipped in cool water, or was it Aghazal who knelt beside me? I took the wet cloth between my cracked lips and suckled.

This time when I dreamed of falling, I let myself fall, for it was more terrible to awaken to dying. I fell into the long funnel of a moonflower, down down to the narrow throat, ivory tinged with violet and apricot. All this time I had been falling toward her and I didn't know it. The flower coiled shut around me, and I lay enfolded like a worm in a bud. The scent was overripe, oversweet, mortifying and fructifying. I writhed and twisted, but I was too tightly bound to free myself.

Sire Rodela sniggered in my ear. "You poisoned me. How do you like it?" I could feel his little fly feet crawling around on the wrong side of my eardrum. My arms were bent and pressed tight against my sides, and my hands were near my face.

"Oh hush!" I stabbed at him with my dagger fingernail and pierced my own eardrum, and the pain made me cry out. Rodela the fly climbed through the torn ear and buzzed about my face determined to annoy me. He landed on my eyebrow and I swatted at him. We were so enwrapped in the flower that he couldn't fly far if he wanted to.

Perhaps I could cut my way out. With the sharpened nail of my mother finger, I scratched a slit in the petal. It was too thick to pierce all at once. At the bottom of the slit a pearl of moisture formed, gleaming in the faint light. I took the sweet dew on my tongue, and found it answered my thirst and my hunger. But it aroused another craving.

My ear throbbed. I set to work on the petal wall, deepening the slit I'd made, cutting again and again with my fingernail. The fingernail would break soon and then what would I do?

"Use a hairpin," Sire Rodela said, landing on my nose. I brushed him off. I searched my snarled hair and pulled out a golden hairpin with a jeweled dragonfly finial, which somehow remained from the last time I'd worn a wicker hairpiece—the banquet at the Court of the Sons.

Wildfire

I scraped the wall with the metal tip. The flower bled droplets and I drank them, and I peeled soft rags of flesh from the wall and ate them. I was growing larger and ever more confined. Beyond one petal wall was another and another, for the flower was pleated around me. I cut my way through the last layer, the tough green calyx that cupped the base of the flower.

I heard Sire Rodela's whine dwindle away, and I was glad. But he came back and taunted me because he was outside and I wasn't. I thrust both hands in the hole and pushed and pulled until I tore an opening, and I wriggled out, sticky with Moonflower's opalescent sap, onto a wide branch.

How had the flower contained me? I was too big for it now. The flower was a single petal with five stiff ribs, and I cut away the damaged part and turned it upside down and wrapped it around me, and fastened my new cloak with the dragonfly hairpin. The funnel throat of the bloom curled around my neck like a ruffled collar, and its ribs clung to my shoulders and arms and spine, adhering to my skin with the sticky sap, and truly there was no difference between my flesh and petal flesh. I spread my skin-petal wings and stepped off the branch into the arms of a breeze. Sire Rodela darted after me like a little dog, yapping wait wait wait for me, and made me laugh.

The flowers in Moonflower's garden were transformed. The heart of a marigold was tinted with colors unnameable. I saw the simple yellow cinquefoil dressed in an intricate new pattern. Every blossom had its unique face and scent, and I was enamored of each one and drawn this way and that in a dragonfly dance. As I flew I rubbed my legs together for the pleasure of feeling skin rasp against skin, and from the desire that suffused me I made a singing sound. "My honey, my sweet," Rodela buzzed, "I always said you were otherwise than you pretended."

I understood why a moth flings itself against a lamp to its own destruction, for I could have immolated myself on this beauty. Perhaps only my pest, Sire Rodela, kept me from doing so: a small grievance in overweening pleasure.

Now twilight dwelled in every walled garden, and lamps were lit within rooms and colonnades. The moonflowers by the portico opened ivory and white blossoms, and though their fragrance was intoxicating, I was drawn to another smell, a musky sweet rot. Pity the thing that dreamed open-eyed under a saffron canopy. Her pupils had shrunk to the size of mustard seeds, and the breath from her open mouth smelled like sour wine. Grandmother Lagas swatted me and said, "Behave!" and I fell into the cavern and the mouth closed and swallowed me up.

Grandmother Lagas folded the canopy and took up a staff topped with a pair of curved, ridged impala horns; between the horns taut strands of gut held small copper disks that made a shimmering sound. She struck the butt of the staff against the ground to shake loose a rhythm. She kept her feet planted in one place and moved her hips one way and her shoulders another, and she shook her head back and forth. Soon her shoulders gleamed with sweat and her garment was soaked between her fallen breasts. She sang a high question in Ebanakan and rattled the disks, and my Sisters danced in the same way and sang an answer. Now and then one of them would uproot a foot and stamp with a thunderous noise. The other women of the house clapped their hands.

I thought their words sounded something like this:

> *Who will, who will help her?*
> *We will, we will help her.*
> *Who will, who will help her?*
> *Grandmother Lagas will help her,*
> *Indigo pot will help her,*
> *Grandmother Shade will help her,*
> *Moon will, Moon will help her.*

All night long I heard them sing, and I was lulled by it and forgot to be afraid. Every time I returned after drifting away, my Sisters and Grandmother were there, promising to help me.

Two days and nights they labored over me, Grandmother Lagas and the kinfolk in the house. First and Second, Aghazal and Tasatyala, were obliged to sing and play and dance incessantly to cure me, because they had caused me harm. Rooster and wren had accused them, and Grandmother Lagas had read the signs, the seeds eaten by the birds and the tracks in the sand.

The birds said that Aghazal had stinted my education; she had been piqued when I ignored her advice and submitted myself to Moonflower's instruction, and had neglected thereafter to offer me counsel or correction. Whereas Tasatyala had afflicted me with her jealousy, because without much effort I'd taken the place she'd worked so hard to deserve.

There was railing and quarreling and weeping when these accusations were made, but I slept through all that. In the morning Aghazal and Tasatyala gave me cherished valuables: from Aghazal, her cape covered with green parrot feathers; from Tasatyala, a carved jade disk and golden cord to fasten a garment, which had been given to her by her first patron. I tried to give these gifts back, but they refused to take them. So I called for my locked casket to be brought to me, and emptied it, giving beadcoins and jewelry and cosmetics to the people of the house, even the tharais bath servant. I gave away my shawls and wrappers. It was as if I had died, and in the Lambaneish way parceled out my precious belongings instead of burning them. But I was given so many gifts in return that I was richer for my generosity.

I sobbed and asked forgiveness of my Sisters; I had been selfish and unworthy, disobedient to Aghazal, disrespectful to Tasatyala, and a poor example to my dear Adalana. We all wept, and were gladdened by it.

Uncle Zubana and Kabara carried me to a small room, empty save for a pallet, the place of seclusion where women of the house slept when they were tharais during their tides. When they left me alone in there, I was frightened. Perhaps they had found me out. But soon the tharais servant came in with rags and a basin of warm water. She washed between my legs and the rags were stained with blood.

A memory came to me that I had lost or hidden. I'd awakened to agony in the night, with Aghazal crouching on one side of me, and Tasatyala on the other, and Grandmother Lagas kneeling between my legs. Grandmother was yanking something from my quim, a knotted clotted rag or cord, and when I screamed at the pain, Aghazal leaned down and said, "Hush now, hush, it will soon be over."

And Grandmother hauled and hauled away and I felt the tug deep inside, and I saw that what she pulled from me was not a single cord but a net or cobweb or roots, sticky and red-black, and I feared she was going to turn me inside out, for these strands were snarled around my inwards. I shrieked and twisted in my Sisters' grasp and they wouldn't let me go, and Lagas would not stop pulling until that thing was all out of me and she had undammed my tides, my tides at last.

King Corvus sent a messenger every day with gifts, and every day I sent the messenger back with answers written in flowers and beads, regretting that I wasn't well enough to receive him, promising fidelity, saying I languished without him, and so forth—no doubt his Lambaneish protocol tutor would interpret them.

I had been fortunate among women to suffer pangs from my tides only rarely, but this flow had been long pent up. It cost me such trouble and pain that I wondered if I were coming apart inside, if Grandmother Lagas, seeking to cure me, had damaged me instead.

The tharais servant came twice a day with broth from Aunt Cook and remedies from Grandmother. The servant washed me and emptied the slops, and I wondered if I disgusted her. I wondered too if Aghazal offered the woman at banquets for the amusement of the patrons in this same small room, which was painted—badly—with images of three of the twelve Abasements. I'd never seen her face.

I said, "We're both tharais now. You can take off your shawl." But she would not. It frightened her to be noticed. People only attended to her when she'd done something that warranted a beating. I gave her two amber beads and she deftly knotted them in a corner of her shawl and bowed out of the room with a basin full of dirty rags.

My tides ebbed on the fourth day, and I left the tharais room on shaky legs and went to bathe. The servant tamed my hair with dragonfly pins, and set a moonflower wreath upon my head. My own flesh seemed to be imbued with the strong scent of the blooms. I would never be able to purge myself of Moonflower, for I'd taken her substance into mine. She'd made me suffer and made me see, and I couldn't repudiate her without repudiating what I'd become and what I'd done.

But I had been mistaken to think of her as my mistress. She was my servant. And if she was, like most servants, not entirely to be trusted, and apt to go her own way when she had duties to perform—well, I was forewarned. I myself had been just such a servant.

I dressed in a magenta wrapper, and Aghazal helped me climb the stairs to the room where her sisters used to sleep. It now had a splendid bed, painted red, with gilding on the scrolled backrests and cushions of blue silk. The king sent it, she said.

I waited for him in the hot afternoon stillness. I got up to close the shutters of the windows overlooking the dining court, then opened them again to let a bee escape, and closed them again for shade. It would be foolish of him to be out when the Sun glared most fiercely. Perhaps he would come in the evening, when it was cooler. I lay down to rest with my hands at my sides, so as not to disarrange my tidy pleats. I had no intention of sleeping.

But when I woke up and propped myself on an elbow, I discovered King Corvus sitting on the other end of the bed, as far from me as he could get.

He gazed at me over his bent knees. "You don't look well."

I sat up with some effort. I couldn't have been asleep long, for the rays of sunlight through the lattice shutters had hardly moved. I covered my face with my hands. "Your pardon, Corvus Rex Incus, Master of Masters. I fear I'm still not fit to be seen."

"Will you be fit in a hand of days, in time for the initiation into the Serpent Cult?"

"I daresay—yes, to be sure." I lowered my hands. Let him see me haggard. Or let him refuse to look, as he was refusing now. He showed me his profile: the long nose, his left eye half closed, veiled by the fringe of his black eyelashes. But he had looked. His stare had awakened me.

I wondered if he would sit all afternoon without speaking, as long as was required for a semblance of coupling. I swung my legs over the side of the bed and stood up, and reached for his arm to steady myself, displaying more weakness than I felt. I opened the door to the upper porch, and as expected found someone waiting to serve us, Aghazal's cousin Gazuf. I murmured requests: refreshments, music, dice for a game.

Aunt Cook had prepared small astonishments for us such as eggs with blue shells that contained an egg-shaped pudding of ginger cream. The king had no appetite, but mine flourished. I ate delicately, bringing food to my mouth under the cover of my left hand. Down in the courtyard Adalana played the cithara and Tasatyala tapped on the fingerdrums. After three dishes, I told Gazuf to bring the wine and nothing further. "He's impatient, ein?" she said. I let her think so.

The dice were of the kind used for snakes and hawks, and made of gold. They came in an ivory casket with wooden counters: rosewood for snakes, elm for hawks. "Shall we play?" I asked King Corvus.

He said, "I heard you're easy to beat."

"You were misinformed. Hazard Chance favors me—they used to call me Luck, did you know that? I always win; it only seems like losing." I warmed the dice between my hands and let them fall on the table-tray, to see which of us would go first. Two numbered sides came up, adding to four.

The king took up the dice. "What stakes?"

"What you will."

He said, "I'll have the stakes my men had," and rolled five.

Without forethought I covered my mouth to hide my surprise.

"I see you no longer pretend not to know what you did."

"I wasn't pretending, truly. I'd forgotten it all, like a man who drinks too much doublewine. But later, when I was ill—I remembered." He believed me, or he didn't. Either way he disapproved. I dropped the dice inside the casket and closed the lid. "You never meant it," I said. "About the stakes." My voice wobbled and I feared my lower lip was trembling. Oh gods, was it possible he didn't know that he was cruel?

"Aghazal said you almost died. She said you were poisoned. Do you know who did this to you?"

"Yes. I did it."

He stared. "Why?"

"You can't guess? Surely I'm not the first—a handsome man like yourself, there must have been others."

"You tried to kill yourself?"

He seemed merely indignant. What was the point of lying if he didn't care? "I didn't say I tried."

"I should be going," he said. "You're still frail, I see."

"You are too courteous, Corvus Rex Incus. You do me too much honor to condescend to visit. I regret I can't accommodate you as I should. Would you like me to call one of my Sisters, Aghazal or Tasatyala? They would be only too glad—"

"This is not amusing. You're too clever not to reckon when you are offensive. Why such malice? Is it for this, your captivity?" He took my left hand and pushed up my bracelet of golden coils to show the pale welts on my wrist left by the manacle. He dropped the hand and it lay where it fell, a discarded thing. I stared down at it.

I was a little glad I'd caused him to waste his time wondering about me. I was also dismayed. To blame Moonflower—to admit I was a mooncalf who thought I could make him jealous—to say I never meant to hurt, or didn't think he could be hurt by the likes of me—all that was true. Yet it was also true that when I dowsed deep I found a wellspring of malice in me, and fury rising like a freshet. "You cast me away," I said. "I helped you and your men to cross the Ferinus and for reward you gave me to the arthygater to be a bondwoman. Or did you sell me? How much did you get for me?"

"I gave you to the arkhon. I emptied my summer palace to give him treasures, but they were received with scant thanks, I can tell you—too crudely made, too provincial. I had to give him something more. I told his factotum you were a seer and a true dreamer, and I expected him to send you to a temple to serve as an oracle. But everything is corrupt in this kingdom, even the seers. He must have thought you would feed the arkhon false prophecies on my behalf."

"Should I be flattered you thought me a worthy gift? I wasn't yours to give."

The king made a swift gesture of dismissal at this foolish statement. "I heard the arkhon had scorned my gift; you can be sure I heard. His factotum was only too delighted to tell me that he'd passed you on to one of the arkhon's daughters. I thought—I hoped—you'd be safe in a woman's service, safer than in mine. Maybe even content."

It had pleased him to think of me content, so he would not have to think of me again.

He stood, and his restless feet took him to a window, where he gazed into the courtyard through the latticework shutter. "Was it your notion to enact the role of Akantha in armor, to set a barb in me? Or was there a message in it from someone else, something I failed to decipher?"

I said, "Aghazal chose the Ode for Second Sister's first enactment, to display Tasatyala's gift for dance. And so Adalana could soar as the skyluck, and Aghazal herself could break hearts with her singing. As for me, my part was mute, so no one had to hear my inferior voice. All I had to do was strut about."

"You're sure no one suggested that particular Ode to Aghazal? Maybe Arthygater Klados hired her to reproach me, because I couldn't keep my wife from risking her life in battle. By the gods, Klados should know her sister better; her mind was impossible to change once she'd fixed on a course."

"I'm certain it was Aghazal's idea, no reproach in it."

"Did you ask her?"

"No."

"Ask her."

"I will—but I think—"

"Ask her."

"I'm such a fool—I should have thought of her, of Queenwife Kalos, when we practiced. If I had, you can be sure I would have told Aghazal to choose a less dangerous Ode to perform, one that would not risk the disfavor of the arthygaters. Or cause you to grieve—though we had no way to know you would be a guest at the banquet." I went to him and put a hand on his sleeve, and he moved away from my touch. "It was only when I lay there, pretending to die, that I remembered the dream of your wife, and regretted I'd been so blind. I never meant to pain you with such a resemblance . . . remembrance, I swear it."

"Oh, what does it matter!" he said, raising his voice. He sat upon the bed and his black brows were drawn together and upright white lines appeared between them.

Either I was spiteful or foolish; no reason he should find one more pleasing than the other. I knelt on the floor and bowed my head, and carefully did not look at him. When a man who prizes composure is bereft of it, he doesn't want a witness.

"You saw it in a dream," he said, "But I *saw* it. It was not a sight I could forget."

I imagined King Corvus seeing the rider emerging from the reeds—a rider lurching in the saddle on a screaming horse, trailing a plume of fire and smoke. And then the moment he recognized her armor—what he'd seen when he pulled off her helmet, the empty socket, the eye clinging to her cheek like a bauble on a string. He had endured that sight, and somehow found the resolve to cut her belly open to save his unborn child, only to find his son already dead.

"Why did she do it?" I asked. "Why risk your child by riding to war? I don't understand."

"Nor did I understand," he said. "She was supposed to remain on the other side of the river with her honor guard. She refused to stay in Malleus, saying it would be unbearable to wait and not to know, and I permitted her, because . . . the oracles foretold I'd have a son—so I thought she'd be safe, even if I fell." He stopped speaking; perhaps he stopped breathing. I looked at him furtively and found him motionless, his head bowed, with shadows in the hollows of his face. His hands were clasped in his lap.

He took a harsh breath and said, "But the oracles misread the signs. When I—when Divine Aboleo said I must save my son, I didn't want to, but I knew it had to be done—for the kingdom. So I—so we—cut her open, and what we found . . ." He lifted his head suddenly and stared as if blind. "She wasn't carrying a child. Something else had grown in her, not within her womb but beside it—a thing, a monstrous twisted thing, a sac of meat and skin. When we cut it open it was full of fat, and it had mats of hair and even a few teeth growing on the inside. Kalos must have known, you see? She must have known all along that my mother had cursed her. And she never told me. An unborn child swims in the womb, she would have felt it kick. This thing was dead, but still it battened on her. I think Kalos chose to die rather than allow the curse to be born." The king let slip a moan. I longed to go to him, but he would flee if I did.

Adalana sang a nightingale song from the Ode of Ouranos, and Aunt Cook scolded someone in the kitchen, but I hardly heard them. I listened to the king fight for breath, his hoarse gasps and shuddering exhalations. I knew he must feel as if he were bound about the throat and chest and belly with a strangling rope. He needed to sob, to rend himself open. He should weep. He must weep. But he mastered his breathing, one breath at a time.

He'd been compelled to speak this horror, to share it with someone, but I feared he'd burdened me with it without unburdening himself. He'd given me an intolerable gift of sorrow. It was not a dull, settled ache, but a weight that bore down on the muscles in my neck and shoulders so that they cramped, and left me struggling for breath against a sharp pain in my side. If this was what he carried every day—had carried over the Ferinus— how had he borne up under it, so long and so far?

I should have touched him, offered comfort that might have allowed him to fight his way to some release, if only for a time. I had been afraid to try. I doubted the chance would come again.

CHAPTER 33

The Serpent Cult

ghazal came to visit me in my new room about sunrise, and woke me up. She had just returned from a banquet with Second, and as usual she was famished and not quite ready to go to sleep. She said, "I missed you, Fourth. Tasatyala is doing splendidly, but still—she's so young, ein? She widens her eyes and gapes, like this, so credulous when a man is boastful. I fear she'll never be a wit, not like you." She poured amber doublewine into a glass for me. "So how was your arkhyios, ein?"

I sat up cross-legged on the bed and covered my shoulders with a morning dew shawl, which did nothing to conceal my nakedness. "Oh, Aghazal," I said. "He is sad."

"Sad?"

"He grieves for his wife, Arthygater Kalos, and I didn't know what to do; I ought to do something, ein? Instead I sat like a—a stump, a lump—useless."

Aghazal took a sip from her glass, and put it down with a tink upon the table-tray and leaned toward me, one arm over the backrest. "So—does this grief make him impotent?"

"Of course not."

"He can do more than glower and sigh, ein? I'm glad. Such a waste otherwise." She leaned closer and brushed aside my hair and took my earlobe between her teeth to give me a nip. When she pulled away, I glanced at her and saw she was only teasing.

I took her wandering hand and held it. "Sister, I fear we caused him sorrow. When we performed at Arthygater Klados's banquet, and I danced as Akantha in armor—we didn't know his wife died that way, in armor, on the battlefield where he lost his kingdom. He found her there and took off her helmet—just as in the Ode, ein? So I wondered why you chose it. Did someone suggest it to you?"

She tilted her head and smiled. "You did, in a manner of speaking. I saw you practicing a song of Pachys in the courtyard, and you were dancing in such an amusing and manly fashion, ein? It made me think we could accomplish Akantha's Ode someday, and I thought no more about it until the arthygater invited us to present a spectacle. And it was so perfect for Tasatyala." I let go of her hand, and she picked up a tiny salted smelt and ate it. "Besides, there was someone in particular I wished to hear me sing Akantha's song, ein? I'm sorry your arkhyios suffered a painful memory, but it did you no harm. Wasn't that the very same night he offered to be your benefactor? Why did he do so, if you caused him so much sorrow?"

She had her secrets—the name of her mysterious beloved, which she so delighted in concealing from the busybodies in the household. I had secrets too, some of which were not mine to bestow. "I've heard it said I bear some small resemblance to his wife. Perhaps—"

"Melancholy Yearning for the Lost Original," Aghazal said. "That's a pity."

"This resemblance—he tries to make me look more like her. He wishes to sponsor me for the Serpent Cult because his wife bore the serpent tattoo."

I expected Aghazal to be amazed, and to congratulate me for having a patron willing to spend five thousand golden beadcoins to elevate me to the cult. I didn't expect her to clasp my arms and say, "Oh no no no. You tell him—with gratitude for the honor he showed you—with humility, with regret, with tears even—tell him you must decline this year. Tell him you're too weak from your illness to be a postulant. Make some excuse, but say no, ein?"

"But why? He asked particularly, and I already said yes, that night in the garden, and he's paid the tithe. I can't refuse now."

Aghazal put her hand on my cheek. "You will try in vain to please him by resembling his wife. The Devotion of a Replacement is a thankless form of love, and you aren't well suited for it."

I shrugged.

"I know, I know," she said. "But the cult—it isn't worth the risk, ein? Didn't he warn you?"

"He said the tattoo would hurt."

"No doubt. But the initiation might kill you, Sister. There are many rumors about the Serpent Cult, and most of them untrue. But that's one I know to be true, for I know women who descended into the mountain and did not return."

"How is it dangerous, this initiation?"

"Who knows, ein? It's one of their secrets. Oh, no doubt it's a great honor to be a member of the cult—and a rare honor for a celebrant. Aeidin has prospered greatly since she became an adept. They are very exalted, very wealthy women, ein? And they look out for each other in business. As for what else they do together, and what they do with serpents—that is Katabaton's business. Do you even worship Katabaton?"

"She has been kind to me," I said, thinking of the shrine in the cave.

"She isn't always kind. Listen, the festival is not many days away. We'll tell him you're ill again, ein?—he'll believe it."

It pained me that I had to ignore her heartfelt warning with no explanation. She was angry and I couldn't blame her. "I see Grandmother didn't cure you of your stubbornness after all," she said.

The Festival of Katabaton's Navel was one of the great celebrations of the year, and women all over Lambanein went on pilgrimage to the sacred Mount Omphalos, which rose from the plains across the river west of Allaxios. It had a high conical peak that kept its mantle of snow long after summer heat had engulfed the city.

In Aghazal's household we were busy preparing for the pilgrimage. The women of the house made a fuss when they learned I was to be a postulant of the Serpent Cult. I would add to the luster of the household name, and everyone was determined to polish me accordingly, even Aghazal, who feared for me.

But one morning I found Aghazal weeping in her room. Our musicmaster, Skolian, had been found dead outside the hindgate of Arthygater Klados's palace; his body had been mutilated, the prick where the tongue should be, the tongue where the prick should be.

"But why?" I asked her. "Because our enactment reminded someone of how Arkhyios Corvus's wife died in armor?" It was a contemptuous Lambaneish punishment for an inferior, the severing of parts. Surely the king's men would not have stooped to such a deed. But Queenwife Kalos's sisters, the arthygaters Katharos and Klados—one of them might have set tormentors to work on the musicmaster. I feared they might start on Aghazal and her Sisters next.

"Not that," Aghazal said.

"What then? Oh no, you can't mean!—I heard a rumor that a singer enjoyed the favors of Arthygater Keros—was Skolian the one?" Would the arthygaters kill him for that? Maybe, if they thought to bend Keros to her duty. If she was refusing to wed the Starling.

Aghazal lay down on the bed and covered her face with her shawl.

I couldn't think of what to say. She knew I disliked Skolian, and I didn't want to sound false. But he'd done nothing to deserve such a death. I said, "He sang so beautifully."

* * *

I went with Second and Yafeqer and Aunt Cook and her daughters to the famous Temple of Katabaton to buy candles for sacrifices. The temple was crowded with women on the same errand. The stout fluted candles looked as if they were made of marble, and sturdy enough to hold up the heavy tiled roof of the temple. I bought two, one that could burn for five days, and the other for three. We prayed before the enormous statue of Katabaton, whose head nearly reached the carved rafters. Her forearms were gilded; her wig was made of red human hair. Ecstatic worshippers kissed her hem and feet, threw flowers, and sang prayers. We too made devotions, but I wished to speak to her alone, in the cliff shrine.

I parted from the others and descended into the markets of the lower town. There I found a good flint striker to make sparks, and chewy cakes of almond flour and figs. In the flower market I bought poplar leaves for courage, hawthorn for hope, heliotrope for faith, and saffron ribbons to twine a garland for Katabaton.

My basket was laden with gifts I'd received from Aghazal's kin and King Corvus, hidden under some leeks. I took small treasures that wouldn't be missed: beadcoins, pots of unguent, swirled glass vials of scented oils, golden bracelets, and saffron wrappers.

I felt Katabaton's presence in the little shrine, as I had not in her temple. I gave her the garland and the cakes, and sparked a fire in a clutch of grasses, and lit the candle that was supposed to burn for five days. I gave Katabaton the flint for the use of any other worshippers who might visit.

I prostrated myself and prayed that she would condone my presumption in offering myself as a postulant for her Serpent Cult. I believed in her, though I didn't hold her higher than the gods of Corymb. I was afraid she knew this. But I told her that I was a true daughter of Lambanein, returned after a long absence, and daily I strove to overcome my strange-ignorant ways.

They say the gods see farther into our hearts than we do ourselves. I prayed that what she saw, she forgave.

In the afternoon there was a lull in the bustle when the Sun shone straight down into the courtyard, and the king came to visit me. Soon I'd be riding from Allaxios with an escort of red-clad guardsmen; or I would disappoint him and refuse to go. Either way there would be no more afternoons such as this, so long, so short, the delicious ache of being aroused and thwarted. I had learned every wile in the list of Flirtations, yet I refrained from all but the subtlest provocations.

The king and I spoke in the High so we would not be understood by others. Certainly we were overheard; Aghazal's cousins Zarfatta and Gazuf had taken turns serving us, and they had teased me often about the lack of moans and cries from the room. I'd lied and said such utterances were considered impolite in Incus.

I told the king that Aghazal had chosen to enact the Ode of Akantha and Nephelin as a message to her beloved. Her songs—Akantha's songs—spoke of love that must be hidden, as Aghazal's was hidden.

"What does a whore have to hide?"

"Her beloved must have something to hide. Therefore it is not a patron. I think it's an arthygater, and an unmarried one at that." I'd puzzled over Aghazal's secret and this was as close as I could come to a surmise.

"Aghazal is an Akanthan, a woman-lover?"

I smiled. "She's fickle. She loves with Lightning Passion, first one person, then another. Aunt Cook says the last time Aghazal was smitten like this, she took up with an Ebanakan guardsman and squandered money on him. But she also falls out of love lightning fast, they say, and *phhtt!*—it's over."

We sat on opposite ends of the bed with a four-legged tray between us that held nothing but a tiny dish of anise seeds, a flask with watered wine, and two glass goblets. The king had refused food. "Is he afraid we'll poison him?" Aunt Cook had asked indignantly.

The king had ceased to listen to me, uninterested in the gossip of the house. Or he found it hard to believe that our performance had been aimed at someone else. He'd been the center of his kingdom, the one everyone sought to please or schemed to harm. He hadn't lost the habit of rule and the conviction of his own importance. Was that why I desired him? So I too could feel important?

I wondered what he was thinking, even as my own thoughts creaked round and round, borne on that wheel of which he was the hub. So we both sat brooding, absurd.

He said, "We've heard some rumors, a disturbing rumor—"

"Your pardon, Corvus Rex Incus—a rumor?"

"Many rumors. It's forbidden for men to witness the mysteries of the Serpent Cult, but men are often drawn to do what's forbidden, for the sport of it. And someone, it's said, once hid inside the mountain and saw women sacrificed to the Serpent, or to Katabaton, I'm not sure which."

"Men who know the least often speak the most," I said. "But I've heard rumors also. Aghazal told me it was dangerous."

"Then you know."

"I *know* nothing. I suppose such rumors serve the Serpent Cult well by inspiring awe and fear. And if these arthygaters do it, how can it be so dangerous?"

"You wish to unde.take the initiation anyway?"

"It would pain me to think of your five thousand in gold going to waste."

He allowed himself to frown at my flippancy. "We might find another way—a painted serpent instead of a tattoo."

"What will the Starling do to me when the paint wears off?"

He was silent. I waited a long time, but he wasn't going to say it; he never would. I said, "You must take me for a half-wit. I know why you're sending me, and what purpose the guards in my escort will serve. You mean to kill your brother—my betrothed. So you must see why I need the serpent tattoo. If your men fail, it will be better for me if the Stark, the Starling, believes I am Arthygater Keros, a real princess. He might hold me for ransom instead of killing me outright. He might even marry me, ein?"

With all the time I'd had to weigh my words in silence, still I had spoken past my reckoning. I knew how much I'd surprised him by the stillness of his face and his measured breath. Angered him. That foolish gibe about marrying the Starling—suppose he believed me to have such ambitions? He'd tell his men to kill me even before they killed Merle, lest I give his brother warning.

"No, listen," I said. "I didn't mean that. I'm grateful for your gift—the way back. I dreamed Sire Galan is alive, and while he lives I can hope to find him."

"You profess to want him still. I don't quite believe it, not since you took so well to whoring. When Divine Aboleo proposed to send you to this house, I thought he was mistaken in your character, for you'd never borne yourself like a wanton. Instead I was mistaken. Your Sire Galan will find you much altered. He will guess what you've become—he'll smell the taint of other men on you."

The king spoke my fear aloud, but how did it serve him to say so? He needed me to go, yet would mock me out of my reason for going.

Unless—I dared think it might be the king who was maddened by the imagined fragrance of other men on my skin. Contempt and desire were so often entwined, the Lambaneish had a name for it on their list. As a celebrant I should know how to use the advantage he offered. But anything I said might send that truth, so inadvertently revealed, back into hiding.

I turned away from him and kept my head downcast. He wanted me to feel shame and I did, and let him see it. My shame was planted deep and could not be altogether uprooted. But I'd been in Lambanein a long time now, and I wasn't as ashamed as he wished me to be.

So I hung my head, concealing joy and defiance. I let his words linger between us. Maybe he would hear what he'd let slip.

Wildfire

"I shouldn't taunt you for clinging to foolish hopes," he said after a while. "I have so many of my own."

We set out for Mount Omphalos before dawn. We women were leaving Allaxios, and all were welcome on the pilgrimage, from the poorest bond-women and beggars to merchants and noblewomen—all but tharais. We crossed the Ouraios River to the western bank over the three bridges, and we were a vaster throng, it seemed to me, than the army King Thyrse had taken to Incus. We sang and danced, played fingerdrums and cymbals and flutes, and talked, of course, and the sound of our songs and chatter, an exuberant commotion, filled the bowl of the Heavens over the plains. Yellow dust billowed around us from the beating of our bare feet.

The Sun rose behind us as we spread out along the road and spilled into the dry fields on either side. It was not long since Moonflower had nearly killed me, but the music and good cheer gave me strength. Never had I seen such a sight as this saffron river of women, and I was glad to be borne along by the current, and held up by my Sisters when I faltered.

It took all day to reach Mount Omphalos, and all of us walked except the very oldest and youngest, and those who were too ill. As we drew nearer to the mountain, the smooth snow-capped peak showed its deep furrows. The stone was dark gray and pitted, and had a forbidding look. Wild gorse, myrtle, and stunted cedars rooted in cindery scree on the slopes.

Aghazal rented shelters of brush and branches from the local villagers, and we made camp in a fold of Omphalos's skirts. We strolled about to watch the singers hired by wealthy noblewomen and merchants to perform enactments. I bought a tin amulet of Katabaton in her Moon boat from one of the many peddlers. Cookfires were forbidden, but everywhere people lit their stout candles to honor Katabaton. Aunt Cook had prepared a feast to be eaten cold, enough for us and for any visitors who chanced by, beggars or acquaintances. I didn't eat, for I'd been instructed to fast for a day and a night before the initiation. I sat on a boulder and rubbed my tired feet, and watched and listened. But I felt as far from my companions now as I'd felt close to them during the march. I'd dismissed warnings about the rites of the Serpent Cult as mere tales. Now I wished I'd believed them.

There were magnificent temples to Katabaton, Posison, and Peranon on the slopes of Mount Omphalos. But one was not magnificent at all; it was ancient, from the beginning of the First Age of the World. The hierophants of Katabaton chose the time for her festival to coincide with the one day a year the first rays of the rising Sun struck the entrance to this temple, a low cave, a maw in the mountain. The soles of many feet over many years had smoothed the stone stairs that led to this portal. We climbed in procession before the dawn, adepts and postulants and worshippers, and we added stones to the cairns lining the way.

We waited on the steps just below the door, the five postulants seeking to join the Serpent Cult. I was the only celebrant among them. I knew Arthygater Keros, and supposed the other three to be wealthy women of the palace district or upper town. We were clad in plain saffron wrappers and shawls; our net caps were strung with gold and amber beadcoins, and about our necks we had pungent garlands of marigolds, which signified prophecy. The adepts wore white wrappers and wreaths of dwale, which in Lambanein meant secrecy. Kin, friends, and curious and devout onlookers waited with us in the dark, in silence; they would not be permitted to follow us into the mountain.

I found by my right hand a swallowwort plant growing from soil caught between stones in a cairn. Such a sign couldn't be ignored. I plucked a stem and smeared the yellow sap on my webeye, the better to see what could be seen. It suffused everything with tinted light, so that even the white robes of the adepts were dyed a most luminous tender apricot, like the sky in the east where the Sun was still hidden.

The night had been cold compared to summer nights in Allaxios, but when I shivered, it was not from the chill. I looked to where my Sisters stood, and found Aghazal weeping. She gazed at Arthygater Keros, who returned her look sorrow for sorrow. And oh yes, I might have savored the discovery at some other time—to find that Aghazal had a Lightning Passion for Keros, and Keros for Aghazal—that First had sung Akantha's song for Keros—and the musicmaster was their go-between, his visits so frequent he'd been taken for the arthygater's paramour himself. It was a tragedy fit for an Ode or even an Epic that Skolian had died for them, and poor Keros was forced to undergo this perilous initiation to satisfy the ignorance of a traitor prince, her betrothed; I wondered if she had told Aghazal what husband had been chosen for her.

I was glad of the distraction of these frenetic thoughts, because I was afraid to be still—afraid to feel fear. Aghazal looked my way and I saw she had tears to spare for me, bless her. Even Tasatyala was crying.

The fiery Sun breached the horizon and sent her red rays across the plains and up the corridor of stones to the portal of the temple, and there the light stopped, and did not enter the mountain. The adepts ululated, and their wild cries went up like birds taking flight in our midst.

Some initiates went before us postulants into the mountain, and some followed, so we couldn't turn back if we lost heart. We descended many stairs in the dark, and crowded into a long room lit with tapers in soot-smudged niches. The temple had been hollowed out of the mountain, and its vaulted ceiling showed crude chisel strokes. Four square stone pillars had been hewn from the bedrock and painted blue. Everything else, even the floor, was whitewashed.

I'd dreamed of this place when I was a captive of the king's. And just as in my dream, there was something missing, something red. But beyond the blue pillars, where an altar would be, stood a figure as tall as a man, shrouded in white silk. An adept pulled away the cloth to reveal a statue of a hooded snake, its head upraised as if to strike. It was tiled in tiny red scales and had obsidian eyes. One of the postulants began to sob. I crossed glances with Arthygater Keros. Courage, we said to each other; we would not be frightened of a statue, no matter how fierce.

We postulants were made to lie down before this statue and cover our heads with our shawls. The noise was painful, all the initiates waggling their tongues to make shrill cries in this stony place, and clacking their fingerdrums. I wanted to cover my ears, but didn't dare. There were grating sounds of something heavy dragged over the floor; water splashing. They prepared some kind of bath behind us, and scented it with mint. These were such ordinary sounds and smells that I was almost giddy with relief. I peeped under my shawl at the base of the statue. Each diamond-shaped red tile was held in place by gold wire.

The initiates fell silent, which was worse than their ululations. A touch on my right shoulder told me it was time to rise. I draped the shawl around my neck and turned, and saw a large wooden vat filled with water, a humble thing like a dyer's vat. But there were snakes in the water. I couldn't tell how many, for they moved with sinuous grace, entwining in curves and coils, and they were ringed with bands of blue and black that confused the eye. They swam like eels underwater, and their tails were flat as fish fins: sea snakes, each as long as my arm.

The postulant who had been sobbing gave a shriek. She looked sturdy, tall and broad shouldered, but her lips had turned pale from fear and her eyes showed white all around. Arthygater Keros gripped her arm and hushed her.

I knew, we all knew without being told, that we would be required to climb in the vat with the snakes to prove our courage. I looked at the adepts who stood all around us, so many women young and old, and among them Arthygater Katharos and the celebrant Aeidin. Each of them had done this. So it must not be fatal, only dreadful.

An adept led forth two white gazehound bitches, lean, long-legged, and graceful, on white leashes. Around their necks were jeweled collars hung with tassels of saffron silk, and garlands of marigolds. Saffron cords were tied around their deep chests and narrow haunches. They trembled, and their dark eyes were mournful.

When the first dog was thrown into the vat, she paddled and kept her long thin head above water, looking to us for salvation. It seemed a long time before the first sea snake bit her flank and did not let go. She plunged and snapped at the snakes, and water rose up in sprays of glinting beads. The other snakes were vexed and struck back.

Three adepts used hooks to catch the gazehound by her collar and the saffron cords encircling her body. As they pulled her from the water, one sea snake hung by its fangs from her flanks, and an adept fearlessly stepped forward and choked the snake until it let go. She flung it back into the vat.

I thought the dog might die at once, but she managed to sit up, her forelegs scrabbling on the stone floor. When she gave a great shake, we postulants were showered with droplets of water. She didn't bleed, and it was impossible to see the marks of fangs on her hide.

Initiates cast the second dog into the vat, and the snakes, already roiling in the water, struck at once. This dog too was hauled out, and the two gazehounds shivered in a puddle on the floor, their marigold garlands and saffron tassels sodden and limp. The dogs had gone to the sacrifice consenting, with never a whimper or a bark—ah, but of course, the gazehounds were mute.

I expected the adepts to cast us in the vat straightaway, but they made us wait, and the waiting was itself a trial of courage. They sang paeans to Katabaton; Aeidin sang one hymn by herself, with the pure perfect tones that had made her famous, and her voice seemed to travel about the temple like a bird caught within the walls.

Arthygater Keros and I bore up the heavy broad-shouldered postulant, and she sagged against us. The other two postulants stood side by side. One was small and plump, with hair the soft brown color of a mourning dove; the other, thin, dark-haired, and resolute, knew all the hymns and sang with the adepts. I wondered why we did not, all of us, turn and flee. But I knew. The bulwark of courage was shame. It no longer mattered why I'd chosen to undertake this trial, or whether my reasons sufficed. All that mattered was that I must not snivel or faint or run, not so long as Arthygater Keros was steadfast. I esteemed Keros for her bravery, and adored her too, because she was worthy of my Sister's adoration.

The first dog lay on her side with her neck outstretched and strove to gulp air; her stiff limbs shuddered but otherwise were rigid. When she died, she released a stream of dark piss. The second dog persisted in living. She sat up with her hind legs splayed awkwardly, and a long thread of drool descending from the corner of her mouth. Her deep chest heaved as if she'd chased down a hare. Maybe the poison killed her later, after the ceremony. I never found out.

The adepts began to hiss a chant, and the sound washed over us in waves. I locked my knees so I wouldn't fall. I felt the chill scratch down my spine that told me a god was present in the temple. Adepts came forward with silver cups full of a dark liquid; Keros was served by Arthygater Katharos herself, and the other postulants by those who knew them, their upholders. I had no upholder and Aeidin offered a cup to me, a gracious gesture from one celebrant to another. The drink was sour and fermented, and among other flavors I tasted moonflower seeds in the gritty sediment I drained from the cup.

The swallowwort made me see everything smeared and refulgent and glittering in the yellow candlelight. We postulants disrobed, and our naked bodies seemed dusted with mica and yellow powder. Our shadows gleamed too, swaying to the praise songs, black and shimmering with iridescence.

Aeidin gestured that I should remove the red cord at my waist. I fumbled with the tight knot, and when the cord slipped to the ground I felt Dread flood into me all at once as if I were hollow. I prayed to the Queen of the Dead to spare me—or to welcome me, if I must die now. I'd forgotten about Katabaton.

I looked to Arthygater Keros and saw terror in her eyes too, yet she didn't falter. Adepts came forward to support the broad-shouldered postulant, who refused to take those few steps to the vat of her own accord, saying, "No, no, no," over and over in a shrill chant. And it came as a surprise and a marvel that, despite the Dread, so unwelcome and so familiar, which caused my legs to shake and my throat to dry—despite all that, there arose in me a Yes. Yes, I will. I will. It must have been a god in me who assented, because I couldn't have done it alone.

The snakes had calmed. They undulated through the water. Sometimes one would show its small head and narrow snout above the surface, or a brilliant banded loop of its back. The dogs had gone in one at a time, but we climbed in all at once, except for the frightened postulant, who balked, and clung to the knees of an adept until they dragged her away. I wondered if the temple would return the tithe to her family, and the thought caused a tiny bubble of mirth to rise in me, which I swallowed. There was no time for such trifles, yet there was all the time in the world; it took an eternity to climb over the wooden walls of the vat and into the water. An adept pressed my shoulder, meaning sit down, and I felt a snake slide past my shin and my legs folded, though I hadn't intended to sit. My chin was just above water and my back pressed against the rough slats. I was horrified that I might be bitten on the face and I covered my face with my hands and squeezed my eyes shut.

The snakes were perturbed again, they darted through the water quick as lightning. One struck my right shoulder a glancing blow; another bit my left thigh and held on. I shrieked and heaved myself to my feet, and for a long moment the serpent dangled there, writhing. It had a small head with a black circle on its brow, and its blue bands were brilliant as lapis. It fell away, and many willing hands helped me from the water. The other postulants too were climbing out; the dark-haired one tumbled backward over the rim of the vat and was caught.

It was over. It had just begun.

There was a whitewashed door behind the blue pillars, and a stair leading deeper into the mountain. Four adepts carrying candles led us, and our shadows wavered over serpents painted on the walls. Down and down we went until we reached a curving chamber, a natural void in the mountain; no one had tried to smooth or polish the rough rock.

We postulants were bidden to lie down on feather-stuffed pallets. Adepts rubbed us with lumps of pumice, snakestones, they said, to take away poison. They said we were not going to die.

The adepts examined us for tiny punctures and scratches; the venom of these sea snakes didn't cause bleeding or swelling or bruising at the bite, unlike that of vipers. I had three bites, the most of any. The stout placid adept who tended me—Horama was her name—plucked out a serpent's tooth from the wound on my thigh and knotted it in my shawl, which had been carried down with my other belongings. She said the fang was a gift from the Serpent Katabaton, and a sign of favor.

Even now it began. My neck was sore and stiff and my right arm and left leg ached. My throat was dry and yet my mouth overflowed with spit, and I was obliged to swallow again and again, and each time it was harder, as my throat constricted and my jaw grew rigid. My tongue took up too much space in my mouth. My left side grew intolerably hot, until sweat burst from my skin, and my right side was chilled. But I couldn't panic. I was drowning in euphoric lassitude.

Horama anointed me with a salve of aloe and grease. My sight was failing now, my right eye rolling one way and the left another, so that I saw the adept doubled as she knelt over me. She appeared as two overlapping hazes of golden light, and all around her shades and shadows undulated from the edges of my vision.

She drew on my body with a burnt stick, zigzag lines from my cleft to the notch at the base of my throat. My neck was rigid, and I couldn't lift my head to see what she was doing, but I felt the tip of the stick scraping my skin, and I knew she limned my serpent. Horama took out a long, shining needle and threaded it with a short thread, and before every stitch she dipped the needle and thread in a bowl of dark pigment. She embroidered the snake, starting at the lips of my cleft and working upward, taking careful even stitches all around the outline. She dragged the thread through the skin, just under the surface, and left color behind. She was a most meticulous seamstress. The needle pricked me entering and leaving, and pain ascended with every stitch. Far worse was the pain of the venom corroding the sinews of my body.

I heard someone else wailing. But Katabaton had turned a key and locked my jaws together, and I couldn't pry them apart to speak or cry out. She has the power to enforce silence. And I had her blessing. She didn't make me numb, but she made the suffering unimportant, ever more distant as I departed.

I sank down and down and at first I believed I was sinking into Sleep, but it was some other sea, one that doesn't grant oblivion. I sank until I realized that all along I'd been ascending, wriggling upward through the umbilicus that unites Mount Omphalos, Katabaton's Navel, to the overworld, where she dwells with her husband and child, attended by meneidon and the shades of the dead and the unborn.

In the overworld only my right eye was useful; my left eye still watched Horama at her work. I was granted a glimpse, I saw but could not *see*, for it was beyond my understanding.

I entered a place—a hall?—a forest?—a forest of pillars, with a sky of honeycombed vaults. This place was crowded with beings who moved swiftly and changed shape like leaping flames. They confused my single eye, for every being, and the place around us, was tiled in intricate patterns such as those found on the skins of serpents; it was hard to tell one being from another, or distinguish them from the surroundings. Perhaps they were all one, flames of a single fire. When these creatures—meneidon I supposed, in their true forms—when they spoke, their words too were patterned with scales, and their song-speech coiled about me, and I was caressed by meanings I couldn't comprehend. I was amazed and baffled to be admitted there, where a mere person did not belong.

My own form was also baffling. I had become elongated, and scaly as a pale snake, a serpent-woman. Some creatures beckoned me to follow, but I was too torpid, my time was thick and slow, while their time was quick; I was too heavy to fly in their darting fashion, and too solid to change shape. I was able to open my jaw just a crack, enough to let out my forked tongue to taste the colorful ribbons of their speech.

But the glimpse was over. That was all I was permitted, and I slipped slithering down through the narrow voids within the mountain to the hollow where drool came from the corners of my mouth and ran down my chin. I took rapid sips of breath, for there was an invisible burden on my chest I could barely lift. My limbs were stiff and still. I thought I was going to die. Horama thought so too. Too much venom, she was thinking. It doesn't matter, I wanted to say. If I die, I die.

Because I'd always thought that when I died, my lonely shade would be all that remained. But that was wrong, all backward. Our bodies are but shadows cast by the one fire, briefly, in this world. But oh, I loved the world and my body in it, the dark and solid shadow—though it might be, like a shadow cast on the ground, but a poor copy of a more splendid self.

The serpent was complete, embroidered on my skin in stitches of fire, and the venom had kindled within me and was burning its way into every cranny, from the crown of my head to the soles of my feet. My sinews spasmed in agony, yet my limbs were stiff as wood. Against my will I let out a gush of piss, and I was cast down again through Katabaton's Navel, though I do not recall that journey or the return.

CHAPTER 34

Adept

ing Corvus summoned me to live with him in the Court of Tranquil Waters. I'd come to look upon Aghazal's house as my home, and upon her Sisters as sisters, and upon her kin as friends, and I never loved them so tenderly as when I had to leave them. Aghazal told me not to weep. Wasn't it a happy occasion that my benefactor wished me to live with him? And we Sisters would see each other often at banquets, and visit back and forth between town and palace.

I said, "I'll try, ein? It isn't the custom of Incus to parade about with one's concubine as it is here."

She teased me, saying she'd be disappointed if I proved less willful toward him than I was toward herself.

The king had not instructed Garrio to give me my own room, so I took one for myself on the opposite side of the courtyard from the king's quarters. The room was full of useless things: stained cushions bursting with tow and inhabited by mice, dusty chipped statues, broken furniture. Garrio ordered mudmen to clean it out, and in the rubbish they found an inlaid and carved bed that had all four legs, though one of the backrests was broken. A tharos maidservant mended a rip in a mattress. Dust flew as they beat the pillows and an old tattered carpet.

I waited in the shade of a pomegranate tree covered with red blooms. I was insulted that King Corvus hadn't seen fit to prepare for me. He surely was mistaken if he thought I would leave immediately. I wasn't fit to go, not yet. I ached in every sinew and my piss was murky yellow—by which I knew I was improving, for it had been brown before, like dried blood. Arthygater Keros too must be suffering from the snakebites and tattoo, though she'd received less venom than I. It would be at least a hand of days before either of us could set forth.

Garrio came to tell me my room was ready. I thanked him, but I didn't wish to move, not yet. Like a serpent, my flesh had grown cold, and I

491

needed the Sun's heat, to bake on warm stone in the courtyard. That's where the king found me when he returned late that afternoon: curled up asleep on the flagstones in my fine silks and gold jewelry. I wore a saffron wrapper with an indigo band on one end in honor of the king. I'd put aside my celebrant garments of magenta and blue and parrot green.

He crouched beside me and said, "Is this the hospitality you were offered? I am ashamed."

I shaded my eyes to look at him, and sat up with a painful effort that required no exaggeration. "Beg pardon, Corvus Rex Incus. It's only that my room wasn't ready, and I fell asleep."

"Your room?"

I pointed to the heap of broken furniture outside my door. "As you have no women's quarters, I told Garrio to put me in that empty room. Was I supposed to—? I thought—it's the Lambaneish custom. This way you can invite me when you have leisure, and when you don't, I won't be troublesome."

"Ah. Quite proper," said the king.

He helped me stand. I waited for the dizziness to pass and leaned on his arm as we crossed the courtyard. A few mudmen had the audacity to cheer and call out my name. Garrio opened the door to the king's bedchamber with a flourish, and gave me a wink behind the king's back. For all his listening at doors, he didn't know his master's use for me.

The king turned to Garrio and said, "Tell Divine Aboleo she's here."

Garrio could be as impassive as his master, when he chose. He bowed and hurried away.

The king sat on his bed cross-legged and asked, "Do you have the tattoo?"

I disrobed before him, and it was not as I had hoped or dared to imagine. I unwound my saffron wrapper, and wondered that I could be troubled by modesty after all I'd done.

I'd removed the bandage the day before, and rubbed the tattoo with the greasy salve I had been given, and looked at the snake backward in Aghazal's small round handmirror. So I knew what the king would see: the indigo outline of a narrow zigzag serpent. Its tail lay between my breasts, and the forked tongue—dyed red with a pigment made from rust—just touched the lips of my cleft. Where I'd been stitched, the flesh was inflamed and swollen and sore.

Divine Aboleo entered the room, and I started to clothe myself. He gestured at me to stop, as if I were a tharais servant who didn't merit speech. He stood too close and peered at the tattoo. My face grew hot even as stipples of gooseflesh rose all over my body. I couldn't seem to teach myself not to fear him.

Wildfire

The king said, "It looks like a lightning bolt, not a snake. My wife's serpent curved around her waist like a girdle and swallowed her navel."

Divine Aboleo sat down across from the king, and I dressed. "Each one is different," I said. "An adept makes it according to her vision, her inward sight. See, I have these three peaks, one for each—" I almost said one for each bite. I didn't mention what Horama told me, that she depicted the creature striking downward because I served Katabaton with the hidden serpent between my legs.

"Merle will not expect it to look like this," King Corvus said.

"He saw your wife's tattoo?"

"At the wedding, when she took off her robe for the consummation. Some took the tattoo as an ill omen—and everyone thought it made her look barbarous."

"Did you think so?" I asked him.

"I assumed it was a mark of her descent from the gods of her people. But I thought at first that it marred her, and she would have been more perfect without it."

At first. I wondered what he meant by that.

Divine Aboleo said, "Did Arthygater Keros receive a tattoo?"

"Hers must be very painful, such tender fresh, flesh." I traced it on myself to show them how the snake looped around both her breasts, and its head swallowed its tail.

"And is yours painful?" asked King Corvus.

"It wasn't easy to come by. I am sorry it disappoints you."

I dined with the king and Divine Aboleo that evening in the king's bedchamber. It was fortunate the king hadn't invited any Lambaneish of consequence to dine with him. They'd have ridiculed him for allowing his cook to serve food so abominably bland and ugly. If I stayed, I'd see to it that the food improved. But the talk was all of me going.

Divine Aboleo said he'd procured two tharos bondwomen to serve as handmaids, young and obedient.

"Did you get a tharais servant too? I shall need one."

"You can have one of ours," said the king.

"You have someone who knows how to arrange a woman's hair?"

"Is that what they do?" the king said. "Perhaps you better purchase one. How much do they cost?"

I had no idea. There was a pause while a servant delivered a dish of potted hare with turnips.

King Corvus said, "My wife had ten handmaids when she first arrived—

magpies, I used to call them. They were always twittering and screeching in those shrill voices. None of them could speak a word in the High."

"What of Arthygater Kalos, could she speak the High?"

The king didn't answer.

Divine Aboleo said, "We've hired an escort of Ebanakans with a Lambaneish captain—an honest chiseler, by all accounts. He came recommended for work of this kind, guarding merchants and their goods, or brides and their dowries. He says it's imperative to leave before the next New Moon to make sure you're across the mountains before the rains start."

So soon? Already the waning Moon was at the half. I said, "I would feel safer traveling with some of your men, trustworthy men. Must I be among strangers?"

The king said, "Merle knows my men."

"Too many spies," Divine Aboleo said. "We cannot send a troop of kingsmen with you, even part of the way. You must leave the city unnoticed and travel to Lake Sapheiros; your escort will meet you there, with the dowry."

I had no appetite, and took tiny morsels of turnip. I was just as frightened as if I intended to do this. "You expect me to go alone to Sapheiros? But that's a ride of many days!" I turned to the king. "The Starling doesn't know your mudmen—please, give me someone I can trust. Give me a jack or some horseboys, give me Chunner and Lame, please?"

The king looked surprised. He knew the names of his horses' ancestors for fifty generations; was it possible he'd never bothered to learn the names of his horseboys?

Divine Aboleo said, "You forgot she was a mudwoman, didn't you? Indeed it's a marvel to see her eating as daintily as a Lambaneish princess. The Ebanakan whore did wonders with her."

King Corvus said, "Of course we didn't expect you to go alone. You may have three mudmen to take to the pass—and beyond, if you wish."

"Which three?"

He made a gesture to show he didn't care.

The priest said, "We've provided you with a protector already, someone to accompany you the whole way. Someone with whom you're well acquainted, I hear." He raised his voice and called to Garrio, who waited outside the door. "Send him in."

I hardly recognized the young priest. Since I'd seen him last, the day of the Hunt, he'd grown a beard and stopped shaving his scalp. The bristle of brown hair on his head was already long enough to obscure his tattooed third eye. Divine Volator. He wore a split surcoat and loose leggings made of the same brocade, in the Lambaneish mode. He bowed to the king and didn't look at me. I wondered if he was being punished for coupling with me during the Hunt, and if the king knew. I touched my cheek and raised my eyebrows, wondering how they'd hide the godsigns on his right cheek, which marked him as a member of the clan of Growan, and a servant of the god Rift.

"He'll have an ugly scar there," said Divine Aboleo.

The young priest slid a glance at me and looked away so quickly I nearly missed it. I said to King Corvus, "So this is the man who will rid you of your brother."

The king asked me to stay in his bed that night. He said his men would wonder otherwise. They didn't care for peculiar Lambaneish customs such as sleeping apart.

I said, "Won't they wonder when you send me away in a few days?"

Likely his men would think he'd already tired of me. But the gossips of Allaxios would find it most interesting. A man didn't spend five thousand in gold to dedicate a postulant to the Serpent Cult only to lose interest in her some days later. If I disappeared, they might think he'd killed me in a fit of jealousy. No matter. I had no family to demand compensation from him. The gossips would wag their tongues and not one of them would care. Aghazal would care, but what could she do?

How absurd—to think of Aghazal fretting about me, grieving over me as if I were dead, made me grieve for myself. It was all planned. They had purchased bondwomen and hired guardsmen, and I merely had to do as I was told. It had been vanity to think I could beguile King Corvus into keeping me. Even if he desired me, he wouldn't hesitate at my sacrifice. Look at how many of his men—men he loved more dearly than he could ever love me—had died for his claim to the kingdom.

The king slept, or seemed to, though I didn't know how he could sleep when I was so restless, turning like a hen on a spit. The venom was devouring me from the inside out—or was this the pain of healing, like that of frozen flesh as it thaws?

I went to the pisspot for the third time; I used the one in the privy closet in the bathing room so as not to annoy the king. I had to step over Garrio going and returning, where he lay before the king's door in the portico. The last time he touched my ankle and said, "Are you ill?"

I stooped and whispered, "Yes."

"Can I help?"

"Have you any doublewine?"

"I'll get you some," he said, and rolled out of his pallet and tiptoed down the arcade. His thin shirt stuck to his back with sweat. Old man. How old was he? His master was—if I reckoned rightly—twenty or twenty-one. I would wager Garrio was twice as old. His legs were slightly bowed and his calves were thin.

I sat with my back against the wall and looked at the dark courtyard. Cool feathers of air brushed my bare shoulders. Garrio returned and we passed the flask back and forth, and soon a pleasant numbness spread from my belly to my limbs. My head felt insufficiently tethered to my body. It kept wobbling.

"Garrio," I said. "I don't want to go, not anymore. I used to want to but now I don't. The king . . ."

"I'll go with you," he said.

"You will? Oh, my brother, you don't mean it. You'd never desert your master." I put my left hand on his bony knee.

"There are four or five of us will go, if you wish. I asked Chunner and Wheezer and Lame tonight, and they're sure Voro will go too."

"You have big ears."

He grinned and poured a libation on the tiled floor of the colonnade. "To Hazard Peril, protector of travelers."

"But I'm not going," I said.

"To Ardor Hearthkeeper then, patroness of staying home." He poured again and passed the doublewine to me. "Not that this is home," he said after a pause.

I crept into the king's bed and curled up with my back to him, but he was already awake. "Do you have to get drunk every night?" he said. "I told you to stay away from my men."

"It's only Garrio. I asked him for doublewine, because it hurts."

"The tattoo?"

"Everywhere."

"What were you whispering about for so long?"

"Nothing. He's homesick." Garrio put me to shame. He had a lodestone in him, always pointing toward home. He'd been telling me about his woman in Malleus and their children, and how he worried, knowing his city had fallen to the queenmother and her Wolves and her foreign allies.

"Aren't you homesick?" the king asked.

I didn't answer.

"Aren't you?"

I rolled toward him. He lay on his back with a corner of the thin linen coverlet over his hips, and the rest of him bare. After the shaven men of Lambanein, it was almost shocking to see the dark line of hair below his navel. His eyes were closed. He opened them a crack and closed them again.

I hadn't bothered to unwind my wrapper. I wished I had, so there'd be less between us. "No," I said.

He was quiet.

"It's unkind of you not to help me sleep," I said.

"If I'd known you were so restless, I would not have invited you to stay."

"I'll go back to my room." I sat up, and he put a hand around my wrist. "Stay here. It will look odd."

I lay down with my back to him again. "Did you truly make a vow?" I asked.

No answer. I smiled, knowing he couldn't see my face. I had made a sort of vow myself, not to be so forward as to frighten the king into rebuffing me. I rubbed one foot over the other as if my ankle itched, so my silk wrapper would rustle. The friction of skin against skin was enough to start the quivering sensation in my cleft, and the heat unfurling in me. I lifted my hair to cool the nape of my neck. To go this slowly was harrowing—and yet there was pleasure in it too, I was even now discovering. Pleasure to linger near the cusp and prolong the waiting.

I wondered about his wife, and how I would compare, and how he would compare to Galan and the other men I'd ceased to count; I wondered whether a consummation so long desired would prove inferior to anticipation.

I felt a pang of longing for Galan then, missing the way we'd greeted each other at night with desire, finding each in the other what we sought and all we wanted. I was artless then, though I fancied myself bold because whores had taught me a few pleasing tricks. But I had learned him. We'd learned each other, there in his bed that moved from camp to camp and yet was always home. The narrow cot in the Marchfield, the wider camp bed in Incus, and yet always we slept touching, and when one turned so did the other.

I remembered we were not always in accord; but better I remembered the way Galan had looked at me sometimes. I was bold enough now to call what he felt, what we felt, by its rightful name: to call it love.

I was still amazed that Galan loved me. What qualities, what particulars had he prized in me that he could see even after Wildfire had struck its blow and made me a stranger to myself? Would he recognize what he loved still, when I came to him in the guise of a Lambaneish princess, bearing on my body the tattoo of a serpent? I might lie about what had happened—the things I'd done—but I would not be able to conceal that I had changed.

Often I had imagined setting forth to return to Galan, but I'd shied from imagining the end of my journey. Even in my Moonflower dreams I'd failed to foresee the moment when we would meet again, though Moonflower had shown me he lived. Did that mean there were too many hazards between us, and I would never arrive? Of all the perils on that perilous road, the one I feared most was that Galan would not love what I'd become. That it would all be for naught.

I could decide later whether to cross the mountains. Step by step, I could choose while I had choice. The gods send us good fortune and bad, and put us to the question of how we will meet our fortune, and what we will make of it.

Nonsense.

My thoughts skittered about as if they had something to do with what I might choose. Ardor Hearthkeeper told me once, *Burn bright, burn fast,* and oh I did burn. I couldn't govern my desires, let alone my fate, which had led me by way of chances and mischances to a foreign city, to lie beside an exiled king. I turned to look at him and found him asleep with his mouth slightly ajar. I didn't mind seeing him that way, so unguarded.

I was truly Lambaneish to desire two beloveds at once. They even had a name for it, the Twinned Heart. Not a heart divided, but doubled. And so it felt: but sometimes one had to choose.

My goat Ruddy had gotten into the kitchen garden again and trampled the hazel sticks that held up the peas and eaten the plants roots and all. The withy fence wasn't sturdy enough to keep her out. I hit her with a stick and threatened to make her into goat stew. She shied away and I chased her out of the garden, and set to work weaving the fence again. She was such a glutton, I was amazed she had enough sense not to eat the moonflowers.

I wondered if the goat was worth the trouble she caused. I asked my cat Gowdylakin what she thought. I had so been looking forward to the first peas.

I could make a fence of stout palings. It would take a long time to cut them and drive them into the ground, but it would serve for years. But there was too much to be done to undertake such a task now. Always too much to do for one person alone.

I went down to the herbary, and picked cockeburr and black lovage to seethe with wine to cleanse my blood of the venom, and borage to make a poultice to soothe the stitches. I did a bit of weeding and straightened up to see storm clouds coming over the Needle Cliffs, trailing the long ribbons of rain. Fork-tailed swallows danced over the meadow and invisible winds trod down the grasses. Thunder resounded like avalanches. Likely the storm would have battered down the peas anyway.

Storms were commonplace here on Mount Sair; I lived in the sky, not below it. Yet I feared the lightning, and woke up.

498

Wildfire

"What did you dream?" King Corvus asked. He was dressed and sitting on the side of the bed. It was well past dawn, to judge by the light through the shutters.

"Nothing of use," I said, and sat up slowly. I rubbed my sore legs.

"An invitation came for you this morning. The messenger went to Aghazal's house first, then came here, so all of Allaxios will know where you are by this afternoon."

"Is this invitation from a patron?"

The king dropped a golden bracelet in my lap, shaped like a coiled serpent with chevrons engraved down its back, and red jasper eyes. "Arthygater Katharos wishes you to dine with her tomorrow evening—no doubt she will ask you many questions, which of course you won't answer. Maybe you can find out when Keros is leaving."

"To dine with her—not entertain her guests?" I put the bracelet on my right wrist and admired it.

"Precisely. This came with the invitation as well." The king crowned me with a wreath. I took it off and found it was made of dwale, like the wreaths the adepts had worn for the rites. I truly was an initiate, accepted as such even by royalty. I put the wreath back on my head and grinned at the king, and belatedly covered my mouth.

He laughed, which seemed to surprise him as much as it did me. "Can you believe it? Five thousand beadcoins to buy a mudwoman, a whore, the privilege of mingling with princesses. Everything is for sale in this city."

"You're wrong," I said. "The gold bought me the right to try. But I, I myself, won this honor by braving the initiation. So don't say I don't deserve it."

He was too pleased to mind being contradicted. He stood up, restless. "Of course you deserve it, I didn't mean to say otherwise. You have courage, I've seen it. In the mountains I used to say to myself that I would endure as long as you did, or die ashamed." He leaned over me and clasped my shoulders. "I know you're afraid of this journey, and with good cause, and you have no reason to be loyal to me. But you have your own reasons to undertake it, don't you? Don't you still?"

I nodded yes. But I let my eyes deny it. I looked at him through a glaze of tears. It would have been coarse, overdone, to blink and let them fall.

The king sat on the bed again. "You told me you dreamed this— dreamed you were standing before Merle with Ebanakan guards. So why do you hesitate now? What do you fear?"

"I had a dream, but not that one."

"Then how did you know our plans?"

"I dreamed you told me. You said it would comfort you to know Merle was dead. But I never had a dream in which I met the Starling."

I expected him to be incensed that I'd misled him, but he appeared stricken. "I took it as a promise, a true foretelling," he said. "A gift from Lynx Foresight, just as you were."

"True dreams are not promises—they prove false if we do something to avert them. I warned you of the Hunt, and you were not harmed."

"Prove the false dream true," he said to me.

Had I time enough, I might convince him he could not part with me for a hundred brothers. There was no time. The next New Moon was in a hand of days.

A hand of days, a hand of nights. I could hope.

I dressed in saffron linen and filled my market basket with things I had taken with me from Aghazal's house: cloth, embroidered and plainweave, lamps, oil, spices, scents, and beadcoins. I carried them to my hiding place in Katabaton's Cleft.

I gave blood and milk and moonflower seeds to Katabaton, in thanks for sparing and welcoming me. I promised her another candle like the one that had burned for five days, and my serpentine bracelet, as soon as I had worn it to the arthygater's banquet. Katharos would expect to see it.

On the wall beside Katabaton's painted image, I scratched a zigzag serpent striking downward like a lightning bolt, in honor of the serpent form she takes when she visits us in the underworld.

I had to sit and rest several times as I climbed the stairs to the wooden door in the cliff. Sweat gathered under my hat and along my spine. I wheezed. No one had said how long these venom pains would last, or if they would ever go away. I wondered who would dress my hair and depilate me tomorrow: what should I wear? I'd failed to send a gift with the messenger—had the king remembered? I snorted and began to laugh and couldn't stop. By Katabaton's soles, I'd rather face the Ferinus again than disgrace myself by appearing ill clad and ill coiffed before the arthygater and the foremost women of Allaxios.

Garrio saw me crossing the courtyard. "Where have you been?" he said. "We were looking for you."

"Errands." I showed him my basket, full of wax, honey, combs, cords, a wicker coil for my hair, obsidian blades, serpent hairpins, salves, plums, and apricots.

"Your servants are here, waiting in your room." He seemed to think this amusing—I suppose I did too.

Wildfire

It was true my new handmaids were young; at a guess, neither above fourteen. One was Lambaneish, and her name was Pousin. Her husband had accused her of adultery and sold her. The second had a shaven head with a fuzz of black hair, which meant she had but lately arrived at the city gate. She was splayfooted, knock-kneed, and skinny. She had pale skin and terrible old eyes, and understood only a few words of Lambaneish, and none in any other language I knew. She stank of fear. They had no shawls, and their wrappers were rags, the saffron so faded it could be mistaken for tharais onionskin dye.

"Who chose them?" I asked Garrio. "I can see they spared no expense."

He shrugged and left me with them.

The bondwomen looked hungry. I gave them my gold and purple plums, and sent them off to get something to eat from the king's cook.

I took a brazier with embers to the bathing room near the king's bedchamber, and melted wax in a borrowed pot, and mixed it with honey and lemon juice to depilate myself. The tiled pool was empty and needed scrubbing. I cleaned it, too impatient to wait for the handmaids. It was furnished with a pair of spouts in the shape of leaping pards, with tongues as stoppers. As water gushed into the pool, I removed the hair of my body, and scrubbed and rinsed myself.

I sat down gingerly in the pool. The water came up to the middle of my chest. It was mountain water from the Kerastes, and it had warmed somewhat on the long journey over the plains in the stone causeway, but it was cool enough to be refreshing on such a hot day. The bathing room was two stories high, and it had been grand once, but now its painted walls were smudged and stained and some of its marble basins shattered. I wondered if a battle had been fought here, or if the court had been abandoned because of ill omens.

Strange to be alone in a bath; it was a place for being sociable. I floated on my back, looking up at the charming dome in the ceiling, inset with globes of colored glass. The water rocked me gently, like Sleep, and I felt as if I could let go and sink without drowning. A dream fish slid along my arm and flicked its tail, and I opened my eyes and settled on the floor of the pool with a thump and a splash.

The king sat on the tiled rim and took off his boots. "You're in my bath."

"Shall I get out?"

A curt shake of the head. He'd been riding, I could tell by the smell of horse and the sweat stains on his kidskin leggings.

"Hunting?" I asked.

"Hawking. Gods, I wish I could get out of this city and go somewhere I could gallop. I'm tired of pretending a garden is a forest, I want a true forest, a green one; I want rain sometimes and animals that are not caged."

He stripped off his clothes and began to step into the pool, and I shooed him away, saying he had to wash and rinse first, or he'd dirty the water. Had he learned nothing of Lambaneish ways?

"Too much," he said, and emptied a basin over his head.

"Scrub too." I pointed at the coarse sack filled with sand.

He threw it at me. What a mood he was in: irked and amused, like someone being tickled who refuses to laugh. He slouched down in the water, facing me. He was tall enough to lean his head on one end of the pool and touch the other with his feet. I moved my hands to set in motion a tiny current. He closed his eyes and I took it as permission to stare. His skin was all over as brown as Galan's face after he'd been tanned by the Sun. His wet hair had divided into neat points, black feathers.

I put my hand on his foot and ran my thumb along the ridge of his anklebone. "Did you truly take a vow?" I asked, knowing the answer already.

He opened his eyes. It was not the look I longed for, but it was plain enough. I moved through the water and knelt beside him. I ran the sharp nail of my mother finger lightly down the dark line of hairs under his navel, and along the length of his prick, which was already rising.

He stopped my fingers from nibbling at him like a minnow and brought my tharais hand to his mouth, and kissed my wrist where the manacle had scarred it. I clenched my fist and he unfolded it and kissed my palm, and I felt chilled, as if all the heat in my body had rushed to my left hand. He marveled aloud that the hand was so hot to the touch. He said Garrio had told him how I'd thawed the hands and feet of his men—he'd seen it himself in the mountains.

He traced the zigzag serpent from the tail at my throat to the tongue at my cleft. Each stitch was reddened, raised proud above the surrounding flesh. He asked if the tattoo still hurt, and it did, it was inflamed in the wake of his touch, but there was pleasure in it too. There'd be no need for him to bite and scratch to mark me. He'd already given me a mark, I would bear it always, and though it was dedicated to Katabaton, I wondered if it pleased him to think it all his own.

I touched the tattoo of his lineage, the godsign above his beard, three stars one above another: Rift. I rose up on my knees to straddle him, and put my palm against his neck so I could feel the life pulsing in his throat. He looked up at me, smiling, and with his hands on my hips he pulled me down. I felt as if I'd eaten moonflower, and emerged from the tough shell of my old skin in some newborn, tender skin that was alive to every sensation, so that I felt again the forgotten imprint of the knots in the red cord around my waist, under the weight of the king's hands. And when I arched backward, ripples moved away from me and returned as caresses, slipping over me as I slid over him. I bent to lick beads of water from his shoulder, and he tasted of cold mountain streams. I wanted to taste his salt, his sweat.

I sheathed him slowly. With Galan I often had been too eager, too hasty, and this time I meant to dally. And it was what the king seemed to want. He leaned against the wall of the pool and draped his arms along the rim, and I understood that he wished me to coax and provoke. He eased himself with me—was that all? It made me feel a whore, and like a whore, I was feigning. Because there was so much longing pent up in me that restraint was a most exquisite torment.

But was there any way he would have taken me but lightly? Never by force, never as a captive; never as a mudwoman or bondwoman who wasn't free to refuse. I'd done as he asked and become a celebrant, and ease was something a celebrant could give, an honorable gift. I should be honored he'd chosen me for that purpose, when he'd let no other console him since his wife died.

He closed his eyes and the smile was still on his lips, but there were creases between his brows and at the corners of his eyelids, signs of melancholy, and I feared he was thinking of her, of his wife. Whether he strove to forget or remember her, I couldn't tell. Whereas I thought of Galan and tried not to. I felt I betrayed him now as I had not done before, with those others—as if betrayal could happen by degrees.

And now the king was all the way home inside me, yet we were not joined, and I couldn't bear the distance between us. I clasped my arms around him, feeling the ladder of his ribs, his sinewy back and the long furrow of his spine, and I pressed against him, chest to chest and belly to belly, until I felt the sting of the serpent tattoo. I sipped water caught in the curve of his ear, and he took my head between his hands and scraped the bedraggled wet hair away from my face and kissed me on the mouth for the first time.

And there at last was what I sought, urgency, and his strong hearthfire blazing up in answer to mine.

Of course the Lambaneish have a name for the first Posture we took, the woman kneeling over the seated man, and for the next, the woman seated on the man's lap, and for other Postures that flowed one into the other in the coupling. But even the Lambaneish have not named everything in their Taxonomies, every posture, every embrace, every utterance, every kind of love.

*   *   *

That night I went to the king's bedchamber without being asked, and he stayed away talking to his men until late at night. When he came to bed, he stripped and lay beside me, but not touching. I stirred to let him know I was awake. He said nothing. I turned on my side and faced him.

"Are you sorry?" I said.

He turned his head my way. "For what?"

"For what we did."

A short laugh. "I have many regrets. That's not one of them."

"But you aren't glad. You think of your wife perhaps. You are sorrowful."

"I'm thinking of you."

"But here I am."

"Yes."

He made a gesture I took as permission, and I moved over to lay my head on his shoulder. He gathered me to him, and his hand clenched my upper arm in a painful grip. I said, "But I thought . . ."

"I know you did. And that I very much regret."

I sat up and reached for the wrapper draped over the scrolled backrest of the bed.

"Come here," he said. "Firethorn, come here." He touched my back. It snared me. Gods, had he ever said my name before?

I'd learned to speak of love with Lambaneish eloquence—easier to speak so when love is not felt. Now I was as wordless as when I was first thunderstruck. I lay under him and he looked down with pity in his eyes, but his mouth was bleak, his kisses unsparing. I was ashamed of the mewling whimpering sounds I made; ashamed to be seen so undone. But even as I grieved I took everything he would give.

Nothing had changed. He still wanted me to go.

CHAPTER 35

Katabaton's Cleft

entered the palace of Arthygater Katharos by the foregate, which I had never done before. In the pavilion next to the dining court, a tharais napkin washed and dried my feet and slipped on silk shoe-stockings, guest gifts from the arthygater. I looked at the napkin's bowed head, hidden under the onionskin-dyed shawl with the brown stripe, and wondered if she was someone I knew, Nephelais perhaps.

I doubted even Nephelais would recognize me. Being without a tharais servant, I'd arranged my own hair on a wicker form shaped like a coiled serpent with its head tucked in. I left curls free around my forehead and down my neck, in a fashion I'd been obliged to use since my hair was too short; it had been copied by others. Over that I wore a net cap with golden beadcoins inset with garnets; over the net cap, a moonflower wreath. On my face, a glittering mask, mica for my cheeks and malachite for my eyelids. My lips were dyed the color of the darkest cherries.

Arthygater Katharos offered the banquet in honor of the new initiates of the Serpent Cult, and the four of us shared a platform near the arthygater's, under the entrance tower. It was cause for celebration that Katabaton had accepted four of the five postulants, all but the coward who had refused to enter the water. Most years only two or three made the endeavor; some years none succeeded.

I'd earned my place here by braving the serpents; we had all been brave, and we postulants shared a bond as partakers in the same secret rites, and I was proud of it. Yet I was cozening them, my fellow initiates. I sat across from Keros, and as we compared our aches from the venom and pains from the tattoo, I was thinking of how the king meant me to steal her place and dowry, and remembering the last time I was in Arthygater Katharos's dining court, serving as a napkin. A day ago I might have felt a secret glee to have such secrets, and taken delight in my daring. But today I enacted a joyless spectacle for the other guests.

I could refuse to go, when the time came. As long as I was here, in Lambanein, I might have a chance. I was not entirely mistaken about what the king felt, I couldn't be.

If I refused, no doubt he'd be furious. He'd turn me out. Aghazal would take me in, but there was no need for her to incur King Corvus's enmity openly, not if I could fend for myself. I'd hoarded enough to rent a lodging, perhaps even to buy a small house in the lower city.

It wouldn't damage my reputation much if the king repudiated me. Some might even say I'd gotten the better of him, persuading him to sponsor me for the cult and then jilting him. Gossips would relish the fact that he'd paid the tithe for my initiation by borrowing against the dowry of his betrothed. The tattoo would raise my reputation and my price, and soon I'd have patrons again and the gossips would have gone on to other rumors.

I could live this way, accepted like Aeidin among the most powerful women of the kingdom; I could rise in the cult, learn its mysteries, perhaps even become a priestess.

Or I could become Arthygater Keros, enough like her to fool a strange-ignorant prince. Wasn't I speaking to her now in the accents of Lambanein, and covering my mouth when I laughed, and winkling snails from their shells exactly as she did? And when she quoted the Epic of Balanos, didn't I find an apt reply from the Commentary of Historian Mnasthan? No matter that the food had no more savor to me than stale bread crumbs, and I could hardly swallow.

I didn't know I would be called upon to speak, but I was. Between the sucked course and the bitten, we new initiates had to stand up before the other adepts and recount what we'd seen during the rite of envenomation. Arthygater Keros went first, describing her vision of Katabaton Milk-giver in the overworld. Katabaton sat in a garden, the most beautiful garden Keros had ever seen, of which the gardens of Allaxios were poor counterfeits; the goddess sat on a throne of shell, suckling the infant Peranon, and her raiment was woven of rays of moonlight, so dazzling it hurt Keros's eyes. Katabaton didn't speak, but she bestowed on Keros the gift of her smile. Keros described garden, throne, raiment, and smile eloquently in verses of six, six, eight, so I was sure she'd been warned of what to expect.

Arthygater Kyma spoke second, recounting a vision like that of Keros, and using some of the same phrases. I didn't believe Kyma at all, for according to the adept who examined her she hadn't even been bitten. She'd swooned from fright, not venom. Which proved to be the worse for her, as she had to suffer the pricking of the needle when the serpent was stitched on her skin without being numbed by the poison. She had screamed and screamed. I'd heard her, but she'd seemed so far away.

Then Gnosin, the devout postulant, spoke in verses of five, six, and seven. She had seen darkness rather than light, for she was swallowed by a giant python, and inside the snake she was bathed in liquid fire that burned and burned without devouring her. She suffered such agony she thought she couldn't endure it, but she was not permitted to die. Winds spoke to her inside the snake, warning her that the arkhon had a wound festering in his entrails, and he was rotting from the inside out. If the wound broke open and allowed wastes to enter his belly cavity, he would surely die. His physicians must see to it that he fasted and was purged and purified, or woe betide the kingdom, for the one who should inherit it was still too young.

It was my turn and I was unprepared, and ashamed of my vision. The place I saw could not have been the overworld, for it was nothing like the garden Keros described. Nor had I been granted a vision of Katabaton herself. But when I stood to speak, I told the truth and told it unadorned. To lie would have dishonored the rite, and I'd suffered too much for it. I spoke loudly and heard my voice echo back to me from the arcades around the court.

> "I thought I was dying,
> sinking, plunging, drowning.
> I descended deep and deeper
> Until I was climbing.
> Up not down, ascending
> through a narrow place, a tunnel.
> I emerged somewhere strange,
> on a threshold, a place
> I took to be the overworld.
> Everything was scaly,
> The walls, pillars, ceilings,
> all covered with scales like serpents.
> The beings too were scaled,
> A gorgeous confusion
> Of patterns bright and intricate.
> I too wore serpent skin,
> But I was slow, too slow.
> The creatures there were swift as flames.
> Swift as lightning they moved.
> One being or many?
> I could not tell—they joined, parted.
> Their speech was bright and quick,
> flickering and winding
> around me like ribbons, long tongues,
> serpent tongues touching me.

It was beyond my ken,
what they said. So I fell away,
down and down to the pain
of tormenting stitches.
I did not belong among them.
Blessed Katabaton
Bound my jaw, forbade speech.
But here, among her worshippers,
I must ask: Where was I?
Who are they, those others?
What were they trying to tell me?"

I sat down on the platform again, and Keros touched my arm briefly in a gesture of friendship. It seemed a long silence after I spoke, but perhaps it was not. Aeidin began to ululate in a high voice that gave me a chill, and another woman and another joined her, until the dining court resounded with their cries.

I didn't truly expect my questions would be answered, not then and there. But I hoped in time I would learn the meaning of my vision from adepts who knew Katabaton's mysteries. In time, in due time.

After the bitten course, a tharos servant approached me and whispered that Arthygater Katharos wished to meet me outside the dining court. I was flattered, thinking the arthygater did me an honor by speaking to me privately. When I reached the corridor, two burly tharais men seized me by the arms. I opened my mouth to scream and one of them thrust a dirty rag in it. They bent my arms behind my back until I feared I might crack at the elbows, and they marched me downstairs and through tunnels I had never seen.

Gnathin, the arthygater's factotum, awaited me in a small damp room with two tharais women. I knew them by their hands: Lychnais from the bathing room, and the taskmistress of the napkins, with rings squeezed onto her plump fingers—she who had threatened to betray me to the arthygater's tormentors if I didn't give her gold. She must have recognized me.

"Let me see her hands," Gnathin said, and the tharais men thrust my arms out in front of me. Gnathin had seen me many times veiled, in the bathing room. She hadn't failed to notice the scar on my left wrist.

"Are you sure this is the one?" she asked the tharais women, and both of them nodded yes. The taskmistress of the napkins scraped powder from my cheeks with the knuckles of her left hand, a gesture that said more clearly than words that I was tharais and not beyond her reach.

One of the tharais men yanked my right arm behind my back again and wriggled his thumb against the inside of my elbow. When I tried to pull away, he wrenched my arm. I didn't mean to kneel, but my knees gave way. Tears stung my cheeks like lemon juice in a cut.

They left me alone in that room, and I had time to consider my own stupidity, how I'd deceived myself and feared all the wrong things. Tormentors were outside the locked door. The room was deep underground and water seeped through the crumbling plaster, and the walls were smeared and spattered with brown stains I feared were old blood.

Arthygater Katharos came to the room after her guests had gone home, in the last passage of the night. She had questions to ask, and she asked them through Gnathin, for she wouldn't speak to me directly. Who was I? Whose thrush was I? She had never believed Arkhyios Corvus sponsored me for the cult because he was enamored of me.

I tried to keep the arthygater's tormentors away from me by talking, and I lied as well as I ever had, and that was well indeed. The lies were all mixed with truth and dreams. Didn't she know I was the king's dreamer, his seer, the one who had found a way for him across the Kerastes when all was lost? The king was impoverished, and he gave me to the arkhon as the greatest treasure in his possession, but the arkhon had disdained his gift. He'd bestowed me on the arthygater—to be a mere bondwoman, a weaver. I told her how Zostra had humiliated me and tried to make me tharais. How could I, a woman of Incus, be tharais? There was no such thing there. It was all a mistake. The taskmistress of the napkins had threatened to tell the arthygater I was a thrush, a false accusation, and I had to flee to the king, what else could I do? He was grateful to me for past services, and he found a place for me with Aghazal. The celebrant knew nothing of my past; she thought I was tharos, an ignorant provincial from the Kerastes.

Arthygater Katharos asked again why the king had sponsored me for the Serpent Cult. What did he hope to gain?

I was kneeling before her. I wanted it, I said, holding up my head and trying to look like someone the king could desire. I wanted to be more pleasing to him, his devoted Replacement.

I shouldn't have made her think of her sister Kalos. The arthygater gestured to her tormentors and one put his foot on my back and the other hauled my hands up behind me with a rope around my wrists, until I felt as if the bones between my shoulders and my neck were twisting hard enough to break, and I screamed because it hurt, and also because I wanted the arthygater to believe she was forcing the truth from me. When the tormentors let go, I straightened up and shrieked at her: You think he isn't besotted, ein? He broke his vow for me. I can make him do anything for me, the whore Alopexin. Now everyone knows it.

The arthygater wasn't satisfied with my answer, and asked again. Such simple methods, pincers, ropes, hands. One tormentor pulled too hard and dislodged my left arm from its socket. I lay on the ground screaming, without any thought of artifice, while they wrenched it back in place again.

When at last I was able to speak, I said of course it wasn't my idea, of course the king asked me to undertake the initiation. Had I known how dreadful it was, I'd never have done it. But I'm the one who is besotted, and I wanted to please him. He scorns me for a celebrant, they have no respect for them in Incus. But he needs me. I am a true dreamer and an oracle, and he offered me to serve Katabaton, the mother. He seeks her blessing and indulgence, he hopes to appease her for an offense he has yet to commit.

When she asked what offense, I said matricide, of course. Because he must kill his own mother, ein?

By daybreak each lie was less plausible than the one before, and at last they were all used up. I told the truth then, about the portrait, and the dowry King Corvus planned to steal, and how he meant to kill his brother Merle rather than his mother, and how I'd served as the king's thrush even in the arthygater's bathing room. And every word was a danger to the king, but I gave way. I gave way to pain and the threats of maiming. They said they'd take my tongue if I didn't speak.

I was ashamed I told his secrets, but I wasn't ashamed to take revenge on the taskmistress of the napkins by telling how she permitted me to spy in exchange for gold. The arthygater didn't allow me even this petty triumph. Of course the taskmistress couldn't be trusted. She was tharais, wasn't she?

Arthygater Katharos was appalled that I'd passed for a tharos celebrant and tainted so many unsuspecting people. But it was worse that I'd sullied the sacred rites of the Serpent Cult. She called into the room a heirophant of the cult and the adept Horama to help question me. They insisted I had not seen the vision for myself—some initiate must have told me what to say. Who was it?

I swore I'd seen it. I said if an initiate had instructed me, surely she would have had me tell about the overworld, the home of the gods with its splendid garden and throne, and not the strange place I'd visited, wherever and whatever it was. They could see my bewilderment. Still Arthygater Katharos had her tormentors press me brutally. I was about to offer a lie to the arthygater, since the truth displeased her, when the hierophant halted the torments.

I owed my life to that vision. I'd seen the overworld in one of its true forms, baffling and terrifying; it was a sight granted to very few initiates, and those few were singled out to ascend step by step into the mysteries. Katabaton might easily have slain me for my trespass during the ceremony, the priestess said, but she had carried me to her jeweled serpent realm. Arthygater Katharos must not take it upon herself to kill someone the goddess had spared.

Instead the arthygater banished me from Allaxios. To make sure I did not and could not return, she had me marked so I would be known as tharais, with or without the shawl over my head. One of the tormentors used his pincers to sever two of my fingers between the top and middle joints: my mother finger, foremost on the left hand, and my father finger, foremost on the right. He knotted the bloody fingertips into a rag and tied the rag around my neck, and he roped my hands before me so everyone could see the amputations. They stripped me of my saffron tharos garments, and made me go naked, without even a shawl to cover my face. By face and snake tattoo and maimed hands I would be recognized and punished if I dared to return to the city. The arthygater found it shameful to reveal that an imposter had been initiated into the Serpent Cult, but it would have been worse to hide it, if it permitted me to deceive again.

I had no way to get word to the king, or to Lame and Chunner, who waited for me at the foregate of the palace with a rented cart. I left by the hindgate with a mob around me. The veiled tormentors had tied a horse's bridle around my head and put the iron bit in my mouth, so I couldn't speak; one of them led me by the reins. The other pulled me along by a rope around my arms, which were tightly bound at the wrists and elbows. The bit galled the corners of my mouth and pressed down my tongue so it was hard to swallow my spittle. I stooped, trying to hide my nakedness, and the tormentor yanked the rope and made me stumble. My blood was on his feet.

The Sun had risen. They let the bondwomen out of the manufactory to see me go. I recognized many, but at least Catena was not among them. Tharos kitchen servants followed to pelt me with rotten fruit, and stable-boys threw stones. Tharais servants were given onions to throw at me. The tormentors led me through the palace district, descending from one terrace to another, and there was such a clamor that many people came out of palaces to see what was happening and join the festivities. They shrieked at me in a fury, and I saw their mouths open and close, the sound like darkness welling from their throats, and I couldn't hear a word they said for the roaring in my ears.

The tormentors pulled in different directions, my head one way and my hands another, so my feet didn't know where to go, and this amused the mob. Dulcis walked behind me, striking my bare back with a stick she'd picked up somewhere, but her little sting was nothing to me. I was in agony from the arm that had been pulled from its socket and put back again. I hardly felt the pain in my hands.

I thought most of the followers would stop at the tharais gate, so as not to suffer pollution, but they accompanied me into the district. Then I understood this spectacle was a warning to all tharais of the punishment for trespassing.

We passed the fountain of the bronze sow Nephron, where I'd so often gone to fetch mountain water, and walked down streets well known to me, past the dyers and tanners and smelters and their familiar stinks. As we passed, tharais residents covered themselves with their shawls, if they had them, or put their hands before their faces if they did not. Some followed, some jeered, but most stood still and silent, watching.

Someone threw weeds at me, and they were bright on my path, dandelions for foresight and poppies for consolation. Tharais stood on rooftops and threw down flowers and sweet-smelling herbs, oleander meaning beware, and irises to say I was too haughty, and incensier for remembrance; even in the tharais district there were many gardens. A daring boy ran up and threw poplar leaves at me: courage. Stones struck my forehead and blood trickled into my right eyebrow.

The stones didn't make me weep, whereas the flowers and leaves nearly undid me. But that well had gone dry. I'd wept all my tears during the night.

There were shades among the living. Sire Rodela jeered, but I paid him no mind. The Dame paced beside the tormentor who led me by the bridle, and Na beside the one who held the rope. I wondered if they'd come to escort me to the realm of the Queen of the Dead, for it was certain I'd never be permitted to enter the Lambaneish overworld when I died. If so, they'd come too soon, for I wasn't going to die, not today.

The guards had closed the huge iron-studded tharais gate in the city wall because of the disturbance. For me they opened the small postern door. The tormentors let go of the reins and rope, and someone, Dulcis probably, gave me a shove. I fell sprawling through the doorway and a guard slammed and locked the door between the mob and me. I was banished.

I walked south between hovels crowded on either side of the road, and naked dusty children stood and watched me. Their parents hid, and no wonder. Misfortune in the city was often blamed on tharais, and those who lived unprotected, outside the gates, were driven away and their shanties burned.

Someone threw a rag at me, a tharais wrapper, torn and dirty. Likely I had never received a gift more precious to the giver, for a rag was a treasure here among the poorest of the poor. I thought people were watching me from the dark huts as I sat down in the road and awkwardly, painfully, freed myself of the bridle and the rope around my arms. I tore strips from the rag and bound up my fingers. They had stopped bleeding, but I couldn't bear to look at them, the ragged meat and splintered bone.

Wildfire

Untying my arms had eased the strain, but as the blood rushed into my numb hands it burned like fire and venom. I moaned as I walked, until I became aware that I was moaning and stopped the awful sounds.

I trudged all alone, dressed in the tharais wrapper. Even the shades had deserted me. I went in the direction I'd been shoved, moving my feet because there was nothing else to do. But in time it occurred to me I was walking in the wrong direction. I turned back toward Allaxios, and saw it again as I'd first seen it, rising terrace upon terrace to the gilded palace that crowned the mountain.

I had remembered I was rich. I didn't have to go naked and poor into exile, to wherever I was going.

I tried to reach Katabaton's Cleft from the south, walking upstream on the riverbank. The city wall was built nearly to the water's edge, and I crossed mudflats and reed beds in its shadow. I passed the marshes and the shallows below the street of dyers where cloth was staked out in the river to be rinsed, and I walked under the arches of the bridge we'd crossed on our pilgrimage to Mount Omphalos. But soon I could go no farther. The terrace walls were too steep, and they came right down to the river's edge. I must go all the way around the city to approach from the north side, and use the current to carry me around the bend in the river that embraced Mount Allaxios.

It was the only thing left to me to do. One imagines in Fate's realm a path that branches, each branch a choice leading to further choices. But sometimes many paths converge on one, the inevitable and only path, and whether one is fearful or fearless, one must take it.

It took a day and a half to walk around the city, much longer than I expected. I stayed far away from walls and roads, and slept in a dry gully and drank water from an irrigation ditch.

Northeast of the city I came again to the river. I found a downed tree with a tangle of gray roots, and I dislodged it with great effort from a sandbank. The current tugged the tree away from shore, and I went with it, my right arm draped over the trunk. I saw the aqueduct high overhead, and the trunk rolled suddenly and I went under. I was nearly caught in the roots, but I dove down, and the tree passed over me, scraping my back, and within the green river I opened my eyes and thought, if I breathe now I will drown. And I almost did. But I kicked and went up to the roil and froth of rapids that pummeled me and tossed me against a heap of boulders, great shards of the mountain, broken teeth in the maw of the cleft.

I crawled out of the water and lay across a flat boulder, gasping. The reeds between the rocks were noisy with frogs and warblers. The river had torn away my rag and I was naked again, and everywhere bruised and scratched. But I lived. Every breath said so.

Mount Allaxios towered over me, turning a stony back to the river, the road of the dead. The Sun had risen over the mountain and she stared down as if amazed to see such a peeled sprawling creature as me. Swallows stitched back and forth between the walls of the chasm, beating their wings to rise, dipping down and rising again.

It was already hot, but I was shivering. I sat up and rested my head on my hands and was startled to discover the moonflower wreath and my net cap with valuable beadcoins. Some of my hair was still entwined around the wickerwork spiral, fastened by serpent pins with obsidian eyes.

I ate three faded, limp moonflower blossoms, such a gift. With Moonflower, pain was not pain, but superb lacerating awareness. Oh why did the gods let me live? For what purpose?

I clambered over the boulders of the cleft floor and the slope that led to the stairs outside the cave; my left arm was almost useless, and all my limbs trembled. I sat on the last stair. Already my throat was dry, my eyes were dry, and I felt a flush rising, the surge of my heart. Vertigo bloomed in me; I clung to the cliff, fearful of swooning, and felt the earth sliding sideways.

When the ground stood still again, I groped behind the tapestry of bluebind and pulled treasures from the cliff. I dressed myself in saffron and fastened the wrapper with the jade disk and golden cord Tasatyala had given me. I used the flint I'd given to Katabaton to kindle a fire in the shrine, and put a clay pot of water on to boil.

What are you doing? Sire Rodela asked, but I ignored him. Of course he had returned. He liked moonflower. I was not at all surprised to see the Dame and Na there too; the Dame watched me gravely, and Na scolded Sire Rodela and shooed him out of the shrine. I'd never been able to dismiss him so easily.

I untied the rag from my neck and spread out the bloodstained cloth. My two severed fingertips looked so strange, so dead. The fingernails were purplish; the skin was yellow and the meat brown; the bone looked gray. I could tell the fingertips apart because the nail on my left forefinger had been trimmed in the beak style.

It made my fingers hurt to look at the parts that had been torn from me. I understood for the first time what Fleetfoot had meant, how the pain was not caused by absence, but by the presence of something invisible; how it pinched and throbbed.

I boiled the right fingertip first. The smell of cooking flesh made my gorge rise, but I didn't falter. When the flesh and nail loosened, I pulled the whole joint from the top of the finger. I rubbed swallowwort sap on the bone to stain it yellow, and I told the Dame it was hers as much as it was mine. I promised to dye it indigo when I could, and invited her to speak through it when it pleased her. The bone of my father finger, my tharos bone, my Blood bone, my rightbone.

Next I put the left fingertip in the pot and watched it bob and boil. I freed the top joint with its splayed knuckle end and notched tip, and colored it with red dye used for lips, from an alabaster jar I'd hidden tennights ago. This bone was to speak for Na, if she wished: the bone of my mother finger, my tharais bone, my mud bone, my leftbone.

Here in Lambanein they divided the left hand from the right, tharais and tharos; in Corymb and Incus they divided mud from Blood. I had been one thing and another, and for a long time I believed I was what people called me. No doubt I would have gone on believing had I been raised by my Lambaneish parents, or lived out my life in a small village in the Kingswood.

I no longer agreed to these distinctions. I wouldn't be bound by them.

I poured the finger broth on the ground as a libation for Katabaton, and it turned dirt to mud. I drew a divining compass in the mud that was two handspans across, twice as large as the cloth one. I wrote the godsigns in their places, sure of the marks and their meaning, sure of their order around the horizon.

Outside the cave, in the brazen heat and light of a summer afternoon in Allaxios, only the insects were awake and chirring. Inside it was dark and cool and silent. Moonflower troubled my sight and made Katabaton's hair of serpentine roots seemed to writhe. I felt, as I had at times before, that other gods watched me through Katabaton's unblinking eyes. I darkened my eyelids with charcoal, as Az had done when she threw the bones for me; I put swallowwort sap in my webeye, as the Dame had taught me. I cast the pair of bones three times to reveal my nature and how I would meet my fate, three times for the past, present, and future, and three times for the gods. The bones touched signs, and the signs whispered and murmured, in a low susurration that did not resolve into speech. I hoped to see images bright and clear as Moonflower dreams, showing some way forward or some way back, for I could go no further on this road.

I thought I deserved foreknowledge. The gods had given me a deed to do with my two finger bones, and I had done it without shirking, despite my horror of it. Why shouldn't my own bones speak to me more clearly than those of the dead?

I bent close to the compass, the better to see and hear. On the very last cast, the yellow rightbone had landed on Artifex, and the red leftbone on the Warrior. This was the ninth throw and I had seen many signs and many patterns. Here I was being asked to worship them both: Eorõe Artifex the maker and Rift Warrior the destroyer.

I would rather owe allegiance to the dead one, Artifex, the one without temples and Auspices; Artifex who made our forebears. Some of the Blood called her the Potter, and disdained her because she'd dirtied her hands with clay. I used to think it a pity she had died, and couldn't protect us from the meddling of other gods. Now I saw her death was necessary. Otherwise we would be her creatures, the making only half finished. She had pinched our ancestors out of clay, like little oil lamps that bore the press of fingers, and she'd breathed into them to awaken their fires, and didn't I too burn with the fire bequeathed to me?

Such a strange gift she had given us all, for the fire had been there already, it was always there. But she had separated it into small buds of flame, in vessels that could be broken—these bodies—so that we loved what was mortal and feared to die. So that while we lived we thought ourselves single and singular, yet we craved never to be alone.

Did Artifex make us just for the pleasure of making something well? She had made us so beautiful that even gods desired us. I saw Aghazal in the kitchen, scolding Aunt Cook Angadataqebay for extravagance, with her thick black hair in a plait down her back and her brown skin glistening, and a damp patch of sweat on the back of her wrapper—just as comely as when she appeared before her patrons in her finery. And there was Mai, with her belly round and pale and perfect as an egg, sleeping between her throes— so dear in her exhaustion, so lovely because she was beloved. And Tobe, the little boy, always in motion, as if the hearthfire of a large man was burning in him and he could not be still, not for a moment, not until he sickened and the fire flickered and went out.

The fire did not go out, it never went out. It was part of the one fire I had glimpsed in Ardor's temple. I used to believe the shade was all that endured, but Sire Rodela had taught me better. The shade lingered, refusing to be joined, but like smoke it dissipated in time. Artifex had given us this perilous gift, and we clung to it even after we died.

But the red bone, the leftbone, pointed to Rift Warrior on the divining compass. Rift for what divided us. Men, knowing they could not live forever, tried to make their names immortal. Sire Galan and King Corvus were both warriors. Did I love them despite that or because of it? To me they shone more than other men, and I felt more alive in their presence, and I had learned to call that feeling by the various names of love, and what was it but the longing to feel the heat of the inward fire, and to be illuminated by its light? Yet I was drawn to what was mortal in them, even the crescent-shaped scar on Galan's back, or the way Corvus's left eyebrow showed his doubt. In me, love had been entangled with rage—rage being another way to kindle a blaze, and now it seemed to me I had sought after it, furious even in desire.

516

Wildfire

I'd given myself over to Galan's wants, and then to the king's purposes, but always imperfectly, in my disobedient, wayward way, so that we would burn brighter and hotter. At times I'd prided myself on serving one important man or another; in my most prideful moments I'd thought I served one god or another. If a god used me, I was not insignificant. Yet I never thought to ask myself whether I admired the purposes I served—whether I wanted to further them.

Did my bones tell me I must worship Rift Warrior, and must I obey them? I'd seen enough of war to know I hated it. Rift Warrior was loose in Incus, and now every kind of cruelty abhorrent in peace was permissible there. I couldn't lend myself to Rift's purposes—nor to the king's and Galan's, not while they served the Warrior.

I'd been given many gifts, the hot left hand and cold right hand, the knowledge of fire, the sharp eye and the webeye, shadowsight and true dreams, and visions of other worlds like veils about our own. I'd been given the gift of healing, and I had neglected it, pursuing Moonflower dreams and other kinds of knowledge, and flinging myself like a moth against Desire's lantern, to be scorched by jealousy and lust.

The power to heal was such a humble gift, maybe that's why I hadn't been content with it. War and plagues and famines killed by the thousands, and a healer saved one by one, staving off, for a little time, a certain end. But even to give a little time was precious, as the easing of pain was precious. It was something I could do, and be glad of doing.

Where war was, there was surely the greatest need for healers.

I scooped up the finger bones and put them in the pouch and drew the drawstring tight. While I'd leaned over the bones to see the signs and listen to their faint whispers, I'd forgotten my pain. Now all I'd held in abeyance came rushing back, and I fell on my side and curled up in agony, and I cried out against Artifex for making us so imperfectly. Why had she given us pain? Why had she made us frail?

Not frail. Look at how much we could endure.

I went on enduring. I spent days uncounted in Katabaton's shrine, in her cleft. My sinews ceased to burn and ache, and my bruises faded, and my left shoulder settled in its socket, and fresh pink flesh covered the naked bones of my fingers. By the grace of the gods, by the labor of life within the marvelous clay, by the hearthfire burning in me, I was healed.

Acknowledgments

Rumor has it that editors don't edit anymore, but my editor at Scribner, Alexis Gargagliano, certainly does. She read this book in several drafts, helped me pare it down, and asked the right questions. I'm grateful to Alexis and to my agent, Merrilee Heifetz, for their faith and patience.

Thanks to those who shared their experiences with me in conversation, Odella Woodson on aphasia and Valerie Windborne on speaking with the dead. Thanks to the midwives Marjorie Horton, Meg Grindrod, and Gina Haldeman, whom I consulted to write the birth scene; any improbabilities remaining are not their fault. Gina especially was midwife to that birthing, and she tried her best to ease suffering, though the sufferers were characters on paper.

When I sent family members and friends a 750-page manuscript and asked for comments, I knew I was asking a lot. For insights and encouragement, many thanks to Carolyn Micklem, Susan Micklem, Meg Kearney, Michael Fleming, Brenda Prescott, Gina Haldeman, and Sharon Kalemkiarian. Thanks to Toi Derricotte, who swapped pages with me, and Kathleen O'Donnell, who swapped stories. Thanks to Cornelius, always.

This book was informed—truly in-formed, shaped inwardly—by many other books, works by researchers, novelists, and people of the past such as Sei Shonagon, a snobbish, observant woman who speaks clearly across ten centuries and the barrier of translation. I try to borrow rather than replicate, but I could not resist one paraphrase: Mox's drinking song is based on a real song I found in *The Autobiography of a Winnebago Indian*, the oral history of a certain "SB," as collected by anthropologist Paul Radin. SB says that when he had delirium tremens, he saw drunken ghosts on horseback singing, "I, even I, must die sometime, so of what value is anything, I think." The song became a popular drinking song.

I want to acknowledge all my influences here, with thanks—even the ones I have forgotten, which are still at work in hidden corners of my imagination.

519

About the Author

SARAH MICKLEM worked at the usual assortment of jobs before discovering that graphic design was an enjoyable way to make a living. After many years as a magazine designer, she began to write about a character called Firethorn, whom she first imagined as a woman alone in the woods. About a decade later, Micklem published her first novel, *Firethorn*. She continues to work as a designer while writing the third book of the Firethorn trilogy. She lives with her husband, poet and playwright Cornelius Eady, in New York and Indiana.

CPSIA information can be obtained at www.ICGtesting.com
Printed in the USA
LVOW12s2137040315

429346LV00001B/123/P